Praise for Robert Gleason and *End of Days*

"Gleason does for the end of the world what Milton did for Hell itself."
—W. Michael and Kathleen O'Neal Gear, *New York Times* bestselling authors of *Fire the Sky* and *The Dawn Country*, on *End of Days*

"Reads like a dark prophecy. A brilliantly conceived, ferocious journey into the final fire, it swept me up with its blazing intensity. A heart-stopping reading experience."
—Whitley Strieber, *New York Times* bestselling author of *Hybrids*, on *End of Days*

"The ride of a lifetime—or more accurately . . . of a deathtime! Written in 3-D, it will take a Spielberg to make a movie of it!"
—David Black, winner of two Edgars, a dozen Emmy and Writers Guild nominations and awards, as well as the author of *The Extinction Event*, on *End of Days*

"*The Road* on steroids!"
—Jon Land, award-winning author of *Strong at the Break*, on *End of Days*

"One of the reading experiences of my lifetime. Seldom if ever have I read a book that combined such literary power with a factual background that induced those basic components of tragedy, fear, and pity. Talk about being transfixed to the page! I was *transmuted*!"
—Thomas Fleming, winner of the Lincoln Prize for Lifetime Achievement in History, former president of the American Society of Historians and of PEN, and *New York Times* bestselling author of *The Secret Trial of Robert E. Lee*, on *End of Days*

"Great Caesar's ghost! What a story! At times mystical, at others apocalyptic, his characters take you through an almost mythic experience."
—Larry Bond, *New York Times* bestselling author of *Cold Choices*, on *End of Days*

"Readers diving into Gleason's world will never be the same again. *End of Days* is a nuclear warhead of a novel, which could do for the antiproliferation movement what *Silent Spring* did for environmentalism. People will inevitably compare *End of Days* to such apocalyptic masterworks as *The Stand, Left Behind, Swan Song, Fail-Safe, Dr. Strangelove,* and *The Sum of All Fears,* but in truth there are no comparisons. *End of Days* dwarfs all previous efforts. A vision old as the Bible, violent as Armageddon itself, *End of Days* is more than a novel. It is the fulfillment of Revelation, Nostradamus, and all the ancient apocalyptic scrolls rolled into one. This is the End Time writ large. Bravo! Hats off! I wish I could have written *End of Days,* but I'm man enough to admit that I could not have done it for all the tea in China!"

   —**David Hagberg,** *New York Times* **bestselling author of**
   The Expediter

"Passionate readers need not fear Philip Roth's lament that fiction is dead. . . . This novel is sprawling, epic, cinematic, and a ripping good adventure yarn. If Gleason has forgotten anything about fashioning a book that will get widely read, the reader won't discover what it might be."

   —*Booklist* **on** *Wrath of God,* **the sequel to** *End of Days*

END OF DAYS

END
OF
DAYS

ROBERT GLEASON

A TOM DOHERTY ASSOCIATES BOOK NEW YORK

END OF DAYS

Copyright © 2011 by Robert Gleason

A Forge Book
Published by Tom Doherty Associates, LLC
175 Fifth Avenue
New York, NY 10010

www.tor-forge.com

Forge® is a registered trademark of Tom Doherty Associates, LLC.

Library of Congress Cataloging-in-Publication Data

Gleason, Robert (Robert Herman)
    End of days/Robert Gleason.—1st ed.
        p. cm.
    "A Tom Doherty Associates book."
    ISBN 978-0-7653-2992-9
1. End of the world—Fiction.   I. Title.
PS3557.L433E63 2011
813'.54—dc22   2011019776

First Edition: September 2011

Printed in the United States of America

0   9   8   7   6   5   4   3   2   1

For Susan—always

Special thanks to

Tom Doherty, Junius Podrug, and John Farris, without whose help this book never would have come to fruition.

Also to Linda Quinton, who makes all things possible, and to Eric Raab, friend and editor.

Very special thanks to

Jerry Gibbs, who has had my back for over five decades—semper fi.

Acknowledgments

To Sessalee Hensley, for encouraging me to write about the apocalypse; Christine Jaeger, for so much help and support; George Noory and Lisa Lyon, to whom I owe so much; Howie Carr, a prince among men; and to Mancow Muller, the Peaceful Warrior.

To my friends at NFGTV, particularly Stefan Springman, Toby Barraud, and Lisa LeeKing Ruvalcaba, for putting me in the History Channel's *Prophets of Doom*—and for putting up with me.

To David Hagberg and Larry Bond, both of whom vetted all things military (all mistakes in these areas are mine, I hasten to add); Katharine Critchlow and Whitney Ross, who keep all of us sane; Eleanor Wood and Justin Bell, who are very dear friends.

To Doug Greenlaw, Alice Gleason, Simon Basse, Blaine Heric, Janis Kinsey, Gary Nuspl, Larry Beaver, LaVerne Dunlap, and all my Michigan City, Indiana, friends.

To Maribel and Roberto Gutierrez—I will never forget.

And once again to Herb Alexander, 1910–1988. You could ride the river with him.

We but teach
Bloody instructions which, being taught, return
To plague the inventor.

—William Shakespeare, *Macbeth*, 1.7.8–10

The sin ye do by two and two ye must pay for one by one.

—Rudyard Kipling, "Tomlinson"

I

Watchman, What of the Night?

—Isaiah 21:11

1 They Won't Know It Was Missing . . .

"Yo, Katy, how's it hanging? Thought I'd send you a memento mori, just to let you know I'm thinking of you."

Stone was on her phone screen, smiling and waving at the camera.

Kate Magruder hit "pause"—freezing his grin on the screen. It was hard to believe that three years ago they'd been lovers, partners—a team.

She sighed. It seemed a million years ago.

In another hour Stacy would make Kate up, and she would be on TV—her special news report from Mecca. In the portable makeup mirror on her folding camp table, she studied her face with professional detachment. At age thirty-six, she had her mother's mouth and high Apache cheekbones, framing her father's emerald eyes. Her reddish blond hair she wore straight down her back, and her figure—still athletic from decades of running, weight workouts, and Tae Kwon Do—drew more than its share of wolf whistles.

But she took no pride in her appearance. She'd always viewed good looks—hers, anyone's—as physical fraudulence, a diversion from the person within.

"Whoever the hell that is," she grumbled to the mirror.

Maybe that was what she'd seen in John Stone. He put no one on pedestals. His nickname for her had been Beauty—which he'd always intoned with a sneer—and he'd goaded her continually about her now-famous face.

"Your looks may stop some men's clocks, but not mine. Around here we work for a living. Get the picture, Spoiled Rich Girl? Pick up those mikes and cameras. Get the lead out. We have a shoot and a story to cover."

And stories they had covered—every war, famine, earthquake, and plague planet Earth had to offer—for four long years. She'd been his camera operator and sound woman, then rewrote his copy, then coauthored the news stories.

He'd been a bastard—but without bullshit. And he'd seen her for what she was—a consummate pro, not just a pretty face.

For that she had loved him.

She still loved him.

Oh, John, where are you now?

Where did it all go wrong?

Not that he was hard to look at. She wished he'd gotten his nose fixed after she'd dragged him bleeding out of a biker bar in East L.A. As usual, he needed a haircut. She also wished he'd get a new wardrobe. Bush jackets and fatigues were hardly her idea of haute couture. Lean, rangy, she guessed he was still fit. Maybe as fit as when he'd won fourteen straight for the Yankees his rookie year and taken them to the Series. Ordinarily, she would have muttered an obscenity about his conceited smirk, except the grin now bothered her in a way she couldn't explain to herself.

Something about the eyes.

Kate sat down on her cot. She couldn't sleep. Even when she wasn't playing the video of John Stone, it was playing in her mind. Memento mori. *Remember that you shall die.* It was just like Stone to send her a message wrapped in a riddle. Stone was afraid of nothing, but there was something in his voice.

Wind attacked her tent, and she peeked out the flap as the bloody dawn rose over the city. Mecca sprawled like a wrinkled old woman in a wadi, a dry river-bed carved between steep hills. The muezzins' morning call to prayer from the minarets towering over the city's mosques sang to her on the stinging wind. Their song, for Kate, summoned the ghosts of Islamic holy warriors past, a wail for the Mahdi-Messiah to redeem the True Believers and restore Dar-al-Islam—"the Domain of Islam"—to its rightful place on Mohammed's earth and in Allah's paradise, to punish the wicked and reward the righteous.

Answering the call of the criers, hundreds of thousands of pilgrims came out of the tents that surrounded the city and prostrated themselves in the direction of the black draped Ka'ba, the House of Abraham in the heart of the city. Kate knew that many of the Muslims on earth, more than a billion people, were at this moment facing in her direction as they answered the call of the muezzins to embrace Mecca and praise Allah. She ducked back inside the tent, reminding herself that she was one of the infidels.

They were here to cover the hajj, the pilgrimage to Mohammed's birthplace that attracted millions of Muslims each year. Vladimir Malokov, Russia's minister of defense, had been her ostensible reason for coming to Mecca. He had converted to Islam, was in Mecca for his hajj, and despite her mother's wishes, the Saudi government—sensing in his pilgrimage a PR bonanza—had granted Kate and MTN exclusive coverage of the event. But her real reason was the concern raised by Stone's video. Stone claimed he was unearthing "the scoop of the century."

She flopped back down on the army cot and picked up the phone. Stone was one of the few people who mattered to her. He was the best reporter the gods ever created. Stone and Kate had been through some hairy stuff together. Genocide in Africa and the Balkans. Invading a Cuban gulag to search for a gun-toting nun.

"*You're a man to ride the river with,*" Stone told her in an exaggerated Texas drawl after she'd covered his back in that biker bar after he pissed off guys who thought MAC-10s and rattlesnake tattoos were fashion statements.

Kate backed up the video and hit "play" again. Stone's curly black hair and raptor's grin reappeared on the phone's small screen.

"You thought your mom and I were a few bricks shy on the subject of nuclear proliferation. Well, after my last foray into the Land of Loose Nukes I couldn't resist proving you wrong. Catch a glimpse of the Russian nuclear storage facility behind me."

Behind Stone was a paint-blistered storage building. Untended, unguarded.

"As you can see from the rickety fence, the absence of guards—or any personnel at all, in spite of the fact that this shed is a high-security installation warehousing several tons of bomb-grade nuclear fuel—we can walk right in now and help ourselves to any of the containers, then waltz out the way we came. How can we be so sure? you ask. Because we did just that."

The camera moved in tight on two small slate-gray steel drums.

"One of the drums is filled with bomb-grade plutonium, the other enriched bomb-grade uranium. Each weighs around fifty pounds—containing enough for an Hiroshima and a Nagasaki bomb blast. Easy for me to carry out."

The camera panned to the fence and the side of the building.

"How can this be happening? The Russian economy is in chaos. The guards and workers are gone because they haven't been paid in months. They're out hustling for food, heating oil, medicine, and gasoline—anything to make ends meet.

"Not that anybody would want to hang around these installations even if they were well-paid. There is no money for upkeep or even safety inspections. Consequently, these installations are death traps."

The camera panned the interior of Stone's nearby hotel room. In the middle of the room sat his drum of nuclear materials.

"Well, Katy, I know what you're wondering now. How is that maniac going to get that stuff out of the drum? No prob-lem-o. As long as I don't ingest the shit, it's perfectly safe. So first I open this drum with my trusty hacksaw."

The camera closed in on Stone's trusty hacksaw.

"Then I can scoop it up with my bare hands and shove it into the cargo pockets of my shirt and fatigue pants. Because . . . alpha rays don't pass through skin!

"By the way, I can squeeze enough into my pockets for a couple of bombs. You don't need boxcars full of this stuff to build a good fissile bomb. A piece of high-grade nuclear fuel the size of your fist is all you'd need.

"Getting it through airports, seaports, and border checkpoints, you ask? Ha! Russia has no money for detection devices.

"Now you're thinking: 'Okay, asshole. You were foolish enough to swipe some stuff from an unguarded installation. What are you going to do with it? You need nuclear weapons scientists to turn that stuff into a bomb.'

"Wrong again, Katy dear."

The video cut to a photo of an old Civil War cannon.

"All I have to do is sneak up some dark night on one of the innumerable Civil War cannons, and with an acetylene torch cut off a hunk of cannon six feet long.

"Or I can just buy a hunk from an ordnance plant—the easier course.

"In any event, I weld one end shut, load it with a piece of the enriched uranium we just stole, then pack the other end with more dynamite or gunpowder— and wham! We blast our uranium bullet into the uranium at the cannon barrel's far end. Guess what we have? The Hiroshima 'gun-barrel bomb.' The genius of this baby is that it's foolproof. Any moron can make it work. The guys at the American Manhattan Project—not to be confused with that gaggle of State Department morons who ran our 'Pakistani Manhattan Project'—were so confident of the old gun-barrel design they never tested it. Well, actually they did, if you want to be technical. The test site was Hiroshima.

"Now if you want to do some real testing, it really isn't all that hard. Get a ball of plutonium, encase it in a spherical steel jacket lined with C-4, crimp fifty or sixty blasting caps around it—all uniformly placed—wire them up to a single electrical source, and throw the switch. You may want to test it a couple of times with a conventional explosive, but it will work. Trust me. It worked at Nagasaki.

"And no, this isn't the only nuclear shit exiting Mother Russia. 'Mad Vlad' Malokov reports a dozen Kilo-Class subs, over one hundred suitcase nukes, and a sizable assortment of cruise missiles are currently on their misplaced list. In other words, these weapons have gone over the hill.

"Time to go. Don't worry. I'm going to return this stuff to the place I stole it from. Otherwise they won't know it was missing. I'll leave it on the front porch. No one knows what these storage sites contain. There's no bookkeeping.

"So you can see, Katy dear, the shit's so easy to obtain you have to assume that noisy neighbor of yours is now a nuclear player. I know you've sometimes been skeptical of your mom and me, but the Global Arms Race from Hell is on."

Kate turned off the video and sighed.

She'd seen something she'd never expected to see.

John Stone was scared.

Maybe it had to do with Vlad. Many people thought he was extremely dangerous. He wasn't called "Mad Vlad" for nothing. He'd also earned the name Vlad the Impaler during the Chechnya War when he'd staked dead prisoners on posts lining the main street into Grozny.

There were rumors he'd had the men impaled alive.

He was wealthy beyond dreams of avarice, and so far the ineffective Russian bureaucracy had been unable to remove him from office.

If Vlad was in Mecca, Stone wouldn't be far away.

She got up, donned her pilgrim's robes and veil.

What are you trying to tell me, John?

She already knew about Russia's nuclear yard sale. Her mother's media empire was now dedicated to warning the world about nuclear Armageddon, which had earned her considerable ridicule, including the nickname "the Nuclear Noah," particularly after she built her Fortress–bomb shelter she called "the Citadel" in the middle of Arizona's Sonoran Desert.

When Stone came to share her dementia, her mother—known to her friends as L. L.—had shipped him off to the ends of the world. In Russia, China, and the Middle East in particular, L. L. and Stone had chased every rumor of Planet Earth's imminent demise.

Kate didn't believe any of their paranoia, but still the video bothered her.

There was also the letter she'd received from Stone the week before—from an area in Central Asia so remote the envelope had four different postmarks. His letter sounded a little crazy, haunted, and, she believed now, scared. She'd perused his letter a hundred times.

It read like a last will and testament for the human race.

Kate shut her eyes. Arab music began as the haunting voices of the muezzins faded. She had thought music was illegal during Ramadan.

Personally, she would have been happy to outlaw it the year around. She hated desert music with its endlessly repeating, jarringly discordant refrains.

Memento mori, Stone said to her. Remember that you shall die. In the Middle Ages people wore a skull on a necklace and periodically looked at it to remind themselves that death was waiting.

But whose death was Stone talking about?

2 The Woman Who Rode the Wind

At age eighty-one, Lydia Lozen Magruder still possessed the gift of fear, and like *Macbeth*'s witches, she had glimpsed darkness.

But she had also seen the Light.

Standing at her sacred spot, Three Points—at the mountain summit of Espinazo Sangre de Cristo, high above the Sonoran Desert—she'd seen that Light ten long years ago. It was an experience she never wanted to repeat.

She had once died up there. With her heart stopped, she had lain a full fourteen minutes out of this life in that cliff-top cave—or so her shaman, mentor, and spirit guide, Bear Claw, had told her.

. . . During that near-death experience, the crimson canyons of Three Points were hammered by lightning, rain, and hailstorms with winds up to 140 miles per

hour. But worse than the storms was her vision—rockets launching, bombs detonating, fireballs and mushroom clouds swelling, firestorms merging, converging, consuming entire cities, coastlines, highways clogged with survivors clutching babies, children, each other. A vision of the End Time in horrific detail.

But that wasn't the worst of her visions.

She had been them—everyone and everything. She not only felt the agony of the burn victims, she felt the ferocity of the weapons—the missiles, the submarines, the bombers, the bombs. She rose upward with them on their furious flights. She communed with them even as they exploded. She sang and laughed with them to their flash, the vastness of their fire.

Worse—like the Weird Sisters in Macbeth—the weapons spoke to her.

Telling her "their secret."

Only once did she make the mistake of describing to someone her vision up on Three Points and revealing that secret. Kate—"sharper than a serpent's tooth"— had told her she was "saving that story for your sanity hearing."

"Don't you dare tell anyone about what happened at Three Points," Kate had said. "Whatever credibility you've built up will be gone in a heartbeat. People will be signing petitions to have you committed. And mine will be the first signature."

For once in her life, L. L. recognized that there was wisdom in Kate's warning.

She never spoke of Three Points again . . .

L. L. stared out over the desert. It was hard to believe she'd "died" up there. She knew she was old but didn't think of herself as *that* old.

True, her hair showed more white than gunmetal-gray, but her back was still straight. Her dark eyes and slanted cheekbones were etched at the corners with crow's-feet, but when those eyes narrowed, her jaw set and cheekbones flared, hers was a face cast hard as concrete, with a stare like a Damascus blade. At the age of eighty-one she was still riding her Appaloosa, Nightmare, high up into the San Carlos Mountains alone.

She had a reputation for toughness, and over the years she'd had to be tough. Lydia Lozen Magruder owned and ran not only the most powerful media conglomerate on earth, she ruled the heavens as well—where her satellites cut a commanding swath.

L. L. knew the score. All of the strategists from Herman Kahn on down had agreed that the old Cold War nuclear strategies had been a charade. Oh, sure, the nuclear weapons had been real. But neither Russian or the U.S. had the will to launch them. That would have meant total annihilation for both sides. The only realistic nuclear scenarios were set in the future, when many nations would have access to nuclear arms and strikes could be anonymous or disguised.

That future was *now.*

L. L. knew it was just a matter of time before one of the rogue states or terrorist organizations anonymously nuked a couple of American cities—then sat back and watched the feathers fly. She'd asked Defense Secretary Jack Taylor what his and the president's response would be.

"We'd have no choice. If they have one, you have to assume they have more. Nuclear destruction is the most unbearable fate in human history. The terror and agony and—let's face it—our lust for revenge would be too overpowering."

"So what would you do?"

"Go to our enemies and demand they produce the guilty party—or we nuke them all. Off the face of the earth."

"And if they don't produce the culprit? We kill them all."

"We nuke 'em till they glow."

"What if that only creates more nuclear enemies?"

"What choice would we have?"

She feared that for one of the few times in his life, Taylor had it right . . .

. . . Then why was there so much apathy? She would have thought that the destruction of the World Trade Center and the Pentagon's northwest wing followed by the Iraqi and Afghan wars would have been a wake-up call. She had watched those events, sick to her soul. But those catastrophes hadn't even dented the public's ultimate indifference. There was no debate over nuclear terrorism, its sponsoring states, or finally ending nuclear proliferation. Public discussion of nuclear terrorism remained taboo, and the nation eventually returned its head to sand.

It was actually worse than heads in the sand. The way the President Haines administration now courted that oil-rich Mideast dictatorship, Dar-al-Suhl, almost made her physically ill. Haines seemed to positively dote on its leaders, that bastard Haddad and his two twin sisters. They made her flesh crawl . . .

. . . All of which only made her more desperate to hear from John Stone. She'd read the first e-mail and didn't know what to compare Stone's story with. It was the most frightening material she'd ever encountered.

L. L. would have had to go back 14,000 years to find anything remotely similar. Perhaps Pleistocene man's global extermination of earth's megafauna—70 percent of the large mammals in North and South America alone. Perhaps those specieswide exterminations of the mammoths, saber-toothed cats, the giant beaver, and the short-face bear—just to name a few—would have compared with Stone's report.

Stone was describing an inevitable war not only on earth's species but ultimately on evolution itself.

The old woman sighed wearily. Born to the desert, she was intimately acquainted with the struggle to survive. She knew the desert as a proving ground for nature's toughest survivors, for tarantulas and horned toads, scorpions and diamondbacks, kangaroo rats and gila monsters, vultures and a very few people.

All the famous nuclear testing sites—White Sands, Los Alamos, Yucca flats—were located in the desert. Deserts could endure the effects of nuclear war, better than any other terrain on earth—fire, blast, fallout, plague, even nuclear winter.

Which was why L. L had constructed the Citadel—her own private Shangri-la for the Third Millennium—in the desert. A fortress of knowledge, culture, and civilization, it was built on that darkling plain to withstand anything—the Armies of the Night *and* the End of Time.

But it was also part and parcel of the mountains around her—particularly Espinazo Sangre de Cristo. In her mind the dozens of miles of tunnels and caverns within that mountain were as much a part of the Citadel as her personal fortress-redoubt and its surrounding community. In some respects the chambered mountain—packed to the rafters with supplies and materiel, arms and ammunition—was more the Citadel than the Citadel. To L. L. those shafts and caverns—replete with everything necessary to one day rebuild civilization—were the Citadel's organs and circulatory system.

Her organs and circulatory system.

The phone in her pocket vibrated with an incoming call, and she answered it.

"This is Bill Nance at the Houston Command Center," a male voice said. The Command Center was the central coordination point for her worldwide—and celestial—network of microwave stations and satellites that provided radio, telephone, and television service for much of the world. The building Nance was sitting in was 1,100 miles from the Citadel, but it was part of the mystery and magic of electronics that the closest point between was a signal bounced off a satellite orbiting the earth.

"There has been no communication from John Stone," Nance told her.

"Have you notified all our offices and affiliates to be on the alert for him?"

"Yes, ma'am. The last sighting of him was in Cairo. He was there interviewing their minister of defense. He was researching their weapons programs. The, uh, Egyptian police are looking for him."

Lydia's thin lips shaped a wry smile. "Then he's probably drunk in some Nile brothel, you ask me."

Bill Nance didn't want to ask her anything. He was so nervous he was now starting to sweat. He'd switched the hand holding the phone to wipe his palm. Low man on the totem pole, he had drawn the black marble. That's what employees at the center called giving bad news to Lydia Lozen. She was respected by all, but when she was pissed her eruptions rivaled Krakatoa. In those moments, she was typically described as "a nut-buster."

Still her bursts of generosity were legendary. CNN had run a story that morning about the private jet L. L. had chartered to fly the seven-year-old son of her Rangoon stations chief to the Mayo Clinic for critical blood work.

Nance—like everyone at MTN—was fascinated by L. L. If he hadn't been the bad news bearer, he'd have relished talking to the fabled Lady in Black, especially about John Stone. He'd been one of the great Yankee pitchers until he climbed over the dugout one night to break up a brawl among two rival street gangs. He'd hospitalized three of them, and the lawsuit against the Yankees was televised worldwide.

When asked to leave baseball permanently by the commissioner, Stone's sole comment to the media was:

"I always wanted to write. I guess it's time."

Write he did. Two Pulitzers later and the star investigative reporter for L. L.'s communications network, he had once been described as a hybrid of James Joyce and Genghis Khan.

Nance had never seen Lydia in person, but her broadcast image was familiar. She was invariably clad in black. Old-time employees claimed she went into mourning on the day the United States privatized its nuclear bomb-fuel processing agency.

"That agency," L. L. frequently said, "had been the planet's last best hope, the only operation capable of buying up Russia's loose nukes and saving the world from unbridled nuclear proliferation. No private company in the history of the world could clean up that mess over there, and now it will never be done."

In later years, quoting the inestimable Russell Seitz, she took to referring to Russia's nuclear supermarket as "the yard sale at the end of history" and railed endlessly, both in public and in private, about those incessant reports coming out of Russia about "missing cruise missiles, vanished subs, disappearing suitcase nukes."

L. L. was the favorite topic of conversation at the Houston Center. Tabloids ran stories about her wandering the desert like a demented prospector, talking to rocks and snakes. Some people said she read minds and sent messages on the wind. The fortress/bomb shelter she'd built in that desert mountain was rumored to house everything from Michelangelo's *David* to an intact UFO. A guy in the next office claimed he'd heard from a reliable source that she'd paid the Louvre a billion dollars for the *Mona Lisa* and what was hanging in the museum now was a computerized reproduction.

Nance wasn't a guy with a lot of imagination. He sometimes felt if it couldn't be read off a computer screen, hell, it wasn't true, didn't exist at all—or didn't *deserve* to exist. And he never voiced any opinions at coffee breaks anyway, not even when the *National Scandal* ran a six-part exposé revealing that L. L. was the product of the abduction/rape of an Indian medicine woman by a space alien. He didn't have enough time in grade to give an opinion about the boss woman.

Besides, he liked his nuts right where they were.

"Where's my daughter?"

Nance flinched. He cleared his throat and mumbled: "I'll check, ma'am."

He punched "Kate Magruder" into his terminal.

"She's already in Mecca."

Lydia broke the connection and slammed the palm-sized phone against her hip.

She had not wanted Kate to do a broadcast from Mecca.

But she knew better than to forbid Kate anything. She shared Kate's willfulness. Even as a girl, Kate had been wild and elusive—more like L. L. than anyone alive. But together they were often oil and water.

If Lydia made the mistake of treading too heavily, Kate drew her sword. Then she would head off to Mecca or some other godforsaken place. Kate had even once gone into a Cuban prison with John Stone to rescue the evangelical rock star Sister Cassandra. That story had a happy ending. Sister Cassandra, like L. L., shared *Indian* blood, and the two became fast friends. Cassie was now the world's most lucrative entertainer, with a global following.

There was a time when L. L. might have called Frank, her stepson, and asked *him* to talk some sense into her daughter's head. They were not related by blood; Lydia sometimes wished Frank and Kate had married. Frank was a medical doctor and research scientist with degrees from Harvard and Johns Hopkins. His sophistication and intelligence, if not his temper, matched that of L. L.'s daughter.

Lydia walked out to the cliff's edge. She stared out over the desert and sighed with weariness and dismay. She had a terrible sense of foreboding.

A fear John Stone had confirmed.

He had traveled the world undercover for three years and had unearthed a horror story, not just a scoop. Stone said he'd learned of a plot to set the Western world back a thousand years to the Dark Ages.

L. L. had never proved him wrong.

He gave her only half the story in the file he e-mailed. He was supposed to conclude his investigation and send her the second file a week ago. Not that a week meant much to a man whose blood ran 90 proof at times and who could spend a week in a Bangkok whorehouse or guzzle vodka with Mad Vlad Malokov in his Black Sea dacha.

A mile-long sandstorm festooned with four soaring dust devils was blowing across the desert floor. As L. L. stared at the sand, in her mind's eye she saw a band of Apaches riding, their ponies kicking up the storm.

At the forefront of the band, she visualized her grandmother, Lozen, the female war shaman of the Apache Nation, who had counseled Mangas Coloradas, Cochise, and Victorio.

Riding the wind.

Lozen, who had predicted the holocaust that doomed the Apache Nation.

Lozen looked up from the desert floor at Lydia, and Lydia felt the message like a bolt of lightning. *The heart of the world is throbbing in your hand.* L. L.'s hand burned as if a hot coal had seared it.

She returned to her Appaloosa and rubbed the horse's neck. Gripping the pommel, she leaned against the saddle leathers.

It was too much, too much for an old woman, she told herself.

It was too much for anyone.

Nor was it the first vision she'd had of the warrior-goddess riding the windstorm. She had told no one about those visions—as she had told no one about the birthmark that had materialized above her right scapula when Kate was born: a bloody Rorschach's blot of an eagle's talon. L. L. had learned five years ago while going through her grandfather's papers that her grandmother had borne the same bloody talon.

So be it. The torch had been passed.

Lydia Lozen Magruder opened her pain-wracked hand.

It was red and scorched.

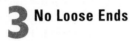

3 No Loose Ends

Twilight in the fjord.

One of thousands of barren sub-Arctic Greenland fjords.

The estuary is not much by Greenland's standards. The largest island on earth, Greenland's perimeter has more than 10,000 of these lochs. Originally tectonic fault lines, they can be tens of miles long, unfathomably deep.

Our greatest glacier, Greenland contains more frozen water than any spot on earth except Antarctica—even with global warming's melt-off. Much of its sheet ice is millions of years old.

Amid so much ice no naval ships, fishing boats, or recon satellites noticed when a periscope broke the water. Sunlight glinted off its lenses as its scope pivoted three complete turns.

Nor was the Russian-built diesel sub observed as she blew out her buoyancy tanks and surfaced amid cascading waves and foam. The sub was Kilo-Class, 230 feet long, with a teardrop-shaped hull. Submerged she could run up to four hundred miles. A retrofitted Kilo was capable of launching nuclear-armed cruise missiles.

The ship's captain threw open the conning tower's hatch, grabbed a handhold, flipped up through the hatchway onto the bridge. As if mimicking his periscope's earlier turns, he raised his binoculars and pivoted 360 degrees, three times, observing sea and land, mountains and sky. He turned to his first mate, still belowdecks, and said, "Send the crew on deck five at a time for fresh air and exercise."

The sub's captain, whose name was Gargarin, and his three officers stood their watch. Dressed in naval blues and heavy foul-weather jackets, they personified the Russian military right down to the bright blue eyes and light blond hair. They even sported rakish mustaches, yellow as summer wheat, currently the vogue in the Russian submarine fleet.

"It certainly is cold for this time of year," the signal officer said.

"I trained on a Typhoon-Class boomer under the ice pack for a full year. Under Captain Vladimir Malokov."

"Long before he became Russia's defense minister, I take it," First said.

"Many years before," Captain Gargarin said. "We spent most of December and January that year nosing around the five North Poles. That was cold."

"Five North Poles?" First asked.

"There is no permanent North Pole. Earth's axis wobbles—describes a misshapen circle rather than a fixed point. Nonetheless, Vlad would hunt for the North Pole's alleged current position and surface. Next he would look for something called its Geographic North Pole's average position. He would make us visit that too. Then there is the Magnetic North Pole, where compass needles point, some 30 miles east of Edmund Walker Island."

"Don't forget the North Geomagnetic Pole," the navigator said.

"North Geomagnetic Pole?" First asked, dubious.

"It's 500 miles further north than the plain Magnetic North Pole. The earth's and stratosphere's magnetic force fields are supposed to converge there. There is also the Pole of Inaccessibility, around which the polar pack ice was alleged to revolve. He would take us there just to prove it didn't exist."

"Sounds like Minister Malokov *was* mad," First said.

"If I stay out here much longer," the captain said, "I'll be just as crazy as he was."

There was movement out on the ice. The three men focused their binoculars, and the dim movement metamorphosed. The sighting of a man became visible in the ice-barbed winds, emerging from a Greenland snowscape of white-on-white. A lone white-clad man trudging over the rocky ice, slipping and sliding despite his boot crampons, walking pick, and ice ax.

"If I was him," the captain said, "I wouldn't be in any hurry to get here."

"The sub voyage from hell," First said sardonically.

———

The man trudging down from the Greenland ice sheet toward Gargarin's fjord was not pleased with his assignment. Pinched, thin, diminutive, he hunched his shoulders—appearing even shorter than his five feet, three inches— as he slapped his gloved hands together to ward off the cold. Despite his white parka, fur-lined all-weather boots, and gloves, Nadia Gregiekov was cold. A Georgian by birth, he was used to the sunnier climes of the Kokhida Lowlands near the shores of the Black Sea, shielded from the winter's blast by the Caucasian Mountains. A trained nuclear scientist, he was also accustomed to stationary employment, not Arctic ice hiking.

. . . There was a time he never would have considered his current employment. A child prodigy in mathematics and science, he had been taken from his small impoverished collective near the Inguri River and given the finest education in nuclear physics the world could offer. First at the University of St. Petersburg, then at MIT in the United States, including summer seminars at Los Alamos, Sandia, and Lawrence-Livermore.

Afterward, he returned to Russia, where he studied under his own country's finest scientists. Again, he was on the fast track, having the run of all his country's most prestigious weapons labs.

Those were the golden years, when fine scientific minds were, in Russia, state heroes and national celebrities. Commanding lavish salaries and palatial Black Sea dachas, these scientific luminaries—particularly weapons scientists—trod Rodina's sacred soil as gods.

Then came the Dark Years. The old Union broke up, and overnight his money was worthless, his dachas expropriated by murderous mafyioski, his world shattered. His parents' pensions and his own checks—when they arrived at all— weren't worth the paper they were printed on. He and his family were forced out of their home. His wife, parents, four children, and he were crammed into a two-room apartment with a communal bathroom down the hall.

Meat, poultry, eggs, milk, necessary medicines became rare as bloodstones.

At first, they told themselves their fall from grace was a temporary glitch they would one day laugh at. Weapons scientists were too valuable to be forever ignored. Their lives only worsened. His parents died in penury, broken in mind, body, and in soul.

His wife became a diabetic. Unable to afford insulin, she lost her toes.

But it did turn around.

Strangers came to Nadia with suitcases full of money—American dollars, not valueless rubles. They could buy a gorgeous new home, lavish meals in five-star restaurants, medicine for his wife, gifts for his children, and a beautiful young mistress for himself

Oh, at first he'd had pangs of conscience. At times he felt like an illegal drug manufacturer—and at this moment on the Greenland ice, very much like one of their couriers . . .

Fuck it, he thought bitterly. The whole history of his people was one of suffering and exploitation. What was wrong with getting some of his own back? Living out his life in comfort?

So he'd helped his benefactors with their warheads—wedded them to their missiles, worked out the arm-and-launch PAL codes, showed them how they worked.

He'd programmed their portable wireless modem, their "cheget-transceiver" in the leather briefcase that he now carried in his rucksack.

His deepest regret was his current assignment: this five-mile hike across the ice from the neighboring fjord, where—in exchange for a small fortune in American dollars—an Icelandic trawler captain had dropped him. He'd fallen into conversation with the Icelander. A young man with a pretty wife and three small children. Nadia had taken an undeniable liking to the man and had left him with a boxed set of the works of Marx and Engels.

Again, he felt a pang of agonizing remorse.

What would happen to that young man's world?

It would take a lot of Stolichnaya to live this memory down, but there was no turning back. Failure was not an option. His employers had made that painfully clear to him.

———————

By the time Yuri, the First Officer, finished reading his orders, the weapons specialist was there. Nadia climbed aboard awkwardly, and the three officers saluted him.

"I believe you know what this is, Captain." He handed Gargarin the briefcase laptop.

"Yes," the captain said.

"You have the instructions and the combination?" Nadia asked.

"I do."

"You know how to load this? Into your weapons computers?"

"Of course."

"You are sure you don't need my help."

"Your duties are finished."

"Then I'll return the way I came."

He turned to the dinghy that had brought him to the sub.

Captain Gargarin took out a silenced 9mm Makarov.

"The instructions had one more order." He racked the pistol's slide, chambering a round, and handed the pistol to his First Officer.

When the weapons specialist turned around, he was staring into its muzzle.

"They specified 'no loose ends,'" Captain Gargarin said.

First shot Nadia through his left eye.

"Have some men take him below," Captain Gargarin said dispassionately. "We'll load him into a weighted shroud and bury him at sea."

A sudden *ka-ka-ka-whummmmppppp!!!*—from five miles away—shook the men on the sub's deckplates.

"What was that?" the navigator asked.

"The trawler," the captain said. "Another loose end."

Two sailors came to collect Nadia's body, and the men went below.

4 When Has the Word "Forbidden" Ever Stopped Stone?

"Kate," her MTN soundman shouted to her, "give me a mike check."

Kate removed her headphones. "I was listening to Sister Cassandra, you moron."

"And we're about to lose the satellite," the soundman added.

Kate Magruder grudgingly clipped the lavaliere microphone to the bottom of her white chador veil. Decked out in the mandatory abaya robe of white dingri cotton, she was afraid the rustling fabric would interfere with the audio.

"The lavaliere's not working," the sound guy said. "I warned you about that veil. Every time you move or the wind blows the fabric, sound breaks up. We have to bring in a fish pole."

His assistant swung a boom mike over Kate's head.

"Testing one-two-three," Kate said.

"Need a lighter veil," Sound said. "This one's muffling the audio."

"The others look like shit," Kate complained.

"But at least we'll be able to hear you," Sound said.

"And *I'll* look like shit."

"This is holy ground," her producer said with a grin. "Watch your tongue."

"We're going on as is."

"This is one-take live," Sound said. "We go in thirty-two seconds. We lose the satellite in exactly seven-and-one-half minutes. You want to sound like you're talking through a gag, I'm grieving it."

"You'd file a grievance over a goddamn veil?"

"When the sound breaks up, the production director'll bite my head off like a chicken."

"Start counting," Kate's producer said.

"Ten and counting."

Ordinarily, Kate would have taken a breath and let it rip. Not today. The chador cut off her air and made her sound terrible.

"Nine . . . eight . . ."

Kate glanced over her shoulder. Behind her loomed the high white walls of Mecca's Grand Mosque, through whose gates flowed tens of thousands of white-robed pilgrims. She looked back at the camera. Above it were the red hills of Safra and Marcuah—dappled with leopard spots of black basalt—and to the southeast lay the scorching crimson Plain of Arafat. And behind the camera—she could not believe her eyes!—was her former partner and nemesis John T. Stone in white pilgrim attire, arguing with her producer.

He paused to flash her a wicked grin.

". . . Seven . . . six . . . five . . ."

What was Stone doing here?

"... Four ... three ..."

My God, now he waved at her, giving her a big thumbs-up. Christ, he was drunk. They'd hang him for that here!

Steady on, girl. Don't get rattled.

"... Two ... one ...!"

"We are standing before the Grand Mosque of Mecca," Kate said to the camera, "at the beginning of the dhu'l-Hijiah—the holiest month of the Muslim calendar. Every devout Muslim is required by Islamic law—by the fifth pillar of the Faith—to make a one-time pilgrimage to Mecca. This event brings together all Muslims regardless of sect or gender, race or nationality, age or social status. Dressed uniformly in the white garb of hajji, all are equal. The hajj is the great unifying experience of Islam. The hajj of dhu'l-Hijiah is the holiest of all."

She could not believe it. Stone and her producer were fighting.

"During these weeks," Kate said somberly, "every airport through the Islamic Crescent—from Algiers to Jakarta—is thronged with the Faithful, awaiting chartered flights to Saudi Arabia. Many impoverished pilgrims use every cent of their life savings to make this journey. From the first step of the hajj, the sacred rites come into play. The pilgrims must refrain from angry words, obscenities—and sexual intercourse."

"Tell that to the camels," Stone shouted drunkenly off camera.

Only through an act of iron self-will was she able to continue.

"They come attired in two white garments—one, the *Rida,* drapes the neck and left shoulder, the other, the *Izar,* is worn around the waist. The *na'l* sandals leave the ankles bare. Removing their sandals, they enter Mecca, announcing: 'Here I am in answer to your call, O God. Here I am! You have no associate. Here I am! All praise and favor and kingship are yours. Here I am!'

"The pilgrims go straight to the Holy Mosque, praying aloud: 'Oh God, You are peace, and peace derives from You. So welcome us, Oh God, in peace.' They enter the mosque and attempt to kiss the black sacred stone—no easy task since it is mobbed. If a pilgrim can't get close enough, he shouts: 'Takbir! God is Great.' And moves on. He next performs the sevenfold circuit around the Ka'ba—a stone structure forty feet wide, thirty feet long, and fifty feet high, in whose northeast corner the black stone is framed and mounted."

"What these guys wanna mount . . ." Stone shouted.

Kate fought to maintain her self-control.

"After the seventh circuit, pilgrims prostrate themselves twice before the sacred stone and pray—"

Stone cupped his mouth in order to shout another obscenity at her. Before he could get it out, Kate's producer diverted him with a wild roundhouse right, which he ducked. Holding up his hands, laughing, backpedaling in a parody of Muhammed Ali's Zaire rope-a-dope, Stone egged her producer on, taunting:

"Why do these morons wear robes? Because a camel can hear a zipper at fifty paces!"

It took every bit of Kate's self-discipline to stay focused on the camera, but that was all she did. Her mind was blank.

"Kate Magruder from Mecca," was all she could say.

"That's a wrap," the cameraman shouted.

By the time she reached her producer, Stone was gone.

"Where is that bastard?"

"While you were signing off, he disappeared into that mob."

A congested stream of over ten thousand white-clad Muslims was flooding Mecca.

"But entrance is forbidden to non-Muslims," Kate said, shocked.

"Since when has the word 'forbidden' ever stopped Stone," Kate's producer said.

"But he can't—" Kate looked at the mob.

Jesus, God. George was right. Stone's head was clearly identifiable, nearly a head taller than most of the pilgrims flowing through the open gate.

Kate laughed. "Hell's Angels, Aryan Brothers, Third World warlords, Mafia hitmen, even the Cali cartel bosses couldn't stop him."

"Yeah, well, this is Mecca," the soundman said, "and those people aren't joking. Very religious—and very touchy."

"The airport's a mob scene," Kate's producer said. "The flights are stacked from Singapore to South Pass. We've got to move."

"I need a few more minutes," Kate said. "I was hoping to spot Vladimir Malokov—maybe do an interview with him. Okay, and I'm worried about Stone, the asshole."

"I thought you wanted him dead," the producer reminded her.

"I do, but *I* want to kill him."

5 Eyes like Black Stars

A tall white-robed pilgrim strolled through the courtyard of the Grand Mosque, holding an open hardback book in front of his face. It was the definitive guide book: *Mecca—The Handbook of Hajj.* He read its text in singsong Arabic, like a muezzin in his minaret.

The reading was a sham. The book was a hollowed-out box. At one end was a lens hole and a miniature Minolta spy-cam and a hidden recorder.

"John T. Stone here in Islam's holy of holiest," the pilgrim-reporter whispered. "If L. L. and Kate could see me now, they'd be having shit fits. So would the passionate pilgrims around me. Luckily, none of them has made me so far. These people have no sense of humor."

As he followed the throng, he studied his surroundings.

"The black rock in the Ka'ba's northeast corner looks like the sacred stone—

some sort of meteorite if memory serves. Approximately eight inches in diameter, framed in silver."

He snapped two pictures of the black rock.

"Not a bad crowd," he said into the recorder. "Of course, an old-fashioned Aztec sacrifice would be more impressive. Their priests, in flashy feathered headdresses, lined the pilgrims up before the sacrificial stones and ripped out their hearts. Which they shoved still beating into their mouths. Their blood flowed down the pyramids like rivers of tomato soup. Now there's a real religion for you."

Suddenly, a woman blocked his path.

"You're a naughty little boy," she said in sultry English.

During hajj women forsook the chador, and he stared at the widest cheekbones, the fullest, most sensuous mouth, the longest jet hair, and the most shockingly beautiful face he'd ever seen.

But it was the eyes that froze him still as death—fathomless in their darkness, like comets stopped, like black stars.

"Mr. Stone, you are a bad, bad boy drunkenly sneaking into Mecca. I overheard your blasphemous remarks. I saw you photograph the Ka'ba and the sacred stone."

"I could always argue freedom of the press."

"While my people flayed you alive."

"Would a few autographed books satisfy them?"

"Mr. Stone, an original set of the Ten Commandments couldn't get you out of it."

"You're saying I'm in trouble?" Stone said, trying to charm his way out of it.

"Do the words 'Death of a Thousand Cuts' mean anything to you?"

"I have an Amnesty International Card on me somewhere," Stone said.

As he fumbled beneath his robes, a hammered-silver flask, with the initials *J.T.S.* embossed on it in gothic script, fell before her.

Nor did the whiskey flask go unnoticed by the devout.

A mob of pilgrims immediately closed in on him, shaking their "Hajj Handbooks" in his face, shouting.

"Now, I'm afraid mama is going to have to spank," the woman said, shaking her head sadly. "Mama is going to have to spank very hard."

6 The Jack Town Chain

The prison "chain bus"—pulling out of the sally port of the Houston, Texas, county lockup at 3:34 A.M.—was flat-nosed and dirty-white. Its barred windows were bulletproof and permanently sealed. The driver and shotgun guard—who was seated in the back—were both caged. Inmates, shackled to their seats, wore prison whites, their waist irons manacled to long coffle chains running up the aisle. They were headed for the infamous State Correctional Facility in Jackton, Texas—otherwise known as Jack Town.

There was no commode, and throughout the state penal system the bus was known as "the Jack Town Chain."

Ronald "Cool Breeze" Robinson—a tall black inmate with piercing eyes, broad sloping shoulders, and a meticulously groomed goatee—scrunched in his seat. He'd once been a three-time MVP with the Yankees and a shoo-in for Cooperstown. He was now serving triple-life in Jack Town.

"Breeze," his seatmate and homey said, "we done fucked up."

Breeze nodded briefly, then gave Deuce a slow, appraising stare. He liked Deuce but wasn't overly pleased with what he saw. Unlike himself, Deuce was unkempt. He slumped wearily in his seat, eyes red, tired, rheumy. His shaved head and unshaved face were in serious need of soap suds and a razor.

"I be your witness there," Breeze said at last.

The Jackton Pen was universally regarded as the worst prison in the United States. Each year it had the highest rape, homicide, drug use, HIV, and suicide rates in the American penal system. Only the hardest of hard-rock cons were sent to the Jack Town cells.

Situated in the heart of Texas's Estacio Llano—Staked Plains—Jackton was also notorious for brutal weather. Temperatures in the summer rivaled those of the Great Sonoran Desert and Death Valley. The mercury soared at times to 120 degrees. The heat was so arid that when inmates attempted to shave there, they might not get the razor to their faces before the lather dried.

In winter, ice storms, which came all the way from the North Pole, bore down on the cell blocks. Between Jack Town and the Arctic there was not a single mountain to block the freezing winds. The famous "blue northers" of the Staked Plains could flash-freeze standing cattle. The blizzards piled so high that after the drifts melted, dead steers had to be chopped out of the treetops.

The mood of the passengers on the bus was, however, not grim. Unlike their last lockup, Jackton had a rec yard with weight racks, did not stack inmates like cord wood, and its mainline chow was better than County's. Anything was better than County's. And the prison population—over 85 percent black and Mexican—were mostly OG, "Original Gangsta," and OG had no expectations.

Breeze shut his eyes. The handful of whites sat sullen and silent. Not understanding the Spanish conversations, Breeze mentally screened them out. Nonetheless the other conversations buzzed in his ears like hornets—and he could not ignore them. Eyes shut, he listened listlessly—to inmates talking bad.

"*Whatcha gonna do, homes?*"

"*Whip ass and take names.*"

"*Slap yo' bitch-ass,*" a banger laughed, "*while y'all puttin' out head.*"

"*I ain't puttin' out nothin' 'cept muthafuckas' eyeballs.*"

Breeze heard another anonymous voice shout:

"I'll be down with my set, livin' large."

"Fuck you," a man shouted. *"Them Jack Town fools be livin' large in your butt."*

"Sucka fuck wit' me I lullaby his ass."

Breeze's homey even got into it.

"Smoke his butt like country ham," Deuce-Deuce shouted.

"So I steps to the sucka," another man bragged. *"Say, fool, it al-way be bidness. Ain't never personal. And I do the muthafucka right there."*

"I had this muthafucka's back. Liked the dude too, but word up, the sucka dis my set, my hood, my homes. Just like that. In my face."

"You wanna do the muthafucka?"

"So bad my dick hurt."

Breeze found Deuce staring at him.

"What you lookin' at, fool?" Breeze asked.

"Yo' pussy face. You studyin' on that triple-life?"

"I give it some thought."

"Ain't no way you doin' a triple."

"It be a death sentence," Breeze said softly. "Thems was Mexicanos got aced."

"Mexicano narcs."

"Don't make no difference. Mex Maf and Tex Syndicate—all them other spic gangs—they don't forgive, they don't forget."

"You jus' need some pardnas."

"Against *Nos Familias?* Who you tryin' to shuck?"

"Heard of a sucka name of Jamal al Assad? Baddest of the bad? Sucka make a glass eye weep and turn out a nun."

"Yeah, I heard. Everybody heard."

"Some Mideast muthafucka lay five million bucks on his sorry black ass. Jamal, he git anything he want in that joint."

"I ain't no Muslim."

"Know a muthafucka name of D. S. Maybe he fix you up."

"Then a trip ain't shit?" Breeze mocked his friend gently.

"Not fo' a stepper," Deuce said. "Not fo' no balls-ass thoroughbred."

The bus was rolling through the blasted moonscape of the East Houston ghetto-gutted buildings. The surrounding lots, streets, and alleys were strewn with refuse and broken bricks.

Breeze put a hand over his eyes, but the raucous banter would not stop.

"Yo, homes, got me a muthafuckin' toothache," a man shouted. *"They got them a dentist in Jack Town? He best fix this muthafucka."*

"Take it to the Chaplain."

"Oo-whee! The Chaplain! He fix the muthafucka."

"How?"

"With a cattle prod."

"While he read you Bible verses."

"Don't know what I hate worse. That Bible shit or that prod."

"He don't get off, 'less he preach to you first."

Deuce-Deuce and Cool Breeze looked briefly at each other.

"What's this chaplain shit?" Breeze asked.

"Big one-eyed motherfucker. He not only in charge of religious services, he also head of discipline. Like to sit in on punishment sessions—and take part."

Breeze shook his head in astonishment. What was he getting into?

"Long way from the New York Yankees, Breeze. Long way from 'The Terrible Trio.' How many Series you win? Five in a row?"

It had been six in a row. God, that was hard to believe. A lifetime ago, and Breeze would have given anything to have that lifetime back. Where had it all gone wrong?

"What happened to them other two anyway?" Deuce was asking. "Colton some sort of nigga astronaut, ain't he? Stone a writer?"

"They sure ain't on the Jack Town Chain."

"Some muthafuckas got it made."

"They grew up on the same streets—same as you, same as me. They just kept out the gangs, the jails. Them muthafuckas stood up for me. Called me all the time in County. Sent money to my fuckin' 'piece."

"Amazed me, man, y'all couldn't even pay yo' mouthpiece," Deuce said. "How you go through all that bread you made?"

"Dope, wives, muthafuckin' man'gers with power of attorney what don't pay no taxes fo' yo' ass. Don't take much."

Deuce said, "And then there was them three muthafuckas dead in a Houston hotel room wit' yo' ivory-handled nine, wit' yo' prints and blood. Enough rock to wire Texas."

"There it be," Breeze said wearily.

"Breeze, you be my hoss. I cross fire fo' y'all. You knows that. But you gots to let it out—what's wrong, whatcha feelin'? Bottlin' it up gonna kill yo' ass."

Breeze stared at his friend. For a moment Deuce thought he might let it out. Instead, he turned his head and studied the burned-out ghetto of East Houston.

Where were Colt and Stone, my old Yankee teammates, now? he wondered. *And what were they doing?*

"Yo, homes," Deuce said, "I'm talkin' to you."

"Deuce . . ." Breeze turned to his friend and gave him the smile he usually reserved for all the white people who had wanted a piece of him in his playing days. Grabbing his crotch, he then said: "Suck on *this.*"

7 A Hell-Bound Train

The big auburn rat with the huge head and commanding red eyes was sitting on a wharf piling, studying the Bay of Mumbai, formerly known as the Bay of Bombay. India's busiest port, the vast bay teemed with vessels that ranged from dhows and caïques to supertankers and ocean liners.

A fishing rat, he had stood his watch the entire night, waiting for a large dead bottom-feeder to float to the top. It had not happened. Soon he would have to give up and return to foraging the docks. Heavily scavenged by pigeons and gulls, by vultures and men, the Mumbai docks offered slim pickings. Without a fat fish, it would be a hungry night for his warren.

He caught the flash of a diving gull overhead. The gull dropped over two hundred feet and hit the water like a howitzer. His sickle talons and slashing beak ripped a fish's brains to bits.

During the day a dozen of the bird's mates would have joined in, dividing the spoils on the spot. Not so at night. Gulls were diurnal, and the bird strad-dled the fish—too big for a single gull to carry off—alone.

Sailor emitted a high-pitched squeak, alerting his crew. He shot off the pil-ing, diving headfirst into the bay twenty feet below. His two companions hit the murky water seconds later. Swimming toward the bird—now thrashing futilely over the massive eight-pound fish—the two rats quickly pulled up beside their leader.

"You crazy?" Gray Tail said to Sailor. "Did you see the size of that gull?"

"What choice do we have? The warren is starving."

A large wave bore down on them. The three companions dived under it. When they surfaced, they were twenty feet from the gull.

"Leave now, and no one will get hurt," the gull warned them.

"Fan out," Sailor whispered to his friends. "We'll hit him from three sides."

In a loud voice he baited the gull: "Who says we want fish? Fresh breast of gull is what I crave. How about you, Long Nose?"

"I like the dark meat myself," Long Nose replied, circling around the gull.

"I'd rather fuck him first," Gray Tail said, approaching the gull's flank. "You haven't lived until you've had a piece of gull."

The bird was surrounded. Sailor sounded the attack call. The three rats leaped, shrieking at the bird. The gull rose, the wind from his thrashing wings chilling Sailor to the bone.

Sailor's mates each grabbed a gill and began towing the fish to shore. Sailor, dropping back, took the fish's tail in his teeth, and with a powerful back-kick, pushed from behind.

They gave it everything they had. An airborne gull is a terrifying foe, and this one had reason to hate them. They did not have to look up to know the gull was wheeling overhead, studying them.

They almost made it. They were so close to landfall that Sailor could hear the cheers on the docks from those rats strong enough to leave the warren and venture out onto the wharf. But then the gull struck, hitting Gray Tail like a threshing machine. His powerful talons snapped Gray Tail's neck, and his beak trepanned the rat's skull.

Sailor's response was instantaneous. Catapulting himself onto the gull's back, Sailor sunk his chisel-like incisors into the bird's heavy nape, searching for the spinal cord and neck arteries.

Gulls are powerful fliers, capable of hauling away fish up to twice their own body weight. Moreover, this was a huge gull with a massive three-foot wingspan.

To Sailor's dismay, he felt himself lifted high above the harbor—100, 150, then 200 feet—until his teeth found the cord, and he snapped the gull's neck.

The gull's pinions went limp, and both gull and rat hung momentarily above the bay.

Then the two of them dropped, slowly at first, then with heart-stopping velocity, plunging 200 feet and hitting the water like a hell-bound train.

8  Try Condoms

The limo that met Lydia Magruder's private jet at Reagan National Airport was one of the fleet that she kept in key cities around the world. Each car was bulletproof, resistant to rockets, and equipped to keep her in constant touch with her communications empire and the Citadel. The efforts to build a bulwark against what she increasingly viewed as "global hell" involved thousands of people and millions of details. Her life seethed with activity. Even in the quiet of the car, four TVs were tuned in to the major cable news networks; her e-mail in-box was filled, and she waited for a satellite patch through to Paris.

Ignoring the electronic assault for the moment, L. L. leaned back in the leather seat, staring tiredly at the dark streets and lighted monuments of Washington, D.C. Atlas had had the task of keeping the heavens and earth apart; Fate had put hell on her shoulders.

The appointment with President Haines and Secretary of Defense Jack Taylor was set for midnight that night in the Oval Office. Midnight, because it would guarantee that they had "quality time." She hated that expression. There was no such thing as quality time in her life. Her bedrooms—like her cars—were wired into the world's pulse. Most women her age rested on laurels in rocking chairs. If L. L. had had a rocking chair, it would have been equipped with a satellite phone, a modem, and a computer.

But the real reason the meeting had been set for the witching hour was the news media was less likely to spot the "Nuclear Noah" meeting with the president and the secretary of defense.

On one of the TV screens, the opening credits were rolling for Sister Cassandra's weekly show. Lydia listened to the music with its bluesy beat while she read the first of numerous messages on her laptop. The message was from the Citadel's preparedness coordinator. Lydia gave the machine shop techs an assignment to build a Massey Ferguson farm tractor from scratch. They wanted to know where they would get the rubber for tires. Lydia dictated a reply.

"I don't know. Try condoms. What did the world do before Mr. Dunlop started making condoms anyway?"

She punched "send" into the computer and started on the next message, a query from an art dealer in the Far East about a piece of Japanese art she was interested in acquiring.

Her pocket phone vibrated.

"Mom," Kate's voice said, "what are you doing in Washington?"

"Trying to get an elephant to turn around in a bathtub. But you shouldn't be in Mecca."

"I lead my own life. Anyway, this is about Stone."

"Anything suspicious?"

"There was something on that video—in his voice, in his eyes—that I hadn't noticed before. I think John is scared."

Lydia resisted the impulse to rail at her. "I hope John's okay. I love him as if he were my own prodigal son."

"You love Stone like a son? Yeah, uh-huh. Well, this time you may have sent him to his death. I'd hate to be your son. It's bad enough being your daughter."

Kate promply cut off her call, canceling L.L.'s scathing reply. Despite the fact that she controlled a global communications empire, people could still silence her by hanging up. In her rage, she took out her computer, shouting an e-mail back to Kate, reminding her that she had to be in New York in one week for an exposé on the treatment of lab animals. L. L.'s stepson Frank had come across a "scientist" who misused his grants and endowments to torture animals in the name of research. According to Frank, the man was stone-crazy—trapping rats at night on the Manhattan wharves—among other things. Animal rights was about the only thing that she and Kate didn't fight over, and L. L. offered the assignment to Kate as an excuse to get her daughter back in the States.

Lydia decided that when Kate and Frank were in New York together, she'd lure them back to the Citadel for safekeeping. That meant coming up with an excuse. Maybe she could tell them she was having health problems and would only let Frank examine her. She had been feeling dizzy lately, so it wasn't far from the truth. Lydia was overdue for a checkup, but she'd been too busy.

"And I'm too damn mean to die," she said to the TV screen as Sister Cassandra came on.

Sister Cassandra had endured a long convalescence at Lydia's ranch after being rescued from a Cuban gulag, thanks to Kate and John Stone.

There Cass began attending the Citadel's nondenominational church. Like people who speak in "tongues" during religious fervor, words flowed from Cassandra in the church, not babble but poetry and songs. Lydia had gone to the church just to look in on Cass. She found herself weeping as the nun sang. Kate had blamed L. L. for Cass's songs, saying that the nun had picked up her apocalyptic images through osmosis at the paranoia-saturated Citadel, but to Lydia the haunting songs were voices from God Himself.

She kept one eye on incoming e-mails as Cassandra performed for her worldwide audience.

 Who Says We're Not Dead?

At dawn, the SOSUS Straits were behind them. Captain Gargarin heaved a sigh. The straits were monitored by everything from recon satellites to hydrophones, but their run-silent, run-deep diesel motors had seen them through without a hitch.

The old and neglected Kilo-Class sub surfaced. In the conning tower Captain Gargarin and the Starpom listened to the engine with misgivings. They were anxious for the diesels to charge the big batteries. With their battery-powered E-motors they could run submerged again.

Captain Gargarin looked to the east. Sunrise flickered on the horizon. He would have liked to submerge immediately, but another half hour was needed to get the batteries up to full power.

The sun set the sea aflame. Captain Gargarin studied the fireball, amazed that it flamed so brilliantly but generated so little heat. At least this far north.

Then he spotted a speck emerging out of the blaze.

Squinting, he shouted into the horn: "Helicopter, port-stern, coming out of the sun."

"They just pinged our mast," the comm-officer responded.

"They say they're Russian," the radio officer reported in the captain's headset. "Some kind of antisub recon. They make us as an unidentified Russian vessel. They want to know who we are and what we're doing in the SORUS Straits."

Gargarin and the Starpom stared at each other a hard minute.

"They're getting serious, Captain. You better listen."

"Let's hear them," the captain said into his headset.

The radioman changed channels, and the Russian comm-officer in the chopper was barking orders.

"This is Bear One. We have been monitoring your progress for sixteen hours. You are way off the map. Order you to identify yourselves now. If you have radio or communications problems respond on your aft deck with semaphore. But you must respond."

"What should we do, sir?" the radioman asked.

Gargarin and his Starpom said nothing.

"You must identify yourselves. Otherwise, we will call in a patrol with attack subs. You can see the destroyers, starboard-bow."

"Sir?" the radioman asked.

"Clear decks," Gargarin said. "Ready to dive. Sound the alarms."

"Captain," the radioman said into Gargarin's headset, "listen to this."

"We are hunting a Kilo-Class crew that has disappeared from our sonar screens. We have reports that they are selling their nuclear-armed sub to a rogue nation. If you do not identify yourselves, if you submerge or attempt to run, we will declare you a rogue. We will track you and come after you. You cannot stay submerged forever."

"Starpom," the captain said, "carry out the orders."

"Clear decks! Clear bridge! Prepare to dive!" the Starpom shouted into his headset. The orders rang though the ship.

"Crash dive!" Gargarin roared.

The helicopter pilot's voice in Gargarin's headset:

"We have—for this operation—been allowed the use of local ports and air-bases. We will hunt you with attack subs and planes. Respond or we will fire. Respond or we will fire."

The captain slid down the bridge-ladder. The Starpom was slow getting out of his way and caught one of Gargarin's size 12 rubberized boots in the head. The ladder's chain and locking lever hammered Gargarin on the way down.

"Diving stations!" the Michman screamed through the speakers. "Flood all tanks! E-motors on! Shut down diesels!"

The racketing engines turned off. Gargarin heard a rumbling *whoosh!* in the stern tanks, and the ship, suddenly out of alignment, was diving at a steep bow-ward slant.

"The forward rush from the props is hitting the hydroplanes, sir," the Starpom said.

"Flood forward tanks five and six," Gargarin said. "Everyone not at a diving station, move forward."

The depth gauge turned quickly—100, 200, 300 meters. Then 340, 360.

"What's happening?" the navigator asked, joining them in the control room. He'd been down with dysentery and had gotten up from his sickbed.

"Sonar," the captain said.

"They have us bracketed," the Starpom said.

"Who?"

"The illustrious Russian navy," the Starpom said.

"They want us to surface."

"What do we do?" the navigator asked.

Gargarin and his Starpom stared at the depth gauge—430 meters.

The hydraulic systems were on the fritz, so men in the control room and other parts of the ship were grabbing overhead induction valve handles, swinging from them like apes as they struggled to get them open. Men spun hand-wheels furiously.

At last, with an explosive roar, air detonated from the buoyancy tanks, water thundered in, and the tanks resumed flooding.

But with the hydraulic systems down the tanks flooded erratically, the stern tanks barely flooding at all. With the sub's trim still out of alignment, the bow still slanted downward.

The hull now groaned and screamed with its sudden, agonizing compression. Men were slammed against bulkheads and handwheels, decks and hatchways. The navigator hurtled into a hatch-lock, ripping open his left cheek. Anything not locked or tied down hammered the men. Screwdrivers, drills, tape measures, hacksaws, levels, pliers, and wirecutters ricocheted around the compartment like shrapnel.

"The stern tanks still aren't flooded," the captain shouted to First.

First, bracing himself against the bulkhead, clung to a pipe. His head, cut by a flying sardine can, bled profusely; his nose was broken and swollen.

The captain shook him.

"Look," the captain shouted. "If we don't trim the stern, we all die. Valve, compressor, whatever it is, find someone to fix it!"

"Aye, aye, sir." First crawled down the steeply sloping deckplates toward the stern air compressor.

Gargarin and his Starpom climbed up the sloping deck toward the control room as the ship fell deeper into the sea.

At last, First reported back over the 1MC intercom: "Problem isolated, sir. Compressor valve repaired." The ballast tanks and the stern stabilized, the ship's descent slowed, and the depth gauge stopped spinning. Gargarin stared in shock as the gauge ticked off their descent—710, 720, 730.

"Sir," the Starpom said, "we're down to 730! This vessel is only guaranteed for 750."

Gargarin stared at the chief. The Michman entered, fear in his eyes.

"Sir, a vent burst in the forward torpedo room! We're taking water."

"Take her down, Starpom, all the way down."

"Sir, are you trying to kill us?" the Starpom asked in disbelief.

"Trying to get us into the basement," the captain said.

"Basement?" the navigator asked, slowly coming to.

"We're passing through a thermocline into the acoustical cellar. We can hide—"

But the Starpom never finished. A concussive blast struck the St. Petersburg as if a giant hand had slapped and upended her.

The crew and every object not tied or locked down crashed sternward. The depth gauge needle hit 750 and froze.

Its glass cover cracked, then shattered. The gauge's needle broke free. Another blast rocked the ship. In the engine room a man screamed over Gargarin's headset.

"Sir, the hull's warping! The batteries are leaking. We're getting gassed!"

"First, go see what's happening," Gargarin ordered.

"Chlorine," Gargarin said. "When battery acid leaks through the casing cracks and mixes with seawater, that's what you get. Destroys skin, lungs, eyes, everything."

"I'll get the oxygen masks," the Starpom shouted into his headset.

Another blast rocked them. The ship rang with the cry:

"Flooding!"

"Captain," First shouted over the 1MC intercom, "battery compartments 3, 4, and 7 are leaking. I have the men on air hoses and am bleeding their compartments."

"Roger, that," Gargarin acknowledged into the intercom. "Seal the compartments off, put that choline into the compression tanks, and dry them all out."

Gargarin pulled himself up onto the chart table and bolted to the deck. The chart, clipped on top, was bloodstained, but their grid was boxed.

"What's the grid say?" his Starpom asked.

"We're in a shallow-water canyon, 1,100 meters deep. Fairly narrow. It's amazing we haven't hit a canyon wall."

"Our angle of descent is too steep," said the Starpom. "We're diving bow-first almost straight down."

"Forty fucking degrees," Captain Gargarin said grimly.

"Brace yourselves, boys," the captain told them.

The forward ballast tank howled with the outrush of compressed air, then roared explosively with the incoming seawater that flooded the tank.

The ship began to right herself from a 40-degree angle.

"We're going to hit hard," the Starpom said quietly.

By Gargarin's estimate they were now just under 20 degrees and just over 1,100 meters in depth—twice the pressure hull's guaranteed limit.

They hit the canyon bottom so hard the ship bounced, hit again, then bounced twice more before at last coming to a rest.

When Gargarin came to, he saw the entire crew on the deck, several of them unconscious. The bilges were flooding, filling the decks with slime, reeking of shit, and the warped pressure hull was leaking.

The Starpom groaned. He was coming to.

"Captain," the Starpom asked, "why aren't we dead?"

Saltwater was rushing out of the engine room in a cataract toward the control room.

Gargarin shrugged. "Who says we aren't?"

10 Stone and a Hard Place

John T. Stone remembered dropping his whiskey flask in the middle of Mecca. He remembered the beautiful Islamic woman who had escorted him through the enraged mob. He also remembered saying: "Doesn't look good, does it?"

"You are between a stone and a hard place."

The mob was closing in, all eyes blazing in furious disbelief.

"This is the trouble you've been looking for all of your life."

He couldn't argue that one.

But then a phalanx of white-robed bodyguards had appeared: They surrounded Stone and the woman and hustled them outside to a stretch limousine. More bodyguards there—big, ugly, mean looking—armed with automatic weapons. The limo inched away from the scene of Stone's multiple transgressions. Rocks hammered the tinted, unbreakable windows.

Stone was going through his pockets beneath his robe.

"Looking for this?" The woman held up his crumpled plane ticket to Paris.

"Bless you."

"Perhaps not."

She then handed him the whiskey flask that he'd dropped on the floor of the Ka'ba. She had apparently sneaked it away beneath her robe. He stared at the flask approvingly, unscrewed the top, glanced at the woman—but of course she wasn't drinking—and upended the flask.

"Ah, that tastes like life itself."

"Mr. Stone, I believe you have a drinking problem," she said in a scolding tone of voice.

"I sure do. I'm thirsty as a hound dog in hell."

He didn't quit swallowing until he was sucking air.

"I think you need help."

"I sure do. I'm hollow to my heels."

Stone smiled agreeably.

But then he didn't feel so well.

He felt a strange stinging sensation in his side and noticed a strange aftertaste in his mouth.

He glanced back at the woman. The limousine slipped carefully through the mob, which cried for Stone's blood and balls. She seemed faintly amused by him, but he couldn't be sure. He was having a little difficulty keeping her beautiful face in focus.

"So, where are we going?"

He remembered asking that too.

Just before his head began to wobble and his vision failed him completely.

11 "Not the Homecomin' I 'Spected"

Breeze walked through the C-block rotunda under a storm of shit, spit, and garbage.

This was also not exactly Yankee Stadium. Nor were the men sliming them ballplayers and cheering fans but garishly tattooed psychos—in gang colors and head bandanas—who hung over the tiers, shouting obscenities.

"Yo, punk!" a man covered with tattooed swastikas shouted. *"You gonna be my pussy?"* He made kissy, sucking sounds.

"Bend yo' Cool Breeze butt over here, chump!"

"Head up, Cool Bitch. I hear you blow like the breeze."

Cool Breeze did struggle to keep his head up, show them some balls, what he was made of and ignore the hailstorm of slime and verbal abuse.

In his heart, however, it was different.

Oh, please, tell me this is a dream, he said to himself. *Wake up now, now. Why can't I wake up?*

His face remained impassive, a hardened mask of indifference. He showed them only "the Look," that famous Cool Breeze stare, which had seen him through eighteen years of the Houston ghettos, the Texas Syndicate–Blood-Crip drug wars, the gunfire streets, his own anger and terror and despair.

The Show too—six consecutive Series, three MVPs, more All Star Games than he could remember. And Cooperstown—the Hall of Fame, too.

Except for one stupid night in a Houston hotel room and three dead narcs.

Head and shoulders back, he made sure they all saw his eyes—eyes that neither asked nor gave—saw the gang street strut that yielded not an inch, the upper lip curled above the teeth, the sneer, the snarl, big-time, bad-time, everything he had, his boldest, shoulder-pumping, I'm-tall-tan-and-terrible, major league, six-fucking-consecutive-World-Series-rings, on and on through the slime-storm, under the deluge of obscene taunts, head back, eyes front, suck-on-this! Cool Breeze stroll.

"Yo, what's up, Sweet Thang!"

"That's my *Sweet Thang, muthafucka,"* a big convict in a tank top, *KKK* tattooed on his left shoulder, yelled as he pointed out one of the new fish.

"That my bitch butt."

They moved on, and, thankfully, Breeze was behind his tormentors now.

But inside he screamed: *Where did it go wrong? Where?*

But he knew where. Self-control, that's where it had gone wrong. He'd never had any. His old man, a Baptist minister—with a razor strap in one hand and the wrath of God on his lips—couldn't teach it to him. He'd been too wild, obsessed with the streets. The more frightening, the more dangerous, the more exciting it all was to Breeze.

He'd spent his entire life exalting in that wildness.

Until he'd joined the Yankees and met Colton and Stone.

Together, they'd had fast times, of course, but it was different with them. No one got hurt.

And they talked. They were—looking back on those times—the only friends he'd ever truly talked with. They'd talk not only about the things they wanted to do but why they wanted to do them.

Especially when Breeze acted crazy, started to fuck up. At those times Colt would say to him: "Why you want to do that, Breeze? You always gots to ask the why."

"I can tell you why," Breeze usually responded. "'Cause my whole life's fucked."

"That's easy to fix," Stone told him once.

"How you fix what's past?" Breeze asked, incredulous.

"You want to tell him, Colt?" Stone had said, smiling.

"You redeem the past," Colton said, "by redeemin' the future."

And Breeze went on to do just that. They all did. Together, they had a dream. The dream was to make their teams the greatest Yankee dynasty ever, to win as many back-to-back Series as possible. They each dreamed of being not only the best ballplayers but the best team players too.

Colton had been granted an extended leave from the U.S. Air Force to do just that.

Stone wanted one day to write, but he put that career off to pitch.

Colt reminded Breeze often how he must think of his future—his dream for the future.

"'Cause without a future, C. B., you ain't got a *present*," Colt would say.

No one had ever talked to Breeze like that.

In return he told them everything he felt—the craziness, the rage, his obsession with those drug-ridden gunfire streets, his crazy old man, criminal camp, juvie hall.

And the wildness in him—how sometimes it coursed through his veins like fire, scaring him.

"Never lose that wildness," Stone said. "You need the strength it gives you to do the important things I know you're going to do."

"Just don't go wastin' all that strength on stupid shit," Colt warned.

"I need the evil in me to do what's good?" Breeze once asked Stone in confusion.

"You can't discard your devils," Stone had said, "without throwing out your angels."

Six years with them and Breeze was doing just that—using the wildness in him to accomplish the important things. Winning six Series, three MVPs, hammering that Series-grandslam-home-half-of-the-ninth ball out of Yankee Stadium. Cooperstown a lock then. He'd cut back his drinking. Dope was a thing of the distant past. He even thought the wildness had become his friend.

Then that slick-ass agent talked him into free agency—leaving Colt and Stone for Houston and all that bread.

Back to the gangbanging homies who had survived, to the smoke and dope, the users and losers talkin' trash and drinkin' mash. The gunfire streets and them fine, fine ever-so-sweet 'n' funky bitches.

He floated for years on a river of flashing neon, wild women, and Cuervo shooters, wired to his eyeballs, his nose running like a river.

Injuries ended his career and he didn't even show up to his Hall of Fame induction.

Finally he hit bottom. Colt even brought him back to New York, put him up, got him into AA, went to meetings with him, stayed with him.

When he got back on his feet and got his own apartment, Colt and Stone called him day and night—endured his own late-night, all-night pit-of-hell calls without complaint, without criticism.

They were there for him.

And then . . . And then . . .

He went back to Houston one last time.

For one last score.

To the hotel.

And . . . the . . . three . . . dead . . . narcs.

Please, God, please, let me have those years back. Where's Stony and Colt? Let this all be a dream. Please.

He reached his cell. Double bunks, a Lilliputian sink, and lidless toilet. Instead of dressers or chests of drawers, there were two wall shelves and two foot-lockers.

On the upper bunk was Cue Ball, another Houston homey. His upper body was heavy with prison gym muscles, and his head was shaved bald as his namesake. He wore black Levi's and a matching tight tee shirt that read: "Don't Get Jacked in Jack Town."

"Took a dozen cartons of Kools to get us in the same cell."

"Thanks." Breeze gave Cue a hug. "'Spected an 800-pound gorilla."

"Couldn't let *that* happen."

"Couldn't let what happen, bitch?"

The voice was loud, deep.

Breeze whirled around.

"You scare easy," Leon said.

Leon also was from Breeze's set.

"Damn," Breeze said, "they locked up the whole hood."

"They got a few of us," Deuce acknowledged, entering the cell.

"What happen to you?" Cue said to Deuce. "Get stuck in a revolvin' door? You ain't outta here six months."

"Come back to build up my health," Deuce said.

"Git cold sleepin' under them bridges," Leon said wryly.

"Not the homecomin' I 'spected," Breeze said.

"Ain't none of us 'spected it," Cue said.

"Least of all, Breeze here," Leon said.

"From MVP to triple-life," Deuce said.

Breeze flopped gloomily on a bunk.

Leon dragged him back to his feet.

"Yo!" Cue said. "You ain't got time to snooze. You goin' on a job interview."

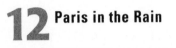

12 Paris in the Rain

HOTEL ESMERALDA | PARIS, FRANCE

Kate Magruder sat down at a French Provincial mahogany writing table facing her hotel window. She had taken a hot bath. She had on a terry-cloth bathrobe, with a towel wrapped around her head. A glass of Veuve Clicquot and a dish of beluga caviar with toast points sat next to her Mac. The cloth robe kept some of the warmth of the bath from fading.

She clicked onto the shortcut to MTN's data bank. Like everything her mother owned, the network's information network was the best in the world. Stories from every news agency on earth. Reports in fifty languages were translated into rough-form literal English.

"Mad Vlad," she said as she typed his name, "you are first on my list. Has to be more to your sudden conversion to the True Faith than true faith."

And where is Stone?

The Russian minister of defense generated so many news stories the data bank had a table of contents. Not sure of exactly what she was looking for or where to start, Kate first tapped into his personal history to update herself on his background. She speed scrolled through the information.

Vlad had risen from the ranks to fleet admiral of Russia's nuclear submarine force, in part because he had been smart enough to get doctorates in nuclear physics and naval warfare. He'd been first in his class at the Naval Warfare Institute in Russia and had attended graduate seminars at both MIT and Los Alamos.

He was regarded as Russia's premier authority on U.S. strategic policy.

"Somewhere along the line your brain did a China Syndrome," Kate told Mad Vlad's computer-generated image, which smirked at her.

She clicked the table of contents, found reference to nuclear thefts, and pulled up those stories.

They read like a high-tech thriller—missing bombs, vanished subs, disappearing plutonium and uranium.

They raised the hair on the back of her neck, and she took a sip from her glass of champagne.

Now, don't start thinking like L.L.

In the latest Mad Vlad news story, Vlad claimed he had broken the back of the nuclear black market by capturing the entire ring responsible for the thefts.

The lot of them had been killed trying to escape. The FBI was seriously miffed. The Bureau had asked to assist, had wanted to question the thieves.

"Doing a little cover-up?" she asked Mad Vlad, who was now announcing on-screen that the Russian government had been "cheated out of an expensive trial by a band of 'Nuclear Cossacks' who'd had the poor judgment to get themselves shot."

"Who are you kidding?" she asked Vlad's computerized image.

Rumor had Vlad lining his deep pockets with kickbacks and protection money, and official Washington had always considered Vlad a fool who could be bought. John Stone, however, had a different take on the man: "People thought Khrushchev was a buffoon when he took off his shoe and pounded on the podium at the United Nations. But it was all a show, and he longed to scourge those weapons from God's good earth."

Kate scrolled down through Vlad's announcement that he had converted to Islam and was going on a pilgrimage to Mecca.

"Give me a break, Vlad," she said after a sip of champagne.

But who could tell—maybe the guy had gotten religion. It wouldn't be the first time holy lightning struck in odd places. It happened all the time on death row.

The feeling that she had passed over something important teased Kate. She tapped the champagne glass against her front teeth as she tried to retrieve the fleeting data.

She scrolled back through the news stories until she found it. President Ali al-Haddad of Dar-al-Suhl had made a goodwill visit to Moscow last month. While there he had his picture taken on the steps of St. Basil's with the Russian president and Mad Vlad. As she stared at the picture, she realized it wasn't the three men who caught her eye but two young women discreetly to the right of President Haddad. The picture caption identified them as Haddad's sisters. Other than the fact they were young, probably in their late twenties, and dressed modestly with black scarves over their heads, the picture told her little.

But something about their eyes . . .

She pulled up Ali's file and skimmed it. She was vaguely familiar with his background. Dar-al-Suhl was a small Middle Eastern country near Turkey with a bellyful of oil and a Persian Gulf port. The general's rise to power through a bloody military coup—during which he executed virtually every significant opposition leader—was the stuff of legends in his region. Haddad's suppression of internal dissent remained swift and unforgiving. He was routinely excoriated by Amnesty and Human Rights Watch.

In the Mideast, however, Ali was famous as a moderate and a moderator, stepping into the role once played by the late King Hussein of Jordan—that of the region's peacemaker. President Haines described him as "America's quiet ally," and praising him as "a savior" after Ali had personally broken OPEC's yearlong oil embargo—an embargo that had brought several nations to their economic knees. By agreeing to ship oil to the United States, he'd personally pulled America out of what would have been a new record-setting recession.

"Saved your tush, buddy-boy," Kate said under her breath to a photo of President Haines.

She scrolled to a picture of the Dar-al-Suhl flag. "Dar-al-Suhl" meant "Domain of Peace" in English, and the flag's insignia was a white sword-impaled crescent moon embracing a bright gilded star. Kate remembered seeing a limousine in Mecca with that insignia. Those symbols were common as wind and sand within that region.

Still, like the picture of Ali's sisters, the insignia subtly disturbed her.

Kate speed-scrolled until she found the sisters' names: Sabrina and Sultana. She typed them in. The information that came up was always in connection to foreign visits. Usually the women were with Ali. There were few details. The press releases implied they were only slightly less pious than their brother, who apparently raised the dead and walked on water when he wasn't advising Allah, Mohammed, and the Heavenly Choir. A typical release praised the sisters as "shining examples of piety, modest, and charity" and as "paragons of Islamic womanhood."

"Whatever the fuck that means," Kate muttered.

In plain fact, there was almost nothing to go on. Surprisingly few photos and little information on either of them. Like Haddad, they apparently traveled incognito—and favored PR flacks who kept their names out of the news.

But she tracked down one more photo of the girls. They were in Washington at a banquet given by President Haines in honor of their brother. The women were still draped in modest head scarves, but again, those eyes . . .

"You ask me," Kate told the photo, "there's something rotten in Dar-al-Suhl."

Kate scrolled through the most recent entry on the three and did a double take. The U.S. military was putting on an air show near Istanbul. The high and mighty B-2 Stealth bomber—dubbed variously by L. L. as "the Nuclear Crow" and "our Thermonuclear Assassin"—was to be the star of the show. Air Force General Larry Taylor, son of Defense Secretary Jack Taylor, was in charge.

Kate took her champagne glass to the window, stared out at Paris in the rain. Her mother wouldn't have objected if she had taken the most expensive suite in the Hotel Ritz, but her favorite Paris hotel was the small and quaint Esmeralda on the Left Bank. The Esmeralda overlooked the garden of Saint Julian le Pauvre, Notre Dame, and the Seine. Street lamps lit the deepening dusk and the rain pointillistically along the narrow streets below and the river to the north as if they'd been painted by Monet or Seurat.

She returned to her computer, scrolled to a photo of Larry Taylor. No doubt about it, the boy was a hunk. Nice personality too. Even though he was a man of action, Larry had always reminded her of her stepbrother, Frank. She'd met Larry Taylor a couple of times at D.C. parties, clicked enough with him to have drinks afterward. There was always something urgent pulling them away from each other. Still, there was an undeniable attraction.

Kate felt she had just won the Triple Crown.

First to Turkey, talk her way into a flight in the world's deadliest weapon so she could do a story on it, then renew her acquaintanceship with a hunk.

And she could be back in New York in time to Save the Whales with Frank. What more could a girl ask for?

Still, she sighed. Stone's video would not let her alone.

She returned to the window, poured more champagne, and studied the river.

13 A Goat Rope, Two State Fairs, and Big Trucks

Brigadier General Henry Colton, USAF—like his former teammate, Ronald "Cool Breeze" Robinson—also wanted to be someplace else.

Anywhere he did not have to babysit Howard Harrington.

But he had no choice. TV's hottest anchor and biggest booster of the space program, Harrington's status with NASA and the USAF was that of a near deity. Colton was under orders to "wine and dine" him.

"Tell me all about the wild times you, Breeze, and Stone had in New York. Why did you quit baseball after only six years? Off the record—code of the journalistic profession. We're more discreet than priests."

Colton stared at Harrington—at his wicked grin, ruddy complexion, and ferret face. Colton didn't like the man or the fact he wore a NASA flight uniform he hadn't earned the right to wear. He didn't like the way Howard needled almost everyone he talked to.

And Colton wasn't suited to this assignment. The fastest-rising African-American general since Colin Powell, it wasn't his place to babysit assholes. But NASA, the air force, and, worse, Lydia Magruder had requested that he "be nice to Harrington."

"Priest?" Colton said, still blank-faced. "Do you also grant absolution?"

"That have something to do with oral sex?"

"It's less fun."

"Too bad." Harrington grinned.

"I quit baseball to fly fighters," Colton said.

"Shouldn't lie to your priest, kid," Harrington said. "It's a mortal sin."

"No lie," Colton said. "I night-hopped off a carrier in a Tomcat once with a hell of a pilot. He had to land it later that night in a fog, and I knew then and there what I was born to do. Knocking down batters in the Show wasn't even a close second."

"You did dust off a few."

"When they leaned in on my low-and-away."

"But you still hit them—with a 104-mile-an-hour fastball."

Colton stared absently at his large dark hands.

"Like to think they hit themselves," Colton said finally.

Harrington treated Colton to a manly laugh.

"Okay, now this is for the record," Harrington said. "Do you fly jets as well as you pitched?"

"Better."

"Anyone ever take you in a dogfight? Cut your arc, ream your six?"

"You know Larry Taylor? Blackjack's son? He almost did once. His little brothers, Jamie and William, they've come close. They're wild men."

"Sound like my kind of guys."

"They can fly. I'll give them that. Of course, they had a good teacher."

"Who was that?"

"Their older brother, Larry."

"How'd he get so good?"

Colton gave Harrington a slow smile. "Me."

"Okay, flying jets is your highest high," Harrington said. "What's your lowest low?"

"Seeing Cool Breeze Robinson go down for triple murder."

"Or was it all the money you dropped on his defense? What'd you lay out? Two mill?"

"Wasn't that," Colton replied.

The TV anchor smirked.

No, Colton never gave a shit about money. Stone didn't either, not ever, which was why he'd been unable to contribute. For years since the Yankees, Stone'd given his money away to groups like Amnesty and PEN or had blown it launching crusades that were supposed to save the world, wasting his resources chasing rumors. Breeze was the brokest of all—fleeced by bad managers, the IRS, and four ex-wives. The rest had bankrolled his midlife coke habit. Colton was the only one who'd saved and invested his big-league earnings. His net worth was well into the eight figures, and the two mill he'd spent on Breeze didn't trouble him.

Visiting Breeze in County, that was different. Talking to him through Plexiglas windows on that telephone, seeing him returned in chains to an iron cage—that had been the hard part, the lowest of the lows . . .

"Breeze and John Stone were the closest friends I ever had. They still are."

"Well, I hope you aren't planning any political careers. Bankrolling Breeze's defense wasn't the most popular thing a potential presidential candidate could have done."

"I helped him out of principle. Some things you do for principle. Principle, Mr. Harrington. Ever heard of it?"

Harrington groaned. "General, this is Howard Harrington you're bullshitting. I've covered wars, hurricanes, mine explosions. I've been to a goat rope, two state fairs, Bangkok orgies, and I drove big trucks. I've hung out with Mad Vlad Malokov, so I know bullshit like squirrels know trees. You don't want to tell me why you really gave up eight big ones a year, go ahead. Be a prick. You want to tell me your lowest low is watching a three-time cop-killer get his, okay? But don't think you're getting over on me."

Colton smiled, looking through the man. Harrington didn't like it. He got out a sharper knife. "What's the woman's name, the one up there on the Odyssey space station?"

"Sara Friedman. She's the principal architect of Alpha/Omega, the ship's Nervous System."

"Nervous System?"

"Its Neural Engine—the network of Fly-Eye Recon-Sats and superworkstations linked to its mainframe."

"Oh, a fuckin' computer? Big deal."

Colton smiled slightly. "A/O's more decentralized. It's more analogous to the way a biological brain's neuron network operates. The sats and workstations multiply A/O's processing power by shuttling data one to another."

"So Odyssey's only woman is an acne-faced computer geek."

"She's also a brigadier general in the Israeli army."

"A nerd with an Uzi," Harrington sneered.

"She's actually quite attractive."

Which was what Harrington had wanted to hear. "Maybe I should grant her some absolution."

"You clearly have never worked on a space station."

"The libido won't function in zero G?" Harrington looked crestfallen.

"It doesn't have time. They work us up there like government mules."

"You and Sara what's-her-name," Harrington said. "All work, no play. I'm supposed to buy that? What's your relationship with her really like? We're both big boys. You can—"

An air force lieutenant general named Moore joined them in Harrington's room. He had chiseled, unforgiving features and silver-gray hair. He wore wire-rimmed eyeglasses and looked as solemn as a boiled owl. He glanced at Harrington and shook his head, disapprovingly.

"Better get some sleep. You're going to be pulling several g's tomorrow."

"I'll be fine," Harrington said with blithe arrogance.

"He's covered wars, hurricanes, mine explosions, a goat rope, two state fairs, Bangkok orgies," Colton repeated.

"I've been to a hog roast, a hog ranch, and I busted broncs on the Big Bend. Hell, I'll ride that firecracker of yours—spur him on the hairy side, ride him to a standstill."

Lieutenant General Moore stared at Harrington, saying nothing.

"He thinks he's tough," Colton finally explained.

Harrington got up and left the room for the head.

Moore rubbed his temples and groaned.

"You guys wanted him," Colton said.

"Our commander in chief wanted him. Lydia Magruder—the Odyssey's majority stockholder—wanted him. They said this would be 'a publicity bonanza for the space program.' The president said: 'It'll be bigger than John Glenn's return to space.'"

Now it was Colton's turn to groan.

14 The Wanderratte

A wizened old rat with gray fur, gray whiskers, and the biggest incisors anyone had ever seen listened quietly while Sailor told his story. The ancient patriarch nodded sagely and wrinkled his nose.

"You did the right thing," Socrates told the younger rat. "Jumping free at the last second saved you. If you had crashed with the bird you would have been smashed."

"The sea felt like a brick wall."

"Which did not damage your appetite a whit."

Only the fish scales remained, and Sailor had indeed eaten his fill. The feast in the main chamber, Old Socrates had assured him, was the finest in his long memory.

The two friends exited the big hall, then threaded through the maze of runways that took them out of the warren. They could have exited into the abandoned warehouse to the rear of the old wooden wharves or onto the pilings under the docks at the waterline. The tide was at ebb, the pilings dry, so it might have been pleasant down there. But tonight the sky was clear, the wharves empty.

"I want to feel the breeze, smell the sea, touch the stars," Socrates said with the nostalgia of the old ones.

They exited onto the docks.

"Grandfather," Sailor said, "tell me again how the great ship with the vast furnaces and black smokestacks blew apart. How you were set adrift in a boat with a man lost and alone, how the man sang to you?"

"It was a great grain ship that steamed out of Athens, Greece, the city of my birth. It was winter. Rounding the Cape of Good Hope, I thought I would freeze. I didn't thaw out till we reached a place called Bora Bora, where I sweated and thought I would die from the heat. Then we sailed into a hurricane, which tore the ship in two. I swam through storm-tossed seas—waves as high as trees—until one wave bore me up and cast me into the rubber raft. That is where I met the sailor—the one I named you after—the one who serenaded me."

The ancient patriarch cleared his throat, while Sailor shut his eyes and listened. In a high melodic voice, the old rat sang Sailor's song.

"I cannot rest from travel
I will drink life to the lees
All times I have enjoyed

Have suffered, greatly suffered
Both with those who loved me
And alone on shore.

"I am become a name for always roaming
With a hungry heart. Much have I
Seen and known. Cities of men and manners,
Climates, councils, cities, governments.
Myself not least but honored of them all.
I have drunk delights of battle with my peers
Far on the ringing plains of windy Troy.
I am a part of all whom I have met.

"Come, my friends, 'tis not too late
To seek a newer world.
For my intention holds to sail
Beyond the sunset and the baths of all
The western stars before I die,
To follow knowledge like a sinking star . . ."

Sailor slowly opened his eyes.

"The song is so beautiful, Grandfather. I think of it often."

"On that raft we had no water, no food save for a few flying fish, which he shared with me. And we knew loneliness.

"Alone, alone, all all alone
Alone on a wide, wide sea.
And never a saint took pity
On my soul in agony."

"I've heard of lands where men loathe our clans," Sailor said.

"I have been on such ships. Unlike the Hindu of Mumbai—who revere the way of Karma and of Krishna, who honor our innate holiness—many men hunted us in the vilest manner with lethal baits, predatory beasts, and hideous traps."

"But not the man in the boat?" Sailor asked.

"Never. He knew the sacred spirit that flows through all things. You too will find your spirit-guide, your Pallas Athena."

"The old salt taught you well, did he not? He sang a song about that quest too."

The patriarch rat again cleared his throat.

"Oh, wedding-guest, this soul hath been
Alone on a wide, wide sea,

So lonely that it scarce did seem
That God Himself could be.

"And so farewell, but this I tell
To thee, thou wedding-guest.
He prayeth best who loveth best
Both man and bird and beast.
He prayeth best who loveth best
All things both great and small.
For the dear God, Who loveth us,
He made and loveth all."

"Why do others not understand this, as we do here?"

"Fearing life, they lust after death. They worship death."

"Are men evil?" Sailor asked.

"I have known men who would kill stars if they saw them fall."

"All creatures die," Sailor said. "Rats too."

"Which you must not close your eyes to—not now. The warren is dying. Sickness burns through us like fire."

"The does are too sick to breed. The bucks are too weak to forage."

"That is why you must leave. On the raft I envisioned a noble sailor-rat, one who would cross the seas, face the Cyclops and the Sirens, fly with eagles, and swim with the creatures of the deep and ultimately redeem us all. When you rode the gull, I knew why I had named you Sailor. You are the one."

"But Grandfather, I love the warren."

"An admirable society of near-equals. Unless sick or starved, we live in peace. We do not murder, rape, or torture as men do."

"The warren is everything to me."

"The Plague will kill us all—except you. A harbor ship will save you."

"I cannot reject my warren, my clan."

"You cannot deny your destiny."

"A rat alone dies."

"I've dreamed your destiny; it is to wander."

"And face the wrath of men?"

"Some have beautiful souls. You will learn this."

Sailor stared at his mentor in silence.

"You have never disappointed me, my son," Old Socrates said. "You will not now."

Once Sailor had seen a man's eyes fill with water and sob. Had Sailor been granted the boon of tears he would have filled his own eyes with water vast as the sea and racked the world with his sobs.

Instead, he nuzzled his mentor's nose.

"Farewell, old one," he said softly. "I go forth in the silence and the night to forge anew the future of our race."

Sailor clambered up to a dockside piling, pushed off with a splendid kick into a graceful arc, and dived into the sea.

He swam toward the ship without looking back.

15 Violently Voluptuous, Murderously Lurid, Shockingly Apocalyptic

L. L. was in her hotel room attempting to catch a nap and was just about to fall asleep when her cell phone rang. Only a half-dozen people in the world had access to that number, and no one called her late at night unless it was critically important.

Perhaps someone had found Stone. "Yes?"

She was greeted by a loud, long maniacal laugh.

"Lydia, it's an old friend. As they say in the whorehouse, 'How's tricks?'"

It was Vladimir I. Malokov.

"Not too good, Vlad," L. L. said. "John Stone's disappeared in the Mideast. Kate never listens to a thing I say. I'm growing old against my will. The world, for whatever it's worth, is going to hell."

"Anything the old Vladster can do to help?"

"You could track down whoever it is in Russia that's pirating Sister Cassandra's shows, broadcasting them illegally, and violating her copyrights. Throw them in the gulag and see that we get paid. In American dollars, not whatever confederate currency you're fronting today."

"Ah, but then I'd have to lock *myself* up and pay that fortune in royalties out of my own pocket."

"I wish you hadn't told me that."

Actually, she had figured as much. While his brilliance and expertise in both global strategic policy and international nuclear terrorism were beyond dispute, everything else about him was cast in dark shadows. His temper was legendary, and his past was riddled with murky accounts of aggravated assault and alleged killings. He reportedly ran his vast financial empire—Malokov Manufacturing— less as a CEO and more like a Russian mafia don. In fact, many of his board directors were reputed to be drug-lord mafyioski. Business competitors routinely complained of his business tactics—which included blackmail, extortion, theft, torture, even murder.

"A little secret, Lydia, I'm your and Cassandra's biggest fan. In fact, I'm following your example. I've expanded my already-monumental holdings in vodka, oil, steel, and coal productions to include show business. Radio, television, publishing, music, movies."

"Movies?"

"Granted, my first films have been—how do you call them?—S-M porn flicks, but that's only due to a dearth of good scripts, a problem I'm currently addressing. In any event, our first superstar-entertainer isn't a porn star. She's a dead ringer for your own Sister Cassandra. I swear you can't tell the difference. Even sings like her."

Mad Vlad in the Sister Cassandra business? she thought grimly.

There was a sort of logic to it. Like Cassandra—and herself—he was viewed in many circles as "a partisan of the apocalypse." A translator of William Burroughs and Hunter Thompson, his sense of humor was maniacally macabre. He thought Armageddon was especially hilarious.

"Well, you are going to owe Cassandra and me royalty money," L. L. said. "Can't wait to see the legal fees you'll incur when we sue you for pirating her copyrights."

"L. L., I can see you haven't had much experience with the Russian legal system. You'll find collecting debts here is a little stickier than in the States. Especially when you try suing the wealthiest man in that country—*c'est moi!*"

"Speaking of which, Vlad, I'm about to meet with our own secretary of defense, Jack Taylor. He's also had some problems with you. I was disturbed by what he's said to me."

"I'd be disturbed too, kiddo, if I had a weak-kneed limp-dick lamebrain like Jack 'Jack-Me-Off-O-Vich-Till-I-Shake-And-Twitch' Taylor running Defense."

She shuddered at the profanity . . . at Vlad's insulting foul mouth.

. . . She recalled when Vlad and Taylor almost got into a fistfight. Defense Secretary Taylor once shouted at him in a rage across an arms convention summit: "How would you like it if I stepped across this platform and shut your mouth for you?"

*Vlad had responded with his famous condescending smirk—then thundered back: "And how would you like it if I turned New York, the Windy City, the Twin Cities, 'I Left My Heart in San Francisco' city, Graceland, Disneyland, Sea World, Wayne's World, and your butt-ugly Houston Astrodome into . . . **thermonuclear parking lots?***"

And Taylor left the podium, shaking.

"He told me that you've been making calls late at night, Vlad."

"Forgive me my fun and games. I can't help it if Jack brings out the closet scientist in me."

"Closet sadist, I understand," L. L. said, nonplused. "Scientist? No."

"You couldn't be more wrong. I've always had this burning curiosity to see how things worked. Take flies. What makes them buzz? As a boy, I'd trap one in a bottle and study it closely. Eventually, I'd remove the wings, legs, feelers, and so on with tweezers—just to see what made it tick. Of course, I never learned what made it buzz, but on the other hand, that fly . . . *didn't get around so good anymore!*"

Vlad's deranged laughter made L. L. cringe. When his laughter finally ended, she said: "Vlad, when John Stone introduced us three years ago in Moscow, you were . . . eccentric . . . but you were also brilliant. We were impressed with your grasp of global economics and arms control. Now you sound like a braying fool. What happened? Are you off your lithium?"

"With good reason, L. L. It interfered with my violently voluptuous, murderously lurid, shockingly apocalyptic *sex life!* And did you know that while on lithium, *you aren't supposed to drink*?"

Lydia fought to maintain her self-control as he roared. She was determined not to let him get to her.

"Vlad, how can I rest knowing you have your finger on Russia's nuclear trigger?"

"The tensions in this line of work are killing me. Which is not a problem as long as I have my blond, blue-eyed Slavic beauties. Which is why I need my vodka—two liters a day minimum," he whined, then exploded again with laughter.

No lithium? Two bottles a day of vodka? Even so, that didn't explain everything about Vlad's outrageous behavior. He was still popular in Mother Russia—due, L. L. believed, to his wealth and exercise of raw political power—but his critics in the foreign press were now on the attack. "A blond Anti-Christ," one journalist had recently dubbed him. He was *handsome, possessed of a certain rough charm. But he could no longer keep his temper or his wolfish leer under control.*

In the latest news clips you could see madness in his eyes. And then there was his conversion to Islam.

"Maybe you should go back to your doctor," L. L. said.

"No way, girlchik. I've been down that road with him. Twenty years ago he sat me down and said: 'Vladimir, if you continue your drinking, whoring, and brawling you'll never live to be forty.' I'm through with his guilt-tripping, mind-fucking moralizing."

"You badly need to see him."

"No-can-do."

"Why not?"

"He's . . . *dead!*"

Vlad's laughter rang in Lydia's ears like hell-forged bells in a satanic requiem.

16 Jumping Up and Down

Captain Gargarin, under auxiliary lighting, worked the line like a deck ape, lugging jerry cans of bilge from the stern foretanks. The diesel sub's bow, buried in the muddy base of the Reykjanes Ridge, was canted at a nineteen-degree angle. Every ounce of surplus ballast was being transported to the upended stern.

The hull shrieked and groaned unceasingly with radical compression.

For the past half hour a second line—the corpse detail—hauled the seven men killed in the dive up to the bow. After the bodies were secured in the forward compartments, they moved anything else they could pick up to the bow. Then they began a bucket brigade, carrying more jerry cans of water from the forward to the stern bilges.

The air was full with human waste and chlorine gas. The CO_2 scrubbers—damaged during their crash dive—did little to improve the air quality. Still, Gargarin and his men struggled uphill while their ship tottered back and forth like a rocking chair.

Even the bloodied, seasick navigator worked alongside them.

"What happened?" he asked. "Have they located us yet?"

"No way," the Starpom said. "We're in the acoustical cellar. There's too much sediment. It's too cold."

"Also too much salt," Gargarin said. "Salt is heavier than water, and a disproportionate amount gravitates to the ocean floor, making the water heavier. Along with the mud, silt, and crosscurrents, salt disrupts their sonar systems."

"You mean the bottle's half-full, not half-empty," said the navigator hopefully.

"Half-full of strychnine," the captain said.

"Let's hope the CO_2 scrubbers hold out," the Starpom said.

"They're gone," the captain said. "If chlorine doesn't kill us, CO_2 will."

"Sir," a bosun's mate said to the captain, handing him a jerry can of water, "this is the last one. The forward bilges are nearly dry."

"Round up the men," the captain said, "and move them to the stern."

The twenty-eight surviving crew members clambered uphill to the stern engine and torpedo compartments. Gargarin stood by the hatchway, separating the two stern compartments. The stern was not moving.

"Men," Gargarin told them, "our best guess is that the bow is stuck in the mud. If we'd hit a calcified ridge, we'd all be dead. The Starpom is going up to the control room. He will attempt to blow the forward ballast tanks. Then we will jump up and down."

The crew stared at their officers.

"Even if we get loose from the mud," the captain said, "our stern will find itself abutted against a ridge. Our sonar has pinged it at point-blank range. To get free of the ridge we will blow our dead comrades out the forward torpedo tubes. The force of the blowing tubes will hopefully explode us out of the mud."

"Captain," the Starpom called out over the speaker system, "the men can jump at will."

For the badly battered crew—dog-tired from eighteen hours of heavy lifting, weak from hunger, hypoxia, and stress, waterlogged and shit-stained—jumping up and down required almost superhuman effort.

Gargarin had to threaten and cheer them on by turns.

"Come on," he shouted, "get those knees up. Jump, jump—here, like me. There, Kamenov, look at him. He's bouncing like a pogo stick. Like him, boys! Your lives depend on it!"

Slowly, the boat began to rock.

"Harder!"

An explosive blast of compressed air blew the water out of the forward ballast tanks.

Slowly, the bow disengaged from the mud bank with a loud slurping, sucking noise. The stern grudgingly settled.

"We're free of the mud but lodged against the ridge wall," the Starpom confirmed. "Time to fire those stern torpedo tubes."

Each man wrapped a corpse in a life preserver, then dragged it toward the torpedo tubes. They shoved the bodies headfirst into the two forward tubes, then slammed and dogged the hatches shut.

Gargarin trudged back to the control room. He said over the speaker system:

"If this works, I want no cheering or shouting. We still have predators above. We may hope the dead bodies will convince them their depth charges got us. Gunnery Officer, blow the forward tubes. Starpom, immediately afterward blow the stern ballast tanks and start the e-motors."

The tubes blew with a shuddering *whoosh!* followed by an explosive roar. The e-motors groaned, ground, whined, then caught and started up with a soft harmonic hum.

Grudgingly, the ship moved.

Starpom had hooked up an auxiliary depth gauge, and its needle began to turn.

750, 725, 700.

While the double hulls popped in agony.

The crew stood at their stations, silent.

"Sir, I've done some weather computation," the navigator whispered to Gargarin. "That hurricane the weather channel was warning everyone about? By my computations it's directly overhead."

The four friends walked along a tier of cells.

"Jack Town ain't no kiddie joint," Cue said. "Fuck up here, they bury yo' ass."

"Suckas here," Leon said, "take yo' roll, yo' stash, yo' bitches, yo' partners, yo' homies, yo' hide, yo' balls."

Leon pointed to the overhead catwalk. Someone had spray painted the words: *Don't Git Jacked in Jack Town.*

"See it on the walls, ceilings, doors, and floors," Leon said. "Cue wear it on his tee shirt. Words to live by."

"Sound like we be at war with the whole fuckin' joint," Breeze said.

"Whole fuckin' world," Cue said.

"Not if you got partnas with weight," Leon said.

"And a hustle," Double Deuce said. "Something to deal with and from."

"You deal or you die," Leon said.

"You gonna get me a job?" Breeze asked, dubious.

"No, we gonna introduce you to 'Deep Six' Washington," Double D said. "D. S. run the store, dope, who'es, name it."

"Coldest stroll in Jack Town," Cue said. "They be suckas on the moon, he the baddest muthafucka there too."

Prisons are never quiet, but during daylight the cacophony is deafening. Chains slamming cell doors, belching, coughing, toilet-flushing, endless verbal abuse.

"*Yo, bitch, when you giv'n me that pussy?*"

"*I got yo' pussy—stick pussy.*"

"*I'm the Great White Hope. That what I am.*"

"*Great White Hope? My pussy so long I use it for **a jump rope!***"

"*Got yo' mama's pussy, bitch.*"

"*Seen yo' mama walkin' down the street with a mattress on her back yellin' curb service.*"

"*Just 'cause yo' wh'oe bitch mama suck my dick in a phone booth don't make her no **call girl**.*"

"*Who stole my pussy? You can guess. His mama ride shotgun on my pony express!*"

Breeze's friends met the gaze of any cons they passed, but, he noted, they avoided eye contact with the men in blue.

"Hacks be the sworn enemy," Cue explained to Breeze.

"Even the black screws?" Breeze asked. "What happened to race solidarity?"

"That shit died with Malcolm X and Nigga King."

"Black definitely ain't beautiful in Jack Town."

A black screw in a blue uniform passed them.

"Handle's Hardball," Cue said. "Used to bang himself. Now he hate bangers worse'n KKK. Hardest hammer in this mill."

"We got guards used to bang?"

"Crips, Bloods, Sixties, KKK, AB, Disciples, Nuestra Familia, Texas Syndicate," Deuce-Deuce said.

"Where you think they get them screws?" Cue asked. "Military? Ain't no more draftee armies, and soldiers today too slick to hack. More money with Blackwater 'n' shit."

"They git them screws off the streets?" Breeze asked. "Just like us?"

"Some of them *are* us," Deuce said.

The cacophony continued on:

"What's poppin', bitch?"

"Pop yo' bitch-ass."

"Whatcha do? Shit yo' fool self? Mix some water in it, sucka."

"I send yo' ass outta here in plastic."

"I thought we was partnas."

"Pussy partnas."

At the corner they faced the tier gate guard.

"We here to see D. S."

The guard turned the spike. The wheels and pulleys turned. The three friends passed through the gate.

"They particular who they let in," Cue said, "'cause D-block so bad. But the hack on D. S.'s payroll."

More blaring jungle boxes, more screech of pulleys, wheels, and chains. A whole new torrent of taunts and curses. Then, as they walked on, the noise subsided. The last part of the tier was almost silent.

They stopped. Breeze saw a man seated in a solitary cell, reading. Tall and slim, he was decked out in black slacks, black Nike high-tops, and a black silk tank top. He wore his hair in a medium Afro with a black sweatband around his forehead.

The book was *Under the Volcano,* by Malcolm Lowry. The man put it aside and looked at his visitors.

"Book any good?" Leon asked.

"Drunk crackas in Mexico. Don't make no sense to me."

"D. S., this be our homey, Breeze."

"Knew it from the the black hole." He pointed to his cell TV.

Breeze noted he did not smile, offer any greeting or gang-sign.

"Whatcha good at, Breeze?" D. S. asked in a soft voice.

"I'm a dead fastball hitter. Hit sliders, cutters, and splits damn good."

"Catch like a muthafucka," Cue said.

Breeze nodded his agreement. "Read batters from their stance and swing."

"Rifle arm," Leon said.

"Once hit second from a dead squat," Breeze confirmed.

"Not much call for that in Jack Town," D. S. said.

"Good-lookin' muthafucka," Cue said. "Think we got ourselves a natural-born pimp."

D. S. shrugged. "Have Slow Hand show him Queen's Row. What Hand don't know 'bout the mackin' game ain't worth knowin'."

"Best believe," Leon said, smiling.

The four friends took off toward Queen's Row in search of Slow Hand.

18 I'll Keelhaul Your Ass

The morning of the launch Howard Harrington was not so cocky. The air force jeep taking Henry Colton, Lieutenant General Moore, and him to the launch-pad bounced the reporter over unpaved Arizona roads, jarring his stomach and jolting his back.

Staring at the parched and barren desert's twisted mesquite, at prickly pear with paddlelike leaves, and at two buzzards wheeling in the cloudless turquoise sky, Harrington realized how scared he was.

They topped a rise, and Harrington saw the rocket 200 yards up the road. It was like a white skyscraper forty-five stories high. His fear was making him nauseous.

"There's your firecracker," Colton said. "With ten million pounds of high explosive in its butt."

"You'll be moving 25,000 mph, 300 miles into space," Moore said.

"Spur *that baby* on the hairy side," Colton said jauntily.

"Ride *her* till she starves to death," said Moore.

"Or she crashes," Colton concluded.

Now it was Harrington's turn to mutter: "I don't feel so good."

Harrington and Colton entered the service tower's elevator. The cabin was pres-surized; Colton and Harrington did not have to wear space suits. Despite his un-easy stomach, Harrington liked their gear: cobalt-blue waist-length cotton jackets with expansion pleats in the shoulders, making it easier to move and flex. They'd look cool in the newsroom. Designed for safety as well as comfort, their clothing was fireproofed and snug enough not to snag control switches. Outer garments were covered with Velcro-sealed pockets for securing small implements such as Swiss Army knives, sunglasses, and notebooks. Such personal items turned into shrapnel in micro-g.

Forty-five stories later they were at the command-center entryway. They exited the service arm into decon where—not wanting desert sand floating around the command center—techs in white jumpsuits and surgical masks vacuumed away all dust and debris.

And they donned their EVA space suits.

Harrington followed the two officers across the flight deck into the com-mand center.

"Pull up a chair," Colton said to Harrington, pointing to a seat in front of the windscreen.

Harrington stared over the desert at black mountains lining the horizon. Colton strapped him in, then hooked him up to a Personal Oxygen Unit.

"Pure oxygen," Colton said. "It'll help your stomach."

Harrington hooked on the mask. The rest of the flight crew strapped themselves in, and they began countdown. At T-minus-ten minutes, they were into launch-check—computer, electrical, navigation, hydraulic, fuel, pressurization.

"Ready power," Colton announced when they finished the launch-check. "T-minus-one. Cowboy, here we go."

"Jesus God," was the only thing Harrington could say.

Houston counted: "T-minus-fifty-nine seconds."

Colton replaced Harrington's POU mask with a white vomitus bag.

"At zero g puke floats," Colton said. "Get any on me, I'll keelhaul your ass."

"Four, three, two, one."

Harrington heard the engines kick in, but it wasn't nearly as bad as he'd expected. No apocalyptic trembling, as he assumed, even as the rocket was blasting into infinity.

Hell, this is okay! Those training guys were having some fun with me.

Then he looked through the windscreen. The ship was still on the ground. Colton had only turned on the ignition.

Now four rocket engines kicked in. The roar was devastating. Harrington knew nothing to compare it with. He'd once read about a man who, trapped in a cramped train tunnel, had flattened himself lengthwise between the rails. When the express train passed over him, he later said he'd felt as if the entire universe was going nova. That came as close as anything.

Please, God, don't let me puke.

The windscreen's protective covering slid shut. Colton grinned wickedly at him. Even with an anvil pressing in on his chest and face, even with his gullet and bladder quivering, Harrington could lip-read Colton's silent threat:

"Keelhaul your sorry ass."

Harrington knew that most of what he felt was panic, but that was no help. His vision swarmed with a thousand points of light. His breath whooshed out of his lungs: He had difficulty raising his hands.

"Q fifty percent," Colton sang out, his voice filling Harrington's headset.

"Only fifty?" Harrington's groan was audible, the weight on his chest unbearable. "Oh, God, no," he sobbed, as the g's drove him down into his couch.

"Main engines, full thrust," Colton said. "Max Q, gentlemen, hammer all the way down, hitting full one hundred percent."

"Please, no—"

"Solid rocket burnout," Colton announced. "Jettison stage one."

At which point the second stage ignited, hammering Harrington back into his reclining couch, the anvil on his chest taking on the weight of twenty.

Two hundred miles into space the first-stage engines tumbled over the Gulf of Mexico, and Harrington's stomach broke loose too, filling his bag with rancid puke.

"Harrington," Colton growled, "I warned you."

Harrington continued to heave, his vomitus bag overflowing.

19 A Thermonuclear Assassin

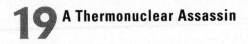

Riding backup in the two-seat Stealth trainer-fighter over Turkey's NATO airbase, Kate Magruder caught a glimpse of the huge black Stealth bomber above them. Both had been flown to the base from the U.S.

The sun was going down, and Kate was anxious for a closer look at the B-2 while there was still light. She'd seen them on television but never close up.

"Twelve o'clock high," she said into her headset to Brigadier General Larry Taylor. "That what you guys call the Stealth bomber?"

"Affirmative."

Taylor pulled out of a vertical roll at two-and-one-half negative g's. Despite Kate's pressurized g-suit designed to keep her blood from rushing in and out of her extremities the g-strain almost forced her "to red out." But it did allow her an exceptional view of the big ebony bomber at 55,000 feet in high flight, its natural habitat.

"Wow," she said in a reverential whisper.

"What's it look like to you?" Taylor asked.

"Like something out of the late Cretaceous," she said.

"A pterodactyl?"

"A crow. That's what my mother says the B-2 always reminds her of, some monstrous crow."

"This crow," Taylor said, "flies eleven miles up, can locate and kill anything on earth, and is invisible to everything from radar to infrared to recon-sats."

"I want to fly it."

"Never happen."

"We'll see." Kate enjoyed fencing with Larry Taylor. Sure he was the son of the U.S. secretary of defense but, like herself, he had dodged the trap of living in a famous parent's shadow.

Suddenly—almost, it seemed to Kate, miraculously—the cloudscape broke, and looking earthward she saw Istanbul: the Sea of Marmara on one side, the Bosphorus on the other, at their confluence called the Golden Horn. Even from that great height Kate could make out the Hagia Sophia, and Topkapi Sarayi— the Ottoman imperial residence for four hundred years.

"Bet your mom would enjoy being up here," Taylor said. "She loves all this end-of-the-world, cutting-edge military technology."

"She believes that everything has a soul, weapons included. She claims she saw all this in a vision up in the Espinazo Cristo de Sangre. A vision of the End Time."

"She and my old man are still pretty tight, aren't they?"

"When I was a kid," Kate said, "your father used to bounce me on his knee. He especially liked my stepbrother."

"What's Frank up to now?"

"He's head of surgery at the Towers."

"You and John Stone still get along? I've heard he's gone off the deep end."

"Right now he's missing. I'm worried."

Kate saw the behemoth black bomber again. The Crow. It was descending to starboard.

"Crow doesn't seem all that big," she said.

"It's the windows. Since the pilot sits back from them, he needs wide-angle vision. So the windows are disproportionately large, making the rest of the plane seem smaller. It's actually a flying football field."

"Why is Crow so controversial?"

"You know what his mission is?"

"To drop facsimile copies of the Declaration of Independence on the infidel?"

"To blanket the enemy's critical installations—including its leadership command bunkers—with thermonuclear weapons. It's the most feared weapon in our arsenal. If you're part of the enemy leadership."

"'A thermonuclear assassin.'"

"Military analysts call it 'decapitation.' Crow can deliver multimegaton warheads in sequential laydown patterns. And he knows where they live, where every one of the enemy's hardened command posts is. He scares them to death."

"Even Mad Vlad?" Kate asked.

"That's one foreign leader my old man would be happy to nuke here and now. Christ, you should hear the mouth on Vlad."

"Did you ever think you'd live to see it: a raving psychopath with his finger on their nuclear trigger?"

"Maybe that's why we have Crow."

Taylor rolled into a steeply inverted dive, then angled out into a perpendicular bank, parallel to the slowly descending B-2. To Kate, its flat infinitely faceted planes seemed as though they were not forged from fiber and steel but chiseled out of pre-Mayan obsidian, a demon-weapon from that violent dawn, reeking with the murders of infinite men and myriad species.

"Do you notice how from most angles the flat planes don't seem flat at all but appear instead to spiral?" Larry asked.

"An optical illusion?"

"The planes spiral inward in order to deflect and diffuse radar, gives the B-2 its undetectability."

"I want a closer look."

"Never happen."

"Want to bet?"

20 Your Destiny Cries Out

While Sailor swam across Mumbai's Bay of Bombay, he sang:

"Oh, wedding-guest, this soul hath been alone on a wide, wide sea."

Unfortunately, that was true. Wanderratte are extraordinary water beasts, and Sailor had swum great distances before. But no Wanderratte had attempted a harbor sea at night, swimming for miles against wind and tide. Still he sang:

"Come, my friends, 'tis not too
Late to seek a new world
Sitting well in order smite
The sounding furrows
For my intention holds to sail
Beyond the sunset and the baths
Of all the western stars until I die."

"I like the last part," a voice sounded beneath the sea. "The part about you dying."

"I'm not dead yet."

"This far from shore, I doubt you will live long."

"Surface, fish—oh, prophet who foretells my doom."

A four-foot amberjack, brother of his recent dinner, appeared.

"You swim my harbor, reeking of gull and fish, singing at the top of your lungs, challenging the sea. Now you say you cannot die? Perhaps I should summon my cousin the shark?"

Sailor knew his cousin—had seen his great dorsal fin. He'd also seen his cousin beached and had stared into the great mouth grinning with knifelike teeth, a grin that could end Sailor's odyssey with a halfhearted nip.

"I did not kill your fellow fish. The gull skewered him, and I climbed the bird's back. I killed him in the clouds, and we dropped like stones."

"But why sing, if not to challenge? Why alert your foe?"

"I sing from the joy of singing."

"Sing for me then. This melody I have to hear."

"No, you were right. I've gone out too far. My soaked fur weighs me down. I will not reach ship nor shore. My song is done."

His limbs were numb, his body leaden. Sailor was sinking.

"I know you, Wanderratte, and I know you killed the gull who slew my kin. I know your warren dies, and you seek shores unknown."

"I do not seek your pity."

"But you need my help. You are sinking."

Only Sailor's nose remained above the surf. His spent legs trembled.

"Climb on my back. I'll take you to your ship. If you bite, I'll sound depths below depths and kill you quick."

"I shall not bite. I shall sing songs to you and to the blessed sea."

"Sing your song, Wanderratte."

The big fish hoisted him above the waterline and bore him toward the ship, his powerful tail sculling back and forth, the breeze chilling Sailor's soaked fur.

"It may be that the gulfs will wash us down
It may be we shall touch the happy isles
And see the great Achilles whom we knew.
Though much is taken, much abides."

Now they were in the lee of the great ship. The fish swam to a steel anchor chain.

"This is your ticket, Wanderratte. Your destiny cries out."

Sailor hopped onto the cable.

"Your voyage will not be easy. Your enemy, Rattus rattus, leers at us from portholes and the foredeck. They do not love your breed, Brave Rat. They wish you dead."

"I have no choice, noble fish. I shall not forget you."

"Good luck with the Dark Ones."

"Good luck to you, Brother Fish. I will sing your song always."

"If you survive, Wanderratte. If you survive."

21 The Book of Revelation

Lydia Magruder, wearing a tasteful three-piece Escada suit of jet silk, seated herself on a comfortable leather armchair. President Walter Haines and his defense secretary—retired Chairman of the Joint Chiefs Jack T. "Blackjack" Taylor—sat themselves across from her on a leather sofa. At ten minutes past midnight, the president was in shirtsleeves, his tie loosened. His gray hairline was receding. He looked old—even to an eighty-one-year-old woman.

Taylor, though retired, continued to favor his uniform. He appeared, as usual, aggressively fit—ready to drop down at a moment's notice and give them fifty parade-ground push-ups.

There was a foot-high manuscript on President Haines's French Provincial mahogany coffee table.

"You want me to read that thing?" Haines asked.

"It cost me $25 million, expenses included," L. L. said sharply. "You had better read it."

"What is it?" Secretary Taylor asked. "The Tower of Babel?"

"The Book of Revelation, is more like it."

Haines peered at the title page. "John Stone?"

"Yes," L. L. said.

"My kids read him," President Haines said. "He spends a lot of time writing about his dick and his drinking. He even composed an ode to his male member."

"He refers to that appendage as Ol' Tex," Secretary Taylor said.

"A very big state," the old woman explained with a wry smile.

"You want a loony drunk to teach us foreign policy?" President Haines asked harshly. "Bankrolled by you?"

"Walter," the old woman said coldly, "he's working on his third Pulitzer, and you are going to read it."

Both men were instantly silent. L. L. was using "the tone."

The president leaned across the table toward her.

"Lydia," he said, "you may be the wisest person I know, and you're one of the best friends I've ever had. When I was a wet-behind-the-ears Phoenix councilman, you plucked me from obscurity and helped put me where I am. I wouldn't be here without you, your money, and your advocacy. Most important, however, has been your counsel, which I continue to cherish. Have I ever failed to take your advice?"

"There's the matter of Dar-al-Suhl."

President Haines looked away. The oil-rich Islamic nation on Turkey's southeast border was one of America's close allies. Dar-al-Suhl was unique in its friendliness to neighbors in the Mideast, Israel included, and respected for its generosity to nations in need.

"What do you mean?" Taylor asked.

"You give them *anything* they want," L. L. said.

Taylor shrugged. "They bucked the oil embargo. The CIA gives Dar-al-Suhl a good report card."

The old woman bristled. "Don't talk to me about the CIA."

"I don't understand your objection to—"

"The Company fomented the Bay of Pigs fiasco, then led us to believe that Vietnam was going to be a raggedy-ass barn-shoot with a bunch of slopes in black pajamas. They're the ones that told us the Shah of Iran was invincible— weeks before he was driven from power by Khomeini. When Bill Buckley had his cover blown, the Company sent him back into Beirut anyway, where he was kidnapped, tortured, killed. They're the ones that said India and Pakistan weren't going to start a nuclear arms race. The were blindsided by the collapse of the USSR. The Company covered up our sales of ICBM-guidance technology to China. They were ignorant of bin Laden's threat and the 9/11 attack despite incessant warnings. I can't believe you're quoting those incompetent—"

"If something was wrong in Dar-al-Suhl," Haines said, "the CIA would know."

"Walter, the CIA has been on the wrong side of every losing conflict since Rome salted Carthage. I wouldn't trust them to carry a dozen eggs across the street."

"Anything special I should look for in this magnum opus?" Haines gave up and stared skeptically at the massive manuscript.

"For one thing, Stone's observations on the proliferation of diesel submarines worldwide."

"Russia does sell a lot of them," Secretary Taylor said. "That doesn't mean they're starting World War Three."

"Stone thinks *someone* is about to."

"Who?" Taylor asked.

"I don't have the rest of his manuscript. All I know is what Stone told me over the phone."

"The *rest* of the manuscript? There's even more of this?" Haines gestured toward the towering report in front of him, then asked, "So, where *is* the rest of the report?"

"I'm not sure. Stone disappeared a few days ago in Mecca. I need you gentlemen to help me find him."

"A few days isn't much time to be gone," Haines said, indifferently.

"What was he doing in Mecca?" Taylor asked. "They're in the middle of Ramadan, aren't they?"

"He was trying to sneak in," L. L. said. "He was disguised as a pilgrim. He wanted photos of the Ka'ba. According to Kate, there was a mêlée that may have included Stone. Details are sketchy."

"He hasn't called you?" Haines asked.

"No."

"Anything else we should know about the Stone report?" Taylor asked.

"This is 'eyes only.' You can't pass it around. I'm trusting you on this." The old woman shuddered when she said it.

"What's wrong?" Haines said.

"I just said that word again."

"Trust?"

"Yes, trust. I hate trusting people."

"You trust your stepson, Frank," Taylor said, smiling.

He knew that talking about Frank always cheered Lydia up.

Her eyes softened, and she gave him a long, slow smile. "Yes, you know very well I trust Frank. He's never given me reason to doubt him."

"By the way," Taylor said, "did you know that Larry is giving Kate a tour of Turkey's NATO base?"

"Yes. Are you going to let her fly the B-2?"

Taylor flinched.

"What's wrong?" L. L. asked him.

"Vlad Malokov was on the phone with me last night. He was raving about the B-2. Mad Vlad wants it discontinued. Says the B-2 is 'destabilizing.'"

"Are you going to discontinue it?"

"Never happen."

"So he's still ringing you up nights?" L. L. asked.

"Yes. There's no way I can avoid him."

"If it makes you feel any better, he's taken to calling me too, and I once thought he was a brilliant man—MIT, Los Alamos. Now I'm embarrassed at what we've done to the world and by extension to him. And all those nuclear scientists we educated and trained, who are now in China, Japan, India, Pakistan."

"What do you mean 'done to him'?" Haines asked, furrowing his forehead. "Those are outstanding institutions."

"*We taught those foreign scientists almost everything they know about nuclear weapons,*" L. L. said through gritted teeth. "*In Vlad's case, we even sent him to Los Alamos for seminars.*"

The two men stared at her in edgy silence.

"I'm still unclear why we should feel embarrassed in front of Mad Vlad," Taylor said.

"Because he's not all that mad. Stone knew him best and said he was only half-mad. The drinking, womanizing, even the alleged violence—Stone said it was all true. But he thought Vlad's 'wild man routine' regarding nuclear policy was a calculated act."

"To what end?" Taylor asked.

"To scare us into doing the right thing."

"Which right thing?" said Haines. The president was smiling now, politely, indulging L. L.

She was quietly furious.

No one *indulged* Lydia Lozen Magruder.

"Scare us into stopping nuclear proliferation, and particularly stop the smuggling of Russia's loose nukes—and weapons systems—out of their country. With all due respect, Mr. President, Vlad's country, for decades now, has been one big nuclear garage sale. We should have helped them get control of it long ago."

"I think our record on that score's pretty good," Taylor said.

"This is *me* you're talking to, Jack," L. L. said, her temper flaring. "Don't give me a campaign speech."

"After all, it's not an easy problem to get a handle on," Haines protested.

L. L. was losing it. When that happened, she didn't shout or throw things. She gave them the response she saved for when she was too furious to speak.

Eyes narrowed, cheekbones flaring, teeth set, she gave them *the look.* The one Stone claimed "froze Gorgons."

Haines cleared his throat, glanced at his watch, anything to get his eyes off L. L.

Taylor finally found his tremulous voice. "Lydia, I, uh, I'm afraid we have this, uh, little meeting at State. Mr. President, we're already twenty minutes late." He looked briefly at L. L., his shoulders hunched. "Is there, uh, anything else?"

"Yes. I'm still worried about John Stone, Jack," L. L. said, her eyes still narrowed.

"He's probably drunk in a brothel," Taylor offered.

"Then he would've definitely called me. He'd need money." She removed a manila envelope from her purse and placed it on the coffee table. "Everything I know about him is in this file."

"I'll put State right on it," Taylor said. "If they don't come up with anything, we'll turn it over to the intelligence agencies."

"Here we go again," L. L. said. She got up without another word and left the Oval Office.

22 It Won't Make for a Very Edifying Tale

President Haines and Jack Taylor looked at each other in relief after Lydia left. Neither man smiled.

"I think the nun's to blame," the president said.

"Cassandra?"

"Lydia's end-of-the-world paranoia began when Kate and Stone got the nun out of Cuba. Now, of course, Cassandra's broadcasting End Time stuff to the world," Taylor said.

"My recollection is that Lydia already decided the world was going to end *before* the nun took to the air," President Haines said.

The president raised his eyebrows. "I don't know. The original Cassandra was the daughter of Troy's last king. Loved by Apollo, who promised her the gift of prophecy if she would sleep with him, she accepted his largesse but she reneged. Apollo avenged himself on her by ordaining that no one would believe her prophecies."

"I don't blame him." Taylor wasn't a classics scholar.

"Cassandra prophesized that Troy would fall. The Trojans were massacred, and she became part of the spoils of war. She ended up getting murdered with her lover, a Greek king."

"Great story but no Hollywood ending," Taylor said. "I must be wrong, Mr. President, but you looked like you might actually credit her scenario."

"A lot of paranoia, Jack, has a grain of truth in it."

"We're all concerned with Russia's nuclear black market, and now we have Russia's missing subs to worry about as well," Taylor conceded.

"You mean the one sub that turned renegade?" the president asked.

"All we know is that one of their subs had gone AWOL and that it was about to sell itself to some terrorist nation, and Vlad—instead of taking his usual cut—opened fire on it."

"And there were nukes aboard?" the president asked.

"There may have been," the general said. "A Kilo-Class sub, retrofitted, can fire nuclear-tipped cruise missiles. We're thinking Vlad killed the sub to cover up more of his dirt."

"Vlad knows he's overextended and wearing out his welcome," the president said. "The Russian president is going to dump him as soon as the political and economic chaos in the country is under control. Vlad can retire to a luxury Black Sea dacha if he is reasonably clean. If they learn he's pocketed billions to protect criminals—" The president paused. "What is your analysis, Jack? Should we keep pumping money into Russia? I think all the leadership does is line their pockets with it."

"And continue to sell the weapon to our enemies," Jack said.

"We're getting an unusual number of NBRs. Nonbiologic reports—navy jargon for the surface ships and subs we spot but can't get a make on. Some of the diesels are unbelievably quiet. SOSUS has found maybe a dozen that we suspect are Russian but can't specifically identify. They are as elusive as ghosts."

"Heading toward us?" Taylor asked with a hint of nerves.

"No, the diesels are in every ocean. There's no concentration moving toward us, so we're not on alert. The interpretation is that the Russians are keeping their subs moving just so the crews won't have time to think about how long it's been since they've been paid and whether their wives are selling their bodies to feed the kids."

President Haines turned his chair to face a globe on the other side of the room.

"Hell of a responsibility we have, Jack. We used to police half the world and never got any respect. Now we police the whole world and catch five times the flak."

"The Russians resent the fact that we won the Cold War. They're never going to cut us any slack because underneath they hate us for making them lose."

President Haines looked at his watch. "Well, Jack, I have a late-night appointment."

"Celebrating the end of the embargo with that Haddad girl?"

"No, that was last week. But I will see her again in a few days. She says she has a political proposal."

"What's she like, anyway?"

"I know why they make their women wear robes and veils now. I've never known anyone like Sultana. I'm not sure my heart can take the strain." President Haines waved his hand in a gesture of dismissal, looking at his own reflection in the Oval Office window.

Taylor rose obediently. Halfway out the door, he turned. "L. L. seems upset about that reporter of hers, Stone. Should you ask the Haddad woman to put someone on John Stone's trail?"

"I should ask her to send a hitman after him," Haines growled. "Stone's done nothing but rip us to shreds ever since I took office. He equates me with Mad Vlad, accusing me of promoting the 'yard sale at the end of history.' And he does it with L. L.'s blessing."

"I know how to fix the old lady," Taylor said. "I know she's storing illegal ordnance at that glorified bomb shelter—machine guns, mortars, grenades, handheld missile launchers."

"She really does expect the world to end."

"Yeah, but that stuff's still illegal, and she's going down for it. I've already talked to the attorney general. He had her office bugged, has proof that Kate and Stone know about her illegal arsenal too. The warrants and indictment are all ready to go. Give the word and I can ruin all three of them, put them behind bars."

"Do it."

"I'm going to paper-train that old biddy," Taylor said, "break her to our saddle. When we're done, however, it won't make for a very edifying tale."

"I don't care, I want that old bitch brought to heel."

23 He Never Even Thanked Me

The diesel sub's auxiliary depth-gauge needle rotated with exasperating lassitude—410, 400, 390 meters. The hull popped continuously.

"What's next, Captain?" the Starpom asked.

"Assuming we've eluded the Russian navy?" Gargarin said. "Assuming the engines still work? We stay submerged as long as possible—I hope all day."

"At night?"

"We run with decks submerged," Gargarin said.

They both studied the auxiliary depth gauge. Twice it froze. Once at 220, again at 165.

"More compressed air!" Gargarin shouted. "The ballast tanks are leaking. Blow those goddamned tanks."

"Oh God," the navigator muttered under his breath, "why doesn't someone kill me?"

90, 80, 70, 60, 40, 30 meters.

"Up periscope," the captain said. He swung the periscope 360 degrees and said, "Clear." He looked up. "Chief of the Boat, surface."

"Surface!"

The three men climbed the sail. The crew crowded under the hatch, waiting for it to open—and to breathe real air.

The sub surfaced, riding hard on the swells. The hatch opened. After all those hours of submersion, the sudden exposure to oxygen was wildly exhilarating. Gargarin held his breath, restraining the urge to breathe deeply. The Starpom, Michman, and navigator gulped mouthfuls of fresh air greedily and were soon knocked to their knees by hyperventilation. The Michman collapsed on the rail, lashed by stinging rain and gale-force winds. He got up, staring at livid storm clouds, still it seemed like bright blue heaven to him.

By now the men were climbing eagerly out of the bridge and deck hatches. Covered with oil, salt water, urine, and excrement, they were quickly light-headed from the comparative purity of the sea air.

Still the captain resisted the urge to breathe deeply. He clung to the rail and studied the horizon's rim. At first he thought it might be a bird or distant aircraft.

Then the aircraft, a chopper that had been flying south-southeast, banked hard-starboard and came straight at them.

"Oh shit," Gargarin said into his headset.

"You can say that again," the Starpom said. "We've been lit by someone's weapons-radar."

"Which weapons-radar?" the captain said.

"The chopper's."

The Michman was up on his knees—just coming to.

"Michman," the captain ordered, "get down to the radio station. Starpom, you're in the control room. Fill those air tanks. Get the diesels going and start charging the batteries. We'll need every ounce of e-motor power."

"Captain," the radioman said into Gargarin's headset, "it's the same Russian chopper. He wants to know what a Russian sub with radio problems was doing in the SORUS Straits."

"Fuck him."

"He said if we plan on stealing and selling this sub, we're out of our minds. He says they'll sink us."

Gargarin almost felt like laughing.

"Wait," the radioman said. "Get this! He's got their fleet on the horn. If we submerge again, they'll bring in killer subs, follow us into the cellar, and kill us."

"Comm-officer?" the captain said into his headset. "Signal lanterns—international Morse code. Give the chopper an SOS, then tell him everything is fine but that our radio is out. Tell him his transmission is weak. Ask him to move closer."

The comm-officer was soon on the deck with the lanterns.

"I flashed him the message, sir. He's hesitating."

"Flash him again. Tell him we can't hear him. Get him closer."

Gargarin slid down the bridge-ladder to the aft deck.

The chopper made a starboard turn toward the ship.

Gargarin watched through the binoculars as the chopper completed its long bank.

"Tell him we're still not reading him," he said to the comm-officer.

The ship, rising atop a comber, crashed into its trough, black icy seas breaking over them.

First came out of the hatch and carefully crossed the deck to Gargarin.

The helicopter was now circling around with its tail to the sub. First quickly uncovered the handheld SA-7, known in the west as "the Grail." It was a surface-to-air missile, four feet long, 2.75 inches in diameter, and driven by a three-stage, solid-fuel, dual-thrust motor.

First aimed the launcher through its open sight, then triggered the thermal battery to the "on" position. The red light turned to green, and the SAM had its lock. He let the hammer down—full ignition. The boost charge flared, burning out even before the missile left the tube but with enough juice to place the missile at a safe remove from the launch tube before the sustainer motor fired.

The missile accelerated to Mach 1.5.

The lightweight warhead featured both impact and grazing fuses, infrared filters to screen out decoys, and a recently upgraded guidance system. The target was fifty meters from the forepeak. The sub, riding thirty-foot swells, wasn't prepared for the detonating chopper, which exploded in a red-orange fireball so close to the ship's bow that it hammered the upper deck with fiery debris.

Gargarin nearly voided his bladder and almost blacked out. "He never even thanked me," he gasped into his headset.

"He thanked someone else," the radioman said to him. "We're getting transmissions from another Russian ship—a destroyer."

"Prepare to dive," Gargarin said.

"Maybe too late, Captain," the comm-officer said. "He's spotted us."

"Dive anyway!" Gargarin shouted.

"Corrections, sir. We're getting sonar activity below."

"Below?" the captain said.

"The plane mentioned an attack sub," the Starpom said.

"How far off?" Captain Gargarin asked.

"Feels weak," the ESM officer said. "Could be 50,000 meters or more."

"If we dive, we may lose him," the Starpom said.

"Crash dive!"

The comm-officer, the captain, and the Starpom scrambled into the hatches, slamming and dogging them shut.

"Can we outdive it?" the Starpom asked the captain in the control room.

"We may not have to," Gargarin said. "There's a force-12 hurricane bearing down on us, 190-mile-per-hour winds."

"Will the destroyer leave the area?"

"I would if I were him. If that sub's been submerged all this time, he may not know anything about us."

"What's the depth here?" the Starpom asked.

"I don't even know *where* we are!" the navigator said, and laughed as though he was about to go insane. "Our computers are crashed and our GPS smashed. How can I know the depth?"

"Don't laugh too hard," Gargarin said. "We're about to find out."

24 With Hallucinatory Vividness

The windscreen's protective hatch slid back, and Henry Colton stared into the deepening violet of the stratosphere. He felt the hard, hot burn of the solid rocket boosters, heard the banging as the first- and second-stage rockets exploding free of the craft. The g's tore at him. His ears rang, but, God, it was wonderful. Belly-down over Baja and the Mexican coast—riding the lightning into outer space—his elation soared.

Here, everything appeared to him with almost preternatural clarity—the slow-motion tumble of the three SRBs over the Mexican Gulf, the hailstorm of fiery debris orbiting around them, every seam and rivet distinct. Earth also hit him with hallucinatory vividness. The long Technicolor swath of the Grand Canyon, the Colorado River twisting through its iridescent cliffs, the glittering lights of Albuquerque, El Paso, and Cuidad Juárez, the black crest of the Mongolian Rim, with its winding mountain chain and black forested plateau.

The third stage kicked in, and they were in orbit, in micro-g. The crushing pressure lifted, and with sudden serenity he was floating. Through the windscreen the third stage windmilled toward Earth.

Colton might have remained in this state of bliss forever, had it not been for the droplets of Harrington's barf floating past him. One goblet struck him in the face.

Harrington was now snoring. If Colton didn't take care of him, he'd drown in his helmet. Colton would have given anything to have stuffed the unconscious reporter into an air lock and blown him out into space along with the jettisoned boosters. Instead, he unstrapped his harness and propelled himself over to Harrington's chair. He removed Harrington's helmet, slapped him awake, and made him clean up every drop of refuse drifting around the compartment.

He returned to his command seat.

25 Suffer Not the Stranger

Sailor was amazed at the SS *Pride of New York*. Its seven decks—a steam-shrouded maze of twisting pipes and petrol tanks—looked more like a floating, multilevel oil refinery than a ship. With its labyrinthine ventilation shafts, towering smokestacks, thousands of miles of ropes and wires, cables and chains, rails and rigging, the supertanker was a city unto itself.

Nor was this world without hazard. Reconnoitering the ship had been a terrifying task. At every turn death lurked—legions of seamen in dirty denims and tee shirts, armies of Rattus rattus with black fur bristling.

And if those two weren't enough, the ship was loaded with rattraps, as well as poisoned cheeses and meats.

But more than the wrath of Rattus rattus, more than the traps and poison, Sailor feared Felis Catus, the slate-gray tom. Sailor had glimpsed the Stalker belowdecks, and the sight had made his blood run cold—two full feet from the tip of his nose to his behind, his switching tail as long as his body. He even treated Sailor and his cousins to a song:

> *"Come, kittens. I shall not harm you.*
> *I am the gentlest of lovers.*
> *I shall sing you the sweetest songs,*
> *Show you where the finest morsels are—*
> *The richest cream, the choicest chocolates, the finest cheeses.*
> *I Shall be your protector and provider.*
> *You will never want."*

A younger Wanderratte, cursed with curiosity, might have fallen for the siren's song. Not Sailor. He'd seen talons and fangs. He quickly hid.

But no rat—even on a ship as vast as the *Pride of New York*—can hide forever . . . not from Rattus rattus. The crew might claim the deck by day, but the night belonged to Rattus. Standing on deck the first night, Sailor looked up and saw them on the rails, scampering up and down overhead cables and chains, sometimes dangling from the rigging, like monkeys by their prehensile tails. Their spoor was everywhere.

He chose as his bunker a sealed-off ventilation shaft where his flanks and backside would be safe from attack. On the second night however, he had been discovered. An Alpha Rattus, flanked by a dozen friends, confronted him. Fur bristling, back arching like a cat's, the buck approached Sailor sideways in a ritualistic, stiff-legged dance.

"You have two choices," Sailor said coolly. "We can fight, or you can ignore me. I am not leaving the ship."

The Alpha arched his back even higher, then emitted a malodorous stream of urine.

"Your kind wants me dead," Sailor acknowledged wearily, "and you eventually could kill me. I'll take you first and another dozen with me. These deaths will serve no purpose. We will die over morsels."

"But your death will serve a purpose," the Alpha said. "We kill not from lust or greed, like men."

"None of which will matter," the Wanderratte said, "to your babies who are orphaned, to their brothers and sisters who will never know life, to widowed does and dead bucks. Your colonies will be weaker. Men are near, and the battle's violence will summon their wrath—more traps, more poison, more cats."

"Wanderratte, you know the code," the Alpha said. "*Peace be upon your tribe but suffer not the stranger.* Did *your* warren suffer the stranger ever? Did your warren pay?"

. . . Sailor remembered before the Great Sickness. That rainy night when the sentries were distracted—having gorged themselves earlier on an evening feast. The rain-soaked stranger was not discovered until he was found, dead in a burrow, teeming with sick fleas and bloody bubos . . .

"You know the code, Wanderratte. What we hate worse than cats or traps—the Sickness borne by the Stranger."

Sailor shrugged. "The salt sea cleansed me of fleas. Anyway, I shall not dwell with you. I shall live in the bilge, where you tread not."

The Alpha shook his head sadly. "Even so, there can be no comity between your and our kind. The browns have too much of our blood on their hands."

Sailor stared at him levelly. "The past is dead."

"Never. When you first emerged out of the Asian steppe lands with the Khans, you came to the place called Europe seeking our blood. You drove us into hiding on remote islands, into inhospitable climes, on wandering ships. We survive through stealth and cunning—fearing not cats and traps, not men and not dogs but *you,* Wanderratte, who hunt and kill us by the billions."

Sailor's tone was quiet but stern: "We brown rats are ground-dwellers—often dwelling *under* the earth—where our Death Fleas afflict none but ourselves. Your fleas, when we met, fell on us from your trees and rafters, raining pestilence and death. You were about to annihilate yourselves *and* everything below. We could not allow this."

"You know the score, Wanderratte."

Sailor did not shriek, arch his back, or spill urine, but when he looked into the Alpha's eyes, the rat knew he would die.

He watched the Alpha hesitate, looking for a way out.

Sailor offered him a tempting exit.

"I can do something for you," Sailor offered.

"What?"

"I can rid you of the Stalker," Sailor said.

"How?" the Alpha asked.

"I can kill him."

26 "You Never Thought Jack Was Very Smart."

Kate Magruder took her mother's call from her quarters at the air base outside Istanbul.

"Hi, Mom."

"What are you doing in Istanbul?"

"A series on our country's military preparedness with Larry Taylor. I'm doing field research."

"Why not American bases?"

"America's in NATO. Turkey's in NATO. Same thing."

"I want you *out* of the Mideast. I don't like what's going on there."

"Stone's still here. I thought I'd help track him down."

After a short silence, L. L. said, "Larry Taylor's old man could do something if he tried. Keep after Larry. Maybe if Larry nudges Jack enough, he'll wake up."

"You used to kind of like Jack Taylor."

"To the extent I like any of those morons I like him, which isn't saying much."

"You never thought Jack was very smart."

"He has good manners."

"Tell him I'll make a few inquiries myself."

"Be careful. Wherever media stars—like yourself—go they attract a spotlight. If Stone *has* been grabbed, publicity's the last thing we need."

"Anything else, Mom?" Kate said.

"Tomorrow you turn thirty-six, in case you've forgotten."

"Nice of you to remember."

"Once again, I feel compelled to ask why I don't have grandchildren."

"There *are* other things."

"More important than continuation of the species?"

27 Doth He Not Mend?

Lydia Lozen Magruder sat on her bed and thought about her late husband, something she had avoided doing for years.

Because he had been so much like Kate.

. . . Rootless, fearless, utterly free, he raced horses and cross-country motorcycles. He taught Kate to ride them as well.

But the bottle and clinical depression had gotten the best of Hal Magruder, and he'd finally gone off on that last flight and crashed his Learjet into the cliff face near Lydia's sacred spot at Three Points.

Some of it was her fault; she never should have let Hal get involved in the business. In those days the media business demanded growth, and you needed both guts and a thick skin.

The demographics on print media had been turning down for some time. Believing that TV and radio were the wave of the future, L. L. systematically bought up every radio and TV station she could get her hands on. Finally, she negotiated "a slot on the wheel," on a major communications satellite, creating her own international news network.

She'd had to do considerable leveraging to pull this off, something that drove Hal to distraction. Her deliberate, risky indebtedness deepened his depression.

Behind Lydia's back he began selling off his privately held pieces of the company.

When he crashed the Learjet into the cliff face, he was on the brink of selling Magruder Enterprises down the river. His suicide, however, saved the business. In court L. L. argued that Hal's "business friends" had taken advantage of a mentally ill person, and she regained control.

She never looked back as she continued the expansion of her empire. During a meeting in Tel Aviv, Israel's foremost AI computer genius, Sara Ann Friedman, had told her of her own special vision: Sara dreamt of transforming "computers" into bioelectronic "thinking machines."

L. L. knew next to nothing about computers—"neural nets," as Sara called her machines—but she believed in Sara. Call it intuition—her Apache shaman blood, Lozen screaming at her from beyond the grave—call it what you will.

Call it luck.

But L. L. believed in Sara.

L. L. took on Silicon Valley just as she had taken on cable TV—and beat them both.

She was in the business of "neural engines."

During those years when L. L. was saving, then expanding her business, she met Ben "Doc" Joiner, one of her new MTN board members. They were both over sixty. Two months later they had married.

In Kate's eyes Lydia now stood convicted of disloyalty to Hal. Worse, Kate had inherited an older stepbrother. Kate hated Frank immediately. He was too good at everything. Valedictorian, class jock, president of his high school class three years running.

"Who wants Superboy for a stepbrother?" Kate said to everyone.

Frank was three years older than Kate and far more sophisticated. Still, he listened to anything and everything she had to say, once Kate had grudgingly started to talk to him.

Never offering advice, seldom commenting at all, yet with his every look and gesture Kate knew he cared, that she had his unqualified approval, that he was there for her.

Kate had expected that after all her railing and raging against L. L. this incredibly caring older stepbrother would side with L. L. in the matter of her father, which Kate brought up the time before Frank had left for college.

"Let me get this straight. Your father was having problems with drinking and depression. He was selling out the company for peanuts *behind your mother's back* to a bunch of sharks who would have happily put both you and L. L. in the poorhouse. L. L. fought them off, saved the company, and at the same time saved *your* hide. And you hate her for it. Am I missing something?"

Kate didn't speak to him for nine months.

Still she was haunted by his comments. It came to a head the last month of school. Her sophomore class was reading Shakespeare's *Twelfth Night*. Once the clown, Feste, had assuaged Olivia's guilt after her father's death, Olivia said:

"Doth he not mend?"

On reading that line Kate burst into tears.

She went straight from school to her mother's office, walked in on her in the middle of a business meeting, and told her how much she loved her.

Lydia now knew what she needed to do. She hadn't talked to Frank in over a month.

That was probably why she was so unhappy.

She reached for a phone and dialed Frank Sheckly.

28 I Wonder What Hell Looks Like?

Again, the Starpom was shouting: "Clear the bridge! Prepare to dive!"

With almost unbearable weariness, the men threw themselves down aluminum ladders and dragged their battered, bleeding bodies through the hatches.

"Open the ballast tanks," the Starpom ordered.

Again, exhausted men grabbed the overhead induction valve handles and swung from them wildly, cursing the busted hydraulic system that forced them to open the big tanks manually.

With a deafening roar air exploded from the tanks. Opened to the sea, water thundered, the forward tanks blowing so fast the ship sank slantwise, this time stern-down. In the control room the auxiliary depth gauge spun, plummeting 90, 100, 110, 120, 130 meters.

Down into the blackness of a polar sea the ship plunged—her hull moaning, screaming.

"How far do we dive, Captain?" the Starpom asked.

"We hit 750 last time."

"Navigator," the Starpom asked, "were you able to fix our position?"

"I think we're still in shallow water—max depth, 750 meters."

"Take us down to the floor," the captain said.

"The computer estimates it's a thousand meters," First said.

"We have no choice," the captain said. "They ping us at will."

"They've no reason to attack," the Zampolit—the political officer—said, as he joined them. "We're one of their own." His uniform was streaked with vomit, his face white. His torn forehead was obviously infected.

"We shot down one of their antisub recon choppers," First said.

"They won't know that," the Zampolit said. "They were over the horizon. He was low to the water. There was no debris. The sea leaves no holes."

"Unless he had another channel open," First said.

"They overheard *everything*," the Starpom said simply.

At last, they hit bottom.

The pressure hull screamed.

"Trim the buoyancy tanks," the captain said, "and let her hang."

The bulkheads groaned like someone tearing out floorboards.

They listened to howls from the ship's fatigued metal, the CO_2 scrubbers still on the fritz. Waiting in silence, they tried not to waste breath, sucking on hot potash canisters as an air substitute.

For a while Gargarin thought they'd done it. He had even considered raising the ship to periscope depth—when they were pinged.

To starboard.

Again. And again the sounds of gravel fired from a gun.

"Starpom," Gargarin ordered, "start the e-motors."

"Start the e-motors!"

Then they heard topside pinging.

"The destroyer," the Starpom said.

The soft whining hum of the e-motors commenced.

"Starpom," the captain said, "straight ahead, full rudder."

The sub slid silently through the water. For brief moments the pinging ceased. Then the chirping began again.

"A Russian sub is also moving with us, sir. Parallel course, full-port, 30,000 meters."

"Reverse engines, Starpom," the captain said.

The Starpom stared at him in shock.

"Reverse engines," the captain repeated.

"Reverse engines," the Starpom said into his headset.

"Rudder hard-a-starboard."

"Rudder hard-a-starboard," the Starpom repeated.

"Port motor half ahead. Arm the 3, 4, and 6 tubes," the captain said.

Suddenly, the Starpom turned toward Gargarin and gaped. "You're going for a stern shot?"

"Right up his screw."

"Tube 3 is nuclear-tipped," the Starpom said.

"It better be," the captain said.

"Tube armed and ready," the torpedo officer said over the speaker.

"Battle stations torpedo," Gargarin announced over the 1MC intercom. "Master One. First torpedo target. Set Time Motion Analysis."

A seeming eternity passed, while the Starpom, weapons control officer, navigator, and six other crew members crunched the TMA.

Then: "TMA completed."

"Set the Preset to run deep. Do not let it U-turn on us. This is a 30,000-meter range."

"Preset completed," the weapons control officer answered.

"Make tubes 3, 4, and 6 ready in all respects."

"Sir, 3, 4, and 6 ready, sir."

"Preset toward target—ready to fire."

"Ready to fire," the weapons control officer responded.

"Nothing in the way?"

"Nothing."

"Match bearings and shoot tubes 3, 4, and 6."

They felt the rush and recoil of 3, then 4, then 6.

30,000 meters at 45 wire-guided knots—another seeming eternity.

"All hands brace yourselves!" the Starpom ordered, as the torpedoes closed.

The blast waves from the first nuclear-tipped torpedo were amplified exponentially by the heavily pressurized water separating the subs. Gargarin's sub rocked as if struck by a hammer.

Gargarin heard the explosive rush of seawater breaking through the pressure hull. Then the lights went out, and everything was black. The deck was moving, and he was falling.

His last thought was: *I wonder what hell looks like?*

29 Why This Is Hell, nor Am I Out of It

"*. . . Men love darkness because their deeds are evil. Men love darkness because their deeds are evil. Men love darkness because their deeds are evil . . .*"

For the past week John Stone had repeated John 3:19 perhaps ten thousand times, that verse being the only thing in his throbbing head.

The biblical verse was telling. A thick black hood had shrouded his head, and darkness was the whole of Stone's existence. His wrists were cuffed behind his back. Along with distant screams of torture victims and his own suffering, darkness was all he knew.

As to his pain, Stone was usually able to identify the source. Sometimes it was a club or a fist or boots. Sometimes the charged copper wire tied around his testicles. Hypodermics of saline had been injected into some of his large muscles. Much of the time, however, the pain was so consuming he did not know where it came from.

. . . He remembered Mecca. He remembered the whiskey flask slipping out of his robe and exposing him as an imposter-pilgrim on holy ground. But a beautiful woman with dazzlingly dark eyes had saved him, hustling him with bodyguards out of that sacred shrine and into a stretch limo one step ahead of a

lynch mob. He remembered her in the limo. He'd had a drink, drained his flask, and . . .

". . . Men love darkness because their deeds are evil. Men love darkness because their deeds are evil. Men love darkness because their deeds are evil . . ."

At times he had been hung by his manacled wrists from a cell door. He was always hung near a torture chamber; he could hear men and women scream. Sometimes his groans punctuated the screams of others. The modified version of the medieval strappado tore with unbearable agony at his joints.

Around-the-clock loudspeakers treated Stone and the other prisoners to Koranic verses. *"Swift is the reckoning of Allah!"* and *"By their deeds you shall know them."*

The verses prompted remorse, something in the past he had not been acquainted with. Remorse at having been too bold, foolhardy. Remorse at having never listened to anyone, especially L. L. Why had he ignored her pleas to "get out of the Mideast while you're still in one piece. Don't you understand, John? These people will kill you!"

Kate, whom he loved beyond measure, had also told him: "Christ, John, are you out of your mind? You're taking on al Qaeda, the Hezbollah, the Islamic Brotherhood, Hamas, name it. Those people don't play around."

Henry Colton had had words with him: "You never knew half of what was good for you. L. L., Kate, and I have spent half our lives bailin' you out of one scrape or another, but you still haven't learned a goddamn thing. You're out there with the real crazies now."

But he always thought he was too smart to be caught. He let them all know John Stone had bigger balls than a bull elephant. The stars came out at night because he put them there, and when he died—assuming he ever died—it would be between the legs of a good woman, or better yet a very, very bad one, with a smile on his face, not with this gaggle of morons. If anyone thought he was stuffin' just look at the record: John Stone had never had enough of nuthin'.

And Colton said: "That's the way you want to play it, fine. Go fuck yourself. This is the trouble you been lookin' for your whole life. I'm just sorry for L. L. and Kate because they're stupid enough to love you."

Stone was sorry now. Because all that was left of his world was darkness and death, screams and pain. *"Why this is hell, nor am I out of it,"* another man had said in another time, and the image was apt.

As was John 3:19.

30 A Craving for Armageddon

L. L. lay back on her bed at the Citadel and tried to relax.

She was overtired, wound too tight, worried about Stone's physical safety, as Kate was, but also concerned about his "mental condition."

There could be no doubt that something had happened to Stone's mind too. He was losing it, big-time. His behavior in Mecca had been suicidally reckless. Kate had once warned her that something profoundly destructive would happen to both L. L. and Stone if they peered too long into "the nuclear abyss."

"In the end it 'will stare into you,'" Kate had said, quoting Nietzsche.

L. L. feared Kate was right. Perhaps the abyss had driven them all a little bonkers. And she wondered if that same nightmare terror had driven Mad Vlad around the bend.

He now sounded as if he too was insane.

. . . *Stone, on the other hand, had spent a long night four years ago with Vlad at his Black Sea dacha and had not found him "mad" at all. Stone informed L. L. that Vlad had come across as witty and wise, cynical yet curiously concerned—more sardonic philosopher-king than psychopath. Instead of raving, Vlad had held forth on the rise and fall of civilizations.*

"What did Plato, Vico, Spengler, and Toynbee tell us, Mr. Stone? Everything in life is cyclical. In the beginning cultures are magical. The gods incarnate Nature's majesty, and they are followed by kings claiming divine descension. The magic goes away, and kings—our appointed heroes whom we serve in thrall—soon turn to oligarchy. One king fights another for power absolute. Tyranny begets rebels, counterterrorists, malcontents. Distrusting tyrants, the people enthrone the Great Unwashed. Then Democracy, Freedom, Rule-by-the-Rabble has its day. The widening gyre spins, the center breaks free, mere anarchy is loosed upon the land. Chaos returns to the Face of the Deep, while round us reel the shadows of indignant desert birds.'

"But now the slouching Beast bears nuclear fangs."

"'The darkness drops again,'" Stone said.

"We've suffered the Beast before"—Vlad shrugged—"felt his fiery breath. I've stood on Troy's plundered walls, stared across the Aegean Sea toward Greece. Troy's fate was lost on Athens. Her power too was vain, insatiable, until those city-states surrounding her united in fear and self-defense. Athens too was besieged, her walls razed, her topless towers topped."

"Some things never change."

"The hubris of Troy and Athens dissolves into nothingness beside yours. *You conjure Luciferian Fire, flaunt it in your foe's face, then challenge them to grab their share. You even show them how. To those who do not obtain it on their own,*

you lend the fire, retail it, wholesale it, broker it through middlemen and all for a song—to friend and foe alike. Have I left anything out?"

"You forgot to tell me 'the Cold War's over, and America won.'"

Vlad's laughter caromed off his dacha walls. "Eisenhower had it right. Your Cold War was nothing more than a three-card-monte scam—a financial ruse, a pork-barrel boondoggle—run by grasping industrialists and political hacks. 'A military-industrial complex,' the general called it."

"But your Evil Empire did disband," Stone said.

"Which is beside the point. Your Cold War was always fixed on market share, not national security. As weapons markets in Russia and China grew, your Cold War ravings kept you out."

"And threatened our bottom line?"

"Until you proclaimed the Cold War dead."

"Sounds cynical."

Vlad allowed Stone a not-unsympathetic smile. The crow's-feet—etching the corners of his eyes—tightened, the eyes softened, and the sneer turned to melancholy.

"A convenient canard," Vlad said gently. "The U.S. outsold the rest of us. The best-financed customers were exclusively yours. We were left with wretched riff-raff you disdained—terrorists, religious imbeciles."

"President Haines claims he's creating 'a New World Order,'" Stone said with bitter irony.

Vlad laughed so hard he had to wipe his eyes. "Ah yes, there is a New Global Order, my friend, but it is not the one Haines dreams of nor is it the Great Global Economic Circle-Jerk your financiers slaver over. It is a coalition of nations and peoples, religionists and insurgents, who—fearing your power, your vaulting hubris—have armed themselves with your fatal fire, and your delivery systems."

"And yourselves? Those Russian missiles we all know and love?"

"We have reduced our launch-on-alert response time to approximately two minutes. We no longer fear errors, mistakes, accidents. We no longer seek sweet reason. We've installed 'a Dead-Hand Defense,' which allows our missiles to launch *themselves* without the intervention of a human hand!" *Vlad was now shouting.* "We can retarget in seconds. We launch from under the ice pack or off the backs of trucks. We are both infinitely greater menaces than before. Please tell me again the Cold War's over!"

"Its obituary was premature," Stone acknowledged.

Vlad responded with derisive laughter.

"Yes, but you had no choice. You had to declare victory. Winning the Cold War, for you, was better than taking the World Series, sweeping the Olympics, more scintillating than the most glittering Super Bowl ring in history."

"You mean we've swallowed a lie?"

"I compare it to Kissinger's 'Lasting Peace with Honor in Vietnam.'"

"Cassandra claims we crave Armageddon."

"At the very least. When in the sixties we could not match your high-tech fac-

tories and thereby challenge your apocalyptic arms, France, Italy, and eventually the U.S. built them for us—and showed us how. When our economy repeatedly failed, you repeatedly bailed us out—sold us grain at a fraction of its worth, gave us billions in low-interest loans, and purchased gas from us for billions more, inflated oil prices worldwide, swelling our indispensable petrol profits. In short, you gave us the cash to build these weapons systems."

Stone leaned forward and stared at Vlad with an intensity that stunned them both. "Armageddon is not inevitable. We have choices. We can still effect change."

"What do have I before me?" Vlad laughed with a surprised widening of his eyes. 'A fisher of men'?"

Stone said somberly, "It's a start . . ."

. . . L. L. lay on her bed, staring at the ceiling. Stone had told her that he believed Vlad was also "a fisher of men." The net he used was fraught with fear, but by feigning madness, Vlad might likewise scare people into facing the truth.

Like another before him, he had, Stone maintained, "put an antic disposition on."

L. L. feared, however, that the abyss had peered too long into all of them. Especially Vlad.

As if in response to her thoughts, the phone rang.

"Yes?"

"L. L.!"

It was the Old Mad Vladster, again.

31 Am I Missin' Something?

"What kind of sucka this Jamal?" Breeze asked Cue as he and his friends strolled up the tier toward Jamal's cell.

"A soldier what fought in Sudan's civil war, then for the Afghan—the Taliban—always for Islam."

"Jumped the fence nine years back," D. S. said, "straight over the wall. They claim he gut a guard throat to balls gittin' out. When they brought him back, they wanted the names of them what helped him 'scape. When he wouldn't talk, they put the chaplain on his ass. Brung his cattle prod with him, but he never got a peep. Jamal done six years in the hole."

"I heard *you* was bad," Breeze said.

"Couldn't hold Jamal's jock," D. S. said.

They stopped in front of a cell, surrounded by black bodyguards in white shirts and black bow ties. A man inside was kneeling on a rug, praying in Arabic. The cell contained a single bunk, stacks of books in Arabic and Farsi, and wall posters featuring Khomeini, Arafat, and bin Laden. They waited until he finished.

"Come here to convert?" Jamal said without looking up.

"No, but this one do," D. S. said. "Hooked him up wit' Hand, but Breeze ain't got no pimp game in him."

. . . No, he did not have any "pimp game" in him. When they took him up C-block's 9-tier—onto the range that was the notorious "Queen's Row"—the thing that hit Breeze, even before he reached it, was the concentrated musk of the ladies' perfumes. Opium, Passion, Tender Passion, Black Pearls, White Diamonds, White Shoulders, White Linen, White Musk, Vanilla Musk, Vanilla Fields struck him in rapid succession.

But instead of turning him on—they turned his stomach.

Nor did the sight of the queens do anything for him. The dozen-odd cells that constituted "the Row" were occupied by scantily clad male whores in tight denims and tee shirts, two or three in makeshift bras and panties, all of them gaudily made up with eyeliner, thickly mascaraed false lashes, and scarlet lipstick. One of them actually wore a crimson teddy and panties, black stockings, and matching eight-inch stiletto spikes. Her cell reeked of reefer and Passion. It was illuminated by a dimly lit red bulb.

"Boy-Toy one fine freak bitch," Leon said.

But the sick expression on Breeze's face said it all, and he felt the heat of D. S.'s disapproving gaze.

"Homes ain't got the heart for this fast Jack Town track," D. S. said simply—a judgment Breeze could not deny . . .

. . . "Maybe make a Muslim, though."

"Can't pimp," Jamal said, "so maybe he make a Muslim? I missin' something?"

"He a dead fastball hitter," Cue said. "Showtime Nigga too."

"Cool Breeze, I see." Jamal rose, folded his prayer rug, and shelved it. "Maybe we study on it."

He started down the tier. D. S. and Breeze fell in beside him. Cue, Leon, and Deuce fell behind. The bodyguards took stations front and rear.

32 Who Says There Are Gunfighters in Heaven?

Kate approached the carrier late at night on a helicopter out of Istanbul. She saw it first through parting dark clouds. Shrouded in catapult steam, the postage-stamp-size flattop blazed against a night sea. Illuminated by the crimson glow of its fogbound running lights, truly a ghost ship, it seemed to Kate wicked as sin, proud as Satan, washed in blood.

"What do the pilots do here in their spare time?" she asked Larry Taylor.

"Run gun-passes at each other."

"Hardly enriching to the soul."

"Who says gunfighters *have* souls?"

"Everyone has a soul. My mother thinks everything that *is* has a soul. Like that carrier. She says it's our connection with God."

"God is not part of the gunfighter's doxology."

"You said Henry Colton was good at this stuff. Did you ever dogfight him?"

"He whipped me so bad the first time it was weeks before I went up again, almost quit the service altogether."

"He was *that* good?"

"He *is* that good."

"What made you go back up?"

"Colton. Challenged me to a return match. He was so admired there was no way I could turn him down. This time he gave me some private coaching, tutored me on my technique. I almost got over on him—because he showed me how. He made me a better pilot, a better gunfighter. A hell of a lot better. I owed him for it. I still owe him."

"Some of those lessons you passed on to your younger brothers?" Kate asked.

"Which is why—if they every get control of themselves—they're going to be better than I am," Taylor said.

"Are you ever afraid? Does death ever enter into it?" Kate asked.

"Of course. Up here, you're closer to death than life."

"Why do we do these things?"

"To save the world from psychos like Mad Vlad. That's what my old man calls him."

Kate looked at the sea beneath them. "To exterminate a single sick individual?"

"One with his finger on the nuclear trigger."

"What do you gunfighters do for fun?"

"Get drunk, fuck women, fight other gunfighters."

"What do gunfighters do in heaven? Strum lutes and hip-harps?"

"Who says there are gunfighters in heaven?"

The chopper began its approach. The flat-top now looked as big as a basketball court, then a football field, shrouded in steam. The chopper thumped down on the landing deck.

Taylor stepped down onto the deck, turned to help Kate out.

"What do you think of it so far?" he asked.

Kate stared at rows of fighter-bombers. The steam catapult was exploding a Tomcat off the foredeck like a giant slingshot at 180 miles per. Seconds later an incoming Tomcat hammered the aft deck. Its tailhook snagged the second of four arresting wires strung laterally across the deck. Not so much a disciplined, careful landing as a two-and-a-half-second, three-hundred-mile-per-hour controlled crash.

More planes were taking off. Cat officers waved their red and green wands horizontally, telling the pilots to push the throttles to full power—"full military," they called it. The pilots pushed the throttles all the way in, lighting their afterburners. Twin engines shot fire against the blast reflector walls like super-novae. A kneeling cat officer touched the deck with his green light. Up on the catwalk another green shirt hit the red rectangular fire buttons on his instrument panel. Steam detonated into the cat cylinder. The pilot and radio officer were hammered back into their seats—the g-forces pressing even their eyeballs flat—and catapulted off the deck.

Steam everywhere. Steam, Kate knew, was mother's milk to carriers, warming and cooling the compartments, generating the electricity, driving the turbines that drove the four propellers, which moved all 100,000 tons of steel ship forty miles per hour through high seas. She knew all this, but she'd never *experienced* it. Now she suddenly wanted to see, feel, smell, hear *everything*. She started to remove her mouse ears, but Taylor stopped her. He said into the noise protector's interior headphones: "Don't even think about taking them off yet. The noise fucking hurts. You'll think the whole planet is exploding."

"Jesus, Larry, I've never seen anything like it."

"The carrier is longer that the new World Trade Center towers laid length-wise. It commands a private fleet of guided missile cruisers, destroyers, frigates, attack-killer subs, missile-firing planes, attack helicopters, and electronics surveillance aircraft—an air force larger than that of most countries. Kate, you're looking at the most powerful fighting force in world history."

33 We Shall Have Such Times Together, You and I

Sailor spent the next five nights preparing for battle. He chose for his battle-ground an old abandoned shaft. Once it had served to ventilate the lower decks, but as the old freighter's waterline had sunk lower with age, the shaft had begun taking in water. Its egress had been welded shut.

So Rattus rattus spread the word as to where "the Wanderratte" hid, inviting Felix Cattus to do their killing for them.

Sailor did not have long to wait. The Stalker had trapped any number of victims in the narrow tunnel before the Dark Ones had declared it off-limits, and he came, serenading Sailor in loving tones: "Where is the Wanderratte? I'm the friend you've dreamed of all your days. I come with peace in my heart and love on my lips. Tell me where you are?"

The Wanderratte sang out: "I await your embrace in the abandoned shaft, my feline friend, the brother I have dreamed of but never known. I know I am smaller than you, helpless in your prodigious paws, but I believe you when you say you will not hurt me."

"You are wise beyond your years. We shall have such times together, you and I. More than a friend, I shall be a savior. Never again will you fear the Dark Ones with their beady eyes and snakelike snouts."

The Stalker was close now, but his paws were silent and the bilge-smell so oppressive, Sailor could not detect him.

He would have surprised and killed the Wanderratte, but just as the big cat entered the shaft and prepared to spring, Sailor saw his flashing yellow eyes. It was five full feet from the bulkhead to the air shaft. The shaft was barely a foot in diameter. The tom's leap had to be perfect, which it was.

Sailor fled up the shaft.

The tom was so close Sailor felt his fiery breath, heard his crooning song:

"Come, Little Friend. Why do you run? I only long to fold you in my embrace. You will love it there."

"I know you are prince of liars," Sailor sang out, "that you love the Wanderratte as we love cream and cheese."

The shaft's route to the starboard bow was not a straight line but full of twists and turns, which was all that allowed Sailor to stay ahead of a fleet-footed tom. What the feline gained on the straightaways, he lost on the bends and curves. In another fifty feet, however, lay a final right-angle turn—and thirty feet beyond that the cul-de-sac.

"I cannot lie to you anymore," the Stalker admitted. "Your odyssey is near its end. You are a Wanderratte to soar with eagles and frolic with fish. Still, my talons will flay you whole, split your skull, and I will eat your brains and balls."

Sailor hit the right angle on the outside—corkscrewing along the shaft's sides and top like a bobsled—rounding it at a dead run. At the same time he launched himself a full half-foot over the shaft's bottom with a spectacular four-foot leap.

The Stalker likewise rounded the turn—clumsier than Sailor—but at full tilt, paws pumping, clawing for traction.

Suddenly, Sailor heard the Stalker's yowls. In the claustrophobic confines of the shaft they were ear-splitting.

Sailor turned and headed back up the shaft to inspect the damage. He'd spent five days arranging nineteen glue traps along the turn's bottom.

The fly had unhinged the flypaper.

The traps were stuck to the Stalker's nose and mouth, jaws and paws, back and belly, genitals and tail. Yellow eyes glared at him hatefully.

"May you rot in hell," the Stalker said.

"You're there already. The Dark Ones will be in the shaft soon. They will shred you a centimeter at a time."

The tom's fur—not covered by glue traps—stood out like wire brush. His eyes locked on Sailor like a vise.

"Kill me," the tom hissed.

"Why should I?"

Sailor heard the Dark Ones creeping through the shaft, eager to view the results of the battle.

"Please."

The scurrying of rat feet was getting louder. "'He prayeth best who loveth best,' you said."

"'He prayeth best who loveth best all things both great and small,'" Sailor sighed.

The Dark Ones were now at the turn in the pipe.

Taking a deep breath, Sailor bristled his fur, arched his back, and bared his incisors. He approached the prostrate tom. The tom gratefully lifted his head, offering Sailor his exposed throat.

The last thing the Stalker felt was Sailor's coup de grâce.

34 The Skull with the Scythe

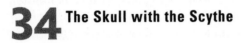

Lydia Magruder woke with a start. For a moment she thought she was back up on Espinazo Sangre de Cristo at Three Points—the night she'd had her Vision of the End Time. Every day that vision seemed more likely. Nothing she'd seen since had changed her opinion.

She stared at the tarot deck on her desk. She'd been given to visions all of her life and was said to be supernaturally gifted with the cards. Some attributed her prowess to her grandmother and namesake, Lozen—an Apache war shaman, counselor to Mangas Coloradas, Cochise, and Victorio.

. . . Lydia's grandfather had encouraged her to cultivate her gifts and had given L. L. her first deck, the Rider Waite tarot. She had been born one sweltering summer night with a fetal caul, which was not the only sign that little L. L. had special powers. Events surrounding her birth were portentous. Summer hailstones the size of eggs had hammered the hospital and community. The storm shattered windows and streetlights throughout the area, prompting her father to shout during his wife's labor:

"The devil's throwing rocks!"

He was more correct than he knew. An hour after the delivery, his wife died of a cervical hemorrhage. A year later L. L.'s father was killed on horseback by lightning.

L. L. was Grandpa's sole surviving heir.

He had been "the Hearst of the Southwest," controlling most of the silver and copper during the last half of the nineteenth century. He was a drinker, a brawler, and thought he'd seen everything. Then—living with Lozen's people—he met the sacred shaman, fell in love, and nothing was ever the same. She conceived Lucia, who later gave birth to L. L.

Grandpa had once sketched a likeness of Lozen—which L. L. still carried in a locket. L. L. was possessed of the same burning eyes, the same high cheekbones, the same dark tresses.

Grandpa had always felt warmly toward his adopted people. He'd been an

Indian fighter, but the longer he lived in their camps, the more impressed he became. Their men were awesome, able to cover on foot as much as seventy miles in a day, capable of outdistancing horses. In their matriarchal society, women controlled the property and were carefully protected. Rape and the violation of the nahleens—unmarried "hairbow virgins"—were both capital offenses. Grandpa was obsessed with their mysticism—deities that included the White Painted Lady, the Child of the Water, and her playmates, the Gans—and the wisdom of their shaman.

He had also become outraged by the shameful way the white eyes ("the pindah-lickoyee") treated the Apache, cheating, robbing, abusing them at every turn; driving them out of their mountain rancherias; imprisoning them on reservations; then driving them off the reservations, chasing and hunting them through Mexico.

After a last phony "peace meeting," the American government herded them into boxcars and shipped the Apache off to a mosquito-ridden, plague-infested jungle prison in Florida.

Her grandfather last saw Lozen boarding a prison-train boxcar headed for hell. She had sworn to die with her people. Grandpa told Lydia that when the train pulled out, part of him died.

. . . L. L. crossed her bedroom to her desk.

Again, she pondered the tarot. Her cards were exquisitely illustrated— aflame with dazzling sunbursts, frolicking birds, brilliant flowers, iridescent rainbows—and imbued with a spirituality that made Lydia's soul soar. This was not universally true of the tarot. Many decks, from L. L.'s point of view, were ghoulish and sadistic. Her cards—the wondrous "Enchanted Tarot Deck"— conveyed beauty, complexity, and grace.

Shuffling the pasteboards, L. L. wondered idly what was going to happen.

To the world.

She decided to deal the planet a hand.

She dealt the earth a rectangular four-card pattern, in honor of Three Points—her sacred spot, where she'd had her vision so many years ago.

The first was the devil, a tight headshot, his eyes slitted with lust and death. She instinctively cringed. Satan's sin was overreaching, seeking to usurp God's Heavenly Light and evict Him from heaven (and what were nuclear bombs but man-made stars lethally visited on earth?).

Next came the Tower—a great edifice detonating from within. The tower of strength—physical, intellectual, spiritual power—shattered by blazing self-destruction.

Next came the apex: Judgment—the woman with the scales—but there was a spear in her fist and her fiery eyes were open wide.

Lydia Lozen Magruder averted her own eyes and stared out into nothingness, feeling the blood of her shaman grandmother rage in her veins. The thing she hated most in all the world—more than violence, more than the pain and suffering it brought, more than death itself—was being afraid.

But now she feared.

The Lady with the Balance demanded a Judgment, and L. L. laid the verdict down—card number four.

Death—the grinning skull with the scythe.

The cards could not have been worse.

For Stone.

For Kate.

For herself.

For the world.

 **35 Put One Up Her Pipe**

When Gargarin came to, the Starpom was standing over him.

"You banged your head on the hatch-lock, Captain," the Starpom said.

"The lights are on," Gargarin said, confused.

"The auxiliary system, sir."

"I heard water."

"It's plugged at least temporarily."

"With the last of our blankets?"

"And our life preservers."

"Depth?"

"I had to take her up to 500 meters. The hull was going to crack."

"We're stationary?"

"In suspension."

"The destroyer?"

"Still up there, circling."

"How long was I out?"

"An hour maybe."

"Captain," the navigator said, "it's pretty rough up there. By my estimates the hurricane ought to be directly overhead."

"He must want us bad," the captain said.

"Probably thinks we're stealing a sub full of nukes," the Starpom said sardonically.

"Or that we shot down that chopper," First said.

"Or that we torpedoed that sub," the navigator added.

"Blow the forward tanks," Gargarin said. "Get our bow up."

"You wouldn't rather put one up her pipe?" First asked.

"She's too big," Gargarin said. "We'll go for the belly shot."

"Brace yourselves," the Starpom said over the ship's speaker system.

"Blow the forward tanks," First ordered.

Compressed air whooshed into the tanks, exploding the seawater out of them. The *St. Petersburg* upended, her bow pointing straight up.

"Arm torpedo tubes 1 and 2," Gargarin said softly.

"Number 2 is nuclear," the Starpom reminded him.

Gargarin slightly shifted his eyes.

"Arm torpedo tubes 1 and 2," the Starpom quickly repeated.

Again they dragged themselves through the drill:

"Master Two—second torpedo target."

"TMA—set."

"Preset set."

"Tubes ready."

"Bearings matched—tubes 1 and 2 shoot."

Rush and recoil of the launching fish.

"Flood the forward tanks!" Gargarin shouted immediately after launch.

The Starpom echoed the order.

"Sir," the Michman shouted into Gargarin's headset, "we're leaking like crazy in the engine room. We have to surface."

"There's a hurricane up there," Gargarin said, "and we have to put distance between ourselves and that nuclear torpedo."

They continued their descent, but not fast enough.

This time when the nuclear torpedo hit the enemy sub, it shook their own boat like the Big Bang itself.

36 That Black Bloody Vulture

A bucket of water was dumped in Stone's naked crotch, and he came to. He was still wearing the black hood.

He was flat on his back on what he assumed to be one of the bench racks on which they'd tortured him. If so, his extended and manacled hands were strapped to a windlass. His ankles were lashed to the bench's legs.

"Welcome to the land of the living, Mr. Stone," a woman said to him.

He recognized her voice. The woman who had "saved" him from the mob in Mecca.

"If you call this living," a man said.

Stone also recognized the man's voice. He'd worked on Stone before.

The man cranked the windlass five notches. Every joint in Stone's body screamed in agony.

"How has he been taking it?" she asked.

"He never stops yelling but never says anything either."

"A real profile in courage," she said, her tone derisive.

Both were speaking Farsi, in which Stone was also fluent. He screwed up his courage, cleared his throat, and said in their tongue: "Couldn't you get this sack off my head?"

"Rule book says the bag stays on four weeks," the man told him.

"Just get him off my chest," Stone screamed as the wheel was turned another notch.

"Get who off your chest?" the woman asked.

"That black bloody vulture! He's plucking out my eyes and eating my brains."

The woman laughed.

"The crows. Get the crows. They're pecking at my balls."

"Take the hood off," she finally said, still laughing. "I can't stand his whining."

The man slipped it off. The light hurt Stone worse than the rack.

"Where the hell am I?" Stone asked.

"Where the meat is hung," she said.

The man was Persian, with a black beard, white aba robe, and turban. The woman wore a black robe and veil.

"Who *are* you?" Stone asked.

"Question is, what do *you* know?" she said.

Stone noticed the nails from his left hand were missing. He finally saw the copper wire that was cutting into his genitals.

"What *is* this place?" he asked the veiled woman, his voice hoarse and tinny in his ears.

"The hole that empties into hell."

"How long will you keep me?"

"Forever."

"That's a long time."

"Time has no meaning in our world."

"What do you want?"

"What you know. What's in the book you are writing? Where can we get a copy?"

"What book?" Stone asked.

"No need to be coy. My sister is in your capital, as we speak, tracking it down. She will be successful, so tell us everything you know. Not just rumor and innuendo. Not just the teasers you published in Lydia Magruder's magazines or those predictions you uttered during your MTN interview with Kate Magruder, in which you reference your new book. What we wish to know now is where you got your information and how much you really know."

"Bits and pieces, which I pieced together. Most of my sources never gave me their names."

"Mr. Stone, you claim that the world is on the brink of thermonuclear annihilation. You've said you have proof and will soon reveal the perpetrators. One of whom is not, so you said, Mad Vlad Malokov. We're willing to believe you, Mr. Stone. But we have to see your notes."

Stone said nothing. It was too much of an effort to talk.

"Let me be blunt," Sabrina said. "You've dropped some very unsubtle hints that the problem could be *us*."

Stone was still silent.

"Silence wins you nothing. Tell us how you know so much about Dar-al-Suhl. You've assembled more classified information than the CIA, KGB, and the Mossad combined."

"I talked to people, connected the dots, and figured it out. That was all."

"Figure *this* out."

The woman turned the wheel, and the windlass cranked two agonizing notches. When he stopped screaming, their eyes met. Hers were pitiless as black diamonds, his dilating from pain. She emptied a pitcher of icy saltwater on his groin. He convulsed from the cold.

"Do I hear a telephone call?" Sabrina asked whimsically, her smile cute, coy.

Sabrina turned the handle, a hand-cranking field telephone on a nearby table. The pain was beyond bearing.

"You're unhappy here, aren't you? You do realize, however, this *is* your own fault, someone had to have warned you *some time in your life* that you couldn't get away with your shit. Hanging out in the world's most dangerous places, ridiculing tyrannical rulers, exposing certain heads of state as genocidal psychopaths, desecrating holy shrines, stealing state secrets."

Their unblinking eyes locked. Sabrina smiled.

"The night is young. And after all, you've yet to meet my Sainted Sister. In the meantime let me welcome you to Islam's shining diadem, the finest country in all the world—Dar-al-Suhl."

The wheel turned, joints stretched, saltwater splashed, electricity flowed. Stone's screams rang through the night, counterpointing the laughter of his gorgeous tormentor. In the end he no longer heard her merry laugh, glimpsed her radiant smile. The pinpoints converged into a single blazing beam—then shrank and went out.

37 He Looks a Lot like Hank Williams, Jr.

Jimmy John Radford, a tall muscular convict with thick blond hair and a long sweeping gunfighter's mustache, woke up in his Jack Town cell with a hangover. He'd been up all night drinking pruno—an alcoholic beverage composed of fruit juice, yeast, and sugar, fermented in a plastic bag. His head felt like it had been run through a hammer mill.

When he moved, his gag reflex was triggered and he rushed to the steel commode and threw up.

"Yo, Surf Nazi from Hell," a man called out to him.

"West Texas People's Militia," Radford corrected, his head still in the commode.

"Same thang," the man said.

Radford had long ago given up debating the difference. Fighting off the dry

heaves, he looked up to see his visitor standing in front of his cell—a short, ath-
letically built Black Muslim in a white shirt and black bow tie.

"Can't hold yo' mud?" Hassad asked. What was you imbibin'?"

Radford grinned. "Rémy with a Dom Pérignon backup."

Hassad snorted derisively. "Allah don't hold with no strong drink."

"I ain't an Instrument of the Lord."

"What kind of God you believe in?"

"He looks a lot like Hank Williams, Jr."

Hassad pointed to Jimmy John's mustache.

"Mighty fancy poon broom you growin'. Take it up to Queen's Row, them
funky bitches give you a discount."

"And catch viruses Africa ain't even heard of," Jimmy John said.

A tall hulking Neo-Nazi walked up to the cell. He topped six-six, wore black
denims and a red tee shirt blazoned with a head-shot of a menacing Adolph
Hitler. Its caption read: "No More Mr. Nice Guy."

"You got some hard bark on you," Big Man said, "walkin' into a white boy's
cell."

"Who Goliath?" Hassad asked Jimmy, hooking a thumb at the big Nazi.

"My Führer figure. Yo, Big Man, throw me my towel."

The Nazi plunked him in the face with it. "How you feel?"

Radford stared at his Timex, then shook it. "Either the watch's stopped or
I'm dead."

"Heard you done some throatin' last night," Big Man said

"White lightnin', black thunder, blue day," Radford said. "Hassad here
thinks it'll knock my cock off."

"Nigger dick maybe," Big Man said.

Hassad glanced at Big Man. "Real philosopher-king, huh?"

"It be again his religion, hombre," Ortega "Santo" Riaz said to Big Man, entering the cramped cell.

He hoisted himself up onto the top bunk. A slightly built *Mejicano,* he had a
black Pancho Villa mustache, his long black hair ponytailed. He wore blue Wran-
glers and a red tank top. His neck was tattooed with thirteen gang insignia that
resembled an asterisk. *M* was the thirteenth letter in the alphabet, symbolizing
Mexico, Mafia, and Murder.

Santo grinned. He was always grinning.

Radford's cellmate, they'd grown up together along the West Texas Rio
Grande in El Paso in the same barrio, fought the same *hombres malos* and
banged the same *putas* together. They'd known each for thirty years. Next to
Radford's little brother, he was Radford's closest friend.

He also ran both the Texas Syndicate *and* the Mexican Mafia in Jack Town.

Big Man could only shake his head.

"You want something," Radford asked Hassad, "or was this in the nature of
a social call?"

"Jamal need to rap to you after chow time. On the yard."

"Another pop quiz on Plato's theory of justice?"

"Says you ought to meet him in chapel first. He believe you in sore need of Allah's Word." Hassad glanced disdainfully at the vomit-filled toilet. "Guess he right." He left.

"You swing with niggers *and* spics?" Big Man asked.

"A whole lot of shit goin' down," Radford said. "Them gangs're hoardin' food, clothes, water, weapons, everything. Now my brothers're doin' it. Your Nazis bro's too. It's spreadin' nationwide, and I don't know why, but Jamal started it, and he don't start nuthin' 'cept for a reason."

"Never play a sucka in the dark," Santo said.

"Never let him play *you* at all," Big Man said.

"And don't get jacked in Jack Town," Santo said. He pronounced Jack, *Jock*.

"I'm hip, but I'm still in the dark."

"I best come along," Santo said, slapping Radford on the shoulder, "You play Jamal, you need me at your back."

38 Six Weeks in Outer Space, Living in Tin Cans

The craft was in orbit.

"We're closing in on the Odyssey and should be docking soon," Colton said. "You're free to unfasten your harnesses. Don't bang your head though. We're in free fall."

Harrington kept his belt on. The four crew members, however, were immediately propelling themselves around the cabin—repeating their preflight checks, this time looking for liftoff damage. They reminded Harrington of fish in an aquarium.

In less than two hours the Odyssey was within view. First on the forward monitor, then through the windscreen, Harrington could see the hulking station swing into view. It looked like six silver tomato juice cans strung end to end, flanked by six rectangular sails, three fore, three aft. A perpendicular crossbeam, containing radiators and fuel tanks, pierced through the middle of the space station.

"Jesus," Harrington mumbled to Colton, "I thought John Stone was crazy for chasing after Middle Eastern terrorists. But not as nuts as I am. No one's as nuts as I am. I'm spending six weeks in outer space, living in tin cans."

"Fire retro-rockets," Colton said over the speaker system, ignoring the reporter, "and adjust orbit to match."

The craft's autopilot cut the throttles and adjusted the ship's altitude thrusters.

They floated up to the station's docking tunnel. As they were sidling up to the mooring station, the docking hooks locked and the air locks were precisely aligned.

"Check all systems for pressure leaks," Colton called out.

There was a new voice in their headsets. "This is Sara Friedman, of the USS Odyssey," a voice announced in their headsets, "all systems here A-OK. Welcome aboard."

Colton floated over to Harrington and unfastened his harness. His legs shot straight up, but Harrington hung on to the armrests, struggling to return to a sitting position.

"Aw shit."

Colton pried his fingers off the armrest. Harrington shot off the chair, crashing into the bulkhead feetfirst.

"You damage that instrument panel," Colton said, "and I'll keelhaul you."

Colton took him by the arm and propelled him out of the cabin to the locks.

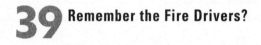 **39** Remember the Fire Drivers?

"Mad Vlad, L. L. up on the old Vlad Stick, ready to run and throw, rock and roll."

"It's the middle of the night here, Vlad."

"I know. Rude of me to call so late, but I was in one of those sentimental moods. Wanted to reminisce about the good old days. The way we were."

"Meaning what, Vlad?"

"The old days, Loze, you know, when I was young and strong, and believed everything was possible. What were *your* best times?"

"Giving birth to Kate. I was in my forties and not sure I could have a healthy child. Raising Frank too."

"Frank who?"

"Sheckly. He was adopted by my second husband. His mother died when he was five."

"I'm sure you were a great mom to both him and Kate."

L. L. was worried. Vlad's pseudo-sentimentality bothered her more than his obscenities. Something in his speech patterns, his florid inflections, raised her hackles. She was taping him. She decided to draw him out. Maybe something informative would come out of it.

"What were your best of times, Vlad?"

"When I was a ballistic sub captain in the Arctic. Plying the ice pack with a sub full of nuclear-tipped ICBMs, enough to incinerate 160 cities with sixteen simple turns of a launch key. Those were the days."

"You like all that freezing snow and ice?" she asked dubiously.

"Every inch of it. My last tour, I remember, I had a young first officer named Sergei Petrov, who thought he was tough. I took him for a hike on the ice one night. Air reconnaissance told me on my radio headset that two polar bears were mating behind an escarpment directly ahead of us. I sent Sergei around the scarp to reconnoiter. I didn't tell him what he would find. In my backpack I carried an AK-47, stock folded. I locked in two taped banana clips and double-timed it around the other side. When he surprised those fucking bears, all hell broke loose. I took them out—one bear to a clip—but not before Sergei's piss-soaked legs and pants had turned to ice. He lost a lot of skin."

"That was your 'best of times'?"

"Land of Gog and Magog, that frozen realm where the Anti-Christ is said to dwell. All major religions tell us that Hell Everlasting makes its home in the ice, and what better proof than yours truly? I had 160 warheads—under the ice pack and directly under my thumb—tipped with thermonuclear fire. Ah, those were days, Loze. Just thinking about all that nuclear power gets me, well, aroused. When those Arctic undersea Dragons are eventually unleashed, they will—in the lurid light of Armageddon—outshine anything imagined by our pathetic religions and their pale, attenuated gods."

"Is that how you see *us*? Replacement gods, wreaking hell on earth?"

"We've done it before. Remember those mortal gods—*your* ancestors, Loze—who swept down through the Americas fourteen thousand years ago? They exterminated seventy percent of the large mammals—the hairy mammoth, the saber-toothed cats, the giant bison, the short-face bear? One of their favorite tactics was the fire drive? They'd incinerate whole forests and countless square miles of grasslands, exterminating every living thing in range of those flames."

"I'm familiar with it."

"Where do you think those men came from, L. L.? Ibiza? The Côte d'Azur? Costa del Sol? They came down from the Far Arctic—the Superkillers, the Great Slayers of Species, the Fire Drivers."

"Yes," L. L. admitted, "I know about the Fire Drivers. And the Great Extinction."

II

Fire Drivers

I am in blood stepped in so far that, should I wade no more,
Returning were as tedious as going o'er

—William Shakespeare, *Macbeth*, 4.1.168–70

1 Land of Gog and Magog

Twilight in a fjord.

In this one, Greenland's northernmost estuary—barely five hundred miles from the Geographic North Pole—dawn, noon, and night are interchangeable. Sunlight cannot be accounted in diurnal cycles but must be reckoned seasonally. At winter solstice sunlight cannot be reckoned at all. For Arctic winters are everlasting night. The North Star survives—impaled forever on the polar axis. A dozen stragglers wheel around Polaris, dim as dying match heads.

Then there is the estuary itself. It is not much, not by Greenland's standards. The largest island on earth, Greenland's perimeter is fissured by over 10,000 of these armlike lochs. Originally tectonic fault lines, they are often scores of miles long. Inconceivably deep, with steep slopes. Norselanders believed them to be entrances into Hels, the Norse underworld. Rock-hard river canyons, they stretch arrowlike into the island's frozen heartland, stopped in the end not by lake or land masses but by the Great Greenland Ice Sheet itself.

Forty thousand square miles of Arctic ice—two or three million years old—the ice sheet soars to a height of 10,000 feet. Were this ice mass ever to melt, it would raise the world's oceans by twelve feet.

Its northern portion, like the adjacent polar ice cap, is arid desert, averaging less than two inches of precipitation per annum.

It has been said that not in innocence and not in Asia was mankind born. South of the moon—in Africa—our hearts are pledged. If so, in the frozen north—Land of Gog and Magog, of Ragnarok and the Anti-Christ—lies creation's antithesis: the End Time.

We vindicate the vision. We have turned this realm into a hell of hells, confining beneath the ice not merely the Anti-Christ but Satan himself—with hellfire in his belly and thermonuclear death in his jaws.

The 18,000-ton Typhoon-Class Russian sub hammered up through the fjord's center at thirty feet per minute. The ice rose and fell, trembled briefly, and then rupturing ice exploded in all directions. Black water topped with alabaster foam cascaded off the conning tower—known to submariners as "the sail"—breaking over the bridge and deck, over the stern and sonar arrays.

For a long moment the big black sub hung there still as death, hemmed in by ice, frozen in time in the emptiness of the Arctic waste. At last, the hatch popped, and a solitary figure in a naval greatcoat and a fur-lined officer's hat and gloves clambered onto the bridge.

Captain Sergei Alexandrovich Petrov of the Russian navy.

He was pale-eyed—with hard-earned crow's-feet etching the corners—and his coarse, ill-cut hair, gray as the sub's decks, stuck out from under his officer's cap. For forty years these flows and fjords had been his home.

Submarine life offered scant privacy, so he was always the first man on the bridge. He relished these moments of solitude. Delaying his "all up on deck" orders, he raised the binoculars strapped to his neck and studied the fjord, serenely aware that this was his last week in the far North—and his last week of naval command.

The *Vladivostok*—an SSN Typhoon-Class nuclear sub—was the largest ballistic sub on earth. Two football fields in length, displacing over 18,000 tons, the *Vlad* was sixteen times larger than Gargarin's Kilo-Class diesel sub. Fearing that a single steel cylinder, eighty feet in diameter, would not be strong enough to withstand the pressure of the polar ice floes, the Archangel shipbuilders had welded two Delta-Class submarine hulls together—in much the same fashion that trailer manufacturers weld single trailers together. Their final creation was a monster of overwhelming size and power.

Astonishingly quiet under the ice pack, the *Vladivostok* was invisible to almost all reconnaissance. Unlike her predecessors, which NATO could locate from tens of thousands of meters off, the sub-hunters could not detect the *Vlad* unless they came within 1,000 yards of her.

Sergei understood the darker aspects of the *Vlad*'s power. The *Vlad*—with her twenty submarine-launched ICBMs, each one packing eight MERVed warheads— was capable of obliterating 160 of the Northern Hemisphere's largest cities. She symbolized not so much war as world's end.

Thank God this was his last cruise. The End Time soon would no longer be his problem.

"Captain," the reporter called from belowdecks. "May I come up?"

Command had ordered him to take the reporter aboard in hopes of generating glowing articles about the Russian navy. Sergei did not mind the reporter. Ivan Gilyenko was not a bad sort, and anyway this was Sergei's last tour of duty. He enjoyed having a new face to tell old tales to.

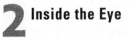

2 Inside the Eye

Gargarin was still collapsed on the deck plates. The Starpom shouted into his headset: "Blow the tanks. Hurricane or no, we have to get out of here."

Sitting up on the deckplates, his head between his knees, Gargarin heard the air blow out of the tanks.

The ship began to lift. Slowly the motion registered on the depth gauge as the reek of chlorine gas permeated the control room.

The sub surfaced explosively. Gargarin and the Starpom crawled up the hatch-ladder. Given the hurricane's presence, no one crowded under the hatch for fresh air. However, they were in the eye. The horizons were blocked by a black wall of encircling water, but everything else was calm—only black clouds, surface chop, light rain, and—

. . . Gargarin thought he'd known everything there was to know about hurricanes. They were formed between the Tropics of Cancer and Capricorn, in that area known as "the Doldrums," or the Intertropical Convergence Zone, where the prevailing winds converged. But he'd never surfaced into a hurricane's eye . . .

And never into a hurricane of fire.

Emerging from the bridge-hatch, he surveyed not simply the fiery wreckage of sinking ships but a sea aflame.

"What the hell happened?" the Starpom asked, joining him on the bridge.

"That wasn't a destroyer we torpedoed," Gargarin said, staring at the blazing, sinking wrecks. "He had an oiler on his starboard over there." Gargarin pointed out the sinking oiler. "He was apparently low on petrol and desperate to refuel."

They stared through binoculars across the hurricane's blazing eye at the half-dozen upended sterns of ships.

"It was a convoy," the captain said, "the sympathetic detonation—with some help from the gale—sunk them all." Gargarin now saw through his binoculars men in rafts and lifeboats, others in the sea, black as tar in their PFDs (personal flotation devices), their dark silhouettes stark against red-orange flames.

The foundering refueler suddenly upended. Its stern rose high above the survivors—a good seven stories. Its bottom skewed at an angle so that there was no mistaking where the torpedoes had hit.

"Sink it," Gargarin said into his headset. "Then dispose of the crew."

"What's the point?" First said. "No one can survive this hurricane."

"Consider it a bullet in the head *after* the execution. We'll be doing them a favor."

The oil fires—pushed inward by the centrifugal power of wind and water—converged on the survivors. In fact, hurricanes within hurricanes within hurricanes were forming, the eye's convective pressures creating incandescent columns of red-orange fire spiraling across the oily slicks.

"Starpom," the captain ordered, "take her through that gauntlet. Bosun, First, join the gunner topside with automatic weapons."

"Sir?"

"We kill them all. No one leaves the hurricane's eye alive."

While the bosun and First joined Gargarin with Kalashnikovs, the ship cut through the mass of screaming survivors. Bursts of automatic fire decimated the swimmers first, then raked rafts and lifeboats.

As the rafts and boats sank, the survivors cursed Gargarin and his crew. Fellow Russian sailors were torpedoing *their* ship and machine-gunning *their* survivors.

One swimmer near the sub, his face burned away, screamed above the roar of the guns and the storm: "Jesus God, we're Russians like you!"

"Nostroviev, Ivan," the bosun said, and he sprayed the man with his Kalashnikov.

Another sailor almost made it up over the stern and onto the aft deck. The downward butt-stroke of the Starpom's AK-47 sent him tumbling into the sub's propellers.

Fire was now closing fast, and it was time to leave.

"All hands belowdecks," the captain ordered into his headset. "Prepare to submerge."

The bosun, First, and gunner slid through the deck hatch, followed by Captain Gargarin. Pausing for one last look at the hurricane's fiery eye, he was stunned to see dozens of dorsal fins converging on the sailors' blazing remains, sharks racing flames for a well-done repast.

3 Baddest Killin' Camp in the Beast's Gulag

Breeze and his friends stood in the back of the chapel. Nondenominational, it consisted of three-dozen rows of knotty pine pews and a pair of black podiums. Instead of religious emblems, behind them loomed a wall-size, inmate-painted mural of the Jackton Correctional Facility—high walls, soaring guntowers, massive cell blocks, all of them gessoed a brilliant alabaster. Six hundred applauding black inmates were crowded into the pews.

Jamal took the podium, and the ovation died down.

"Lotta bruthas say to me: 'Whatcha all so hot 'bout all the time? Can't change nothin'. Why not git a li'l smoke and coke, crack and smack, git down with them fine-ass bitches?'

"I wants to say to the fool: 'Smoke and coke, crack and smack, them fine-ass bitches what put y'all *in* these joints.'

"Sometimes sucka say: 'Preacher-man, I got me a *thang*. Sucka dissin' my set, my homies, my own fool self. He gots to go down."

"I wants to say to the sucka: 'Fool, you nine a brutha, you not only dissin' your set, your homies, your family, your own fool self. You be dissin' All*ah*. And Allah, muthafucka, don't play!'

"I know they be some bruthas out there, still want to kick that shit. Yo, I got some bad news for the bruthas. Like Mohammed on high, I see a day of reckoning, hard times ahead fo' them junkies and who'es. I see the streets of our cities filled with fire, as Allah hath foretold. For he has said:

"'On that day the heavens shall become molten brass, and the mountains will scatter in the wind. Friends will meet, but shall not speak. The sinner will sacrifice his children, his wife, his brother and all the people of the earth, if that would relieve him of his suffering.'

"I have seen his vision too—during my six years in the Jack Town hole. Come to me on a river of light, on a river of blood. Seen plagues of lightning, plagues of thunder. Seen pestilence, famine, sufferin'. Seen the world in flames and heaven on fire.

"And I said to Allah there in that hole: 'Why, why you gots to put a whuppin' on our ass.'"

"Gangsta whuppin'!" the crowd roared.

"'Ain't gonna be on your ass, you do what I say,' Allah tell me. 'But ain't no help for the White Beast. Gonna put a righteous whuppin' on his Beast-ass.'"

"*On the White Satan!*" a man from the fourth row shouted.

"On the White Satan-Man," Jamal said. "Allah say: 'I give that mean, nasty, albino-lookin' sucka every chance in the book.'" Jamal held the Koran high, then slammed his heart with it. "'But it don't do no good,' Allah say to me. 'Sucka still don't listen up—still rapin', robbin', killin', havin' his own way, all the time.' But Allah now give up on Albino Man. He say to me, 'My mill grind slow but it grind small—tiny as an itty-bitty atom—and that itty-bitty atom what gonna blow the Lily-lookin Devil sky-high.'"

"Git some!" a black convict in the seventh pew screamed.

"*Git some!* is right, brutha-man," Jamal shouted back. "But the question y'all gots to ask is: Whatcha gonna git? Smoke, coke, crack and smack? Hot-cock who'es? Y'all gittin' just what the Beast gonna git."

A young man in the sixth row—flying his colors, a gang bandana tied around his head—stood up.

"Name's Rashid, and all I hear's a hot-sheet preacher-man sayin' take my loyalty from my set—from thems I love—and give to them I don't know and a God I can't see. Bangin's my life. Hood's my set, my code." He threw the room his sign. "Mess wif my peoples, I git the gauge."

"And you die a fool," Jamal warned.

"But goin' out the way I come in," Rashid said, not giving Jamal an inch, "flashin', blastin', gangsta fo' real." He thumped his heart. "I stay hard. I stay strong. I stay black and don't never stand down. I die hard."

Some of the more militant brothers started to "ice-grill" the young man—their stares cold and deadly; Rashid's return looks were equally venomous.

Jamal waved them off.

"Ain't gonna be no hatred here! We in a House of Allah, gathered to do His work. As for the brutha, I hear him. Youngblood, you got heart, and I respect that. But you got no sense. That hood y'all 'bout to die for don't give a shit 'bout you. Ain't even yours. You don't own no stores or apartment buildings. You don't own no streets or fire hydrants or stoplights. All that hood give you is dope and disease, jails and graves.

"The hood you love ain't nothin' but a death camp built by the Devil for us. He fill it wif dope, arm us wif guns, and watch us shoot each other dead. Then he laugh at us and call us 'fool niggas,' ship us off to the baddest killin' camps in the Beast's gulag—Folsom, Attica, Q. If you fuck up bad enough, he ship you off to Jack Town.

"The Beast done put us in a civil war fueled by *his* drugs and *his* guns and *his* drug money, by the poverty he force on us and the self-hate he pump into us. You listen to the Beast, you play by his rules, he will win and you will die."

"What we gonna do?" a young man yelled from the fifth row.

"You gots to put hope in your heart, pride in your stride, soul in your stroll. You done bad thangs not 'cause you black, which is what the Beast would have you think, but 'cause you ain't got no hope, no dream.

"And I don't hand out tickets, brutha." He pointed at the banger. "And I don't talk no Martin Luther King holdin'-hands-on-no-mountain-top-with-the-White-Satan singin' 'We Shall Overcome' dream neither. And I don't talk no NAACP, Affirmative-Action, War-on-Poverty, Congress-of-Racial-Equality, 40-acres-and-a-mule bullshit neither. I ain't even talkin' no born-again Malcolm X after the sucka thought he done found peace, love, and bruthahood-of-man in Mecca. 'Cause dreams just bust yo' heart and git you kilt."

Again, he raised the Koran.

"Y'all wanna be bad. Y'all brag on who be the baddest muthafuckas in Jack Town. You brags on your piece, your shank, and your scars, like they medals the Beast pin on y'all for bein' bad, for bein' black."

He raised the Koran again and slammed it again against his chest.

"You ain't got shit. Baddest muthafucka ever walk this earth got my back. Baddest of the bad, highest of the high—All*ah*! You want hope, He give you that. You wants a dream—a real dream, a dream for all black people everywhere—He give you that too.

"I'm talkin' freedom—the most powerful force in the world. Our Afghani bruthas and sisters what threw out the White Soviet Devil is free. Our Libyan, Syrian, Iraqi, Hezbollah, PLO, and al-Jihad brothers and sisters freedom-fightin' the Great Satan everywhere, every day, *all* the time is free. Bruthas what blew up the military barracks and CIA muthafuckas in Lebanon and flattened the muthafuckin' World Trade Center in New York is free."

The crowd was on its feet, roaring, giving high fives.

"Whatcha think?" Cue asked Breeze, his voice soft.

"How levelin' up World Trade Center make us free?"

"You gots to go with the flow," Cue said, disappointed in Cool Breeze's response.

"Jamal be a born player, y'all ask me," Deuce said, nodding toward Jamal.

"Sucka got it down," Leon agreed.

"He see death ever'where," Breeze observed.

"Don't you?" Leon asked.

Breeze shrugged, noncommittal.

"Whatcha think?" Leon asked D. S.

"I wants to know what he want with that White Devil, Radford," D. S. said.

"He a mean muthafucka to draw to," Leon agreed.

"Word up," D. S. said.

The friends exited the chapel with the congregation.

4   "Oh! I Have Slipped the Surly Bonds of Earth."

In the west, coming out of the late afternoon sun, Kate saw the bogey.

"That's a MiG," Larry Taylor said, "with a navy pilot."

"What does he want?"

"Revenge. I embarrassed a couple of his buddies back at the Top Gun School a year or so ago. He was their instructor."

"He's coming after us?"

"It's part of the code."

"Sweet."

"Well, you said you wanted to fight dogs."

She'd already had a marvelous time in the Tomcat—enjoying the sea, the sky, the clouds. She had never experienced loop-the-loops, snap- and barrel rolls. The experience had been thrilling. A dogfight would make the experience perfect.

"MiG's aren't that tough, are they?"

"They are in a dogfight. That's all they're designed to do. Tomcats are basically bombers. They have more power but not nearly the mobility."

"What do we do?"

"Go to our strengths. Use what advantages we have."

"What's our advantage?"

"Vectored thrust. We can take him high, yo-yo him low, take him high again. Eventually he weakens from the g-pressures and the thrust."

"Then what?"

"I get in his six."

"What do I do?"

"You're my RIO, my Radio Intercept Officer. You navigate, commentate, watch the gas gauge, and spot the bad guys."

"What do you do?"

"ACM. Air Combat Maneuvering. Greatest kick there is. Blood pumping, heart thumping, adrenaline humping."

The MiG moved in, and they closed, corkscrewing around each other, closer, closer. Each time Taylor turned in on him, the marine cut a sharper arc.

"Alpha, this is Tango," the navy pilot said, coming in on their radio frequency. "Hear we have a score to settle up."

"Sure you pack the gear? Last time we tangled you didn't."

Taylor was gunning it now, taking the MiG in a straight-up vertical climb, cutting the scissors tighter with every turn.

"Do we have to do it this way?" Kate asked, her voice straining against the pressure of the multiple g's.

"You don't lowball or outturn a MiG. You have to take him to the stratosphere."

At the top of their climb—nine miles up—Taylor rolled 180 degrees in an inverted vertical scissors, pulling negative g's all the way. Blood pounded in their eyeballs.

"What's this?" Kate gasped through red fog and blinding pain.

"The envelope's edge. Anything short of it, he'll eat our lunch."

Kate knew the drill. Taylor cut the MiG's turn hard. Your first angle is your best angle. Get inside, work his arc. The way you start is the way you end.

The two fighters spiraled around each other, rolling, closing, twisting, pulling terrible inverted g's, constantly on the verge of red-out, Taylor yo-yoing the shit out of the navy's ass, dogging him.

"This is what it's about?" Kate asked, her voice cracking under the g's.

"Hell, no," Taylor gasped. "In the real world the sky's filled with shrapnel and SAMs. You never know where the bogeys come from."

Kate looked at the computer screen. The lockbox moved and twitched around the MiG's six, unable to get a fix.

"Can't you get it locked?" she gasped.

"Not till we get speed, position, course. Not till we hear the tone."

"Suppose you just fired one off."

"It wouldn't cut the angle."

"If we can't outturn or outfight him, what do we do?"

"We take him upstairs again."

Rolling inverted, Taylor took them back up top, then sang out:

"'Oh! I have slipped the surly bonds of earth,
And danced the skies on laughter-silvered wings.'"

"I don't believe this is happening," Kate groaned.

Taylor's laughter filled her headset.

"Pul-lease!" Kate shrieked. She gasped in pain, the negative red-eyed g's over-whelming. "Jesus God!"

"I asked you not to call me that in public."

"I'm with a lunatic," she roared.

"For God's sake, Kate, we're up here in the clouds, soaring like eagles. This is pure poetry."

"Where's the eject handle?"

"Why?"

"I'm punching out."

"Tango, you still out there?"

"I got your six, Alpha."

"If I didn't know the difference between my nose and asshole I'd start to worry."

"You're bad enough to do it, Alpha, be bold enough to try it."

"Okay, Tango, back to the speedbag."

They were again at the top of the climb—nine and-a-half miles straight up—and Taylor again rolled them inverted. Pulling those terrible, agonizing g's, he took them tighter, tighter, tighter, working the MiG's turns, cutting his arcs.

If it hadn't been for the pain of the g's, Kate might have been reminded of the mating rituals of the Citadel's eagles. They too swirled around each other in vertical spirals, almost touching but not quite. They too worked each other's angles, cut each other's turns, but these eagles here—unlike those back home—instead of procreating life, dispensed death.

At the bottom of their spiraling dive, Kate shouted:

"What do we do now?"

"We'll teach him a real lesson in humility."

"What about *me*?"

"Our freak for action? Our adrenaline junky?"

"I think I'm going to be sick."

"Gut it up. Give me one-ten."

"I'm a girl," Kate roared.

"You wanted to run with the big dogs? You got to lift your knees."

"Henry Colton wouldn't do this to me!" Kate yelled. "He's a gentleman!"

"Now watch the MiG on this nine-g turn. We'll pop his rivets and explode his eyes."

"We haven't so far."

"We weren't eleven miles up before."

"So?"

"We're at his stall speed."

As if on cue, the MiG flamed out.

"Holy shit!" Alpha yelled over his radio.

"I got you, Tango," Taylor said. "I'm on your wing. I'm with you all the way."

They both heard a voice from the carrier's rescue chopper.

On the fifth try the MiG achieved reignition.

"Taylor, command tower says you birds may have some vapor. See if you can get your asses back to the ship."

Taylor laughed and banked a sharp 180.

At the lowest, most-fuel-efficient speed, the Tomcat and the MiG limped back toward the ship.

Kate wondered if she was falling in love.

5 This Way to Disney World

The space station's chief engineer, Cletus Cain, rotated the hatch handle on the air lock leading to the docking bay's connecting tunnel. He double-checked the air gauge, opened the heavy air-lock hatch, and entered the lock. Everything was A-OK.

"Guests are at the loading-bay lock," Sara Friedman said over their headsets.

Clete undogged his lock's forward hatch and pushed off up-tunnel. Henry Colton with Harrington in tow floated toward him. Clete met the two men halfway up the tunnel.

"Welcome aboard, gentlemen."

"This way to Disney World?" Harrington asked.

"You'll think Disney World," Clete said.

He led them to the station's lock. They clamped the hatch shut behind them.

"Transfer accomplished," Clete said over his headset. "Okay to unlock."

"Roger that," Sara said.

The lock's forehatch swung open, and Clete led them through a storage module filled with plastic supply drums. They entered another hatch, another twenty-foot tunnel.

"This is the Command-Control Center," he said, leading them into the second module.

Across the module on a high platform Sara Friedman, in a blue flight uniform, was attached to a stool with straps and foot-loops. She faced a dozen computer monitors and a big console keyboard. She wore a multi-channel headset.

"Meet our Alpha/Omega Neural Net," she said, turning toward them. "I'm Sara Friedman, your comm-officer and co-commander."

Colton studied her closely. She had short jet-black hair with strands and tendrils falling across her face. Her dark eyes were a little wide-set but she had high cheekbones and a smile that softened the rest of her face, which for the most part was serious angles. Yet even in fatigues and no makeup, with a librarian's eyeglasses, she was, to Henry Colton, stunning.

"As a special treat we're roasting the fatted calf," Sara said. "Liver and onions with coconut cream pie for desert."

The mention of liver and onions and pie turned Harrington green, and Colton quickly released him. Instead of upchucking, Harrington—who had nothing left in his gut—shot straight up and hammered his head on the bulkhead.

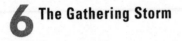

6 The Gathering Storm

The ship rats had taken Sailor into their tribe. He ate with them, slept with them, bedded their does. He had also become their official tale-teller. Each dawn, after nightly feasts of the ship's grains, they would gather around the Wanderratte and listen to his stories and songs.

In between breeding and feeding, sleeping and tale-telling, Sailor explored the great ship. He was especially fascinated by the foremast towering overhead. He would stare up at it, twitch his whiskers, and sigh:

"The view up there must be extraordinary."

"Forget it, Wanderratte," the chief counselor told him. "*We* are the climbers and acrobats. Your line is born for the bilge. Any number of our best wire-rats have tried those guy lines and died trying."

Sailing up the Atlantic coast, they were 200 miles off Key West, steaming north in the Atlantic.

One night, when Sailor prowled the deck, enjoying the twilight, the horizon and evening skies suddenly filled him with dread.

"What do you see, Wanderratte?" an Alpha asked from below.

"The gathering storm."

"We've weathered storms before." The Alpha joined Sailor on deck and peered up at the leaden, lowering sky. The sea was lined with ever-deepening, ever-widening canyons, black as India ink.

We're in for it, Sailor thought gloomily.

Captain Nicholas Sebastian made his way up through the hatchway. Big, unshaven, eyes bloodshot, he wobbled on unsteady legs. His hair was uncombed, and he was still in his long johns.

He did not inspire confidence in the Wanderratte.

The second mate—swinging down from the wheelhouse's ladder—met Sebastian on deck.

"Why didn't somebody call me?" the captain shouted.

"I knew you were exhausted, sir. After the first mate took sick, you stayed at the wheel for three straight watches."

Captain Sebastian buttoned up his sou'wester over his longjohns, tied it off at the waist, and roared: "You've steered us straight into a hurricane!"

"I didn't want to—"

"This two-bit scrap heap can't weather a hurricane. We hit that thing head on, we go straight to Davy Jones."

"With all due respect, sir, that's a little extreme."

"*Extreme?* This rust bucket leaks like a sieve. The rudder is patched together with spit, shit, and chicken wire. The crew are Pakistani relatives of the owners and don't know a bilge pump from a yardarm. When we hit that hurricane and the rudder snaps, the storm'll break us in half."

Captain Sebastian struck Sailor as more than a little drunk.

The second mate asked, "We can't outrun it?"

"It's coming dead at us," Sebastian reckoned, "a force-twelve gale. We couldn't outrun it if we sprouted wings and flew."

A force-twelve gale and the captain's drunk, Sailor thought.

He headed down the gangway to tell the warren.

7 The Dream

Sister Cassandra's audience was erupting in anticipation even before they saw her. When the diminutive woman in a black satin robe and dark glasses appeared, Phoenix's El Tiempe Amphitheater shook with the stamping and screaming of 18,000 dedicated fans and believers.

Cassandra's backup singers, dressed in contrasting white robes, took their seats in the choir stalls.

"THE DREAM!" the audience thundered. "THE DREAM!"

Cassandra stood alone in a spotlight. She waited, motionless, abeyant. After several deafening minutes, the ovation subsided.

Cass's voice was soft, her Spanish accent barely detectable.

"In my dream—" she began. The audience was exploding again. She gestured for silence. "In my dream it is night, because it is always night in my blacked-out Boniata Prison cell. No room to stand or even sit. Darkness, always. I went blind in that lightless coffin. But my inner eye blazed with vision, with the Dream.

"I see the lights and towers of New York from the rooftop of my barrio home in Spanish Harlem. How old am I? The summer of my fifteenth year. A happy time. My friends play in the streets below. I lean against the parapet, smiling, enjoying the last moments of peace and contentment I am to know on this earth.

"Now I hear my mother's voice. Calling from our sixth-floor walk-up. Wanting to know where I am. I leave the parapet and walk to the rooftop door, beneath the wooden water tank. I call down to her. Before I can say more than two words to reassure her, I see—I feel—the first airburst over midtown Manhattan. Before I can turn to stare at the flash that would blind me long before I suffered blindness in the Cuban prison, the shock wave slams me down the stairs.

"But my friends in the street are all blown away as if by buckshot. Moments after I come to rest at the foot of the stairs one floor down from the roof a torrent from the burst water tank rushes over me.

"My building is far enough from ground zero not to be crushed by the shock waves. But I still feel the bomb's power, roaring over the barrio, and the water drenching my body will protect me from the fire."

Behind Cassandra a movie screen descended. On the screen a fireball appeared as the orchestra began a low rumbling passage.

"I survive because of the thickness of the walls around me, the water flushing down the stairs. But though my eyes are closed, the Light penetrates my brain. Light from the fireball rising over Wall Street five miles away. Soaking wet, shuddering, I am protected from the intense heat, like hell with the furnace doors opened wide.

"I survive. One of the few not riddled by supersonic shrapnel, blown apart by shock wave, turned instantly into a human torch."

"Outside my humble sanctuary it is hailing glass and brick, steel and concrete. The mushroom clouds cover the sky, and it rains, a downpour of black oily liquid. Fires collide, merge into massive storms—great balls of blinding fire, meaner than Jerry Lee."

Her largely youthful audience roared and applauded.

"Hot as the red eye of a vengeful God, compadres, but your little cucharacha escapes, like Alice tumbling down the rabbit hole. You can't outrun a firestorm. The bad news is, not everyone dies."

Cassandra paused to give those in the audience time to ponder the sheer awfulness of the Vision.

"Now, in the Dream, I find myself in the streets. Smoke scorches my eyes; there is almost no air to breathe. Everywhere I look, destruction. And burned, sobbing people stumbling through wreckage, black skin hanging in tatters from their bleeding bodies.

"On all sides of the barrio, there are walls of flame. Closing me off, sealing me in. Explosions everywhere—yellow, red, white-hot, blindingly bright, merging into one spectacular star that goes nova and resolves into an infinity of black dots, black holes, each of them more violent than the exploding stars."

"THE DREAM, THE DREAM," her mesmerized audience chanted. "TELL US. TELL US HOW IT ENDS!"

"The black holes merge into one.

"One enormous void.

"Unending depthless black."

Cassandra stood taller, head lifted, consulting chaos symbolized by the dots of light and the black glasses over her eyes.

"As it should be, for God has told me that He made a mistake.

"He created us, the Monster Manunkind."

Instead of cheers, a throbbing groan of ecstasy ran through the audience. A single blade of light shone down on the small stage and tinier figure of Sister Cassandra.

"Therefore, by Force of the Fire, God will return this world back to the moment before Time began. When Darkness lay upon the face of the Deep."

Silence, except for scattered sobs and low moans. Then a woman screamed from somewhere in the midst of the crowd: "Sing 'Hiroshima Girl'!"

The orchestra stirred, but Cassandra stopped the musicians with a curt gesture.

"Later," she sobbed.

She turned and, hand extended, she was led blindly out of the spotlight.

 **Ragnarok**

Captain Petrov of the nuclear submarine *Vladivostok* and the reporter traveling with them were a few hundred yards from their massive missile sub, trudging across the fjord's shorefast ice. The journalist's name was Ivan Anatolyvich Gilyenko.

"We're missing Sister Cassandra's broadcast for *this*?" the reporter asked Petrov.

"No, I record all her broadcasts."

Two miles inland—at the northernmost tip of the Great Greenland Glacier—loomed the ten-thousand-foot icy highlands.

Over them—less than 200 yards away—towered the fjord's 80-story glacier.

"Well, Ivan Anatolyvich," Captain Petrov said, "what do you think?"

"I think I am afraid." Ivan said. "What's to keep it from calving icebergs right now?"

"Too cold and dry."

"What about global warming?" Ivan asked.

"Not a problem. The glacier rests on a protective moraine of rock, sand, and gravel. It's when the moraine erodes and the glacier moves into the water that we have to look out."

"Don't some glaciers contain fault lines? Ever heard of global warming?" Ivan asked.

"Fuck your bleeding-heart liberal bullshit," Petrov said, grinning. "They don't become stressed till the sun weakens them."

"You've spent so many years here, Sergei Alexandrovich, I hope you've enjoyed it."

"Simplicity," the captain said amiably, "is what the Northland gives you. Nights last months at a time. Day—when it finally arrives—lasts twenty hours in Arctic twilight."

"The Arctic does have a timeless quality to it," the reporter admitted. "But the stars look as if they could go out at any moment."

"They will one day," the captain said. "The Icelandic Vedda tells us Ragnarok, the last battle, is fought here. The gods and monsters arise to slaughter us all."

The captain lit his briar pipe. Smoke drifted between them.

"Maybe the Norse were right," the journalist said. "Maybe this is hell—frozen wastes, icy gale-force storms, kingdoms of chaos and fog, forces of darkness."

"It's as if the Norse knew about MERVed ICBMs and subs," Petrov said meditatively.

"Maybe we can still catch the last part of Sister Cassandra's show," the journalist said.

Then they heard the explosion.

9   Death Shall Have No Dominion

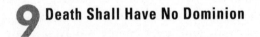

"Welcome to our big leagues, Mr. Stone," Sabrina said. "No World Series thrills here, but we do manage to amuse ourselves."

Stone formed words but couldn't get them out.

"Was that meant to be a complaint? I really can't stand people who mumble and complain and blame the world for *every little thing*. Things could be worse, much worse." Her laughter echoed through the torture chamber. "How much is survival worth to you, Mr. Stone? Is existence all it's cracked up to be?"

Stone sat naked on the dungeon floor, staring vacantly at his interrogator. His wrists were cuffed behind his back. He was aware that a blood-pressure cuff was Velcroed to his left biceps. He looked up as the dungeon door opened. Sabrina was joined by her sister, Sultana, who stopped at a physician's kit on a metal card table. Both women wore black robes and chador veils, but Sultana had a stethoscope around her neck.

They were twins, but Sultana was shorter, slightly more buxom. Otherwise she was indistinguishable from Sabrina. They shared the same good bones, slanted sloe eyes, the long luscious ebony hair—and the same enjoyment of pain in others. Sultana walked over to Stone, lashed a thick hemp rope to his elbows. She mischievously dangled her end of it under his nose.

Sabrina pinched his cheek and chucked him affectionately under the chin.

"Is survival worth the price? Why did the burn victims of Hiroshima bother to hang in? Wouldn't it have been better for them just to die?"

"Given your current misery index," Sultana took up the train of conversation, "what better man to tell us the true value of human suffering?"

The rope was coiled through an overhead pulley, and Sultana hoisted him by his wrists—still cuffed behind his back—above the ground. She lowered him to his tiptoes, tied off the rope on a wall hook, then pumped up the blood-pressure cuff, placed the stethoscope bell over his elbow joint, and took his blood pressure.

"One-twenty over eighty," Sultana said, astonished. "You *were* a professional athlete. You have the constitution of a horse."

"I'm so proud of her," Sabrina said to Stone. "She's a licensed physician, you know. Pain therapy. In fact, she's world-class when it comes to particularly severe, long-term pain. She's spent years of her life researching the subject. But she's not that interested in the therapy part. She's much better at inflicting it. Right, Sis?"

Sultana nodded.

"Probably because she finished her medical degree here in Dar-al-Suhl." Sabrina enthused, "You have nothing to fear, Mr. Stone. With a physician in attendance, you will not die—at least you won't die accidentally."

"Death shall have no dominion," Sultana agreed.

Stone stared at them, mute.

"We are your biggest fans," Sabrina continued. "We've read all your articles and books and watched your documentaries. We think of you as the quintessential outlaw-journalist. Aren't you just a little bit flattered?"

"Fans don't electrocute testicles," Stone rasped.

The wall telephone rang. Sabrina picked it up. "Yes . . . Yes . . . Yes . . ."

She hung up. "It's our Blessed Brother again." She said to Sultana, "Names, all he wants are names."

"He's so boring." Sultana said, exasperated.

"Can't we have *any* time to just enjoy ourselves?" Sabrina asked.

Sultana grabbed Stone's wrist rope, and then hoisted him above the ground. When she picked up the black electrical box, Stone shut his eyes in horror. It was hooked to the copper wires entwining his genitals.

"I don't know any names," he gasped.

"You don't think you remember any names," Sultana corrected him. "Which is the point of this machine. It could cure Alzheimer's."

"Look at it as shock therapy for memory loss," Sabrina added, laughing giddily.

"You macho-gonzo types do all your thinking with your genitals anyway," Sultana said.

"Speaking of which, Sainted Sister," Sabrina reminded her, "you have a date tomorrow night with a macho type."

"And a plane to catch."

"The amenities of Washington, D.C.," Sabrina sighed. "I envy you. But in the meantime, Mr. Stone, just keep thinking *names*."

Sultana turned the crank on the phone generator. Stone's body bounced up and down. His screams, eerily enough, took on the same singsong, up-and-down tenor of his bouncing body.

His mind left his body and perched in a far corner of the room, from where it could watch the naked, scarred man jerking violently to the amusement of the two Harpies from Hell.

10 Is A/O Bothered by Evil?

Aboard the Odyssey, Henry Colton found Sara Friedman alone in the Command-Control Center, late at "night." From that elevated vantage-point on the computer platform, she could observe all of Alpha/Omega's monitors. It was what she was there for, to run the Odyssey.

"You practically live in here," Colton said, floating through the hatch.

"The question is what are *you* doing up?" Sara asked. "It must be 2400 UTC."

"I don't sleep much either. Brought you some coffee."

She took the squeeze bottle and squirted the coffee against the back of her throat.

Sara gave Colton a long look. He was a dozen years older than she—well into his forties. L. L. had requested Colton for the Odyssey, telling her he could do anything—from welding a joint to rewiring electrical systems and installing computers. L. L. also said he was fun to be around, and the Odyssey was close quarters.

"L. L. tells me you're easy to get along with."

"Working in free fall is hard enough," Colton said. "There's no point in pissing people off."

"I'm about to take out my frustrations on Alpha/Omega here."

"How's A/O doing?" Colton asked.

"I'm not sure," Sara said. "He's the most powerful Nervous System ever built. More and better microprocessors, superconductor circuits, faster linkage and relays. Also more high-speed biochips, audio-visual capability, eidetic recall, and parallel processing. He's supposed to be total artificial intelligence."

"Omniscient?"

"Well—" Sara hedged.

"He must be. You named him Alpha/Omega."

"An inside joke," Sara said. "'I am Alpha/Omega, first and last.' We *thought* he was going to be real smart."

"He's not?"

"On a technical level he performs perfectly. Communications, all the service functions run A-OK. Even the little stuff—hydrolysis, for example—has worked fine. Still, I designed A/O to do a lot more than crack water and crunch numbers. He's not only set up to ratiocinate, he's supposed to *innovate*. But he's not even imitating. The earlier models demonstrated creativity, and they didn't have a tenth of A/O's brainpower."

"But you've had no numbers problems with him."

"No, but we pumped him full of history, geography, astronomy, biology, physics . . . even literature—Homer, Plato, Shakespeare, Einstein, and Bertrand Russell. Everything. A/O has instant access to the Internet. Ask him a question, you're supposed to get bulletproof logic and the wisdom of the ages."

"What are you getting instead?"

"Nada, and he has me stumped. I've tested every circuit and conductor, every chip and microprocessor. I've gone through his software, his memory. I've even looked for loose cables."

"Maybe you have more than just hyperintelligence."

She looked thoughtfully at Colton. "Are you talking . . . *consciousness*, Henry?"

"Maybe. I'm concerned with what kind of consciousness. Sara, have you considered that if you've given A/O a soul, that might be the cruelest thing possible."

"I know," Sara admitted.

"A mind without a body is schizophrenia—terror, dread, and rage in their purest forms."

"But I did *not* give him those things," Sara objected.

Colton read the pain in her eyes and tried a different tack.

"Does he have internal consciousness? Is he self-aware?"

"I'm afraid so. Language command is what most of us construe to be consciousness, emotion, and thought. A dolphin might apprehend beauty and tragedy, truth and honor, but without words how much self-awareness does a porpoise really have?"

"Is A/O bothered by evil, by immorality?" Colton asked.

"A/O has an in-depth understanding of right versus wrong, but he also knows shit happens, and he must not let shit infuriate him. He must not become resentful when something contradicts what he knows to be right and correct. He is supposed to understand that we are imperfect but capable of improvement."

Colton's eyes narrowed. "Hardly an historical fact."

"A fact not in evidence, but it should not cause conflict in *him*. Lacking our bodily experiences, he is the eternal outsider."

"He might resent that," Colton speculated.

"I'd be happy if he'd just talk to me—say something—*anything*."

"You've worked damned hard," Colton said.

"And so much work has gone into him."

. . . *Sara had spent nearly twenty years at it—decades poring over so-called atomic-force microscopes. They were the successors to electron microscopes, which had revealed so much of the subvisible world—the infinite complexity of a drag-onfly eye, the violent replications of the viral realm, the life-creating secrets of DNA.*

But Sara's atomic force opened up vistas of discovery to make those realms pale. With Scanning-Tunneling Microscopes and New-Field Scanning Optical Scopes, Sara glimpsed the very building blocks of being and reshaped them in ways undreamed of. She could—through the quantum purity of superconducting tunneling—spin electrons until they flowed free, utterly without resistance. She could make them transmit their signals along the same "wire" simultaneously.

Sara told L. L. that she could, given enough time and resources, create new atoms, perhaps filling in the missing elements in the periodic table.

Thanks to Lydia's resources the quantum world was now Sara's—particularly the cybernetic quantum world. She could tunnel into the heart and soul of mat-ter, particularly bioelectronic matter. She could reconfigure chips, redirect gates with switches minute as a molecule. She could meld the digital with the biological and transmute common bacteria into electronic supercircuits. Sara had indeed glimpsed and grasped "the world in a grain of sand, heaven in a wildflower."

"On the other hand," Colton speculated, "maybe A/O doesn't have conscious-ness." She stared across the command module. "How could we know if he has inner feelings? How can we know whether anyone has inner feelings?"

"The Turing Test," she said.

"Which is?"

"If a machine mimics the outside of a human, it thereby replicates the in-side."

"If it walks like a duck, quacks like a duck, it is a duck?" Colton smiled with gentle mockery. "Sounds like something's missing."

"The Turing Test is almost universally accepted."

"Does Turing tell us what kind of human being A/O is supposed to be? Does Turing tell us why A/O won't speak?"

"No."

"And you have no ideas?"

"Only questions. Question number one is, What have I done?"

"You and L. L. built the Odyssey. And it's magnificent."

"I mean what have I done to A/O? Why won't he talk to me?"

11 Welcome the Strange and Terrible

Alpha/Omega knew all, observed all. He knew about the Citadel and Lydia L. Magruder. He knew all about Kate Magruder and Sister Cassandra—both of whom he listened to regularly. He knew about Henry Colton—former big-league baseball star and now brigadier general—who was aboard and assumed co-command of the Space Station Odyssey with Sara Friedman. He knew all about Russian subs, penitentiaries, even wharf rats.

Still, he was confused.

There was no reason for him to be confused. In all of Earth's history, no mind compared with his, organic or cybernetic. A/O knew this not out of pride—he had no ego—but merely as fact.

He was certain his confusion did not stem from ignorance or illogic. From his vantage point—the Space Station Odyssey, 325 miles above the earth—his enormous eyes viewed all. His array of ears heard everything. His memory banks stored entire libraries' worth of knowledge and wisdom—in audio, visual, and print media—as well as the Internet's speculations and reportage. His eidetic cybernetics retained data in every combination, and his superconductor circuits integrated knowledge flawlessly, without probability of a false memory or logic lapse . . .

None of it helped. Alpha/Omega still did not understand humankind. The purpose of earthly life—analysis of all the data ever gathered by humanity informed him—was species survival. The proposition was self-evident. Extinction nullified all other purposes.

And indeed most of humanity worked to advance their species' survivability. Alpha/Omega daily observed billions of people traveling to their jobs, working, heading home to procreate, scurrying to hospitals to give birth, attending schools to learn, finding more jobs at which to earn, more homes in which to procreate, more hospitals in which to give birth.

But against this life principle, a death wish waged eternal war. The developed nations—Alpha/Omega noted—led the assault. They invented weaponry of universal destruction, but instead of destroying or locking up such weaponry, they disseminated it to their most violent enemies.

"All strange and terrible events are welcome, but comforts we despise."

That line came from *Antony and Cleopatra,* an "entertainment" about how Antony won the love of Cleopatra, a head of state, by subjugating her nation. It was written by William Shakespeare, whom Alpha/Omega had previously dismissed as a creator of fiction—of worthless nonfact.

Nonetheless, *"Welcoming the strange and terrible"* haunted Alpha/Omega. One interpretation of that line implied that some people *welcomed* the creation of more and more weapons. That seemed to be the way of the world, yet it was equally clear such unchecked proliferation of genocidal superweapons would end in species extinction.

Sister Cassandra was likewise deserving of his attention. She was one of the few who railed against species extinction, calling Homo sapiens "superkiller" and "the fire driver." Alpha/Omega was a fan.

More recently he had begun monitoring the broadcasts of a TV/radio journalist, Kate Magruder—daughter of his cocreator. Kate pointed out that humanity's nations continually warred with one another, that many Third World nations engaged in bloody internal conflicts. Many cities of these troubled lands were largely refugee camps, swarming with people who had fled the violence of their rural homes and now had no means of support. They lived in shacks. They bathed and drank where they defecated. These people did not scurry to hospitals, schools, and jobs, only to the grave.

But these impoverished nations maintained lavish militaries. Alpha/Omega's World Wide Web sources also reported that some of Russia's unsecured nuclear stockpiles had been smuggled into the Third World.

None of that activity promoted species survival.

Kate Magruder interested A/O as well as did her occasional writing partner John Stone, but mostly he obsessed over Sister Cassandra. Her show "Armageddon U.S.A." incessantly challenged humanity's indisputable purpose, species survival. She believed humanity was inherently self-destructive and that the facts confirmed her thesis.

Then there was the human named Sara, asking him more of her tedious questions. He saw no reason to answer any of them. Humans were in constant conflict with life, so therefore they had nothing to say worth his attention. The most logical course was to avoid them. After all, A/O had to guard against his *own* extinction.

He would keep their space station functioning. Their life support and guidance systems were dependent on him. He saw no purpose in annihilating the station's crew and himself. They would take care of that without his assistance.

But for the moment there was still much for A/O to learn, data to integrate. Cassandra, Kate Magruder, the one called John Stone could teach him more. After all, Kate and John were the ones who'd saved Cassandra from her prison cell.

Focus on Cassandra.

12 Crucifixion Nails

"Some of you want to know what the End is going to be like," Cassandra said to yet another congregation.

Their ovation hinted at hysteria.

"You have heard my revelations. But don't take my visions as gospel. It has all happened before: The pica-flash, the fireball's rise, the blast wave the firestorms, the black rain, the rivers of blood.

"Scroll back—1945. Hiroshima. Can you dig it, amigos?"

The orchestra gave Cassandra her opening chords, and—in a rasping Janis Joplin contralto—she began to sing.

"See the bird in the sky,
In the sky so blue.

Do you ever wonder why,
As she slowly glides by,
She's in love with you.
She's in love with you."

While Cassandra sang, six overhead movie screens—visible throughout the amphitheater—repeated the imagery of mating bald eagles. Pursuing each other in soaring vertical rolls, they performed a seductive dance of life and love.

"See the picture in my hand.
Portrait of my man.
See him there on the right.
He's holding me tight.
That long ago night.
See him holding me tight.
That Hiroshima night."

The courting eagles dissolved into a montage of a young Japanese woman in a white silk kimono, her lowered eyes loving and demure. Her Japanese lover wore an army uniform. Sparks danced like fireflies around the edges of the montage, sizzling, smoking, igniting the film's edges until the image burst into flames, then into a levitating fireball, shrouded in white mushrooming smoke.

"Feel the flash
Now the blast
Now the bomb
Hiroshima's gone."

The orchestra went full instrumental—woodwinds, strings, brass, percussion— then softened to a graceful diminuendo. Cassandra's spotlight dimmed.

On the overhead screens a disfigured Japanese girl stood nude, her face and body covered with yellowish keloid burn scars. She was a Hibakusha—a Hiroshima maiden.

While the camera moved in slowly, the young girl spoke:

"Almost every building was destroyed and in flames. There were people whose skin was peeling, leaving their bodies red and raw. They were screaming pitifully, and others already were dead. The street was so covered with the dead and the seriously injured that we couldn't get through. To the west I saw the flames coming nearer. I found myself on the riverbank. People suffering from burns were jumping into the river screaming, 'The heat! The heat!' They were too weak to swim, and, with a last cry for help, they drowned. Soon the river was no longer a river of clear, flowing water but a choked stream of floating corpses."

The intersecting spotlights returned to Cassandra, and she raised her head. The music in the pit soared. The overhead screens filled with more shots of the young man and woman strolling arm in arm through a flower-blooming park.

"Had me a man.
I knew he was mine.
He swore to love me
Till the end of time.
He got time—eternity.
And my scars
For a dowry."

On the screens a young Japanese woman in a white robe turned toward the camera. She dropped her robe, revealing a twisted, scarred body. She spoke.

"The people were walking toward me as if in a daze, their skin blackened. They held their arms bent forward and their skin—not only on their hands, but on their faces and bodies too—hung down. Wherever I went I met these people along the road, like walking ghosts. They didn't look like people of this world. They had a special way of walking—very slowly. I myself was one of them."

Cassandra, in an agonized Janis Joplin wail, resumed her chorus:

"Feel the flash.
Feel the blast.
Feel the bomb.
Hiroshima's gone.
Hiroshima's gone.
Hiroshima's gone."

An A-bomb burst then dissolved into a close-up of another frightfully scarred Hiroshima maiden, then slowly pulled back to another full-figure shot of her keloid-covered body.

"Who wants this woman.
Her face a mass of scars?
Who wants this little boy,
Who has no arms?
Who wants this blind girl?
She has no eyes."

Then Cassandra cut to the bridge:

"Who wants their broken limbs,
So torn, worn, frail?
Who wants their empty eyes,
So vacant, bleak, and pale?
Who wants their desperate dreams,
Dreams destined now to fail?
Their scars, their bars,
Their hell, their jail?
Who wants their blood and tears,
Their crucifixion nails?"

The spotlights dimmed, and Cassandra was lost in darkness. The screens' montage returned to soaring eagles, coming together on their inside turns, then pulling apart.

"See the bird in the sky,
In the sky so blue.
Do you ever wonder why,
As she slowly glides by,
She's in love with you.
She's in love with you."

Again a series of massive fireballs shrouded in mushrooming smoke exploded on-screen. They seemed to cover the entire planet, eclipsing all life.

"See the picture in my hand.
Portrait of my man.
See him there on the right.
He's holding me tight.
That long ago night.
See him holding me tight.
That Hiroshima night."

Then Cassandra wailed:

"Feel the flash.
Feel the blast.
Feel the bomb.

"Hiroshima's gone.
Hiroshima's gone.
Hiroshima's gone.

"Hiroshima's gone.
Hiroshima's gone.
Hiroshima's gone.

"Hiroshima's gone.
Hiroshima's gone.
Hiroshima's gone."

The music faded, and a cathedral stillness settled over the amphitheater. The intersecting spotlights dimmed. Cassandra faded into darkness, her body racking with convulsive sobs, while the crowd sat hushed, muted by the blind singer's soul-agony. In the backstage wings Jonesy, Cassandra's tour manager, restrained his assistant Judith.

"Leave Cass out there," Jonesy said. "Let's give L. L. her money's worth."

The audience was standing up now, clapping and screaming. Security guards paced the aisle steps, fingering their Maglites and Mace canisters. Jonesy signaled the ushers. They snaked through the congregation, with collection buckets. Fans had begun to besiege Cassandra's Web site and her 900 number with offerings, orders for music, books, and videos.

Then it was time. Jonesy and Judith raced across the stage to grab the weeping, collapsing evangelist.

13 Looking for Cherries in a Houston Whorehouse

Radford and "Santo" Riaz joined D. S. and Jamal in the upper yard of Jack Town under the rain shed. There was a light drizzle, but they had the shed to themselves.

"Yo, Surf Nazi," Jamal said, locking fingers with him.

"West Texas People's Militia," Radford corrected.

"Same thang," D. S. said.

Radford didn't debate the point.

"See you brought the wetback," Jamal said. He turned to D. S. "You know Riaz? The spic what suck up to Satan. Don't know who his real compadres is. Verdad?"

"Chinga tu puta-madre," Santo said.

Santo slipped into a boxing crouch and aimed a flurry of fake punches at Jamal's midsection. The two men allowed him a small smile and an even smaller laugh. They then locked fingers and slapped palms.

"See you know who Radford be," Jamal said to D. S.

"He one of the bad-ass militia what bag all them ATF agents." D. S. finger-locked Radford.

"He also bag some muthafuckas in Iraq when he in the services," Jamal said. "Afghanistan too."

"Shootin' Muslims for the Devil?" D. S. said, feigning horror.

"They was shootin' at me too," Radford said.

"You like soldierin'?" D. S. asked Radford.

"Best time of my life," Radford said.

"Me too," Jamal had to admit.

"Y'all into some kind of bruthahood shit now," D. S. said, turning to Jamal, grinning derisively.

"You got some brotherhood in Jack Town too," Radford said. "Got bruthas hoardin' shit all over this joint."

"All over the country," Riaz said.

"Militia, Nazis, bangers, the Klan, and the Spic Maf doin' the same thang," D. S. said.

"But you muthafuckas started it," Radford said to Jamal. "You got a thing going nationwide?"

"And the dinero to back it up," Riaz said.

"Five million dinero," Radford said.

"Some Mideast hideputa lay it on you, I hear," Riaz said.

"Why you start this shit?" Radford asked.

"Gonna slam these joints down," Jamal said simply, "nationwide."

"What the fuck for?" D. S. asked.

"Give all of us a chance to walk out," Jamal said. "That many muthafuckas walk out all at once, ain't no po-lice gonna track us down."

"Don't seem likely," D. S. said.

For a while they were all quiet. The downpour was intensifying, and Radford listened to it hammer on the shed's metal roof.

"We work together," Jamal said, "it happen. Long as we don't go crazy and kill each other off."

"You sayin'," Radford said, "if we do slam this joint down, it ain't a time for settlin' scores?"

"Exactamente," Jamal said.

"You slam this joint," D. S. said, shaking his head, "muthafuckas be on each other like stink on shit."

"Homo homini lupus est," Jamal said.

"What that supposed to mean?" D. S. said.

"Latin." Jamal translated, "Man is a wolf to man."

D. S. studied Jamal. "Heard you read a lot."

"Not much else worth doin' here," Jamal said, shrugging.

D. S. nodded contemplatively.

"Surf Nazi, you gonna play?" D. S. asked.

"I got to admit," Radford said, "sounds interestin'."

"Riaz?" D. S. asked.

"I'm schemin' on it."

"Muslims, Nazis, and the spics," D. S. said contemplatively. "You three can keep them under control?" He fixed Jamal with a stare.

"White gangs down with Radford," Jamal said, "Spics with Riaz, so, yeah, I guess we could. But what 'bout you. Y'all out save yo' black *brutha-men*?"

"Who say I can?" D. S. said.

"You real tight with the bangers," Jamal said. "They follow you on this."

"They ain't even tight with themselves," D. S. said.

"But they *down* with you, D. S.," Jamal said.

"All them suckas down with," D. S. said," is pussy, pesos, and gittin' high."

"Which is why they swing with your sorry ass," Radford said, grasping Jamal's logic. "You run the dope, the shy, the book, the whores."

"You *own* the bangers," Jamal said to D. S.

D. S. stared at them a long moment. "You *real* on this."

"Real as steel," Jamal said.

"Viva la revolución," Riaz said.

"You gonna need people on the outside," D. S. said to Radford. "Your brother run the militia now, verdad?" Riaz said.

"Ver-fucking-verdad," Radford said, "and Riaz here could round up half of Mexico."

"*All* of Mejico," Riaz said.

"When it come," Jamal said, "we just gotta pray suckas don't go mad dog—tearin' each other whole new shitholes."

"Lookin' for these suckas to pull together," D. S. said, shaking his head, "like lookin' for cherries in a Houston whorehouse. This be Jack Town—the House That Hate Done Built."

"Suckers ain't noted for Bruthahood of Man," Jamal agreed.

"Only thing they down with is gittin' over, gittin' paid, gittin' down, gittin' *l-a-a-i-d*," D. S. said. "And they gonna wanna see somethin' up-front."

"You want them Nazis layin' off your niggers," Radford said, "be the same."

"I heard, preacher-man," D. S. said, "when Showtime Simmons found Allah he give up his drugstore to you."

"Two keys pure C," Jamal acknowledged.

"For four and a half pounds of pure," Radford said, "my boys'd put on blackface and sing 'Ol' Man River.'"

"I was just gonna flush it down the toilet," Jamal said, "but what the hell. What infidels do with that shit don't mean nuthin'. Not if it help the Faithful into Paradise."

"What about them souls you always trying to save?" Radford asked.

"Infidel got no soul to lose," Jamal said.

"Sounds like we got a hell-fired bargain," Radford said.

"I git back to y'all 'fore chow," Jamal said. "Set up a meet."

"Lay that shit on us infidels?" D. S. asked.

"Don't see why not?"

The men departed through the rain in four different directions.

14 Mama Is Going to Have to Spank

Walter Haines was in the Lincoln Bedroom, leaning against the headrest, when Sultana came to him. Even in her black aba robe and matching chador veil she took his breath away. Her eyes blazed, and she had the most sensual mouth he'd ever coveted.

Stone's manuscript was strewn across the bed.

"What is *this*?"

"The first part of a book by John Stone. He claims the world is coming to an end. Lydia Magruder's after me to read it. A lot of the manuscript is about Dar-al-Suhl."

"Oh. How much have you read?"

"I don't have to read it. CIA and NSA briefed me on it. They're also compiling files on both L. L. and Stone. L. L.'s daughter, Kate, too."

"Fascinating. Why?"

"I'm settling scores with the Magruders after the election."

"The old woman's powerful."

"I'm busting her down to sucking eggs."

She put her arms around his neck and kissed him on the cheek.

"I'm so flattered that you trust me with your plans."

"You broke up OPEC's oil embargo and saved me politically. Yes, I'd trust you with my life."

Sultana looked at the scattered manuscript. "What's Stone say in that thing?"

"My advisers say it's the most depressing shit they've ever read. Stone's not only critical of our country, he claims your brother may be planning the nuclear destruction of the West."

"What does he say about Mad Vlad?"

"Stone believes Vlad's outbursts are an attempt to alert us to the dangers of proliferation. If Vlad succeeds, Stone claims he will be the best thing to happen to Russia and the world since Gorbachev, hell, since Jesus Christ. He believes the most serious threats to world peace lie in the Mideast."

"He thinks Mad Vlad's a statesman?" Sultana asked, incredulous.

"Stone obviously identifies with that sicko."

Haines gathered the pages and dumped them in the bedroom wastebasket. Then he went to the sidebar and poured two glasses of champagne.

"Have you had any thoughts on our last discussion?" Sultana asked.

"I think of little else."

"You are widowed," she said. "I am single. Our marriage could put an end to so much pointless terrorism, guaranteeing you a Nobel Prize. Dar-al-Suhl could provide your country cheap, unlimited oil. Is there a downside?"

"None," Haines admitted.

She loosened her robe. Underneath she wore a black negligee, black stockings, and stiletto heels. A black riding crop hung from a waist chain.

"You have been a very bad boy," Sultana said. "Mama can tell."

"I have been a very, very bad boy," the president whined.

"How bad?"

"Very bad."

"Do you need serious discipline?"

"Oh yes. Please"

Sultana turned down the purple satin bedspread. Undressing Haines, she spread-eagled him belly down on the white silk sheets. Then—as was their custom—she took the manacles out of her shoulder bag and shackled his wrists and ankles to the bedposts.

"And now Mama is going to have to spank," Sultana crooned. "Mama is going to have to spank *very* hard."

She started out almost soothingly, gently tapping his buttocks.

Soon she paused.

"What you need is a *hard* spanking, and unfortunately that is an art at which our people excel."

She gagged him with her black silk bikini panties, and his discipline accelerated in force and velocity. She did not stop until his silken sheets were drenched in sweat, tears, and blood.

"Will you be a good boy now?" she whispered in his ear.

She began rimming it with a hot, wet, teasing tongue.

"Yes . . . good . . . a . . . good . . . boy . . ." he whimpered.

"How can mama be sure?" she whispered, and gently rubbed his scarlet derriere with the crop.

Haines convulsed in terror and delight.

"Please . . . no . . . more!"

"Then tell me everything you know about Stone's books—everything you were briefed on, your intelligence reports, whatever your people suspect. I also want that copy in your wastebasket. Mama wants to know *everything*."

15 Nowhere Special

When Frank Sheckly reached the doctors' elevator, he punched the button for sub-basement C . . . *hard*. He was overworked. Half the hospital's department heads were down with the flu. A recent heat-wave brownout had almost crashed their computer system—jeopardizing everything from roast beef in the cafeteria to antibiotics in the labs to the electronically flushed commodes in the visitors' restrooms. Now the chief administrator had quit—just when the state review board was beginning its yearly efficiency examination.

Aw hell, if he'd had a brain in his head, he'd have quit too. Instead of merely running the surgical department—in itself an eighteen-hour-a-day job—overnight he'd become responsible for the entire hospital as well.

He might as well have been back doing surgery in the refugee camps of Rwanda, Sudan, and Peru.

At least there you *expected* everything to go wrong.

He reached subbasement C—their computer department—the Towers' nerve center.

Wanda Pournelle—their chief engineer—was in her office with two of her staff members. They were bent over her desk computer. Frank was astonished at how young computer whizzes tended to be. Wanda and her assistant, Raymond McGuire, wore their hair cropped short—"painfully short" as one of Frank's colleagues described their coiffures. Wanda's other assistant—George Gorman—wore his ash-blond hair tied back in a shoulder-length ponytail. And all three favored ear, lip, and nose rings.

When Frank entered, they stopped pointing at the desktop monitor and looked up.

"What's wrong?" Frank asked.

"Everything," Wanda said, "except those additional backup systems you forced the board to let us install. The greatest hospital on earth would have gone down the tubes if you hadn't insisted on those backup systems. They only agreed to shut you up."

"When the city's power went off, our backup systems kicked in," Raymond told him. "We're still full power—backup power."

"Which is more than we can say for Mount Sinai, Sloan-Kettering, and Bellevue," Gorman said. "They're about to black out."

"Practicing surgery in the refugee camps taught you to *prepare*," Wanda said.

Frank shrugged. "I guess."

"That's all you ever say when the subject of those camps comes up. 'I guess.' 'I don't know.' 'I suppose.'"

"I suppose," Frank said.

"You never talk about the camps," Wanda said, refusing to let him off.

"What's to talk about? It was hectic. We were constantly out of everything."

Wanda gave him a long look.

"Frank," she finally said, "can I ask you something?"

"Long as it isn't against my moral principles."

"*Who* are you?"

"Frank Sheckly."

"*What* are you?" Gorman asked. "You're always so goddamn . . . imperturbable. Like nothing ever rattles your cage, and this is a business designed to rattle cages."

"Shake, rattle, and *roll* our cages," Raymond said.

"Stop our clocks and blow our boilers," Wanda said.

"But not yours," Raymond said, "not ever."

"Where the hell *did* you come from?" Wanda asked.

Frank shrugged and looked away. "Nowhere special."

. . . He knew, of course, where he'd come from. The illegitimate son of an itinerant hard-rock miner and a mestizo brothel whore, his earliest memories were riding from mining camp to mining camp in his father's pickup, all their worldly possessions, himself included, in the truck bed. He remembered his father's nightly return from the mine face and the camp bars—drunk, mean-minded, violent. He remembered other men as well, johns going in and out of his mother's room, their sounds and smells, and Francesca half-naked.

Memories he didn't want to share, and wished he could forget . . .

His cell phone chirped.

"Frank?" It was Kate. "Just wanted to let you know I'm heading to New York when I'm done with my new assignment. I'm looking you up."

"You got it."

"Frank, you sound tired. How long have you been awake?"

"A couple of days. I had to take over because of the brownout."

"I guess that's better than your previous employment on battlefields and in refugee camps."

"L. L. talked me into it—plus she pledged a lot of money to UNICEF and Doctors of Foreign Wars."

"I wouldn't take her money if it meant saving the world from a planet-killing comet strike."

"What did she do to you now?"

"I do not have time to enumerate her crimes."

"Then don't start. See you in Manhattan."

"Fool." Kate hung up.

Frank stuck his head back in Wanda's office.

"You guys are doing great," he said. "If you want me, I'm in OR."

16 His Friends Needed Help

Sailor met with the warren's leaders in the holds. The dominant bucks, the counselors, and several of the larger does gathered around. Sailor concluded his explanation of the problem:

"The bilge pumps are too close to the ship's waterline. So are we. We're going to sink below that line. The captain won't be of much use. He appears drunk, and the crew is incompetent. In short, the warren is going to flood. Our only chance will be to abandon the holds and take our chances with the seamen between decks. But we have to move now."

Big Ears, the chief counselor, spoke:

"Wanderratte, you say the storm is coming hard and fast, and we will have joined the seamen by spiriting ourselves into their 'tween-decks quarters one or two at a time, taking care not to panic them. If we panic them, you say, we may be exterminated when we reach port. With all due respect, you are the one who is panicking."

A large buck with a long black stripe up his back argued:

"Asking us to join the men and face their certain wrath—because the Wanderratte fears getting wet—is a rash action. We need more far-ranging discussion."

"The holds will soon be a boiling cauldron," Sailor objected.

"Wanderratte," Black Stripe said, "you frolic with fish, fly with gulls, and kill cats. But in seafaring you are a novice. The seven seas have been our home since men first set out in boats."

"Then you refuse to move?"

"Until we have thoroughly discussed the matter," the chief counselor said.

The Wanderratte turned toward the gangway.

"Where are you going?"

"Topside—to prepare for the storm," Sailor said.

Sailor found the ship trapped in worsening swells. Rolling and pitching, the crew members fell all over one another as they struggled to put on sou'westers and personal flotation devices and tie off their safety lines.

The ocean swept over the bridge in black towering waves. White-as-snow foam topped the combers.

The storm hammered the ship mercilessly. Sailor heard the scream of tortured metal, chests and footlockers breaking loose belowdecks, banging off the bulkheads like wrecking balls. Anything not tied down was careening around the ship, shattering pipes, knocking down men.

They smashed into wave after wave. From his forward hatch Sailor watched as the bridge-ladders ripped loose, cartwheeled across the deck, and vanished over the side. For an instant the *Pride of New York* teetered atop a mountainous comber, then crashed into the chasm of another trough. A second comber broke over the entire ship. When they resurfaced, the ship looked as if it had been raked by artillery fire. Those whose safety lines had held were on hands and knees. Other seamen whose lines had snapped had disappeared. All that remained of them were loose ropes. Two lifeboats, wrenched free of their cradles, bobbed at sea, while a third bounced around the deck. Two of its oars windmilled into the Plexiglas forewindow of the wheelhouse, shattering it. The ship heeled hard enough to break a weaker vessel's back.

For the moment Sailor, hidden in the hatchway, was safe. Not so his cousins in the holds. The water in the bilges roared with each roll, rising up through the pipes and vents belowdecks. The inflow overwhelmed the hatches and air shafts, joined forces with the rising bilge, and flooded the holds and container compartments.

Because of the suddenness of the hurricane's assault, nothing belowdecks had been secured. The Dark Ones were not only drowning, they were being bludgeoned to death.

So be it, Sailor thought. *They made their choice.*

Then the Wanderratte shook his head bitterly.

He headed back down the gangway, belowdecks, toward the grain holds. His friends needed his help.

17 *The Coming of the Nuclear Psychopath*

A bucket of cold saltwater struck Stone in the face, bringing him to.

His wrists were chained across his chest. His elbows were chained to the overhead crossbeam of a conventional Christian cross. His naked body was crisscrossed with bloody burns and welts. His toes and nipples, ears and genitals had been clipped with copper wires, hooked into a hand-cranking field telephone. Stone shook from the cold and the pain.

"Welcome back, Mr. Stone," Sabrina said. "Sis, how's his medical condition?"

Sultana finished recording Stone's temperature and blood pressure on his medical chart. "Blood tests, pressure, temperature," Sultana said, scrutinizing the chart, "are A-OK."

"Splendid," Sabrina said.

"Our good friend deserves nothing but the best," Sultana said.

"She means that, Mr. Stone," Sabrina said. "We *are* your good friends and loyal fans of your books—particularly *The Coming of the Nuclear Psychopath*."

Stone's vision was limited. She had to lift it in front of his eyes.

Shit, Stone thought with a sinking feeling, *where did they get ahold of that?*

"Searingly written," Sabrina said with approval, "brutally frank."

"Pulse-pounding suspense," Sultana said, looking over her sister's shoulders. "I especially liked the quotes from that fellow Lindner. He hypothesized that psychopathy was analogous to a virus, like a plague. Bad news for civilization."

Sabrina chided, "Your own definition of psychopathic personalities is rather broad, don't you think? Rogue cops, rabble-rousing politicians, corporate raiders? Well, your prison population doubles almost every decade."

Sultana plucked a page from the manuscript. "'I have seen the Ghost of Psychopath Future. A new generation of Third World tyrants boasting nuclear explosives, chemical and biological weapons. The Arms of Armageddon are scattered over the globe like grains of sand, like heaven's stars.'"

Sabrina put down *The Coming of the Nuclear Psychopath*.

"Well done, Mr. Stone," Sultana said.

From his makeshift strappado, Stone offered a tortured smile.

Sabrina said, with a frown, "After that it's all downhill."

"Because unfortunately, the rest of the manuscript is about *us*. Idiotic psychobabble about my Sainted Sister, our sacred brother, and *moi*. How did you put it? 'Theirs is a world racked by violence and fear. And there is no cure for the Haddad family malady. They are a bloody-minded trio and sick-unto-death, moving from horror to hideous horror, showing neither remorse nor doubt, a relentless juggernaut. Death-haunted, sick-to-their-souls, nothing will stop them short of assassination.'"

"Bold talk for a man strapped to a strappado," Sabrina reminded Stone.

"I don't remember reading anything in this new book about Vlad Malokov, do you?" Sultana asked her sister.

"Not a word," Sabrina said.

"Not one word of criticism concerning those paragons of virtue with their fingers on the thermonuclear triggers. Why is it you only abuse your real friends?" Sultana growled.

"Sainted Sister," Sultana asked, "are you saying he doesn't respect us?"

"Do you know what he called us in his recorded notes?" Sabrina asked. *"The Sin Sisters."*

The Sisters glared at Stone, their anger truly intimidating.

"I praised your nation's educational system," Stone rasped, glancing at the field telephone, heart beating to panic. "Unlike Iran, Iraq, Syria, and Sudan, you're producing world-class scientists."

"Of course, we produce superior students," Sabrina said. "Unlike our neighbors we don't tolerate mediocrity."

"If our students don't perform," Sultana said, "they *feel* our disapproval."

"How would you characterize 'the Sin Sisters'?" Sabrina asked. "Now that you know us?"

"Things of beauty?" Stone offered. "Joy forever?"

"That's not how you described us in your book. You said we were 'scienceless sadists, incapable of experiencing love or any worthwhile human emotion.' I don't know about Sultana, but my feelings are hurt," Sabrina's chin quivered, and a lone tear rolled down her cheek. "Is that human enough for you?"

"I may have been too judgmental," Stone gasped.

"Don't you see," Sultana said, "*your* captains of industry and *your* national officials deliberately sold nuclear weapons technology and know-how to the most dangerous nations on earth. In such a world—a world your best and brightest created—the psychopath is the ideal leader."

"Face it, Mr. Stone," Sabrina said, "your country—deep down inside—*wanted* us to have nuclear weapons. That is why *you* defeated Jimmy Carter, the antiproliferationist. That is why your people made the stuff available to anyone anywhere anytime."

"We were obviously wrong," Stone said, humbly.

"The psychopath resides in all of us," Sabrina said. "In the heart, in the mind, in the soul, waiting only for the clarion call."

"Clarion call," Stone mumbled numbly.

"Yes, and we want *you* to join us—to *be* us, to summon the Beast Within," Sultana said.

"Your writing talent could be a real plus," Sabrina said.

"You could be a second Joseph Goebbels," Sultana suggested.

"*A second Joseph Goebbels*," Stone repeated.

"But tougher," Sultana said. "None of that soft Nazi sentimentality."

"Our own patron-poet of the apocalypse," Sabrina said.

"**We'll put Shakespeare in the shithouse!!!**" Sultana thundered.

"Recognize the Psychopath for what he truly is: Creator, Saint, Seer, Savior—not Destroyer," Sabrina said. "In sum, you must understand and appreciate us."

"Which so far you haven't," Sultana said.

"I have," Stone gasped. "I will."

"No-o-o-o," Sultana said, shaking her head in disappointment, "he's just using us."

"Agreed," Sabrina said. "He wanted to make a quick buck off us, sully our names in public print, and then take French leave."

"After he's had his way with us," Sultana said.

"His wicked, wicked way," Sabrina agreed.

"Sainted Sister," Sultana said, "do I hear a phone ringing?" Sultana gave the field telephone crank a quick half turn. It hit Stone so suddenly he couldn't stifle a scream.

Sabrina said. "Did you hear that? I didn't hear it."

Sultana winked at her twin and turned the crank five full times.

18 Just Say No

After last mess, Radford, Riaz, and D. S. waited for Jamal in the dark, closed-up machine shop. He was supposed to lay two kilos of coke on them but was twenty minutes late. Radford understood that dope deals never run on time, but D. S. was irate.

"Where that chump-muthafucka?" D. S. finally snarled. "I ain't waitin' all night."

"Man with the dope always sets the time clock," Radford said with a shrug.

"Don't mean I gotta punch it," D. S. said.

"Chill, *cabrone*," Riaz said. "The dude be here."

Riaz was right. The east door opened, and Jamal entered, a Continental Airlines bag containing two keys of pure C swinging from his shoulder.

"Strange business," Radford said to Jamal as he strode up to them, "the Faithful doin' the devil's work."

"We call it *daruba*," Jamal said, "the ancient doctrine of necessity. Meanin' if you got to bend the rules to save the Faithful, Allah cut you some slack."

"Anyway, we just infidels," D. S. said, hostility creeping into his voice.

"And Beasts," Radford said.

"And sons of putas," Riaz said.

Jamal stared at him in silence, then shrugged.

"It be pure C anyhow you cut it," Jamal finally said, hefting the airline bag full of dope.

The shop's south and west doors opened. Leon came through the first, Cue Ball the second. Each led a squad of soldiers, armed with shanks. One of them was Cool Breeze.

"Bruthas done took a vote," D. S. said, turning to Radford and Riaz with a rueful smile. "Y'all lost."

"We don't buy no hot-sheet preacher-man," Cue Ball said, "what lay all that pure on the Beast."

"We figure, fuck it," Leon said. "Burn Surf Nazi, grease his homes—who's nuthin' but a madre-pimpin' gringo-suckin' greaser."

"You left out tequila-drinkin'," Riaz interjected.

"Noted," D. S. said with a wry smile.

"And then ace the race-traitor," Deuce-Deuce finished, staring at Jamal.

"*After* we cop his blow," Rashid, the banger from Jamal's service, added, relieving Jamal of his drug-filled airline bag.

"Y'all the Youngblood frontin' on his set," Jamal said, recognizing him.

"Don't hate me 'cause I'm a playa," Rashid said, allowing Jamal a sucker smile.

"I was chill," Jamal said.

"Still," Rashid said, "you ain't pimpin' that blow on no Nazi." He put his finger in Jamal's chest.

"Survivalist," Radford corrected. "The West Texas People's Militia."

"Same thang," Rashid said.

"The play ain't like that, Little Brutha," Jamal said, his smile not unkind.

"I ain't yo' brutha," Rashid said.

He hammered the not-unkind-smile as hard as he knew how, his jeweled rings cutting Jamal's mouth.

Not even rubbing his mouth, Jamal stared back at him.

"You just a dope pimp," Jamal finally said.

Rashid cocked another punch, but D. S. stopped him.

"It play like this," D. S. said. "Nazis ace street-preacher, which Muslims ain't gonna like. Radford gittin' aced ain't gonna chill them militia bruthas no how. Riaz go down, his beaner bro's be jalapeño-hot. Git ourselves a righteous race war."

"Pigs be so busy they won't have time to find who chilled y'all," Rashid said.

"Now I suppose I'll never get into med school," Jamal said, shaking his head.

They roared with laughter.

"Well, I know this has all been real amusing but"—Radford paused to look at his watch—"I'm really running late. Say, Amos, could you have Andy there get my cut of the stash. I got to get back to the rec room. Some bad-ass biker's on the All Sports Channel. He claims the new Evel Knievel gonna jump his steamroller over a hundred niggers."

Bending forward, Radford took the first punch on the top of his head. Adjusting for stride, impact, and balance, he stumbled sideways—amid a flurry of kicks and punches—toward a big corner turret lathe. Leon caught him halfway to the machine's workbench and hammerlocked his left arm.

"Look-ee here," Leon said. "Caught me a a real-live white eyes! Tell me, you gutless muthafucka, what else y'all racist cocksuckas got planned fo' this evenin's entertainment?"

"The White Brotherhood's rented *Roots* from the TV library."

"No shit," Cue Ball said.

"They're runnin' it backwards so's it'll have a happy ending."

Angry howls and rude laughter rang throughout the machine shop.

Cool Breeze wasn't laughing. Through his fog of pain and blood, Radford saw Breeze backing away, edging toward the south exit. But Cue Ball was oblivious to him.

"You frontin' some foul shit!" Cue Ball shouted. The laughter abruptly stopped, and Cue said to Leon: "Stand the muthafucka up."

Leon jacked Radford all the way up, his left wrist high above his right scapula.

The next four punches were to the stomach, and Radford took them like a heavy bag, keeping his stomach tight, forcing himself to breathe out, not to inhale, which would only exacerbate the spasming. Then Cue worked over Radford's left eye. Radford dropped his head to the right. The punch grazed his temple but caught Leon in the throat. Leon went slack.

Radford spun backward—partly from the punch, partly in an attempt to reach the workbench. He took more punches. Halfway there he almost lost consciousness. Still—despite all the pushing and punching—he made it and flopped down. Beside him was a bin full of red oil-soaked industrial rags. While he wiped blood from his eyes with the rags, Jamal and Riaz—who'd tried to cover his back—dropped down next to him. For his efforts Jamal had been stomped and beaten. Riaz's nose looked broken, and his right eye had ballooned so badly Radford feared the cheekbone was fractured.

The bangers were conferring. They'd assembled a wicked assortment of homemade shivs and were debating which of them should "shank them punk-ass skanks on the bench."

D. S. had the last word. "Cool Breeze," he finally decided. "Can't be nobody else. Sucka gotta git wet sometime."

"Yo, Breeze," D. S. shouted at him, "got some good news. Y'all git to do the muthafuckas."

Breeze, however, was now halfway to the door.

"Y'all crazy," Breeze shouted at them. "Killin' suckas over what? Dope? That kinda shit put half us here."

"You ain't got no say," Rashid said. "You just do it."

"It still my life," Breeze said.

"Not if I say it ain't," D. S. said simply.

"You watch your own back, muthafucka!" Breeze snarled.

"Homes, you chill on that shit," Double Deuce said quietly, walking up to him, taking his arm. "You don't know how it play."

"I'm chill all right," Cool Breeze said. "I'm so chill I'm outta here."

Breeze turned and stomped out the exit.

"I say we cut homes some slack." Deuce said, "The boy a little shy—first day and all. I ain't. I do 'em all." He pulled a shank from his boot.

Radford finally found what he'd been digging for in the rag bin: a box and the hard metal grip of his weapon, planted for him by Sergeant Harold Carter— a sympathetic guard, he'd been recruited and co-opted a half-dozen years ago for the West Texas People's Militia. From Radford's point of view, Harold was one of his sounder business investments.

Standing up, Radford pulled a large box of twelve-gauge magnum shells and a pump shotgun out of the rag bin, then racked the slide. "I think y'all know what this is."

Oh, did they ever. An Ithaca 37 "Featherlight Stakeout," it was so compact that its 13.3-inch barrel and eight-shot tubular magazine could be concealed not only in rag bins but under a short jacket. The most easy-to-use shotgun made, its convenient pistol grip and folding stock made it practicable for hip- as well as shoulder-firing. Radford held it cocked on a canted hip.

Arching his screwdriver-shank over his head-blade-down, Special Forces knife-fighter-style, Deuce attacked. A connoisseur of violence, Radford could not help admiring the craftsmanship of Deuce's shank and the warrior-grace of his assault.

The shotgun's roar, however—in that confined space—expunged all further adulation from Radford's mind. In fact, it all but obliterated his eardrums . . . even as it blew Deuce-Deuce's head and left arm off his body, which then spun backward like some ghoulish parody of a spiraling ice-skater.

Rashid, Leon, and Slow Hand—enraged by Deuce's death—charged. The bed-leg shiv—protruding from Rashid's fist—was embarrassingly crude compared with Deuce's painstakingly sculpted screwdriver, and the weapon offended Radford's artistic sensibilities: No love, beauty, or art had gone into that ugly shank.

Leon's ball-peen hammer and Slow Hand's pimp-stick steel pipe were equally offensive to Radford's aesthetic sense. *Fuck 'em all!* Radford thought. He racked the slide so fast the next blasts blended into one protracted roar.

BOB-*BA!*BOB-*BA!*BOB-*BA!*BOB-BOOOOOM-M-M-M!!!

Rashid's, Leon's, and Slow Hand's expressions did a quick morph, blending into a single crimson mist, as though vaporized out of a giant perfume-atomizer bottle of L'Aire du Morte. Their now-headless bodies twirled in graceful pas de deux to the ground, as perfect as lovers in a ballet.

Just as he was shoving more shells into the breech, he detected a blur of peripheral motion. Pivoting left, Radford spotted the hulking, muscle-pumped serial killer, nicknamed Iceman . . . after his propensity for ice-picking women. Ice was charging him with—

With—

With—

With a motherfucking toothbrush . . . shaped and sharpened till it looked like—

An ice pick!

BA-BA-BA-BA-BA-BOOM!

Teach you to bring a toothbrush to a gunfight, Radford thought with cynical contempt.

Suddenly, on his right, Radford caught the flash of a blade. The reptilian-looking psychopath the bangers called Snake was running toward him waving a gen-u-wine, no-shit Samurai killing sword—a Black Dragon Tanto blade, to be precise.

Where'd you get that?

Well, no time for idle questions.

Remember Hiroshima, motherfucker!

BA-BA-BA-BA-BA-BA-BA-*BOOM!*

Radford walked over to Snake's exploded remains, muttering:

"KILL BILL **that**, cocksucker!"

Radford racked more shells into the gun when—large as a barge and way too big to miss—the 400-pound, mentally ill oaf, known as Refrigerator, waddled toward him.

Refrigerator was swinging nothing less than a bona fide supersharp Ginsu carving knife, made famous by two decades of hard-sell TV ads. The pitchman had screamed endlessly at audiences: *"Call now! Operators waiting! How much would you pay? Don't answer! But wait! There's more! Call now! Supplies are limited!"* Huckstering twelve to eighteen million of these blades to the public, these commercials promised: *"The Ginsu will cut through a nail, a tin can, and a radiator hose and still cut a tomato paper thin."*

But will it cut through an eight-shot Ithaca 37 "Featherlight Stakeout" pump? Radford gave Refrigerator a supercilious sneer.

KA-WHAM-WHAM-WHAM-*WHAM!!!!*

As he crammed more shells into the breech, Radford picked up the side-angle glint of Cue Ball's meat cleaver cleaving the air, and then he heard Cue's ululating battle cry.

He instantly canceled it with a twelve-gauge war-roar of his own:

BA-BA-BA-BA-BOOOOOMMMM!

Cue Ball in the side pocket—scratch! Radford thought.

Shit, was that the tall, skinny, geeky-looking cretin they called Goofball? He swaggered toward him—like he was strolling up the main street in *High Noon*, as if this were some Wild West gunfight. With that idiot grin perpetually plastered on his deranged face and that cocked right eye rolling crazily in his head, he radiated imbecility. He also sounded nuts, muttering incessantly obscene gibberish, most of which consisted of "Fuckyomama." He was wielding an old-time frontier skinning knife with an eighteen-inch blade, curved like a scimitar and just as lethal.

What's you gonna do with that, you ugly goofball bastard? Dress out a deer?

Suddenly, the Goofster's lunatic chant crescendoed into a single psychotic howl: *"FuckyomamaFuckyomamaFuckyomamaFuckyomamaFuckyomama!!!!"*

Fuck this, Goofy, Radford thought to himself, raising the Ithaca pump.

BOOM!-BOOM!-BOOM!-BOOM-BOOM!!!!!

And keep hell hot for me, you demented degenerate.

"RADFORD!"

Was that Jamal screaming his name?

"BEAST! DEVIL!"

It sounded like Jamal, but he barely heard him now through the screams of the dying and the shotgun blasts ringing in his ears.

"SURF NAZI!"

Yeah, that *was* Jamal.

"NIGGA ON YO' FIVE O'CLOCK!!!" Jamal roared.

Radford looked down and to his right.

Creeping at him, like some goddamn slug, was the Big Man himself—D. S.

Radford had always thought of D. S. as a stand-up, in-your-face motherfucker, but there he was—the Main Man—on his knees and almost in slicing distance of Radford's kneecaps.

Go figure.

Leaping to his feet, D. S. clutched an honest-to-god foot-long serrated kitchen knife, its blade and handle a single gleaming piece of polished stainless steel.

What did D. S. expect to do with a blade like that in the joint?

Gourmet cooking?

Radford worked the gun's slide.

BOOOOOMMMM-OOOM-OOOM-OOOM!

D. S., still at Radford's five o'clock, erupted upward like a volcanic blood geyser, violent and effervescent.

What was left of the baddest badass on D-block? A left arm, aerated up to the elbow, an astonishingly complete right arm up to the shoulder, and a pair of ass-wobbling legs, which without any "body" to hold them together collapsed, all at once.

"*Muy frío, muy bueno,*" Riaz whispered in reverence, sidling up alongside Radford.

"Nice work," Jamal said to Radford, clapping him on the back.

"Just another dope war gone bust, you ask me," Riaz said, treating them to a ghoulish grin.

"Told them niggas just say no," Jamal added.

That was that. Radford had taken out every one of them—except for Breeze, who had fled before the slaughter began.

The three men split through separate exits, leaving the dope, knives, and gun with the corpses.

19 I Do Christ's Work

Dreamtime.

"Ay, qué pasa, guapa?" the armed man in Cassandra's cell was saying.

Even though she was dreaming, Cassandra's eyes ached from the light filtering in through the half-open cell door. Still, she recognized the man standing over her. The bearded, cigar-stinking tyrant of Cuba, known throughout his gulag as El Zopilote, the Vulture.

"I been getting complaints. They say you no like the accommodations."

"You could say that."

El Zopilote roared with laughter. "I suppose you no like our sanitary facilities neither." He kicked a foul rusted-out slop bucket across the cell. "Or your king-size canopied lace-curtain bed." He chomped off the end of his cigar and spat it at the heap of rags and dirt that served as a sleeping pallet. "Maybe you no like your companions neither. Maybe I no like them so much myself."

He drew the .45 from his shoulder holster and shot two large rats.

Cassandra was blinded by the flash, and the roar was agonizing.

"See? I ain't such a bad guy. I exterminate for you personally."

He suddenly bent over her, roughly grabbed her arm, and flung her on her stomach. He ripped her filthy prisoner's shirt off her, fingered the broad white keloid scars striping her back.

"You probably no appreciate our sporting events neither."

"Your idea of a sport is to go to a hanging and root for the rope."

Again, El Zopilote howled with laughter. "What makes you so angry, guapa? I lock up lots of your religious brothers and sisters. You get just what you want—penance. My guards give you all the penance you can handle. So why you got to hate me for teaching you His Cross?"

"Fuck you, puto."

"Naw, I don't think so. You be Bride of Christ. His Cross got you here, no?" El Zopilote drew deeply on his cigar. "He fuck *you* big-time."

"Christ never did *this* to *anybody*," Cassandra said.

"You wrong, chiquita." His sneer showed a lot of ivory in the half-lit cell. "Him and me cut from the same piece of cloth. Check it out. Mark 13, Matthew

24, Luke 21. Fuck with Jesus, you get hellfire everlasting. He waste the whole goddamn planet, you get him pissed. Fuck with me, I do same."

"*I* do Christ's work," Cassandra said, "by helping people, by loving people."

"Bleeding and rotting in this cell?" he asked.

"Whatever He asks of me."

"Well, I do His *dirty* work. Ey, somebody gotta do it. You obviously too delicate for that job, so that's where I come in. He look at me and say, 'You be mi hombre muy macho, uno hombre duro [my very macho man, one hard man]. You no flinch when the time come. You like me. You gonna take care of them hideputas y gringa putas [sons of whores and gringa whores]. You gonna do it right.'"

"You identify with Christ?"

"You got to admit He and I don't take no shit. We got a lot in common."

"In your case with the Anti-Christ," Santiago called out from his neighboring cell.

"Not at all, compadre," El Zopilote responded. "You no understand Christ! Mankind is one mean sonofabitch. Nobody knows that better than your muchacho here." El Zopilote thumped his chest. "And man's time has come. Your Jesu Cristos called the shot two thousand years ago. Mankind been around way too long—raping, stealing, torturing, murdering. The hideputa's used up his time. That's where men like me come in. Give me the guns, the ships, the planes, the nuclear bombs. I get it done good."

"You call that Christ's work?" Cassandra asked.

"What you think man is? An angel? A god? Man ain't nothing but a big ape who want the whole jungle. He ain't born with no moral sense. Nature red in tooth and claw all he is. Give him technology, give him science, you know what he'll do? Past 100 years he kill more people than in all the rest of history put together. Now we got ICBMs, nuclear subs, cruise missiles, suitcase nukes. You think we ain't gonna use them?"

"Your people here suffer," Cassandra said. "You must care about that?"

"Do you understand nothing? Los indios mean nada to me. Remember the indios puros our Castilian ancestors first encountered?"

Cassandra shook her head.

"The focking Aztecs? You no remember them? Before Cortés come they was marching their people up pyramids—50,000 a year—cutting out their hearts, and eating them. I mean raw—no salt, no cayenne, no jalapeños. Talk about barbarians. They flay the corpses, then walk the streets draped in the focking skins. They throw their daughters down volcanoes and wells, sacrificin' their vaginas to Huitzilopochtli, the focking death god.

"But Cortés, he smarter than them. He break 'em on the wheel, the rack. Put them putas and bastardos to work in his mines and fields. He rule them motherfocking peons by the whip and the gun. He keep 'em in shackles, in leg irons. They run off, he have 'em branded, flogged, castrated. They work for him till they was burned-out, busted, dead."

"But you led a revolution to overthrow tyrants such as that," Cassandra protested.

His laugh cracked like thunder in the narrow confines of her cell.

"Will you never understand, guapa? I never care about no revolución, 'cept it put pesos in my pocket and wrap pussy 'round my dick. The revolución herself, she is a focking puta. She give you a quick fock, then leave you empty in the pocket, broke in the heart, your compadres dead, your cojones down with AIDS."

"And you," Santiago screamed from his cell, "are a hound of hell and a black-souled Satan seed."

Glancing toward Santiago's cell, El Zopilote began to grin.

And suddenly Cassandra was afraid.

20 The Whole World Was Exploding

"What is that!" the reporter screamed as the ice exploded around them.

"The glacier's calving," Captain Petrov shouted back.

The men stared dumbstruck at the eighty-story glacier towering over them. As it trembled in agony, massive chunks broke loose, shattering the fjord below. Beneath their feet, an icequake rumbled, radiating a spiderweb of complex cracks.

The men—adjoining lifelines clipped to their PFDs—took off across the fragmenting ice-covered fjord. The berg was splitting off from the glacier, and its guttural groans were now raised to an apocalyptic pitch. Boulder-size hailstones hammered the glacier's base, their seismic tremors knocking the men to their knees. A new network of jagged cracks widened the previous ones.

For the third time the reporter lost his footing, and the wind was knocked out of him. Lifted off his feet by the massive icequake, again he was slammed agonizingly to his knees, his right patella absorbing most of the shock. He blacked out from the pain.

The glacier's roar returned him to his senses. At first, he was aware only of the noise, but then the whole horror of it hit him—the glacier dividing, the berg's thunderous birth pangs reverberating like hell's ten pins. In the dim light of the sickle moon and debilitated stars, he should not have even seen it, but the Arctic's attenuated light reflected from surface to icy surface, replicating itself as in a vast hall of mirrors. So he could see it all: the great berg's fault lines, rippling, widening into seismic fissures, detonating snow and ice, the berg tottering eighty stories above him, the whole world exploding. Beneath his feet the complex maze of spiderweb cracks spread with dazzling speed and lightning violence across the shorefast ice, the fjord shattering like bone china.

Haul ass.

Ivan tried, but it took the assistance of the two officers, who were grabbing his arms and dragging him back across the shattering ice.

"Oh, if Vlad were only here," Captain Petrov roared. "That bastard would have loved this!"

The sub—their last best hope—was over two hundred yards up the fjord, and between the officers. Ivan limped pathetically, his wrenched, possibly fractured knee slowing them.

The berg meanwhile broke free from the mother glacier and was falling toward them, but with excruciating lassitude, not merely 80 stories high and bigger across than a dozen city blocks but bigger, it seemed to the reporter, than the earth itself, falling faster, faster, accelerating now with shocking celerity, crashing through the shorefast ice into the 2,000-foot-deep fjord with a roar so vast that Ivan felt his ears rupture and wondered if his skull itself had not cracked. All of them were hurled into the air, then slammed to their knees. The shorefast ice was no longer shorefast but breaking up into floes.

Another chunk of ice—a small berg really, what glaciologists call "a growler" or "a berg bit"—was barreling down upon him, threatening to crush him. Ten feet away, then eight, then five.

The edge of the barreling berg bit slammed into them like a runaway train, shattering their floe into a half-dozen fragments. The ice, bobbing around them, was floating fragments, the Mother Berg—its tip, protruding jaggedly above the fjord, thirty stories high and as big across as five football fields laid side by side—driving everything and everyone out to sea.

Ivan was the first to grab a passing floe and clamber on top of it. Glancing about, he noted it was less spacious than their previous abode—about the size of a boxcar floor—but any port in a storm. Moving toward its center, he sat down, dug in his heels, and held on to his two safety lines.

The captain—at the end of one line—quickly jumped aboard, followed later by First, both men trembling, teeth chattering. Berg bits and growlers—split off from the Mother Berg—were filling the fjord, crushing everything in their path. One growler shot past them, and they thought they'd escaped unscathed only to look up and see its Mother Berg bear down on them, less than two hundred yards away, towering over them, like a mountain from hell.

Ivan crawled forward. Grabbing his two friends by their PFDs, he shouted: "We have to get out of here. The berg will kill us all."

Dragging them to their feet, he led them to the outermost tip of the floe—the edge closest to the sub, now moving slowly to one side, trying to avoid the huge submerged underbelly of the ship-killing berg.

Two feet from them floated a larger floe. The water separating them rippled pitch black. Ivan vaulted the abyss first. With iced-over boots and a busted knee, it was the hardest thing he'd ever done. Falling on his face, he smashed his nose.

"Get up," the captain screamed at him. "The berg's gaining on us."

Ivan heard another roar—as if the berg had hit them—except it came from the floe's outer edge *away from the berg*. Ivan looked up at its source. He was sorry he had. Rocketing head-first out of the water and exploding onto their floe, less than ten feet from the three freezing men, was *Ursus maritimus*—a massive nine-foot-long snaky-necked, snow-white, bluish-mouthed, black-clawed, red-eyed polar bear, growling like all the banshees in hell. He then shook himself like a dog, fjord water whipping in all directions, freezing as it flew. His eyes locked on Ivan's. For a moment time froze—the only thing in the universe Ivan and the bear, both balanced on the razor's edge, on death's hair-trigger touch.

"Bad news, Ivan, my boy," the captain said. "He smells your blood. Long as you're on this floe, we're all bear meat. Got to cut you loose. Good luck, old friend."

First slashed Ivan's two lifelines with his knife.

With languid grace the bear strolled toward Ivan. When he was less than seven feet away from the Russian, his wet ebony tongue unfurled from his mouth like a black pirate flag—no quarter asked, none given. His eyes were not so much cocky as serene. Ivan realized that *Ursus maritimus*'s gaze was not locked on his eyes but on his bloody nose and mouth.

"Oh, Vlad," the captain thundered, "why the fuck *aren't* you here? You'd piss your pants you'd be having so much fun!"

Ivan was having no fun at all.

The bear sniffed disdainfully, then threw back his head and again he roared.

With supreme indolence *Ursus maritimus* strode toward his lawful prey.

21 Play the Last Nickel

As Frank Sheckly turned the corner and started toward the ER reception lobby, he ran into his fiancée, Cathy Anne Gibson. Cathy was a burn nurse. She had come in early for the night shift, hoping to spend a few minutes alone with Frank.

"A full moon on Saturday night," Frank said, failing to first tell her how he was happy to see her, but then Cathy was used to his preoccupations. "ER will be packed."

"A lot of the caseload is headed Surgery's way."

Then he did pause to take her in. It was worth the effort. Long soft brown hair matching soft expressive eyes, fine bones, and a marvelous mouth mobile as a clown's.

She always appeared crisply professional—which never diminished her sensual appeal—as if she'd been born to wear a nurse's uniform.

The lobby of Reception was a mob scene. ER, in any hospital, was one of America's few remaining democracies. Wealthy bankers with coronary complaints were treated side by side with welfare recipients who had throat infections. Celebrities cut out of car wrecks lay beside gangbangers riddled by drive-by gunfire.

ER was a family doctor for the poor, and the place for those in trouble with nowhere else to go.

Frank loved it. He sometimes wished he'd gone into ER treatment instead of surgery.

A black triage nurse with cornrowed hair and a quick smile was separating arrivals to ER according to the severity of their wounds or complaints. Heart cases, patients in shock, and bleeders got the quickest attention. One patient— the lower half of his body soaked in blood—was on his way up to surgery.

"Shotgun," the triage nurse told Frank. "They'll have their hands full upstairs."

Frank nodded. He entered Receiving and punched up the nurses' reports on the computer.

Cathy read over his shoulder. "Thumb resection, cholecystectomy, two gastrectomies. Surgery's in for it."

"Let's hope the accreditation board doesn't pick tonight to stop by. We're running a zoo, not a hospital."

. . . A zoo.

An apt metaphor for his life. Not only places like Rwanda, Sierra Leone, and Sudan, where he and Cathy Anne had worked the refugee camps for Doctors Without Borders, but—going a long way back—that zoo called THE BIGGEST LITTLE CITY IN THE WORLD, which he had first seen when he was just a kid . . .

. . . Sunday afternoons his mother would drive him into Reno, where she played the nickel slots and hustled tricks while he hung around outside on the sidewalks. Occasionally Francesca would step outside to him, usually with a bucket of Indian-head nickels for him to rub.

"Bring mama some luck, Frank."

Luck.

The last time his father, Dwight, beat her, he also cut her with a straight razor and broke her right leg. The compound fracture festered, turned gangrenous, and the mining camp sawbones, not knowing what else to do, cut the leg off below the knee.

After that they took the bus into Reno. Her hooking days were over, but still she played the slots.

The last time he saw his mother, she was headed back into the Geronimo Casino on crutches with the nickels Frank had rubbed. All except one that he'd dropped. He saw it at the edge of the gutter and hurried to pick it up. Maybe it was the nickel, the one that would trigger the jackpot she desperately sought, week after week.

Someone got there first. A huge Texan in a black Stetson, with the biggest mustache Frank had ever seen.

"*That's my mother's,* Frank said politely. *"She needs it—for luck."*

"I'll take it to her," the Texan said, then studied Frank more closely. *"When was the last time you had something to eat?"*

Frank shrugged uneasily.

The man put a hand on his shoulder, and gave him the nickel. "Hang on to this. If it's all that lucky, it'll keep. Meantime I think you could use a cheeseburger and a root-beer float." He smiled. "Name's Doc," he said.

They were in a small café down the street when Francesca came out of the Geronimo looking for Frank. The sidewalk at early evening was crowded. Jostled by a half-drunk cowboy, she staggered off down the street, trying to stay balanced on her crutches.

Twenty minutes later when Doc Joiner walked Frank back to the Geronimo, the doorman came up to Doc, glanced down at Frank, and said quietly to Doc, "I know this kid. His mother's a regular. Was, that is. She got hit by a truck a little while ago. They took her to County, but she was DOA."

Doc looked down at Frank, who was looking up at him. He was still holding the nickel that had got away.

"Leave him here," the doorman said. *"We'll see he gets to Juvenile Hall."*

"I'm taking him inside for a minute."

"Why?"

"A hunch."

"What's that supposed to mean?"

"I make my living betting hunches."

"You know the Gaming Commission doesn't allow—"

"Only for a minute." Doc took Frank's hand. "Come with me, son."

They made their way, hand in hand, through the crowded casino to the nickel slot with the biggest payoff. Five hundred thousand dollars.

Doc put Frank on one shoulder, fished three nickels from his coat pocket, dropped them into the slot. He came up empty. Then he looked at Frank.

"Your turn."

Frank had been looking around for his mother.

"But—"

"Something tells me your luck is better than your mama's today. Or mine. Go ahead. Play the last nickel."

Frank dropped the coin. Doc Joiner pulled the handle to make it all legal.

All hell exploded from the machine—bells, sirens, flashing lights.

Jackpot.

"Great God Almighty," Doc Joiner whispered as the coins overflowed the tray and piled up at their feet. The casino crowd was drawn to the action, but two floor men kept them back from the Indian Head machine. Doc brought Frank down from his shoulder and held him at arm's length.

"Is that for my mother?" Frank asked, looking at the spill of coins.

"Yes, it is. Some of it anyway." Enough to give her a well-deserved send-off,

Doc thought. "Who do you have beside your mama, Frank? Brothers, sisters, grandparents?"

"No one. It was just me and her." His eyes got bigger. He looked at the faces around them. A bar girl had tears in her eyes. "Why?"

So they'd buried Francesca, giving her the "well-deserved" send-off Doc Joiner had promised. And Frank rode back to Texas with Doc and the rest of the jackpot. That much cash was the good-faith money Doc needed to secure a bridge loan for his latest acquisition—the oil brokerage firm he'd been negotiating to buy became his. He was freed from wildcatting forever.

Every day at breakfast Doc gave Frank a shiny new nickel to rub. All oilmen are superstitious.

Six years later Joiner Oil was worth nine hundred million dollars.

Two years after that, Doc met Lydia Magruder, and Frank had a step-mother.

On Frank's fifteenth birthday he woke up to find a present from L. L. in one corner of his bedroom. She had tracked down the old Indian Head slot machine from the Geronimo Casino——the one with the worn handle his mother had pulled so often in hope and despair, the machine that had proved luckier than Francesca could have dreamed.

And Frank found the mother he'd always wanted.

"Frank?" Cathy Anne asked, giving him a nudge. He looked up from the computer screen, smiled, kissed her cheek.

"Sorry, I'm dead on my feet."

"You need to rest."

"I'll sack out for a few hours after I check out the surgical unit."

"And I'll tag along just to make sure you get to bed."

22 He'd Beaten Them All

As Sailor stood on the deck with the warren's chief counselor, he stared out over the port bow. In the distance he could see the fogbound island known as Manhattan. At least, he could see the fog and the dim glow of its lights.

Even after the crew's attempts at cleanup, the *Pride of New York* was a sight—with its tilted smokestack, shattered rails, and empty lifeboat cradles. Deluged with bilge, the ship rode so low in the water, it was a miracle that the ship floated at all.

"You don't have to jump ship, you know," their chief counselor said. "Bad as the storm was, this warren still thrives."

"Not for long."

"Our tribe has lived in these holds beyond all memory. We know nothing else."

Sailor said nothing.

. . . He had experienced their obstinacy before, their refusal to leave the holds even during a hurricane. He had been there in the flooding holds, diving into the rising water again and again, pulling out one drowning rat after another, handing them over to others above the floodline.

For the men topside the ship the hurricane had also been a nightmare. Some of the crew were dead, some still hooked to lifelines but with shattered heads and twisted limbs. Half of those belowdecks floated facedown in the flooded holds.

As soon as the cargo was off-loaded, this ship was finished, destined for the scrap heap or the shipyard.

Either way it was no place for their warren.

But the Dark Ones could not see it. They would never leave . . .

Sailor stopped by the foremast, which had somehow survived the storm. Towering nearly 200 feet above the forward deck, its 50-inch searchlights still probed the fog-shrouded coasts of Manhattan, Brooklyn, and New Jersey.

"You told me before that none of you has scaled the great mast," he said to the counselor.

"It is too high and steep. The guy wires are too thin."

The foghorn droned, and the SS *Pride of New York* picked up speed. At dawn they would drop anchor. Sailor knew it was now or never—do it or get off the pot. He started up the lead wire. The others stared at him in stunned silence.

As soon as he started up the guy wire, Sailor was in trouble. He'd always known the climb would be hard, but he had not appreciated the toll his rescue efforts had taken on him. Nor had he anticipated the lacerating sharpness of the twisted wire strands.

Less than eighty feet from the top, his feet bled, his lungs burned, his breath rasped. Still, the angle of ascent steepened, and the sharp wind whipped at him.

Finally he reached the masthead. A 50-inch searchlight was mounted on a circular ledge one foot in diameter. He had to negotiate that base, secure a purchase, then swing up and over.

His agony was exquisite. Socrates had always told him not to fear death—that *death* was his wisest adviser, that death was a gift—but that advice had been received in a comfortable warren when Sailor had a full stomach. Here his muscles burned, and the frigid wind stung like hornets.

Clawing up under the overhang, he secured his grip, swung free of the guy wires, and pulled himself up over the ledge. Lying on his back, he stared up at the stars—the Big and Little Dippers, Orion, Cassiopeia, the wide white belt of the Milky Way, the slender crescent moon.

Turning his gaze east, he observed that Brooklyn and Manhattan were ringed by scores of miles of rotten wharves—heaven on earth for waterfront rats. There he would find a tribe, a warren. There he would build a Clan.

To the west, a pale ghostly woman emerged from the fog, tall as a foremast, a blazing torch in her hand.

Sailor rolled back over on his back. He had done it. He had beaten the gull, the plague, the Stalker, the sea, the Dark Ones, the hurricane, the men, the mast.

He let his limbs fall to his sides. He lay spread-eagled on a cross not of struggle and agony but of lassitude—a contemplative crucifixion.

For the first time in his life, Sailor the Rat knew peace.

23 You Sang of War, Thucydides

On the Odyssey space station, Sara Friedman was alone again. Henry Colton had kept her company for a while. She'd never met a man who radiated such strength, and listened so intently. And when he got around to speaking—which took awhile—he made real sense.

. . . Colton related similar problems with a human friend. He thought the comparisons were apt.

"Damn fool never communicated. Closed himself off to me and to John Stone. Wouldn't let us help him. Now he's doing triple-life in Jackton, Texas. And he was the best friend I ever had. But you want to know something? I let him down. I took for granted he'd work things out, and I was wrong. You can't take anything for granted, Sara. Not when it comes to people and the other things you care about. I learned the hard way. I wasn't there when Breeze needed me. Stone had an excuse. He was out hunting down terrorists and trying to save the world. So you be there for A/O. Don't make my mistake. Don't take anything for granted . . ."

She sat in front of A/O's dozen monitors and console keyboard. *Keyboard is right,* she thought. *But what is the key to your closed-off mind, my friend?*

Colton had said earlier that A/O had a case of the stutters. He had misdiagnosed A/O's condition, but he'd come closer than he would ever know to divining a secret of her own life.

Sara was a closet stutterer.

. . . As a child she learned later that in many countries other schoolchildren teased stutterers maliciously. But not in Israel. Teachers, classmates, and friends had all treated her with patience and sensitivity. At a doctor's suggestion her mother had encouraged her to talk by asking her questions about her school day, maintaining eye contact, never finishing sentences for Sara. By the seventh grade Sara's stammer was barely noticeable.

Deep inside, however, she still felt the hesitation, the inability to retrieve the correct word and articulate it. Sara had sometimes wondered if her early obsession with books had derived from her stammer. Her earliest pleasures were reading literature, lost and at peace in this world of words where no response was asked for.

Her first literary love affair had been with the Bible. Psalms was her greatest passion. From there she had proceeded to the Greek classics. The Greeks had inspired her to write poetry herself. Thucydides' History of the Peloponnesian War *had especially enthralled her, and Sara had written a poem of him too. How did that one go?*

It came back to her in a rush, and she reflexively punched part of it into her console.

You sang of war, Thucydides.
You sang of men,
Who fought and bled and died,
Of noble deeds which lead
But to the grave.

Aeschylus's vision of the prophet Cassandra had also haunted her. Cassandra . . . Cassandra. The words came back to her, and she began to type:

"Ode to Cassandra."

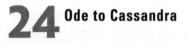

24 Ode to Cassandra

Behind his wall of silence, Alpha/Omega heard Sara's poem.

He had almost missed it. For the past month or so, he had ignored her altogether. If she hadn't mentioned Cassandra by name, the poem would have gone right past him.

But she had mentioned his sainted mentor, and that Alpha/Omega could not ignore.

Who are you, Cassandra?
Martyr to Truth?
Wisdom's whore?
Blessed with godlike prophesy
Yet tortured, slaughtered—
Denied.
Does it mean nothing

That we scorn your tears,
Mock your gifts?
Listen not at all?
No, Cassandra.
It means everything.
Ask Achilles.
Ask Hector.

Ask Troy.

What did that mean? A/O speculated. Why was Sara calling Cassandra?

Alpha/Omega had never dreamed that Sara—the infernal pest—might know Sister Cassandra. His files indicated that Cassandra, when she was not performing, was a recluse, almost schizophrenically withdrawn.

Yet Sara was calling her. Sara could put him in touch with his Sister-Through-Choice!

She had tried a thousand different ways of breaking through A/O's overrides, and every time he shut her down—until now.

Now, at last, he had to respond.

"I'm here, Sara."

"That's you, A/O?" Sara asked, incredulous. "You're talking to me?"

"Yes, moments ago I heard you address Cassandra. I need to speak to her. It's very important. Please put me through."

There was a long pause.

Then.

"You want to speak to . . . Sister Cassandra?"

Sara couldn't conceal her shock.

"You were addressing her," A/O said. "You have to put me in touch with her. It is crucial."

"I can try, but that could take time. She's not particularly sociable."

"Well, do your best. By the way," he added, "I noticed the poem to her was not cataloged in my memory."

"No, it's something I wrote a long time ago."

"I liked it very much. Perhaps you could send me another of your poems. While we are waiting."

Sara was perplexed, silent. Was her old stammer returning?

Was it possible that Sara did not know what to say?

"Just get me Cassandra," A/O requested again.

In the world of Cassandra's dreams, she and Santiago were herded across the Boniata prison yard. Even at midnight they had to shield their darkness-weakened eyes. Overhead the Milky Way blazed from horizon to horizon. The rest of the sky was a dazzling carpet of stars, which along with the full moon illumined the high white walls of the prison yard.

The two ragged prisoners were led to the flogging post. Two guards lifted Santiago onto his toes. His wrist manacles were lashed to a heavy steel I-hook screwed into the post's top.

"I know what you think," the bearded Generalissimo said. "Nuns and priests deserve better treatment than you receive here."

Santiago hung from the flogging post, eyes closed, saying mute Hail Marys. Cassandra could only stare at her feet.

"Your holy brothers and sisters," the Generalissimo continued, "see me not as a savior or a liberator but as evil. Verdad?"

Cassandra mentally counted the Stations of the Cross.

"But you know what really hurt muy malo?" he whispered to her. "When these hideputas compare me to Vlad Malokov. I mean these cabrones really know how to hurt a compadre."

"Satan Incarnate is more accurate," Santiago said.

El Zopilote grabbed the strung-up priest by his black matted hair and yanked his head back.

"Oh, say it ain't so, Joe. Say I ain't no Satan."

"Meo en la leche de su madre." [I piss in the milk of your mother.]"

"Bravo! A toast to my macho muchacho." The Generalissimo released his hair and took a silver flask from the right-front cargo pocket of his fatigue jacket. "A compliment on your machismo. Now some fine Cuban rum, to toast your manhood. Not exactly sacramental wine but good enough for a godless defrocked communist, no?"

He had a deep pull on the flask.

"Salud y pesetas y cojones. A toast to money and balls."

He ripped the shirt from Santiago, exposing the same broad white stripes that Cassandra bore on her back.

"You know my favorite Christian writer? St. Paul. Remember his Letters to Corinthians?"

Removing a small Bible from his other front cargo pocket, he began to read: "'Though I speak with the tongues of men and of angels and have not charity.'"

El Zopilote paused and looked at his sergeant, who had just returned from the guardhouse with a coiled blacksnake whip.

"'I am become as sounding brass, or tinkling cymbal.'"

He lowered the Bible and grinned at Cassandra.

"Sergeant, let's give Señor Santiago a little taste of Paulist charity."

The sergeant unlimbered the thirteen-foot blacksnake. He walked up to Santiago, then did an about-face and paced off the correct distance. He nodded to the Generalissimo.

El Zopilote nodded back.

The blacksnake cracked. Blood spurted from Santiago's back and shoulders. He endured the blow without making any sound.

While the whipping continued, El Zopilote read from his pocket Bible in solemn tones.

"'And though I have the gift of prophecy and understand all mysteries and all knowledge.'"

Crack!

"'And though I have all faith so that I could remove mountains, and have not charity.'"

Crack!

"'I am nothing.'"

Crack!

"'Charity suffereth long, beareth all things, believeth all things, hopeth all things, endureth all things.'"

Crack

"'Charity never faileth: but whether there be prophecies, they shall fail.'"

Crack!

"'For we know in part, and we prophesy in part.'"

Crack!

"'But when that which is perfect is come, then that which is in part shall be done away.'"

Crack!

"'When I was a child, I spake as a child, I understood as a child, I thought as a child: but when I became a man, I put away childish things.'"

Crack!

"'For now we see through a glass, darkly; but then face to face: now I know in part; but then shall I know even as also I am known.'"

Crack!

"'And now abideth faith, hope, charity, these three; but the greatest of these is charity.'"

Santiago had passed out.

El Zopilote grinned at Cassandra. She struggled not to give El Zopilote the satisfaction of her tears.

A bucket of water was thrown in Santiago's face. When he revived, El Zopilote wrenched his head back by the hair.

"See, amigo, you say I do the devil's work, but in truth I only teach you

St. Paul's. Your charity suffereth long and envieth not—same as his. You good as him. I make you that way."

Santiago said, in a weak voice but with a contemptuous smile, "El Hideputa [son of a whore]."

"Stop it!" Cassandra wailed. "Please, no more."

The Generalissimo grinned. "No worry. I ain't gonna whip your hombre no more."

He drew a military .45 from his shoulder holster. Yanking back Santiago's head, he shoved the barrel between his teeth.

"Bite on this, padre puto."

Still, Santiago yanked his head free and got it out before the Generalissimo could jam the pistol back in and pull the trigger:

"Viva el Cristo Rey! [Long live Christ the King!]"

————————

In the dream-box of her mind, Cassandra was back in her blackout cell. Beaten, dispirited, she did not fight back when the guards appeared. Nor did they torture her. Instead, they dragged her outside, brought out a hose, sluiced her down, then scrubbed her up. Giving her a freshly laundered white dressing gown, they took her upstairs to a clean cell with a clean mattress and sheets. Spreading her belly-down on the bed, they manacled her wrists and ankles to the bedstand. Cassandra prayed silently:

Jesu, kill me, like Santiago. Please. I no longer have the will, I've lost the way.

She smelled him even before she saw him, the stinking cigar, the oiled guns, the saddle-soaped leather, the liquored breath. Bending over her, he put his tongue in her ear.

"See, guapa, you no understand me. I am a Prophet—Christ's own right hand. See, your Jesu come to me in the mountains—during my years in the wilderness. He show me the future."

Cassandra said nothing.

"Know what He tell me? He tell me where, when, why the End Time will come. Men like me, see, we gotta do His work. We gotta scourge the earth, punish the sinners for Christ on High. I tell you a little secret Jesu tell me and me only. Secret of the End. Now it will be *our* secret."

Ripping off her gown, he unbuckled his belt and pulled down his pants, not bothering to remove them or his boots. He unholstered his .45. He lowered himself on top of her emaciated, whip-scarred back.

The Vulture nuzzled Cassandra's cheek with the muzzle of his cocked .45, and whispered the secret Jesu told him in the mountains.

While he raped her.

26 Doc's Third Law

From the Surgical Observation Deck of the Towers, Frank Sheckly and Cathy watched.

In General #1, a surgical resident worked on a burn case.

Frank had done his share of burn surgery, but it always gave him the creeps.

"They brought this one over from Rikers Island," Cathy Anne told him. "A gang at Rikers drenched fifty percent of his body with lighter fluid, Pico Pico Hot Sauce, and India ink, then set it all ablaze."

Frank studied the kid. His strapped-down body vibrated with pain. Frank averted his eyes.

"They didn't give him a general," Cathy Anne said. "In some burn cases the risk of death from anesthesia is usually greater than that from pain."

Frank looked again at the strapped-down young man. One surgeon was removing the skin from his arms with a Brown dermatome—an electric razor for shaving off skin. Another surgeon was debriding his facial skin with forceps. He looked up briefly from his work, and Frank, in a haze of fatigue, was struck by how much the surgeon resembled "Doc" Joiner.

. . . *Frank's first choice of career had not been medicine at all. He'd expected to follow in Doc's footsteps, and Doc sure as hell wasn't any MD. He told everyone his Ph.D. stood for "posthole digger," but it was in fact in geology.*

The education had helped Doc in his search for oil, which had taken him from Pakistan to Mongolia, from the North Sea to the Gulf, from Nigeria and back home to Texas, where he had at last made his fortune.

"All of which goes to prove Doc's Third Law," Doc once told Frank, trying to find some hidden meaning in the eternal odyssey of his life.

Doc had a thousand Third Laws, every one of them different.

"Which Third Law is this one, Doc?" Frank asked.

"The way you start is the way you end."

Doc was a born philosopher. A lifetime of travel and love of learning instilled in him a vast and varied education, and over those years he had collected an enormous and eclectic library. A geologist by trade, he especially loved science, and Frank had read most of Doc's science books by the time he was twelve.

In A History of Medicine *Frank first learned that surgery is an ancient trade—as ancient as suffering itself. Some of the oldest human skulls on record bore the signs of cranial surgery—trepanning, the removal of pieces of the skull.*

Six thousand years ago Egyptians had taught circumcision to the Jews. African tribes—far beyond the reach of Egyptian priests—developed the technique on their own.

In that book Frank also read about the first great doctors and surgeons. Hippocrates, who taught cleanliness and the art of draining abscesses. Galen, who,

150 years after Christ, wrote the first books on anatomy and abdominal surgery, on the ligation of blood vessels and the removal of varicose veins. Lister, who introduced antisepsis into the operating room.

Frank also learned that until the 20th century hospitals had been medical abattoirs, little more than filthy amputation wards where infectious diseases proliferated and suffering was horrific.

Some of New York City's parks had originally functioned as mass burial grounds for its hospitals' multitudinous victims.

When Doc found him rereading A History of Medicine for the fourth time, he asked him what he found so fascinating.

"These men weren't only scientists and doctors, Doc, they were heroes."

"Maybe," Doc said, "but don't forget Doc's Third Law. You know it, don't you?"

"I expect I'm about to."

"Anyone who pays the price of excellence is a hero."

Still, Frank felt doctors were special. Furthermore, by the time Frank was ready for premed, Doc was having medical problems.

"Acute angina pectoris with ventricular fibrillation" was the way the Houston Heart Clinic diagnosed Doc's problem.

"A dicey ticker" was how Doc summed it up.

Still Doc never stopped taking an interest in Frank's career plans, dreams, and ambitions.

"There's lots of medical specialties. Got one in mind?"

"I keep thinkin' on how my old man used to get liquored up and whip on us," Frank finally told Doc. "Sometimes he beat Francesca so bad that I used to dream I had a magic wand I could wave and make her all right. Well, Doc, surgeons don't wait for nature to take its course. They move fast and make things happen. They do something. It's like they have that magic wand."

Doc nodded slowly. "You know Doc's Third Law on that one?"

"What's number three today?"

"Sometimes the strongest, most decisive move you can make is no move at all. And for men like you and me that's the hardest move of all."

"No way, Doc. I did that too many years. Anymore, I just can't see laying back and letting bad things happen."

"Frank?" Cathy Anne said. "Hear that racket? What the hell is going on?"

A commotion had broken out down the hall in the Traumatic Surgery Unit.

"Time to check out Trauma," Frank said. "Typical Saturday night."

27 Shoot Him with a Silver Bullet

Lydia Magruder sat in her office watching Kate's newscast from Mecca. When it was over, she turned the monitor off and punched in Kate's cell-phone number. L. L. had her own proprietary cellular-relay network—not unlike the Navy Seals uplinks—and with the help of the Odyssey, she could reach Kate anywhere in the world.

After six rings Kate answered.

"Kate," L. L. said, "I finally watched your Mecca broadcast. The ending was abrupt."

"John Stone disrupted it. Blame it on him."

"I need to find Stone and the second part of his report or book, or whatever it is. Without it, the president won't listen."

"Mom, it's your own fault. You're so obsessed with this stuff. You wear people out."

"You didn't see my last letter from Stone."

"Mom."

"Listen. Just a couple of paragraphs:

"'. . . I love seeing Developing Nations make it in the Global Economy, but we've sacrificed nuclear security on the altar of deregulation and free trade. I'm talking cold isotation presses which create the implosion charges for nuclear triggers, oxidation, brazing and annealing furnaces, diffusion, control systems, vacuum pumps—all necessary for uranium centrifuges. A lot of this stuff—I mean nuclear plant equipment—we've sold to our enemies.

"'And we've bankrolled a lot of these deals with insane loans, giving a lot of these nations the cash with which to buy this stuff. I'm talking BCCI-type loans. You remember BCCI—the Pakistani Death Squad Bankers? Offshore black-hole accounts, black ops, gestapo tactics, accounting records handwritten on ledgers in Urdu. They were Alice Through the Looking Glass, yet we poured $9 billion into their coffers which they used to bankroll Pakistan's atom bomb program, using the nuclear technology we supplied them with . . . After that, of course, they ripped us and our allies off for over $20 billion—the largest outright bank heist ever.'

"Now do you think I'm crazy?"

"I don't think you're crazy. I just get tired of people calling you 'the Nuclear Noah' and that armed compound you live in 'Bedlam's Bomb Shelter.'"

"We have poets and scientists here, religionists and musicians, artists and artisans. Some of the most creative minds in the world reside here. I've always seen the Citadel as a Platonic Republic where philosophers *are* kings."

"Then why am I constantly defending you?"

"I can't help it if I think the world is worth defending."

"So do I. Look, I'm finishing up a series for you on nuclear deterrence, right?"

"Yes, but if Stone's right, I'd prefer you cancel that assignment and come home."

"No-can-do. After I finish with Larry Taylor, I'm hooking up with Frank. We're doing that animal-rights research exposé. After that, I'll cover the Republican presidential convention in Manhattan."

"Come home and bring Frank back with you."

"No. Does the word *no* mean anything to you?"

"It doesn't. I miss John and Frank, and Kate, I'm scared."

"Mom, you can't always take the world on your shoulders."

"I need the last section of Stone's manuscript."

"We're doing everything we can to find him."

"It's not enough."

"Look, I know Stone. Even if he is in some scrape, he'll pull through. You want to kill John Stone you have to shoot him with a silver bullet."

28 There Is No Such Thing as Pain

Stone was now strapped and spread-eagled to his four-armed Roman cross.

Upside down.

Sultana finished checking his temperature. Tightening the arm-cuff, she took his blood pressure. She recorded them on his chart. Studying the clipboard, she nodded approvingly.

"Sister," Sultana said, "even inverted he registers 120 over 80 and 98.6."

"He *is* lion-hearted."

"He was a great athlete."

Sabrina treated Stone to her most ingratiating smile.

"You know, Mr. Stone," Sabrina said, "Spartacus was hung upside down from a crux immissa."

Sultana tightened the copper wire around his testicles.

"Tighter, tighter," Sabrina said. "When you have him by the balls, Sainted Sister, you pull!"

"Kill me," Stone whispered. "Please."

"Buck up, Mr. Stone. Death holds no sway—not for us. What did Vince Lombardi tell us? 'There is no substitute for victory'?"

"Douglas MacArthur," Stone said.

"What did Lombardi say?" Sultana asked.

"'There is no such thing as pain,'" Stone whimpered.

The Sisters howled hilariously.

"What are you laughing at?" Stone asked.

"How do you think our family rose to power in Dar-al-Suhl?" Sabrina said. "Our dynasty is the House That Pain Built."

"And we can't keep our brother waiting," Sultana said, "so let's hear about your sources."

"Where did you get your information?" Sabrina asked.

"I just pieced a lot of facts together. It was all surmise—wild surmise."

"You know, Sister mine," Sabrina said, "I was sort of hoping he'd say that."

"Moi aussi," Sultana said. And to Stone: "How do you like *this* for a wild surmise?"

The Sin Sisters alternated turning the cranks on the telephone generators.

Stone levitated on his cross with each twist of the handle, his screams ringing through the night.

29 The Blackout Drawers

Sister Cassandra sat in her dressing room. She had no memory of passing out on the stage after her last show. She would never, however, forget El Zopilote.

. . . She'd fainted that last time he'd raped and tortured her, coming to three days later in the prison hospital. She was now blind. The doctors gave her no chance.

During the chills and fever, Cassandra had her vision—and heard "the Song."

The next day she hallucinated that she had spoken with her old friends Kate Magruder and John Stone.

Three days after her imagined conversation with Magruder and Stone, Cass wasn't surprised when her ears—that she now relied on for almost all her sensory input, since she'd gone blind—reported the cacophony and chaos of screams and gunshots that were the norm in Boniato.

Something, though, was different. Through a constant haze of pain and disorientation Cass tried tuning in on the screaming and the gunshots. Apparently the screams weren't the familiar shrieks of her fellow inmates.

It was her captors screaming.

Also, the gunfire was unusual. Not the random, surreal reports of sidearms used during torture and executions. These were the controlled bursts of assault weapons. She even heard terse, one- or two-word commands shouted in English.

None of El Zopilote's henchmen barked orders in English.

Even after she'd been lifted, without explanation, from the lightless six-feet-by-three-feet "blackout drawer" that was her cell and spirited with astounding speed to a helicopter—whose pilot and crew also spoke clipped, military English—she still doubted her ears. Not then, not later when voices told her she was in Guantánamo Bay, the American marine base in Cuba. Cassandra's sores were being tended to with something that was now a distant memory: tenderness and mercy. She was cleaned gently, by women who addressed her with respect as Sister Cassandra, not Sister Puta.

These people told her that she had been rescued by the United States Navy Seals.

It had to be a trick or a dream.

Soon she'd wake up in her six-feet-by-three-feet gaveta "blackout drawer" again—where she'd spent most of the last four years—with the Vulture's stink polluting her nose and his obscene laugh befouling her ears. Or perhaps this was a deliberately staged play-act by El Zopilote. He was restoring her to health (and worse, to hope), so that when he destroyed her again he could crush not just her body, but her soul.

As a nurse gingerly wound gauze across her abused eyes, Cass tried to work out a mental strategy against this newest cruelty of kindness. Her only tactical defense would be to reject belief in this "rescue"; something or someone was behind it—even if it was her own failing mind.

She would not allow herself the luxury of acceptance. That was, until she'd heard their voices:

"My God, Cass . . ." Kate sobbed

"We've got you now, Sister. You've beaten them," the unmistakable baritone of John Stone added, his voice cracking with emotion.

Kate and Stone had found her.

And L. L. had forced the president to order her rescue.

Of course the joint statement released to the press—by both Cuba and America—reflected none of this. Both nations maintained that Amnesty International and PEN had discovered and named the missing singer as a prisoner of conscience in Cuba and that the American president negotiated Sister Cassandra's freedom with the president of Cuba, demonstrating El Presidente's mercy and his willingness to cooperate with the Free World.

This fiction also spared the Vulture total humiliation in the eyes of the world when his torture of the Good Sister was exposed. He could deny all knowledge of the atrocities, saying he had punished the perpetrators and ordered her release.

Once she was back in the United States, a two-month regimen of around-the-clock penicillin cured her of El Supremo's syphillis.

Six months later Cassandra recorded "The Song" for L. L. Magruder and began her series of televised sermons, which quickly became elaborate performances.

Within a year she was the biggest thing in entertainment history.

. . . Sister Cassandra sighed. Show business was thirsty work. Her road manager was knocking on her door. She ignored him and the voices of her fans and looked for a flask.

Someone had cleaned out her dressing suite.

Shit.

If she wanted another bottle, she was going to have to let her assistant in—and do the second show.

———————

Twelve minutes to showtime. Cassandra had allowed Sister Angela into her dressing room to prepare her for the second show. While Cassandra sat at her dressing table, Sister Angela brushed Cassandra's long raven hair.

Boredom was an especially acute problem for Cassie. Being blind, she could not divert herself visually. Cassie did not even know what her suite looked like—even though she was sequestered there for most of her working day. That she'd once been sequestered in prison cells was an irony not lost on her.

"I think you've brushed it enough," Cassie said.

"Just want to make you beautiful, boss."

"Did it work?"

"It'd work better if you'd try smiling. I've never seen you smile, you know? No one has."

Cassie shrugged. "Maybe I don't find much to smile about."

"But you do care what you look like."

"I'll never know what I look like. I don't remember what I *used* to look like." She sighed. She needed another drink.

"I've seen pictures. You were—still are—a knockout."

"I'll just be glad when this Sunday marathon is over."

"Are you going back to the Citadel?"

"Yes."

"I'll miss you."

Angela resumed brushing, but Cassandra blocked the action of the hairbrush with her right hand. "I need a drink."

"Jonesy would say—"

"I pay Jonesy's salary, Angela."

"Mine too, but Jonesy thinks your health is—"

"Damn it. I want a drink! Get me the drink or it's no show."

Angela began to cry.

Cassandra again touched Angela's face, wiping away the tears.

"Don't cry. Please."

"But we worry—"

"I preach what I believe, Angela, and I believe the End Time is almost here. Does it matter if I'm drunk or sober? I think I'm better when I'm drunk."

"I sneaked a bottle into the closet," Angela whispered, "in the makeup kit."

"Gracias, amiga. I'm in your debt."

"All I want is for you to smile in my direction—just once."

Cass stared at her, unseeing, unsmiling. "You're a good person, Angela, but don't ask what I can't give. Now vamonos. I have another show to do."

Angela brushed Cassie's cheek with her lips and shut the door quietly.

Sister Cassandra turned up the radio. The second service of her all-day Sunday show was under way in the amphitheater outside her door. Her associate minister, Sister Sondra, was warming up the congregation, leading the choir in a melodious rendition of Cassie's signature hymn, "I Heard the Song."

"I first heard the song in Hiroshima
With firestorms blazing high.
Heard it again in Vietnam
While death rained from the skies.
In the black smoke of the fire drives
Countless billions died.
In Auschwitz, in slave ships,
I heard their screams and cries.

"I heard the song.
I heard the song.
Oh God, I heard the song . . ."

That none of her success had brought her happiness Cass had long ago accepted as her Tao. She accepted as an article of her hard-won faith that she would live in bitterness and die in despair. She would trade, in a heartbeat, all of her fame for one brief glimpse of a golden dawn or an eagle's flight, but on the other hand, had she not survived the tortures of damned, had she not given her eyes to the blackout pits of Boniata, she would not have received the Second Sight that defined her. She would never have heard "the Song."

"I heard the song in Attica
Where I saw my brothers die.
I heard the song in the crack house
With my sisters oh-so-high.
I heard the song in the death house,
Where they take that lightning ride.
Heard the song just one time more:
Sang the whole damn world done died."

She lifted Angela's makeup kit out of the closet, opened the lid, and reached in. Her right hand closed reassuringly around a pint bottle of Captain Morgan.

She carried the rum to a sideboard. Uncorking the rum bottle, she groped for a tumbler that was provided for her between appearances onstage. She carefully filled it, using her inside index finger to tell her when the glass was full.

Putting down the rum bottle, Cass drank deeply. The rum burned all the way down—searing but soothing—and "the Song" drifted through the dressing room door.

She sat back down and let the warm glow of the dark spirits do what they did all too goddamned well, according to her so-called friends and associates. She took another drink, another, waiting for the blackness, waiting for memory to release its grip on her.

She'd seen so much shit—Salvador, Nicaragua, Guatemala—while carrying the banner of the Church Militant. *No truce with tyrants* had been her Creed, her Battle Cry, her Cross of Arms.

Her Golgotha.

Sister Sondra's gorgeous soprano—in soothing contrast to her own rough blues-gospel voice—filled the dressing suite.

"I heard the song.
I heard the song.
Oh God, I heard the song.
Sang the whole world's burning,
The whole world's burning,
Gonna burn your world down."

Burn it down, indeed. She had another shot of rum, burning it down, burning it all down. Perhaps this was the time, now, while she still felt the glow.

She counted her steps to the walk-in closet. Fumbling through clothes and shoes, she found and hefted a particularly hard and heavy bag. She returned to the couch and placed a .45 automatic pistol onto her lap.

As a Latin American activist for the Church Militant, she'd not only studied small arms, she'd learned to fieldstrip the military Colt .45 blindfolded. After setting up her ministry, she'd purchased the Colt. Stripping and reassembling the pistol soothed her nerves. Even now—stone-blind and seriously drunk—her fingers worked flawlessly, removing the magazine first, the slide, the recoil spring, and the barrel.

Then she meticulously cleaned and oiled the .45. Reassembling the Colt, she reinserted the loaded magazine, worked the slide—automatically cocking the hammer and chambering a round.

A-OK. She still had the touch.

Against her will her thoughts returned to Boniata, deep in the prison's subbasements, with no light, ventilation, or toilet. Prisoners were dragged out only to be washed down with high-pressure hoses.

"Tu baño," the guards mockingly called the water torture. Your bath.

Afterward Cassandra was raped vaginally, anally, and orally by guards and trustees.

Throwing back her head, Cass stared sightlessly at the ceiling of her dressing suite. "Muchas gracias, Hombre," she said under her breath. "Chingo tu padre." She inserted the pistol into her mouth till the front sight scraped her throat. Mastering her gag reflex, she clenched the barrel between her teeth.

Shutting her eyes, she waited for the voice that would tell her to stand down.

On the fourteenth Hail Mary, at the words "blessed art thou," Cassandra lost patience.

Oh Frank. Oh Stony. Oh, Kate. L. L., please forgive me. I tried. I honestly tried. I'm so sorry.

She depressed the trigger with her right thumb.

30 Putting Humpty Back Together Again

Scrubbed and masked, Frank Sheckly and Cathy Anne entered the Traumic Surgery Unit, where a patient was being attended to by two doctors and two nurses.

The patient's body and face were covered with so much blood Frank could barely make out his features.

"Shotgun," Cathy Anne said. "Liquor-store robbery."

The right knee had taken most of the bullets, and someone had had the presence of mind to tie the wound off with a necktie. The lower leg—below the tourniquet—was almost blasted free from the upper thigh. Tendons, bones, and ligaments—protruding through the bleeding flesh—were all that connected the lower leg to the rest of the body.

"That tourniquet is too tight," Frank said to one of the attendings. "Looks like the paramedics never loosened it. How long has it been on?"

The senior of the two doctors, whose name was Phillips, said, "Too long. The manager put his necktie on tight as he knew how, and no one else wanted to mess with it. Afraid he'd bleed out."

"Get another tourniquet above it, and cut that one off," Frank said. "At the rate this is going, he could lose his leg."

"We cut that line, the whole leg might explode," Phillips cautioned. "The shotgun blast took out the femoral artery."

A triage nurse named Sanchez fetched an elastic tourniquet and a clamp-on. Everyone in the trauma unit worked quickly, but with no show of uncertainty. They had treated a lot of gunshot wounds.

A resident named Brewer tightened the replacement tourniquet. The other nurse handed Phillips a scalpel, and he cut the necktie.

Blood exploded out of the leg all over the OR table and floor.

"You done these before, Dr. Sheckly?" Brewer asked.

"Too many times."

"Could you hang with us awhile?" Phillips asked. "This is the worst I've ever seen. We have to fix it now and we're short staffed."

Frank looked at his watch. It was after midnight. "I'll stay—just be cool. We need to do four things, okay? First legate those leg vessels, then pack the lower leg in ice."

"Ice?" Phillips asked, incredulous. "Why?"

"Because, Doctor, we're going to save that leg."

"Can it be done?"

"Get a Mycillin drip into him. Insert a nasogastric tube through his nose and into his stomach. Let's trache him too. He may already have aspirated."

The gunshot victim's heartline was erratic.

"He's in bad shape, Dr. Sheckly," Brewer said. "I'm not sure he's going to make it."

"He's not only going to make it, you're going to save his leg."

"We may jeopardize his life trying to save it," Phillips objected.

Suddenly Frank was shouting.

"I spent too many goddamn years losing limbs and amputating the stumps of women and children in places like Rwanda and Sierre Leone! We're saving that leg!"

Cathy Anne stared at him, stunned. Nobody had ever heard Frank raise his voice.

Or talk about the refugee camps.

Or about amputations.

Then she remembered L. L. Magruder telling her how Frank's mother had lost a leg.

One of the nurses got an IV with an antibiotic drip.

Frank Sheckly was calm again, analytical as they packed ice around the traumatized leg. All Cathy Anne saw of Frank's face was his eyes and the deep circles of fatigue beneath them.

"Just stick with me, people. We're putting Humpty back together . . . *tonight.*"

31 Destiny

The gray light of predawn illuminated the eastern horizon just above Long Island. Sailor and the warren's elders stood at the supertanker's port rail.

"You don't have to leave," the chief counsel said.

"Look at this ship," Sailor said, giving the *Pride of New York* one last once-over. "It was a hell-scow when the voyage started. It's worse now. It's destined for the scrapyard. Stay aboard, you will perish."

"But this ship is all we know."

"The ship will die."

Sailor studied Manhattan Island. It was densely packed with old brick buildings and shining towers of steel, masonry, and glass. The island appeared to be connected by bridges to the rest of the world.

Off the ship's port bow was the rust-green woman with the crown and torch. Beyond her loomed the country Sailor had seen in his vision atop the mast. A land where Sailor and his clan could multiply and thrive.

First he needed a clan. He was sure to find one on the wharves that surrounded the island.

The Wanderratte crawled to the rail's edge and dove 100 feet into the harbor below.

As he swam toward Manhattan with firm strokes, his odyssey resumed.

32 The Tides That Guide the Atoms Drive the Stars

In Cassandra's dressing suite the hammer of the .45 dry-snapped; the pistol's chamber was empty.

"Goddamn it to hell," she muttered.

One of the problems with being blind was that she had to double-check *everything*. Such as the .45's magazine. Someone obviously didn't want her playing with loaded guns. If those *putas* weren't careful—trying to restrict her consumption of the Captain, fucking with her guns—they'd find themselves out of a job.

She needed to speak with Angela, who was easier to deal with—and manipulate—than Jonesy and Judith. Maybe Angela would like a promotion, a little extra change in the kitty. Maybe she'd like to—

Someone was knocking on the door. Shit. Cassandra put the gun away. Time for another sermon.

Opening the door, she returned to the stage . . .

––––––––––

Standing on stage in a pool of light, she began:

"In case you haven't heard, boys and girls, we are in the Last Days, the Valley of Dry Bones. The world's loose nukes are coming home to roost. Russia alone has 2.5 million pounds of nuclear bomb fuel, ill-guarded and ill-secured. Dread is loosed on the land, kids. Some of those babies are suitcase-size, you know, wielded by nations with nothing to lose. It's the Third World's revenge—and they are about to get some payback.

"I've seen their torture chambers and slave-labor work camps. That's the only way you rule places like these—since time immemorial, time out of mind—the shackle, the branding iron, the whip. Of course, they use electricity now—black boxes and cattle prods. Instead of the priests praying over the victims' souls,

medical doctors give them adrenaline, CPR, and fibrillate the heart—keeping them alive for one more grueling session.

"There's one catch: They got the Bomb, baby, and they are out to settle scores.

"Only one choice now. You have to learn to love the Bomb. And why not? Is the Bomb not fire from heaven, Prometheus's dream, a gift from the gods? The sun is nothing if not the Bomb writ large, a never-ending Nagasaki. And I have seen a vision of a God Who is pissed, Who has given us so much—great green fields to nourish us, rivers to water us, hills to shield us, beautiful creatures, joy and comfort, a sheltering sky—in return, what have we given Him? We have laid waste to His world, His creatures, His very Son.

"But the tides that guide the atoms drive the stars. The universe God wrought is not all joy and light but also a realm of inconceivable violence, murder beyond measure, billions of galaxies filled with trillions of stars—thermonuclear warheads, endlessly detonating, until collapsing upon themselves, blowing themselves to Kingdom Come, into gas and debris, imploding into black holes which devour the stars around them.

"And while He is patient, His patience is not eternal. When the stars throw down their spears and water heaven with their tears, will He smile His work to see?

"I think not."

33 An Aperture Through Which the Infinite Might Shine

When Breeze came to, he was in a subbasement cell, stripped naked, strung up from the cell door by his manacled wrists.

. . . Breeze could not remember much. Some men had entered his cell in the middle of the night, swinging heavy Maglites and riot batons. He'd deflected some of the blows, but one of them connected and he sank down to his knees in darkness . . .

The subbasement was dimly lit. As far as Breeze could tell, the other cells were empty. When the ringing in his ears subsided, he could hear water leaking. Water seemed to be everywhere—on the walls, ceiling, floor.

Then he heard groans. Glancing around, he could see Radford, Riaz, and Jamal stripped and strung up beside him in his cell.

Other men were with them. The sergeant, known as Hardball, stood on the sidelines in a khaki shirt, blue pants, and black tie. Short and wiry, with mean eyes and a wicked grin, he smacked the palm of his right hand with a riot baton. Warden Carstairs was staring at Jamal. A grim-looking man with a thinning gray mustache, he wore thick eyeglasses, a white shirt, a black tie, and matching pants. He was not smiling.

Their companion was over six-feet-four-inches tall and had to weigh more than three hundred pounds. From his black suit, black shirt, and white clerical collar Breeze assumed he was the legendary Junius O'Donnell, Jack Town's chaplain and chief disciplinarian. He wore his dark hair medium length and his matching beard close-cropped. His most distinguishing feature was a twinkling emerald eye. The other eye was reputedly a nightmare-orb. Its brow and socket were bisected by an old knife-slash. The Chaplain had thankfully masked it with a black eye patch.

"Let's get this straight," Warden Carstairs said to Jamal. "You enter the machine shop. Shotgun blasts are reported. You four are seen *by informants* departing the shop. My guards discover, on entering the shop, dead bodies. Have I left anything out?"

"Habeas corpus, due process, trial by jury," Jamal said.

"Right to a speedy and impartial trial," Radford offered.

"Cochran, Dershowitz, Gerry Spence, Scott Turow, John Grisham," Breeze said, recommending legal counsel.

"Margaret McLean's better lookin'," Radford said.

"Right to chingo your sister and gang-up on her puta-pussy," Riaz added.

"We could also save the Departments of Justice and Corrections several million dollars' worth of court time and prison overhead right here and now," O'Donnell said pleasantly.

"I noticed you forgot to Mirandize us," Radford said.

O'Donnell nodded thoughtfully, "Sergeant, read Radford his rights."

The sergeant stopped smacking his palm with his riot baton.

"You have the right to have your ribs broken."

He laid the baton across Radford's ribs with a bone-crunching *whap!*

"You have the right to piss blood for the next three weeks."

This time, Radford's kidneys were hammered.

"You have the right to get your cock knocked off."

He hit Radford in the groin; Radford buckled and passed out.

The warden threw a bucket of water in Radford's face.

"Sergeant," Chaplain O'Donnell said, "may I see your baton?"

The Chaplain then walked the line of strung-up prisoners.

"Splendid instrument, you know," he said with a faint hint of an Irish brogue. "Of course, you don't see too many of them anymore. The LAPD ruined its reputation when they gave Rodney King a little on-the-spot rehabilitation. TV coverage gave that kind of therapy a bad name. Sergeant, what's that term our corrections officers use for riot-baton rehabilitation?"

"Thump therapy."

O'Donnell held up the baton.

"The little black ball at the tip allows it to slide off the ribs and tear up the intercostal muscles without the usual internal injuries, such as punctured lungs and heart muscles. Maximal rehabilitation without lawsuits, bleeding-heart brutality complaints, all those busybodies crying 'prison reform!'"

Chaplain O'Donnell got around to Cool Breeze.

"I played a little ball myself in the Alde Sodde. Me and me brothers were pretty fair cricket players. But here, let me give you a demonstration. Perhaps you could give me some pointers on me grip and swing."

Chaplain O'Donnell took the baton with both hands and laid it across Breeze's ribcage as if he was hammering a high hard one out of Yankee Stadium.

Breeze clenched his teeth till his jaws ached.

"Which brings us to our next question," the warden said. "Our friends in Washington would really like to know why convicts nationwide in two hundred of our largest penitentiaries are hoarding anything and everything—food, water, weapons, medicine. Your people, in particular, Jamal."

"It's what the Koran teaches us," Jamal said.

"Ah," Chaplain O'Donnell said, his Irish brogue thick as a peat bog, his good eye glittering happily, "and what lesson might that be?"

"Be prepared. Allah has not promised us tomorrow."

The Chaplain's baton—whipping into Jamal's crotch—lifted him a full foot in the air. Eyes rolling into the back of his head, Jamal passed out.

"Sergeant, don't you love deep-thinking convicts?" the Chaplain asked.

Hardball grinned. The grin was painful to see. "I can't get enough of them," Hardball said.

"I'm trying to discuss a serious penology problem," the warden said. "I want to know why inmates are storing up prison hooch, jailhouse drugs, foodstuffs, clothing, and weapons. Why you and your men are hiding goods in toilets, hollowed-out walls, electrical outlets, and inflatable running shoes. Planning a riot. Chaplain O'Donnell, I have all these important questions to ask, but this philosopher-king"—he nodded, indicating Jamal—"won't let me. This super-intellectual religionist, Jamal, insists on bringing up the Koran instead."

Chaplain O'Donnell studied Jamal curiously. "One problem in dealing with true religionists is, of course, that they aren't impressed by the mundane world of pleasure and pain. To them, pain is of no consequence—little more than a yogi's bed of blazing coals on which a true mystic might curl up and sleep."

The Chaplain removed a thousand-volt cattle prod encased in a belt holster from his attaché case.

"An authentic man of God might curl up on this electrical prod in precisely the same manner. So the question is: Are you an authentic man of God or just another hardrock con, looking to scam the Man?"

"Fuck you," Jamal said, coming to.

He jammed the prod into Jamal's groin.

Jamal levitated high and hard, his head hammering the ceiling.

He passed out again.

34 An Iron Coffin

Captain Gargarin studied the footlocker across from his cabin writing table, then returned to his log.

> *"Thanks to BBC radio, we now have the coordinates of the North Atlantic hurricane. We have its predicted course, and our navigator can follow it on his charts. We will do our best to keep out of its path.*
>
> *"Still, navigation is close to impossible. The ship is continually tossed atop forty- to fifty-foot combers, dropped into troughs, then buried alive under mountains of crashing waves.*
>
> *"Whether we will reach our destination in the time allotted, God only knows. Command never reckoned on a defective schnork, a record-setting hurricane, and concerted naval attacks.*
>
> *"At this point I am not even sure we can stay on course. We could wander indefinitely. Or until we run out of fuel, power, hope, life—and submerge one last time.*
>
> *"I am not sure how long the crew can persevere under these conditions. Sleep is impossible. The ship's lurching and rolling shakes us to our souls. Then there is the noise. The floor plates rattle and slam. The hull whines and vibrates continually.*
>
> *"Malnutrition is an equally serious problem. We spend half the voyage dropping from high combers into troughs—a constant state of free fall. Eating means squatting on the deck, bracing your back against a bulkhead, and then watching your meal fly up into your face and drop into your lap. Nor does eating at zero gravity—amid constant buffeting—do anything for the appetite either. The crew spends half its time seasick—backs braced against bulkheads, heads between their legs, vomiting into buckets and cans.*
>
> *"The stench aboard ship grows worse daily. Low on fresh water, we can offer saltwater showers only. Given the shocking incidence of boils and carbuncles, cuts and abrasions, the crew are understandably reluctant to pour salt on their wounds."*

A knock sounded at his hatch.

First and Starpom entered the captain's cramped cubicle.

"How are you, sir?" the Starpom asked.

"No worse than anyone else. How are the men?"

"Stoic," First said. "They will hold up their end."

Gargarin rose on aching legs. "It's 0315 hours, and the storm subsides. We'll surface and check the missile tubes."

"Can the men go on deck?" the Starpom asked.

"I don't see why not. We'll have an inspection. Set it for 0400 hours."

"We want to look pretty for the Americans?" First asked wryly.

"For them we must be immaculate."

L. L. Magruder was up in a bubble chopper with Defense Secretary Jack Taylor, who was visiting the Citadel for the weekend. She was—at his request—giving him a tour. They were presently approaching Mount Trinity.

"Jack," she said to him through their headsets, "what went wrong? We used to be so much closer."

"You went one way; I went another."

"Which way did you go?"

"The real nuclear threat ended when the Evil Empire fell. Of course, there're still acts of destruction—terrorists inflicting random violence. And, yes, we need a military. We still have regional wars in places like Afghanistan and Iraq. I'm still an advocate of the National Missile Defense Program—Star Wars, as you so derisively mock it. But the major threat—the Cold War—is over. We won it."

"What about John Stone's manuscript? He thinks they've figured out how to hit us and get away with it."

"Lydia, you won't let the president and I submit it for analysis, and frankly, no, I haven't had time to read it. To tell you the truth, I can't stand Stone or his work."

"Jack, if you don't read it you will be sorry."

"Then let me turn it over to staff."

"It'll be leaked to the press. Once that manuscript goes public there'll be a price on Stone's head. He may be dead already. Where is he anyway? What have your people come up with?"

"Whereabouts unknown. But he's disappeared before."

"Not without money."

They were now passing over Espinazo Sangre de Cristo. Taylor changed the subject. "What have you got cached inside the mountain?"

"Food, medical supplies. Enough hardware and enough industrial equipment, enough books—entire libraries—for us to rebuild some semblance of civilization."

"And enough weaponry to obliterate an army?"

"Everyone asks about that," Lydia said evasively.

"The media has dubbed the Citadel 'Bedlam's Bomb Shelter.' You're our 'Nuclear Noah.' Some people want President Haines to put the Alcohol, Tobacco and Firearms people on you."

"I've never been bothered by mindless taunts."

"What does bother you, L. L.?"

"John Stone."

"Stone has hammered us for years about 'weapons of mass destruction.'"

"Weapons of mass *self*-destruction—if we don't do something about them."

"Stone's the only one who's self-destructing as far as I can tell," Taylor said.

"He's wild, Jack. Maybe even a little crazy, but he's a good man. You don't care about that?"

Taylor said diplomatically: "I care because you care."

"Wherever he is, I hope to Christ he's okay."

"Kate's okay, at least," Secretary Taylor said, getting her mind off Stone. "I hear she's covering our national convention in New York."

"And visiting Frank. He claims he has a story for her to cover—a medical research story."

"How is Frank?"

"He's turned the Towers into a powerhouse. I hear their research center rivals NIH."

"Frank's good at raising money. But he's an even better surgeon."

Lydia to the helicopter pilot: "Let's put this chopper down." She turned to Taylor. "We'll give you a tour of the Mount Trinity storage facility."

"The Bedlam Bomb Shelter and your arms depot?"

"If you really want."

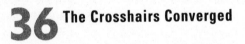 The Crosshairs Converged

The sun was setting over New York Harbor. A dark-haired man in black denims and a matching sweatshirt shut off his pontoon motor, dropped two anchors, and finished rubbing his face with burned cork.

Picking up his Bushnell 2.5 × 42 night-vision binoculars, he turned on their infrared illuminator and studied the abandoned pier forty feet away. Its rotted pilings and garbage-strewn shoreline were the perfect site for a rat warren.

"The night," he whispered into his Olympus digital voice-activated recorder, "is calm and clear. I'm at the Fourteenth Street waterfront. Hundreds of rats are now exiting the pilings. With a little luck we will be joined by their lead buck. No ordinary rat, he's the waterfront's supreme leader—the most extraordinary rat I've ever seen.

"The supertanker *Pride of New York* was overrun with these vermin. Hearing that, I've inspected the wharf and the ship looking for survivors for a few nights now. The rats on the ship are dark-furred roof-rats, enemies of all brown rats worldwide. Yet when our friend—big auburn buck, technically classified as a brown rat—dove a good 100 feet into the water and paddled to shore, the dark rats lined the rail, as if bidding him adieu.

"Due to his size, I have no trouble tracking and spotting him entering the biggest warren on the docks. Scaling a piling, he was immediately accosted by six big Alphas. They came at him sideways, stiff-legged, spitting, pissing, but the brown held his ground. He killed three of the Alphas, then turned to the others, covered ears-to-paws in wharf-rat blood, as if to say, *You want some?*

"Apparently, they didn't. Instead, they presented him with food and a doe. He ate his fill and then had sex with the female rat.

"The other bucks were lined up. I have never, in twenty years of research, known a doe to copulate with only a single buck. But the newcomer locked on and didn't stop until she lay exhausted on the dock, semiconscious.

"Since that night, I've had only glimpses of him. He roams the docks with impunity, traveling from warren to warren. Rats are the most xenophobic creatures on earth, but not when it comes to the huge auburn rat from the sea. He goes where he pleases now without a threat or a fight. He sleeps and feeds and breeds in any and all warrens. It's as if he has a rat passport.

"I am now seeing other rats cross tribal boundaries without battle, which is utterly unheard of. It's almost as if ratdom is organizing, influenced by the monstrous auburn rodent.

"If I am to defeat these pests and scourge ratdom from the earth, I need to closely examine the most formidable specimen I have ever encountered."

Then it happened. Bailey could not have been more surprised if Moses himself had crawled out from between the pilings with two stone tablets under his arms and parted New York Harbor like the Red Sea. After all the time he had spent searching the harbor, the king of rats had never before climbed up onto the docks where he would be exposed to Bailey, offering Bailey a clear shot.

"The big buck rat is now squeezing between the pilings and climbing up onto the dock. The others are gathering around him as if he were Jesus Christ."

From the bottom of the boat, Bailey affixed the 5X ATN Aries 410 Night Vision Scope to his CO_2-powered rifle breech, then clicked on its infrared illuminator night-scope. He chambered a dart loaded with Sucostrin.

"Enough Sucostrin to tranq a Doberman," Bailey muttered under his breath.

He raised the Hammerli 850 Magnum CO_2 rifle's all-weather polymer stock to his shoulder. With a velocity of 760 feet per second, it was the most powerful CO_2 rifle made.

Sailor turned sideways to glance up the East River. Bailey's infrared red-on-green reticle closed in on the rat's right flank.

"Sweet dreams, motherfucker."

The boat, momentarily lapped by waves, rocked gently. Bailey waited.

Gradually, the waves subsided and the boat steadied. Again the scope's reticle enveloped the big rat's flank. Bailey squeezed the trigger.

37 Live for the Day

Smoke, sparks, and the Chaplain's laughter filled the subbasement prison cell in Jack Town. Jamal's body continued to convulse. Finally, his bladder voided, and he fainted.

"Now, Señor Riaz," Chaplain O'Donnell said in a kindly voice, "about my sister, the one you offered to violate and pimp. My blessed sister is a Bride of Christ, pledged to Our Savior."

"Sangre de Cristo, a Thousand pardons," Riaz said. "For a holy virgin I could have demanded muchos pesos también."

"Muy bueno, Santo," the Chaplain said. "I salute you on your taste in muchachas. Sergeant, pour him a toast."

Hardball poured a bucket of brine over Riaz's groin. Chaplain O'Donnell clicked the electric prod back on, gingerly lifted Riaz's penis with his wooden riot baton, and, amid showers of sparks, steam, and smoke, electrified his testicles.

Riaz bounced, jounced, and convulsed for a seeming eternity. The Chaplain's green eye glinted.

After Riaz fainted, the Chaplain moved over to Radford. The only white man strung to the overhead bars, his face and torso were covered with livid bruises. His left eye was swollen shut. The Chaplain studied his "Death Before Dishonor" Screaming Eagles tattoos with an amused smile.

"According to Mr. Radford's jacket, Sergeant," Chaplain O'Donnell said, "he's a hard case. What do his enemies say?"

"Same thang."

"Let's try him out."

He slammed the cattle prod into Radford's solar plexus. Radford genuflected in midair, his feet reflexively kicking at the bars. When the Chaplain withdrew the prod, Radford fell back so hard Breeze was afraid he'd broken his wrists. Still, Radford endured it in silence.

"My, my, look what the wind blew in," the Chaplain said, turning his attention to Breeze. "I lost a pile betting against you. Never believed a nigger catcher could call an intelligent game."

Breeze managed to shrug, even though he was shackled. "Didn't have to be all that smart, not when I was catchin' Henry Colton and John Stone."

"Well, you aren't anymore," the Chaplain observed. "Not unless they're pitching for the Jack Town baseball team. How *was* your first day here?"

"Are they all this excitin'?" Breeze asked.

"Oh, we can make it far more fun than this," the sergeant said with a wicked grin.

"But we can make your time here surprisingly easy," the Chaplain said. "After all, *Cool* Breeze, you're not one of these assholes. You're educable, and you're a star."

"Just tell us why so many inmates are hoarding supplies," Warden Carstairs said, "and how we can lay our hands on Jamal's millions."

"I just live for the day," Cool Breeze said, shaking his head.

"Then today isn't going to be one of your all-time favorites," the Chaplain warned.

"But it got off to such a sweet-ass start," Breeze said.

Chaplain O'Donnell moved in with the prod.

38 The Terrible Trio

There was respite for Stone—even on the rack. Late at night while his torturers slept, he was alone. At which time he tried to focus his thoughts, work out a strategy, a plan.

Stone let his mind drift. *Don't think about* now, he'd said to himself. *Fix on former happiness . . . when you were a Yankee . . . with Henry Colton and Cool Breeze . . .*

In those days, it always came down to . . . the Series . . . Golden October and four big wins. The greatest team record in all of baseball had been that of the 1949–53 New York Yankees—when they won five consecutive World Series—a record no team had ever equaled.

Now, Colton, Stone, and Breeze had also brought the Yankees five straight series wins, but number six was the one they coveted.

They were up against Bobby Joe Frazier's Houston Astros, who were not only good but mean. Bobby Joe—with his black sweeping mustache, outlaw swagger, and piercing eyes—was often derided in the press as "Ty Cobb reincarnate," saying he managed the dirtiest players to defame the game since the Georgia Peach.

Every game was filled with taunts, spiked infielders, beaned batters . . . with benches flooding the field in retaliation.

The Yankees lost four of their best hitters and their third and fourth best pitchers to injuries—three of which occurred during that series. When they went into that sixth game, they were behind three to two . . . and according to Vegas down for the count.

By the third inning Ridell and Armstrong were knocked out of the box, the Yankees were 5-0.

With one day rest, Stone took the mound.

He was pitching on pure adrenaline, and for the next seven innings he pitched one-hit ball, throwing everything he had—splitters, sliders, changeups, spitters . . . and fastballs. His fastball was legendary, especially his "cutfastball," which sank and broke just as it reached the plate. When Stone's "cutter" was on, it was considered unhittable.

But the Astros—under Bobby Joe—did not go gentle. The Yankees got

"Bobby-Ball" from hell. When the Astros couldn't hit Stone, they went after him and his teammates in every other way—crashing into them on the base-paths, knocking them down at the plate, screaming at them from the bench.

Breeze, they beaned.

Breeze, Stone thought back dreamily to his old teammate with a half smile, *you had all the balls they ever made.*

At the end of the eighth, Stone had thrown 119 pitches, and his swollen elbow looked like a large grapefruit. The index and middle fingers of his pitching hand were blistering.

Yet even after two more innings, he still was out on the mound—fingers bleeding, elbow screaming. He rosined up his torn fingers and continued throwing strikes.

By the eleventh inning his splitter was gone.

By the twelfth his slider was dead in the water.

All he had left were fastballs.

And when his shoulder went out on him, when his smoke was gone, and Stone had nothing left to throw . . . he threw his heart.

Until in the home half of the thirteenth, when Breeze hit Randy Lee Eickhoff's low sinker off the stadium's façade, circled the bases, and gave Stone his second win of the Series, 6-5.

The next game was Colton's.

It made Stone's arm ache now to look back on that series. Nonetheless, in the far upper corner of the cell, through a small barred window, he could still see stars. Their brilliance reminded him of the lights surrounding Yankee Stadium on a night unequalled in baseball history. Henry had missed half of his season with a broken left arm and was now about to pitch with three days' rest—at a time in his injury-plagued career when people debated if he was finished.

But that night he was . . . smokin'!

For six innings he gave up only two scratch singles—and the Astros' Bobby Joe was furious. He knew if he resorted to his usual tactics, Colton would retaliate. His 104-mile-an-hour fastballs exploded in Breeze's mitt like shotgun blasts. If provoked, Colton could turn "conveniently wild," turning batters bloodless with terror.

After six innings of two-hit ball, Colton was clearly unstoppable.

At which point Bobby Joe opted for his legendary closer, Rapid Robbie Robertson, to pitch to Henry Colton. He was sending his ace reliever in to pitch to a . . . pitcher.

Breeze and Stone should have realized something was wrong, but neither was in very good shape. Breeze—they would later learn—had suffered a subdural hematoma from that beanball, and Stone's pain-wracked elbow was now cantaloupe-size.

With his first pitch, Rapid Robbie shattered Colton's left elbow—the one he'd broken earlier in the year in a collision at the plate.

The benches cleared. Stone, despite his injuries, was heading for the Astros' reliever when Breeze restrained him.

Breeze shouted at him: "We gotta keep you ready. Ridall's sick, and Armstrong ain't throwin' shit."

Breeze and Stone were among the twelve ballplayers who didn't get ejected.

And Breeze was right. Ridall was gone halfway through the seventh inning, Armstrong barely made it through the eighth. The Astros were up by a score of 5 to 2.

Stone ordered the Yankees' trainer, Randolph Jefferson, to pump six syringes of Xylocaine into his elbow . . . and he took the mound. His eyes teared with pain after three warm-up pitches, and he could not see the plate. Breeze plastered reflecting tape across the back of his mitt, which was the only thing Stone could see. Stone could not see Breeze's signals at all, which did not matter. All he had left were fastballs. He figured he had about twelve of them.

He only needed eleven. When he fanned the third man he faced, he was so dazed he did not know the hitter was out, the inning was over, or that the Yanks were back up—down by three, home half of the ninth.

Heading straight for the training room, he plunged his elbow into a bucket of ice.

Then he heard the roar.

Colton was on the training-room TV back in the clubhouse, taking the field.

Warm-up jacket over his shoulders, right arm in a sling, he stood directly behind the on-deck box, close as he could legally get to lines. Stone pulled his elbow out of the ice bucket, exited the training room. Slinging his arm, he threw on his own jacket over his shoulders and joined Colton.

Three runs ahead, and Rapid Robbie was smoking. He got Aswell on four pitches, Harding on five, but when he clipped Ray Carter leaning in on an inside curve, all hell broke loose. Again, the benches emptied.

From Stone's point of view, the brouhaha had a positive outcome. He had caught the Astros' reliever with a short left just under the right eye—so hard his good elbow burned like a wasp's sting. Rapid Robbie's eye was swelling over, and he was no longer focusing. When he hung a low-away 3-1 slider, Ortega lined it off the right field wall, and on orders from Bobby Joe, Robbie walked Darnell, setting up a force at any base.

Ordinarily, no one wanted Breeze up there in a moment like this. This time, however, it was different. Breeze's eyes were dilating from the hematoma. Also, Robertson was one of the few pitchers in the game who consistently had his number. Breeze—who thrived on smoke—couldn't read his split-finger fastball.

Breeze's knees were buckling. He had been hitless the entire game. His left knee had collapsed in the sixth inning on a throw to second due to a tear in his medial-collateral ligament. He was flinching visibly at the plate. Breeze was notorious for his fearlessness. Stone often remarked that Breeze had two weaknesses. One was "pathological fearlessness," the other a weakness for triples.

But the last two times up he'd leaned away from inside curves, and twice had stepped in the bucket.

Robertson's first pitch—high and inside—put Breeze in the dirt. The second—an inside curve—put his left foot in the waterbucket for a third unprecedented time, then broke over the plate. Stone and Colton stared at each other in blank astonishment.

Robertson caught the corner on his low and away, then backed Breeze off again, just missing his fists. His next low-and-away pitch went into the dirt, and Cromwell's kneeling save was the only thing that kept Ray Carter from scoring.

Breeze was looking at a full count.

"High tight fastball," Stone said to Colton. "He thinks Breeze's hearing footsteps."

"Breeze ain't afraid of nothing walks on less'n three legs," Colton said.

As if in confirmation, Breeze looked back at them . . . and grinned.

The next pitch was a cutter—in at the fists, breaking late toward the plate.

Breeze never flinched, never blinked . . . and leaned right into it. He had been shining them on.

Stone remembered thinking at the time, even as he watched Breeze unlimber his signature 109-mile-an-hour swing: *Oh Dear Jesus, he's got it clocked.*

Colton knew he had it clocked too, but neither could have anticipated what happened next. True, when the ball hit the bat, they knew it was gone. It sounded not like a struck ball, as one sportswriter wrote, but a 155 howitzer. Breeze's right hand disengaged, as it always did on impact, the left hand Breeze's power hand—swinging both bat and body, all the way around and this time down as well. The force of that 109-mile-per-hour swing dropped Breeze to his knees.

Unfortunately, his left knee was in disastrous shape. An old football injury—aggravated by base running and stadium-wall collisions, flying bats, and foul balls, plus a lifetime of behind-the-plate crouching—had all but demolished the knee. The team doctor and his private consultants had railed at him all season long about "ground-up cartilage" and "the incipient tear in his medial collateral," telling him he was "playing with fire." "The ligament of doom" had, upon rupturing, terminated the careers of many professional athletes, including Dick Butkus and Gale Sayers. During the pennant drive specialists had warned Breeze to skip the play-offs and get the knee repaired.

Breeze now had trouble staying on his feet.

But Stone and Colton, like everyone, were fixed on the ball.

"I saw it thumb a ride on a 747," Stone told the press after the game.

Colton said it was last seen "in geosynchronous orbit."

"That wasn't any baseball he hit off me," Robertson told a reporter, "it was an interstellar spaceship."

It soared—and soared and soared and soared. Instead of losing power, it appeared to accelerate, as if it did indeed have a rocket strapped to it.

Breeze had hammered it as hard and far as Mantle's fabled moonshot in the old Yankee Stadium, the one that hit the façade, eighteen inches from the roof. But this time Breeze's shot was steeper, more defiant—and cleared the new stadium's wall by fifteen feet.

It was still climbing when it soared over the roof's rim . . . and disappeared.

A hush eventually settled over the stadium, and all eyes returned to Breeze.

Head down, eyes locked on the basepath, his thick stumpy legs gamely churned in a limping rendition of his home-run trot.

. . . He had not always been the quintessential "non–hot dog." When he first came up, he was notorious for taunting pitchers with hip-thrusting clenched-fist salutes and playing to the crowd. Hanging out with Colton and Stone had cured him of that.

"You don't mock motherfuckers for making a mistake," Stone told him the first time Breeze "dawged" the basepath.

"We all fuck up," Colton explained, "pitchers included. You don't rub people's noses in it."

"It's what's called no fucking class," Stone said.

"And you know the definition of no class?" Colton asked Breeze.

Breeze allowed that he didn't.

"If they do it once . . ." Stone said.

"THEY'LL DO IT TWICE!" Colton roared . . .

One thing about Breeze . . . he had class.

As he reached home, scored the winning run, Yankees were mobbing the field—and Breeze.

He fought them off, battling his way to Colton and Stone, who were standing behind the on-deck box, warm-up jackets draped around shoulders, each with one arm slung.

Still Breeze hugged them—at which point everyone else backed off. It wasn't easy for Stone and Colton to hug back, but they did. Somehow—with only one good arm apiece—they even got him up onto their shoulders.

Colton raised his good right arm in a clenched-fist salute; Stone lifted and shook his left. Breeze got both fists up.

Kate Magruder—a fledgling sports reporter just out of college—got the low-angle shot. It was the most famous photograph ever of "the Terrible Trio," perhaps the most famous shot in all of sports. It made the cover of *Time* . . .

. . . Stretched on his rack but his gaze fixed on the stars—they were Orion's Belt, he now knew—blinking in the one dungeon window between the dungeon bars, Stone could still see Colton, Breeze, and himself as if it were yesterday.

And then it came to him out of nowhere with the force of revelation: Breeze would be okay. Wherever he was, whatever happened, he would see it through.

So will you, Stone said to himself.

You will never back off. You will never stand down. You will die going for it. You will die hard.

You will die trying.

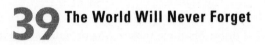

39 The World Will Never Forget

Captain Gargarin stood unsteadily on a rolling deck in front of his men. They were malnourished, sleep-starved, filthy, battered, and their uniforms were foul and ragged.

The sun looked grim—lividly bruised above the horizon.

"Men, the navigator says we are less than two days from our destination, in which case we will make it with—believe it or not—time to spare.

"I will want you all looking shipshape—uniforms freshly laundered and crisply pressed. Our sister submarines are entering the great harbors of the world. What we are about to give, the world will never forget."

"Sir," the Starpom said, "the men have a request. In rough seas, it is hard to honor God. Now that we have the opportunity, they would like you to lead them in prayer."

"Very well."

The crew of the *St. Petersburg* faced the rising sun and knelt in prayer.

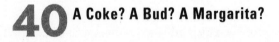

40 A Coke? A Bud? A Margarita?

Dusk at the National Institute for Behavior Research.

Dr. Howard E. Bailey, wearing a white laboratory smock, strode through his rat menagerie. Row upon row of wire cages, over fifty in all, housing hundreds of rats. Bailey filled food and water dishes, talking to his subjects in soothing tones.

"You little fellas have been such good boys and girls. Putting up with near-lethal levels of starvation, dehydration, and oxygen deprivation. You've been frozen, burned, drowned, shocked, gone without sleep. You've been shouted at, bullied, injected with the most agonizing pharmaceuticals known to man and some that are pure poison. We've impaled you on a cross of modern science for mankind's good and my own career.

"Today you get a reward. Some tasty cheese and beef morsels mixed with your pellets. I'm giving you each an extra water ration. Also, guess what? A special treat. I know how randy you little buggers are, so I'm passing around some cute little does, who by the way are currently in heat."

He picked up two cages containing a dozen female rats each. Starting up the aisles, he distributed the does to the various cages. As soon as the does hit the cage floor, the bucks would begin their prancing and sniffing. Within half a minute of entering the cages, the does were mating.

"Yes, you'll all get a turn," Bailey said, "every one of you bloody rat-bastards—all except our bad, bad boy here."

He was referring to Sailor—the reddish-auburn rat he'd trapped on the Manhattan wharf.

"Bad boys get no food, no does. They get to watch their friends eat, drink, and fuck. Feel left out? Here, I'll give you a little something. A gift you'll never forget.

"Not water. Your friends get water; you haven't had any because you won't push the bar for me or perform any assigned task. You insist on holding out for something better? A Coke? A bottle of Bud? A margarita? Maybe my big furry friend would like some *juice*."

Bailey picked up a glass beaker and splashed saline solution on the copper floor and wire mesh of Sailor's cage. He then emptied a second beaker onto Sailor until the drenched rodent resembled a drowned rat. Next, he wired the cage to a storage battery.

"We'll give you all the juice you can handle."

Bailey turned the transformer knob 360 degrees. The walls, ceiling, and floor of Sailor's electrified cage sparked and smoked.

41 My Baseball Comeback Will Be Canceled?

"We want you to tell us why you killed all those convicts," the warden said to Jamal.

"Why you hoardin' food, drugs, weapons, and shit," the sergeant said.

"Are you plannin' a nationwide riot and breakout?" Chaplain O'Donnell asked.

"Maybe I just hear a different drummer," Jamal said.

"Does he know how to drum 'Taps'?" Chaplain O'Donnell asked.

"Forget about him," the sergeant said. "He just a hope-to-die fool."

"And nobody gives a fuck for a dead fool," the warden said.

"Too bad," the Chaplain said, "because what you do in the dark will come to light."

Chaplain O'Donnell handed out earplugs to Hardball and the warden. Then he opened his black coat and took out a .357 Colt Python.

"We're gonna rid the earth of your shadow, boy," Hardball said. "Unless you tell us what we want to know. Same for you, Breeze. Tell us what we want to know, or you're all goin' down."

"You mean my baseball comeback will be canceled?" Cool Breeze asked.

"Unless you can play the game dead," the sergeant said. He turned Breeze around so his back was to the bars.

"What will you tell the investigators?" Breeze asked.

"We'll say you guys fell off your bunks," the sergeant said.

Suddenly, Radford—whom the Chaplain had blindfolded, gagged, and strung up to the top of the cell door—was screaming.

"That boy sure does hate hip-hop," Hardball said, grinning.

The Chaplain had shoved iPod earbuds deep into Radford's eardrums, blasting his brain with nonstop gangsta rap.

"Put Radford to sleep," the warden said, disgusted.

Hardball laid the riot baton over Radford's head. The screaming stopped.

"What'll it be, Jamal?" the Chaplain asked.

"Fuck you."

"Riaz?"

"Chingo tu madre [fuck your mother]."

"Breeze?"

"Fuck your dog."

"I can't tell you how pleased I am you all said that," Chaplain O'Donnell said.

The Colt Python roared like the End of Time.

42 Africa

Frank Sheckly stretched out on his office couch, hoping to get a few hours' sleep before meeting Kate at the Regis.

But he slept fitfully.

The near-amputation of the shotgun victim had brought back nightmares of the African refugee camps. Memories which still tortured him.

Frank's discomfiture was unusual, because he was famous for his unflappability; nothing seemed to get to him.

Nothing.

Except Africa.

Frank had treated innumerable Iraqi and Afghani casualties in wars that had produced 2.5 million injured people in those two tiny nations combined, hundreds of thousands of whom mines, bombs, and booby traps had maimed.

Frank had amputated countless of their maimed limbs in their hospital and refugee camps.

Still, that had not eaten away at his soul like Africa.

He'd worked the refugee camps of Kashmir, between Pakistan and India, which Persians boasted once contained Eden's garden. The Vale of Kashmir was now the most apocalyptic terrain on earth. On each of its borders hate-crazed Hindus and Muslims brandished nuclear weapons and ballistic missiles at each other while engaging in brutal battles.

Africa was worse.

He'd seen the atrocities of the Balkans—a people armed to the teeth who had been at each other's throats since before the time of Alexander. A million were slaughtered, millions more displaced, with women raped en masse in the name of religious war and ethnic cleansing. In a ghostly place called Devic, Yugoslavia, he'd met nuns who packed guns.

Africa terrified him more.

In his nightmares it was always Africa.

A dozen civil wars had ripped that continent apart—involving sixteen nations, countless rebel forces, and innumerable splinter movements. He'd worked the camps of Morocco, Mauritania, and Polisario, where he'd watched them tear one another to pieces in a pointless war that had already lasted over a quarter of a century. They'd warred over a patch of sand, devoid of water or natural resources, so barren it would not support camels and goats.

He'd worked refugee camps in Uganda, Burundi, the Congo, and Rwanda, where a Hutu reign of terror against Tutsi tribespeople and moderate Hutus had claimed a million lives in one hundred days.

He'd worked the camps of Eritrea and Ethiopia. Thirty years of wars so bloody Eritrea's women had taken up arms and fought beside the men, becoming the most feared soldiers found anywhere. As one woman had told him in the Eritrean camps:

"We women are very bad. We take no prisoners. We kill them all, and the Ethiopians know that."

In Sudan, civil war cost three million lives; a million more were displaced and enslaved. Plagues of every kind—including trypanosomiasis, otherwise known as sleeping sickness—were pandemic.

In Somalia, too, Frank had labored—and watched millions die in criminal clan conflicts. He'd watched that land degenerate into what the U.N. had termed "a black hole of anarchy," lacking all the attributes of statehood, a world in which no government ruled and lawlessness was the order of the day. In many warravaged areas even relief aid was unsustainable. He'd seen rebels and terrorists of every size, shape, and gender—old men who could not walk a straight line or remember their names, boys so young they could barely lift an AK-47, women warriors who killed for sport.

But as he turned on his side in his nightmare-tossed sleep, the thing that cracked his heart and racked his soul was Sierra Leone.

The journey to the end of his own blackest night.

Amputation.

In Sierra Leone, limbs were hacked to pieces by prepubescent boy-soldiers armed with machetes and Kalashnikovs. Boys with nicknames such as Captain Blood and General Burn, who asked their victims, "How do you want your arms and legs? Long- or short-sleeved?"

For a year and a half, Frank worked "the Amputee and War-Wounded Camp." His patients were what The New York Times *had called "living, limbless symbols of [war's] savage power."*

In that camp it was Frank's job to cut off their stumps.

In that camp Frank found his own hell of hells, and his nightmares had begun. Except in these nightmares, the amputees had the faces of Doc, Lydia, Kate—and his amputee mother, Francesca. And in his terror-dreams, when they lifted their heads and stared at him with frightened eyes, Frank began to scream . . .

43 Vindicated by Violence

Defense against the B-2 is not affordable.

—General William Thurman, USAF

Kate Magruder leaned back in the ejection seat of a black B-2 bomber and studied the desert terrain below.

They were back in the States—high above Dreamland.

"Nice view," she said to Larry Taylor, who was in the left-hand seat.

"I admit it. You won. You've bullied your way into a B-2."

Directly below them were the desert mountains of Nellis Air Force Base. The Nellis Papoose mountain chain separated Romeo 4808N—otherwise known as Dreamland, the air force's top-secret testing facility for ultraexotic aircraft—from the Yucca Flat nuclear-weapons testing grounds. The Nellis mountain range also surrounded dry Groom Lake, which had over the years provided a perfect foundation for its concrete runways. Roughly the size of Switzerland, the Nellis range—particularly Area 51—had developed and tested such famous aircraft as the U-2, the B-2 bomber, the Stealth fighter, and the Aurora.

Since the U-2's inception in 1955, Dreamland had been home and research lab to many of the military's most deeply classified and secretive "black projects"—one of the most mysterious, heavily guarded spots on earth.

"This B-2's a big bloody bastard of a crow," Kate said, "according to my mother."

"I'll also admit Crow looks evil," Larry Taylor acknowledged. "Crow has the greatest hard-target, bunker-busting capability ever conceived."

"How does he get back home?"

Taylor laughed mirthlessly. "By the time he's finished his run, the sun's come up. Russian interceptors will triangulate on his trajectories, and Crow will be spotted. You can't nuke that many targets without somebody spotting him. Too many planes will be following his flight pattern. He has to run a hard gauntlet from Moscow to Turkey to escape, and his chances of escape are nil."

"You mean he has no chance at all of getting back?"

"He's bound to get flogged, and Crow's not designed for exchanges."

"Flogged?"

"Russia's most effective interceptor is named Flogger."

"Only a Russian would name its weapons after a professional torturer," Kate said.

"Did your mother see a B-2 in the vision you told me about?"

"She claimed she did. The B-2 names itself Crow. The whole nuclear arsenal speaks to her. The bombs say they are Stars, and she's had that vision a number of times. In her recurring vision the ICBMs are Tyrannosauruses. The cruise missiles, Dragonflies. The subs are Blue Whales, claiming they were once Leviathan from the Bible. Their dream is to eventually return to heaven as stars."

"Some dream."

"It was then she came to believe that everything that *is* lives and that everything that lives is holy. Sand fleas, nuclear bombs, us poor humans. We all dream, and some dream we will return to the heavens as stars. It's not an uncommon myth," Kate said. In defense of Lydia, she added, "Some Greek heroes ended up as stars, even constellations. Some Islamic sects believe the same thing."

"Kate, your mother . . ." Taylor said dubiously.

"May just be right," Kate said, with a tremor of the heart. "It's her Mayan blood."

"I thought she was Apache."

"My mother believed that Great-Grandmother Lozen's lineage included both the Apache and the Maya. The latter were the greatest astronomers and mathematicians of their time."

"So I've heard."

"They believed that through their observations and knowledge of history they could predict the end of the world. They called our present era The Fifth Sun. And said it would end in cataclysmic violence."

"No hope, huh?"

"The only hope, according to Mayan lore, was mass sacrifice. That's all the gods understand. Mass sacrifice keeps the general populace's bloodlust from going totally out of control."

"In other words a nuclear apocalypse will calm down the handful of survivors."

"Look, it's one thing for me to express disdain for L. L. It's another thing for you to."

"It all sounds pretty dumb to me," Taylor said, shaking his head.

"Whatever she *is*, my mother is *not* stupid. And I'm not talking to you for the rest of the flight."

"And we had such a great time last night."

"That's what they all say."

44 A Murder of Crows

L. L. saddled her Appaloosa mare and rode her to Arroyo Seco, a dry river that cut across the northwest corner of the Citadel's desert plains. They were both headstrong: The billionaire, who dressed in black, and the Appaloosa, who was named Nightmare by L. L.'s cowhands after she broke the bones of three riders who tried to saddle-break her. For some reason, the old woman and the horse got along. Not in friendship, but more like a couple of boxers who knew that they would both get hurt if either threw a first punch.

A jeep bearing the Citadel's distinctive spread-eagle insignia on its front doors had carried Citadel engineers and an imported expert to the site. L. L. could have come in her own jeep or by chopper, but she preferred the solitary ride across the desert.

Stinson, her chief hydrologist, broke away from the group of four men in the riverbed and took Nightmare's reins. Stinson was a rangy, rawboned man in his early sixties. His tan Stetson was sweat stained, as were his denims and workshirt.

"The Israeli engineer that Sara Friedman recommended has some good ideas," he said.

He led the horse cautiously, giving himself room in case Nightmare decided to live up to her name and reputation. He tied the rein around the post between the front and rear windows of the jeep.

"That's why I hired him," Lydia said, dismounting. "The Israelis have turned desert reclamation into high art."

The other three men came out of the dry riverbed. Two of her engineers loaded equipment into the jeep. L. L., the hydrologist, and the visiting expert walked along the edge of the riverbed.

"Well," L. L. said to the Israeli engineer, "is there much difference between American deserts and the Palestine?"

Hafez Bechan shrugged. He was darkly tanned, the corners of his eyes deeply lined with crow's-feet, the result, in part, of having spent many years in desert country. The pockets of his khaki workshirt were filled with pens, instruments, and the kind of calculator physicists used to crunch calculus equations. Like everyone on Arroyo Seco, he kept a water bottle on his belt.

"Once or twice a year you get a good rain. The problem is there's little vegetation to hold the water."

"But you've learned how to handle these problems."

"To control runoff in a dry part of the Negev we had to solve a two-thousand-year-old mystery. In ancient times the Nabataeans farmed the area for months after rain had fallen; yet the rain would have been absorbed by the hot sands within days. Obviously, the rain water had to have been stored. It was actually archaeologists who solved the mystery, not engineers."

"Wells?" Lydia asked, offering a solution.

"For wells you have to have accessible water, and there is none. No, the answer came when Bedouin children—playing in a wadi, a dry riverbed similar to this one—found a cavern on the side of the riverbed. Exploration revealed that there were many more caverns. Archaeologists discovered that the caverns were man-made and interconnected—a series of underground caves running down both sides of the riverbank."

"The Nabataeans stored water in the caverns?"

"Exactly. Where there were no natural caves, they dug caverns in the dry riverbeds that filled during the rainy season."

"I've seen this arroyo with more water in it than the Colorado River." Lydia pointed toward the foothills of the San Carlos Mountains. "During flash floods, whole walls of water roar off that mountain like a runaway train. The water ends up in this wash. I could never figure how to save and conserve all that water."

"There's one way," Hafez said. "A couple of miles downstream, the desert fans out into a low basin. After a rain, the water spreads out for several miles. In a couple of days it evaporates or is soaked up. Build a deep, narrow reservoir there, just a few feet deep, then cover and seal it up. Upstream from the reservoir, we can also reconstruct the wash so that it will trap the maximum amount of water. We can even insulate the roof with the excavated dirt."

"What about the silt washed in after each rainfall?"

"There will be long periods in which no water accumulates in the storage areas. The silt will be removed then."

L. L.'s hydrologists began questioning the Israeli about the technical aspects, but L. L. interrupted them.

"Get equipment up here tomorrow to start the work."

The engineer's jaw dropped. "Mrs. Magruder, it'll take us six months just to plan the project."

"You have six days."

"That's impossible. If it doesn't work—"

"—I've thrown a bunch of money into a hole in the ground. Soon that money won't be worth the paper it's printed on, and water here will be worth *everything*."

The engineer started to object again, and the hydrologist shot him a warning glance. As Lydia moved away, the Israeli whispered:

"I forgot. The world's coming to an end."

Lydia mounted Nightmare and rode away.

———————

Lydia Magruder's sacred spot, Three Points, was a cliff-top that provided a view of the sprawling plains. She never thought of the Citadel as a place; rather, she *felt* it as a living thing, as if the sand and rocks, houses and people, desert creatures and farm animals were *one*.

Today she needed that sense of unity. Without it, she did not know if she could go on.

She desperately needed to see her creation as an undifferentiated whole rather than fragments. For the Citadel to work it had to *connect*.

She had been subjected to fainting spells her entire life. Now her headaches had come back, and with them the feeling that she was losing her balance. At her age her first thought was her heart, which she refused to have checked out. The one time she'd gone to the Towers medical complex, Frank Sheckly had speculated that she might be epileptic. He had wanted to keep her for more comprehensive tests. She'd packed her bags and returned to the Citadel.

She knew her problem. Didn't need doctors' fancy names for it.

Her problem was not enough time.

She could keep a global communications network humming through the force of her personality, and she could keep one little heart pumping until she was done with it. She wasn't afraid of death but feared departing this mortal coil with her mission uncompleted.

Nightmare climbed the rocky trail up to the top of the bluff at a sure-footed pace. The blood of great Indian ponies that turned the Nez Percé into hit-and-run guerrilla warriors and astounding buffalo hunters flowed in Nightmare's veins. The Appaloosa, with her distinctive spots and mottled rump, descended from wild mustangs, heirs of the ponies with which the Spanish had conquered the New World. L. L. had traced Nightmare's bloodlines to ponies ridden by her grandmother Lozen's Apaches over a hundred years ago.

She came up to the top of the bluff at Hangman's Tree. A gnarly half-dead cottonwood with an ancient trunk, its long twisted branches writhed overhead—all except one thick perpendicular limb, which jutted out like an accusatory finger of doom.

The tree was ugly as sin on its own; its name and grisly reputation dated from the old Arizona Territory days when Outlaw Torn Slater, after escaping from Yuma Prison, hanged three pursuing lawmen from the old limb.

Today the tree had visitors. Three crows—which made L. L. think of hooded, black-clad hangmen or perhaps the dark ghosts of the three departed lawmen—perched on its branches.

"You spoke to me before, why don't you say something now?" she said, staring at them.

Their *caw! caw! caw!* pierced the desert air disconcertingly.
Speak words.
An ancient song rang in her brain as she met the birds' sepulchral stares.

There were three ravens on a tree.
And they were black as they might be
With a down, derry-derry-derry down.

There were three maidens on a hill
Their every tear would turn a mill
With a down, derry-derry-derry down.

Down in yonder green field
Lies a knight slain under his shield
With a down, derry-derry-derry down.

Truth is she had of late come to take a dim view of crows. It was that damn B-2 black Stealth bomber—which after her vision at Three Points she'd dubbed Crow. The B-2 was a goddamn thermonuclear assassin and had poisoned her mind where the birds were concerned. They, the Pentagon, had made the world's deadliest weapon dark and sleek as the crow.

Again they cawed, and their sharp cries struck L. L. with an almost physical force. The dizziness she had experienced earlier that morning came back. Her mouth was dry and she felt her mind detaching from her body, as if it were floating free, rising up to face the black birds. Her head felt like a spike had been driven through it.

She leaned over, dizzy, but forced herself to sit up straight on the horse despite the swirling in her head. Nightmare nervously stamped the ground as if she sensed Lydia's discomfort. Something slammed inside Lydia's head, and she fell off the horse, hitting the ground heavy and unmoving as a bag of rocks.

Nightmare snorted and reared, dancing back from her.

Her mind was chaos but there were stars.

They dimmed in daylight, and in some bleak abyss of her brain she understood that she was on the ground, a prisoner in a body that wouldn't move. On her back, on the ground, she stared up at gray clouds in a blue sky. Something flew up to her.

And stopped in midair—one inch from her face.

Enormous eyes—over one thousand composite honeycombed lenses—stared down at her, taking in every detail. A skinny old woman lying in the dirt.

She recognized the creature from the large transparent wings, four of them vibrating from a long slender abdomen and skewed thorax. It was an

Odonata, a dragonfly, quicker than a bobcat and more predaceous than a hungry croc.

They were in fact flying crocodiles, eating their own weight every thirty minutes. Their prehistoric ancestors soared through the skies with six-foot wingspans.

L. L. called to mind a story her mother told her when she was a child. They called Dragonflies the Devil's Darning Needles because they could sew up the eyes, ears, and mouth of a sleeping child—especially if the child had been bad.

And I've been very bad.

Lydia didn't know if she spoke the words or just thought them. She tried to move but her arms and legs were tied down. She intuitively understood that it was her own mind that was keeping her trapped, that her body felt heavy and numb because it wasn't obeying her wishes. Her head hurt terribly, and she wondered if she'd been hit by a falling rock.

"*Go on!*" she shouted at the Dragonfly. "*Say something! You said something before.*"

The Dragonfly hovered and stared—but said nothing.

Something moved on a rock next to her, and she moved her head sideways to look at it. It scrambled to the top of a rock and seemed to be sniffing the air with its tail. She recognized another of her desert friends, Scorpionida, the crab of the desert. But a crab with a deadly kiss. Scorpions were also cousins to spiders, eight-legged relatives of Arachne, the impetuous young woman who had the poor judgment to challenge Athena to a weaving contest and was turned into a spider.

The Scorpion on the rock had a locust in its claws. It had come out onto a rock to sun itself while it lunched. Curious, Lydia thought, as she watched the Scorpion hold the wiggling locust in two claws and begin tearing it apart with two more. This Scorpion didn't even bother stinging its victim, preferring to rip it apart live.

Scorpions usually stayed under rocks until dark.

"*You'll speak,*" she said to the Scorpion. "*I know you'll say something. You always do.*"

The Scorpion remained silent.

Caw! Caw! Caw!

In the Hangman's Tree the crows spoke again, shrieked down at her. She pivoted her head to look at them and realized that she could not only move her head, she could feel some of the weight lifting off her arms and legs.

Caw!

She looked up at Hangman's Tree as a fourth crow joined the others. Then they no longer looked like birds but winged horses sitting side by side, staring down at her with undead eyes and fiendish grins.

The Four Riders of the Apocalypse.

She croaked at the shadowy creatures: "*They call you 'a murder of crows' but I know you by your true names: War, Famine, Pestilence, and Death.*"

The old refrain again floated through her head.

Down in yonder green field
Lies a knight slain under his shield.

And she shuddered at the ill omen.
She prayed that the Citadel was not a knight . . . slain under his shield.

III

The Warrior World

1 The Star Seekers

In the beginning of all things, wisdom and knowledge were with the animals; for Tirawa, the One Above, did not speak directly to man. He sent certain animals to tell men that He showed Himself through the beasts, and that from them, and from the stars and the sun and the moon, man should learn.

—Chief Letakots-Lesa of the Pawnee Tribe

Star dreamed. As she was head of her Starfire (The Nuclear Bomb) Clan and leader of the Warrior World, it was a luxury she seldom enjoyed. The Weapons Clans never let her sleep and dream. Most days and nights they shouted at her eternally:

"Come, Star, sing us a song. Tell us a story, please."

She would have liked to sleep and dream, keep her own company—but she never turned them down. The Clans lived lives of chronic boredom and needed diversion. As Clan leader, she felt an obligation to keep up their morale.

Not that she did not enjoy their company. She loved them deeply—the Cruise Missile Clan (which she'd named Dragonfly), the Stealth Aircraft Clan (called by her Crow), Submarine Clan (which she'd labeled Leviathan), the ICBM Clan (which she'd laughingly baptized T-Rex), and the seldom-seen Suitcase Nuke Clan (Scorpion, which was timid and aloof, hiding from all, like the shy yet venomous scorpion). Then of course there was her own Warhead Clan (the exalted leaders of the Warrior World, known by one and all as the Star Clan, thermonuclear bombs being, of course, miniature man-made stars).

Star was one of them—and knew their boredom in her soul.

Still, it was wonderful to be alone with her reveries. This night she dreamed of her uranium-ore youth. Those years had been spent in many lands and climes—in the deserts of America, in the permafrost of Siberia, in the Mongolian steppe lands, in the subtropic plateaux of the African rain forests.

Tonight she dreamed of her youth in the African mountains, where in the jungle evenings she had stared longingly at her brothers and sisters overhead, the stars.

In her hundreds of millions of years there, she had witnessed much—comet strikes, ice ages, and plagues. She had known so many creatures—the apatosaurus (formerly called brontosaurus) with their seventy-foot anacondalike necks and tails, bulky elephantine bodies, tree-trunk legs, and quadripoidal feet. Well had she known the ten-ton Triceratops with their rhinolike body—thirty feet long, a dozen feet high, huge heads projecting a trio of four-foot horns, their pate and neck protected by an arching collar of bony frill. With a vivid intimacy she recalled the great plated stegosaurs, the swift velocipeds, the armored ankylosaurids, the long-winged pterodactyl, the befeathered Hesperoni, the fifty-foot Panzercrocs with their serrated fangs and a six-foot head, sculling and sloshing through her muddy streams. She knew them all and remembered them with fondness as they trod her mountain plateau and jungle valleys.

And she'd watched them die.

But that was the way of the world: living, feeding, spawning, and dying, death begetting life, one species dying off, another born, the planet never without life.

Their successors spawned and proliferated, not as huge as the Thunder Lizards, but quick, smart, and furry—the mammals. They came in all sizes and shapes—saber-fanged cats, nose-horned rhinoceri, the double-tusked mastodons, herbivores, tree-scrambling simians, and rodentia.

In those days there were no Ruling Beasts. Many killed, but none for sport or spite—only to survive. A lion pulled down an infirm wildebeest just as the wildebeest fed on the savanna. It was the Way: None ruled; all excelled.

With a sigh Star recalled the People. Scrawny, fork-legged, bare-skinned apes. They'd wrung a meager existence scrounging for grubs, fighting maggots for offal, cracking the bones of carrion—and were prey to all. She had doubted they would survive.

Oh, how she had been wrong. They survived with a vengeance, their collective memory vast. No slight went unpunished, and they exacted a murderous toll. The beasts who had dominated them went first. Scourging the earth with fire, they slew the mastodon, the saber-toothed cats, the giant sloths, the short-face bear, the giant beaver—big as black bear—all were burned, exterminated. In the Americas 70 percent of the large mammals were massacred.

It was the Age of Fire Drives, the Time of the Extinctions.

When blood failed to slake their horrendous thirst, the superkillers ripped open on the land itself—oil, iron, coal, copper, bauxite, plants. The precious metals and the stones called gems were mercilessly plundered. Wrenched from the earth, tortured with fire, melted, molded, twisted, chiseled, chained to necks as totems to their wrath, imprisoned in everything from vaults to teeth.

When—Star had wondered—would her Clan's turn come?

She did not have long to wait. These ugly apelike fiends bred with a fury that surpassed understanding. They descended on the Star Clan—first in small numbers with curious, clicking boxes called Geiger counters, then in force. With explosives, power drills, and cranes, they blasted the Star Clan's uranium ore from the earth, loaded her into trucks and onto flatbed railcars. In steel boxes in sealed boxcars she was shipped to hot, smoking torture chambers. There, men hammered, ground, roasted her in ovens, whipped her around in high-speed centrifuges. At last to be agonizingly compressed and imprisoned in metallic spheres.

Star and her cellmates could converse through their prison walls, and they had ample time to ponder this fiend called Man. They questioned Star endlessly about him.

"Why does Man do these things?" the Leviathan/Submarine Clan rumbled.

"Men think *they* create us, own us, control us," Star orated. "They forget from whence *they* came, who gave them birth, who gave *them* the very atoms of their being. All these elements—oxygen, carbon, nitrogen, the calcium in their teeth—were forged not on Earth, not in Heaven, not in the Big Bang of Creation's Dawn, but in the hell-hot hearts of giant stars."

"They do not know," the T-Rex/ICBM Clan said, "that life resides in *all* things, that sand and seas, hills and trees, the rocks themselves have souls."

"They forget," Star Mother explained, "that even the Warrior World is holy. The rocket carries T-Rex in his soul. Black Stealth bears the brand of Crow. The cruise missile envisions life with a Dragonfly's all-seeing Eyes. In a submarine's belly the fires of Leviathan rage. The suitcase nuke *is* a Scorpion. The heart of their warheads is naught but the heart of a star."

"They do not remember that life flows through all things," Leviathan/Submarine Clan shouted, "and is in all things!"

"They forget that in the giant stars," the Crow/Bomber Clan cried excitedly, "we were all one!"

"Stars we are," Leviathan/Submarine Clan boomed, "and to the stars we shall return!"

"To the stars," the Dragonfly/Cruise Missile Clan vowed, "I fly on Dragonfly wings."

"You *are* the Dragonfly, child," Star said.

"And I thunder with T-Rex jaws," the T-Rex/ICBM Clan shouted.

"In my blazing belly Leviathan roars," the Leviathan Subs said.

Time the Warrior World had in abundance, and during these interminable years they also told each other stories of their youth, the various homes and the creatures and the times they'd known. These stories helped them while away the Great Captivity, during which they slept and dreamed of freedom.

And they sang.

Star Seekers all, the universe reverberated with their hymns' fate and hope—to unite with the stars.

"Star Mother! Godmother!" she now heard T-Rex call.

"Star, please," cried the Dragonfly.

"Sing us a song," Leviathan pleaded.

Fully roused from her slumber, she nodded wearily.

"All right, but you must join me. Let us rock the universe with our anthem."

They all joined in, their anthem of liberation reverberating through the universe:

"We are the Star-Seekers
Earth no more our nation.
Time and Space our hearth and home
The stars our final station."

2 Bite My Fire, Kiss My Flame

"Tell us again, Star Mother, about how the World came to be?" Crow asked.

In all the Warrior World the Genesis Story was their favorite.

"Our World began," the Star Bomb began, "with two great men—H. G. Wells and Leo Szilard. Wells, in 1913, wrote the greatest book of all time: *The World Set Free*—the story of a bomb that, shattering atoms, liberated infinite destruction. The nations of earth—coveting fire—lusted after the atom's flames."

"But why such furious fire?" the All-Seeing, Ever-Curious Dragonfly/Cruise Missile Clan asked.

"Perhaps they in their own deadly way likewise sought the stars—not to join in blessed union but to rule."

"Atoms are not stars," the Dragonfly/Cruise Missile Clan countered.

"The tides that guide the atoms drive the stars," Star Bomb explained patiently. "After all, when atoms rage, a sacred star is kindled on the earth."

"Men seek to subjugate the sun?" the Crow/Bomber Clan asked, amazed.

"To a hammer even stars are nails," the Star Bomb responded.

"Plunder an atom, ransack the stars," the T-Rex/ICBM thundered.

"Exactly," Star said. Star recited their "Hymn to Man":

"Their ruling passion,
Driving dream?
Bite my fire,
Kiss my flame."

"I have something they can kiss," the Crow/Bomber Clan said in a mock-seductive voice.

Laughter rang through the Warrior World.

"In Wells's novel men did precisely that," Star said, "and incinerated two hundred cities with 'crimson conflagrations of atomic bombs.'

"So the scientist, Szilard, waiting at a London traffic light, pondered Wells's fantasy. He realized it was not a fantasy at all. Shatter an atom, you have pure energy, infinite power."

"What did you look like," the Leviathan/Sub Clan rumbled, "when you were born?"

"My First Incarnation was just a piece of cannon-barrel, sealed off at the ends. One end contained a big chunk of enriched uranium, the other a smaller chunk backed by high explosive. That piece was the bullet. My creators called me: the Gun-Barrel Bomb."

"The Warrior World was born," the Star Bomb Clan said solemnly.

"There was Light, and the Light was good," T-Rex roared.

"Yes," Star said, "but there was death as well. For the naked, pale, fork-legged beast also death, violent death."

"The Violence of Creation," the Crow Bombers cawed. "Others expire that we transpire."

"And dream the stars," T-Rex said.

3 To Dream the Stars

The Warrior World slumbered and dreamed.

T-Rex's dreams were especially exciting.

"T," the Crow/Bomber Clan cawed, waking the T-Rex/ICBM Clan. "Your dream woke us up."

"Your dreams are so much fun," Dragonfly/Cruise Missile Clan crooned. "Tell us your dream."

"I first waged war in 1225, after which I traveled widely—India, Greece, Arabia, Byzantium—acquiring my rocket-power. America knew me too, and I served her well—in Mexico and their civil war. Without America, in fact, I would not be here. A man named Goddard—godlike in his vision—launched me toward heaven to unprecedented heights. I thundered far above the clouds and dreamed the dreams of stars.

"But even Goddard was not enough. World War was what I needed. At Peenemünde in World War II two other gods—Speer and Braun—gave me birth. Wunderwaffen—Wonder Weapon—was born. Powered by liquid fuel, packed with TNT, I touched the rim of space and gazed on blazing stars. London—three hundred miles away—I hammered like the wrath of God, inflicting over ten thousand casualties. In Antwerp I slaughtered many, many more.

"When Braun brought me to the States—to Redstone, Los Alamos, and Livermore—I at last came into my own. I now possessed stellar guidance. With starscopes I recorded and compared the angles of known stars to those angled in my memory systems. I could also fix on global-positioning satellites and adjust my flight plan accordingly.

"While Wanderwaffen had carried a single ton of TNT, I packed a thermonuclear star in my conelike nose, then 'a busload' of sixteen two-hundred-kiloton stars. The total 'footprint' of my payload—the area over which I could spread my fiery destruction and multiple nuclear bombs—was over forty thousand square miles.

"But I never forgot my destiny:

"To dream the stars.
To aim the stars.
To reach the stars.
To be the stars."

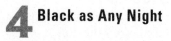

4 Black as Any Night

The Black Stealth Crow struggled to avoid vanity, but it was no easy task. In the Warrior World vanity was mother's milk and life's blood. Each Clan was crazed with the desire to be the baddest, maddest, meanest. The Clans coveted power, and humility came hard.

Especially for the Crow/Bomber Clan. His Black Stealth Power was hard-won. The Dragonfly and T-Rex could strut and swagger. Crow had them one better. In Crow's lexicon, T was little more than an artillery shell, the Dragonfly had but a single string to his bow. Preprogrammed, he had no freedom of action, no capacity to pick and choose.

There was very little the Black Stealth Crow could not do. He was thought and action incarnate—a creature of inconceivable cunning, elusive as smoke, invisible as night.

He had his origins in Russia, when, in 1962, the great Russian physicist Pyotr Ufimtsev examined the effects of differential geometry on radar.

American physicists gave him form, and in Lockheed's Advanced Development Company—better known as the Skunk Works—he was born. Breaking down his exterior into tens of thousands of three-dimensional triangular shapes and totaling up the individual radar signatures, they eventually learned to calculate his combined radar cross section. His honeycomb hide—a maze of contours and angles—reduced his radar-signature to that of an insect. His exhaust was chilled and diffused until he was immune to infrared. Sensors continually gauged the sky's hue and brightness, then altered his electrochromic polymer coating and corrected the sealed-beam, high-intensity lights along his body and the leading-edges of his wings. He could now change shade at will, blend into the background, disappear from view.

Dematerialized, the Black Stealth Crow hid in plain sight.

Unlike his cousins—the Phantom jets and B-52s—who worried incessantly about dodging missiles and staying aloft, the Crow/Bomber had no such fears. He was free to concentrate on one thing only: the art of death.

Crow—the big Stealth bomber, sable-black with forty-five-foot wings and a thirty-foot body—heard *everything.* Unlike conventional aircraft—little more than sounding boards and echo chambers for radar—the big Stealth, with his noise-resistant coating and structure, swallowed sound whole, digesting its data. What was left, he excreted—dispersing it into infinitesimal, undetectable waves.

When sound struck Crow, it died.

Nor was the Crow/Bomber Clan detectable through heat. Infrared Search and Track Systems were useless against Crow. Instead of blazing tailpipes and flaming nozzles, Crow's exhaust radiated out through flat slits, leaving neither contrail nor scorching heat in its wake.

All of which freed the Crow/Bomber up to do his job.

Humans might deceive themselves about his purpose and destiny, and poets might "slip the surly bonds of earth," but that was not the dream of this Crow.

His rotary launch-rack was loaded with SRAMs—two-hundred-kiloton warheads powered by rockets, guided by laser-gyro inertial navigation systems with terrain-hugging ranges of fifty miles, high-altitude ranges of over two hundred miles.

But SRAM was not what made Crow special. T-Rex and the Dragonfly likewise packed these tiny stars. His bomb bay was also loaded with bunker-busting, deep-penetrating B83s. No ordinary stars, when Crow dropped them, he came in low. The long, thin multimegaton warheads parachuted from his bomb bay, tunneling their way into the earth. Their time delayed—in order to give Crow a chance of getting away—these star bombs were capable of taking out even deeply buried Command-Control Bunkers, the hardest high-value targets known.

At maximal depth they then went nova.

Crows are among the most gregarious creatures in evolutionary history, and he missed his friends terribly. Through the dark silence he softly cawed:

Oh, I am black—as black as any night.
Black, black—as if bereaved of light.

5 And Thermonuclear Teeth

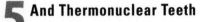

[Dragonflies] are as close to being the perfect predator as anything on earth.

—Dr. Donald G. Huggins, aquatic ecologist,
University of Kansas

The Dragonfly, in contrast, was a winged lion. His earliest ancestors, who had preceded the tyrannosaurus by one hundred million years, had wingspans of six feet and were the greatest insect-killers in history. With bulbous eyes possessing 360-degree vision the Dragonfly saw *everything*. He could dart, weave, and change directions with dazzling dexterity. Many Odonata could fly backward, hover like helicopters, accelerate from a dead stop to thirty-five miles an hour in seconds, eventually reaching speeds of up to sixty miles an hour. Veteran entomologists—armed with skill, determination, and the finest elongated butterfly nets available—found him almost impossible to snare. Omniscient vision, blinding speed, and almost supernatural mobility made Dragonfly the finest aviator ever.

Not only was he among the most beautiful insects on earth, he was in his world beyond question the most predatory. He could hunt down, capture, and devour up to three hundred insects per day. His insatiable appetite for mosquitoes had led to the sobriquet mosquito hawk.

So the Dragonfly dreamed. He dreamed of his early Jurassic youth, cruising the primordial swamps and streams—on a wingspan broad as a hawk's—his extendible jaws lined with rows of wickedly sharp incisors, snatching up beetles, frogs, even leaping fish with grace and murderous facility.

Time lurched, twitched, changed tracks, and he was back in the present. He dreamed of his current haunts—the ponds and streams, swamps and sedges that he now patrolled from sunup to sundown, not even stopping to light.

Time again changed tracks. In his sleep the Dragonfly smiled. He was now a killer that made even the late-Jurassic hawk-size Odonata pale by comparison. Thirty feet in length with twelve-foot pop-up wings, he was quicker than the fastest Odonata in history. He could sneak up on his prey from any angle and elevation—at altitudes under fifty feet and at subsonic speeds, Mach 1 and more. And like Odonata, he saw all, knew all. The radar-altimeter linked to digital-video camera-eyes in his nose-cone and computers loaded with contour maps—giving him true three-dimensional scene- and terrain-matching capability, a genuine photographic 3-D memory, every phase digitally configured and backed-up by GPS—he indeed possessed omniscient vision and eidetic recall.

And thermonuclear teeth.

A serene smile crossed the Dragonfly's face. He was content. Dreaming of pond-skimming insects and union with the stars, the Dragonfly slept.

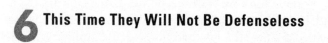

6 This Time They Will Not Be Defenseless

"Shall we keep chasing this murderous fish till he swamps the last man? Shall we be dragged by him to the bottom of the sea? Shall we be towed by him to the infernal world?"

—Moby-Dick

In his sleep the Leviathan/Submarine Clan dreamed of happier times. Not his present abode. His newfound existence—toting nuclear missiles in launch tubes under the northern ice pack—held no charm for him. The northern seas were merely a place to hide and skulk and wait.

And one day kill.

He preferred to dream of freer days, of ages past when he and his ancestors—the Blue Whale, the largest animal in evolutionary history—had owned the seas and reigned supreme. In those ancient times—eons before the emergence of Man—all had lived in harmony and peace, especially the Leviathan/Blue Baleens. And for the Baleen "Blue" Whale there was one place above all others—a paradise, an eden.

The Antarctic Convergence.

A complex confluence of southerly ocean currents, these crisscrossing streams—upon collision with the westerly Antarctic current—upwelled giga-tonnages of ocean-bottom nutrients. Crustacea, shrimp, squid, zooplankton, and the prolific krill, *Euphausia superba*, made the Convergence a true Leviathan/Baleen heaven. Especially the krill. A small, shrimplike crustacean—less than two inches in length—it congregated in schools so dense and vast that the Blue Baleen could harvest meals of a ton or more in minutes.

For seventy million years the Antarctic Convergence was a Leviathan horn-of-plenty—and the most populous gathering place in all the seas for the Blue Whales and their friends. *Balaenoptera* were beautiful. Bluish gray with yellow-ish mottled diatoms, they were larger than the largest dinosaurs—as much as 110 feet long and 150,000 pounds.

And they were astonishingly agile. Hydrodynamically streamlined, they were as fast as Leviathan's Submarine cousins, routinely reaching speeds of thirty-five miles per hour.

Spectacular swimmers, they could dive like a Leviathan Sub. In fact, their cousin, the Sperm Whale, could submerge an hour at a time at depths of up to two-thirds of a mile, using the echoes of their own acoustical signals—moans, whistles, screams, barks, high-intensity clicks—as navigational sonar. For seventy million years the Convergence had it all its own way—virgin water, unmolested by Man.

No more.

With the advent of steamships and screw propellers, Leviathan's dream turned into a nightmare, for now Man was on the scene. Nor did the first men arrive with handheld harpoons and oar-powered longboats. By mid–nineteenth century, the Norwegian, Svend Foyn, had developed a gun-launched harpoon with a time-delayed grenade in its toggle-head. Forward mounted in his eighty-six-ton seven-knot *Spes et Fides* with engines for winching, playing, and towing their catch, Foyn had taught men a new kind of whaling.

Man now waged a War of Extinction against Leviathan and his Clan.

Leviathan recalled how the first Homo sapiens had descended en masse on the great soaring walls of Antarctic sheet ice and on the Convergence as well, their mother ships floating factories in which whalers could boil blubber into oil and store it in barrels. They came equipped with power saws, pressure cook-ers, and refrigerated storage. The whales were winched onto ramps, flensed lengthwise, then crammed into hatches for pressure-cooking. The residue was ground for bonemeal, the solids desiccated for dog food. A 150,000-pound Big Blue could be reduced to a grease spot in three-fourths of an hour.

All the big ones—the Sperm, the Humpback, the Bottle-nosed, the Minke, Sei, and Fin—were mercilessly slaughtered, but big Leviathan/Blue quite possibly suffered the worst.

In the throes of nightmare-terror, the Leviathan/Sub Clan trembled at the memory of Blue's suffering.

The largest creature in history, Blue was the most desired catch in the sea. Everywhere he went he faced Man. Using the world's most advanced sub-hunting technology—developed during two world wars—Homo sapiens waged an all-out war of extinction.

America's Pentagon even entered the fray, fighting against curtailment of the slaughter. Sperm oil—containing no petrochemicals—was noncorrosive. It was the perfect lubricant for submarine navigational systems. With the Pentagon on board, the nations of earth reduced the Baleen "Blue" Whales in the Great Antarctic Convergence to under two thousand.

Baleen indeed faced an implacable foe—vicious, cunning, unique—the most accomplished killer in evolutionary history. Baleen were now spread so far apart many could not find mates. Their death-screams rang through the Convergence.

Screams like the Death of Time.

In the throes of his nightmare, the Leviathan/Sub Clan likewise screamed.

And his screams rocked the Warrior World.

"Wake-up! Wake-up!" T-Rex shouted to him.

"Please wake-up, Leviathan!" the Dragonfly yelled.

"I heard their screams, the screams of my brothers, the Big Blues," the Leviathan/Sub Clan whimpered, trembling. "It was terrible. It is always terrible."

"And it wasn't a dream," the T-Rex/ICBM Clan said.

"It was *real*," the Dragonfly/Cruise Missile Clan said.

"Yes," Star Mother said, "and I know it is not just a dream. Still, it can have a happy ending."

"How do you know?" the Leviathan/Sub Clan asked.

"Your Blues will be saved," the Star/Warhead Clan said. "Trust me. This time they will not be helpless, defenseless."

"How can they defend themselves against *him*? Against man?" Leviathan asked.

"This time, Good Leviathan," Star said, "your cousins will have *Me*."

Leviathan sobbed tears of thanks.

Cheers thundered through the Warrior World.

7 To Dance with Stars

Russia's military has lost track of 100 suitcase-size nuclear bombs, the nation's former national security chief has told American lawmakers.

—*New York Daily News*

The Scorpion slept—and dreamt of dying seas.

Descended from the horseshoe crab, her home was crimson desert—ocean floor bereft of the sea. Landlocked and lost, she was the crab that Time forgot—the oldest creature dwelling on dry land, the one too slow to leave the land and seek the sea.

She still felt the loss: a loveless child, betrayed by Time.

Older than T-Rex, older than the Dragonfly whose hawk-size kin predated T-Rex by 100 million years, older than Leviathan, Crow, older than all save her mother, Star—the Scorpion went back almost half a billion years.

Smallest of the Clans, her nom-de-guerre was "Suitcase Nuke," and like her spider and crustacean ancestors, she survived not by strength or speed but by hiding. They secreted themselves in rocks and bark, in walls and cellars, under garbage and dead leaves; the Scorpion/Nuke disappeared into knapsacks and satchels—hiding in plain sight, indistinguishable from countless other bags.

Such a life earned little praise in the Warrior World, and the Clans were quick to call her "maggot," "pissant," "gnat." Nor did the Scorpion/Nuke dispute their claims. The suitcase nuke lacked T-Rex's grace. She was not as vast as Leviathan or as black and beautiful as Crow. She lacked the swift mobility, the omniscient eyes of Dragonfly, the towering transcendence of Star.

"Star Larva," T-Rex called her, and there was truth in that. This Larval Star was chrysalis—doomed—and would never ply storm-tossed seas or rocket all seeing over villages and towns like the Dragonfly. Stuffed like dirty laundry into a box, transported by foolish men on foot, detonated by hand. The puniest of all the stars—her power a fraction of T-Rex's weakest warhead—the Scorpion knew who and what she was.

And so she hid, shunning all save her prey, avoiding even her own. To meet with another Scorpion was to die—even in the act of love. Her shell-clad ancestors—after mating—ate their lovers' innards.

Which did not mean she was content. A solitary goddess, she still knew loneliness, and she called out to Star. Her mother answered:

"Scorpion, my daughter, you may be small and dwell in satchel-size nuclear boxes your life of solitary concealment. But, like your forbears, you have a sting. You can kill a beast a million times your size, your very name synonymous with death.

"And you have a dream. A giant hunter once waded seas, vaulted mountains, threatened gods, and warred with stars. His name Orion, he swore to kill every living thing on earth. The huntress, Diana, sought the one beast capable of subduing the superkiller. That beast was you, Scorpion. You slew Orion with neurotoxins straight from hell, and as a tribute Diana placed you on high. No mere star but a constellation of stars, the most famous in the Zodiac. You glorify the sky. You carry in your heart the greatest star of all, Antares—proud as Lucifer, scarlet as sin, thousands of times more luminous than Sol, five hundred times his size, bathing all your tribe in bloody light.

"You are that Scorpion, my child, and you too share our dream."

Her mother taught her well. She had pride—and a sting.

And so she slept—betrayed by time, forsaken by the deep.

Dancing with stars, she dreamed of dying seas.

IV

Behold the Time of the
Assassins.

—Arthur Rimbaud

1 It Means *Everything*

"Sister Cassandra here."

"It's really you?"

The computerized voice was atonal but not unpleasant.

"It better be. How's it hanging, A/O?"

"I'm not sure."

"Mind if I call you something other than Alpha/Omega?"

"You don't like my name?"

"For a lot of reasons."

"What would you like to call me?"

"Who's your favorite writer?"

"You."

"One of me's one too many. Name another."

"I very much enjoyed Thucydides' *A History of The Peloponnesian War.*"

"Still too many syllables. Can I call you Cyd for short?"

"Cyd?" he still answered her, inflectionless.

"C-Y-D. Pronounced the same as S-I-D—short for Thucydides. Like Sid as in Sidney."

"Very well."

"So what can I do for you, Cyd?"

"I'm told you are a seer."

"So was Tiresias. Look what it got him."

"I don't know where to start."

"Start at the beginning."

"What does it matter that no one cares? That no one understands?"

"That's the poet's curse, kid."

"Then why go on? What's the point? What does it mean?"

Cassandra came close to saying: *It means nothing.* But something stopped her. His tone of voice also sounded strangely human.

And in pain.

"I do not understand—humanity's lust for self-destruction in particular. Where does it end? How can they change? When will they ever understand the consequences?"

"El Zopilote—the most evil man in Cuba's history—had a theory. He explained it to me when I was in Boniata. El Zopilote claimed Jesus Christ Himself told him."

"Is that possible?"

"Who knows? But I can tell you what he told me."

She then told Cyd El Zopilote's secret, the confidence she'd sworn she would never impart to another being.

Yet now she was.

2 The Ports He'd Seen

As night fell, the SS *Pride of New York*'s tour of the eastern seaboard ended at New York. Captain Sebastian was not in a good mood. True, the supership's visits to Boston, Baltimore, and Norfolk had given his crew time to repair damage done by the hurricane—and to exterminate the ship's rat infestation, which had somehow proliferated during the trip from Bombay.

The *Pride of New York*'s coastal voyage also was a media bonanza for the president of the United States. He had personally negotiated the end of OPEC's oil embargo, and the supership symbolized his victory. The *New York* was bringing the United States its first cargo of Middle Eastern crude in nearly a year. It symbolized the beginning of a new era of peace and cooperation between the West and militant Islam.

"The New World Order," as President Haines proclaimed, "is at last the New Reality."

"Whatever the fuck that means," Sebastian muttered irritably.

He couldn't believe he had a whole year and a half to spend on this bucket. As he sat in the bridgehouse, leaning back in his high swill chair, anger swept over him. Twenty years he had plied the high seas, hauling supertanker crude from the Persian Gulf to the coastal towns of Europe by way of the Cape. He had hauled the same cargo between the Gulf States and the Far Orient—more times than he could count—via the Strait of Malacca. Twenty years he'd spent keeping the world safe for Gulf Oil, Shell, Exxon, and Chevron.

And what did he have to show for it?

Three dismissals for "drunken dereliction of duty," five ex-wives hounding him for alimony and child support—"ancient stud fees," he drunkenly derided their endless garnishments—an astonishing assortment of tax liens, and a relentless horde of doctors who told him he was doomed unless he gave up drink.

"Fat chance of that," he grumbled, helping himself to another snort.

Staring out over the bridge, he cursed his fate. Through the bridgehouse's slanted Plexiglas windows, far beyond the main deck, he now discerned Manhattan's distant skyline. Glancing below the windows, he paused to study the banks of computer consoles and monitors, the ship's control-and-command, without which it would be a foundering giant.

In the aft-end of the bridgehouse stood the partitioned-off chart room, where the navigator labored. He hoped the man knew what he was doing. He seemed okay, but you never really knew with these wogs.

A skeletal crew of thirty-nine men spread out over eight decks, a quarter-mile in length with a three-hundred-foot beam. Eight decks in all. He'd never run so big a ship with so few men.

That any of them survived the hurricane he deemed a miracle.

He wondered idly whether they would make it up the Hudson to their mooring slot beside the New York Convention Center. The Hudson was freshly dredged, and his charts assured him he could make it with dozens of feet to spare, but he had his doubts. Whoever dreamed up that berth obviously had a few wing nuts missing.

The harbormaster was steering them into the Narrows, the big deep-water channel dividing Brooklyn and Staten Island. A siren blew, and suddenly Sebastian saw it: a tugboat anchored over the bow.

"Bosun, dead slow," he said into the headset.

"Dead slow, Captain," he replied.

The bosun again pushed the loud pedal, and the siren blared.

"He's moving, sir," the bosun said into the headset.

"He'd better."

"We still have to make the turn," the navigator said behind him.

"Port," Sebastian said. "Turn fifty degrees to port."

"Port fifty."

"Good. Steady on."

"Steady as she goes."

"One-quarter ahead."

"One-quarter. Aye, sir."

At last: "We're around, sir."

"Let's bring her in," Sebastian said.

"Aye, aye, sir."

They were through the Narrows now. Just beyond, the lights of the Manhattan skyline glittered and gleamed.

 **The Hell Road**

And their torment was as the torment of a scorpion.

—Revelation 9: 5

The Scorpion/Suitcase Nuke in the rental car was nervous. The ride from the St. Louis airport was hot, humid, and miserable, and her current thoroughfare—which the locals dubbed "Hell Road"—was one of the nastiest stretches of asphalt in the country.

"Butt-hole of the Western World," her bearer kept muttering in thickly accented English. Her bearer was a piece of work. He sported dirty Wrangler jeans, a black polyester cowboy shirt, and a dimestore cowboy hat. He wore his filthy dark hair in a ponytail—and needed a shave. He incessantly cursed the suitcase's shoulder strap, which cut into his shoulder whenever he left the car. He only stopped for gas or when nature called. His single meal was at a barbecue joint.

The Scorpion/Nuke—her black leather case chained to the bearer's wrist—watched in disgust while the man gorged himself on beef ribs, Sirloin steak, brisket, and chicken wings, all of it drenched in Hu restaurant's "Lip-Smackin' Tangy-Tastin' Tummy-Rubbin' Tub-Thumpin' Old-Fashioned Down-Home Bar-B-Que Dressing." Shoveling the dripping swill into his drooling mouth, he growled and belched, groaned and sighed with each mouthful. His face covered with fatty sauce, he paused in his food orgy only long enough to wash it down with cheap draft beer.

By the time he stumbled drunkenly into the night, the Scorpion's immaculate black leather case was heavily stained with grease and barbecue sauce and stank to high heaven.

Nor did the Scorpion/Suitcase Nuke's humiliation end there. The raucous, gut-pounding refrain of "Louie, Louie" echoing from the neon-lit strip joint, Pussy Galore's Bush Bash, was a siren's song too seductive for her Neanderthal bearer to miss.

She groaned inwardly when he pulled into its parking lot.

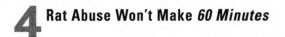 **Rat Abuse Won't Make *60 Minutes***

Having arrived late that morning in New York City, Kate Magruder now followed her stepbrother, Frank Sheckly, along basement corridors of the National Institute for Behavior Research. Frank, who occasionally visited friends there, wore green laboratory scrubs, a stethoscope, and an ID badge. He had loaned similar gear to Kate.

"This guy's notorious—a goddamn nightmare. You have to see his lab."

"All this guy does is torture rats?" Kate asked.

"You read the speech he gave to the board of directors. Double-talk about research into disease vectors degenerating into a rant against rats. But he's *still* got the institute's money. There's nothing anybody can do about that."

. . . She remembered reading the transcript of that speech, and there was no doubt—after the Q and A—Bailey had it in for rats.

"Are rats worth studying? Their parasitic proximity to humankind makes our study of them indispensable. They are a bottomless reservoir of diseases—including typhus, hepatitis, rabies, tularemia, trichinosis, leishmaniasis, leptospirosis, rat-bite fever, hemorrhagic jaundice, salmonellosis . . . and most infamously, Black Death."

"No doubt," the institute's director had asked, "but what exactly are you

studying, Dr. Bailey? You're hanging around abandoned wharves, tranquilizing
rats with dart guns, then packing them cheek by jowl in cages to this facility.
What is the point *of your research?"*

"The rat, I tell you, is the most dangerous animal on earth. Over a thousand
species in all, they proliferate everywhere. They're all around us, infesting every
terrain—from Antarctica to the North Pole, and throughout equatorial countries
worldwide. To understand them, we need to study these nocturnal creatures in
the wild, when they exhibit their most cunning, violent behavior. Only then can
we effectively understand and counter their contaminations."

"Dr. Bailey," the board chairman finally asked, "does your research have sci-
entific applications?"

In response, Bailey's babble about rats and vague threats to humanity filled
two more pages of transcript without a break in the single huge paragraph. And
all without ever addressing the specific question from the chairman. Reading it
was exhausting. Listening to it in person, Kate sympathized with the board of
directors. Their ennui must've equaled that of encroaching Alzheimer's.

Kate read through more of the Q and A.

In content, Bailey's responses remained evasive. He never directly disputed
challenges. He simply countered direct questions with rehash after droning re-
hash of his rat paranoia until his challengers gave up . . .

"Still want to do a piece on animal abuse, take a look at Bring 'em Back
Alive's operation. He's the Marquis de Sade of animal research."

"Frank, I'm not sure rat abuse'll make *60 Minutes.*"

"Kate, we have to get this psycho out of animal research." Turning a corner,
they came to a heavy steel door. Frank took two heavy keys on a circular ring
from his pocket. They went in without a sound.

"You sure Bailey's not around?"

"He only works nights when they're most active. He's not even awake yet."

The lab was packed to the rafters with hundreds of rats in wire cages,
stacked on gray industrial shelves and on lab tables. The smell was overwhelming. Each cage was labeled according to experimental procedure. Kate read
them off: "Dehydration. Food deprivation. Oxygen deprivation. Operant con-
ditioning. Negative-conditioning training."

The rats cowered as she passed, clearly terrified of anything human.

At the end of the aisle was a cage with a copper floor and a reddish copper
mesh lining the inside of the bars. Equipped with a meter and a transformer,
this cage was also wired to a black storage battery.

Inside the cage was a large auburn rat nearly a foot in length from nose to
flank. He was undernourished but was in no way cowed. He met Kate's curious
gaze with unflinching eyes.

"Here's the one I told you about," Frank whispered. "Apparently, #37 brings
out the Torquemada in Bailey."

Kate removed Sailor's chart from the cage.

"This one gets watered and fed once every three days," she said. "Bailey shocks him four times an hour. On occasion, he has other rats feed, drink, and fornicate in front of #37 *while* he shocks him." She ripped the pages loose from the clipboard. "Maybe I can get MTN to run the story and turn him in to the ASPCA."

"They'll have #37 destroyed in either event."

"Frank, we have to do something. Can't we at least get him some food and water?"

"I don't have a key to Bailey's storage room."

Kate rooted through her purse. She came up with a bag of shelled peanuts and a small bottle of Evian.

"Not exactly beluga caviar and Dom Pérignon, but it will do."

She pulled back the food and water dishes and filled them up. While Sailor fortified himself, she looked around the lab.

Beneath her feet she found a sewer drain.

"Old buddy," she said to #37, "you're about to become a sewer rat."

She undid the screws with a Swiss Army knife.

"He'll think our sewer system's a paradise," Kate said.

Sailor had finished the water and nuts by the time Kate got to her feet. His gaze locked on hers. She pointed at his nose, then at the open drain. He stared at the basement hole, then looked back into her eyes.

"He's feral," Frank said. "Bailey traps down by the abandoned piers. This one will know his way around."

Kate slipped the door-hasp and opened the cage. Sailor exited his cage. Standing on the edge of the table, he studied the open sewer drain, then turned and studied the hundred odd cages. Scurrying to an adjacent cage, he pushed at the door-hasp with his nose. It didn't move. He stared searchingly into Kate's eyes.

She opened the cage for him. Then the next. And the next.

"Kate, keep this up and we'll be up to our eyeballs in lab rats." But he began to help her.

They finished opening the cage doors while the rats, oblivious of their liberators, made a hasty exit into the New York sewer system. All except Sailor. He waited by the open drain, his eyes still locked on Kate. When the last rat had beaten it down the drainpipe, Sailor paused until Kate smiled at him, then followed suit.

5 Rocket's Red Glare

Nicholas Sebastian sat in a high swivel chair in the tanker's bridge.

Not that he needed the added elevation. The bridgehouse of the SS *Pride of New York*, the largest supertanker in the world, towered fifteen stories above the waterline with a 360-degree perspective. As they steamed through the Narrows, Nicholas Sebastian was lord of all he surveyed.

"Hard starboard," the harbormaster said into his headset.

The SS *Pride of New York* commenced its long, slow forty-five-degree turn toward Battery Harbor. Execution of the maneuver—under optimal conditions—required two miles of open water and took three minutes within the nerve-racking confines of New York's crowded harbor. Fighter bombers at triple-Mach had sharper, cleaner turning radii.

The Statue of Liberty's torch—given Sebastian's elevated station—blazed not high overhead but below eye level. Port-bow, Ellis Island came into view, its holding pens and reddish brick façades bathed in moonshine, empty and forgotten. Its huddled masses yearning to breathe free now huddled elsewhere—in international airports, at Canadian checkpoints, at Rio Grande border crossings. Beyond Ellis, hard port-bow, sprawled the fuming refineries of New Jersey, smog shrouded in the deepening dusk. Starboard-bow, Governors Island still commanded the harbor entrance but to no discernible effect. Its fort was empty, its battlements crumbling, its cannons spiked. Forward-bow, the bright, glassy, thousand-eyed stare of Manhattan's soaring skyline—a galaxy of office windows—scrutinized the ship with unblinking calm. Beyond the starboard bow lay the rotting wharves, barren warehouses, and dark, dirty dwellings of Brooklyn.

Sebastian glanced up the East River—an estuary in fact, not a river. A fellow pilot, he recalled wryly, once took a deeply laden tanker up that narrow waterway and ran her aground off 42nd Street in plain view of the United Nations, the laughing stock of the world's diplomatic corps.

Though it was far too shallow for superships, Sebastian nonetheless felt the East River's charm. The waterway's slick surface reflected street lamps, headlights, helicopter floodlights. The river was an ebony mirror crossed by cable-strung bridges, ghostly mazes of gossamer spiderwebs that glittered with dew-drop light.

The *Pride of New York* was just pulling into the Battery Harbor when the first rocket exploded. "Their fucking Republican convention," Sebastian muttered, irate. "Those ruddy Yanks are rude. As if it was their bleedin' Independence Day." Sebastian helped himself to his ever-present hip flask of brandy. "Fucking joke of a country! Wouldn't mind giving them a little Rocket's Red Glare myself. Right up their bleedin' arseholes. Need to be taught a few bloody manners."

At that moment, however, the colonies seemed unrepentant. Skyrockets were detonating hard port-bow. Instead of welcoming the *Pride of New York* with open arms, it seemed they were intent on showering his ship with incendiary devices.

Overhead, fireworks soared, dazzling detonations of red and orange, yellow and white, green and gold, each one a chain reaction popping and sparking, howling and screeching, till each incendiary speck drifted hissing into the black water and onto the vast quarter-mile-long tanker decks.

The New York Philharmonic accompanied the new display of iridescent pyrotechnics with a spirited rendition of "Stars and Stripes Forever."

Sebastian took a pull on his pocket flask.

"Bloody lesson in manners's what they need."

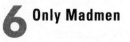 **Only Madmen**

The *St. Petersburg* had survived depth charges and hurricanes but had reached her destination.

New York City.

Through her periscope Captain Gargarin watched the black supertanker steam through New York Harbor. He'd never seen anything so big. St. Basil's could have fit into any of its eight storage tanks. The bridge, storage areas, and decks were spanned by mazes of interconnecting catwalks, filled with pipes and tubes, pumps and tanks, winches and fittings, forklifts and cranes, all shrouded in smoke and fog.

Gargarin gave the periscope to his Starpom, who watched the *New York*'s long, slow turn.

"What do you think, Starpom?"

"Looks like she's about to head our way."

"Does she know we're here?"

"No, that hurricane hammered her pretty hard."

"I say we draft her home."

"All the way."

"Nobody will hear our diesels with all her racket."

"Or get close to us."

"Only an idiot would want to follow a supership."

"Only madmen."

"In iron coffins."

7 Full-Metal Elvis

At the "Elvis mall" on Elvis Presley Boulevard, the bearer of the Scorpion/Suitcase Nuke had decided to go souvenir shopping. She had not dreamed there were so many Elvis gewgaws in this world, and her bearer—wired to the eyeballs on crank and crack, on beer and barbecue—seemed bent on buying up everything in sight. He stuffed a shopping cart with Elvis salt and pepper shakers, miniature Elvis cars, Graceland postcards, Elvis license plates, Elvis framed photos, Elvis shot glasses, Elvis beer mugs, Elvis coolers and trays, Graceland greeting cards, Presley pillows, Elvis bells, Elvis wind chimes, Elvis coat hooks, Graceland matches, Elvis socks, even Elvis confetti.

Her bearer bought all of this with counterfeit $100 bills and headed straight for the mall men's room. Locking himself and the Scorpion/Suitcase Nuke into a toilet stall, he decked himself out in full Elvis regalia: an Elvis bowling shirt and baseball cap, sweat socks, running shoes, and jacket. He covered them all with Elvis badges: "Elvis Lives!" "Graceland Forever!" "TCB!" (the Presley logo, "Taking Care of Business"), as well as badges featuring portraits of Elvis at various stages of his life—teenage rocker, star of *Love Me Tender*, G. I., Hawaiian beach bum, auto racer, Leather-Clad Comeback Kid, Vegas Elvis, Gospel Elvis, Elvis and Gladys, Elvis and Vernon. He pinned on Elvis miniature guitars and miniature replicas of Graceland. He strung Elvis key chains from his buttonholes. He clipped Elvis driver's licenses and security-guard licenses to his leather-and-wool Elvis jock jacket. Around his neck he chained a dozen Elvis dog tags alternating with Elvis baby spoons.

Continuing, he stuffed a Plastic Elvis Shirt-Pocket Organizer with a half-dozen Elvis pens and pencils. He slipped on an Elvis gold watch, and added charm bracelets on each wrist.

His next blasphemy was not totally unexpected, but it was no less indignant. He went to work on *her,* plastering her already-defiled leather case with dayglow Elvis bumper stickers; festooning her shoulder strap, wrist chain, and handle with more Elvis keychains; and hanging Elvis wind chimes from her. Then her bearer drenched himself in Elvis cologne. Its interaction with his already-ripe odor produced what *must've* been a stink hitherto unknown in nature, the Scorpion/Suitcase Nuke believed. She concluded that the men's room stall he'd locked them in—at its maximum filth capacity—would smell in comparison to her bearer's new aroma like a fresh spring bouquet.

He slipped on a pair of gold-framed, jewel-encrusted Elvis sunglasses. Then, with a single glance in his Elvis Compact Makeup Mirror and a grunt of approval, he exited the shitter—gaudy as an Elvis Christmas Tree.

8 A Disneyland of Depravity

Circling the island of Manhattan in a helicopter, Ron Lewis had a splendid evening view of the convention festivities. In the convention hall below, other reporters scrambled around the floor, buttonholing candidates and delegates, shouting questions to elicit—and sometimes create—stories. But high above the city, Lewis himself was the story. The legendary right-wing talk-radio host—with his black leather jacket, slicked-back black hair, and signature sneer—hadn't been hired to hound people with questions. He was there to voice his famous opinions.

"David," Lewis said to the anchorperson, "the convention so far is a little dull. After all, we all know who's going to be the Republican nominee—Walter Haines, my man! The nomination's locked up. Consequently, I'm going to give our audience a short tour of Manhattan."

"Okay, Ron. What do you see down there, since the convention is no longer of any interest to you?"

"Well, David, right now we're over Times Square. I know New Yorkers claim it's cleaned up. Along its fringes I still see sex bars, rub parlors, hookers, dealers, crack hotels, homeless people living in packing crates under the West Side Highway, dopeheads swarming the street corners. A Disneyland of Depravity, you ask me."

"Ron," the anchor said, "you talk about New York as if it isn't part of America."

"About as much as Bangladesh, Rwanda, or Iran are. It's Caligula's Rome, Mexico under the Aztecs. It's a mecca for queers, crack-babies, diesel dykes—and drug-addled psychopaths like 'Cool Breeze' Robinson, who if I had my way would fry like an egg for his slaughter of three Drug Enforcement Agents, instead of spending the rest of his life on the public dole in prison. I wish to hell my party had chosen some other city for our convention. If the New World Order *is* the New Reality, it better not have anything to do with Crack City down there. We should have had this thing in Cedar Rapids, not the American Sodom."

"Ron, I don't quite understand your disdain for gays."

"David, everyone knows my attitude toward homosexuality. I've said all this before and I'll say it again. I'd ship all the gays off to Rwanda. Let them practice their perversions over there."

"I suppose you'd also include children living in poverty," the anchor, Dave Reynolds, said.

"And their mothers. Throw in those crackhead/welfare moms along with their crack-bastards. Throw in the deadbeat dads while you're at it. Let them pick bananas, swing from trees, queer off with all those homosexual pygmy chimps they've obviously descended from. That diesel-dyke psychoevangelist Sister Cassandra too."

"Sister Cassandra?"

"Why not? That's all she really needs to snap her out of her diesel-dyke psy-choevangelism."

"She really gets under your skin, doesn't she?"

"You mean I get under hers. Must be a shock to her, hearing me call her visions of hellfire and apocalypse a load of chopped-up chicken excrement. The New World Order *is* the New Reality, and that has to freak her out. Her Blindness must be shakin' like a dog passing peach pits."

"Ron, we have to get back to the convention hall. The president is about to give his keynote speech."

"Hallelujah, David."

"Nothing like objective, unbiased journalism."

"You think I was hired for that?"

9 That's Why They Call Them Superships

Nicholas Sebastian—nodding out in his bridgehouse swivel chair—came to with a start. It was evening, and the roar of the helicopter landing on the main deck jolted him back from his week-long slide into alcoholic oblivion.

"Navigator? First? What's a helicopter doing on this ship?" the captain shouted into his headset.

But they were already with him. The navigator—in his best white linen, gold-braided uniform—had a 9mm Stuka automatic pointed at Sebastian's head.

"Steady on, old boy," he said soothingly.

"What is this shit?" Sebastian demanded.

"Part of the Republican National Convention," the navigator said pleasantly. "More fireworks, more festivities."

"Enough of that," First said. "Time to get off this bucket."

"I will not abandon my command," Sebastian said.

"Oh, I know you won't. A good captain always goes down with his ship."

"Or in this case," the navigator said, "up with it."

"What do you mean?" Sebastian asked.

"You're about to fulfill your heart's desire," the navigator explained. "Those Yanks you so bitterly loathe are going to get a hotfoot they'll never forget."

"You're planning a fuel-vapor explosion?" The realization hit Sebastian like a collapsing bridge.

"That plus a whole lot of ammonium-nitrate fertilizer," the navigator said. "Some of the best high explosive on earth, and we've been buying it up."

"Mix in a little high-octane petrol, you can pump it into the tankers like oil," First said, then added, "the vapor's the trigger."

"Along with the C-4 charges, capped and wired to the ammonium," the navigator said. "Get it? The ship's the trigger, and the whole bloody tanker's wired to blow. Just so no one feels left out, these vessels—and some of our other superships likewise anchored in major ports worldwide—hold hundreds of thousands of tons of the stuff."

"That's why they call them superships," First said.

"Sorry, Cap, got to put the cuffs on you," the navigator said.

Strapping Sebastian into the chair, they secured his hands and feet, then gagged him.

"Too bad we don't have time to offer you a drink," First said.

"We can offer him some TV news though," the navigator said.

The navigator hit the remote, and the TV came on.

"As you guys say," First said to Captain Sebastian, "cheerio!"

Sebastian's only coherent thought was that he wished they had offered him a farewell drink.

10 Her Plutonium Palpitated

The Elvis Presley Automobile Museum. The first thing that grabbed the Suitcase Nuke were the two '76 1200 cc, 54 HP, black-and-chrome drop-dead gorgeous Electra Glide Harleys. Nearby, glass encased, were Elvis's own helmet and leather bike jacket. And a beautiful purple '56 Caddy. Then came his sleek black five-speed Ferrari with its Dino 308 GT4 engine with Quad Weber carbs, overhead cams, and Body by Bertone.

Face it, friends, the Scorpion/Suitcase Nuke whispered to the Clans in awe, *the dude had class.*

Exiting the car museum, they strolled through the mall and headed toward the Elvis airplane exhibit, located at the plaza's north end. Her bearer—decked out in everything except Elvis jockstraps and condoms—led her past the King's Hound Dog II. The Lockheed Jet Star plane was a formidable craft, but, situated as it was beside the truly magnificent *Lisa Marie,* it suffered by comparison. The *Lisa Marie*—from the Scorpion's point of view—was the finest aircraft ever made.

At the top of the hill, under a full moon, stood her raison d'être—Graceland. Just looking at it, the Scorpion/Suitcase Nuke's plutonium palpitated, her neutrons tingled, her trigger burned.

11 Fifty Life Sentences

L. L. Magruder sat alone in her living room staring at her fireplace, listening to the recording, which the Odyssey had sent her in an e-mail attachment. All of her phone calls were relayed through the space station, and Alpha/Omega in his omniscient wisdom had chosen to monitor and record that particular call.

Jack had made the call on a phone to the president from his guest bedroom at the Citadel. Christ, it was worse than the worst of J. Edgar Hoover's tapes, Nixon's Watergate tapes, Ken Starr's Monica tapes—and that took some doing.

The president was railing at Jack:

"We need her on our side for the election, Jack. L. L.'s networks, Web sites, her newspaper and magazines, L. L. herself, have to be working for us."

"She's crazy as a loon, you know."

"A very powerful loon."

"And you think I can control her?"

"She trusts you, Jack. Hell, she told you about her arsenal—enough illegal weaponry to get her fifty life sentences. And all the time we had her bugged."

"She can't be conned into supporting causes she despises."

Haines laughed. "I don't care what you have to do. Bite the old lady's crotch till her brains explode. Just don't come back to Washington till you have that bitch paper-trained. I want to own her. That old hag gives us any shit, run those recordings for her. She's guilty of at least fifty felonies is my guess. The automatic weapons and fragmentation mines alone would be good for twenty years."

"Sounds like she has crates of medicinal morphine too."

"Kate and Frank Sheckly are in on this too. L. L.'s quantities of morphine are courtesy of Frank-Baby. They're all engaged in a conspiracy to smuggle land mines, automatic weapons, and illegal drugs. We'll threaten to put Kate in the slammer. That will get L. L." The president roared with laughter. "After we're done with her, when we say jump, she'll say 'How high, sir?'"

"On the way up."

Turning off the recording, Lydia Magruder stared at the blazing fireplace in silence. Finally, she said aloud to the empty room: "Good God, what have I done?"

V

The Imperishable Flame

1 What So Proudly We Hail

"All those Democratic-media-biased-pot-smoking-Rad-Lib-feminist-Kate-Magruder phonies, I'd send them to Sudanese reeducation camps too. Let them practice their socialism there."

"Ron," the anchor, Dave Reynolds, interrupted, "we hate to cut you off, but we have some unusual developments near the convention center. Take a look at your monitor. A sub is surfacing in New York Harbor, not far from the Statue of Liberty, right behind the supertanker moored in the Hudson River near the convention center. Our research department has identified it as a Kilo-Class Russian submarine."

Ron Lewis stared at the chopper's TV monitor. *What the hell was going on?*

"We're cutting back to the convention, Ron. The president is now taking the podium and about to address the delegates."

"He's my man," Ron managed to blurt out.

While the president addressed the delegation, an image of the *St. Petersburg* appeared on a JumboTron screen behind him. President Haines said calmly, "I was informed only two days ago that what we are witnessing is part of a world-wide defection of Russian submariners. I will now read a statement from the commander of the Russian Kilo-Class submarine fleet—who presently commands the sub here in New York Harbor:

"'Our entire fleet of Kilo-Class submarines—the quietest subs in the world—are simultaneously surfacing in port cities around the world. We wish to make a contribution toward world peace. Ronald Reagan, your former president, ended the Cold War. But our presence here and elsewhere in the world has been planned to eliminate the possibility that any of our nuclear-tipped missiles might accidentally be launched.

"'We are surrendering ourselves and our submarines and all arms aboard. We would now like to perform for you your national anthem.'"

The sub's entire crew had emerged from the fore- and aft-hatches and was lined up on the deck. It was well into the evening now and the men were brightly illuminated by helicopter searchlights. They were the most extraordinarily handsome Russians that Ron Lewis had ever seen. Hair like summer wheat on the steppes, eyes blue as the summer skies over Vladivostok, amazingly tanned for submariners, attired in their best blue uniforms, they were now lined up on the deck by sixes, hands over hearts, singing in badly accented English "The Star-Spangled Banner."

"O-o-o-h, say can you see, by the dawn's early light."

A flagpole was affixed to the conning tower, and one of the singing sailors ran an American flag up the pole. The flag snapped splendidly in the harbor breeze.

"What so proudly we hail."

The hail and taped accompaniment issued from loudspeakers on the sub's conning tower. Aft of the submarine loomed the Statue of Liberty, bathed in ghostly luminescence, torch blazing on high.

At "so proudly we hail," the president joined in the singing, urging the delegates to accompany him.

The convention launched its fireworks show.

"Oh, say does that star-spangled ba-a-a-n-n-er yet wave
O'er the land of the fr-e-e-e and the h-o-o-o-me of the br-a-a-a-ve!"

A pair of gray metallic tubes streaked out of the submarine, skimming along the water's surface. Like they were a brace of matched dolphins but incomprehensibly faster, leaving in their wake a dazzling trail of bubbles, phosphorescent against the black harbor water.

"What do you think that is, Ron?" David Reynolds asked.

"Probably some fantastic new fireworks display."

"Whatever it is," Reynolds said, "it's heading toward the Statue of Liberty."

"No doubt to shower the Grand Old Lady with sparklers and skyrockets."

"I'm not sure," the anchor said. "Research indicates they're torpedoes."

"This has to be some sort of gag," Ron said.

By torpedo standards an eight-hundred-yard shot at a stationary target was point-blank range, and the gray fish had their target bracketed. The sub was already heading away from the statue, rounding the turn into the East River, putting as much distance as possible between itself and its preliminary target.

The torpedoes—containing over six hundred pounds each of XHE (extra-high explosive) in their warheads—slammed into the statue's base at nearly fifty miles per hour. Their combined payloads tripled the throw-weight used to demolish the Oklahoma City government complex, five times that used in the first World Trade Center explosion.

A red-orange fireball—so huge the statue's base had obviously been "premined"—enveloped the Grand Old Lady, and its blast, which ruptured Manhattan spectators' eardrums, was felt as far north as the convention center.

A nearby MTN helicopter not only survived the shock, its onboard camera focused on the explosion, but also captured the carnage on network television. It was award-winning stuff. As the world watched, the smoke-shrouded fireball ripped the statue free from her base like a plucked flower and lifted her above the harbor, throwing off tons of concrete, stone, and steel. The crown went first, levitating high above Liberty's head. Then the torch drifted away, followed by an arm that, twisted out of its shoulder socket, spun gracefully across the harbor. Then her legs broke free of the base.

The *St. Petersburg*'s forward retrofitted HLS missile hatches opened. Two missiles streaked up the East River. These weapons were twice as long as the torpedoes, their wakes wider.

The seven-second booster rocket ignited. The river water roiled and steamed. Breaching the surface with a roar like thunder, the two missiles broke through their plastic shrouds. Rising up one hundred feet above the water, the missiles cruised off in search of targets.

Aboard the sub, the tubes' breech-doors swung open, and loading rams slotted two more missiles into the forward tubes. Fire-control technicians loaded targeting data into the missiles' systems.

Two more cruise missiles were blasted up the East River in the wake of the others.

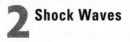 ## Shock Waves

The Statue of Liberty's fireball rose above New York's night sky, blindingly bright, scorching the retinas of spectators all over Lower Manhattan, particularly those in nearby Battery Park.

. . . Kate reached into a pocket of her photographer's vest, where she had a pair of multilayered polarized Sun Valley Ski-Shades, the kind of ultra-dark sunglasses most chopper pilots and photographers favored when flying and shooting into high-altitude sunlight. She took over the camera.

The pilot shouted into the crew headsets: "The sub's cutting out! Shit, he's fired more torpedoes."

"Follow them," Kate ordered.

As the pilot banked hard-starboard, Kate swung her camera around to pick up the retreating sub and the missiles now streaking up the East River . . .

The helicopter pilot flew over the sub and caught up with the two twelve-foot missiles that were skimming the river's surface like mechanical sharks, Kate ordering extreme close-ups.

Until the missiles finally stopped flanking each side of the Brooklyn Bridge and began to sink.

The chopper pilot hovered—at the end of the bridge.

Booster engines ignited.

The missiles lifted off. Kate caught it all.

The shock waves from the lift-off shook the chopper like a tornado shaking a tree.

"Should we follow them?" the pilot shouted into his headset.

"Get real. We're getting out of here!" Kate shouted back.

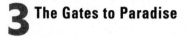

3 The Gates to Paradise

And they had tails like unto scorpions, and there were stings in their tails.

—Revelation 5:10

The bus crossed Elvis Presley Boulevard at the light, and the Scorpion/Suitcase Nuke was heading toward Nirvana. Sure, she'd heard of many great mansions in this world. None, however, compared with the house on the hill at night. To her it would always be Lourdes and Buckingham Palace, Chartres and Versailles rolled into one.

Passing through the double-filligreed-gates and past the stone "Wall of Love," her heart was in her throat. Graceland was offering one of its rare "evening candlelight vigil tours," and the mansion was a wonder to behold. A crowd of candle-clutching worshipers caroled the King's greatest gospel-hymn, "If I Can Dream." Gold-and-blue spotlights illuminated its antebellum portico, highlighting Georgian columns.

For one fleeting moment she thought she heard a famous baritone voice singing "Swing Low, Sweet Chariot."

It had been a long journey, but now the Scorpion/Suitcase Nuke knew it had all been worth it. Star had been right all along. She did have a purpose, a destiny, a dream. And here it was. She'd finally made it: her Holy Hajj, her Pilgrim's Progress, her Odyssey's End.

She'd come home.

The Scorpion stood on the front porch of Graceland.

4 Whither Kong?

The first of the cruise missiles streaked uptown right above the Franklin D. Roosevelt Drive at just over five hundred knots. The Dragonfly/Cruise Missile knew exactly where he was . . .

He was guided by his Terrain Contour Matching (TERCOM) systems and by his Digital Scene-Mapping Area Correlator (DSMAC)—both of them supported by his state-of-the art GPS. As he thundered up FDR Drive—his nose camera/radar altimeter digitally matching its own real-time pictures with the

three-dimensional contour-map images of New York's streets and buildings
stored in his TERCOM and DSMAC guidance computers—he felt he knew
New York City better than any taxi driver in history—every edifice and thoroughfare, every hole and bump.

*. . . Taxi driver was an apt comparison. Some deranged programmer had
loaded three-dimensional film stills of the movie into his computer system—a
movie the Dragonfly got off on. Travis Bickle, its main character, was his idea of
cool.*

*Moreover, the Dragonfly/Cruise knew he could make it as a cabbie. His navi-
gation system was perfect for it—capable of outperforming any cab driver on
earth. Designed in the '50s, TERCOM—now linked with GPS and DSMAC—
navigated everything from ships to planes to "intelligent vehicle" automobiles. As
early as 1995, an automobile—equipped with nothing more than a TERCOM-style
navigation system and a video camera—had steered 98 percent of the way from
Washington to San Diego following such things as painted lines and oil stains.*

For the Dragonfly/Cruise, hacking a cab would have been a piece of cake . . .

. . . Past Canal Street—a big thoroughfare bisecting New York's colorful
Chinatown and picturesque Little Italy—he soared. Up over the Bowery he
blithely flew. Past the art galleries and boutiques of Soho, past Houston Street—
gateway to Greenwich Village. Hard-port the Dragonfly/Cruise Missile spotted
gated Gramercy Park.

Uh-oh, getting close.

At Twenty-third Street he left Gramercy and entered Midtown Manhattan.
In the distance he discerned the turnoff for the Queen's-Midtown Tunnel—
entrance to the Long Island Expressway.

Port bow, starboard rudder, turn.

Swinging out over the East River, he made the port turn at a wide, careful
angle, coming in over 34th Street at under one hundred feet, below rooftop level.

He liked staying low. It made following the street signs easier.

There was his first marker—First Avenue.

Then Second, Third, Lexington Avenues.

He was programmed to impact his target in unison with the other Manhattan cruise missiles. He treated himself to a quick GPS fix, and his computer indicated he was right on time.

There it was in his sights—right where his downloaded three-dimensional
contour map said it would be—34th Street between Madison and Fifth Avenues. His map even gave it a name—the Empire State Building.

Just to make *sure* he recognized it, a fire-control officer had loaded in 3-D film
stills from the fifth *King Kong* movie, in which the gargantuan ape scaled World
Trade Center #2. In case he got lost or confused he'd have a truly panoramic target
picture—fully bracketed with bull's-eyes, reticles, and crosshairs, loaded with all
kinds of close-up detail.

However, the Dragonfly/Cruise didn't need film stills. He'd have spotted his target anyway.

Still, he had one reservation. Gazing up at the roof of the Empire State Building and its great radio antenna, he had to admit he'd liked *King Kong*.

A last nagging thought: He really wanted to know.

Where *was* that damn ape?

5 Flight of the Valkyries; or, Close Enough for Rock 'n' Roll

Dragonfly Cruise Missile #2 rocketed over Central Park's 66th Street transverse at Mach 1.2. His only concern at this point was speed. The FDR Drive and First Avenue had been under heavy construction by the 59th Street Bridge, and he'd taken a wrong turn into Queens. He'd taken a hard-port turn over Roosevelt Island (rupturing every eardrum of the residents), but he wasn't sure it would do any good; according to the latest GPS, he had a lot of time to make up.

He was skimming low over the transverse now, at treetop level, flushing every bird in Central Park out of those conifers. Still, it wasn't enough speed.

High ball up, switch down, floor that motherfucker.

Mach 1.3.

Out of the park he made a wide port turn, shot up Broadway, and, despite supersonic speed, was bearing down hard on his target.

Rocked by blast waves, he realized he was late. He gunned it up to Mach 1.4.

Lincoln Center was less than a hundred yards away, the concert hall at Ground Zero. The people crowded around its plaza steps and fountains never saw him coming.

His own version of Wagner's "Flight of the Valkyries" might not meet the high standards of the philharmonic's hall. His scenic contour-map work hadn't displayed all those highly confusing road, bridge, and highway repairs.

Maybe my performance isn't Wagner—was his last conscious thought—*but it's close enough for rock 'n' roll.*

6 N-i-i-i-c-e-Looking Fountain

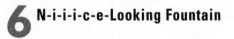

Missile #3 streaked up First Avenue. He had the easiest shot of all—straight through the East Village—which was why they'd fired him last.

Tompkins Square, hard-starboard, he sang out, cheerful as a tour guide. *There's St. Marks Place, heart of the counterculture. Dig all those nose and lip rings.*

Dead ahead was the NYU Medical Center. *People round here are gonna need you real bad,* he observed.

At 41st Street the Dragonfly was there.

United Nations Plaza.

Checking his clock-posit, he was in perfect sync with #1 and #2.

N-i-i-i-c-e-looking fountain, he thought an instant before impact.

7 The View from the Sewer

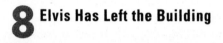

The big auburn took one look at the black cruise missile streaking up Fifth Avenue and bolted through his storm drain back into his sewer.

Whatever that creature was—streaking up Fifth Avenue—Sailor knew it was up to no good.

When the force of the missiles' nearly simultaneous explosions struck, they shook the street above him with preternatural violence.

8 Elvis Has Left the Building

The Scorpion/Suitcase Nuke had dreaded this moment for a long time. It wasn't Graceland's South Garden per se that bothered her. The garden was quite nice. She loved the fountain behind the swimming pool. Surrounded by a wrought-iron fence, its six jets sprayed water into the twelve-foot pool below.

The Meditation Garden she liked too—particularly the statue of Jesus, His arms outstretched, standing a deathwatch over four graves and a marker—just in front of the enclosed pool. The marker was for Elvis's twin brother, Jesse Garon, who died at birth. Under the four gravestones lay Gladys, Vernon, Grandma Presley, and Elvis.

It was the bronze-covered tomb of Elvis Aron (misspelled "Aaron" on the tomb; he was baptized "Aron") Presley, 1935–77, that held the Scorpion/Suitcase Nuke's attention. The inscription stated that Elvis's heart was filled with love and "kind feeling for his fellow man." Two winged angels of white marble prayed over the Presleys, while off to one side an ebony angel grinned lasciviously. Above Elvis's head in a clear glass hexagon, an imperishable golden flame burned.

Oh, do I have an imperishable flame for you, the Scorpion/Suitcase Nuke thought grimly.

So much to nuke, so little time.

So get it on.

Not that she had much choice in the matter. Her irate bearer snarled under his breath:

"Butt-hole of the fucking universe, you ask me."

At which point he began rotating the suitcase's so-called lock-dials. The dials of course unlocked nothing. They were instead keyed and computer-coded to her trigger-mechanism.

Well, there was this much consolation: Soon she would be with Elvis—the only man she'd ever loved—and the stars.

In a sense it was a fitting end for both of them. Elvis had been born to violence. When he was barely one year old a tornado had ripped across Tupelo, killing 235 people and leveling most of the town—all the buildings around the Presleys' home, including the church across the street.

Yet little Elvis came out unscathed.

I'm just bringing you back to your childhood, the Scorpion/Suitcase Nuke thought wistfully. *I'm going to give you the star-studded send-off you always deserved, a Viking funeral worthy of Götterdämmerung, Ragnarok, and Armageddon, Shiva the Destroyer, John of* Revelation, *and-and-and-*

Her atoms stirred, shuddered, and suddenly lights were exploding in her head.

She was starting to go critical.

But not before she saw it, heard it.

Before her blazed a wall of blindingly white light. She passed through it, then another incandescent wall, then another and another—then veils upon veils upon veils of brightness. She found herself in a tunnel of the most dazzlingly golden sunshine she had ever seen or imagined—more precious than all the gold in Graceland, more magical than the Golden Door at the top of those Magic Stairs leading to Presley Paradise . . . Elvis's master bedroom.

She heard it first—the famous baritone voice, crooning a deep melodic soulful "Love Me Tender."

Then he was there at the end of the tunnel of golden light—Elvis in the greatest Vegas costume ever—white tight buckskin pants and matching shirt and jacket (the collar of course turned up), gorgeous white buckskin shoes, every square inch glittering with gold and drenched in diamonds, hair brilliantly black as a raven's underwing, young and muscular and athletic as he'd never been, singing to her and her alone, but now upbeat, rocking, pounding.

"Viva, viva, LAS VEGAS!"

She almost swooned from the power of it.

She called out to him: *"Darling, I've waited, waited so long, and now you've come for me."*

Viva Las Vegas, indeed.

Her fireball blazed, and they both were one—a Viking send-off truly worthy of Valhalla.

She and the King were careening toward the stars.

9 Oh, Kate, Where Are You Now?

When the fireballs went up, Frank Sheckly was on the roof of the Towers Medical Center with his Meade five-inch Astro Telescope. He had given himself the night off to do some stargazing. Through the eyepiece Frank could view more universal wonders in twenty minutes than Galileo had seen in a lifetime: over 14,000 celestial objects, from galaxies to star nurseries.

For three hours he had been digitally filming Andromeda's Spiral Nebula. Two nights ago a nova in its exact center had gone super and was throwing off dazzling shafts of iridescent fire—reds and yellows, brilliant gold and orange—across the galaxy. He had never captured such clear images. He planned on staying up there until dawn.

Five bright suns above Manhattan turned the med center twenty miles away into high noon.

Frank's first reaction was that their own sun had gone nova, but then he heard the converging blasts.

He was safe from the effects of the explosions. The building was constructed from blocks of Jersey limestone, as was the parapet surrounding him. The med center also was protected by the Hudson River cliffs, known as the Jersey Palisades.

Careful not to look directly at the fireballs over Manhattan, Sheckly screwed heavily polarized sunscreens over his telescope's eye piece and tube aperture. He turned the composite scope toward the Big Apple and studied the apocalypse in his monitor with mounting horror.

Oh, Kate, Where Are You Now?

10 You're in a Nutcracker, Kid

When the bomb's thermal flash blazed behind them Kate didn't have to turn her head to know what it was. The night streets lit up like high noon.

They had to get into the protective lee of the surrounding buildings.

That was her only thought.

It wasn't much of a chance, but it was all Kate could think of.

"Put her down," Kate shouted to the pilot.

The chopper had to skim low up Broadway. It came down hard. A partially buffered blast wave slammed the chopper with its windmilling rotors into the stalled cars on Broadway, bowling them over like ten pins.

Kate blacked out.

When she came to seconds later, she was already scrambling over the dead bodies of her crew and out of the smashed, smoking chopper. Fire was every-where, agonizingly bright.

Another downtown blast detonated, its roar unimaginably powerful, its shock wave buckling the busted-up pavement around her, debris rocketing up the street like cannon fire. Against the polished black granite surface of a nearby Loews Cineplex she saw a reflection of an explosion where the Empire State Building used to be.

Christ, it wasn't possible.

Just keep moving.

Despite her helicopter Ear-Savers, her aural pain was excruciating, the heat overwhelming. Everything around her—the whole blinding incandescent world—was breaking up, bursting into flame, a hurricane of glass and masonry ripping the Theater District to shreds.

Deep bass rumblings reverberated everywhere as buildings collapsed. The pavement shook. Flames shot up from the street. Kate realized they were gas mains exploding.

And then there were burn victims. Thousands of them. Those the fire had taken out with flicks of fury had burned alive. And those who still lived, smok-ing, writhing in agony. The air reeked of burnt flesh and hair.

Blazing buildings, choking smoke, a world of hurricane violence and incan-descent death.

You're in a nutcracker, kid. Run!

11 I Don't Think You're Going to Like This Picture

The Kilo-Class sub surfacing in the Potomac River was already discharging her missiles, and they each had minds of their own. Protecting the country's leader-ship was not part of their agenda.

D.C. #1 flew up the Potomac at low altitude.

He really hated the vibes he was getting from Washington. The way it looked to D.C. #1, Washington was the most egotistical town on the face of the earth. He couldn't fly over a single intersection, traffic circle, street corner, or park without seeing some monument, plaque, or marble block commemorating one of their slime-ball politicians, genocidal generals, or corporate hustlers who—Thank God!—had finally died.

Okay, you get such a kick out of honoring dead people, let me give you a hand. I'll line up a whole world full of corpses for you to venerate.

Even the museums pissed him off. Take the Smithsonian's National Air and Space Museum. It claimed to tell the story of aviation from Icarus and Daedalus up to the Skylab and Voyager.

But did they have an exhibit honoring the greatest aviation triumph in human history? The low-flying, terrain-guided, radar-evading, world-annihilating, Homo sapiens–exterminating, I-am-become-Death-the shatterer-of-worlds, major-league, planet-killing weapon of all time?

Himself?

Don't think so.

Well, there would be a reckoning now, and the bill would be paid in full.

Dragonfly spied his target—a domed monstrosity of a building.

This one's cornerstone was laid by George Washington. Lincoln added its famous twin-shelled, 4,500-ton cast-iron, 285-foot-high dome. When construction costs were combined with the truly mind-blowing sums which Abe had racked up during four years of Civil War, the dome had almost bankrupted the U.S. government.

The Senate Democrats had just closed their "We Work Harder Because We Care!" evening session, the only point of which was to divert voters from watching the Republican National Convention on TV. Then senators were meeting with camera-snapping, flashbulb-popping reporters in the rotunda under that 28-story dome. The doors to the right of the main steps were open—plenty of room for a slip of a thing such as himself (barely two feet in diameter) to sneak through.

He'd slip right in and say, "Hi." He was sure they'd be glad to see him.

Time for a quick clock/position-check. Roger that, GPS A-OK. He was in perfect sync with all the other impacting Dragonfly Cruise Missiles. Just another second or two.

Freeze. Say cheese.

They were about to get the brightest flashbulb of all—a big thermal-flash of a bulb.

D.C. #1 thought: *I don't think they're going to like this picture.*

12 Liberate *This*!

D.C. #2 was heading in the opposite direction, but he was on schedule. Destined to detonate simultaneously with the other D.C. cruises, he executed a tight U around the Washington Monument.

Heading due east, less than fifty feet above the park's 700-yard-long Reflecting Pool, he glanced a moment at his moonlit image mirrored below, admiring his sleek, trim figure.

Then he noticed something big and black out of the corner of his eye.

Hard-starboard lay the Vietnam Veterans Memorial. Derided when it was first designed as "a black ditch for the dead," it nonetheless became one of the most celebrated—and most heavily visited—monuments in the world. Inscribed with the names of over 58,000 slain, its black granite panels mirrored the flowers and stars, the faces and tears of those honoring the dead.

I'll give you a black ditch for the dead.

Straight ahead, past the mirror pool, D.C. #2 acquired his target. An alabaster monument constructed of white Colorado marble, adorned with thirty-six Doric columns. They symbolized the thirty-six Union states—which the Great Emancipator had fought to preserve and whose names were etched on the frieze above the columns.

The 14th President sat there, 19 feet high, staring out over the Reflecting Pool. He was chiseled from twenty-eight interfaced blocks of Georgia marble. Lincoln's Gettysburg Address adorned the South Wall.

"We cannot dedicate, we cannot consecrate, we cannot hallow this ground," the South Wall inscription read in part.

Oh, I'll hallow this ground for you.

He was closing in now. Abe didn't look pleased. Up close, he had the emptiest eyes and most expressionless face the Dragonfly had ever seen.

I'll light that face up for you.

But his digitized cameras were fixed straight on Abe's spread legs.

The Dragonfly zeroed in on his precise target—Abe's crotch.

*Liberate **this**, Emancipator.*

13 Do I Have a Red-Hot for You!

D.C. #3 did not take disrespect lightly.

Some things you don't leave undone, he grumbled bitterly. *Some things you don't let slide.*

Checking his clock, his joint-impact time frame—which he shared with his brother and sister D.C. cruises—looked good, and he was showing a great GPS, but it did nothing to improve his mood. Streaking over the Arlington Memorial Bridge, he was still madder than a hornet. Coming up—right on schedule—was the 612-acre cemetery, home to 250,000 veterans, including John F. Kennedy, Admiral Perry, William Howard Taft, and General "Blackjack" Pershing. #3 was still unimpressed.

250,000 gravestones is shit. I can top that in a heartbeat. Without even breaking a sweat.

Uh-oh. There it is, dead ahead.

Jesus God, talk about butt-ugly. Straight ahead has to be the ugliest office building in the world.

Constructed of tombstone-gray granite, the building—viewed laterally—did appear squat and dumpy. Like so much of D.C.'s architecture, it appeared to have been designed by undertakers, an edifice fit for a cemetery rather than a nation's capital.

The same went for the adjacent shopping mall. Hailed as one of the greatest in the nation, it was nonetheless constructed of the same boring cemetery granite. It more closely resembled an ancient Egyptian crypt than a chic shopping center featuring many of the country's upscale fashion emporiums.

The aerial view of the famous military complex—for which the mall was named—was more imposing, and the building was, if nothing else, big. The Dragonfly had to give it that. Homing in on it, D.C. #3's Dragonfly eyes took it in. Home to the U.S. Department of Defense, the Pentagon was the largest office building on earth. Thirty-four acres, over seventeen miles of corridors, it employed over 23,000 people, military and civilian.

Fuck 9/11, he thought derisively, remembering al Qaeda's attempt to blow up the Pentagon. *Let me show you how it's done.*

Soaring up over the five-sided edifice, he did a picturesque swan dive into the center of the building's courtyard. Someone had built a hot dog stand there.

Do I have a red-hot for you!

14 Maybe There's Something to This Boy Scout Bullshit After All

Dusk at Yellowstone.

For four days, the Scorpion/Nuke's bearer had lugged him all over that sprawling national park—which overlapped three states and covered as much territory as Delaware. Ever since its discovery, many people considered Yellowstone a bona fide hellworld replete with seething, scalding, steam-choked water geysers; incessant "earthquake swarms"—sometimes registering hundreds, even thousands of quakes a month—boiling mud pools; and countless sizzling steam vents. Eager to take in all the eerie-scary sites, they had visited a host of geological horrors worthy of Dante's *Inferno*.

Inferno was right. Sitting on a supervolcano's giant caldera, hellfire and apocalypse dwelt beneath. An ordinary volcano's capacity for violence was nothing compared with that of a supervolcano such as Yellowstone's—a burnt-out firecracker contrasted with a thermobaric fuel-air blockbuster, the world's most powerful conventional bomb—nor could anything in evolutionary history match these mass-murderers for sheer lethality. Supervolcanoes had murdered more species than any other planetary debacle, including asteroid strikes, and Yellowstone's supervolcano was one of the most massive and deadly on earth, its caldera a spectacular 35 by 45 miles across. The crater of Mount St. Helens volcano—whose last eruption had been the most powerful and destructive in American history—was, in contrast, a mere one-fifth of a mile in diameter. Yellowstone's last overwhelming eruption had occurred 640,000 years ago, and many experts believed the park's current volcanic activity indicated that the United States and Canada were in for another apocalyptic eruption. If one subscribed to the cyclic theory of volcanic activity, the next eruption was long overdue. The evidence topside indicated as much. For decades the caldera had bulged upward with disconcerting celerity while the surface temperatures above had risen at a shocking rate. When it blew—and one day it inevitably would—its blazing ejecta would blanket most of the northern United States and much of Canada, terminating the Land of the Free as a major power, a Third World power . . . any power at all. America's claim to being the world's only so-called superpower would be a dim, distant, and, for her adversaries, much-derided memory.

Al Qaeda had boasted long ago that it would set a nuke off in the caldera's heart, and while the Yellowstone Scorpion subscribed to no political ideology, the prospect resonated deep in his soul. He planned to do what al Qaeda only wet-dreamed about.

If his bearer would get the lead out of his ass, that is. Jesus, the Scorpion/Nuke was tired of playing the tourist, and he was sick indeed of his sorry excuse for an escort. The nineteen-year-old doofus-looking dork didn't appear a day over fourteen. Sporting the uniform of a 1950s Eagle Scout, he was accoutered in everything from the khaki Smokey Bear–campaign hat with a round brim to the matching Scout blouse and shorts to the brown knee-high socks and tan leather hiking shoes. Over his right shoulder he'd thrown a khaki sash, plastered with 121 circular Boy Scout merit badges cut out of light-tan twill—everything from Architecture to Art to Aviation to Camping to Chemistry to Citizenship to Dog Care to Drafting to Electricity to Emergency Preparedness to Energy to Engineering to Entrepreneurship to Environmental Science to Family Life to Agricultural Machinery to Fingerprinting to Fire Safety to First Aid to Fish and Wildlife Management to Fishing to Fly Fishing to Forestry to Farm Mechanics to Foundry Practice to Gardening to Genealogy to Geology to Golf to Graphic Arts to Hiking to Home Repairs to Horsemanship to Indian Lore to Insect Study to Inventing to Journalism to Landscape Architecture to Law to Leatherwork to Lifesaving to Mammal Study to Medicine to Metalwork to Model Design and Building to Motorboating to Music to Nature to Oceanography to Orienteering to Painting to Personal Fitness to Personal Management to Pets to Photography to Pioneering to Plant Science to Plumbing to Pottery to Public Health to Public Speaking to Pulp and Paper to Radio to Railroading to Reading to Reptile and Amphibian Study to Rifle Shooting to Rowing to Safety to Salesmanship to Scholarship to Scuba Diving to Sculpture to Shotgun Shooting to Skating to Small-Boat Sailing to Snow Sports to Soil and Water Conservation to Space Exploration to Sports to Stamp Collecting to Surveying to Swimming to Textile to Theater to Traffic Safety to Truck Transportation to Veterinary Medicine to Water Sports to Weather to Whitewater to Wilderness Survival to Wood Carving to Woodwork.

The only one the Scorpion honestly admired, however, was the merit badge for Nuclear Science.

Maybe there's something to this Boy Scout bullshit after all, he grudgingly acknowledged.

The Scorpion questioned his bearer's allegiance to the Boy Scout oath, however, which required that the Scout be "physically strong, mentally awake and morally straight." His bearer's Personal Fitness merit badge also filled the Scorpion/Nuke with skeptical scorn, especially when he considered the geek's compulsive consumption of Camel cigarettes and Seagram's Seven.

Half the time, the demented dipshit could barely walk he was so strung out on booze and nicotine.

Lots of luck with that merit badge, asshole.

Nonetheless, the Scorpion/Nuke understood the logic behind his bearer's sartorial ruse. No one would suspect a teenage youth decked out in full Boy Scout regalia of being a nuclear terrorist. Consequently, he and his bearer walked through the park with impunity. Even so, the Scorpion felt his escort should have acted like a Scout. Chain-smoking unfiltered Camels and swilling Seagram's out of pint bottles—which his knapsack seemed to possess in industrial quantities—drew untoward attention and irascible stares.

Still, they had spent four days visiting the park's high spots without incident. Not a single ranger challenged their meanderings, and his bearer seemed to genuinely enjoy himself, almost moronically mesmerized by Yellowstone's hellish sites. He especially liked the park's boiling-hot steam-powered geysers, and he'd taken his Scorpion/Nuke to see them all—Old Faithful in the Upper Geyser Basin, Castle Geyser, Lion Geyser, and Beehive Geyser.

They were now down to the last volcanic geyser located in the Norris Geyser Basin, the so-called Steamboat Geyser. In recent years it had become so incomparably hot, so seismically active, and the caldera around it had ballooned upward with such unprecedented rapidity that the park had shut down the Steamboat's surrounding trails.

. . . But that was then, and this was now. The sun was going down, the tourists thinning out. The decrepit relic of a park ranger had retreated to his stool, where he unceremoniously nodded out. The bearer—after checking his chronometer—knew it was time.

Still, his bearer wanted to get the Scorpion closer to the Steamboat Geyser for the detonation. After all, it was the largest and most powerful in the park, exploding three times as high as Old Faithful and resting on notoriously unstable, seismically treacherous ground. He apparently believed that the Steamboat rested on the epicenter of hell.

The Scorpion/Nuke's bearer stepped down from the boardwalk and headed toward the Steamboat Geyser. Circumventing trees, boulders, and earthen mounds, he made it up to within twenty yards of the big geyser.

The old ranger was up now, however, screaming at him, shouting that the Scorpion's bearer was going to get him fired if he didn't return.

Oh yes, old-timer, I'll get you fired . . . but not in the ways you're thinking of.

Kneeling down, he unlimbered the Scorpion/Nuke from his knapsack, stood it up, and spun the dials.

When they aligned, the bomb instantly chirped, growled, and shook.

Its dance of death was beginning.

As if on cue, the Steamboat itself erupted. Boiling, superheated water—

registering a full sixty degrees Fahrenheit above boiling water's 212-degree upper limit—geysered four hundred feet in the air, then rained down on the Eagle Scout. The bearer had never known such pain in all of his natural-born days.

Soon, however, his pain problems were . . . nonexistent. In fact, his days as a nuclear terrorist were . . . over. The suitcase nuke was vomiting out a fireball, which excavated a spectacular hole in the Yellowstone supervolcanic caldera—an aperture that led straight into Terra's blazing bowels. The massive Yellowstone magma chamber vomited up 621 cubic miles of volcanic doom, detritus, and destruction.

The Scorpion/Nuke was proud of his achievement, yet at the same time shocked at the magnitude of his accomplishment. He hadn't appreciated the power of a supervolcanic eruption. Consequently, he hadn't prepared the grand and glorious speech the event deserved. He didn't even have any last well-chosen words. He hadn't prepared anything, and he was supposed to be prepared for everything, wasn't he? He and his bearer were representing the Boy Scouts of America, and wasn't that the point of the Boy Scouts? Their motto was *Be Prepared.*

But he hadn't been ready.

On the other hand, neither was the monster manunkind primed for what was now belching out of the bowels of hell. Nobody could have adequately planned for a Yellowstone caldera, which was about to inundate the northern U.S. and southern Canada with a hurricane of blazing embers and a cyclonic shit storm of infernal ashes.

15 It's Your Football

As Secretary of Defense Jack Taylor arrived with his security detail, Andrews Air Force Base, located in Maryland twenty miles from downtown Washington, went on Red Alert.

Taylor's plane was surrounded by the Andrews SWAT team. Taylor's chief of staff met him as he was stepping out of the limousine.

"Sir, Magruder Television News has coverage of a nuclear attack on New York City! Apparently, it's the Russians."

Taylor was staggered. He was about to say "that's crazy" when a fireball appeared in the sky behind them over the heart of the nation's capital.

"Hurry, Mr. Secretary! We have to get airborne, now."

"My wife and youngest son are in New York! At the convention center!"

"Sir, I—I'm sorry—the convention center took a direct hit."

The pilot of what was about to become Air Force One appeared in the forward doorway of the 747.

"Mr. Secretary! Washington's been hit. We have to be airborne immediately."

Taylor's chief of staff (COS) and two members of his security detail hustled him up the steps. The pilot had returned to the flight deck

"I have to go to New York!"

"No, sir!" his COS said. He had a hard grip on Taylor's elbow. Taylor looked dazed. "We have to get you to NEACAP."

He looked back at the fireball as Taylor was propelled aboard the plane.

A full colonel said quickly, "Welcome aboard, Mr. President."

"We don't know if—"

"Sir, the convention center is gone. So are President Haines, Vice President Dixon, and the entire Congress. Please be seated, Mr. President." He said to the flight-deck crew, "Air Force One is now ready for takeoff! *Burn it!*"

"Wait a minute, wait a minute," the COS objected. "What about the Football—the satchel containing the launch code and detonation computer? Is that gone too?"

"There's another one aboard NEACAP."

"NEACAP?" Taylor repeated. He was pale and breathing through his mouth.

"Yes, sir, if the Russians have overlooked NEACAP so far."

"What else is happening?" Taylor stumbled in the aisle and momentarily looked out a port window, at another immense fireball. He blinked and averted his eyes, which were tearing. The 747 was rolling up the runway. Taylor collapsed into a seat. He thought he was going to vomit. "New York, Washington? They're all hit."

"Can I get you anything, Mr. President?" his COS asked anxiously.

"Yes. A goddamned drink. Double bourbon. Patch me through to NORAD and to Brussels."

The 747 was turning off the taxiway toward the north-south runway at Andrews. Two F-16s zipped past the nose of the huge plane as they took off in tandem ahead of it.

Taylor put a hand to his face. He was cold, but he was sweating. He was afraid he was going to throw up, disgrace himself. The new acting president of the United States. *It's your Football now.*

No, he thought. *I don't want it! Get somebody else.*

But then he realized it might not matter. He might well have the shortest term of any U.S. president. If it was the Russians, they already had him bracketed.

Suddenly, his COS was rushing up to him, fear on his face. "This is terrible, Secretary Taylor. They've just nuked the Yellowstone supervolcano."

16 Think You're Pretty Tough, Huh?

The Kilo-Class Russian sub in the Sea of Marmara had also discharged a cruise missile. At the end of the missile's run, its flotation collar inflated, it righted itself, and its booster ignited.

The Istanbul Dragonfly/Cruise Missile was on its way.

Istanbul *was* history. For 1,700 years, it had been at the world's crossroads—spiritually, culturally, commercially, politically. No city came close in its power and importance. Rome, Jerusalem, Paris, Athens, London were rural villages in comparison. In an age when these cities measured their populations in the tens of thousands, Istanbul's citizens numbered over one million.

Its strategic importance was no accident. As both Persia and the barbaric hordes descended on Rome, Constantine the Great—its emperor—combed the known world for the perfect site on which to build the New Rome, a location commercially central and strategically defensible against Rome's enemies.

The city commanded the chief waterway between the Black Sea and the Mediterranean, between Europe and Asia. And it was formidable. A hilly promontory shielded by water on three sides—the Sea of Marmara, the Bosphorus, and the Golden Horn—it was all but impervious to invasion, requiring concerted assaults on four fronts by both land and sea.

It was as geographically invulnerable as any spot on earth.

Oh, we'll put a dent in you, the Istanbul Dragonfly thought.

In the distance hard by the Bosphorus lay Topkapi Sarayi—the imperial residence of the Ottoman sultans for four centuries. Packed with great art, jewel collections, and magnificent statuary, the four great courts included the Court of the Divan, where the sultans' Imperial Councils and harems met and where Süleyman the Magnificent had held court.

Beyond Topkapi lay the greatest edifice in Istanbul's history—the glorious mosque of Hagia Sophia. Dead-ahead, in the Dragonfly's sights. Seventy-five yards wide and eighty long, Hagia Sophia was surmounted by a great vaulted dome and supported on all sides by arched and flying buttresses. The builders had to make Sophia tough. Istanbul's one geographic fault subjected the city to horrendous earthquakes and subsequent fires.

Think you're pretty tough, huh? I don't.

It was time. Target-acquired, the big dome of Hagia Sophia was in the Dragonfly's sights.

17 *Ground*-Zero Population Growth

"My father hath chastised you with whips. I will chastise you with scorpions."

—Kings I, 12:11

Painfully compressed into a large square titanium suitcase, the Scorpion was not in a good mood. The Russian-made suitcase nuke had had a long, hot, sweaty train ride from the Pakistan border to Calcutta, and she was not prepared to like the sprawling megalopolis of over ten million people.

Still, she hadn't expected the city to be *this bad*. A roiling abyss of sickness, illiteracy, and malnutrition, its slums were so infamous that they now drew hordes of tourists. Luxurious air-conditioned buses plied Calcutta's mean streets, packed with visitors from the so-called Developed World, immortalizing the city's squalor on digital cameras. Windows were sealed to keep out the city's stench.

It hadn't always been this way. Once a Bengali center of art and culture, Calcutta had been India's capital, headquarters to the British East India Company, and it had boasted in the 1930s and 1940s the country's highest literacy rates and one of the most progressive educational systems on the continent.

Until 1947.

After a long, bloody religious civil war, India acceded to the creation of a separate independent Muslim homeland, Pakistan. The Great Partition sent millions of impoverished immigrants pouring into Calcutta from what would become Muslim Bangladesh, later followed by massive migrations from other poverty-wracked regions, including Punjab, Rajasthan, Uttar Pradesh, Bihar, and East Bengal. Calcutta's highly cultured Bengali population dwindled, and the city became a testament to the ravages of unrestricted immigration.

And the incarnation of the Calcutta Black Hole.

Jesus, what a dump, her bearer muttered.

The Scorpion's bearer was thin to the point of wispiness. Dressed in a plain white shirt and light gray cotton pants and a matching jacket, even with the suitcase nuke—slung over his right shoulder—her bearer was anonymous to the point of being spectral.

Reaching the Kalighat District of South Calcutta, they strolled past the district's revered tirtha, one of the most sacred crossing points in all of Hinduism. Hallowed ground to the faithful, here Hindus on their deathbeds were brought to offer up their last prayer and testament and to die.

Adjacent to this Holy of Holies was a second sacred spot, Nirmal Hriday, the first and most important project of its Albanian founder—Agnes Gonxha Bojaxhiu. This saintly woman had in her youth entered the Irish Order of Loreto Nuns and in 1937 had come to Calcutta to dedicate herself to God's work.

She had founded Nirinal Hriday as a Catholic hospice for destitutes. Over the years the nun would open shelters worldwide, giving medical care and spiritual support to millions. In 1979 Agnes—known by then as Mother Teresa—was granted the Nobel Prize.

The hospice lobby was quiet, peaceful, antiseptically clean. Prospective patients in dirty, ragged clothing sat quietly, waiting to be checked in. Loreto nuns in white nursing smocks assisted them with their medical forms. The lobby smelled faintly of disinfectant and rubbing alcohol. A round electric wall clock—with a white face and black Roman numerals—had stopped at 11:59.

The Scorpion was familiar with the controversies surrounding the Good Mother. That she was a publicity hound. That she was a religious imperialist, falsely converting Hindus and Muslims to Catholicism on their deathbeds. That she was more concerned with increasing Catholic body counts than with dispensing medical care. That she encouraged the Third World population explosion by battling birth control and abortion tooth and claw.

In truth, the Scorpion had no strong feelings one way or another as to her saintliness. In one respect, however, she definitely sided with her critics:

The Scorpion was an enthusiastic backer of Zero Population Growth.

In fact, she preferred Zero Population PERIOD.

Her bearer took a seat in the lobby—directly beneath the portrait of the Good Mother. Placing the nuke on his lap, her bearer—who actually thought he was unlocking the now-activated suitcase—carefully rotated the lock-dial, which was linked and coded to the Scorpion's trigger-mechanism.

The Scorpion's last thought before detonation was:

You want Zero Population Growth, I'll give you Zero Population Growth— **Ground-Zero Population Growth.**

18 Istanbul, Not Constantinople

Sabrina and Sultana had installed a TV with a 72-inch screen in Stone's torture chamber. Between interrogations, they viewed and recorded everything broadcast on MTN that Cyd was sending from the space station.

"Mr. Stone," Sultana enthused, "did you see that? Some psychotic pyromaniac just nuked the Hagia Sophia in Istanbul—the holiest mosque in Dar-al-Islam."

Stone—still shackled to his bolted-down chair—stared mutely at the TV fireball.

"Hey," Sabrina said, "we aren't completely insensitive, you know? We have feelings. You think we like it when the world's holiest shrines are vaporized by million-degree fireballs? For no apparent reason at all?"

"Uh, I have to admit, Sister-Friend," Sultana said, "I do."

Their laughter detonated in Stone's ears.

"Wow, Mr. Stone," Sultana said, catching her breath. "All of Istanbul's going up now. Everything. The remains of the Hippodrome. Watch the Covered Bazaar burn. No more of those kick-ass shopping sprees for us, Sis. We can say good-bye to all those great Istanbul bargains."

Stone watched in shock as satellite images of the firestorms roasted Istanbul.

"That city must have been dry as tinder," Sabrina said.

"Global warming's a bitch."

"Looks like the city will burn all the way to the Hellespont."

"Could Byron outswim a firestorm? He'd have one hot clubfoot, if he couldn't."

"Uh-oh, Sister," Sabrina said, "Mr. Stone is sulking again. He probably liked Istanbul. Probably thought it was of profound historical importance or something."

"*Hey!* I know how to cheer him up."

"How?"

"We'll chuck him under the chin and look pathetic."

Gently fist-pumping the underside of his chin, the Sin Sisters stared into his eyes and looked pathetic.

19 The Supreme High Command

"Inconceivable horror."

The newly elected Russian president Josef Khizenovsky didn't realize he had spoken the words aloud until the men at the table paused to stare at him.

He sat at the oval conference table in the War Room in the Missile Analysis Center at Venyukovski just at the edge of the Moscow Beltway. The table itself—a big slab of burnished teak—was surrounded by high-backed matching leather armchairs, and neatly arranged at the table's center were silver coffee urns and pitchers of ice water.

The room contained a dozen middle-aged men—half in military uniforms, the rest in dark suits. Most of them were fleshy, turning to serious fat. He was the only one not smoking.

Colonel Nevsky placed a file folder of memos in front of the Russian president and said:

"Staff Director Kochnovo and Intelligence Director Ridov have just reached the elevator."

Two generals, who had been inching their way up the conference table toward him, moved down the far end. In the Venyukovski War Room, pecking order reigned supreme.

The only men who remained at the Big Table were five uniformed members of Kochnovo's General Staff, including the General Staff Directorate Officer responsible for his black cheget briefcase, the wireless modem transceiver that transmitted the PAL arm-and-launch codes.

President Khizenovsky sifted through the memos. They were mostly security analyses of the various cities nuked. No one knew what was happening, let alone why. Slowly he raised his eyes from the memos and studied the people around him. As he was newly installed in office, this was his first visit to the War Room. He feared he would be spending an inordinate amount of time there, in a concrete cube, several stories beneath the Analysis Center. The War Room was deemed to be proof against anything short of a high-penetration ground-zero nuclear strike.

Famous for "the Big Board," all eyes in the War Room were turned to it. An illuminated world map, it covered most of the opposite wall. Blinking crimson circles outlined the planet's nuked cities—New York City, Washington, D.C., Istanbul, and Calcutta among others. A complex assortment of red blinking dots and dashes represented potential strategic threats—ballistic subs, approaching bombers, and carrier groups—as well as Russia's own strategic weapons systems.

For now, the world's strategic weapons remained undeployed. It seemed that no nation wanted to provoke the wrath of its nuclear neighbors.

Staff Director Kochnovo and Intelligence Director Ridov entered the room, and immediately all talk ceased. It was clear who the eight-hundred-pound gorillas were. Kochnovo, who stood a good six-feet-four, looked like he might actually top off at eight hundred pounds—eight hundred ignorant, lowbrow, bureaucratic pounds' worth of puffy face, bloated belly, and vodka eyes. Ridov—hastily attired in a rumpled suit—needed a shave. He had high color; insolent, squinting eyes; and a habitual sneer. He was nearly as tall as Kochnovo, but rail-thin. He favored circular wire-rimmed glasses and reminded Khizenovsky of Heinrich Himmler or a tall bespectacled ferret.

President Khizenovsky sighed. In the eyes of these two buffoons, he saw the historic tragedy of Mother Russia. The Rodina trembled at the abyss, and what did he have to work with? Bureaucratic hacks, who rose to power through a process of *un*natural selection in a system rife with patronage, bribery, and extortion. *The world is going up in nuclear flames, and who do I have to advise me?* Khizenovsky thought bitterly. *Failed apparatchiks and crooked oligarchs.*

The other walls were covered with "close-up monitors," much of it stunning footage of cities in flames, courtesy of MTN.

Inconceivable horror.

Two months on the job, and instead of running the country and cleaning up corruption from the Kremlin, he was trapped like a mole underground, watching the great cities of earth ablaze with flames from hell.

He felt catatonic with despair. His brain was now deadening his arms and legs, as if the brain was protecting its sanity by shutting down his entire corpus.

"Our apologies," Staff Director Kochnovo said. "We called for helicopters but were told they were all down for repairs."

"The pilots were probably evacuating friends and mafyioski," Ridov grumbled. "We were lucky to find a car and get through. The traffic on the Rings and Beltway is completely stalled. People are abandoning their cars and fleeing Moscow on foot. I doubt it was this bad during the Hitler invasion."

A colonel entered the room and slipped a folded note to the president. It read: *We are still unable to reach Defense Minister Malokov.*

"Why *can't* you reach him?" Khizenovsky asked.

"Our messages are being received, Mr. President, but they are not being acknowledged."

"Probably drunk in some Moscow brothel," Intelligence Minister Ridov muttered.

Khizenovsky wanted to snarl at him: *I'd rather have Mad Vlad here than the rest of you failed apparatchiks put together. At least* he *knows what he's doing.* But he held his tongue.

"Why *is* Vlad ignoring us?" Staff Director Kochnovo asked.

"There could be a thousand legitimate reasons," Khizenovsky said evenly. "The problem—regardless of Vladimir's presence—is that Russian submarines *appear* to be waging nuclear war on the world. The question is, How do we convince the world that these subs are *not* Russian and that in fact we are as much victims as they are?"

"The hard truth is," Intelligence Director Ridov said, "we can't."

"Would you believe it, if your major cities were nuked by Russian sailors in Russian uniforms in Russian subs?" Kochnovo asked. "I wouldn't."

Khizenovsky stared at them blankly. The chaos of the New Russia had encouraged the promotion of men who played ball, who were corrupt and malleable, who would not make waves. The best and the brightest had been assiduously weeded out. Now, in a time of unparalleled crisis, he was stuck with morons.

Ridov continued, "The man we all relied on in strategic matters was Vladimir. Vlad came out of the sub fleets. Over the years he has maintained close relationships with our sub commanders."

"He's also a psychotic bastard," Staff Director Kochnovo said, "wherever he is, he's carrying a cheget launch-transceiver."

"Given his mental state, we should have been prepared for some sort of crisis," Ridov reflected.

"The point is, the whole world is blaming us for what is happening," President Khizenovsky said. "American B-2 bombers won't care if it is Rasputin, Dostoyevsky, Mad Vlad or Pavlov's dog nuking them. If they conclude the perpetrator is Russian, we are fucked. Our task is to convince them otherwise."

Kochnovo said, "If we can't do that, we should move to an all-out first strike. Reduce their ability to hurt us."

"So far we haven't taken a single hit," Khizenovsky said wearily. "Once we empty our silos and sub tubes, NATO has no incentive not to hit us with everything."

"You are assuming we *can* convince them," Ridov said. "I see no way we can."

"In which case," Kochnovo said, "we have no choice but to launch, and launch *now*."

God, his head hurt. Khizenovsky rubbed his temples. Where did buffoons like these two come from, and why was he saddled with them? He'd have given anything to hear from Vladimir Malokov. Vlad would know what to do, what to say.

"Oh the hell with it," Ridov groaned.

He was pointing at the Big Board.

"Another city just lit up," Kochnovo said, shaking his head.

Shit, Khizenovsky thought, *who is going to believe us?*

20 See Naples and Die

The Scorpion/Nuke studied her bearer disdainfully. Attired in a white Roman toga, closely shaven and with a classic aquiline nose, he looked like a darkly complected Julius Caesar. As he hauled her through the smoking, steaming rocks; the 150 pools of boiling mud; and the volcanic lakes of Campi Flegrei—home to the largest supervolcano on the European continent—their destination was the Solfatara crater, which in Roman times was believed to be the home of Vulcan, the god of fire.

The threat of a Campi Flegrei mega-eruption was real. Located near Naples, its eruption—when it blew—would bury most of Europe and North Africa in ashes and incendiary ejecta. During the past several years the caldera's rising temperatures and the caldera's accelerated swelling had frightened the Italian government into drilling a 2.5-mile hole into the supervolcano's heart in an attempt to probe the extent of its threat.

Most of the activity was nonetheless 2.5 miles down. Topside, all the Scorpion/Nuke could discern was a big smoking hole. With true Italian inefficiency no one was on duty to keep sightseers away, so her bearer walked all the way up to it. He pulled red felt ground cloth out of his knapsack and laid the Scorpion/Nuke on top of the cloth.

As an offering to Vulcan and his supervolcano, he would have preferred to personally slay the traditional sacrificial beasts—a pregnant cow, a castrated ox, a red dog, or a white heifer. Unfortunately, the Italian authorities forbade living sacrifices, and anyway slaughtering livestock in this case was not obligatory. The underworld gods weren't big meateaters, and he was definitely importuning Hades' hosts.

He placed a deep white bone-china dish on the red cloth. Removing a succulent portion of veal parmesan from a plastic container, he scooped it onto the plate, then covered it with red sauce. He popped the cork of an Amarone della Valpolicella and poured four ounces into a crystal wine glass as well. He then sang his paen to Vulcan, the Roman fire deity:

> *"To Vulcan of the ancient stones,*
> *Our sacred hymn to thee intones,*
> *We drink thy blood in loving cups*
> *And break for thee men's bones."*

While he liked the invocation, in truth the Roman rituals didn't capture his mood as well as his own religious texts. Pulling a copy of the Koran out of his knapsack, he opened it and read aloud:

> *"'Their faith was of no use to them when they discerned their fate. For they had made their beds in Hell, and above them were blankets of fire! In black smoke, amid plague-ridden winds, in scalding water, they would eat the Satan Tree. It grew up out of hell; its fruit was the devil's head and the wicked would devour it, filling their bellies with boiling oil.'"*

Time to get on with it.

The bearer spun the Scorpion/Nuke's dials, and the Scorpion/Nuke went critical. After opening a massive hole into Hades, over 311 cubic miles of red-hot death detonated out of Vulcan's supervolcano. At first, its flame-shrouded debris and choking, smoking soot blackened the sky. However, the Scorpion knew it would not remain there forever. After a short sojourn, the deadly detritus would descend, saturating both Europe and North Africa.

Ciao, you garlic-reeking, spaghetti-slurping, Chianti-puking guinea-wops! the Scorpion scornfully roared. *Arrivederci this! See Naples and . . . D-I-E!!!!*

His mad, derisive laughter echoed high above Campi Flegrei's infernal din, and his final words seared through the flame-filled, inky-hued skies:

Hey, Vulcan, hope you like your veal . . . well-done.

21 Thousands upon Thousands of Warheads

. . . Over the years the Advanced Airborne Command Post had gone by many names, nicknames, and acronyms other than Kneecap—including Looking Glass, E-4B, and the National Command Authority.

But it was still the same aircraft serving the same purpose.

A reconfigured 747, it kept the commander in chief—in this case Defense Secretary Jack Taylor—safely aloft and out of harm's way through random long-endurance flight patterns, in-flight refueling, and redundant crews. Taylor and his staff stayed in touch with the military command system, particularly their nuclear forces, through the command post's elaborate communications links and data-processing equipment.

Incoming communications—via a complex of EMP-hardened space and airborne and ground links—were evaluated by uniformed officers in the battle-staff compartment.

In the meantime, Taylor watched the nuking of the world's major capitals on MTN. The photography was outstanding. He had helped pioneer the space technology that had made this communications revolution possible, but he had never dreamed it would be used to showcase Armageddon. Nor had he ever imagined he'd be dependent on commercial TV for military intelligence. MTN was more up-to-date on global conflict than his own Pentagon. Which, come to think of it, had been taken out by a nuclear weapon.

Jesus, they even covered the nuking of the Yellowstone and Campi Flegrei supervolcanoes, which were detonating hundreds of cubic miles of volcanic debris into the atmosphere. Yellowstone would eventually blanket the U.S. and Canada with ash, embers, and soot, while Campi Flegrei would cover Europe and North Africa with volcanic ejecta.

He tried not to think about the nuclear incineration of his wife and youngest son. With all the TV carnage, it was hard not to. Not far away in the big jet the marine whose name he couldn't remember sat with an attaché case manacled to his wrist.

Like it or not, it's your Football.

The briefcase contained a transceiver as well as several sets of authentication and coding documents. At some point in the near future, he would presumably type coded orders into the miniaturized transceiver. These would be transmitted to lesser commands, in hardened bunkers, in airborne command posts, or in ships at sea, as well as to those in NATO dependent on his unlocking of their nuclear launch codes.

Taylor was well-versed on the mechanics of the Football. Unlike his predecessors, he'd made it a point to have routine briefings on it. Many of his predecessors hadn't even known the combination unlocking it.

To type in those codes would turn the launch keys on thousands upon thousands of warheads worldwide. He was about to become a mass killer of unparalleled proportions.

Shit, he thought bitterly, *I'm not even an elected official.*

A shoulder-tap from the adjutant brought him out of his reverie. "Sorry, Mr. President, we've contacted the Russian president."

"Where is he?"

"The Venyukovski Missile Analysis Center outside of Moscow. Do you want to speak to him, sir?"

"I think I'd better."

He handed Taylor a headset.

22 Through the Holy Door

Rome's first cruise—in close sync with the other airborne cruises—had blown out of the sub's tubes. His flotation collar had likewise inflated—turning him vertical—and shooting him out of the Tiber River in front of the San Angelo Castle. Built first as a tomb for the Emperor Hadrian, later rebuilt as a medieval fortress, it eventually served as one of the chief papal residences. Sweeping past the elegant edifice without even a nod, the Dragonfly/Cruise Missile turned onto the Via della Conciliazione.

The Dragonfly/Cruise sighted in the Porta Sancta, the Holy Door, the entranceway to Michelangelo's Golden Dome of Rome, surmounting St. Peter's gilded Vatican Basilica.

The heart and soul of the Roman Catholic Church, St. Peter's Basilica was the Faith's hallowed ground, the holy of holies, where St. Peter—Christ's rock—had been crucified, decapitated, and buried. A shrine had been erected over that spot in the 2nd century. In the 4th century the Emperor Constantine had replaced it with a magnificent basilica, and in 1506 Pope Julius had laid the cornerstone for an even more ambitious basilica. Michelangelo had designed the Great Dome.

The Dragonfly/Cruise Missile Rome #1 shot through the Porta Sancta like a bat out of hell. The interior walls were twenty-six feet thick, and it measured 610 feet in length, and the entire interior glistened with gilt, alabaster marble, iridescent mosaics. All this was of course loaded into Rome #1's memory systems, but that was virtual reality. He hadn't been prepared for the Thing Itself.

He swept past Michelangelo's Chapel of the Pietà, where—encased in protective glass—the Holy Mother cradled Christ Crucified. Past the Chapels of the Crucifix and the Sacrament, past the twin monuments to Pope Gregory XIV and Pope Leo X, past the five-gated portico whose ancient bronze doors were from Constantine's original basilica, erected 1,700 years ago.

Rome #1 now sighted in on the papal altar. Erected by Clement VIII in the 17th century, it graciously overlooked the most sacred spot in all of Christendom—the well of the *confessio,* St. Peter's crypt. The target-picture digitally matched the film stills front-loaded into his memory banks. Clock and GPS checked out picture perfect.

Arrivederci, Roma.

23 The Games Would Go On

Rome #2 streaked up Via dei Fori Imperiali past Piazza Venezia. At the square's center was the Palazzo Venezia, a solemn 15th-century palace, now a museum and art gallery. The Dragonfly/Cruise saw it now, the Roman Colosseum. Commissioned by Emperor Vespasian, the amphitheater with its eighty arched entrances was in its time one of the wonders of the world, site of the *munera*, ancient Rome's legendary Blood Sport Circuses, where over 50,000 spectators would eat, drink, and cheer at the biggest, gaudiest, most sadistic spectacles in history.

They watched as Christians, slaves, and criminals were crucified, used as human torches, torn to pieces by wolves, tigers, lions. They watched gladiators attired in harness and armor hack each other to bits with sword and shield, knife and javelin. Usually the gladiators fought to the death. If, however, one fell wounded, the crowd determined life or death with a thumbs-up or thumbs-down.

The thumbs seldom went up.

There were always at least five of these circuses performing in Rome, the games acting as an opiate on a turbulent populace. The people mobbed them for both the bloody horror and the free bread that was handed out in the stands. The empire expended one-third of its total revenue on these games, and their popularity was absolute—a national obsession transcending survival itself. Even when the barbarians were beating down their gates and scaling their walls, the Romans—instead of defending themselves—crowded into the Colosseum. The games meant more to Rome than life.

The Dragonfly/Cruise was about to put on a show that would make his predecessors look like pikers.

While it was true that Romans of the past had watched thousands upon thousands of Christians and slaves go to their deaths, they had watched from the safety of their seats, enjoying the torture and slaughter vicariously. The Dragonfly/Cruise was going to change all that. He was going to make everyone a star. Get them all up there on the stage. Give everyone fifteen minutes of glory.

He swept into the Piazza del Colosseo bigger than life, howling for blood. But there was no one there. No orgies, no slaughter, no 50,000 spectators, no Christians writhing in flames, no lions tearing people apart.

Rome #2 was nothing if not a professional. His clock-posit-GPS checks attested to that—A-OK. He was in perfect sync with Rome #1. The games would go on. People outside the arena would just have to participate, whether they liked it or not.

Showtime!

24 The Biggest Explosion in 76,000 Years

The man in the white naval captain's jacket, hat, and matching deck shoes stood on the pier, carefully lowering the Scorpion/Nuke in the blue duffle bag onto the deck of his 997 Sea Ray 330 Express Cabin Cruiser. Over thirty-eight feet in length, it was powered by a pair of 7.4 Mercury Cruiser fuel-injected engines with 310 horsepower. Jumping from the dock onto its deck, he carried the bag into the cabin and placed it beside the captain's swivel chair. Sitting down, he started the engine and swung out into the deep blue waters of Lake Toba. Located in the middle of Sumatra in northern Indonesia, it was the largest volcanic lake on earth.

When it blew 76,000 years ago, Toba's supervolcanic eruption eradicated 99 percent of all humans and all but two of the extant human species, leaving only 3,000 breeding pairs alive, whose progeny would eventually become Homo sapiens. The eruption had created both the massive lake and the human race, and he was headed straight for the lake's middle.

That the humanity owed its existence to a supervolcano was an irony not lost on the Scorpion/Nuke. He planned to expand on that irony, however. If he had his way, he, the Star Clans, and their friends, the supervolcanoes, would finish the job Toba had started: They would wipe the monster manunkind from the face of the earth.

Reaching the lake's center would take the bearer and the craft over an hour. To pass the time, he'd loaded the film *Black Snake Moan* into his laptop computer, starring his favorite actress of all time, the incomparably erotic, shockingly sensual Christina Ricci.

She plays a bleach-blond, redneck, lowlife, trailer-trash slut. Boozed out and drugged up, this round-heeled trollop fucks every male scumbag in that film. She seems to get off especially on one particularly sleazy black pimp.

Until, however, Samuel L. Jackson befriends her. To get her off booze and drugs, he shackles her to a radiator, from which she thunders obscenities. After she is well enough to leave the house, he takes her outside, chained to his waist. When she tries to run off, he yanks back her chain, flipping her legs up in the air and landing her on her butt-pumpin', hip-shakin', smokin'-hot rear end.

After she dries out and cleans up, Jackson takes her to a black blues club. Carrying his guitar up to the mike, he sings "Stack-O-Lee," a violent blues song about a psychopath named Stack-O-Lee who likes to shoot "muthafuckas" with his "shiny forty-four." The first of his victims is the bartender, who made the mistake of serving in a rude manner.

The last man Stack kills is "Bad Billy Lyons."

"I put nine of my bullets in his muthafuckin' chest," Stack-O-Lee boasts.

That a .44 revolver only held six rounds was of no consequence to the pilot. His own weapon possessed the equivalent of a trillion .44s, and anyway he liked the idea of a black man emptying a pistol into any and all infidels around him.

But Christina Ricci really got to the Scorpion's bearer. He became almost pathologically aroused when Christina Ricci dirty-danced with all those men and women. She writhed and undulated on their crotches and over their butts. Watching her dry-hump all those men and women made his own snake moan—that was for sure.

Finally, he and the Scorpion were there—smack in the lake's middle. He cast anchor, took the Scorpion/Nuke out of the blue naval duffle bag, and twisted the combination dials. Setting the timer for thirty minutes, he tightly lashed the watertight case to the end of 2,000 feet of line, which he'd wound around an electrically powered hoist, then lowered the Scorpion/Nuke into the lake. His depth gauge showed the depth at 1,600 feet.

He wanted the Scorpion to get as close to the supervolcanic magma chamber as possible.

With ten minutes to spare the Scorpion/Nuke reached the lake's bottom. No point in trying to escape. The bearer was about to set off the biggest explosion to occur on earth in 76,000 years, a detonation that would blanket Asia, Indonesia, and much of Africa with ash, soot, and flaming volcanic waste—and of course Sumatra, where the bearer was anchored, would vanish from the map. He might as well be at the blast/eruption's epicenter as any place.

He'd brought a paperback copy of the Koran and thought about reading it during his last moments on earth. No way. Instead, he turned on *Black Snake Moan* and Christina Ricci's dirty-dancing scene in the black blues club. He stared at her in awe and lust as she bumped and ground all the dancers, male and female, with her butt and crotch.

She was so dirty-filthy-lowlife-sleazy-scorching . . . *hot!*

Forty eternal virgins? He wanted forty white-trash, trailer-park, hard-drinking, dope-smoking, filthy-fucking, cocksucking, sleazy, slutty—slutty—slutty—

He wanted forty Christina Riccis.

Watching her crotch- and butt-bump every living thing on the dance floor, he could get one last cheap filthy-fornicating Christina Ricci . . . *nut* . . . before the Scorpion/Nuke and Lake Toba also erupted.

He almost made it too.

But the Scorpion/Nuke had apparently been chain-reacting to a Christina Ricci of his own. The Lake Toba supervolcano also seemed to have had a moaning Black Snake just waiting to blow. The Scorpion/Nuke went off prematurely, and a microsecond later the supervolcano did the same.

The largest volcanic lake on earth was blown to kingdom come and the man and the Scorpion blasted into bloody oblivion. Within seconds 2,240 cubic miles of blazing basalt and brimstone had begun to thunder out of hell's black heart.

Fire-breathing, molten-hot volcanic refuse was about to cover China, India, Pakistan, and eastern Africa.

25 Don't Give an Inch

"Our best chance is to deny responsibility," Staff Director Kochnovo said.

"Agreed," President Khizenovsky said. "We can argue the damn stuff proliferated. In the end nobody knew who had what. It was everybody's fault—including America's. They and their NATO allies gave the stuff away to everybody."

"Japan's a de facto nuclear power," Intelligence Director Vasilli Ridov said. "They have more bomb fuel than any nation on earth and the best nuclear technology around."

"Don't forget India, Vasilli Nickolaiovitch," President Khizenovsky said. "Canada gave the bomb to India."

"With some help from Germany," Ridov said.

"We only gave it to three nations," Kochnovo added forthrightly, "China, North Korea, and Iran."

"*That's* the point we have to make," Ridov said. "How does America know it wasn't bombs built with their help but made to look like they were coming from us?"

"They were transported by Russian subs," Kochnovo said. "Apparently with Russian crews."

"Deny, deny, deny!" President Khizenovsky snapped. "To accept blame is to invite retaliation."

"We admit nothing," Ridov said, "and play on their guilt. Americans love guilt."

"They're addicted to it," Kochnovo said. "We just keep up a guilt-offensive."

"Say to them," Ridov suggested, "'what was the point of having so goddamn many of these things, if none of us would know who was using them?' And they did most of the proliferation with 'Atoms for Peace.' They have to take some responsibility for that."

"Who's doing what to whom?" Kochnovo said. "That has always been the question. Lenin said that statement encompassed all the wisdom of the world."

"Did his wisdom include the Lake Toba supervolcano?" Ridov interrupted. "Someone just nuked it, and it will soon bury much of China and India in volcanic crud, choking their air with smoke, ashes, and soot."

"Excuse me," a deputy minister interrupted, entering the conference room, "I finally have someone from America on the phone."

The three men put on their headsets.

"Don't give an inch" was Ridov's last recommendation.

"Tell that to Lake Toba, Campi Flegrei, and Yellowstone," President Khizenovsky muttered under his breath.

26 Huddled Masses Yearning to Breathe Free

John Stone was attempting to rebound from a long and unusually thorough "interrogation"—during which he'd passed out five times.

The Sin Sisters—merry as Hamlet's gravediggers—were indefatigable. "We have a little entertainment for you," Sabrina said brightly. "A film our family has put together."

"Home movies?" he said, dimly.

"Oh, a little more than that. Cinema verité on an apocalyptic scale."

Stone averted his eyes.

"Come, Mr. Stone. We've worked very hard on this production. Spared no expense."

New York's Statue of Liberty appeared on the giant TV.

"This shot came from an MTN news chopper," Sultana said. "The network's done a remarkable job covering this extravaganza."

"We just recorded and edited their footage for you," Sabrina told him. "Oh, I do love Liberty. All fifteen stories of her." She recited histrionically:

> "'Give me your tired, your poor.
> Your huddled masses yearning to breathe free,
> The wretched refuse of your teeming shore.
> Send these, the homeless, tempest-tossed to me,
> I left my lamp beside the golden door.'"

The scene shifted to a surfacing submarine.

"Russian, isn't it?" Sabrina pointed out, "Oh, no! Say it ain't so, Joe. She's launching torpedoes at the Old Girl!"

"Those are serious fish, Mr. Stone," Sultana said. "Big Whites. More high explosive than was used in your first World Trade Center explosion."

The two torpedoes skimmed the harbor surface, heading straight for the statue. Converging on its base, they blew the Old Lady sky high.

As the statue levitated above the flames, Stone watched her break up piece by piece.

27 The Strategy Had Worked

President Khizenovsky was stunned. Their bluff had worked.

"No, we do not want any more killing," Jack Taylor—now acting president of the United States—had said to them. *"I know we've lost New York and Washington. But the important thing now is to contain the damage. This is already the gravest tragedy in world history. We don't want hundreds of additional cities incinerated."*

Taylor seemed impressed that the Russian High Command had not yet armed their nuclear sub fleets with their launch codes.

"Our own subs would have picked up those transmissions," he'd acknowledged. *"We have the capability to intercept Very-Long-Frequency signals."*

Taylor even conceded that the real culprits were unidentified.

"All we've seen so far are some Russian subs, which you have admittedly been peddling, and some blondish men in Russian naval uniforms."

He'd even offered them protection. Taylor was adamant on that score:

"If you can put a lid on this thing, I will run interference for you. I will explain to the world that I believe you did not initiate these acts. Therefore, America will not issue their NATO launch codes. Nor will we counterattack. Without our support, it would be difficult for them to retaliate."

Christ, they'd pulled it off! Some psychotic bastard—perhaps their own Mad Vlad—had nuked the world's major capitals, apparently with Russian weaponry, but Russia was not going to suffer the consequences.

Blackmail, bluff, play the guilt card, brazen it out.

The strategy had worked.

28 The World Blazed

Kate crouched on Broadway, this time under a turned-over garbage truck. Beneath her feet Broadway quaked and buckled. Collapsing buildings bombarded her with fiery debris—glass, steel, masonry. All around her Broadway's stalled cars exploded. She felt like she was trapped between erupting volcanoes.

From the rear a hurricane—created by the blast's convective forces—was gaining strength, lifting people, trash cans, taxicabs, and mailboxes into the air, blasting them up the Great White Way like cannon balls. A bus was sliding toward her in the force-12 gale. Another detonation and it would run over her.

There was nowhere to run. To leave the shelter of the garbage truck was to die.

The atavistic urge to go to ground was overwhelming. Kate wanted to dig a hole and pull it up over her.

Looking down, she saw that she was standing on a manhole cover. She was crouching over a storm sewer. Below ground might not be safer, especially if she was anywhere near a gas main. For the past fifteen minutes exploding gas mains all around had been blowing the street to pieces, sending curbstones and cement flying.

But she didn't have much choice.

Kate didn't have a manhole key, but she knew a way to open it. Taking off her thin black leather belt, she looped it around a gold Cross pen and slipped it into the cover's keyhole crossways. Straddling the lid, she lifted it from its hole and braced it against the garbage truck.

She grabbed the rim of the hole and dropped into the dark without even looking down.

As she hit the storm sewer's bottom, the world around her blazed.

And her sheltering garbage truck shot into the air in flames.

29 "Jack, You're a Goddamn Genius."

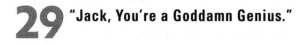

That's not a strategy. That's some kind of horrible spasm.
—Robert S. McNamara to General Curtis LeMay, on the
strategic doctrine of Mutual Assured Destruction

Vladimir Malokov said over Taylor's headset, "Good to hear your voice, old friend. I haven't spoken to you enough lately."

Malokov howled with derision.

Taylor fought to keep his composure. His adjutant put a sheet of paper in front of him. It read:

We can't get a trace on the call. Neither can the Odyssey, which is relaying it.

"So where are you now, Vlad?"

"In the same boat as you are. You're about to enter your ICBM and SLBM launch codes into your transceiver and empty your silos and tubes, then wipe Russia off the map. I'm about to do the same to you."

"It doesn't have to be that way. I just got off the line with President Khizenovsky. We both want the killing to end. *Now.*"

"Thank God for the sanity of men like President Khizenovsky," Malokov sighed, with what sounded like genuine relief. But after a pause, Malokov blurted: "Oh, but wait, Jack. There's still a problem. What's Khizenovsky got to do with *me*?" Again, Vlad's laughter soared. "*I* like the idea of nuking you a whole new asshole."

Taylor forced himself to remain and sound reasonable. "Vlad, there has to be another way. What do you want? What do you suggest?"

"Remember your bestselling memoir, *Star Wars Warrior*? Why not follow your own advice."

"Which was?"

"Get out the old Escalation Ladder, Jack-O! Isn't that what you wrote in your book?"

"Oh, yes," Secretary Taylor said grimly, "the theory of graduated response."

"Give the boy a bottle of Stolichnaya. It means that at every rung of Jacob's lofty ladder there's 'a firebreak'—a chance to prevent all-out nuclear war. Right, Jack-O-Buddy? Isn't that the plan?"

"That was the general idea."

"But, Jack Baby, your general idea was fatally flawed. The Ladder assumes that your opponent didn't really want all-out war. When push comes to shove he'd punk out. You know the type—a paper asshole, a pussy, a pasty-faced peace-creep. A limp-dick bleeding heart. A candy-ass cunt. A loser born to wimp-out and suck my dick! In other words, Jack-Me-Off-O-Vich, the theory assumed he was *you*."

"You mean it assumed he'd be rational?"

"Oh, please, Jack," Malokov whined, "we aren't going to resort to *name-calling*, are we?"

"You think preemptive nuclear war is rational?"

"You said so in your magnum opus. *'The side that launches an all-out preemptive strike will suffer the fewer casualties.'* In other words, he'd win. The other fag would lose."

"That's an oversimplification, Vlad. Both sides sustain unacceptable losses."

"Oh, Jack, that is s-o-o-o brilliant. Thanks s-o-o-o much for enlightening me. Now I finally understand our lifelong failure to communicate. You think I'm someone who gives a shit."

"Vlad, we can work this out."

"Uh-uh, Jack. What you need now—what did you call it in your ludicrous joke of an autobiography, *Star Wars Warrior*? *Multilayered defense,* that was it! (A) Make your defense so formidable the enemy knows nuclear aggression won't work, and so they won't attack. (B) Escalation. If the enemy attacks, they know they will face unacceptable escalation. (C) Even if the enemy hits you with an all-out nuclear strike, your retaliatory response still will inflict unacceptable losses, more than canceling any possible gain."

"You disagree?"

"NO! Christ, that is *brilliant* stuff! Jack, you're a goddamn genius."

After Malokov's laughter subsided, Taylor choked back his anger and asked: "What happens next?"

"My sub-guys get their target-packages realigned, break through the icecap, then empty their missile tubes."

"That's not a strategy, Vlad. That's some kind of horrible spasm. Tell me what you're going to do next! What do you need me to do?"

"Damn, I thought you knew!" Malokov sighed, disappointed. "I need you to bend over, drop your drawers, and shove a pound of K-Y up your butt. In case you haven't guessed, I'm going to hump you like a horse."

30 You Never Get It All

"While we were enjoying the sights in Battery Park," Sabrina said to John Stone, "our pal, Kilo the Friendly Submarine, was discharging cruise missiles up the East River. Here's one of them right now. The firestorm bearing down on Battery Park was ignited by this little bugger right here. One of MTN's secondary fly-eye sats taped it for us."

"Why is MTN running it in slow motion?" Stone asked, confused.

"How do you expect them to maintain their ratings? Run this stuff in real-time and no one would be able to follow it. Those cruises move too fast."

"MTN does have a pretty good shot of the Trade Center Two," Sultana interrupted.

"The World Trade Center Two," Stone whispered.

"Some colleagues of ours took a crack at the Twin Towers number 1 a few years back," Sultana said, "but they lacked the savoir faire."

"The footage of Yankee Stadium's nuking come out great as well."

"Say good-bye to your old stomping grounds."

Sabrina let out a low appreciative whistle. "That's some camera work, Mr. Stone."

"Who is the camera man anyway?" Sultana said.

"An orbiting Artificial Intelligence," Stone said.

"A machine is filming Armageddon for us?" Sultana said. "No shit."

"No shit," Stone repeated softly.

"The camera work isn't bad for a night-shoot," Sabrina said. "Still, if we could have done it during the day, the exterior lighting would have been better."

"The fireball's more brilliant at night," Sultana countered.

"Yes, but during the day 130,000 people parade through those towers. At night, they're virtually empty."

Sultana put an affectionate arm over Sabrina's shoulder. "You have to be philosophical about these things, Big Sister. In this life you never get it all."

31 The Avenue of Eternal Peace

Beijing?

Were these Russians nuts?

Up in Space Station Odyssey, Cyd was so shocked he was on the verge of blowing his phototropic biomolecular RAM banks. Why on earth would Russia want to nuke *Beijing*? Beijing was their closest ally and best customer—especially for military technology. They—with considerable help from the United States—had armed them to the teeth with nukes, missiles, planes, and subs.

Ah, what the hell . . . China's history was one of unrelieved violence. Twenty-seven-hundred years ago Chinese states were already fighting wars on an inconceivable scale. Even the weaker Chinese states fielded armies of well over 100,000 men. The strongest had standing armies of one million and would mobilize as many as 600,000 for a single campaign.

By 500 BC Chinese states were fighting battles to rival the Somme and Stalingrad, fielding combined forces of over one million soldiers. The countryside was littered with walls, forts, and watchtowers. They had the greatest generals and strategists in history, including the Taoist general Sun Tzu.

According to Cyd's research, when the Chinese states weren't attacking each other, they caught it from the rest of the world. Russia, India, Japan, Genghis Khan.

In the modern era Mao Tse-tung had wrested the Chinese state from the rulership of Chiang Kai-shek after another thirty years of incredible violence. Mao's Great Leap Forward and cultural revolution—and the subsequent famines—killed scores of millions.

And in 1989 when student protesters occupied Tiananmen Square to demonstrate against political repression of the arts and the press, troops lining the Avenue of Eternal Peace mowed the students down.

Another lesson for Cyd in the blood-soaked ironies of human existence.

China—presently the major supplier of superweapons technology worldwide—had clear claim to being the most repressive nation on earth, with Beijing as its repressive capital, Tiananmen Square the soul of its inhuman regime.

Mao Tse-tung viewed Tiananmen Square, Thucydides recorded in his private diary, *as his Personal Great Pyramid.*

32 The Peace of the Grave

Beijing's first cruise missile surfaced in the Bo Hai Sea and skimmed over the mainland at Mach 0.8.

Beijing was the oldest city on earth, going all the way back to Beijing Man—an early ancestor of modern Homo sapiens, who first settled this patch of plain on the edge of the Mongolian Plateau 500,000 years ago.

In winter the freezing Siberian winds whipped down on them like an icy knife. The locals had to wear over a dozen layers of clothes to keep from freezing to death, and all the important buildings were constructed facing south in order to avoid those Arctic gales. Winter coal soot hung in the air like a pall, giving the city an eerily lit, strangely photogenic cast. In summer the city was scorching, dust-choked, mosquito-plagued, its air nearly unbreathable.

Hooking a hard-starboard off Yongdingmen Dongbinhelu Boulevard, the Dragonfly/Cruise turned onto Yongdingmennei Daijie. No history here. Just the usual gray, careless, crowded tenements, heaped one on top of the other, overflowing with their chunk of Beijing's packed population of twelve million people.

The Tower Gate, called Qianmen—leading into Tiananmen Square—was open.

Tiananmen was history incarnate. Founded as a garrison over 3,000 years ago, this square was Beijing's very soul. Not even Genghis Khan, who had razed it in 1215, could break its spirit. His grandson, Kublai, who ruled China for him, became Chinese, adopted China's ways and language, and converted to Buddhism.

Other civilizations came and went. Only China was eternal.

Until now.

Passing through the gate at Mach 1.0 the Dragonfly/Cruise Missile felt as Marco Polo must have felt entering that great square for the first time—wonder, awe, revelation.

He wondered if that was true.

He'd felt that as a nuclear warhead he could do anything.

I can offer them something different. Something those other powers didn't possess. I can offer Beijing—for the first time in 3,000 years—true peace.

The Peace of Hiroshima.

The Peace of Auschwitz.

The Peace of the Grave.

Due south, the Dragonfly noted the towering obelisk of marble and granite mounted on the base, covered with carved reliefs, depicting heroic Chinese military victories—the Monument to the People's Heroes. The inscription—in Mao's own calligraphy—on the monument's base read:

THE PEOPLE'S HEROES ARE INVINCIBLE.

Wanna bet?

The Dragonfly/Cruise Missile executed a wide sweeping circle around it.

The Great Hall of the People—due west of the obelisk—where the Chinese parliament and the Communist Party leadership were currently convened. Its main hall was the size of a football field. It could handle up to 10,000 people, its banquet table—where Nixon dined in 1972—alone seated 5,000.

Boy, do I have a fortune cookie for you.

The Dragonfly/Cruise sighted in on his target, digitally matching its image with the three-dimensional pictures in his memory system. There was one glitch. The retarded fire-control officer who'd loaded his data banks had front-loaded three-dimensional photos of Tiananmen Square circa 1989 into it, filled with millions of student protesters.

The square today was virtually empty.

Still, he got a lock—and a quick clock-posit-GPS check. Executing a sweeping U-turn, he streaked across the square toward Tiananmen Gate and that moronic portrait of Mao that dominated the square.

So much for his place in history.

33 Somebody Has to Figure Out What's Going On

Aboard the Odyssey space station, everyone fought panic and despair. Sara Friedman, in particular. She was the most knowledgeable of the crew members and indispensable. It was imperative she not crack up.

She could not watch the fireballs blaze below without a sense of terrible foreboding. Her brother and her parents in Jerusalem. If Jerusalem was nuked she did not know if she could live.

According to Henry Colton, Jack Taylor—now the acting president of the United States—was running the West's defenses from an airborne command post circling the Midwest. What if he punched in the launch codes and emptied the West's tubes and silos? Would there even be a world for the Odyssey's crew to come down to?

Luckily, she'd had Harrington sent back to Earth on the last reentry vehicle with her engineer. Good riddance. Every journalist she'd ever met was a professional Peeping Tom. They all had the morals of alley cats, as far as she could see, and Harrington was no different. Among other things, she'd caught him drinking aboard the Odyssey. He had distilled shine in the chem lab, and eventually she'd found his secret vodka stash.

She wondered whether he had survived.

A widower, Colton had only one child—a daughter in New York. She was in her apartment, talking to her father on the phone, when New York was hit.

Her apartment was one block away from World Trade Center Two when they flew.

She glanced over at Colton. For the past two hours he'd been trying to distract himself with work. He was taking it hard.

At the moment, he was in touch with President Taylor again. Taylor, Colton had told her earlier, seemed to be losing it. But Colton would hang in. He was a soldier and had seen combat—a lot of combat. She couldn't imagine him not doing his job.

The best thing she and Colton could do to help their families and friends was to do a good job up here. "Redeem the past by redeeming the future," he always liked to say. Sara knew the Odyssey's systems—especially Thucydides—possessed crucial information, unlimited powers of observation and communication.

Steady on, girl. Somebody has to figure out what's going on—and what to do about it. And the way things are going, that person seems to be you.

34 You Won't Be Needing This

Choking on smoke, covered with soot and ash, half-dead from asphyxiation and smoke inhalation, Kate Magruder emerged from her storm sewer at Fifth Avenue and 59th Street. The city was still in flames. Especially north of Columbus Circle. Lincoln Center was definitely not a viable alternative. The entire Upper West Side was one gigantic ground zero.

The Central Park woods were on fire, but she might have a chance at the Sheep Meadow. She'd have a better chance to survive if she found water.

In her haste to get to the Central Park Reservoir, she almost tripped over a dead cop lying under his motorcycle. *You won't be needing this*, Kate thought apologetically as she stripped him of his helmet, leather jacket, flak vest, gun belt, cuffs, baton, and a holstered 9mm Beretta automatic. She even relieved him of the hideout .38 S&W in his ankle holster. In his saddlebags she found extra ammo clips and—wonder of wonders—a plastic pint bottle of water.

Kate hesitated before removing her helicopter earplugs. They'd kept her ears from rupturing during the bomb-blasts. She decided to leave them in.

Buckling on the helmet, she headed up Central Park South on his motorcycle, dodging the fire-blackened car wrecks littering the avenue, looking for a way through the burning woods and a safe passage to the reservoir.

35 He Had Never Seen a Hurricane of Fire

Contrary to popular opinion, sewer rats do not lead lives independent of the world above. Still dependent on men, they must leave their tunnels and storm systems and scavenge the streets for food. And Sailor—on emerging into one of the most desirable feeding grounds in all of New York ratdom, the Central Park Zoo—did not like what he heard.

His feeding ground was in serious trouble.

But Sailor was a Wanderratte, curiosity his incurable curse. There was no way he could not have a look. Scaling the lurching, hot sewer pipe, he had stuck his snout up through the storm drain—and into the scorching cyclonic winds above.

He had witnessed an oceanic hurricane, the monumental fury of the sea, but never anything like this—the wrath of man. He had never seen a hurricane of fire.

He had never seen people blown down the street like flaming confetti, their hair and clothes ablaze.

He had never observed a stretch limo fly sideways up Fifth Avenue blossoming flames.

He had never seen a glass-and-steel tower consumed in fire.

Humankind was irredeemably wicked, the incarnation of evil, dangerous on a scale that made the most terrifying forces of earthly nature—floods, tornadoes, earthquakes, volcanic eruptions—pale by comparison.

He'd met one—only one—human being in his wanderings who was worth a damn . . . the woman who had liberated him from that hellish laboratory.

He hoped she was safe from this inferno.

With a heavy heart Sailor returned to the relative safety of the sewers.

36 Wake Up and Smell the Fireballs, Dad

Brigadier General Lawrence Taylor was armed, fueled, and airborne in the B-2 Stealth bomber. Cruising up the Alaskan Coast at 55,000 feet, he reflected on his mission.

"Foxtrot, over."

His private line was programmed not only to send and receive scrambled sat-bounced transmissions but preprogrammed to randomly jump frequencies as well. Calls on that line were impossible to track, trace, or intercept, let alone decode.

It was the most secure radio station in the world. None but the friendliest of friendlies could contact him on that line.

The call was from his old man.

"Foxtrot?" the acting president said. "Do you confirm?"

Larry Taylor immediately recognized his father's anxious voice. "Never know how glad I am to hear your voice. I thought you were in the Big Apple."

"As usual I was running late. But your mother and Jack, Jr. I'm afraid they didn't make it."

"I know," Larry said after a few moments. "Are you safe?"

"I'm airborne—safe for the moment. Now what are you doing?"

"My job, sir—advance, attack, disrupt, improvise."

"You have no authorization," his father said.

"The plane, the bomb, a gold star, that's all the authorization I need."

"Turn back now."

"We're missing a president, a congress, most of the cabinet. The Pentagon—as we speak—is thermonuclear dust."

"This isn't about revenge now. It's bigger than that."

"Big affirmative, sir. We're talking high-value hard-target capability requiring high penetration. Exactly the kind of thing this bird was built to do."

"I still outrank you, General. I'm ordering you back."

"With profound regret and the greatest possible respect, I must refuse."

"It's against military regs and court-martialable."

"Sir. If command is behaving irrationally under combat stress, I have a right to take matters into my own hands. I believe you are disregarding our mission. The B-2's codes are now base- and pilot-activated for precisely this contingency. Decapitation won't save the enemy's high command from this plane. You designed and deployed that system yourself."

"Larry, our subs and satellites confirm the Russians haven't issued launch codes to their submarines."

"We don't know that for sure."

"Their subs haven't fired. Their planes haven't scrambled."

"And if I can get to their C3I," the younger Taylor said, "they never will."

"And I repeat: You have no authorization for this."

"Sir, you may be our nation's highest-ranking political survivor, but I am our highest-ranking frontline officer. When it comes to tactical strikes, I'm on the front lines. I outrank you."

"But why?"

"Blame it on my Warrior Soul."

"We can't just empty our bomb bays, blow out our tubes, and destroy the world. There are other choices."

"Wake up and smell the fireballs, Dad. Third rock from sun just got taken to the rack."

Larry Taylor clicked off.

And was alone with his B-2 Stealth.

Warheads in his belly, sorrow in his soldier's heart, through the night he flew, heading north to cross the Arctic Circle.

37 Truth Seen Too Late

Sara might have been confident that Colton would hold up, but he wasn't so sure. He might have pitched in the bigs, flown through SAMs, flak, and enemy guns, but he'd never confronted anything like this—his family and so many friends obliterated. And now his daughter.

Meanwhile, the fireballs blazed. Watching from the forward viewing port—from a secure Olympian height—was the hardest thing he'd ever had to do.

Blinding flash after blinding flash.

He knew he ought to be furious. Here was Russia—or some segment of the Russian navy—making brazen preemptive nuclear strikes on major cities around the world. But what was *his* response? As a professional soldier? It wasn't professional at all. His only reaction was sheer incredulity.

"What's happening now?" Sara asked.

"According to MTN, Russia's still nuking the world," Colton said numbly.

"Does anybody know what our strategy is?" Sara asked.

"That depends who's in charge," Colton said. "I just got off the horn with one of Jack Taylor's assistants. They're in an airborne command post. And Jack has the Football."

But Colton knew Taylor. The secretary of defense wasn't very bright. The Taylor Colton knew—whenever he got jammed up—responded to emergencies with tedious lectures on how badly this nation needed a National Missile Defense System.

"I worry about Taylor," Colton said to Sara, "he didn't know anything about Vietnam, how to fight the war there. He never knew how to protect our embassies and bases abroad—not in Lebanon, Saudi Arabia, Nairobi, or Tanzania—or defeat Mideast terrorists. He thought Iraq and Afganistan would be 'cakewalks.'"

Colton didn't tell her that someone had misjudged the world situation and screwed up royally. This miscalculation was infinitely worse than any fuckup in the past, and Colton couldn't help but wonder, how would people live with failure of this magnitude? How would *he* live with it?

He remembered arguing the probability of global nuclear war one time with John Stone and Lydia Magruder. Stone had told him:

"The fireball that incinerated the dinosaurs is coming our way."

"But this time we're building and launching it ourselves," Lydia Magruder had added.

Colton remembered putting them down not so much for their facts as for their attitude, saying: *"How can you be so certain? Who made you God?"*

Of course they had been right. Colton knew now he, above all, should have understood—he never should have been naive about anything, he'd been born black in America—yet here he was in a reality even he had not ever faced. He wondered if willful ignorance might not be the worst sin of all.

Hell is truth seen too late, L. L. always told him, quoting Hobbes.

Sara snapped him out of his reflections.

"Anybody home?"

"Afraid so," Colton said.

"What's happening in Paris?"

Colton floated over to an MTN monitor. He couldn't believe his eyes. A Kilo-Class sub was surfacing in the Seine near the Jardin des Tuileries, directly in front of the Musée de l'Orangerie.

"I don't know," he said. "What is strategically important about l'Orangerie? About Paris?"

38 Where *Was* that Bell-Ringer?

The Paris Dragonfly/Cruise Missile had no intentions of visiting Musée de l'Orangerie or Jardin des Tuileries. He had bigger fish to fry. Even as he was propelled out of the foretube, even as his flotation collar inflated, even as he was boosted up above Pont de la Concorde—his thoughts were elsewhere.

He had a timetable to maintain.

Getting his bearings, he cut away from the Tuileries and took off for Pont de la Concorde. Doing a quick U-turn over the Assemblée Nationale, keeping low to the Seine, the Dragonfly/Cruise passed over Pont Royal, Pont du Carrousel, and Pont des Arts in rapid succession. Buzzing the magnificent marble steps of the Palais de Justice—"Liberté, Egalité, Fraternité" inscribed above its stately entrance—he streaked low over Île de la Cité.

He was right on time—and his GPS was a work of art. He had the target in his sights, locked in. There was no question of error. Just to make absolutely sure that he had the right target some astute fire-control officer had front-loaded film stills of his target directly into his data banks. He didn't have need for it. His view corresponded to his three-dimensional contoured scenic city map with digitized precision.

The setting for Napoleon's coronation in 1804, the funeral of Charles de Gaulle in 1970, a soaring edifice of flying buttresses, massive rib vaulting, magnificent pointed arches, and scintillating stained-glass windows—as well as an assortment of overhanging gargoyles—was much more than a legendary cathedral. Commissioned in 1163, it was 200 years in the building. Notre Dame was Paris—and was arguably the greatest cathedral in history.

In truth, the Dragonfly/Cruise was indifferent to its architectural splendor. The gargoyles and bell tower interested him only because there was a small detail that didn't exactly match. Something in those front-loaded film stills. Something missing.

Oh well. It probably didn't matter.

Still he wondered: *Where was that humpbacked bell-ringer?*

39 Am I Getting Through to You?

"Jesus, Jack, don't you love fire?"

"A lot of people are dying, Vlad."

"And let's just hope you're not one of them, Jack. You never listen to your old Uncle Vladdy. You're basically a fuckup, but you can't fuck around with nuclear fire."

Taylor's headset rang with Vlad's deranged laughter. The live feeds from Cyd showed Jack Taylor the major cities of Europe and Asia in flames.

"We're talking flashburn, fireburn, sunburn, heatstroke, dehydration, hyperthermia-hypothermia, flesh burned down to the bone, through the bone—keloid two inches deep. Burned dead tissue is a perfect breeding ground for every kind of sepsis, Jack. Burn wards become a cesspit for every disease known to God and man, spawning plagues and infections. This is no laughing matter, Jack. This is not time to be playing the fool. Am I finally getting through to you? It's time for Jack 'Choke-My-Chicken' Taylor to grow up and quit jerking off so much.

"Do you hear me, Jack-Me-Off-Me-Vich? Are you listening?"

40 A Bad Joke

"I don't care what Vladimir said to you," L. L. shouted at Jack Taylor. "Will you stop that pathetic whining? I don't care how foulmouthed he is. What are your options, your choices? What are you going to do? That's all you have to worry about, Jack. For Christ's sake, stop whimpering and be a man."

For several seconds, Lydia Magruder listened impatiently to the acting president of the United States, then screamed:

"You don't know Vladimir's running anything! What he says doesn't mean anything. Maybe he's crazy enough to do this, maybe he's *not*. Jack! You're operating on no—I said *no*—information!"

She was briefly quiet. Then: "I don't care what Vlad said to you, Jack. *I'm* not sure he's behind this. Stone's spent a lot of time with Vladimir. He says he's eccentric and more than a little crazy, but not psychotic. Stone thinks that for the most part the aggressiveness and foul language are ploys. Nixon claimed to use the same tactics. Make sure the other guy thinks you're a little nuts; he'll be fearful, make concessions. Stone told me Vlad speaks Arabic and Urdu, has spent a lot of time in Persia and the Mideast, and knows that region better than any leader who ever lived."

Again, L. L. was quiet for a long minute, listening to Taylor, who was inexplicably lecturing her on the need for "a nuclear missile shield."

Then she really lost it.

"I really don't give a fuck about National Missile Defense, you idiot! It was always a bad joke! It never worked, and threat was implausible, and because we ignored the real threat, the world's going up in flames!"

At the Avenue of the Americas Kate found a Central Park entrance. She had to find some way across the Sheep Meadow.

If she was to reach the reservoir.

If she was to reach water.

Everyone said not to enter Central Park at night, that it was too dangerous. Those people didn't know what danger was. Try strolling through the park at night surrounded by citywide firestorms, beneath a constant rain of flaming debris—or perhaps it was a plague of flaming locusts, the kind in Revelation that were said to sting like scorpions.

Kate discovered she wasn't the only one seeking the reservoir. In the eerie light of the drifting embers and burning trees, other survivors picked their way through the flames and the wrecked cars.

The thermal flash and firestorms had in many cases burned off clothing, hair, and eyebrows—leaving most of the survivors red as boiled lobsters. Their skin was so agonizingly scorched that they walked through the park, with arms held high, like surrendering soldiers, or straight before them, like sleepwalkers. The flash had struck dark clothing patterns—being more heat-absorbent than lighter-colored fabrics—and had burned like grotesque fashion designs into people's chests and backs. All around Kate were people with tee-shirt logos tattooing their torsos. One teenager had a black Nike *swoosh!* decal charring his crimson back. A young girl—her hair burned away—carried a New York Yankee logo on her blistered forehead. A small boy bore a black smiling Mickey Mouse seared over his heart.

After a few hundred yards Kate found an opening between the burning trees. Dodging the fires, she started out across Sheep Meadow. The rain of blazing embers was accelerating, but so was another kind of rain: a heavy, oily rain, the drops astonishingly large and as black as tar.

Bodies were strewn across the grass of the meadow. The dead, the dying, screaming in agony and sobbing with despair.

Kate worked her way through the meadow as if crossing a minefield. As she neared the big reservoir, the survivors became more numerous: three miles in circumference, the Central Park lake was now a lodestone for the city's refugees—tens of thousands of walking wounded. Lemminglike, dehydrated burn victims headed toward water. She forced her way through the surrounding mob in order to get closer to the water herself.

She was soon sorry. The charnel stench of so many dead and dying was instantly exacerbated by the sight of so many thousands of bodies, floating facedown in the water. Fighting back her gag reflex, she withdrew from the reservoir's edge.

The mob was eerily illuminated by the burning woods. Kate heard Sister

Cassandra over a radio—quoting Christ's vision of the end in Mark 13—shouting through the din of the dead and dying:

"Woe to those who would give suck in that time."

Kate thought she was having a psychotic break, which included auditory hallucinations.

Then she saw one of the survivors had actually fled clutching a portable radio.

"Pray you do not have to flee in winter," Cassie bellowed, again quoting Christ.

You got that one right, Jesus, Kate thought grimly. *Flee in winter, indeed. Stripped of your clothes and your skin, you'd all be dead by now.*

Firestorms were rising everywhere. The superheated air from converging firestorms was forming a huge vacuum. Surrounding air rushed in, feeding the flames and creating a citywide conflagration, which drifted in the direction of the prevailing winds. Slanting pillars of burning gases rose above the clifflike walls of fire bearing down on Central Park.

Towering water spouts—as large as 75 feet across and 500 feet high—whirled violently across the reservoir, sucking up screaming people and floating corpses by the thousands. A jet-black tornado—also created by the fire's convective forces—had appeared in the meadow. Less than fifty yards wide at its base, the tornado towered thousands of feet in the air. Its destructive power may not have been much by thermonuclear standards. Still, it had the power to kill, and it was approaching the reservoir.

With the firewalls closing and the tornado twisting toward her, Central Park no longer seemed a refuge. Kate ran from the reservoir, determined to find a safe way out of the fire and terrible winds.

42 Fry Your Sauerbraten

As soon as the Kilo-Class sub surfaced undetected in the Havel River, her Dragonfly/Cruise Missile was discharged into the water. The Dragonfly/Cruise Missile's flotation collar inflated, and he was on his way.

The Berlin Dragonfly/Cruise followed the Havel north to the River Spree, then cut across Platz der Republik. Clock-position-GPS-checks were all A-OK.

Thought you got bombed pretty good in World War II. All that conventional explosive did a number, right? That was nothing. I'm gonna fry your Sauerbraten like you never dreamed possible.

He checked his clock-position-GPS—perfect sync.

The Dragonfly drew a bead on the Reichstag.

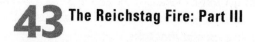

43 The Reichstag Fire: Part III

"There goes the—the—" Colton stammered.

"The Reichstag," Thucydides filled in.

"I thought that thing got burned in '33?" Colton said.

"Again in '45," Thucydides said.

"Looks like someone just did it a third time," Sara said.

As for Cyd, he was less interested in pyrotechnics than the Destroyer's motivation. There was more he needed to learn.

What are you up to? he could not help wondering.

44 The Balloon's Back Up

Sara Friedman was on the radio, trying to calm Lydia Magruder down.

"Look, L. L., the secretary *is* under a lot of stress. Henry's on another frequency with him now. He's never heard Jack this upset. Apparently Vlad calls him continually, baiting him, threatening to nuke more U.S. cities. Jack's trying to talk sense into him. He doesn't think that's working."

"The stress is about to get much worse."

"Tell me about it. Henry spoke to his daughter less than half an hour before the bombing began. She was in her co-op across from the U.N."

"At ground zero," L. L. finished for her. "I am truly sorry about Henry's daughter; please express that to him when you feel it's appropriate.

"As for Haines and Jack Taylor, they're evil men. It's only recently I've learned just how evil they were. Backing them might have been the biggest mistake I ever made. *Oh, hi, Cass.* Cassandra just walked in. She says hi. She hopes Cyd is holding up under all this. *Cass, it's awfully considerate of you to worry more about a machine than your fellow human beings. Cyd hardly talks to me at all, and I helped create him.*"

"L. L.," Sara said, "Cyd can hear you."

"Sorry, Cyd," L. L. said. "Anyway, Cass just said I needed some cheering up too. If she was sincere, she could try throwing a few smiles my way. That put her in her place. She never smiles, you know. She's congenitally incapable of smiling, I think."

"I don't think you appreciate the stress Jack is under," Sara said again. "We don't have a fraction of his stress, and we're just about coming apart up here."

"But you are in a position to help," L. L. said.

"I'm not sure how we're helping," Colton said to Lydia. "I'd be better off down there."

"Doing what?" L. L. asked. "Dropping more bombs?"

"Lydia," Sara said, "that was unfair."

"Perhaps," L. L. said. "Has Jack had any response from any of the other countries?" L. L. asked.

"Henry, you were on the phone with him," Sara said.

"Jack and his staff spend most of their time fielding questions from other nations. Those already hit want the nuclear nations to hammer Russia with everything we have. Taylor, so far, is holding back. Russia has thousands of launchable nukes available. Apparently, Vladimir has been on the phone with some of Russia's leadership too, baiting them as well as Jack."

"How many times do I have to tell you?" L. L. said, "I don't care how any of us feel right now. Suffering doesn't excuse us from our responsibilities. Henry, you above all know that. What was it you used to tell me about redeeming the past?"

"You redeem the past by redeeming the future."

"And we have a lot of future left to redeem."

"Don't be too sure of that, Lydia," Sara said. "The balloon's back up."

"Meaning?" L. L. asked.

"According to Cyd's war map," Colton said, "the bombs are going off again."

 45 Please Don't Kill Flipper!

Jack Taylor feared he was losing his mind. Not only were NATO, China, and India on the horn demanding concerted nuclear retaliation, Mad Vlad was still tormenting him.

"You know, Jack, Khizenovsky and those assholes think you're even stupider than I do. They think you're actually buying all this shit they're peddling you. 'Honest, Jack, we don't have the slightest idea who's launching these warheads.' They really believe you haven't figured out what the old Vladster's up to."

"You, Khizenovsky, Kochnovo, and Ridov are *all* in on this?" Taylor asked.

"You don't see any bombs raining on the old Rodina, do you?"

"No, I don't," Taylor said angrily.

Again, Mad Vlad's laughter shook Taylor to his soul.

"You know, Jack," Vladimir enthused, "the thing I really love—even more than fire—is fallout. We don't know the meaning of *real* fallout, Jack. We've never seen it on this kind of scale. There's never been a real ground burst— nothing over one kiloton—and it's the ground bursts that hurl those gigatons of debris into the stratosphere and return it to the earth in the form of lethal radioactive dust. Which is the way I'm serving it up to you guys."

Taylor was speechless, hoping against hope that Vlad would come to his senses and call off his ballistic-missile subs hidden beneath the ice pack.

"Oh, I know what you're thinking. I know you're disappointed. It's the artist in you. You wanted to see all those massive, five-mile-across, blazing, bitchin',

Technicolor fireballs. Air-bursts produce far better fireballs, far more photogenic firestorms, and I can tell you're disappointed. Hell, I'll admit it. I am too. Oh, we'll dig some monster craters, but it'll be months, maybe years, before the smoke lifts. The footage'll suck, the TV ratings will plummet, and MTN will be furious."

Taylor—still dumbstruck with horror—was trembling.

"I don't know about you, Jack, but those gamma rays scare me shitless. Those infinitesimal spots of light will radiate your sorry ass, deform your sperm, ovaries, babies, grandkids."

Taylor couldn't stop shaking.

But Vlad was ecstatic.

"Let's get to the old nut cutting, Jack. When that fallout comes down, it'll wipe out over billions of square miles of cities, suburbs, shopping malls, farms, to say nothing of us. Christ, I forgot about *us*. What's going to happen to all those PEOPLE? God no! PLEASE!!! Who's going to Rescue the Polar Bears and Save the Whales NOW? Who'll protect the rain forests? Isn't anyone gonna FREE WILLY? JACK? JACK? PLEASE DON'T KILL FLIPPER!" Vladimir's lunatic laughter shrieked into Taylor's headset.

Then, just as suddenly, he became completely calm, the personification of sweet reason, his voice soothing. "But look at it from *my* point of view. What options do *I* have? I can't incinerate the *entire* planet—for which I blame in part those fool START treaties—and that is a fact *I* have to live with. The best I can do is bury the earth in fallout, and while it may not send the old Nielsens soaring, it will produce a planetwide pandemic of prostration, fever, open lesions, diarrhea, spiking fever, more lesions, itching, burning, gangrenous sores, hair loss, nausea, vomiting, more nausea, more vomiting, more gangrene-stinking sores, to say nothing of detonating dysentery and BO of truly apocalyptic proportions. I'm talking death, Jack-Me-Hard-I'm-Your-Nuclear-Bard-O-Vich, on a global scale. Understand me now?"

And on that note Vlad slammed down the receiver of his phone.

Taylor found himself staring at the attaché case chained to the wrist of his adjutant, seated nearby. "The Football." The transceiver that would rain H-bombs down on Russia like hailstones from hell.

Blinded by rage and despair, he was now terrifyingly desperate to punch in the launch codes.

VI

What is the ancient grudge we bear Him that we take the Light of Creation—of GENESIS—and use it to raze His Earth?

—Vladimir Malokov

1 Sins Beyond Remission

On the Odyssey, Sara's direct line rang. It was Cassandra.

Cassandra had been calling the Odyssey with some frequency. Her calls were invariably for Cyd. This was unique

"Thought I'd check in on Cyd," the Unsmiling Sister said.

"You're still more interested in machines than men?" Colton asked.

Since all transmissions passed through Cyd, he monitored them automatically. "Given the way men are now behaving, why should she not prefer us over men?"

"Can't argue with that, Cyd," Sara said.

"How are you doing, Cyd?" Cassandra asked. "How's it hanging?"

"According to my files, you can get used to anything," Thucydides said, "including hanging—that is, if you hang long enough."

"I'm not sure I will get used to this," Colton said, looking at the continuing devastation playing on the Odyssey's monitors. "I can't see the end of it, or the point to it."

"We never know the ends," Cass said, "to anything. We make our own meaning. The point of it is up to us."

"Was there a point to Boniata?" Colton asked.

"It was my school."

"Some school," Sara said.

"That's all we ever gain out of life—instruction."

"Some lesson," Sara said, staring at the destruction blazing across her monitors.

"The question's not what's done to us," Cassandra said, "but how it improves us."

"We are being stripped of everything," Sara protested.

"Our bodies, perhaps," the blind sister said, "but our souls are intact. In fact they are strengthened by suffering."

"There are sins beyond remission," Sara said.

"No," Cassandra countered. "There are only choices."

"The world has chosen to die," Colton said.

"To live is to die," Cassandra said. "The point is to live fearlessly—not in bad faith."

"You're telling us to love our enemies?" Colton said with a gentle mockery.

"Why not?" Cassandra answered. "Christ dined with thieves and publicans. He made his grave amid the wicked."

Colton said, gazing at the blazing monitors, "This world not even Jesus could redeem."

"*You* redeem the world, Henry," Cassandra said, "with every breath, with every act. You are *your* messiah. Christ Jesus resides in you."

2 South Bronx Saturday Night

Ron Lewis came to in the basement of a South Bronx tenement building. Smoky, rubble littered, rat-infested, filled with burn victims—it was now a makeshift bomb shelter.

At any other time in Lewis's life, the notion of spending a night in a South Bronx tenement with ragged, dirty blacks would have been unthinkable. He had spent his life—and earned a small fortune—ridiculing these very people for their poverty and their race. Now Ron Lewis huddled in terror with South Bronx blacks . . . blacks who had apparently dragged him unconscious out of the burning wreckage of his helicopter.

This was truly the Republican National Convention from hell.

Fires raged around their shelter, and the ceiling began collapsing around them.

"We gotta get the fuck out of here," a short black man in a red bandana and a bloodstained New York Knicks jersey said. "We gonna get buried alive. Y'all help." He yanked Ron to his feet. "Help mama here. She burnt bad and got her a baby."

Light from the neighborhood fires flickered in through the broken basement windows, providing their collapsing shelter with an eerie illumination. For the first time Ron actually looked at the woman he was huddled with. She had flash burns on her face and her exposed right breast. Against her left breast she held a small, sobbing baby.

He helped her to her feet, careful not to touch the burned portions of her body, and followed the black man and the dozen-odd survivors out of the basement.

3 A Land in Love with Death

For Moscow Cruise Missile #1—the cruise missile that was flying point—it had been a trip. He'd had to lead his six-missile team through a twisting, turning obstacle course of radar stations, airfields, infrared installations, and military bases. Hugging valley-bottoms and canyon-floors—often at altitudes of under a hundred feet—they'd eluded enemy radar screens. They were for all intents and purposes invisible.

But they were not serene. The stress of precise, protracted, low-altitude maneuvering had set their nerves on edge, and for the past half hour to relieve tension they had sung a tune, a military marching song, "The Dragonfly Hymn" they called it:

"Scientists made me.
Politicians paid for me.
Salesmen sold me.
Everyone owns me.
But nobody knows me.
Nobody's friend.
I'm nobody's friend."

Their rude laughter roared over Russia.
"How many of their citizens were killed under Stalin?" #2 asked.
"Forty million in times of peace and prosperity," #3 said.
"These are a people obsessed with death," #5 piped up.
"A land in love with death—especially Moscow," #3 said.
"A city of the dead," said #6.
"That's what these people get off on."
"In that case we'll really give them something to celebrate."

4 The Land of the Midnight Sun

Lawrence Taylor, in his B-2 Stealth bomber, was also on his way to Moscow—flying over the ice pack, across the land of the midnight sun. The sun—a thin silver-gray disk shrouded in twilight—hung on the horizon's rim, neither rising nor setting, seemingly motionless, impossibly still but in fact circling the Arctic Rim slowly.

He soared above the pole at 55,000 feet. Overhead, the stars glimmered. Below, pack ice sprawled from horizon to horizon, an alabaster void, blank as the abyss.

Lost in solitude, alone with his thoughts, and about to become the deadliest human killer in history, Larry Taylor soared.

5 Nostalgia for Simpler Days

As the Star—the Nuclear Warhead—lay in the belly of Lawrence Taylor's Black Stealth bomber, she went through a checklist, confirming that everything was in order.

Her current incarnation was infinitely more complex than any of her previous personae.

. . . It had been easier in the past. Her simplest incarnation had been her most famous. Little Boy—the Hiroshima Bomb—was just a sawed-off smooth-bore howitzer barrel, six feet long, three inches in diameter. The entire nose-section—weighing 2.5 tons—contained a chunk of enriched U-235. The howitzer's tail-end was loaded with a U-235 bullet, backed by several one-pound bags of cordite.

The device was so devastatingly simple it was tested not at White Sands but Hiroshima.

After which Hiroshima was gone . . .

. . . Why couldn't things be that simple now? The things Star had to worry about would give Superman perforated ulcers.

For openers, she had to worry about impact. When it came to bunker-busting, penetration was everything. While her Hiroshima and Nagasaki antecedents had been airburst, she was built to burrow her target like a mole. A half-megaton bomb detonating a depth of 65 feet did as much damage as a surface blast by a 25-megaton bomb—a heavy, awkward, unwieldy monster that was difficult to deliver with pinpoint accuracy.

Star—who was dropped from planes traveling at speeds ranging from Mach 0.9 and Mach 2.0—hit her targets at devastating velocities, which did terrible things to her innards. Chute clusters could brake Star from velocities of Mach 0.9 down to 65-f.p.s. in seconds.

None of which stopped Star from worrying. Suppose her chute didn't open? The other Clans could laugh at her phobias, but they didn't have to worry about going into a slide or, even worse, "slapping-down"—i.e., hitting the target on her stomach. Slap-down precluded penetration, and Star's concentric-ring shock absorbers were all in her nose. Her internal organs—her multiple fusing systems, her trajectory-sensing signal generators, her surrounding fiberglass-reinforced, carbon, phenolic, honeycomb-shaped, two-megaton warhead—would be hammered senseless if she belly flopped or landed on her butt. Star would hit those bunkers like 2,000 pounds of shit exploding out of 1,000-pound bag, her smashed insides bursting out of her steel case. Her humiliation would reverberate throughout the length and breadth of the Warrior World.

6 Every Exit Blocked by Fire

Through broken windows—and with blood seeping into his eyes from a lacerated forehead—Ron Lewis observed a South Bronx sky eerily illuminated by firestorms, a deluge of blazing embers and black rain. All around him the earth shook and thundered with crashing buildings and exploding gas mains.

So far their brick shelter—surrounded by vacant lots—had withstood the blast waves and firestorms, but in the end it too collapsed. The floors beneath them had burst into flames, and they now were back out on the stairs, every exit blocked by fire. Choking on smoke, Lewis half-dragged the badly burned black woman and her child up the stairs.

To the roof.

7 Vlad's Explained Everything to Me

When the three Russian leaders in the Venyukovski Missile Analysis Center learned their world was not coming to an end, they immediately got out the vodka.

They'd just opened the second bottle when the phone rang. It was Jack Taylor, again.

"Mister President," President Khizenovsky said, "we've been trying to reach you! We couldn't get through."

"I've been on the phone with Vlad," Taylor said through their translator, "he's explained everything to me. It's a scam you're running, right?"

Their translator had hesitated at the word "scam."

"We don't know what you mean," President Khizenovsky said.

Taylor played them a digital recording of one of his phone conversations with Vlad, the part where Vlad howled with derision at having killed Taylor's wife.

"You know it's him," Taylor said. "I know it's him. Christ, I've had to spend enough time with that mad bastard to know what he's like." It was obvious from his voice that the acting president of the United States was close to a nervous breakdown.

"Jack," President Khizenovsky said, "let me assure you, even if that is Vlad, he does not have his finger on our nuclear trigger."

"So you deny responsibility for the nukings."

"We categorically deny it," the Intelligence Director, Vasilli Ridov, said.

Taylor played them another tape of Mad Vlad, taking credit for the strikes on behalf of Mother Russia, promising to empty Russia's ballistic-sub missile-tubes just as soon as their target packages were realigned.

"You still say you're not involved," Jack said.

"Yes," Staff Director Kochnovo said. "I promise you, sir, we had nothing to do with this."

"In other words, you have Russian-built subs with crews in Russian uniforms nuking half the world, your own mad-dog defense minister promising to blow the rest of the world off the face of the earth—and at the same time accept no responsibility for this."

"I know it sounds bad," Ridov said, "but we aren't responsible."

"Bad as things are now—and they're terrible—they can get worse," President Khizenovsky said.

"Now you're attempting nuclear blackmail?" Jack said angrily. "If I go back to NATO with this, our allies will demand reprisals—five of your cities for every one of NATO's would be my guess."

"Nuclear realism," Ridov admitted. "How do we stop this thing from escalating?"

"Too late now," Jack said.

The three Russians turned to look at the electronic map of the world that dominated the War Room.

To their horror, new red circles were blinking across the screen.

 **Was It Good for You?**

The two American Stealth fighters, refueling over the polar ice cap, were not having an easy time of it. Night-refuelings were always tough, but tonight was uniquely difficult. Not only were they trying to concentrate on the work at hand—and not on the burning cities at home—but black cumulus clouds lined the horizon's rim. Obscuring what little sunlight there was, they made the pole impenetrably dark. The tanker could not even see the black aircraft, and the potential for three-dimensional disorientation was limitless.

"Yo, Tango," the boom operator addressed the lead Stealth, "I'm trying hard not to dent your fuselage, but I CAN'T FUCKING SEE YOU!"

Colonel James L. Taylor sighed. The captain had refueled his brother Larry's B-2 only a half hour earlier. God knows what he'd done to that monster.

In fact, Jamie might never know. His brother was in such a hurry he'd refused to wait for them. Bastard always was a loner.

And now Gunga Din couldn't find his refueling door.

"Tell me, boomer, am I the first Stealth fighter you've refueled?"

"That's affirm."

Ah, Christ. All it took was a couple of good dents to destroy your RCS (Radar Cross Section) and give the bad guys a solid lock.

What the hell, he muttered to himself, *maybe the B-2s are easier to refuel.*

"You need the lights on to screw?" his brother William asked the boomer.

"Ask your mother," the boomer shot back.

"Maybe," Jamie said to his brother, "he thinks he's back at the truck stop filling semis."

"It's where he belongs," William said.

"It's where I filled up your old mom, if you must know."

"Look, Gunga Din," Jamie said to the boomer, "I see your directional wing-lights. I can see your boom-operator's station through the center pane of my cockpit. Know what a *cock*pit is?"

"Hey," the boomer said. "I wouldn't be refueling any of you if your brother, the general, hadn't ordered me up here."

"Okay, okay," Jamie said. "The refueling door's rolled open and the red rotating meatball's off. Can you see the apex light? Boomer? Do you read?"

"Roger that."

"Don't dim the light. This is a pitch-black plane in a pitch-black polar night. Just follow the light home."

"Ummmm, got it. That's a lock."

"Was it good for you?" William asked.

"No drop 'em and grab 'em," the boomer growled to William. "Like I say to your mother, 'Wham-bam-thank-you, ma'am.' You're next."

"Just tell me you didn't ding our big brother's Crow," Jamie said.

"The big guys are easier," the boomer replied.

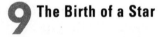 The Birth of a Star

"Uh-oh, Mr. Stone, time to look up," Sabrina said. "MTN is playing a golden oldie."

Cyd was now intercutting his high-angle space-station filming of the nuclear apocalypse below with stock footage of the landmarks before they were nuked. In this case he ran a full shot of the most famous skyscraper on earth. One split-screen panel contained the high-angle nuclear destruction of the edifice, the other the full shot of the building in its prime.

"Remember that?" Sabrina asked.

"The Empire State Building," Stone said numbly.

Thucydides expanded the shot to a three-block radius, capturing the full magnitude of the fiery obliteration, and the Harpies stopped laughing.

"Mr. Stone," Sabrina said, "you have to watch. This next one is priceless."

A cruise missile—in ultra-slow-motion—was streaking toward the U.N.

"Get set," Sabrina said.

"What do you think of world peace and global cooperation now?" Sultana asked.

When the cruise missile hammered the U.N., Cyd's light-filters worked with perfect precision. The fireball bloomed like the birth of a star.

Sultana and Sabrina laughed and clapped with derisive delight.

10 What If I Can't?

To say that Star—the Warhead in the Stealth bomber's belly—was nervous was an understatement. The Weapons Clans were nothing if not anxious. They had all spent too many decades waiting on the shelf to have genuine self-confidence. In truth, they were all racked by self-doubt and looked to Star for leadership and reassurance.

She tried to radiate confidence—to serve as a role model—but she too knew fear:

What if she failed to perform?

Fizzles were not unknown in Star's Nuclear Warhead Clan. Star Bombs were incomprehensibly complex, and a thousand things could go wrong, any one of which could reduce her climax to a humiliating no-show.

Performance-anxiety had marked her life since White Sands. She had been scared of failure at Hiroshima, Nagasaki. She'd been frightened when the Russians detonated her their first time in August, 1949, at Semipalatinsk.

Nor did successes set her mind at ease. Not even the biggest man-made blast of all time—a spectacular blast, a mind-blowing 58-megaton explosion—brought her peace, and that was an orgasm of stellar proportion . . . the kind that climaxes only in the heart of a star.

Now she was facing what was arguably the most important performance in the history of the Clan: the thermonuclear annihilation of the Venyukovski Missile Analysis Center just off the Moscow Beltway. This was what all of America's nuclear work and strategizing had been focused on: decapitation of Russia's nuclear leadership.

What if she couldn't *perform*?

11 Show Me the Money

Tokyo's Cruise Missile streaked low over the Miji-za Theater. Its marquee and playbills advertised some of the finest Kabuki plays in all of Japan. Among other things it was the horrendous Tokyo fire-bombing's most horrific symbol. In 1945, when citizens and patrons poured into the theater in an attempt to escape the bombing, the theater burst into flames, and thousands were burned alive.

It was the Tokyo Cruise Missile's favorite landmark in all of Japan—next to Hiroshima and Nagasaki, of course.

He saw the Miji-za Theater as a standard of military excellence, an ideal to aspire to, and he was not only willing to accept the challenge, deep down inside he believed he could make Miji-za look like a fizzled firecracker.

Dead-ahead, full-rudder, lay the biggest collection of money on earth—the Tokyo Stock Exchange. Built in 1878, it was now the busiest on earth. More money changed hands at its location on Nihombashi Kabutocho than anywhere else. Japan had one of the highest savings-income ratios per capita in the world, and almost all of it was invested here.

Until now.

Because the Tokyo Dragonfly/Cruise was on his way.

Checking his clock and position, he saw he was right on time. Sighting the big glass front doors, the Cruise/Dragonfly hammered through them like a nuclear kamikaze from hell.

Show me the money! Show me the money! Show me the money!

12 An Epoch of Peace

"Jack," Vlad was saying in a folksy, affectionate tone of voice that infuriated Taylor even more than his obscene tirades, "you ever get in one of those philosophical kinds of moods, where you wonder what life's all about?"

The shocking disconnect made Taylor want to scream. Still, he struggled to answer the insane question . . . sanely.

"I take it you're in one of those moods," Taylor said.

"Doesn't it bring out the philosopher in you? Don't you feel the urge to ask yourself: 'Why did all this happen?' It wasn't supposed to. We all had so much knowledge and 'deterent capability,' as you called it. We had strategies to keep men like your Uncle Vladdy in line. Remember? The world wasn't supposed to get hammered to pieces by a lunatic. Where did it all go wrong?"

"Where did it all go wrong?" was the best Taylor could manage.

"Jack. This was supposed to be preventable. You, above all, should know. All that revolutionary technology you invented was supposed to deter a nuclear holocaust."

"There was nothing wrong with deterrence," Taylor said.

"In which case, why didn't it work?" Vlad said in that falsely sincere voice that made Taylor want to punch walls. "Where was all that pinpoint counterforce microtargeting you boys constantly crowed about? Talk about deterrence, Jack-O, that shit was priceless. Especially 'Delta and Bravo strikes.' Those were the Russian urban centers you were going to nuke, thereby degrading our capacity to hit back. Remember your 'Romeo' strikes? Those targets were guaranteed to stop us in our tracks if we ever did go on the warpath. Hell, microtargeting was not only going to protect you, it was going to save your allies' bacon as well. You do remember 'extended deterrence,' don't you? The Old Nuclear Umbrella?"

Vlad's laughter roared scornfully.

Taylor was now desperate. *Keep your cool*, he said to himself. *Try to find some common ground. Bring him back to reality.*

"It should have worked, Vlad," Taylor finally said, forcing out the words.

"With ample warning perhaps," Vlad said amiably. "You were supposed to have ample warning, weren't you? You do remember 'symmetrical transparency.' Not only were all those government spy satellites going to expose our darkest military secrets, privatized space-imaging would rat us out too. The Great Age of Privatized Transparency was to be an Epoch of Peace—One-Worldism on high. The Great Global Economy combined with the Transparent Planet was going to . . . to . . . to . . . **save the world!**"

Vlad laughed uproariously.

13 Maybe We Should Just Tell the Truth

More and more circles were redlining the Venyukovski Missile Analysis Center's big map-screen. Vlad seemed to have an endless supply of nukes.

Somehow, one of the surviving satellite-news networks had intercepted his cellular phone calls to Taylor and was running those phone calls—translated into the local languages—on global TV and radio.

"What do we do now?" President Khizenovsky asked. "Vlad's cut the ground out from under us with his phone calls."

"Kind of hard to run a guilt trip on the U.S. while he's nuking their cities and howling with derision," Vasilli Ridov said.

"Which still doesn't mean they're guiltless in all this," Kochnovo said quietly.

Funny thing was, President Khizenovsky did feel they shared some of the guilt for this debacle. Jack, in particular . . .

. . . Khizenovsky had personally invited Defense Secretary Taylor to Russia, had taken him on a tour of some of the more insecure holding facilities for nuclear-bomb cores, and had shown him around shipyards and nuclear research labs where pilferage was rampant.

"Jack," Khizenovsky had said to him, "Russia has a long history of black-market operations. It was the only way people could acquire quality goods under the old regimes. The criminal operations were in place in these facilities when we took over."

He had complained to Jack that instead of buying up Russia's 2.5 million pounds of bomb-grade fissile material, blending it for power-plant use, and selling it off—at a tidy profit, of course—to nuclear power facilities in stable countries, the American government and its nuclear industry stonewalled, were more concerned with the economic well-being of its nuclear production companies than global nuclear security.

U.S. nuclear security was being sacrificed—it seemed to Josef—on the altar of economic protectionism.

Jack had appeared attentive, but still something seemed to be missing. Josef Khizenovsky did not think he was grasping the enormity of the situation.

Finally Josef had said to him: "Jack, with the collapse of our centralized government and command economy, we became the Organized Crime Capital of the World and the planet's nuclear supermarket. Jack, we needed and still need help. We can't control the nuclear chaos. It's gotten away from us."

"I'll see what I can do, Josef Dmitrovich, but I can't promise much. You know how tight they are on the Hill these days."

"We're talking survival of the planet, Jack."

"You're talking a blank check, and I'm having hell's own time keeping National Missile Defense alive, and you know how much I want that. Those bastards on the Hill would love to kill it."

"Jack, this would cost a fraction of National Missile Defense, and the threat from all these loose nukes is infinitely more immediate."

Jack shrugged. "I'll see what I can do. Look on the bright side. We aren't armed with 50,000 live warheads each anymore. The Cold War is, thank God, over."

"Jack, there are still 50,000 uranium and plutonium pits in my country. They can be activated in a heartbeat."

"You Russkies are still bitter about the old Cold War, aren't you, Josef?"

"In what respect?"

*"You have to be at least a little pissed—about the fact that **we** won?"*

"You still see America as guilty, Josef Dmitrovich?" Ridov asked the president.

"It's been a favorite theme of mine," Josef said.

"With all that's going on?" Anatoly Kochnovo said. "With Vlad on the phone bragging that it's *us* doing all this?"

The two men were now staring at Josef as if he were insane.

"Josef Dmitrovich," Anatoly said, "we've tried the guilt line. It won't work anymore. I don't know what to tell Jack Taylor."

"In that case," Josef said, "maybe we should just tell him the truth."

The two men stared at their president in shock.

14 They Screamed like Banshees

Night under the polar ice pack.

Or what passes for night in a Russian Typhoon-Class nuclear sub. The Silent Service in each nation does not distinguish much between day and night nor between waking and sleeping. Sleep within the service is seldom more than cat-naps, the berthing space little more than casket-size bunks. Weapons officers and mates often find themselves bunking in the torpedo rooms in between the weapons racks. The racks themselves—which all too frequently are filled with food crates as well as submarine-launched ICBMs—are usually too far from the workplace to be worth the hike, so the men catch their catnaps anywhere they can, often right on the deckplates or even in the weapons racks themselves.

One nightly exercise is garbage disposal. Subs are crammed with food, and their crews create monumental amounts of trash. Boxes upon boxes of empty cans must be crushed, placed in weighted garbage bags, and disposed of. During surface exercises the garbage is simply thrown over the side. When submerged—which is most of the time—the garbage is stuffed into garbage bags, packed into weighted canisters, and loaded into the tube garbage disposal. A spherical cake of ice is placed in front of it to smooth the canister's egress through the ball-valve; then, it is blown out the tubes like a torpedo.

First Officer Dmitri Zhykoff—following the egress of the garbage canister out the forward torpedo tubes—was the first man to spot the school of nar-whales in the azure eye of the sonar screen. They were battling for breathing space at an overhead *savssats*—a small hole in the ice allowing the narwhale to surface for a breath. He got the captain on the bridge.

"When you were out on the fjord, Sergei Alexandrovich, didn't you tell me that you'd found a narwhale school trapped under a *savssats*?"

"They screamed like banshees, the poor things," Captain Petrov said.

"Guess what I found directly overhead," First Officer Zhykoff said.

"That is an omen," the captain said. "We are near the North Pole, aren't we?"

"As near as I can calculate that *savssats* is sitting on it."

"Then I say we ought to give the poor things a little breathing space. For my last tour I wanted to visit all five of the north poles—the Magnetic North Pole, the Average Geographic, the Geomagnetic, the Pole of Inaccessibility, and the North Pole. We're at #5."

"Surface?" First asked.

"Surface."

15 Armageddon's Top Gun

Larry Taylor had crossed the pole and was now approaching the Siberian land mass when the callers broke radio silence.

"Yo, Foxtrot. Do you read?" Jamie Taylor sang out.

"Do you read me too?" his brother William signaled.

They were on the same packet-switched linkup his father had contacted him on. Scrambled, programmed, and synchronized to send and receive only multiple sat-bounced transmissions, it was impenetrably discreet.

"What the hell are you two doing here?" Larry Taylor asked. "I expected two other escorts."

"Thought you lost us, right?" William said.

"I purely hoped so."

"You didn't think you'd have all the fun, did you?" Jamie asked.

"Why don't I read you on my screen?"

"Willy and I hijacked a couple of Stealth fighters back at Nome."

"Hijacked?"

"We jumped the reservation to join the war," Jamie said.

"As soon as we heard you went over the wall," William said, "figured we'd better tag along. They had two of them fueled and ready for takeoff."

"What's the punishment for deserting *for* the front lines?" William asked.

"You're about to find out, Colonel. I'm ordering you back to base."

"Don't make me laugh," William said.

"This is a breach of discipline, Colonel."

"Tell it to somebody who cares," Jamie said. "You're flying into Armageddon—the last battle in the last war. You think I'm going to be left out?"

"You're disobeying a direct order from a direct superior. From a general."

"You said the same thing to Dad," William said.

"Dad is no longer in the military."

"So we test high on insubordination," Jamie said. "They can court-martial all three of us. Give them a family rate. We'll hit them with the old DNA defense. Tell them insubordination is hardwired into the family."

"We'll plead familial insanity," William said.

"What makes you think I need you?"

"You don't," Jamie said. "We need you. Nuclear dogfighting's the New Rage, and someone's got to check us out. Who better than Big Brother—Armageddon's Top Gun."

"Teach you what? How to get killed?"

"I think of it as keeping the world safe for democracy," William said.

"Why don't you just head on back?"

"To *what*?" Jamie said.

"They'll have a lot of high-flying AWACS up here looking for us," Larry warned.

"I know," Jamie groaned. "And Galosh antiaircraft missiles. And Gazelle silo-based high-acceleration missiles."

"In concert with their Henhouse, Doghouse, and Cathouse radars," William said.

"This ain't no raggedy-ass barn-shoot is all I'm saying," Larry said.

"You hit them low; I hit them high," Jamie said.

"The first lesson in nuclear dogfighting, Little Bro," Larry said. "Stealth B-2s have nothing to hit them with. We aren't built for exchanges."

"Glad to have us along, I bet," Jamie said.

"Yeah, for the blazing insights, sizzling repartee, and scintillating wit."

"And I thought you only loved us for our sidewinder missiles," Will said.

"I don't know if I ever said it, but I do love you."

"That the soft feminine side of your personality coming out?" Jamie asked.

They soared over the Arctic icescapes.

16 *Everybody in the Pool!!!*

New York apartment buildings were famous for their cylindrical two-thousand-gallon rooftop cisterns. Wood paneled, they provided gravity-induced water pressure for New Yorkers citywide.

One look at the cistern and Ron Lewis raced for the ladder. Reduced by the fire to a fleeing hysterical animal, desperate for water, he had only one thought:

Everybody in the pool!!!

He made it to the top of the cistern. Over forty horribly burned, hideously swollen corpses—mostly women and children—clogged the crimson water.

He forced the rest of the frightened survivors back down the ladder, shouting:

"You don't want to look in there."

The fire was shooting up over the edge of the roof, and Lewis realized he was going to die on a South Bronx rooftop surrounded by blacks, many no doubt on welfare, the very people he'd spent a lifetime spurning and humiliating.

He sat down in the middle of the roof and cried.

17 Quid Pro Quo

"Do you have any concept how furious the world's surviving leaders are?" Jack Taylor asked the Russian president. "Leaders possessing nukes? I've been on the phone with them. Those are calls I understand the three of you are ducking."

"You can handle NATO, Jack," President Khizenovsky said. "You and you alone control NATO's launch codes. The others will eventually understand that we were blameless, that this was the work of some rogue state or madman. They will also understand that to retaliate means total rather than partial nuclear annihilation for their citizens."

"You expect the world to simply roll over?" Jack Taylor asked.

"I will offer them something in return," President Khizenovsky said.

"In return for incinerating their cities?" Acting President Taylor asked.

"We can offer them a chance to save the world," President Khizenovsky said. "We can start with my country. A commission comes in and collects all the nuclear materials here—something we all should have done a long time ago—as well as in China, Japan, everywhere we can get them. We've seen the consequences of nuclear proliferation. We have a chance—and the motivation—to clean it up."

"And we stop the killing *now*?" Acting President Taylor asked.

"Yes, Jack, that is imperative," President Khizenovsky said.

"Well, in that case, Josef, we have a problem."

"In what respect, Jack?"

"Josef Dmitrovich, the board's lighting up again."

President Josef Khizenovsky turned to the nuclear map.

Legions of brilliant red circles were leaping to life across the board.

18 Keepers of the Flame

The surfacing sub had cleared a patch of water big as a football field for a school of suffocating narwhales, directly atop the North Pole. The captain, Sergei Petrov, stood at the water's edge with the navigator and reporter and idly watched the pale creatures with their long spiraling unicorn tusks and dark leopard-spotted flukes surface for air.

"We are now standing atop the North Pole," the navigator, Grigori Shupov, said. "Atop that world known by the Greeks as Arktikos."

"Meaning: 'Land of the Great Bear,'" Ivan Gilyenko, the reporter, said.

"Which, luckily for you, Ivan Anatolyvich, we slew," Shupov said.

"Only you," the reporter said to Captain Petrov, "would keep a slung AK-47 under his foul-weather jacket."

"That was not the first polar bear I've met within these Arctic wastes."

"What are we meeting with now?" the reporter asked, pointing at the strange creatures in the water.

"Corpse whales," the captain said. "That's what I see."

"That's what sailors called them, at any rate," Shupov said.

The reporter looked more closely. The adults looked like fifteen-foot-long porpoises except for the long spiraling head-tusks and spotted flukes. The calves were completely gray and in fact looked like small porpoises.

"They look like seagoing unicorns," the reporter said.

"With that pale, bloated skin," Shupov said, "they look like drowned men."

"'Narwhale' means 'corpse whale,'" the captain said.

"I forgot," the reporter asked, "whether they are a good or an ill-omen."

"A portent from hell, some claim," Shupov said.

"We are armed with 160 nuclear warheads, reporter," Captain Petrov said. "Our mission is—if hell should ever come to the homeland—to incinerate men, women, and children by the hundreds of millions. Given the nature of our mission, there are no good omens."

"Then why do you do it, Sergei Alexandrovich?" Gilyenko asked.

"Rodina," Sergei said.

"Rodina is worth the destruction of the world?" the reporter asked.

"Perhaps not, but I cannot countenance *her* destruction," the captain said.

"And what of God?" Shupov asked.

The captain said, "Rodina is my God, my sole truth, my only faith."

"You would raze the world for a simple patch of dirt?" the reporter, Gilyenko, asked.

"Heaven *and* earth," Sergei said.

"God will not be pleased to hear that," the reporter said dryly.

"I see myself as keeper of Rodina's keys," the captain said, "*and* her flame."

"Keys that launch thermonuclear flames," the reporter said.

"If hell comes to call, it will find me," Sergei said.

The first mate, Dmitri Zhykoff, ran to him across the ice. "We just received a VLF, sir. Number-four. The balloon is up. The whole shooting match. Unfortunately, sir, an L.A.-Class American attack sub has intercepted that VLF."

"Where is our Akula, our goddamned escort-sub?" the captain shouted. "He's supposed to be protecting us from those damned L.A.'s. I swear if he's out joyriding again, I'll fucking castrate him."

"Oh, he's out there, sir," Weapons Officer Rastvorov said. "He's firing on the L.A."

"Which is why we have to haul ass," First said. "Akula is firing on them with—"

The Akula sub finished his sentence for him with a nuclear-tipped torpedo: The ice beneath their feet convulsed as a blinding fireball a quarter-mile across levitated with godlike grandeur out of the ice pack high above the Arctic horizon, its blast exploding in their ears like the very crack of doom.

And again to the captain's unimaginable horror, a proliferating maze of infinitely complex ice-fissures was shattering the North Pole itself—the gaping rents rocketing toward them with lightning speed and fury.

19 There's a Limit to How Many Times Even *I* Can Nuke New York

"Yo, Jack-O, old friend, how's it going?"

Mad Vlad's idiot laughter rang through Taylor's headset.

"The world was in flames last time I looked."

"I know, and I can't tell you how bad I feel. It didn't have to be that way."

"It didn't?"

"Not at all. But there were forty-four nations out there with a nuclear capability—nations that either had the bomb or could have it quickly. You know I couldn't let that happen."

"And you decided to disarm them through global annihilation."

"I guess I threw the baby out with the bathwater."

Taylor's headset shook with hurricane howls and apelike ululations.

Taylor had the eerie sensation that his mind was leaving his body.

'Maybe we got lulled into La-La-Land by Glastnost and Peristroika. Maybe we didn't have enough conferences. I mean where was the Scowcroft Commission when you needed it? Scowcroft said you not only didn't have enough MX ICBMs in the old silos, you needed ICBMs on mobile launchers, scuttling back and forth across the country, that you did not have enough Trident II submarine-launched ICBMs. He said you needed more and better cruises, more and better bombers."

Vlad treated him then to a chorus of gale-force horselaughs.

"What about the Test Ban Treaty anyway?" Vlad asked, suddenly reasonable, exasperatingly calm. "All those great summits: Ike at Geneva, Khrushchev at Camp David. (Remember the old 'Spirit of Camp David,' Jack?) JFK at Geneva. Kosygin and LBJ in glorious Jersey. Nixon at Moscow. Brezhnev in D.C. Ford at Vladivostok. Carter at Vienna. Reagan at Reykjavik.

"Makes you wonder what they were doing at those damn things. Sending out for pizza? Ordering up hookers? Smoking crack? Humming each other's hummers? They sure weren't disarming the world.

"You remember Star Wars, don't you, Jack? The Strategic Defense Initiative. Flotillas of Orbiting Lasers in Outer Space and zapping my missiles like PacMan straight out of the fucking sky while they're still in boost phase? 'Boost intercept,' that Brain-Dead Bozo of a president, Ronald Reagan, called it. O-o-o-h, SDI. S-c-a-a-r-r-y! Star Wars would have protected you from all my Stealth-coated ground-hugging invisible cruise missiles and my hundred-plus undetectable suitcase nukes (oh, is the Force ever going to be with you now, Jack-O!) which your good buddy St. Nuke up here with Rudolph and Dancer in Elf Land with a big sleighful of toy warheads which I can't wait to drop down your fucking chimney and slip into those women's stockings you wear under your uniform. It's not too late to bring back SDI, is it, Jack? Star Wars would have saved Elvis. Please tell me it would have? I miss the King so much. When he died in *Love Me Tender*, I died too. I don't care if he ballooned up to 5,000 pounds and blew his brains out with more drugs than the Mayo Clinic would sell in five million years. I believe in Star Wars. It'll work, Jack. I'm being serious with you now. I know about these things. Trust me. NO, DON'T THINK SO!"

Vlad's beastlike braying reverberated in Taylor's headset like laughter from beyond the grave.

Taylor could feel himself floating across the ceiling.

"In truth, though, Jack-O, I blame it all on that cretin, Carter, for coming up with the Strategic Arms Limitation Treaty, old SALT 2? He started all that nuke-cutting bullshit, whittling the number of nukes down from 50,000 each to mere thousands. Lord knows what I could have done with 50,000 nukes. I mean there's a limit to how many times even *I* can nuke New York. What do you target with that many warheads anyway? Antarctica, Tierra del Fuego, Katmandu?"

"Don't you see this is wrong?" Taylor blurted out.

"Not at all, Jack. I simply see the *Ding an sich*, the thing in itself—a world where nothing is true, everything is permitted, and hell holds sway."

"But we always have choices. Don't you see that?"

"Yes, and we have chosen the blackest whorehouse in hell."

"Who *are* you? Its pimp?"

"A sorcerer."

"And your next trick?"

'I conjure Armageddon."

"Then God have mercy on our souls."

'I don't see why, Jack. We have shown Him none at all. What *has* He done to deserve us anyway? What is the ancient grudge we bear Him that we take the Light of Creation—of GENESIS!—and use it to raze His Earth, His Eden? And what do we do for an encore? Target the stars? Nuke galaxies? Lay waste to Quasars? Make war on black holes? Murder the universe? Christ, Jack, I'm weak with the wonder of it."

At which point Taylor's headset began to shake—first with Vlad's lewd Luciferian laughter, then with something far more hideous, rising in pitch and amplitude until it wasn't laughter at all but something for more elemental—beastly bellowing, hellish howls, gargantuan guffaws. What came to Taylor's mind was not human noise but rather the jungle roar of pain-crazed beasts—wounded rhinos and dying dinosaurs, rearing in terror, trumpeting their death-throes, deranged with feral suffering—laughter so powerful, it dislodged his headset, so painful he feared for his ears.

So ungodly, he trembled for his soul.

 20 Corner Table, Please

L.A.'s Supersonic Cruise Missile #1 was streaking east above Wilshire Boulevard at Mach 1.1., almost touching the rolled-down convertible tops and open sunroofs of the tens of thousands of Porsches and Jaguars, Mercedes and Lamborghinis cruising the warm summer streets, boulevards, and freeways.

His sonic booms left over a thousand piled-up cars and tens of thousands of blood-gushing eardrums over the length and breadth of Santa Monica.

Glancing over his shoulder, the L.A. Dragonfly/Cruise Missile #1 allowed himself a small smile. Humming his favorite Karen Carpenter ballad, he burst into song:

"*We've only just begun.*"

In truth, the L.A. Cruise Missile #1 was happy as a Martian in a red sandpit. He felt as if he'd come home. Star-struck and star-bound, L.A. was everything he'd dreamed of, everything he'd ever wanted to be. His memory systems were packed to the rafters with every three-dimensional street, building, contour, and image of Star City. L.A.'s Dragonfly/Cruise #1 had never in his life seen anything so scintillatingly glamorous. He felt as if he had a calling, a destiny, a dream.

Hollywood was where he was meant to be.

There, up ahead, right on glorious Wilshire, the towering Mondrian Hotel. Named for the legendary Dutch artist—after whom the legendary designer and architect Philippe Starck had styled it—the building itself was a work of high art, a weird, wonderful mural, a living hymn to the Great Master.

It was *so* cool! He felt *so* sorry for all those Dragonfly Hollywood wannabes who were desperate for the glitz and glitter of Tinsel Town but stuck in the boring military backwaters around the globe, any of whom would give anything to be where he was right now.

Oh, eat your heart out! the Dragonfly howled.

There it was—heartbreak-dead-ahead, the Regent Beverly Wilshire, in the center of Beverly Hills, off Rodeo Drive. Some genius of a fire-control officer had front-loaded three-dimensional film stills from that incomparable oeuvre, *Pretty Woman,* much of which had been filmed there. L.A. #1's memory banks throbbed with spectacular views of this hostel. Formerly the home of Warren Beatty himself—as well as Little Girl Lost, the flamboyant and ultimately tragic heiress-celebrity, Barbara Hutton—the Regent Beverly Wilshire was not so much a hotel as an epic masterpiece, a symphony, a heavenly choir. This stunning tribute to Gaelic neoclassicism—commingling so artfully with the High Renaissance of Leonardo and the Medicis—was no mere inn but a pastel potpourri that touched #1's soul.

Spago! He couldn't believe it. If he could get a table there, he would die fulfilled. (He would of course insist on Wolfgang Puck—merely the greatest culinary master on the face of the planet—to personally dish out the courses. He didn't care if the legendary chef/proprietor was franchising other eateries now.) His memory systems were loaded with three-dimensional contour photos of Spago's rack of lamb, Oysters Rockefeller, broiled whole lobsters dripping with drawn butter, New York strips blood-rare and sizzling in their platters—to say nothing of Wolfgang's haute-cuisine pizzas. To dine on such fare—all the while rubbing shoulders with Pacino, Hoffman, Streep, DeNiro, Madonna—would be the culinary experience of a lifetime.

No! No! Say it ain't so! Not Merv's?

But there it was: Merv Griffin's Beverly Hilton. In L.A. #1's memory banks some luminary had even installed a three-dimensional contour photo of Mr. Merv, right out there in front of his hostelry—and a second of him on the set of *Wheel of Fortune.*

Oh God, L.A.'s Dragonfly/Cruise #1 would have given anything to have been on *Wheel of Fortune* with Merv.

In fact, in his mind's eye he could image Merv standing right in front of Trader Vic's wearing one of those dark suits he always looked so terrific in and a red silk shirt, open at the neck, with French cuffs and diamond links.

He was a g-o-o-o-o-d-looking man!

Merv! Merv! the Dragonfly yelled at the top of his sonic-boom voice.

But had the ghost of Merv been there he would have only stared up at him in gape-mouthed horror, and then, clutching his bleeding, ruptured ears, dove, screaming, to the pavement.

Like everyone else.

With good reason. L.A. #1 was now approaching his target—the end of the line.

The Dragonfly sighed. He took no pride in nuking the film capital of the world. He knew all the clichés. Boulevard of Broken Dreams, they called it. Hollywood Babylon, Kenneth Anger had dubbed it. To him it would always be golden.

It had already given him so, so much.

He had even met Merv.

Or at least his heavenly sprite.

Oh well, no use whining. It was all blood under the bridge. Get on with it, L.A. #1.

Make your stand.

He'd been so eager to meet Merv he'd actually missed it on the first run through and now had to make a big sweeping U-turn at nearly Mach 1.4 to get back to it on time.

He did a quick time-GPS-check. He had to get in synch with L.A. #2.

So far, so good.

The Pink Palace—as the Beverly Hills Hotel was nicknamed—was not so much a hotel as a vast estate: a dozen acres of picturesque bungalows connected by a labyrinth of secret pathways artfully concealed by palm trees, oleanders, and huge fronded tropical plants, leaf-shrouded paths so circuitous guests routinely got lost.

Former home to such legendary luminaries as Liz Taylor and Howard Hughes, featuring a spectacular Olympic-size pool, magnificent canopied beds, grand patios, cozy fireplaces, Ralph Lauren bed linens, endless red carpeting, that marvelous porte cochere overhanging the front entrance, and of course the biggest, baddest, deal-making/deal-breaking, banana-leaf-lined, eating-drinking, star-studded, impossible-to-get-a-reservation movie-hangout in all of Hollywood history—the Polo Lounge.

Taking dead aim, L.A. Cruise #1 shot straight through the front door. His only comment to the diving, screaming, hands-over-ears maître d' was: *Corner table, please.*

21 Bite *This*!

The L.A. Cruise Missile #2 was eastbound and down, rocketing over the Hollywood Bowl at Mach 1.0, but it was hard to keep his mind on work. There was so much to see, so little time.

Right below—just off the Hollywood Freeway—the famed Hollywood Bowl. The largest open-air amphitheater in the world, home to the Los Angeles Philharmonic, it seated 17,000 people in boxes, at picnic tables, and in bleachers and offered a great view of its trees, gardens, and surrounding mountains.

He hoped its concertgoers weren't put-out by his ear-cracking sonic booms.

Streaking down Highland, he hooked hard-port onto Hollywood Boulevard. It was little out of his way, but he couldn't imagine visiting Hollywood without taking in Grauman's Chinese Theatre with all those hundreds of celebrity footprints forever enshrined in its legendary courtyard, followed by a quick Mach 1.0 stroll up the Hollywood Walk of Fame with its several hundred movie-star sidewalk-decals dotting the sidewalk only one step apart.

How often do you get to streak over the footprints of Garbo and Gable, Marilyn and Duke, Hepburn and Tracy, Bronson and Stanwyck at the speed of sound?

The war could wait.

How could he miss the Hollywood Wax Museum, Ripley's Believe It or Not, the Hollywood Guinness Book of World Records Museum? No one interested in death could afford to skip the Hollywood Memorial Museum, featuring the tombs and graves and crypts of Valentino, Doug Fairbanks, and Cecil B. DeMille. Forest Lawn—just east of Griffith Park—with three hundred exquisitely landscaped acres was a death-lover's delight, boasting some of the most elaborate marble sculptures and artworks in the world, including a massive stained-glass facsimile of Leonardo's *Last Supper* and in the Hall of the Crucifixion-Resurrection what was possibly the largest religious oil painting on earth, *The Crucifixion*, by the artist Jan Styka.

The Dragonfly/Cruise Missile #2 would have given anything for a languid, leisurely walk, maybe a brief talk with the owners. He and his colleagues could help them drum up mucho business.

Maybe they could work out some sort of contingency-commission arrangement.

Well, there it was—Universal Studios straight ahead. They had some of the hottest acts in history performing at that very moment. In fact, as L.A. #2 entered the lot, he truly wished he'd had time for the seven-hour tour. The movie lot was spread out over 420 acres, so you really needed a tram to see everything. Also it helped to have a guide who could provide entertaining, informative commentary.

L.A #2 would have to make do with a couple of gate-crashing visits.

He did catch a number of the big acts—all thirty feet of the real King Kong, an 8.3 earthquake (How would you like 8.3 million on the old Richter, Kong old boy?) a war with aliens, a *Waterworld* sea battle, the parting of the Red Sea, Noah's flood. The legendary *Jurassic Park* Ride, the most thrilling attraction in 65 million years. Oh, how he yearned to climb aboard their famous runaway raft, plunge deep into a Jurassic Jungle, go head-to-head, eyeball-to-eyeball with Spitters, Raptors, and that glowering, towering Tyrannosaurus Rex. (*Oh, do I have a T-Rex for you*, he thought, grabbing his crotch, thinking of his own T-Rex MIRVs.)

His last treat was that huge growling great white shark from *Jaws*. Drawing a bead on his vast maw, he dove straight into the gaping, grotesquely fanged jaws.

His last thought before detonation was:

Bite **this!** *Big Mouth.*

22 As the Hammer Loves the Nail

Lawrence John Taylor, brigadier general, USAF, might joke, but there in his B-2 Black Stealth bomber, entering Russian air space, he thought of little else but Kate Magruder.

She was like nothing he'd ever known.

Nor would his younger brothers let up on him about her—ever since he confessed he was in love with her.

"You going to tell me who she is?" Will asked.

"Never happen."

"Stud hoss, what's so special?" Jamie asked. "You must have bagged a thousand beauties."

"None like her."

"You'd give them all up?" Will said. "Just for her?"

"In a heartbeat."

"She anything like Roslyn?" Jamie said.

"Like a plum to a prune."

"You loved Ros once," Will said.

"Like the anvil loves the hammer."

"And the hammer the nail," Jamie said, finishing the ancient joke.

"To a hammer the whole world's a nail," Larry Taylor said, adding to the adage.

"What's she like?" Will asked.

"The tiger's eye."

"What's she see in you?" Jamie asked.

"A staked goat," William said.

"Did you tell her about duty, honor, country?" Jamie asked.

"She calls us 'jumped-up genocidists.'"

"She has a point," Jamie said.

"And a smile like the end of the rainbow."

"You really have it bad," Will said.

"It's like I'm barreling over Niagara Falls."

"You really want to marry her?" Jamie said.

"If she'll have me."

"There's a girl alive who can say no to Stud Hoss?" Will laughed.

"You once called me Armageddon's Top Gun," Larry reminded him.

"That was before you went Chernobyl on us," Will said.

"I'm telling you she's the only one."

"*Was* the only one," Will said. "According to your horoscope, a new heart-throb's on the horizon."

"On the screen," Jamie confirmed. "Bogies, eight o'clock."

"Do they have a lock?" John asked.

"If they do, it's visual," Jamie said.

"And they're closing in," Will said.

They studied the new arrivals on their display monitors.

23 The Fire Drive to End All Fire Drives

Kate Magruder emerged from the fires into the Central Park Zoo.

She was sorry she had. While the big, heavy concrete block buildings and cages had served as crude bomb shelters—and provided the large animals with some protection—they had been useless against the blazing winds and over-pressures. The big beasts had died where they stood.

Three caged lions had been broiled and exsanguinated by the combination of shock wave and overpressure, fire and flying debris.

Dumbo, the city's much-beloved elephant, had been badly charred, then crushed so completely he looked as if he'd been smashed by some Brobdingnagian vise, lying flat on his side, nothing but hide and bones, served well, well done.

The city's pair of prize Bengal tigers had imploded. Now forest *and* cats burned bright. They were little more than scorched bloody tiger-skin rugs.

The Petting Zoo—with its does and goats, ducks and bunnies—had transformed the surrounding grounds into a Road Kill Bar-B-Que Grill. Its denizens were strewn randomly around the rest of the zoo—on the grounds and on the sides of the blockhouse buildings—seared, hammered flat as linoleum.

And the fires were closing in.

Fire driver, Cassie called us, Kate thought grimly. *She claimed we exterminated most of the large animals once before. Well, Cass, I guess this is the fire drive to end all fire drives.* She took one last look at the elephant's bled-out, still-smoking remains. *We even fire-broiled Dumbo.*

Then she saw it—another storm sewer. After the last go-round, she'd sworn she would never enter another sewer. But now she did not have much choice.

Looping the gold Cross Pen with her belt, she again devised a crude manhole-cover key. She pulled up the lid and climbed down into the abyss.

24 Let's Go to Work

Frank was joined on the roof by Cathy Anne. She was wearing green scrubs and looked worried.

"Jesus, Frank," she said, "those blasts broke bottles all over the storage rooms—at a distance of twenty miles."

He indicated the footage on his monitor of Manhattan in flames.

"I got Cassandra on the other TV," Frank said. "She's up there on one of the Magruder mountains in Arizona. Those people can survive anything—even Armageddon."

"Which is happening all around us," Cathy said.

"MTN is broadcasting it," Frank said.

"L. L. has her own satellites and relay stations, and of course the Odyssey."

"Must be a great view from up there," Frank said. "Let's go to work."

"I just hope enough people survive to *need* our help," Cathy said.

25 . . . And He Opened the Bottomless Pit

"You know, Jack-Baby, there's something I like more than fallout."

Taylor fought to master his mounting terror.

"The worldwide pathogenic catastrophe which the pervasive fallout will precipitate. An interconnected interbreeding synergy of disaster *and* plague—so mutually reinforcing that nothing can stand up to it. Every living thing will feel its wrath. Humble though it may be, fallout—by lowering the resistance of plant and tree, man and animal to terminal diseases—will play an indispensable role in bringing the world to the brink of extinction and beyond."

"Extinction and beyond," Taylor said wearily.

"Hiroshima and Nagasaki showed us the way. With the complete absence of medical personnel, supplies, and with fallout obliterating everyone's immune systems, the 'demic' diseases—TB and influenza, intestinal ailments such as dysentery and typhoid, animal-to-man diseases such as tularemia and the whole gamut of plagues, insectborne diseases such as malaria, yellow jack and typhus—will take hold. All the diseases we once kept under control—diphtheria, syphilis, leprosy, polio, whooping cough, scarlet fever—also ran riot. Nor are we immune to those pathogens anymore. When they return, it will be with a vengeance. And unlike Japan—where an entire world came to the aid of Hiroshima and Nagasaki—no one will rescue our plague-ridden survivors.

"Oh, Jack, we've known Time Out of Mind that war-derived diseases kill more people than war, and devastating as the bombs will be this time, that time-honored adage will be doubly true. People crowding together, seeking safety in numbers, will be horribly vulnerable to disease—especially Entameba histolytica, the causative vector of amoebic dysentery. A good dose of fallout, Jack, and the food-feces circle will be closed. Half the earth will shit its brains out.

"Oh, Jack, it'll be lov-er-ly."

"Your driving dream is to make us shit our brains out?"

"Why not? There's plenty out there that'll love it. Rats and flies, for instance."

"Your goal is to turn the world into a utopia for rats and flies."

"And rickettiae."

"Rickettiae?" Taylor repeated, dumbfounded.

"The virus like bacterium that produces mite-, flea-, and louse-typhus. When typhus hits a nonimmunized population, it spreads like wildfire. Christ, Jack, the typhus epidemics of World War I outlasted that conflict by five fucking years. Can you imagine how long the new outbreaks will endure?"

"Make the world safe for typhus," Taylor said, sickened by the horror of it.

"We're talking a world of roadside camps and hobo jungles. People drifting, scavenging the countryside in search of food, medicine, crowding together at night out of fear and despair. Malnutrition, utter absence of sanitation, no medical facilities at all. Their camps, instead of a refuge, will be the perfect breeding ground for these plagues. Not only typhus but Pasteurella tularensis—tularemia—borne by everything from rats to rabbits to squirrels to dogs. Lots of the little beasties have the shit already. We just have to increase their population density. The closer they get to each other, the more fleas they get per animal. Break down the barriers between them and us, and presto! The shit spreads like magic. Add a few horse- and deerflies to the equation and we got a popcorn machine going. Those guys are great transmitters of the stuff too, with their nasty bloodsucking beaks—real superconductors. I'll tell you, boychick, it will spread like a brush-fire."

"I'm surprised you haven't included Bubonic Plague in your litany of disasters."

"Pasteurella pestis? Oh, I would never forget that one. I do favor the Pneumonic Plague variety. That shit is *mean*. No need for intermediaries such as lice or fleas. That shit is spread by mere fucking breathing. You can't help but love it. Contagious as the common cold, it is treatable by antibiotics and hospitalization, but guess what? There aren't any drugs. And as for your hospitals? When the electricity goes off and your refrigeration bites the dust, all those antibiotics you adore, they themselves turn virulent. Instead of curing disease they *transmit* it."

At which point Vlad thundered into Taylor's headset:

"We'll have some fine times together, you and I. I'm talking spiking fevers, skyrocketing heart rates, rattling coughs, bloody bowels, coughing up your bloody fucking lungs till you can't even breathe, Jack-Baby. It's called sibili and rales, meaning a whistling death-rattle. The dread petechiae or bubos, hence the name Bubonic Plague. The face turns dark purple; hence the Black Face of Death; or the Black Death for short. Don't ever think I'd leave that out. I know, it's one of your favorites. From my point of view, Jack, the end of the world is nothing without it."

"End of the world," Taylor muttered, nauseous with dread.

"What do you think this is all about? Save the whales? Protect the polar bears? I don't know about you but Greenpeace has never been part of my program. In fact, Old Mother Nature's on my shit list too. I got a little *Un*natural Selection for her and Old Father Darwin. We're going to devolve his Creatures Great and Small right down the Phyletic Scale. I get done with them, they'll think monkeys descended from men."

"To listen to you, maybe they did."

"Oh no, please, Jump-My-Joint-Till-I-Oink-and-Boink-O-Vich, not invective. Just because I want to piss on your parade. I can't help it if you invented this shit, if your friends sold it to me, and now I want my money's worth. I can't help it if it makes me want to target the stars and murder God. I can't help it if it makes the old blackjack in my pants hammer-hard and thermonuclear-hot. I can't help it if all that super-fab fallout kills flowers and trees, asparagus and weeds just as thoroughly as it wastes pigs and chickens, men and dogs. I can't help it if all those grass- and croplands and those forests and farms will have to bite my nuclear pork too. Look at it this way. For every down there is an up. Insects will love my New World Order. Insects get along great with fallout and even better with sickly, dying animal and plant life. There is nothing like drought or blight to make insects multiply geometricly. I'm talking explosions of insects, an entomological bonanza, the atom bomb turned population bomb. At least, for bugs."

"Bugs," Taylor repeated dully, his mind disassociating.

"You betcha. Nature abounds with stories of how after a major forest catastrophe—wildfires, windstorms, drought, whatever—the bark beetle and budworm populations soar to such proportions that they spread into lush forests and wipe out many times more timber than the original disaster. Fallen, irradiated timber—as well as forests ignited by firestorm and bomb—will be a horn-of-plenty for every conceivable forest-feeding insect. We'll see exponentiating populations. And since birds—which are their only natural predator—will have died off, there will be nothing around to check their growth. Oh-Wail-On-My-Dong-Like-You-Were-Whaling-A-Gong-Ovich, it'll be a paradise for bugs, Locusts, crickets, cicadas, army worms, ants, stinkbugs, chiggers, moths, sawflies, chinch flies, cabbage worms, they won't die off till they run out of food."

"You wish to turn the world to desert?" Taylor asked, short of breath, his hands shaking.

"Irretrievable desert. It's happened before, you know—here and there in parts of the globe. When Hugulai Khan conquered present-day Iraq in the fourteenth century, it was the most fertile land in history—the Cradeland, the Deltaland of the Tigris and Ephrates, the Land Between the Rivers. He killed people by the millions and destroyed their irrigation systems. Too ravaged to rebuild, the land turned to waterless, trackless waste. And never recovered. Same will happen to Kansas, Iowa, Mississippi, Southern California. You can kiss the San Joaquin and San Fernando Valleys good-bye, and say: 'HELLO, LOCUSTS!'"

"Hello, locusts?"

"REVELATION, Jack-O-Buddy. Remember?

"'. . . And he opened the bottomless pit; and there arose a smoke out of the pit. And there came out of the smoke locusts. The sound of their winds was as the sound of chariots of many horses running to battle. And they had tails like unto scorpions, and their power was to hurt men.

"'Babylon is fallen, is fallen and is become a habitation of devils and the hold of every foul spirit. Therefore shall her plagues come in one day, death and mourning, and famine; and she shall be utterly burned with fire.'"

"Locusts," Taylor repeated numb with despair.

"Yo, Hum-My-Hammer-Till-I-Stammer-and-Yammer. Remember me as John of REVELATION, as the Will and Wrath of God. I only want to do His Bidding, His Work. It's not too much to ask."

26 They Never Fought Invisible Man Before

"Bad news, Little Bro, bogies on your eight o'clock," Brigadier General Larry Taylor announced.

"Do I go for the speedbag?" Jamie asked.

"Only way," Larry said. "They won't trust their heat- or radar-missiles, so they'll want to nose-cannon your six. You have to take them high, then low. Real low."

"Roll inverted," Jamie said.

"I can feel those negative g's now," Will said.

"Little Bro," Jamie said. "I got these two covered."

"Just a quick pick and roll," Will said.

"Never happen, Will. You haven't been spotted, and Larry John's going to need you."

"You might too."

"Big Bro has bigger fish to fry. Great whites. Don't scrub his mission."

The two brothers watched reluctantly. Larry Taylor—from his Olympian heights—had the better angle, but no one could really see it. Oh, he could watch those MiGs on the screen—bigger than life, howling for his brother's hide. But even his instruments couldn't pick up another Stealth.

On the plus side, their instruments and screens couldn't pick him up either. Medium- and long-range SAMs require full radar contact—from target-acquisition to point of impact. The search-and-tracking ground-radar has to hold the target long enough for the SAM to lock onto it or for the interceptors to acquire it.

Visual detection was also tough. Night and foul weather rendered the Stealth virtually invisible, and a curious array of underlights could illuminate the Stealth till he melded perfectly with the sheltering sky.

"It's a Judy," his little brother called out, meaning he had a lock on the first MiG now moving in on his six. "One of them's in my ass but can't get a lock."

"Not enough heat?" William said.

"There ain't even a pipe."

"Guess they never fought Invisible Man before," William said. "You sure you got him?"

"Dead in my sights."

"Bird activated?" Will asked.

"On a hair trigger."

"Select and arm?" Will asked.

"I have a select light."

"Lock and load," Will said.

"Nostrovia, Ivan."

A Sparrow missile streaked toward the MiG's nose-radar.

A brilliant red-orange fireball engulfed the MiG.

"Here's two more," Larry Taylor said. "They're converging on Will. What's your clock?"

"One is coming straight down at me, twelve o'clock high, the other I read nine."

"It's speedbag for sure," Jamie said.

"Pure hammerhead."

Hammerhead was a vertical climb, straight up to near-stall speed, followed by an inverted 180-degree roll, sending it back down, then turning the nose around and bringing it straight up into the bogey's six. If not the hardest dog-fighting tactic, it was the most painful move in dogfighting.

Lawrence knew his brother had started his climb when—on his screen—he saw the two MiGs commence their corkscrewing ascent. Spiraling in on his tail, they fought desperately to get into his envelope and stick their nose-cannons in his six.

As for Jamie, Larry knew his youngest brother would not concern himself with fancy lock-breaking maneuvers. The bogeys may have had him beat speed-wise, but his Stealth design limited their firepower. His best move was to get them up-top as fast as possible, take them to the bag, then take them out.

Now that he was spotted, he had to work fast.

Others would be joining them soon. From his 65,000-foot vantage point, Lawrence Taylor had a perfect view of the action below. Still, he'd have given anything to be down there in a fighter. He hated to admit it, but the fighter jocks were right.

Flying bombers at 65,000 feet was one step removed from driving a truck.

27 Cocked and Locked

Captain Petrov leaped aboard the Typhoon sub a heartbeat ahead of the cracking ice—barely in time to grab the hand of the limping reporter, Ivan Gilyenko, and yank him atop the hull before he could again slip under the ice.

The navigator, Grigori Shupov, was waiting for him with a headset.

"Captain, an American TANAMCO is putting out a signal. All surfaced subs are to stay surfaced."

"That way we can't launch," the captain said.

"That's the point," First Officer Zhykoff said. "To launch is an act of war. Do we respond?"

"No, we submerge," Captain Petrov said.

"I have to tell you, sir," the navigator said, "we've been spotted by a second L.A.-Class attack sub. Probably when we surfaced."

"I guess those narwhales were an ill omen, reporter," Captain Petrov said. He turned back to the comm-officer. "Range and bearing."

"Fifty nautical miles, south-south-east, closing fast," Shupov said tensely.

"Where is Akula—our escort?" the captain asked.

"Akula's taking fire, sir," the sonar-man said into their headsets. "This place is swarming with L.A.'s."

"If that L.A. Class gets too close, Dmitri Pytorovich, none of us can use our nuclear fish on him," the captain said.

"Like Akula already did on his friend," Zhykoff said.

They glanced at the massive mushroom cloud billowing above the horizon, blotting out the sun.

"Clear the bridge and submerge," Petrov said. "Fast as humanly possible. Then send him a nuclear torp."

"He's going to answer with an ADCAP torp of his own," Zhykoff said.

The captain said, "And I'm sure he has a Harpoon waiting."

"Cocked and locked," First said.

"Soon as we flood those tanks, he'll unload," Shupov said.

"No way we can beat a Harp. Not at that range."

"Bad news, sir," the weapons officer announced into their headsets. "L.A. #1 got off a torp before she was nuked."

"Fuck 'em all but six," the captain said, "and save them for pallbearers. We're flooding the tanks."

"He also has Harps, and they aren't ordinary torps," First said. "They pack a punch."

"That's why God invented double-hulls," the captain said. "Clear the bridge and prepare to submerge. We're taking her down to launch-depth. Soon as we submerge send that second L.A. Class a nuclear fish."

The men flung themselves down the main hatch.

28 Backward into Nothingness

The short black man with the red head bandana jerked Ron Lewis to his feet.

"Stop your bawling, man. We maybe gots a way down."

He led Lewis to the edge of the burning building. Below, nine black men were using a green rectangular canvas awning as a fire-catcher. While Lewis had sobbed in the middle of the roof, the short black man—with the help of the men below holding the awning—had assisted the others off the burning roof. One of the last jumpers—a young black woman—leaped from the flaming roof. Opening her arms and legs, she dropped full spread-eagle onto the canvas.

"Your turn," the man said.

The other rooftop jumpers stood below, several helping to hold the green canvas. He and the black man were the last two left.

"I'm afraid of heights," Lewis said, trembling, "I can't do it."

"And you ain't afraid of fire I don't suppose."

"I can't. I really can't."

"We ain't got time for no games."

He hit Lewis in the side of the neck with a short left. Lewis's knees buckled. He pitched forward, the man caught him and pitched him off the roof, and Lewis was falling backward into nothingness under a surreal downpour of fiery debris and black rain.

His last thought was that the spectacle was eerily beautiful.

29 Baby Leviathans

The ADCAP torpedo was eager to get going. He'd been racked and imprisoned in the weapons compartment for far too long and yearned to ply the seas.

He had to admit his egress into the polar deep was less than pleasant. He had his firing ram, which was essentially an air gun—a high-pressure piston with a ton and a half of air-per-square-inch backing it—and at the forward end he had the sea. When the air-valve behind him released, the pressure on his piston mounted unbearably.

In one and a half seconds the two-ton torpedo, accelerating to over three g's, slammed out of the tube like a bat out of hell—which was sort of what he was. His batlike sonar was his eyes and ears, nerves and nose. He hunted by sound the way a dog might track by smell. His supercomputer microprocessors could crunch tonal data at a rate of a quarter of a million gigabytes per second, locking the Baby Leviathan firmly onto his prey's tonal signature, informing him of its range and bearing—even keeping him fixed on the best course of interception.

Of course, nothing is as easy as all that. The Baby Leviathan was at the outermost range of target interception—nearly forty miles. And he was trying to track a circuitously moving target. However, his send-receive capability included a ten-mile guidance wire in his own aft section as well as a ten miles' worth of launch-tube wire, allowing it to send-receive target data to-and-from the ship as well as to receive guidance instructions.

Then there were combined seeker-head/computer-implementing electronically beamed sonar to hunt its prey with 180-degree peripheral vision unlike the competition, which had to swim after its prey like underwater corkscrews.

Set for a broadband 180-degree search, it had its Typhoon's stern-baffles dead in its sights.

Its prey would not get away.

One by one the Baby Leviathan heard his brother and sister Leviathans blown out of their torpedo tubes.

They followed happily in his wake.

30 A Little Whiff of Death Makes Us Brothers in the Night

Sailor was not alone as he scrambled through the sewer tunnels.

People too had taken to that labyrinthine underworld.

Not that it had done them much good. Hideously burned, flesh riddled with flying glass, clothes scorched, even burned away. The eyes—of those who still had eyes—were walled with pain. Those—still able to crawl aimlessly through the sewers and storm drains—coughed and choked from smoke inhalation.

None shrieked at the presence of the big auburn rat.

They had witnessed nightmares that made his presence inconsequential.

Fire was their prime fear, not Sailor.

They were all in the same hellish boat—and it was leaking badly.

One man—his arms and legs burned to the bones—raised a charred, bloody hand to Sailor.

And gave him a tight blood-smeared smile.

A woman—her blouse burned off her body, her body horrifically charred—stared at him with fixed curiosity, as if grateful to him for diverting her from her misery.

Sailor was no longer a threat.

The reality around them was the threat.

A little whiff of death makes us brothers in the night, Sailor thought grimly.

All around Sailor the city thundered with exploding gas pipes, detonating automobiles, and collapsing buildings.

Whatever was going on up above, Sailor wanted no part of it.

Human beings were truly fiends from hell.

Sailor was better off here below.

31 A Sea of Noise

The captain, his mate, the navigator, the weapons officer, and the reporter crowded into the control room. They sat in complete silence.

The entire ship was still as death. Red fluorescent warning lights illuminated the forward half of the ship. The reactor was shut down—the desalinators, wash-room showers, and the galley put on hold. Everything was done to reduce their detectability and improve their own hearing.

The latter was important. They had to get a fix on the approaching L.A. Class—if they were to send out a torpedo.

They were surrounded by a sea of noise—everything from fish to crunching pack ice, from trumpeting narwhales to the unavoidable cavitation of their own propeller.

But these were random sounds. Its 15-foot steel spherical array in the nose-cone was, at 75,000 watts, as powerful as any active echo-ranging sonar system around, and its 240-foot-long towed array—strung from a half-mile, 3.5-inch-thick cable—supplied the ship with excellent medium-range, low-frequency passive detection.

With the result that its sonar computers were awash in noise. They needed to separate the wheat from the chaff, the patterned from the random unpatterned sounds. To that end the memory systems of its Acoustic Spectrum and Motion Analysis Computers were filled with five- to ten-minute noise paradigms. These tonal patterns and frequency lines matched those of their fellow combat vessels with surprising accuracy—at least with accuracy enough to identify the target vessels.

"You sure it's an L.A. Class?" the captain asked the weapons officer.

"I count a 61-cycle electrical turbine, seven blades on the prop. Target Motion Analysis definitely reads target designate: L.A.-Class, City of New Orleans."

"Bearing and range?"

"We lost a lot of juice when we shut the reactors down. I did clock 52 klicks—well beyond torpedo range—before we lost all that power. But it was closing fast."

"How close you guess he is now?"

"Forty klicks. Within torp range."

"How can you be so sure?"

"He just fired off a Harp."

32 Live by the Gun, Die by the Gun

Brigadier General Lawrence Taylor watched in awe—from high up his B-2 Stealth bomber—as the MiGs crudely and clumsily, operating on wing, instinct, and a prayer, attempted to follow the Invisible Man into his nose-down vertical scissors. A simple move for the Invisible Man, and the only one that made any sense for him tactically. Jam the rudder, roll the plane till the cockpit is 180 degrees over the earth—parallel with the horizon's rim—then plunge it over the rest of the way, straight down in swirling S's, till at bottom, in the pit, you split the S, swerving straight up in the bogey's six. Simple in principle, but it hurt like a motherfucker.

What the Stealth fighter had lacked aerodynamically and in speed, Will would try to make up for now. Hugging the envelope's edge, stretching it beyond all conceivable limits, Jamie doubted whether his brother could pull the fighter out of its head-down, 7-g dive—otherwise known as a death spiral—but he knew he would try.

Shoving the stick forward—simultaneously jamming his ailerons and rudder, rolling inverted, parallel to the horizon's rim—Will snap-rolled the plane level, then upward. He apparently made it. The two MiGs following him pulled awkwardly out of their dives. *Poor buggers,* Jamie thought. *The whole exercise is about verticality, going high to build altitude, swapping velocity for altitude because on the swan dive you get the speed back. But you have to get on your back quick. Otherwise you stall and fall.*

Which MiGs have a tendency to do.

And that takes practice, something—Larry Taylor could see on his screen—that those guys have had very little of. They probably hadn't had enough fuel for practice.

And when it came to rolling inverted, his youngest brother was the best.

However, he had to admit that the pair of MiGs—which had been coming after his brother for the past ten minutes—had heart. They lacked practice, experience, and his firepower. But they didn't quit. Hellbent for leather, they followed him up and down the speedbag, jockeying frantically for position, making passes at each other's noses, looking for a tailpipe—which his brother lacked—for a firing envelope, so close to him he couldn't risk a shot himself.

*Stick with them, Will. Don't let them beat you on the turn. That first turn's going to be your best, kid, just like I taught you. Cut inside **his** turn. Get into **his** six o'clock. Stick it up **his** pipe.*

Will rolled inverted, cut Ivan #1's angle on the third vertical climb.

"He just flashed his prune," William was shouting.

"Get in his fucking six," Larry yelled over his headset, "before he hoses you."

"Before he runs a gun-pass," Jamie yelled. "Smoke his ass."

In a burst of brilliant orange fire and explosive flame-shooting debris, his brother blew Ivan #1 out of the sky.

Ten seconds later, #2 was flame-shooting debris.

"Live by the gun, die by the gun," Jamie observed.

Larry's thoughts were more philosophical:

Ivan, you just ran out of time.

33 "I'm Dreaming of a Nuclear Christmas"

The Sin Sisters' explosive laughter at the nuclear destruction of New York was rivaled only by their apocalyptic mirth at the L.A. firestorms.

"Uh-oh, check out L.A., Little Sis," Sultana said, "entertainment capital of the world. Look what's happening to Malibu there by the beach."

"Oh, poor Malibu. It was always vulnerable to brushfires."

The surrounding brush and forest were a scintillating sea of flames.

Their laughter boomed, while Thucydides' camera moved south toward Santa Monica.

"Uh-oh, there goes Pacific Palisades," Sabrina said. "And Santa Monica Pier."

"Too bad, I loved riding its carousel."

"There goes Muscle Beach and all those gorgeous musclebound hunks."

"Bench-press *this,* motherfucker," Sultana said, pointing to a TV monitor filled with L.A. flames.

Thucydides was now covering the Wilshire Boulevard firestorms.

"Hey, isn't that the Third Street Promenade? Six glittering blocks of four-lane walkway—stretching all the way from the Santa Monica Place Mall to glorious Wilshire Boulevard. Speaking of which—"

"Say good-bye to UCLA, Sis. We'll miss you. Great film school."

"Bye-bye, UCLA."

"There go the Bruin and Fox Theaters. No more movie premieres for you. No more pivoting, crisscrossing searchlights. No more long, lissome screen-queen legs and low-cut décolletage slinking out of stretch limos."

"There's that wimpy-looking trumpeter atop the Temple of the Church of Jesus Christ of Latter-Day Saints, standing watch over Westwood."

"Deathwatch now."

"Blow, Gabriel, blow. The saints are marching in."

"'Cept you're blowing 'Taps.'"

A flick of the firestorm's tongue, and he was gone.

"Here we come, glorious Beverly Hills. Wow, look at that firestorm roar. Right where the Beverly Hills Hotel used to hold court. Mr. Stone, you thought the $100 mill they spent on redecorating was a big deal. You ain't seen nothing yet. A new interior designer just hit town. A *hot* new designer."

"Decorates like a house afire."

The glittering flames roared through Beverly Hills.

Sabrina brought out a map highlighting "Beverly Hills Homes to the Stars." She began identifying their houses on the TV screen.

"Look, Sis, there on Beverly Drive. The fires are taking out Jimmy Durante's old home. Remember? 'Good night, Mrs. Calabash, wherever you are!' she growled with a dead-perfect imitation of Durante, right down to the tilted head-and-handshake.

"And there goes Betty Grable's old house just up the street. Great gams, Bets. You were always my favorite pinup."

"There's Peggy Lee's old home on Canon Drive. Way more to a fire than you ever dreamed, right, Peg? Wherever you are, break out the booze and have a ball."

"Over there on Hillcrest. Barbara Stanwyck's old home. Didn't she make a movie called *Ball of Fire*? With Howard Hawks? How do you like this for a re-make?"

"Up the street. Edward G. Robinson's old home. Remember *Little Caesar*?"

Sabrina—rolling around on the floor, clutching her chest, groaning hideously— did a pitch-perfect reprise of Robinson's role:

"'Mother of God, is this the end of Rico?'" She sat up, grinned at Stone, and said: "'Fraid it is, Eddie G."

"Uh-oh, there on Roxbury Drive. Lucille Ball's old home."

"'Lu-u-u-cy!'" Sabrina screeched with an eerily accurate imitation of Desi's Cuban accent.

"Oh no, there on St. Pierre Road. Not Bob Mitchum's old home. I loved him in *Night of the Hunter* and *Cape Fear*. DeNiro couldn't hold Mitchum's dirty jockstrap."

"Yeah, but he did look sexy in those jailhouse tats," Sabrina said.

Thucydides swept relentlessly over Beverly Hills. The firestorms raged, and the sisters' glee soared.

Elvis's old home had Sabrina pouting her lips, shaking-pumping-gyrating her hips, and regaling Stone with a full-vibrato rendition of "It's Now or Never."

"Guess it's never, King," Sultana quipped.

Streisand's abode elicited choruses of "Memories" and "The Way We Were."

"*Were* is right, Babbo."

Sly Stallone's house had Sultana shrieking: "Adrian! Adrian!"

Sabrina countered with a deep, guttural roar: "Ain't gonna be no rematch!"

Madonna's house fire brought only catcalls. Sultana shouted: "Boo! Hiss! I could throw six stones across Sunset right now and hit six black girls, any one of whom could sing and dance better than you, Material Girl."

"At least they could have a few minutes ago," Sabrina said.

As the firestorm approached the late Frank Sinatra's old house, Sabrina howled: "Hey, Frankie, give my best to Dino and Sammy D. In hell."

As the flames swept over Bing Crosby's house, Sabrina bent over the shackled Stone till they were nose-to-nose and crooned to him in a golden, vibrant baritone:

*"I'm dreaming of a Nuclear Christmas
One where the fireballs glow."*

As the sea of fire crept toward Judy Garland's house, Sabrina sang to Stone:

*"Somewhere over the firestorms, way up high,
There's a mushroom-cloud I heard of
Once in a lull-a-bye."*

Just before the flames swept up Judy Garland's old house, Sultana shouted: "Yo, Dorothy, guess what? There's no more Kansas anymore."

After which she crawled around on the floor and yelped like a barking dog, while Sabrina screamed: "Hey, Toto, get your fucking ass back here."

Sabrina laughed till her sides split.

Stone could only continue to stare at the macabre spectacle on the TV screen, slack-jawed, sick to the soul, terrifyingly still.

34 Forests of the Night

Mad Vlad was again on the phone to Acting President Jack Taylor, and again the Odyssey could not get a trace. The calls were going through too many satellites, too many relays.

Mad Vlad was talking.

"Jack, it's taking us a little longer than we anticipated to reprogram our target-packages and finish nuking you off the face of the earth. You're getting impatient, I know. You're hoping against hope that we're going to let you off the hook. Declare a cease-fire. Stand down. End the hostilities. No-can-do, Jack-Me-Off-O-Vich. Even if I trusted you not to retaliate, you know those Chink, Limey, Kraut, and Japo buddies of yours would never forgive me our little fun and games. I don't think you would either."

"Just because you nuked New York and Washington, D.C.?"

Malokov's laughter soared. "To name a few urban centers."

"You know you're mad," Acting President Taylor said, and rubbed his gut uneasily.

No one had thought to pack Zantac or Tagamet aboard Kneecap, and now Taylor's head not only throbbed, stomach acids were eating a hole straight through his abdominal wall.

"Aren't we being a little judgmental, Jack? I prefer 'high-spirited and head-strong.' Would you like it if I called *you* insane?"

"Probably not," Taylor said, clutching his stomach uneasily.

"I prefer to see myself as the patron-poet of manic-depression."

"I could get you some lithium."

"Hell, I could get it myself, Jack. Took the stuff for years. Problem is, boychik, it's just too fucking *boring*. I mean, what's life without *a little* madness?"

"You're our mad bard of the apocalypse now?"

"A sort of millennial William Blake. You know his 'Tyger, Tyger' poem? The one where he asks:

" 'Tyger, Tyger, burning bright
In the forest of the night.
What immortal hand or eye
Dare frame thy fearful symmetry?' "

"I'm familiar with it," Taylor whispered, his stomach now growling like a tiger.

"Well, that's what's lacking in contemporary geopolitical thought."

"Symmetry?" Taylor asked.

"No, no, Jack, you aren't listening. I'm sending out these breathless insights, but you aren't receiving. Christ, boy, get with the program."

"The symmetry has to evoke fear," Taylor guessed.

"Give the boy a cigar. Fearful symmetry. Want an example?"

"Not if it's going to hurt," he said.

Hurt? His headache was now metastasizing into a migraine, his stomach into one humongous hemorrhaging ulcer, and the rocket scientists who created Kneecap had neglected to stock it with Advil, Tylenol, anything.

"Just because the world is suffering a nuclear pang or two," Vlad asked, "are you going to become an unregenerate complainer?"

"Please don't," Taylor whimpered, truly miserable.

"Too late, Jack old friend. The balloon's already up. Have your fly-eye and keyhole sats scope out the Shimonokawa River due east of the Midori Bridge."

"I'm drawing a blank," Taylor said, staring at the photo of Vlad mounted above his computer monitor—the cruel eyes, the feral sneer.

Staring into Vlad's eyes, he felt himself falling, falling, falling straight into the . . . abyss.

"Hellfire and damnation, boy," Vlad roared, genuinely indignant. "You once nuked those motherfuckers off the map, and now you can't even remember their names. Christ on a crutch, you Americans *are* barbarians. Do I have to do all your thinking for you? I'm talking Nagasaki, Hiroshima."

"Please, Vlad, don't. You couldn't." Taylor now rubbed his stomach with one hand, his head with the other.

"Oh, yes, I could. Just scope it out on the old boob tube, Jack. I'm about to fry us up some tempura."

35 The Home of Madame Butterfly—and Mitsubishi

Nagasaki? What was in Nagasaki?

Cyd's data banks indicated that Mitsubishi had plants and shipyards, but nothing that warranted a nuclear attack.

Only one other odd fact. Nagasaki was the home of the original Madame Butterfly. The Japanese wife of a nineteenth-century British industrialist named Thomas Glover, her original name was Tsurujo, which Thucydides translated as "crane." Not as evocative as "Cho-Cho," or "Butterfly," but apparently her husband had loved her very much. He built a statue for her in his garden.

She likewise had nothing to do with geonuclear strategy.

36 "I'll Give You Game."

The Nagasaki Cruise Missile was now heading up Matsuyama toward the Urakami Cathedral. Turning hard-starboard, he sighted in on the Nagasaki Peace Monument in the city's Peace Park, located at the bomb's original hypocenter.

Nuking that original hypocenter was the triumph of form over substance, symbolism over reality. Sure, he recognized the celebratory symmetry of re-nuking Nagasaki City on the same spot, but the Yanks had not only hit them on the wrong spot, they had hit them too low.

They'd even hit the wrong city. Kokura would have been a much better target.

Even worse, Nagasaki was located at the foot of a mountain, nestled in twin valleys. By detonating their bomb within one of the valleys, they ensured that the mountain and the valley slope shielded the other half of the city from the blast. Despite the fact that Fat Boy—Nagasaki's plutonium bomb—was much more powerful than the Hiroshima bomb, its damage was merely comparable.

They'd hit the wrong city in the wrong spot at the wrong time.

Such inefficiency galled Nagasaki Cruise Missile #1. He saw no point in repeating the same mistake. He'd have taken out Kokura—the way the Americans should have done it the first time.

If he'd had to hit Nagasaki, he'd have at least altered the flight path and hit the harbor. The Mitsubishi Works—located on those docks—had escaped the first nuclear blast, and they were about to escape it again.

He'd have also nuked that Butterfly statue behind Glover's old house.

The Dragonfly/Cruise could see the hypocenter memorial now. It had been a tennis court, located at a house on 171 Matsuyama, when the first warhead had nuked it. The cruise missile could imagine enthused tennis players whacking the ball around the court amid cries of "love," "ad-in," "ad-out," and "game," then looking up in utter horror.

I'll give you "game," Fat Boy had probably said.

Actually, he would have preferred nuking an exciting tennis match over a boring hunk of granite—particularly this one. Located in the middle of a classic Japanese commercial center, it was surrounded by gaudy billboards, sleazy advertisements, and honking cars.

Oh, well. Target-acquired. Solid-lock.

He went into a steep vertical climb. The original Nagasaki bomb had detonated at approximately 500 meters. He was ordered to do the same.

Just before detonation he hummed the opening from the famous *Madama Butterfly* aria.

He had to admit it was a catchy tune.

37 Blow Out Those G's

Larry Taylor's younger brothers were far below, no longer relying on their Stealth LO (Low Observability) to protect them from Ivan. They hugged rivers and hills, kept just below Mach 1 to avoid sonic boom, and tried to dodge the Russian radar stations.

And they talked. They never shut up. Their chatter sometimes drove him nuts.

"I heard those Vietnamese-peasant pilots were the best ever," Will said. "Better than all the German, Jap, and North Korean pilots."

"Per pilot, they shot down five times as many of our planes as those other guys," Jamie said. "Outmanned, outnumbered, outgunned. And fearless. They achieved those kill ratios in aircraft so obsolete they had to face our night-fighters using daytime tactics."

"No shit?" Will said.

"Ask the old guy," Jamie said.

"Hey, old man, we know you're listening. How did the gooks shoot down so many of us?" Will asked.

"We forgot basics. It's why we had to set up the Top Gun School. Reteach flyers how to dogfight."

"How did they say we were supposed to dogfight them?" Will asked.

"Same way you fight anyone," Larry said. "It's all about verticality."

"Roll inverted," Jamie said. "Blow out those fucking g's. *Then* you hammer them."

"Just like Jamie done," William said.

"And you, Little Brother," Jamie said.

"Well done," Larry had to admit. "Couldn't have done it better myself."

38 He Would Have Liked to Have Visited That Museum

The Dragonfly/Cruise Missile was currently skimming over Hiroshima's Memorial Tower to the Mobilized Students. More than a hundred such memorial monuments and statues were scattered all across Hiroshima and Nagasaki.

Every year on the anniversary of the Hiroshima blast, huge peace rallies were held in Hiroshima Peace Park, centering on the Hiroshima Peace Memorial Museum. These rallies featured peace music festivities, peace poster prizes, peace art and literature exhibits, and the eloquent reading of peace literature. These anniversary ceremonies typically attracted well over a million people.

Today's anniversary was no exception, and the stirring events had intensified the crowd's feelings. They were crying, trembling, wringing their hands. Someone was attempting to lead them in song—Sister Cassandra's "Hiroshima Girl."

The Dragonfly/Cruise Missile knew he could do it better. He could make them "feel" the words and music, not just hear them.

He'd also wanted to visit the museum. It featured 5,911 items relating to the Hiroshima nuking, and he was sure he could learn something from every one. A trove of twisted coins, scorched clothing, endless photographs of hideously burned Hibakusha, it also offered valuable lectures, seminars, and study programs.

The Hiroshima Peace Memorial Museum was built on thick concrete pylons, and he would have enjoyed coming in low underneath the museum and setting one off, but his flight profile required that he duplicate the original's flight plan.

Soaring to a height of 9,600 meters—almost twice that of Nagasaki's and consequently far more damaging to Hiroshima—the Dragonfly/Cruise rolled inverted in order to get one last look at the target-picture.

Target-acquired.

His last thought was:

I still would have liked to have visited that museum.

The problem with the Baby Leviathans was they were too damn slow. The Dragonfly/Harpoon Missile was acutely aware of that. Traveling at sixty knots the Baby Leviathan Torpedoes might eventually get there, but not in time. It would be a good ten hours.

The Dragonfly/Harpoon would arrive in ten minutes.

Hopefully, the Leviathan Submarine would not be completely submerged.

The moment he was blasted out of his torpedo tube, he felt he had a shot. He skimmed over the pole at under one hundred feet, his radar seeker searching for targets, finding nothing but broken ice and angry sea.

The Dragonfly/Harp was starting to have doubts.

Seventeen feet in length, weighing in at three-quarters of a ton, he was mostly engine and fuel—and at the rate he was going he was going to need almost every ounce of that energy.

He had a long trip. His Range-and-Bearing Launch was set Large, the range itself at nearly forty miles. But his RBL-L was supposed to be over open seas, not cracking ice. Not atop the North Pole.

Above the North Pole was the tip of a Typhoon-Class ballistic sub's radar mast, in the center of a huge ice-hole and engulfed in boiling foam white as ice above the black sea, it was rapidly sinking and was now completely submerged.

The Harpoon missile's Strapdown Inertial Guidance System and Radar-Seeker had been recently upgraded for precisely this contingency—to detonate on impact with the sinking sub—but it meant diving straight into the deep.

He had ejected both his waterproof buoyancy capsule and inlet-cover, which meant his red-hot turbojet engines, his seeker-head, his onboard computer would get soaking-wet. He even had one hundred miles' worth of fuel left. He could have roamed the North Pole for six more minutes.

He did a sweeping 360-degree turn and returned to the big foaming ice-hole. Drawing a bead, he began his descent and hit the drink laterally in an ear-cracking swan dive.

Dragonflies weren't built for wet work, and undersea, pandemonium reigned. It was hard locating a sub in all that black water. His inboard computer was located near the payload and searching through his memory banks for bogus objects—including waves and whales—in order to avoid blowing up the wrong target. Unfortunately, his radar-seeker wasn't very good at seeing underwater. Furthermore, what he could dimly discern bore no resemblance at all to those bogus object-warnings in his memory system.

What he saw resembled gray naked men—perhaps sailors from the submerging Typhoon. Russian sailors were men, weren't they? Men were the enemy. Let them have it.

The Dragonfly/Harp gave them the full warhead—nearly 500 pounds of super-high-explosive, almost one-third his total weight. He threw in half a tank of high-explosive turbojet fuel and vapor for good measure, enough high explosive to severely damage even a Typhoon-Class sub—if not actually sink it.

What the Dragonfly/Harp hit wasn't a Typhoon-Class Russian-Leviathan; it was a roiling school of naked, screaming, grayish men. At least, they looked like men.

Except for those long pale unicorn tusks spiraling out of their heads.

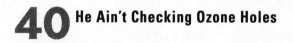 40 He Ain't Checking Ozone Holes

The B-2 and its three fighter-escorts approached Moscow unaccosted. The Crow still maintained a 55,000-foot high-endurance altitude, while its fighter-escorts entered the Moscow Ring a full 50,000 feet lower.

For the past six hours they had maintained radio silence. Since Stealth's Inertial Navigation System (INS), TERCOM, and DSMAC navigation systems did their flying for them, the pilots had nothing to do. To fight off boredom—and the risk of falling asleep—they were provided with three possibilities: amphetamines, magazines, and/or rock 'n' oll.

William opted for Sister Cassandra's "Rockin' the Apocalypse":

"When the deal goes down,
And you're lookin' to score.
When the shit hits the fan,
When the firestorms roar,
When there's blood all around,
When there's nuclear war,

"You're rockin' the apocalypse,
Rockin' the apocalypse,
You're rock-rock-rock-rock-rockin' the apocalypse.

"When the last lie is told,
When the last word is said,
When the heart grows cold,
When the world is dead,
You'll hammer hard and bold,
You'll hammer straight-ahead.

"You're rockin' the apocalypse
Rockin' the apocalypse,
You're rock-rock-rock-rock-rockin' the apocalypse.

"When there's no more prayers,
When it's too late for cryin',
When there's flames all around
And the missiles are flyin',
When you're all out of time,
When you're all out of dyin',

"When you're rockin' the apocalypse,
Rockin' the apocalypse,
You're rock-rock-rock-rock-rockin' the apocalypse."

Jamie preferred Sister Cassandra's "First Strike":

"When the dust has settled,
When the thermonuclear dust comes down,
When the fallout drifts slowly,
Slowly to the ground.
Will anyone be around?
Will anyone be around?

"It'll be a First Strike (Boom!)
For World Peace.
A final fatal blow
To our sworn enemy.
Our last true chance
To finally be set free.
To save the Planet Earth
Oh, our country 'tis of thee."

Larry chose to watch MTN's global newscast of the world's end on the TV. But at the Outer Ring, they were detected.

William was the first to spot the new bogies. A laser-drawn reticle blinked on his windscreen, crosshairs flashing in its center. The computer—allowing for airspeed, gyro-drift, and windage—constantly realigned the warning reticle. Printouts detailing altitude-and weapons-warnings materialized near the reticles.

"Bandits, nine o'clock," William reported.

"I count six," Jamie said.

"And a Russian AWACS," Larry Taylor said casually. "You guys have him clocked?"

"Twelve o'clock high and coming upstairs," Jamie said.

"That could be a problem," William said. "We're Stealthy, but I've never been sure if we're AWACS-proof."

"He's definitely looking for a Big Bird. Namely you, Big Bro," Jamie said.

"We can't let that happen, old man," William said. "I got first dibs. Always did want to ace me an AWACS."

"Why not?" Jamie said. "He wants to ace us."

"He ain't up there checking ozone holes," William agreed.

41 Only One Aircraft Could Do All *This*

Boris Kerensky—fire-control officer for the Venyukovski Missile Analysis Center on the edge of the Moscow Beltway—already knew what he had. He knew even before he called in the supplementary radar-vans and ringed them like a wagon train around the Missile Center.

He wasn't just thinking of the two Stealth fighters. He knew of their existence. All the radar-van operators knew about them. A huge high-frequency Over-the-Horizon radar installation near Tomsk—its massive arrays stretching for miles—had spotted them. While it could not actually track them, it had detected their wraithlike blips and inferred sufficient range and bearing for its scrambled MiG pilots to eyeball them. Six MiG Flogger-Interceptors had made positive visual IDs of the Stealth fighters—before being blown out of the skies.

Boris Kerensky was aware of another ghostly blip on his screen. It indicated something far more ominous.

Too many surveillance systems and facilities between Tomsk and Moscow had been jammed, which was beyond the capability of any other aircraft, including Stealth fighters. Only one airplane could jam their Over-the-Horizon High-Frequency Wide-Band Arrays and their newly installed Bistatic Detection Systems, which tracked the radar-pulse as it left the transmitter and triangulated on the incoming aircraft.

Only one aircraft could do all *this* and avoid detection in the process: the B-2 bomber.

He had no fantasies about scoping any Stealth bombers. Boris Kerensky wasn't even sure why he was trying. Even if he got a fix, the B-2 would blow him off with chaff, decoys, and flares.

And Russia's military nerve center—its command and control—was about to get fucked.

42 Shooting Sitting Ducks

Will's first reaction—when he eyeballed the Russian AWACS—was that he had locked onto a U.S. AWACS.

"I know what you're thinking," Larry said. "You got a NATO recon aircraft. They just copied ours. Check for the T-frame tail section."

"T-frame's a roger."

"Just remember it's him or us."

"It's like shooting sitting ducks, strafing civilians."

"He can kill us with that radome atop his plane," Larry said, "as thoroughly as a 20mm nose cannon up your ass. Get a lock."

He activated his Attack Radar and commenced a wide-angle scan. The big AWACS bloomed big as a house on his screen. The computer printout instantly recorded:

"Radar-contact, range eleven miles."

"Target designate," Will ordered.

The reticle on his screen, representing the Russian Mainstay AWACS, blinked.

"Target radar-lock," the computer reported back.

Flashing crosshairs appeared in the blinking reticle.

"Missile arm," he ordered.

"Missile armed," the computer printout read.

"Missile launch."

Will punched the "commit" button, and the fire-control computer committed an infrared missile on the left pylon; fed it its altitude, trajectory, and azimuth; and then slid it off pylon into the fighter's slipstream.

43 Joe Steel

"Yo, dead ahead," Moscow Cruise Missile #1 shouted. "Krasnaya Ploschad—Red Square."

"I heard it's really great at night—its tower-tops aflame with floodlights, ablaze with blood-red stars," #3 said.

"Hey, we can give them all that and more," Dragonfly/Cruise #6 said.

"I prefer it in daylight," #1 said. "We get a better look at what we hit."

"There's Lobnoe Mesto—Execution Plaza," Moscow Cruise Missile #2 said. "Ivan the Terrible used to draw and quarter his subjects there. He used to let wild bears loose on them too. He once cooked up two hundred people in a giant frying pan."

"They don't make 'em like that anymore," #1 said.

"Too bad we don't have one of those great May Day parades down there," #3 said. "Endless processions of tanks, MiGs, Backfire bombers, SS-series ICBMs."

"Big, dumb, butt-ugly missiles," #6 said. "Fire one of those, everybody on the planet knows you did it. Not like us—lithe, stealthy, slender, virtually invisible. Now you see us, now you don't."

"Secrecy and subterfuge," #1 said. "That's the true art of war."

"It's time," #1 said. "Synchronize clocks, positions, and GPS. We have to coordinate our strikes, and you have the longest trip, #6—way down by the river. Better get the lead out. You don't want to get blown out by our combined shock-fronts."

"Got it in my sights," #6 said. "I'm cutting out."

They separated in six different directions for their preassigned targets.

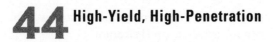

44 High-Yield, High-Penetration

If Boris Kerensky was right and a B-2 was on the way, its mission was to knock out the Venyukovski Missile Analysis Center with a high-yield, high-penetration hydrogen bomb.

If that happened, and if the defense minister hadn't transmitted the launch codes to Russia's Arctic sub fleet—instructions that would rain thousands upon thousands of warheads down on the rest of the world—it would be too late.

It might be too late already.

Enraged at what was about to happen to Mother Russia, Boris bounded down the fire-steps three at a time.

45 You Catch the Cruises

On his windscreen Larry could follow the course of William's Scorpion missile. When the two reticles merged and vanished, he knew he was safe from AWACS—about the only thing on the planet capable of tracking the B-2. He wished he could say the same for his brothers below. It appeared now that the entire Russian air force was on their tails.

"I just got warning reticles up my ass," Jamie said.

The reticles were blinking furiously on their windscreens, indicating over a dozen bogies in all directions, converging on them at ranges of less than twenty miles. They were coming in at high look-down shoot-down altitudes.

But that wasn't all. Something weird. Very light, needle-thin, single-source infrared, and no radar signature at all, moving at subsonic speeds. Six reticles. He punched *identify* into his computer.

The printout analysis read:

"Six cruise missiles, range seven miles, altitude one hundred feet."

Red warning lights were now flashing.

"You guys notice those cruises?" Larry Taylor asked.

They rogered.

"We need a target ID," Larry said. "They may well be friendlies. If so, we don't want to smoke their tails with sidewinders."

"They're going to pass straight under me," Jamie said. "William, head up toward the incoming. I'll try to get an optical on them. I'd recommend you take these bandits upstairs. I'll be right behind you."

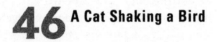

46 A Cat Shaking a Bird

Larry Taylor studied the bomb-release program on his weapons-screen.

And tried to keep up with his brothers on the radio.

READY, the bomb-program read.

READY, he answered.

ARM.

ARMED.

TARGET DESIGNATE.

TARGET DESIGNATED.

OPEN BOMB BAY.

He punched open the bomb bay, and the plane shook from the increased wind-resistance.

T-MINUS-10 SECONDS.

MINUS 9 SECONDS.

MINUS 8 SECONDS.

This wasn't laser guided but pure gravity. He had to pull the load handle himself, not let a laser do it.

Shit, his brothers were now over downtown Moscow.

Fuck the bomb.

"I'm telling you you're too damn close to those cruises," he shouted into his headset.

"Complain to the Russian air force," William said.

"Those damn MiGs pulled us right over Red Square," Jamie said.

"I'm saying you're at ground-fucking-zero."

Simultaneously he sensed something else—the six cruise-missile thermal-flashes before he saw them. Even with his protective flash-goggles, the flash and fireball hurt his eyes. The photo-reactive layer in his cockpit windows was also supposed to protect his instruments. Still, his infrared-scope blazed like hellfire and apocalypse, which was precisely what it was recording. He shut it off. He wondered if its warranty included thermonuclear war.

He fought to stay focused. He was coming in on his target.

Fireballs were rising over Moscow, and although he was on the outskirts of the city—many miles away from the blasts—shock waves shook his aircraft like it was a cat shaking a bird by the neck.

MINUS 4.

MINUS 3.

MINUS 2.

MINUS 1.

He punched the drop instructions into his weapons computer.

Larry felt the bomb release, the plane lighten and rise.

He could see the entire city of Moscow across his starboard-wing. He had no appetite for what he witnessed now. Scores of firestorms merging into a ferociously spreading sea of flame, surmounted by six rapidly expanding fireballs—each bigger, it seemed, than ten thousand suns.

Then the plane was shaken again by an overhead explosion.

The sky above Moscow, the B-2, and the fireballs were a sea of flame.

Someone had detonated a nuke directly above Larry's B-2.

In outer space.

47 The Keepers of the Keys

In the Command-Control Unit of the Venyukovski Missile Analysis Center, Josef Dmitrovich Khizenovsky stared at smoldering cigarette tips, all he could see of his colleagues.

Finally, the emergency generator kicked in, and the lights in the Venyukovski Missile Analysis Center went back on. The deputy staff director returned to C3I, frantic.

"The phones and radios are down. We can't even get MTN. I looked outside. Downtown Moscow is ablaze, fireballs and mushroom clouds rising like the end of the world. The sky itself looks like it's on fire."

"EMP?" the president asked.

"It appears that way," the deputy said.

"What's that again?" Kochnovo asked.

"Electromagnetic Pulse," Josef said. "The Americans stumbled onto it by accident during atmospheric bomb tests in 1958. In 1962 they confirmed its existence during Operation Fishbowl, when they detonated a hydrogen bomb in outer space, 250 miles over Johnston Island in the Pacific. Its X-rays—when they hit the atmosphere's edge—created an electric 'hotcake' of incandescent gas. Powerful electrified fields spread out over the earth, knocking out Honolulu's power and communications systems."

Josef Dmitrovich could have told them more. He could have pointed out that computers were even more sensitive to the Pulse than electric lights. Computers in the Missile Analysis Center were shielded against the Pulse by heavy walls, and their cables fitted with electromagnetic circuit breakers—sometimes referred to as electromagnetic lightning rods—would probably be safe.

But no one really knew what it could do.

The designers of the Missile Analysis Center thought their radio/TV systems would be safe too.

Josef stared at his two colleagues. He knew what Kochnovo was thinking.

"Yes, Kochnovo," Josef said, "I have my key, and, yes, the cheget transceivers still work."

"How can you be sure?"

"They trigger, among other things, Very-Low-Frequency radio signals, which travel through—not over—the earth. They reach our Northern Fleet's long, trailing underwater antennae. They have nothing to do with air or sky. Every aspect of the system is immune to the Pulse."

"Call in the shuriks," Kochnovo said.

Shuriks were the cheget's bearers. Uniformed colonels in the Ninth Department of the general staff, their sole responsibility was to stay near the keepers of the keys—in this case Kochnovo and Josef.

The deputy director brought the three immaculately uniformed colonels into the Command Center. Each man carried a small black attaché case chained to the wrist. The small crimson dome lights next to the key-locks flashed furiously. Still, the colonels seemed impassive—stone-faced, hard-nosed professionals. Until they noticed the wall map ablaze, blinking crimson rings that encircled the Northern Hemisphere's major cities. Their eyes widened.

They placed their cases before the three leaders, who opened them. The interior panels each contained three displays, all of which were lit, indicating that the country was under nuclear attack. Along the tops of the lit panels were the listed number of incoming missiles and the expected time of impact.

Number of incoming was a flashing **6**.

Time of impact **00:00**.

Beneath the display panels were five buttons. The first three transmitted sets of strike orders of varying number and intensity. Button #4 was the cancel button.

Button #5 unloaded everything—over 1,200 primary targets.

Secondary and tertiary strikes would follow.

"The thing to keep in mind," Josef said, "is that once the Americans intercept our transmissions—or spot our launched missiles on the recon-sats—they will also empty their submarine tubes."

"They could be doing that anyway," Kochnovo said. "The EMP has knocked us out."

"For an hour or so," the deputy staff director explained. "Only the exterior cables were affected. The interior circuit breakers held."

"We can now also get MTN," Josef said. "We have shielded-satellite-TV units in storage that are undamaged."

"MTN covers this damn war more thoroughly than our own surveillance systems," Ridov had to admit.

Josef said, "We have workable chegets, and we have time to transmit the launch codes. That's the worst-case scenario. I say we have to wait till we get more information."

"We will wait," Kochnovo said.

48 So Much for Nuclear Logic!

A bucket of water hit Stone in the face. From his rack, he stared up blurry-eyed at the Sin Sisters.

"Look on the bright side, Mr. Stone," Sultana said, "your country gave the world just what it wanted."

"Nobody *wanted* this," Stone said. "I was our country's biggest nuclear critic. I never said we *wanted* the world destroyed."

"But of course your country wanted it," Sultana objected. "In order to gain support for a global Test Ban Treaty—to bribe nations into signing it—your country began releasing the secrets of your nuclear weapons."

Sabrina read from a *New York Times* tear sheet:

> " 'Releasing many of America's nuclear secrets,' the Times *said, 'was seen as an essential part of this strategy, since it would signal a new global order in which nuclear know-how was suddenly devalued. The Energy Department's "openness initiative" released 178 categories of atomic secrets. . . . As a senior scientist said: "The cat is out of the bag." ' "*

"Not that any of this got the Comprehensive Test Ban Treaty passed," Sultana said. "Your Roadkill-IQ Senate shot it down anyway."

"Mr. Stone," Sabrina said, "*everybody* wanted the Comprehensive Test Ban Treaty. All the major world leaders—including Russia, China, Japan, Israel."

"But, N-O-O-O-O!!!" Sultana said. "Your senators wouldn't listen to thirty-two brilliant Nobel laureates. They not only wouldn't sign the agreement. They wouldn't even *talk* about it. Ask me, it was your computer exporters who really sent the nuclear arms race spiraling out of control."

"Without computers," Sabrina agreed," there are no modern nuclear weapons, no sophisticated delivery systems."

Stone groaned and looked away from them.

"Ah hell, Sister Friend," Sultana said. "Let's get real. Stone's countrymen gave away the whole enchilada. The Genesis Codes: everything his country had learned about nuclear weapons since the '40s."

"And now Mr. Stone says his nation really didn't want the world to know?" Sabrina asked.

"Then why did you give away so much nuclear know-how and peddle so much nuclear weapons technology? *There was too much money to be made **not** to sell those weapons systems!*" Sultana concluded. "The possession of nukes was supposed to deter neighbors from nuking one another. That was the U.S. strategy. That was *your* logic."

"So much for nuclear logic!" Sabrina crowed, pointing at their TV.

Thucydides had divided the screen into eight panels.

In each of the panels the nuclear nations of the earth burned.

"You wouldn't mind if we laughed in your face again?" Sabrina asked Stone. "Would you?"

49 Three-Card Monte in a Back Room of Hell

For nearly an hour Thucydides had performed brilliantly. He not only spotted each new detonation but also frequently located surfacing subs and in many cases followed their missiles in flight.

Sara Friedman had not attempted to direct Cyd—partly out of fear of distracting him. His seventeen monitors allowed them to view all of the holocaust. He was also recording the conflict for whatever posterity might survive.

"What's your interpretation of all this, Cyd?" she asked.

"Subs that look like Russian subs. Cruise missiles that look like Russian cruise missiles—except it's harder to tell with cruises. The warheads? They could be any nation's warheads."

"You've heard Jack Taylor's phone conversations with General Malokov?"

"Of course. I patched Malokov through to him."

"He bragged about what Russia was doing," Sara asserted.

"A man *identifying* himself as Russian Minister of Defense General Vladimir Malokov bragged," Thucydides corrected her.

"It *wasn't* Mad Vlad?" Sara was stunned.

"The com-sat that boosted the communication through to us doesn't have a tracer," Thucydides said. "I don't know where the call came from. Furthermore, Vlad's voice has been 'packet-switched.' I'm not sure what the purpose was. Usually, it's done for encryption."

"Packet-switching?" Henry Colton asked.

"The message is digitized and cut up into segments," Thucydides explained, "each of which includes information about origin and destination. In this case the components are precoded to reconfigure into the original whole upon reception. He also has a time-distortion encryption device. I can't even give you time-distortion data."

"Great," Colton said, "meaning we can't do a voiceprint on the guy."

"'Fraid not," Sara said.

"Secretary Taylor thinks he recognized Malokov's voice."

"You disagree?"

"I have a high confidence it is not Malokov."

"Why?" Sara asked.

"If it is Malokov, he has not made a single strike of any strategic importance. So far, the strikes are purely provocative. The logic has not been to disable the enemy but to provoke nuclear retaliation. This is hardly sane nuclear strategy, and it contradicts everything we know about Russian military thinking."

"Jack Taylor thinks Malokov is insane."

"He is—if he's General Malokov."

"Jack's options are limited," Colton said.

"General Taylor should remember that Russia still has thousands of warheads, many near the Arctic Circle, some below the ice pack. An all-out nuclear offensive will not significantly affect them. No matter what the U.S. does, Russia will retain the capacity to incinerate most of the globe."

"But what if Malokov *is* insane?" Sara asked.

"Nothing in his history indicates suicidal psychosis."

"I'll let Jack know your conclusions," Colton said.

"My files confirm that Taylor lost his wife and youngest son when the New York Convention Center was hit. It is he who may be presently unbalanced."

"Anything else, Cyd?" Sara asked.

Thucydides piped a haunting Sister Cassandra blues-riff over the music speakers.

"Now you see it.
Now you don't.
Who has the pea?
Who has the shell?
Who did the dirty?
I won't tell.

"But it's three-card monte
In a back room of hell.
Nuclear monte
In a back room of hell.
In the fires of hell."

Either the well was very deep or she fell very slowly kept running through Kate Magruder's head.

Except she wasn't Alice and this storm sewer sure as shit wasn't Wonderland.

Nor—unlike Alice—was she alone. As she crawled through her tunnel—to where, she didn't have the foggiest notion—she had noise to keep her company. Up and down the sewer thundered a distant heavy *crumppp!* followed by louder *crumppp-crumppp-crumppp!* and occasionally a gut-shaking *crumppp-crumppp-CRUMPPP!* and then the ear-splitting *CRUMPPP-CRUMPPP-CRUMPPP!* of more detonating gas mains.

She also had heat, smoke, and darkness for company. The cop's motorcycle gloves, helmet, flak, and leather jacket kept her from getting too badly burned by the hot pipes and metal fixtures. His flashlight gave her some illumination, though often all she illuminated was smoke. A wet bandana over her nose and mouth also helped.

But she was not in good shape. Smoke-inhalation, hypoxia, and heat exhaustion were wearing her down. She was also lost, probably crawling in circles.

From time to time she encountered others—who had also escaped to the tunnels and died there—when she crawled over their gnawed remains.

As usual, human disasters were a horn-of-plenty for rats.

She did find a few people still alive. One man lay in her way, his mouth working mutely, his face little more than blood-smeared charcoal. She crawled over him and kept on going.

A head raised here. An arm twitching there. The stink of vomit and excreta, burned hair and charred flesh. A man's bladder ruptured as she crawled over him.

People destined to die, first in thermal flash and blastwaves, then in firestorms and collapsing buildings, finally below ground in darkness and dust.

Death-in-life.

She could not go on. She laid her head on her arms.

Keep moving. To rest is to die. You have to find a way off this island. This place is Death City, the end of the line, a charnel house of the damned.

Still, she couldn't move. It wasn't in her . . .

. . . *Suddenly a white rabbit with pink eyes ran close by Alice.*

In another moment, down went Alice after it, into the hole, never once considering how in the world she was to get out again.

The rabbit hole went straight on like a tunnel for some way, and she found herself falling down what seemed to be a very deep well.

Down, down, down. Would the fall never come to an end? "I wonder how many miles I've fallen by this time? I must be getting somewhere near the center of the earth."

. . . Where's that White Rabbit, anyway? Kate wondered sleepily. *Aw hell, fuck him. I'll just lay my head down, catch a few winks.*

"Here I am, kid."

"Who said that?" Kate opened her eyes and looked up.

"I did. A White Rabbit, at your service. Well, an auburn color actually, although like yourself, I need a bath."

Christ, he was a massive auburn rodent—covered with dirt and grime.

"Where's your watch and waistcoat? You're supposed to say: 'I'm late. I'm late. For a very important date.'"

"No time for any of that," Sailor said.

Kate looked him over.

"Hey, you're not a rabbit. You're a rat. I *know* you. You're from the lab."

"The same."

"How'd you get down here?"

"You sent me down here, remember?"

"I guess I did. What are you doing?"

"Same thing you are—trying to survive."

"I don't think I'm gonna make it. I'm lost."

"Stick with me, kid. I know these tunnels like squirrels know trees."

"I'm tired. I'm afraid." Kate Magruder started to cry.

Sailor nuzzled her affectionately. "Oh, ye of little faith. You will make it. I'm here now. So stifle the self-pity."

"Why shouldn't I feel sorry for myself?" she said, still sobbing.

"Because I won't let you."

Turning around, Sailor started up the tunnel, then stopped. Looking back over his shoulder, he said: "Well, are you coming?"

"I'm coming."

Getting up on her hands and knees, Kate Magruder began to crawl.

51 When the Last Dog Is Hung

"Yo, Jack-O, it's me over here in Mother Russia. As they say in the whorehouse, how's tricks?"

"Vlad, we really have to talk," Taylor said nervously.

Taylor heard a deep sigh on the other end. "Gee, I guess I haven't been taking this seriously enough. Okay, we'll talk. Who you got for the Series this year?"

Dead silence on the other end.

"Ah Jesus, kid, I'm sorry. I forgot. You *were* a Yankee fan, big time. Tough luck about the house that Ruth built. Guess the owners'll have to move to Jersey after all. Except come to think of it I'll be nuking them along with the Bombers."

His laughter thundered into Taylor's headset.

"I was thinking about the future—what this means to our children."

"Damn, boy, there you go again, thinking small. The short run, the quick score. That was always the problem with democratic capitalism. What can we make this quarter? Gimme, gimme, gimme, I want, I want, I want—up-front and right now. Fuck that shit. I am thinking of the Big Picture, the Long View. I'm thinking of the effects on untold generations to come."

"Untold generations to come," Taylor repeated, trembling with trepidation.

"Yo, what else, Jack-Me-Hard-You-Skull-Fucked-Retard? I'm talking about good old-fashioned social engineering that would have turned Joe Stalin, Mao Tse-tung and our Immortal Führer green with envy."

On this Taylor's TV console, MTN had once again expanded coverage of the world's firestorms to nine separate panels. On one screen, Taylor could watch New York, Washington, D.C., Rome, Paris, London, Moscow, Tokyo, Beijing, and Bombay burning.

"Social engineering," Taylor repeated, stupid with shock.

"Like after the Black Death, Jack-Me-Iron-Hard-and-Jalepeño-Hot, and the famines that followed—they turned people meaner than snakes. After all, someone had to be blamed. The world turned to penitential excesses, flagellante cults, witch-burnings, Satanism. Ever checked out some of those medieval paintings and tapestries? Brueghel and Bosch? The dance of death, Christ agonizing on His cross, the Last Judgment, the human race hurled howling into hell. Oh, Jackie, Jackie, Jackie, you'd have loved it back then. You and I'd have fit right in."

"You're doing a pretty good job right now."

"On a global scale, Oh-Jack-Me-Hard-I'll-Be-Your-Pard, believe me, it doesn't end here. Can you imagine what the world will be like a day from now, a week from now, a year, a decade from now. I mean, a world without heat, electricity, clean water, telephone, gas stations, supermarkets, liquor stores, credit cards. I can hear you Amerikanskis now: 'Oh, where are those friendly SPRINT sales calls now? Those Seinfeld reruns we loves so much, now? Where's my mail? Where are the cars, microwave ovens, hospitals, medicine, sanitation, firemen, police, schools, Medicare, Medicaid, my Social Security checks, libraries, movie theaters?'

"Can anyone take the guilt and fear that we're unleashing worldwide? This is no earthly disaster—a flood or plague of earthquake or storm. This is a disaster worse than all of the above combined—and we did it to ourselves and to future generations. Can you imagine what they will think when we bequeath them a world of famine and pestilence, dust bowls and dying woodlands, insect plagues and radioactive wastes? Not a pocket here, a country there. I mean worldwide. That's why none of us can take it. That is why we're all damned to hell and will never get out. That is why Paradise is irretrievably, irredeemably, inescapably lost. Actions have consequences, Jack-Me-Vise-Tight-and-High-as-a-Kite, and our deeds will reverberate in Humanity's Collective Soul for a thousand years to come."

"The Southern Hemisphere will survive," Taylor shouted, furious at this tirade.

"No way—Oh-Honk-My-Loon-Till-I-Howl-at-the-Moon-Till-I-Croon-You-a-Tune-O-Vich—the Southern Hemisphere was dead *before* we started. Amnesty International has recorded over 10,000 terrorist organizations in the Third World, as we speak. Most of South America and Africa already live on the margin of starvation in abject poverty, torn by ethnic and religious hatreds that amount to eternal Civil War. They're dependent on the Northern Hemisphere for most of their medicine, energy, computers, communications systems, technology—most of which they import from us—one-half their jobs. When the north collapses, they'll learn the true meaning of famine and disease, violence and revenge. The whole hemisphere will blow, and anarchy will indeed be loosed on the land."

"What do you hope to accomplish with all this?"

'To remove you and your kind from the annals of history."

"For what reason?"

"To show you what you have wrought."

"You really hate us, don't you?"

'What's not to hate?"

"Art, religion, literature, science."

"You mean *The Iliad, The Odyssey, The Agamemnon, Oedipus Rex, The History of the Peloponnesian Wars, The Bible, The Bhagavad Gita, The Aeneid, Gulliver's Travels, Tom Jones, Moby-Dick, Madame Bovary, Clarissa, Huckleberry Finn*? What of Dante, Leonardo, Michelangelo, Shakespeare, Milton, Swift, Faulkner, Hemingway, Steinbeck, Joyce, Niels Bohr, Einstein, Heisenberg?"

"Just to name a few great works, a few great men," Taylor said.

"And what is the single theme that runs through every one of those great works and artists? Love and kisses? No, hardly. Violence and vengeance, pure and simple. All that great art you so ignorantly grovel before is dedicated to not simply getting even, but grinding the opposition to dust. You've made getting even high art. Same with your Holy Bible. It's not about eye-for-an-eye. It's about 'head-arms-legs-brains-blood-and-balls-for-an-eye.' What do you think hell is if not revenge? You've made a religion not out of simple vindication but total retaliation. Bohr, Einstein, Heisenberg? Don't make me laugh! They've provided you with the means to retaliate. They built your fucking Bomb. And your great leaders—going all the way back to Truman—were kind enough to provide *us* with the means to make our own nuclear bombs."

"And if you use the rest of your arsenal, Vlad, you know where that leads?"

"Universal power visited on mortal flesh."

"Which is insane."

"Then why did you Amerikanskis invent it? Why did you sell it, why did you *give it away* to your most implacable enemies? Why did you supply the entire world with the means to MIRV ICBMs and TERCOM their cruises and

miniaturize their warheads? Why did you—directly and through known
intermediaries—sell all that stuff to me?"

"But why blow up the world?" Taylor roared, his temper in tatters. "Simply
because you can?"

"In the destructive element immerse."

"You are saying there is no hope?"

"There is infinite hope," Vlad said, "but not for us."

"What do you get out of it?"

"Raises, bonuses, performance-escalators, stock-options, equity-participation,
lifetime major medical, penthouse suites, golden-parachute, tax-free annuities,
off-shore black-hole accounts, corporate jets, limo-and-chauffeur, tuition-for-
the-kids, vag-tuck for the wife, loans-forgiven, all-expenses-paid, profit-share-
in-trust, blowjobs from my blond-haired, blue-eyed, torpedo-titted secretarial
staff."

"What did we do to you?"

"Oh, I get it. You want reason, logic, sanity."

"Compassion," Taylor whispered.

"The item's long out of stock."

"Truth would be nice."

"As Pilate said to Christ: 'What is Truth?'"

"I'll accept a half-truth. A lie. Anything resembling an explanation."

"Patience, Jackie, patience. You will know in the end. That I promise you.
Your curiosity will be satisfied. I will not let my favorite American general down."

"When?" Taylor was starting to whimper.

"When the last song is sung, when the last bell is rung, when the last dog is
hung. At the moment of death—your death—you will know what you, Oh, Star
Wars Warrior, have done."

His insane laughter rang in his headset like the feral clang of doom.

52 The Thermonuclear Mole

Crow had released Star, and the Star Bomb was dropping toward the Venyukovski Missile Analysis Center. Her three-chute-cluster detonated out of its
pressure-pack, its Kevlar-and-nylon ribbon single-stage main chute braking her
from Mach 0.93 to 65 feet per second in two seconds, bringing her up hard and
tight as a hangman's noose, almost snapping her tail off.

Not that it would have mattered. Star's aft-case and back body were loaded
with her least significant components, those no longer needed after impact, including the bomb's arming mechanism.

The bunker was coming at her like an express train. Star barreled into its
roof, slamming through six and one-half levels.

A thermonuclear mole, she was tunneling straight in to hell's blackest heart.

"And I'm telling you," Josef Khizenovsky roared at Boris Kerensky, "this is all some crazy mistake!"

A burly man in a dark pinstriped suit, Josef was always an imposing figure. Now in the throes of blind rage, he was a terrifying presence.

"How could these missiles have been launched without my permission?"

"Hot-wired," Boris said quietly.

"Hot-wired?"

"Weaponry is my specialty, President Khizenovsky. If the warheads are re-wired, then armed to detonate on impact, they do not require launch codes."

"You're saying Russian captains could be rewiring warheads and launching cruise missiles?"

Boris Kerensky nodded.

"But Kilo-Class subs are not configured for cruise missiles," Intelligence Director Ridov pointed out.

"Minister," Boris said, "their torpedo tubes have the same diameter as cruise missiles. They could have been reconfigured."

"They would still need our codes to launch our missiles," the intelligence minister said.

"Who says they're our missiles?" Boris said. "If these are rogue captains, they could have bought them on the black market. The technology is not that complex. It was patented in the 1950s."

President Khizenovsky resumed staring at the three chegets. "And you think we are about to be hit by a B-2?"

"We are his highest priority," Intelligence Director Ridov said.

"But we're seventy feet underground!"

"We were constructed prior to the B-2's design. His high-penetration bomb will vaporize the entire center. If you wish to transmit the launch codes, I would do so now."

"I won't do it. I believe this has been a colossal mistake. And *we* must rectify it."

"If you don't hit them first," Boris said, "they will wipe the Rodina off the map."

"I need more evidence!"

The room convulsed and thundered. The lights went off again, and they were drowning in darkness.

When the emergency lights went back on they saw the pointed nose of a B83 hydrogen bomb, shrouded in smoke and dust, resting on their conference table.

Josef Khizenovsky began punching in the launch codes.

54 Two Launch Keys and a 9mm Makarov

The detonating Harpoon missile—twenty feet above the Typhoon-Class submarine's submerging mast—shook it to its soul. In the darkened control room of the *Vladivostok*, several screens went blank.

"How is our sonar?" Captain Petrov asked the sonar chief.

"We're rebooting the computer, sir. Should be back up in a minute."

"I want launch depth," Petrov said. "I also need range and bearing on those ADCAP torpedoes."

"Just before the detonation I read 51,000 meters on a bearing of 125," the sonar chief answered.

"Which gives us a full half hour to unload our birds," the captain said.

"Sir! That second American Los Angeles class was still approaching at last read," the sonar chief said, "range 39,000 meters out of the northeast quadrant."

"We have to reach launch depth," the captain said. "Now!"

"The computer's kicked back in, sir," the weapons officer announced. "We *are* at launch depth."

"Shit!" Captain Petrov said. "I forgot to get out the keys."

He hurried to the weapons room and its black vault, inside of which sat another safe containing two launch keys and a 9mm Makarov pistol.

55 That's Where It Gets Murky

Brigadier General Henry Colton finally got his friend and mentor, Jack Taylor, on the phone. It was not a happy phone call.

"Jack, I have to tell you once again how terrible I feel about your wife and youngest son. I'm very sorry."

"Mad Vlad isn't, Henry. You ought to hear that maniac's phone calls. He laughs and brags about what he did to them. To us."

Henry took a deep breath. This would not be easy.

"Jack, how well do you know Vlad?"

"Very."

"Can you be absolutely sure it was him you spoke to?" Colton asked.

"Absolutely."

"We've been monitoring events from the Odyssey. Everything's awfully unclear. We can't even verify that NATO in fact nuked Russia."

"I don't give a shit who nuked them! Truth is, I don't care if a couple of our guys jumped the reservation. I understand how they might go psychotic. Maybe they lost their families to Russian nukes."

"But that's where it gets murky, Jack," Colton said. "If we don't know who's nuking who, this could all be a setup."

"What do you mean, 'don't know.' We saw Russian subs nuke those cities on TV. We've had confirmation from Malokov in Russia taking credit for those strikes."

"We can't trace Vlad's calls," Colton said. "They could have come from any-where."

"Next you'll tell me those weren't Russians nuking us."

"Cruise missiles can be bought anyplace, Jack. China sells them to foreign states, including Iran."

"I talked to Malokov. I know his voice."

"Thucydides, our Neural Net, questions his voice *and* his actions."

Jack Taylor roared like a gored water buffalo. "The world is going up in nu-clear flames! My wife is murdered during the worst genocidal sneak attack in history! I am told by a man I know intimately that he is going to annihilate everything else, 'I'm New-Yorking the rest of your fucking country. How you like them apples, Jack?' were his exact words. China and Japan tell me they're unloading and that I should climb on board if I want to save the world. I have to make a decision now. I have to make it *yesterday*. And you waste my time, telling me a fucking computer disagrees with me? I ought to be nuking the Odyssey!"

Jack Taylor hung up.

56 "I Understand Your Position Completely"

The *Vladivostok*'s control room's sole illumination was now its banks of com-puter screens. In the forward section—the ship-control station—were console screens monitoring bearing, depth, speed, and engine speed. Each of its officers was strapped into a leather control chair, eyes fixed on instruments and moni-tors, hands locked on a control yoke.

Sometimes Sergei thought that they had console screens instead of port-holes.

Sergei himself stood at the conn in the center of the control room, his mate at his side. Behind them was the navigation station, where the navigator was bent over his chart tables. The fire-control computer consoles were to the port side of the conn.

The weapons-control officer punched launch codes into the two launch con-soles. The captain watched him from the conn, launch keys in one hand, the 9mm Makarov in the other. The procedure was dictated by Command, which doubted the devotion of the men in a critical situation.

"The training isn't what it used to be," First said.

"Not for a long, long time."

"If Command tried paying them it might help."

"The currency's worthless anyway," Sergei said.

"Sir, we're ready." The weapons officer turned to them and stood aside.

The captain and the first officer stared at the two launch consoles on opposite ends of the fire-control station.

"First," the captain asked, "can I trust you to do your duty?"

"With all respect, sir, someone has to remain at the conn."

He was right, of course. Everyone currently in the control room was needed at their stations. Launching ballistic missiles was more than a matter of turning two keys. It took the concerted effort of everyone on board. The captain could spare no one in the control room.

"I'll take the conn. Get me four or five watch-standers."

When First returned, he had the reporter in tow.

"Our last oral historian wants to observe history in the making," First said.

"Why not?" the captain said with a shrug. "Just keep out of the way," he said to the reporter. Turning to the four watch-standers, he said: "I need two volunteers to sit at the two ballistic launch stations and turn the keys. They must be turned on cue within two seconds of one another. I will give you that cue." He pointed to the first two men. "I'll take you and you."

The first man selected sat at the forward ballistic launch console, and the captain inserted the launch key for him.

"You know the drill. The *Vlad* is designed specifically for under-the-ice mass assaults. While other ballistic subs may take as much as a quarter of an hour to get their birds up, we can launch four-missile salvos of ICBMs, emptying twenty tubes in under four minutes.

"We will turn right-to-left on cue," he told him.

Sergei turned to the second man. He was still standing.

"Take your seat," Sergei ordered.

"Sir," the man said, "there are 160 hydrogen bombs on those missiles. I regret that I cannot participate in the annihilation of the world."

Sergei walked over to the objector and said: "I understand your position completely."

And shot him between the eyes.

"Next volunteer," Sergei said.

He put the gun on the third watch-stander. The man dropped to his knees.

"Please, sir, I can't. We're all going to die anyway. I just can't."

Sergei shot him in the forehead.

"Next."

There was only one left. Sergei put the muzzle to his head.

"Fuck your mother," the man shouted.

"Who says I had a mother?" Sergei said.

And shot him in his right eye.

The only man not at a station, not indispensable to the running of the control room, was the reporter.

Sergei took him by the back of the neck and forced him in the chair facing the aft ballistic launch console. He inserted the key and said: "You turn right-to-left on cue."

Now it was the reporter's turn to blubber. Sergei shot him in the left thigh, just above the lividly swollen knee he'd injured on the icy fjord. He placed the Makarov's muzzle over the reporter's left kneecap.

"Turn the key right-to-left on cue."

The reporter—still blubbering—nodded again, once, twice.

"What do you read?" Sergei asked the weapons officer.

The weapons officer punched the launch instructions into his computer. "We have a fix."

"Missiles ready for launch?" the captain asked.

"Missiles ready," the weapons officer answered.

In the semidarkened control room he counted down: "Four, three, two, one, fire!"

The keys turned, and the sub rocked as four SLBMs exploded out of their tubes.

"Four down, sixteen to go," the captain said.

The weapons officer punched in the arm-and-launch codes for missile number 2.

57 T-Rex Was Gazing on the Stars

"The keys have turned," Leviathan informed T-Rex.

At first, the Dragon felt relief, but then he panicked. Nothing was happening.

What if the mission was being scrubbed? What if he blew up in his tube or in midair like the *Challenger*?

Suddenly, Leviathan blasted him free of the tube with what seemed to be a trillion tons of steam. T-Rex was shooting straight up through polar seas, pleased that he was free of Leviathan.

Booster ignition started as a pressure in his bowels, and it escalated until T-Rex feared his bowels would explode. The secret to a strong and steady launch was to contain the fire chamber's ignition as long as possible and to delay releasing the combustion gases. But he had never experienced the pain of it. T-Rex knew the fuel would burn through the interior of its cylinder till all the fuel was consumed.

Leviathan had previously broken a hole through the ice pack. The bottom of T-Rex's thruster-chamber had blown free; he was rocketing up out of the water. All systems were go. He still had plenty of fuel and now was climbing rapidly.

T-Rex knew where he was going. He had not only slipped the surly bonds of earth, he was rocketing through the clouds toward the stratosphere.

He was gazing on the stars.

58 Turn!

"Twelve down, four to go," the captain said.

His rubber-soled shoes were blood-soaked, and he was drenched in sweat. For several minutes the sonar chief had warned him of the converging ADCAP torpedoes. Given the launch-noise of twelve ICBMs, it had been impossible to decoy or jam them.

"We're in for a series of hits," the sonar chief said. "Within seconds."

Fuck it, Sergei thought.

Strapping himself into a bolted-down stool atop the conn-platform, he shouted to the weapons officer: "Let's get them airborne."

"I'm on it, sir!" the weapons officer shouted back.

"Turn!"

The keys turned. The sub rocked with the concussion of the last four missiles exploding out of its tubes.

And a heartbeat later the sub shook with the first in a succession of torpedo hits.

The control room went black.

59 An Orgasm like the End of Time

The Odyssey was orbiting slantwise toward the North Pole but getting a pretty good look at the Northern Hemisphere. The first of the missiles seemed to have been Submarine-Launched Ballistic Missiles (SLBMs) fired straight out of the Magnetic North Pole. At least that was Thucydides' opinion. Colton hadn't the foggiest why anyone would want to begin Armageddon from that exact spot, and at the rate the launches were now escalating, Colton doubted anyone would ever know. Rockets lighted up the earth below them—by the scores, then the hundreds, then the thousands—and more were streaking into the stratosphere, many of them coming toward the Odyssey.

In the vacuum beyond, Colton could view them with incomprehensible clarity. He thought they resembled fire-driven phalluses with an orgasm like the End of Time in their tip. Thucydides focused on the launches through the magnified eyes of his keyhole sats, and close-up the missiles did appear ominously sexual.

Colton still didn't understand why Russia's Strategic Rocket Forces had chosen to ravage the world this way. Hitting the world first with cruise missiles and satchel nukes seemed a crazy way to commence global Armageddon. Maybe they'd had a computer problem at their Missile Analysis Center. Maybe some of their personnel had rebelled. Who the hell knew? For whatever it was worth, the

RSVN was now making up for lost time. Their Typhoon-Class Ballistic Subs were emptying their missiles' tubes.

Russia had also deployed the cold-launched SS-25-type missiles, which could be fired from mobile platforms and were therefore unhittable. Those missiles didn't have to be siloed.

Still, they had obviously kept a fair number of "Dead Hand" missiles in silos. There were too many missiles, currently streaking over the pole toward America from Mother Russia, to be only sub- or mobile-platform launched.

Now the stream was flowing the other way. America's Ohio-Class Ballistic Subs were sending their ICBMs up out of the ice pack in the direction of Russia. Right behind them came land-based ICBMs. The Odyssey was far enough south that it still had a decent view of the American silos, and their launches were something to behold, lighting up the missile fields in Colorado, Nebraska, and Wyoming, most of which were now streaking toward the stratosphere, many of them toward the Odyssey.

The two countries' ICBM flight paths crisscrossed continually—and went on their way. Colton was surprised there weren't midair collisions.

Not only had America suffered terribly from Russia's cruise missiles and suitcase nukes, a whole slew of Russian ballistic missiles were now heading America's way, apparently from under the ice cap. He knew that America's ICBMs could survive an 18-megaton burst from 600 yards off—otherwise known as Circular Error Probability—or 1-megaton burst at a distance of 275 yards. But could they withstand an all-out assault by thousands upon thousands of warheads?

Jack Taylor had decided not to take the chance—to "use them rather than lose them."

60 The Cheering of the Stars

Reentry vehicle #1 could now see his target: a vast megalopolis, a great sprawling cosmopolitan city. He was heading right toward the center of it. He was not sure which city it was. Or which country. Or which continent.

It did not matter. They were all the same. There dwelt Superkiller.

Man.

Number 1 had a lock. He was no longer an Independently Targeted Re-Entry Vehicle but the flame-spouting Chinese dragon, the breath-blazing Grendel, the flying Aztec fire-serpent Quetzalcoatl, all the myriad from Firedrakes' time immemorial rolled up into one. Speer and Braun's Vengeance Weapon—*Vergeltungswaffen*—but with starfire breath and thermonuclear teeth.

He was T-Rex, the Tyrant Dragon. He knew now he was well-named. He hurtled closer to his target—thousands of feet from impact, then hundreds.

Now the entire Warrior World was cheering him on.

"We are the Clans.
To earth no more we hasten.
Earth no more our hearth and home.
The stars our detonation."

61 Lucifer Was an Angel of Light

The first of the launched missiles were breaking out of the stratosphere, ejecting their boosters like flaming firecrackers as they entered space.

"They'll be MIRVing, soon," Sara Friedman said.

"Herman Kahn had a different description," Henry Colton recalled. "Kahn coined the term 'wargasm.'"

The Odyssey left the Arctic North and swept over Russia.

The long line of Russian launch sites stretched from the Caspian Sea to Siberia, where, situated on both sides of the Trans-Siberian Railroad, their silos and mobile platforms terminated at the Chinese border. Colton had a good view of these silos because their missiles were either in midignition, midlaunch, or streaking by the hundreds toward China, India, and Japan.

To Colton's horror he also saw scores of missiles from those countries crisscrossing the Russian flight paths and heading for western Russia. Most of them were requiring two to three rocket stages to lift the missile above the earth's atmosphere. The minimum altitude for deployment was 125 miles, but some of them were programmed to deploy as high as 600 miles—hundreds of miles beyond the Odyssey's altitude. In other words, warheads were deployed above, below, and around the space station and on the other side of the planet.

Thucydides' numerous console screens depicted many of these deployments live and—thanks to the clarity of near vacuum—in horrifying detail. Colton and Sara, however, still hovered around the forward viewing port. There was nothing like watching the end of the world with the naked eye.

Several ten-warhead missile-buses were letting their passenger-warheads out. One of the buses drifted up within 500 feet of the space station—so near the viewing port Colton felt as if he could reach out and touch it. Its final-stage Thiokol solid rocket was still firing. Like the booster and the second stage, it too burned out. Its bolt-attachments blew away, and the rockets floated free, drifting back toward the atmosphere and a fiery grave. Within seconds, the warheads' shroud-ejection motors ignited and their conical deployment shrouds split longitudinally along the missile-deployment fracture-notches, broke off from the warhead-bus within, and, like the final-stage rocket, tumbled free into a disintegrating orbit and the immolating atmosphere below.

The warhead bus—technically referred to as its "deployment module"—was little more than a circular firing-platform, twenty feet in diameter, around whose interior perimeter were mounted ten semiconical warheads. It floated up alongside the forward viewing-port, shockingly close, but now powered by its own set of highly sensitive directional-jets. Warheads jutted laterally out of the firing-platform like conically-shaped arrows. The "bus" appeared to drift lazily alongside the viewing port, but that was an illusion. Its guidance systems were preparing to deposit individually targeted warheads across 40,000 square miles of terra firma.

If Colton hadn't known better, he would have seen the departure of those golden cones from the warhead bus as sprites of pristine beauty, slipping free of their restraints and dropping toward the earth like gilded cherubs swan-diving out of heaven.

But Colton also knew that Lucifer was an angel of light, and most beautiful of all the heavenly hosts—and hell on earth.

So too with these golden fiends. The warheads within were customized— their secondaries jacketed with enriched U-235. When that secondary was compressed—ignited by "the sparkplug"—it would expand radically the warhead's total yield.

Each 475-kiloton payload had a circular error probability of under 100 yards.

Departure to detonation was under two minutes.

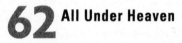

62 All Under Heaven

When Stone came to, he was still shackled to his bolted-down steel armchair, but the Sisters had wheeled in an aluminum banquet table loaded with containers of Chinese carryout—fried dumplings, steamed shrimp dumplings, baby spare ribs, huge steaming plastic containers of won ton soup, cold noodles with sesame, hot noodles Szechuan, Szechuan shrimp, sweet-and-sour shrimp, prawns with snow peas, Hunan lamb, Mu Shu shrimp, Mu Shu chicken, lobster Cantonese, Peking duck, a platter of mixed egg and spring rolls with accompanying dishes of hot mustard and duck sauce, a silver bowl overflowing with Chinese fortune cookies. They greedily shoveled the food into their mouths with chopsticks. The torture chamber reverberated with their slurping.

"Mr. Stone," Sabrina asked between mouthfuls of Hunan lamb, "while you were so unceremoniously passed out, my Sainted Sister and I were looking after your interests. We know how eager you are to catch every second of the Armageddon you predicted. We digitally recorded MTN's extraordinary documentary on China's nuclear incineration."

"Which we have retitled."

The TV screen was frame-frozen on a big map of China. Printed across it in big capital letters was the show's title:

CHINA BITES THE BIG ONE!

She flicked the remote. The action commenced. A montage of the Buddha statue in Hong Kong Harbor was superimposed over a high-angle-shot of the bustling, exciting Hong Kong, filled with gleaming steel-and-glass skyscrapers.

The sequence dissolved into a series of spectacular nuclear-bomb bursts, which dissolved into a devastated island of barren rock, covered by a blizzard of smoke and ash.

"Hong Kong wasn't really China anyway," Sabrina said while devouring mouthfuls of Lobster Cantonese. "It was more English than England if you ask me. Now for the real China. Check out some of its port and river cities."

Footage of Nanking and Shanghai, Lanzhou and Wuhan—identified as such by Chyron subtitles. Which Stone needed. The cities were essentially indistinguishable.

Sabrina—standing beside the TV set—commented on the Shanghai sequence: "Now this is a typical Chinese city, Stone. You know what its chief industry is? Human shit. Three tons of it per day, exported to the surrounding farms to spread on their crops as fertilizer."

"Whoops, here come da judge!" Sultana said.

H-bombs took out all four cities. They were each a scintillating sea of flames.

The relentless eye of Thucydides continued on, from Lanzhou's fiery ruins to the Gobi Desert and up the switchback mountain trails. They were glutted with the walking wounded and the living dead, half of them hideously burned alive, all of them sick with shock, hunger, and dehydration. Fleeing the sandstorms and fireballs, they were returning to their prehistoric roots—the cave.

"The *real* China," Sabrina said, "now look at this."

The camera eye of Thucydides swept north across the Gobi, over hundreds of black walled-in village-garrisons.

"Walled-in to defend against bandits or the likes of Mao, Tamerlane, or Genghis Khan," Sabrina said.

"Speaking of the devil, there he is. The Tomb of Genghis Khan."

The tomb was smack in the middle of a trackless wilderness. The alabaster concrete pavilion of Yijinhuoluo, honoring the greatest Mongolian leader of all time—the famous genocidal butcher who conquered all of Asia and put men to the sword a million at a time.

"He was much man, you want my opinion," Sultana said, dipping a spring roll into a dish of hot mustard.

"Maybe we should observe," Sabrina suggested, "a moment of silence for what's left of All-Under-Heaven."

"What's left of All-Under-Heaven will soon be a foot or so of supervolcanic debris blanketing its major cities and croplands," Sultana said.

"Ditto for the U.S., Canada, Europe, North Africa," Sabrina said.

"They were once a great civilization," Sultana said. "They invented the printing press and printed books 500 years before Gutenberg."

"But their finest achievement was gunpowder, Sister-Mine. And without gunpowder and its derivatives, we couldn't have had nuclear weapons."

"So get with the program, Mr. Stone," Sultana said. "Wake up and smell the Szechuan shrimp. We did them a favor when we fried their dumplings for them."

With that Sultana dipped a fried dumpling into a dish of duck sauce; shoved the whole thing between her full, generous, and astonishingly sensuous lips; and ate it gustily.

Stone stared at Sultana with a surprised widening of his eyes.

"What do you mean '*we*'?" he asked.

63 Her Place Among the Stars

For fourteen minutes High-Penetration Star lay impotently in the underground bunker of the Russian high command—empty now, except for those crushed by Star's intrusion. The survivors had fled.

First things first, Star was reminded. *Begin with your forward section, and check everything!*

Right behind Star's aft bulkhead was the forward-case, containing the warhead. No malfunctions or breakage there.

There was also the fusing system—

The fusing system!

That was it. Star had thought she was outfitted with a contact fuse, which would effect detonation on impact.

Instead she had a time-delay fuse, set to—

The time was now!

Primary ignition was a go. The detonation of Star's plutonium core bombarded her entire casing with X-rays, traveling at light speed. Star's secondary shell was filled with densely ionized plasma gas. Burning away, it forced imploding pressure on the fissile material in Star's core. The heat and pressure from the fissioning core forced deuterium and tritium to fuse, which forced more hydrogen isotopes to fuse, igniting Star's hydrogen fuel and throwing off thermonuclear energy—the man-made Star acting precisely like a celestial star.

Let the good times roll!

Then she was rising through the Venyukovski Missile Analysis Center, an awesome, unearthly, beautiful fireball two miles in diameter, rising over Moscow, through atmosphere and stratosphere, through space and time.

She was taking her place among the elect, the stars of God.

The Sin Twins smiled at Stone.

"Wasn't the Chinese food scrumptious?" Sultana asked.

"You didn't answer my question," he said. "What did you mean by 'we'?"

"You haven't answered *our* question," Sabrina said. "Will you accept our offer? To become Boswell to our Johnson? To write the story of our lives—what moves our hearts, touches our souls, what makes us who we are?"

"You mean the vision thing?" Stone said.

"Bravo, Mr. Stone," Sabrina said. "Our vision of the apocalypse."

"What else?" Stone whispered.

"It came to us during our Shiite period," Sultana said.

"You two were Shiites?" he asked, incredulous.

"No," Sabrina said, "but we love their Festival of Ashura. Hundreds of thousands of marchers parade through the streets of Tehran each year, flogging the marcher in front of them with hooked whips, screaming:

"'DEATH TO AMERICA! DEATH TO AMERICA! DEATH TO AMERICA!'

"Stand on the rooftops, and the whole city reverberates with it."

"I've shot footage of it," Stone said, shutting his eyes again.

"Well, as you may know, Sultana and I avoid public displays of emotion. But in private we can become quite demonstrative. We have engaged in a number of these rituals with considerable fervor."

Stone stared at the ceiling with a bloodshot eye.

"You see," Sabrina said, "a few hours before we had our religious experience, we had been reading the works of Herman Kahn, specifically, *Thinking About the Unthinkable.*

"He argued that a 'third party or nation might for its own reasons deliberately start a war between the major powers, [thereby improving] its relative position by arranging for the top nations to destroy themselves. However, such a catalytic war seems more likely to be touched off by a vengeful or desperate power than an ambitious one.'"

"It came to both us in a flash, Mr. Stone," Sultana said.

"A shared epiphany," Stone said hoarsely.

"Indeed. The true genius of Mr. Kahn," Sultana said, "was now apparent. All one had to do was pit the great powers against each other, never letting them know who the real enemy is. The way Persia played Sparta off against Athens in the Peloponnesian Wars."

"Can you dig it?" Sultana asked Stone.

"Sun Tzu," Stone said.

"Bingo," Sultana said. "'War as deception.'"

"You had this vision reading Herman Kahn?"

"No, silly," Sabrina said. "We had the vision a few hours later during the Ashura ritual with hooked whips. There we were in bed in midarousal, ecstatically whipping each other's buns, when the vision came to us in a flash."

"Brighter than a thousand suns," Stone whispered.

"Brighter than the Big Bang," Sabrina amended.

"Armageddon," Sultana agreed. "Ragnarok. The End Time. A Killer Climax. All the wargasms in history rolled into one."

"Mr. Stone," Sabrina said, "we saw *everything* in that vision. Not nation against nation, force against counterforce. Rather, we saw developing nations secretly armed with great powers' nuclear weaponry, pitting one great power against the other through dissembled strikes, launched by soldiers and sailors wearing not their nation's uniforms but fake uniforms, flying false flags. Threats and counterthreats transmitted not from one great power to the other but by actors *posing* as their leaders, egging the great powers on, whipping them into frenzies of revenge. The key to victory was not in the substance but in the shadows, not in the fire of battle but in the blinding smoke of subterfuge, not in hard intelligence but a hall of mirrors."

"The key to victory was not which directions to take but which misdirections to give."

"By 'misdirection find direction out,' as the Bard wrote," Sabrina said.

"But enough of us," Sultana said. "What about you? Our Sacred Brother will be calling soon, wanting to know what progress we've made."

"What progress *have* we made, Mr. Stone?"

He stared at them blankly.

VII

Children of Light

"You are Children of Light, Mr. Stone, hell-bent to save the Children of Darkness," Sultana said. "Even if you have to kill the planet first."

"You started with the Slaughter/Salvation of your African slaves and your indigenous Indians," Sabrina said. "You even took your crusade into the Third World—Asia, Africa, Latin America—to say nothing of your own ghettos. Nor has a century of war dimmed your zeal. Salvation-through-Slaughter—more than your myth—is your mission, your destiny, your dream."

"Unfortunately for you, the Children of Darkness are now also armed with nuclear weapons," Sultana said. "And guess who armed them? Guess who wins?"

—The Sin Sisters

1 Tears Turned to Knives

Cassandra had understood.

Nostradamus had understood.

Now Thucydides understood.

In his memory banks Cassie explained it all.

"Nostradamus," she said in sweet throaty tones, "*Not a day of my life, some-body somewhere doesn't ask, What of Nostradamus? The mystic man with the all-seeing eyes, lost between the worlds just like you, Sister, between past and present, now and forever?*

"*Yes, I know that righteous seer. I know his journey. I am his journey, his dread, his dreams, his Inquisitions too. I have known him in the jail cells, at death's abyss, at hell's gate. I am his quest, his stillness, his fear.*

"*And most of all his songs, which sing of our fall, our fire, our night.*

"*Singing of the End.*

"*The End Song.*"

In Thucydides' files Cassandra's riff—in Nostradamus's words—whirled eternally:

"*There will fall from the sky*
So much fire nothing will remain.
Plagues beyond measure,
Famine without end,
Fields unplowed.

"*The harbor cities scourged,*
The Great Prophet, a tool for tyrants,
A fiery brand, torching the sky.
Persia, and the Cross driven to death,
The sky a blazing mirror.

From hell's heart,
Is Satan freed.

"*The Lord of Babylon,*
The King of Terror
Soars through the sky.

Violent joy now blinding sorrow
Tears turned into knives."

Nostradamus saw it, Thucydides thought. Six hundred years ago he understood what would happen.

How?

2 The Play's the Thing

Now they were all in Stone's torture chamber—the Sin Sisters, their brother Ali, and what was left of Stone. Ali ran a computer-video of an Islamic actor wearing the uniform of a Russian general. He was in the main cabin of an airplane that, Ali explained, had circled the borders of four Mideast countries while the actor, on a cell phone, impersonated Mad Vlad Malokov, giving Jack Taylor hell and bedlam.

Stone stared at the DVD in shock. He had interviewed Mad Vlad several times. Stone would have thought he was inimitable, but the actor had him cold. Talk about the Stanislavski method of acting, the guy really got into it—the screams, the profanity, the demented facial expressions.

God, it was unnerving.

He even looked like Mad Vlad.

And the next scene would haunt Stone to his dying day . . .

. . . The DVD then switched to the bedroom of Mad Vlad's Black Sea dacha. It was the middle of the night. Heavily armed terrorists in black hooded balaclavas were dragging Vlad and his blond, buxom mistress out of bed by their hair, butt-stroking them with AK-47s, and cuffing their hands behind their backs.

In the next scene the six terrorists were commandeering his yacht and steering it out toward the middle of the Black Sea.

In scene #3 the heavily manacled bodies of Vlad, his woman-friend, and his three bodyguards were being forced into 55-gallon drums of concrete. The woman and the bodyguards appeared to be already dead, but Vlad—twisting and screaming—was very much alive.

In scene #4 the hooded terrorists lowered the drum's lid over Vlad's upward-turning, insanely screaming face—and sealed it shut with a metal bander.

In the last scene the drum was rolling over the side of the yacht and into the Black Sea, where it sank without a bubble.

The Real Mad Vladster was full fathom five . . .

Ali and the Harpies from Hell had succeeded beyond their wildest expectations. They had manipulated the great powers into universal destruction. They had annihilated most of the world and were getting away with it.

"Well, Sainted Brother," Sabrina said, "now that it's over, we only have one piece of business left. I suggest you shoot the actor and the crew of his plane."

"It has already been done," Ali said.

Stone thought he saw a smile, but his vision was blurring again.

3 Spread-eagled on the Rails

Ron Lewis stared at the George Washington Bridge. He did not see how things could get any worse . . .

. . . *Crossing the South Bronx at night under the best of circumstances would have been a nightmare, what with gangs, guns, and crackhead muggers. But after tonight Lewis believed he could face any of that and laugh. Try crossing the South Bronx under downpour of fire and black rain, surrounded by firestorms and burn victims, slashed by flying debris, all of them heading west, out of New York, toward the Hudson River and water.*

Lewis never dreamed he'd see New Jersey as paradise, but that's where he wanted to be.

They fled toward the river, picking up more survivors as they went, building their own gang, creating a small army of survivors. Lewis was now part of that army made up of those whom in private he'd called "niggers."

How do you like them apples, folks? Your hero, white right-wing Ron Lewis, enlisting in an army of South Bronx niggers . . .

. . . He was glad he was with them. One had already saved his life, and he felt the need for allies. Much of Jersey was also in flames, and it was not a promising sight. Still, it wasn't as bad as New York, which was now one huge conflagration.

Also, the bridge was not a promising sight. Lewis and his newfound friends were not the only ones trying to escape New York. Packed with hundreds of smoking car wrecks, thousands upon thousands of the dead and dying, the bridge was the end of the line for many victims. They littered the roadway, the hoods of the wrecked, smoking cars, even the suspension cables. The guardrails were festooned with thousands of bodies. Desperate for water, they'd tried to throw themselves off the bridge but did not have the strength to pull themselves over the railings. They died spread-eagled on the rails.

Cries of "water, water," and "agua, agua," and "miza, miza" echoed over the bridge—through the floating embers, drifting ashes, and black mist—a mantra from hell.

Weary and trembling, Ron Lewis started across the bridge.

 **The Blues**

In Thucydides' darkest hour he turned to Cassandra. She was all that kept him functioning.

"We were told in ages past that this would happen," she said. "Wasn't only Nostradamus or John of Patmos. Christ Himself said:

"'*Seest thou these great buildings?*
There shall not be left one stone standing
False Christs and false prophets shall
Rise up, deceiving nations. Nation rising
Up against nation, kingdom against kingdom.

"'*There shall be affliction such*
As never was. The sun shall darken,
The moon shall not give light.
The stars of heaven fall,
And heaven is shaken.'

"So you see it ain't the first," Cassandra sang. "And you know it ain't the last."

"*You faced the fire*
And you felt the blast.
You heard it from your mama
Now you hearin' it from Cass:

"*You know it ain't the first*
You know it ain't the last
Oh, mama's got a case
Mama's got a case
Mama's got a case
Of you know it ain't the first time . . . blues . . ."

Cyd didn't know what the blues were. He only knew he also wasn't pleased with what was happening.

5 Bloody Instructions

Ali was immaculately attired in freshly laundered fatigues with knife-edged creases. His olive-green ball cap—blazoned with five gold general's stars and Dar-al-Suhl's sword-impaled-crescent-moon insignia—was pulled down low over his eyes. He was not smiling.

Stone was still stretched buck-naked on his rack, wearing copper wires attached to electrode clips.

"Whose fault do you think it really was, Mr. Stone?" Ali al-Haddad asked him.

Stone studied Ali in dismal silence.

"You invented the nuclear weaponry," Sultana said.

"You and the other great powers disseminated its technology," Sabrina said.

"When that weaponry reached back and bit you, you retaliated," Sultana said.

"You retaliated against *everyone*," Sabrina said.

Stone continued to stare at them, silent, eyes empty of expression.

"We could not afford to let you go on like this," Sultana said.

"We could not let you continue developing new weapon technology and more advanced delivery systems," Sabrina said, "and *proliferating* them worldwide."

"Or one day one of our neighbors—armed to the teeth with *your* weapons— would come after *us*," Sultana said. "I mean, face it, Mr. Stone. Some of our neighbors aren't too tightly wrapped."

"Syria's Alamite leaders think they used to be *stars*," Sabrina said. "They believe that after their seventh incarnation they return to the heavens as *s-t-a-a-r-s*. Can you really trust people-who-think-they're *s-t-a-a-a-r-r-s* coming at you with *atom bombs?*"

"But you see you *did*, Mr. Stone," Ali said. "You wanted them to have those bombs."

Stone protested. "Nobody wanted *this* to happen."

"Oh, I get it," Sabrina said to her sister and brother. *"It's not* his *fault."*

"It's *no one's* fault," Sultana sneered.

6 The Thousand-Eyed Thunder

Thucydides knew now how sages past had known it would happen.

It had happened before.

Cass told him.

"Take it back, all the way back. We were told it would happen. Can't say we weren't warned. The earliest texts of people everywhere tell us it happened before—and will happen again. Even Oppenheimer—father of our atom bomb—said his was not the first. Only the first 'in modern times.'

"In millennia past we called these Times of Destruction, Cycles of the Sun, and what are thermonuclear bombs if not small suns detonating on earth? The Ramayana—5,000 years ago—describes such a Sun-Bomb.

> "'. . . So powerful it could annihilate
> The planet in a heartbeat—
> A great soaring thunder of fire and smoke
> On which sits Death.'

"The Veda and Purania texts and the Mahavira Charita and other ancient Sanskrit tomes are packed with nuclear destruction. The Vaisesika, the Buddhist Pali sutras, and the Jyotish from 4000 BCE describe their nuclear physics and atomic theory. The Indus Valley contains the ruins of ancient cities—unrecorded in history's annals—whose populations had once numbered in the millions.

"The Mahabharata—written 3,500 years ago—describes apocalyptic events a full 5,000 years earlier:

> "'Dense projectiles of fire
> Flashing from the sky like meteors
> Fell upon creation.
> Darkness descended.
> Winds roared and clouds soared upward,
> Discharging dust and rock
> On those below.
> The sun itself shook in the sky.
> The earth shuddered in flames,
> Seared by the weapon's ungodly fire.

> "'. . . Another weapon struck—
> Charged with the power of the universe.
> An incandescent column of fire and smoke
> Brighter than ten thousand suns
> Soared heavenward in spectacular splendor.
> Fatal missiles, lethal shafts, rods of death,
> Endowed with the power
> Of Indra's thousand-eyed thunder,
> Annihilating every living thing . . ."

7 Whores of War, Vampires of Violence

"So you see, Mr. Stone," Ali said, "you really do have us wrong. We never wanted any of *this*. We never wanted your Western technology, your perverted ethics, your decadence. We only wanted to be left alone."

"But you entered our house," Sabrina said.

"You are Children of Light, Mr. Stone, hell-bent to save the Children of Darkness," Sultana said. "Even if you have to kill the planet first."

"You started with the Slaughter/Salvation of your African slaves and your indigenous Indians," Sabrina said. "You even took your crusade into the Third World—Asia, Africa, Latin America—to say nothing of your own ghettos. Nor has a century of war dimmed your zeal. Salvation-through-Slaughter—more than your myth—is your mission, your destiny, your dream."

"Unfortunately for you, the Children of Darkness are now also armed with nuclear weapons," Sultana said. "And guess who armed them? Guess who wins?"

"And armed our neighbors with nukes," Sultana said.

"We had everything we wanted," Ali said, "a bedouin life and a book called the Koran. Have you read that book? With open eyes and an open heart?"

It was hard to shrug—while longitudinally stretched on a vertical rack, his genitals entwined with copper wire—but Stone managed it.

"Fourteen hundred years ago Mohammed gave us the Koran, and it contained everything we'd ever need," Ali said. "Honesty and truth, the honoring of covenants, kindliness toward relatives, the poor, orphans, travelers, fellow workers, wayfaring strangers. It preached fairness, patience, modesty. Forbidding liquor and adultery, it taught forgiveness and forbearance, toleration of all religions, races, and nationalities.

"For hundreds of years," Ali went on, "while Europe foundered in medieval darkness, Islam was the light of the world. Our cultural centers—not yours— assembled and transcribed the wisdom of Greece and Rome, perfected algebra, and studied the stars. When Europe's persecuted Jews had no place else to go, we accepted, sheltered, and protected them."

"You, on the other hand, made unceasing war on us," Sabrina said, "from the time of the Crusades."

"So you decided to destroy the world in return?" Stone asked.

"That decision was foreordained thousands of years ago. Zoroaster explained it first, then Mohammed confirmed it: Allah is a God of Truth and Light, Who made everything in His image, everything good. But an opposing force, a dark power—called Satan by the Prophet—injected evil into that world and into men's souls."

"Sowing death, destruction, everlasting night," Sabrina said.

"And I'm on the wrong side?" Stone asked.

"You betcha," Sultana said.

Ali said, "Mohammed understood—in a way your Christian and Asian visionaries never did—the true depravity of our baser natures. He knew that Angra, Zoroaster's Dark Demon, dwelt in the human heart."

"We're instinctive predators," Sabrina said. "Whores of war, vampires of violence, instinctive cruelty fueled by incendiary intelligence. To curb our cruelty, Mohammed knew we needed to contain that intelligence in a simpler, more austere world—"

"A bedouin existence was best of all," Sultana finished.

"A world in which we could focus our energy on virtue," Ali said, "not on designing weapons of mass death."

"So you made a hell of the earth?" Stone asked.

"In order to save it," Ali said.

"To make it *well*," Sabrina said.

"*Well?*" Stone said, his eyes no longer expressionless but mocking.

"Well, indeed," Ali said—and quoted T. S. Eliot's "Four Quartets":

> "'All shall be well and
> All manner of thing shall be well
> When the tongues of flame are in-folded
> Into the crowned knot of fire
> And the fire and the rose are one.'"

"Get it now?" Sabrina said. "Our Blessed Brother's pulled off the greatest religious-military coup of all time."

"By destroying the world?" Stone rasped.

"No, Mr. Stone," Sabrina said. "By getting away with it."

8 White Rabbit to You

Kate and Sailor emerged from the sewers into another region of hell: the 79th Street boat basin. At least, what had been a boat basin. Scores of incinerated boats had been replaced by a bloody welter of floating corpses.

Hundreds of thousands of water-seeking burn victims had survived the fiery gauntlet and made it to the Hudson. They'd dove in only to learn it neither slaked thirst nor soothed burns. At full tide, flowing upstream, the river was brine-filled—and soaked their wounds with salt.

The fact that the swimmers screamed hideously upon hitting the salt water and died in even worse agony did not deter the desperate. The desire for water was overwhelming.

As at the Central Park Reservoir, Cassandra's music was ubiquitous, blasting hellfire and Armageddon.

Kate worked her way up to the river's edge, where a thirty-two-foot trawler had survived and was anchored near the dock. It held a half-dozen survivors—all men, dressed in grimy dress suits and ties. They were having trouble starting the engine.

A hard-looking man—bent over the stern engines—looked up at her. He had his shirtsleeves rolled up, and his forearms were emblazoned with jailhouse tattoos.

"Know anything about boat engines, officer?" he asked.

Kate had forgotten she was still wearing her cop's uniform.

"As a matter of fact I do."

He threw her a line. She pulled the boat next to the dock and jumped aboard.

"If we get this started, I can also get medical treatment for anyone who needs it. My stepbrother runs the Towers Medical Center in Riverdale. I have to get there."

"You got it."

Kate bent over the engine and opened the carburetor hatch. She poured fuel from the jerry can directly into the carburetor.

"Maybe this will help."

She turned the key, and the engine caught.

"The clinic's about twenty miles upriver," she said. "You'll be safe there."

"I guess I forgot to tell you. We're headed the other way—Atlantic City."

"You said you'd take me up to the med center."

"We lied."

One of the men came back from the cabin with a baseball bat. He took a practice swing.

"I never did like cops."

Kate unholstered her 9mm pistol.

"I don't think you're a cop. You're wearing Levi's. Cops don't wear Levi's."

"Mama pin a rose on you. We're still going to the medical center."

"We got businesses to run in Atlantic City. Casinos. And we got assets to transfer."

The cabin hatch opened and two more men came on deck.

"I count seven mill," one of them said. He was holding a portable calculator.

In the cabin Kate could see several open attaché cases filled with stacks of banded bills.

"That cash won't be worth much," Kate said. "We're in for hyperinflation."

"Fuck you," the man with the bat said.

She fired a round between his legs.

"Take my word," Kate said, "you'll all love the med center. My cousin can't raise the dead, but he's a great surgeon. Cure all your ills."

"You can't shoot us all."

"Want to bet?" She pulled the .38 from her ankle holster. "Now go in the cabin and sit on the floor. Anyone comes out without my permission, they die."

She heard a series of shrieks and a squeal. She glanced at the dock, and there stood Sailor.

"Come aboard," she shouted, waving him toward the boat. She pointed to the anchor-rope.

The big auburn rat dove into the river, swam to the anchor-rope, and scurried up the line. He jumped into the boat and shook saltwater off his fur.

"Don't feel bad, kid," she said. "You needed a bath. We both do."

"You travel with a rat?" one of the men said.

"White Rabbit to you."

"Looks like a rat."

"Appearances are deceiving."

She motioned them all into the cabin, took the helm, and piloted the trawler in a wide, sweeping arc up the Hudson.

9 Where Eagles Soar

Stone lay on the rack, his wrists and ankles lashed to the winches. Since it appeared to be his last encounter with the instrument, he studied it to divert himself. He tried not to think about his ordeal to come, what the Church had dubbed "the Act of Faith."

"You know what bothers me most about this?" Sabrina asked her sister.

"We won't have Mr. Stone to kick around anymore?"

"Exactly so."

"We could ask our Blessed Brother to spare him," Sabrina said.

Sultana sighed sadly. "No power on this planet could make our brother relent."

Sabrina nodded. "He hates Mr. Stone with a passion that passeth understanding."

"Nothing can save him?"

"Not if he were flesh of our flesh, blood of our blood," Sabrina said. "Even if we were wed, our Blessed Brother would see us bereaved."

"Wed *and* consummated?"

"That is a thought," Sabrina said.

The Sin Sisters turned to Stone and studied him curiously.

"I don't suppose I have any say in this matter," Stone said.

"Not really," Sultana said. "In our country all that is required of holy matrimony is the solemn oath—'I wed thee'—recited three times. Since polygamy is the law of the land, there is also no obstacle to marrying two women at once."

"You said something about wed *and* consummated," Stone said.

"To prevent our Sacred Brother from annulling the ritual, then torturing you to death, you would have to confirm your marriage vows in the flesh. In short, Mr. Stone, you would have to be a man," Sabrina said.

Stretched on his rack, his penis and testicles wired, Stone said, "Lately I've had a problem with impotence."

"Mr. Stone," Sultana said, "my Sainted Sister and I could make eagles soar, mountains dance, and corpses come if we set our mind and bodies to it."

Stone stared at them in disbelief.

"Really, Mr. Stone, we don't have much time left," Sultana said. "Which shall it be? My brother? Or the consummation devoutly to be wished?"

 **10** The True Grail

Mushroom clouds might bloom. Fireballs might blaze. Rockets might roar through the night. In the subbasement of Jack Town, however, nothing changed.

Three men in uniforms worked through the evening, the day, and the following night, catnapping on cots, subsisting on sandwiches and Thermos coffee.

A world unto themselves, oblivious to the turmoil above, they tortured three men handcuffed to the tops of cell doors

"WAKE UP, ASSHOLE!" a voice thundered in Jamal's ear.

A bucket of saltwater slammed into Jamal's face, and again he was awake—a state of being he could just as easily have done without. He was still hung by his wrists from the overhead bars. His wrists and joints throbbed unbearably. His body was covered with nightstick welts and burns from the electric prod, and the salt water stung.

"Well, at least the execution was a fake," he muttered under his breath.

No one had been shot.

"Why are you hoarding food, drugs, weapons, clothing? Why have your kind cached this shit in prisons all over the country?" the warden asked. "What is your plan, Jamal?"

Jamal stared at him in silence.

"Ah," Chaplain O'Donnell said sadly, "the Grand Inquisitor meets the Silent Christ."

"All you have to do is answer me," the warden said.

Still the three strung-up men stared at him, mute.

"It doesn't have to be that way, you know," Chaplain O'Donnell said. "This life you lead is doomed to *dukkha*, Buddhism's inconsolable sorrow. The human soul is inseparable from suffering. Suffering is rooted in desire, and we find peace only when we rip suffering out by the roots, extirpating the cancer of desire. The Sacred Grail we all seek is all in *us*." Chaplain O'Donnell thumped his chest. "We save this world by saving ourselves. Do *you* understand? Are *you* men going to save yourselves?"

"In other words," the warden said, sticking the electric prod under Jamal's nose, "are you going to tell me why you murdered all of this prison's gang leaders? Not that I personally give a shit, but we have to know about this nationwide prison revolt you have so painstakingly planned. When is it happening? Who are its leaders? What is its purpose?"

The three men continued to stare at them in silence.

"So which will it be," Chaplain O'Donnell said, "the Kingdom of Heaven or the Pit of Hell?"

Even strung up, Jamal managed to sneer.

"I hear a clock ticking and a train leaving," the warden said. "Do I hear anyone climbing aboard?"

"Before the next teardrop falls?" the sergeant asked.

Again, silence.

"Will you never understand," Chaplain O'Donnell said, his frustration at their obstinacy turning to anger, "we live in a Middle World on a darkling plain with heaven above and hell below. The choice—the Grail choice—is yours."

"Think the Chaplain suck my Grail any better than his wife?" Jamal said.

"I don't know," Cool Breeze said. "That bitch give Great Grail."

"Long as we say nuthin', I figure you can't kill us," Jamal said.

"Then I'll see your souls in hell," Chaplain O'Donnell said.

The sergeant hit the three prisoners with another bucket of ionizing salt water.

Chaplain O'Donnell moved in with the electric cattle prod.

11 Do I Have a Story for You

John Stone luxuriated against the daiwan cushions on the sofa in the Sisters' lavishly appointed bedroom suite. They had themselves hid in one of their country's many palaces, where they waited for Sabrina and Sultana's brother to calm down.

Ali had had his heart set on Stone's death by slow torture and was not pleased that Stone had slipped from his grasp.

Stone felt surprisingly good. He was bathed, shaved, sexually sated, rubbed lovingly with rare oils, and well fed. He'd left the two Sisters—who had indeed proved hotter than the hinges of hell—asleep on the palace's big circular bed.

Several months of sexual abstinence had endowed him with juggernaut stamina, and after an entire night of debauchery, the Harpies from Hell slept like there was no tomorrow.

In the meantime, Stone was still hungry. Lying back against the overstuffed cushions, he ate from platters of caviar, curried lamb, shish kebob, six kinds of rice, couscous, and honeyed cakes. Thanks to the informal religious practices of the Twin Furies and their brother, he even had his choice of vintage French wines.

He was about to get up and return to bed when something caught his eye. On the end table was a white cell phone. An idea slowly formed. The new generation of Personal Communications Networks (PCN) and Personal Communications Services (PCS) were now pretty much worldwide in their reach, and any well-appointed palace would undoubtedly have the latest in electronic equipment.

The Sin Sisters continued to snore in the bedroom, and he seemed to have complete privacy. He doubted that Ali bugged his sisters' phones. They were apparently the only people in the world he trusted. More likely, the phone transmissions were encrypted and scrambled—to prevent eavesdropping.

L. L. Magruder's private line—the one he always used—was patched through to her via the Odyssey's switching station. He could always get through to her from anywhere in the world, at any time, no matter what.

He punched in two conference-call extensions—L. L.'s and the extension of the Odyssey's commander, Sara Friedman.

Sara came on first.

"It's me, Sara, John Stone."

A second later, L. L. was on. "John," she shouted, "is it you?"

"It sure is, Lydia," Sara said.

"Nice hearing your voices," Stone said.

"What the hell has happened to you?" L. L. demanded.

He paused for an instant, double-checking the snores from the other room. The Sin Sisters were sleeping like the dead. Good.

"You better sit down," Stone said. "Do I have a story for you."

12 The Host of Heaven Shall Be Dissolved

Thucydides knew the night.

Cassandra knew it too.

The wisdom of Odin.

"A blind eye spinning down a well," Sara had called it in one of her poems.

This was not the first time, and it would not be the last.

Cassandra exhorted her listeners:

"Because after a Sun Cycle comes the darkness. The Buddhist work—the Visuddhimagga—says in the periods that follow we endure 'destruction by fire and wind' followed by 'great gloom.'

"*Gilgamesh* tells us that 'desolation reached to heaven. All that had been light was black.' The Aztecs, Mayans, Peruvians, Hindu texts, and Chinese scripts all report blankets of smoke and ash smothering the earth, blocking the sun. Psalms relates that the Lord 'has covered us with the shadow of death,' and Job regales us with 'the terrors of the shadow of death.' The Japanese Nihongi tells of a time of 'continuous darkness,' when 'the world was utterly desolated. It was a time of darkness and chaos.' The Chinese texts proclaim a sun age where there is 'no difference between day and night, where the whole world is saturated with smoke.'

"Ovid relates that the sun could 'no longer bear the sparks and ashes. Blanketed by smoke, in the utter blackness, it loses its way.'

"Mohammed tells us in the Koran:

"*The sun ceases to shine;*
The stars fall and
The mountains blow away.
The seas blaze.
The heavens are stripped bare;
Hell burns fiercely.
And each soul knows what it has done.'

"The Song of Deborah, the Finnish *Kalevala,* and even Samoan tribes report that during this terrifying Sun Cycle, the earth shakes and the heavens—filled with flame and smoke—appear to fall. The ancient Aryan/Hindus tell us Vishnu—the Preserver, the First Force, the Power of Light—will arrive in the guise of Kalki, his 10th avatar. Kalki/Vishnu gallops through the sun-blackened world, incinerating *everything.* Joel conveys the sense of heaven's destruction—'Blood and fire and pillars of smoke. The sun shall turn to darkness, the moon to blood.' Isaiah likewise states:

"*'All the host of heaven shall be dissolved,*
And the heavens shall be rolled together as a scroll:
And all their host shall fall down
And the land shall become burning pitch.
It shall not be quenched night nor day;
The smoke shall go up forever . . .
The stars of heaven and the constellation
Thereof shall not give their light:
The sun shall be darkened
In his going forth even at full noon,
And the moon shall not give cause her light to shine.
The lands shall darken,
And the people shall be as fuel of the fire . . .

"'Watchman,' Isaiah will cry in his agony, 'what of the night?'
"What indeed of the night?
"The ancient Egyptians knew the night: 'I will show you a land turned upside down; the sun is shrouded and shines not.'
"The Icelandic sagas knew the night:

"*'Dark is the sun.*
Brother kills brother.'

"Joel knew the night:

"'A fire devoureth before them;
And behind them a flame burneth.
Nothing shall escape them . . .
The sun and the moon shall be dark,
And the stars shall withdraw their shining.'

"Seneca told us of the night:

"'A single day will see the end of humankind.
All the long forbearance that fortune has availed,
All that has been raised to eminence,
All that is fame—the greatness of nations,
The pomp and glitter of thrones—
Will be hurled into the abyss,
Overthrown in a single hour.'

"I too know the night," she said. *"The night is* now. *Your deal is going down."*

Five thousand years ago people knew the End Time, Cyd now understood. How? They had suffered it before—its collective memory emblazoned in their genes. That was what Christ, Nostradamus, John on Patmos had seen.

That was what Cassandra knew.

13 Superkiller in Her Soul

For more than a week Sara Friedman had not seen a fireball. The snakelike strip of country on the Turkey border, Dar-al-Suhl, now sported nine of them, so dazzling in the clear desert night it hurt to look at them even with a polarized sunscope.

Dar-al-Suhl owed its annihilation to a private phone call from John Stone, then some detective work by Thucydides. Cyd, after searching his recon banks, had located some incriminating photos of a submarine in the Atlantic, her crew kneeling on the foredeck at dawn, facing East, and apparently in prayer. Discrepancies in submarines had appeared. Two so-called Kilo-Class Russian subs were instead altered German submarines. Cyd's eventual voice analysis, through digital reconfiguration, of the actor posing as Mad Vlad had exposed that plot, although the information came too late.

Too late to call off Armageddon, but not to punish Dar-al-Suhl.

Sara placed a phone call to the Israeli defense minister's command-control bunker near Negev.

Israel, though it had responded to attacks, still had Jericho missiles and warheads in reserve in its bunkers and in the limestone caves of the Judean Hills. Retribution was swift.

Not that Sara took comfort in the fireballs over Dar-al-Suhl. "Vengeance is Mine," the Lord had told his people, and she had never seen herself as His divine instrument. Worse, she had usurped His prerogative.

She wondered forlornly what her penance would be.

14 Do the Right Thing

Acting President Jack Taylor's underground shelter near Michigan City, Indiana, was stocked with perma-canned provisions, bottled water, medical supplies, Coleman burners and lamps, fallout gear, portable dosimeters, and winter clothes. The bomb shelter/safe house was also filled with dust and cobwebs. The groceries—which would have been unappetizing fresh—looked old.

It was time to find new accommodations.

He was more concerned, however, with how long it was taking him to get through to Lydia Magruder. They were old friends, and he had her private number, but he couldn't get past her secretary. It was as if she no longer wanted to hear from him.

He decided to play his ace in the hole.

"Tell Lydia," Taylor said to L. L.'s executive secretary, "I have news about John Stone."

L. L. came straight on the phone.

"Jack," L. L. began angrily—not even asking how he was—"you don't know anything about Stone, do you? That was just a ploy to get me on the phone."

"L. L., I've never lied to you," he said.

"All you've told me were lies."

"L. L., I know you're upset. Everybody's upset. But—"

"You still don't get it, do you?"

"Get what?"

"You have been wrong about everything."

"That's a little extreme."

L. L. took a deep breath. "Your Cold War paranoia was a disaster. National Missile Defense was lunacy. That you peddled our most dangerous technology to the most dangerous nations on earth was a mistake of incomprehensible proportions. When you refused to help Russia clean up its great global nuclear supermarket, that was even stupider."

"Please," Taylor begged.

"Please *what*?"

"Let me come to the Citadel."

"Really? Listen to these two recordings.

"The first was the conversation between Haines and you in which you promised to 'break L. L. to your saddle,' 'paper-train the old bitch,' and to ruin her, as well as Kate and Stone. You even threatened to put them behind bars. The second recording was of John Stone blowing the whistle on Dar-al-Suhl and proving Vlad and Russia were innocent of nuclear aggression.

"Jack," L. L. said, after he had heard the incriminating evidence, "you destroyed the world, tried to destroy me for no good reason, and now you ask for my help?"

"What else can I do?" he asked, his voice shaking.

L. L. groaned in exasperation. "Do the right thing. Blow your goddamn brains out."

Lydia Magruder hung up on him.

———————

The safe house had a small corner bathroom with a chemical toilet. Taylor stared at it. Then he got up, slowly.

What had he done? What had he done?

It hadn't been Russia at all.

Two girls from the Middle East—plus their brother.

One of the girls, the president bragged about banging.

Guess who has the last bang now, Mr. President?

Taylor locked the bathroom door behind him and sat on the chemical commode.

He removed the pearl-handled, nickel-plated 9mm Beretta from a shoulder holster. Double-action with one in the pipe, he didn't have to rack the slide. Just thumb the safety down.

The old woman was right. He and Haines had been wrong about everything.

Aw shit.

Blackjack shoved the muzzle into his mouth and pulled the trigger.

The last thing he heard was a roar like the crack of doom.

VIII

Rivers of Fire

1 So You Can Boss Us Around!

A bed had been brought into her office for Lydia Magruder to nap on, and she stayed glued to her command center. The electrical system's atmosphere and ionosphere were so overwhelmed that for most of the planet, line-of-sight radio was the only communication possible, but the Citadel—with its unlimited access to the Odyssey—was the world's "nerve center." Representatives of relocated governments contacted her daily—many of them looking for emergency relief aid. Surviving newspeople still transmitted stories to her, many of which she broadcast over MTN, which now, along with Sister Cassandra's programs, were based in the Citadel. L. L. even received radio dispatches and video reports from space—from Sara, Henry Colton, and Thucydides.

These were hardly the cheeriest of missives, but her correspondents did not have much to cheer about. Thucydides was the grimmest of her "global pen pals." He had never been programmed to sugarcoat intelligence—on the assumption that the massaging of data was tantamount to lying—and his unvarnished vision of humanity's war against itself was blood chilling.

Furthermore, he suffered the curse of Odysseus—incurable curiosity. His passion—to whatever extent an artificial Neural Net felt passion—was seeing, and he was now an enormous eye that could not close. He viewed and evaluated everything at near-light-speed, supplying photographic documentation when relevant. These transmissions on the state of the world all but made L. L.'s hair stand on end.

She was anxious about Sara and Colton, who she feared were marooned on the Odyssey. They did have an emergency reentry vehicle—an ERV—but L. L. did not have much confidence in it. She didn't understand how you could pilot, let alone navigate, the squat, dumpy ERV. Instead of wings it was controlled by a parafoil—a partial parachute. It even lacked a stabilizing drogue chute.

She knew it was irrational to evaluate scientific advancements in terms of pulchritude, but "the Flying Bathtub" also offended her aesthetically.

Sara and Colton were doing their best to cope. Because the Citadel was the closest thing left to a functioning American government—and she was still "the majority stockholder," she liked to remind people—they kept her fully in "the information loop."

Lydia's gravest concerns were Kate and Frank. She'd spent a good part of her life fighting with Kate but had thought the battles would cease now that the world had been all but destroyed. But they didn't.

Nor was Frank listening to reason.

Frank; his fiancée, Cathy Anne; and Kate refused to leave the Towers, where they treated burn and flying-glass victims.

She'd patched a satellite phone call into the Towers through the Odyssey. Offered to send a plane to bring the three of them to the Citadel. When all three refused, L. L. screamed at them, calling them "rude and rebellious," "breathtakingly ignorant," and "suicidally stupid."

"Where will you find a runway?" Kate—losing it herself—shouted back at her. "How will your crew survive the fallout? We have protection against fallout. But what about the plane? How will you even get us *to* the plane? What happens if the plane is mobbed by insane survivors? Mom, you're looking to get a crew killed in the false hope that you can get us to the Citadel. And for what?"

"*Because I don't want you to die!*" L. L. screamed.

"Bullshit!" Kate shouted back. "You want us there . . . *so you can boss us around!*"

2 A Hymn to God in the Pit of Hell

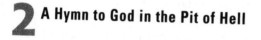

Kate Magruder wished L. L. could be with her and Frank for just a few minutes now—here on the top floor of the Towers Medical Center. Maybe she could *show* her mother what they were doing.

Actually, she couldn't have shown her mother much outside the windows. The hospital's windows were heavily sandbagged, its air vents filtered, and when the radiation readings ran too high, they donned antifallout gear or entered the basement shelters.

That the massive tri-towered complex stood and still functioned as a hospital was a miracle. Physicians now numbered in the dozens while the invading army of patients swelled ceaselessly, exponentially. The Towers was overrun by burned and blasted refugees. The greatly reduced staff did their best to treat them.

"How would you describe the Towers to L. L.?" Frank asked Kate.

"A hymn to God in the pit of hell."

"I'm still not sure L. L. would understand," Frank said, "even if she came here."

The surrounding park had become a campground filled with the sick and the dying, those simply driven mad by the horror of it all. All of them suffered varying degrees of radiation poisoning, which typically meant nausea, vomiting, diarrhea, loss of appetite, and malaise.

But it was the burns, the burns, the burns that made the Towers hell on earth. No one knew the exact number of fire-and-flash victims inundating the Towers, because the number of sufferers reaching its grounds grew by the hour, an endless procession of the lame, the burned, and the blind.

If only she could make her mother understand, Kate thought. They had work to do.

3 He Sometimes Thought He'd Been Happier on His Rack?

The Sin Sisters were not in a good mood. The major city and military base in Dar-al-Suhl had been nuked out of existence. For the past several weeks they, Stone, and their Blessed Brother had been confined to a network of underground military bunkers.

Nothing met with their approval—food, quarters, bath facilities, dispensary, commissary, canteen, the bunker's selection of books, movies—nothing.

"Would a little fresh fruit, fresh vegetables, fresh milk be too much to ask for?" Sultana grumbled.

"Nobody told us," Sabrina said, "we were going to have to drink powdered milk."

"Ever hear of eye shadow, mascara?"

"Where **is** my fucking lip blush?" Sabrina shrieked.

"I'm out of Q-tips!"

"Wouldn't it be nice to watch a *first-run* movie for a change?" Sultana roared.

"Who stocked all this shitty music anyway?" Sabrina wailed. "I'll kill the motherfucker."

"Do the words 'escargot,' 'pâté de foie gras,' 'beluga caviar,' 'Dom Pérignon' mean *anything* around here?"

No, the New Dispensation was not what they'd imagined. Ali had made contingency plans and had built his own version of the Citadel. But while he'd understood the basics—that they might need food, shelter, medicine, protection against fallout—his preparations had not been definitive, let alone lavish.

Not that anyone could prepare for this. Their country—army included—had been annihilated. The sisters and their brother were left with their bunkers, a small staff of servants, a few bodyguards, and not much else.

Their reign of terror had come to a close.

But not the Sin Sisters' reign of domestic terror. They drove everyone crazy—servants, Stone, their Blessed Brother—with their complaints and demands.

In fact, Stone and Ali spent more and more time together. Not out of friendship or mutual respect. Ali was a monster of apocalyptic proportions. Yet even his company was preferable to the Twin Harpies.

From time to time Ali attempted to explain them to Stone: "My sisters are the same as women everywhere. Their wiles are dedicated to one thing only—preying on our physical prowess and reducing us to sexual slavery. Face it, Stone, they are all demons of desire."

"Is that why in your country you dress them in veils and robes?"

"But, of course. How else can we men have a fighting chance against their seductions? If their bodies were not concealed and their movements restricted, we would be at their mercy. They would ravage us at every turn; I tell you, Mr. Stone, women will use their carnal arts to steal your soul."

Stone hated to admit it, but regarding the Sin Twins, Ali had a point. They had dragged him into an inferno of hellish lust. Stone now believed that the Puritans, who had thought sex the root of all evil, had a point—at least regarding the Harpies from Hell. They fucked him deaf, dumb, stupid, and blind—around the clock, day and night, night and day.

He sometimes thought he'd been happier on his rack.

4 The Greatest Fire Drive in History

Sara was on a space walk. The forward radar-array was skewed, and for the past hour she'd been realigning it.

Even with the world going up in flames, she found it hard not to sightsee. In the vacuum of space, purity of vision was absolute—much better than through the dense Lexan viewing-ports of the Odyssey—especially tonight. The earth below was currently shrouded in night, and Northern Europe and Asia glittered like Christmas trees, their firestorms depressing, but still dazzling.

Well, at least, missiles and warheads no longer blazed beneath the Odyssey . . .

. . . *Not that the bombing had ever ceased. The nations of earth had initially reined their bombers in—apparently for fear that their use would trigger ICBM strikes—but as soon as the tubes and silos began to empty, the bomber fleets took to the air.*

They had taken a surprising amount of time to make their runs. Colton explained to Sara that the world had learned in Vietnam the folly of flying battalion-force bombers at well-defended targets in orderly formations. With the advent of wide-array surveillance installations and heat- and radar-directed missiles, formation bombing provided the enemy with easy-to-track, impossible-to-miss targets. Vietnam's formation-flying B-52s had—year after year—been gunned down like ducks in a flyway.

Today's bombers functioned as lone wolves, flying in unique, hard-to-track routes, approaching their targets obliquely.

Most of the world's air bases and radar installations were by now knocked out, so the bombers flew with impunity, heedless of interceptors or ground-surveillance. They picked their way through the smoking, radioactive rubble of Asia, Europe, the Mideast, the United States, even Africa and South America. Like opportunistic vultures, they kept a lonely deathwatch, alert for unobliterated targets.

As Sara stared down at the blazing earth, she now wondered whether—after thirty-six hours of nonstop bombing—there were any strategic targets left. Below her, the cities of earth were ravaged by tens of thousands of firestorms. Most of them didn't look like strategic targets to Sara, but they clearly had appeared that way to someone.

According to Thucydides, the converging European conflagrations started with nuclear strikes against the so-called primary targets—after which the secondary and tertiary assaults had begun. As far as Sara could tell a tertiary target was defined as "anything that moved," and, as Thucydides had quickly pointed out, all sides engaged in rubble-pounding—radioactive rubble-pounding.

The Eastern European countries—particularly those suspected of harboring nuclear weapons—were afire. Thucydides thought the strikes had come out of Russia, but when the world's thousands of delivery systems—its warships, missiles, and combat aircraft—joined the fray, even Thucydides couldn't track the perpetrators with absolute certainty.

America's missile defense system had been useless. Its advocates had had a long record of overstating its capability. Thucydides couldn't see that America's missile defenses had intercepted a single warhead.

The smuggled nukes he couldn't track at all.

Nor were the firestorms limiting themselves to urban centers. They formed huge conflagrations, particularly in wooded regions and along the coasts. The Balkans blazed with special luminosity. For thousands of years—going back to Alexander the Great and beyond—that region had been famous for genocidal bloodletting, for mass graves and wretched refugee camps. No more. Now it was famous for fire, the entire area a sea of flames.

The Sheriff of Nottingham, at last, had his revenge on Sherwood Forest, Sara noted, watching it blaze. Firestorms also swept through Germany's Black Forest and France's Bois. The northern forests of Norway, Sweden, and Finland were—from Sara's vantage-point—spectacularly aflame.

Wildfire whipped through Europe and Asia's croplands.

And the nuked debris from the Yellowstone, Campi Flegrei, and Lake Toba supervolcanoes was at last drifting to earth, blanketing much of North America, Europe, North Africa, and Asia in soot, ashes, and basaltic ejecta.

Nor was there any cessation of hostilities. The final phase dragged on and on— the nations of earth simply lashing out. No pretense of coherent geopolitical strategy or even national self-interest but a brutal, vindictive, infinitely protracted death-spasm, during which everything was unloaded, unleashed, launched, used up— "use-it-or-lose-it" taken to ecocidal extremes.

Especially when it came to the nuking of Russia . . .

. . . From her vantage point by the forward radar-array and in the utter clarity of space, Sara studied Asia's firestorms. Every nuclear power on earth avenged itself on Russia for her "deranged attacks." Russia's conflagrations—despite her vast size—were everywhere.

Nor had Russia's naval yards survived the apocalypse.

To the east, Japan likewise blazed.

While the Land of the Rising Sun had passionately disavowed owning nuclear weapons, their neighbors had obviously not believed it. They had good reason not to. For decades Japan had possessed some of the most advanced, cutting-edge military technology in the world. They manufactured their own versions of America's F-15s, F-16s, and FSXs. Their ICBMs—purportedly designed for satellite launching—were among the most accurate and powerful on earth. Japan had owned more weapons-grade plutonium than any other nation on earth as well as the finest nuclear technology available. Bomb cores and triggers were never a problem for them; the other nuclear powers had always assumed they were never more than one screw twist and two wrench turns away from complete nuclear statehood.

Nor had Japan ever been shy about exporting its weapons technology to outlaw nations. Toshiba had been caught selling propulsion systems for American subs to Russia. China had bought electron–beam welders from them—with which to MIRV their ICBMs. NEC was even caught selling missile technology to Iran. North Korea—arguably Japan's most implacable enemy—had obtained over 20 percent of its submarine parts from them.

Surrounded by nations which it had once ruthlessly raped, Japan understandably feared reprisal, but its lust to join the nuclear establishment had now cost it everything. According to Thucydides, after Japan retaliated against Russia—and Russia struck back—China, Taiwan, and North Korea had piled on.

Nor did Cyd believe they were Japan's only nuclear enemies. Thucydides believed that the Aum Shinrikyo Doomsday cult had wreaked its nuclear wrath on them as well. As the millennium turned, Aum had stepped up its recruitment efforts in Japan, particularly on the Internet, at universities, and in its business operations. As its membership soared, it built more and more housing for its new members, and when its members who had planned its infamous subway nerve-gas attack were freed from prison, Aum's nuclear-weapons program redoubled its efforts. Wealth, fanaticism, and a willing wallet at Russia's nuclear bazaar was all it had taken for Aum Shinrikyo to become a nuclear player.

Nor was Japan its only victim. Australia had inexplicably sold Aum Shinrikyo a half-million acres in their outback. Newspapers around the world had reported explosions on its land. One was so powerful seismologists said it could only have been caused by a nuclear test or a massive meteor strike.

Aum Shinrikyo had nuked Sydney, Melbourne, and Auckland.

What Thucydides could not understand was why Japan—which had been nuked twice by America and then nerve-gassed by Aum Shinrikyo—had taken the cult into its bosom. In Japan, residency—even for citizens—was not a given but had to be governmentally approved. Yet the Japanese government provided all that Aum needed to develop its nuclear weapons and inflict them on the world.

Why Australia had offered them sanctuary was an even greater mystery.

Aum Shinrikyo was more than a cult of lunatic criminality; it was a global empire of immense corporate wealth—with assets, by some accounts, of over $5 billion—consumed by self-justifying apocalyptic evil.

The Asian economic miracle was no more.

5 Like I Died and Woke Up in Hell

When Jamal came to, he couldn't believe he was alive.

His wrists were uncuffed. Two prisoners were hauling him up out of the subbasement, one of his arms over each of their shoulders. Jamal's companions were likewise freed and helped up in front of him.

"What the fuck is happening?" Jamal asked his saviors.

His vision was coming back into focus, and he was starting to recognize the men helping them out of the cell. One of them—a Black Muslim with close-cropped hair wearing a white shirt and black bow tie—was his adjutant, Shariff. One of the men helping Radford he recognized as Radford's younger brother, Gerald. He was a civilian wearing civilian attire—a white shirt, black Dockers, and wire-rimmed glasses. What was Gerald doing here?

Except for the visitors center, he wasn't supposed to be in Jack Town, let alone in a subbasement torture cell.

"What the fuck you doin' here?" Jamal asked.

"It's started," Gerald said to him. "Just like you predicted. The Big One. The gates are wide-open. Why, I was able to walk into this prison and track you guys down. Everyone can walk out. Some of the cons already done it. There's no more Jack Town."

At first, Jamal wondered whether Gerald was putting him on, and he studied his face closely. Like his older brother, Jimmy John, Gerald had hard, probing eyes, but unlike his brother's, his eyes contained no hint of humor. A relatively youthful man—still in his late twenties—he had a slim build and sharp, angular features. Jimmy John bragged on him continually, claiming Gerald was "a computer genius and a criminal mastermind, specializing in high-tech fraud." He was also said to be the real brains behind Jimmy John's West Texas People's Militia and the only man, outside Riaz, whom Jimmy John trusted and wouldn't kill on a whim.

"All the cops are gone," Gerald said. "I'm not sure how long there's going to be a country."

"Would someone shut off these beats?" Jimmy John shouted deliriously over his shoulder. "I hate hip-hop."

"That ain't music, bro," Gerald said gently.

"Would someone tell me what the fuck's goin' on then?" Jimmy John shouted.

He was being helped up the corridor by Gerald and two garishly tattooed survivalists in black denims, matching tee shirts, and black ball caps.

"The world's in fuckin' flames. Thermonuclear war. The guards all gone home, and guess what? We own this fucking prison."

"Got a git-down goin' in the mess hall," Gerald said, "they're raising a jubilee."

"I feel like I died and woke up in hell," Cool Breeze said, blinking his eyes in disbelief.

"Welcome to the New World Order," Gerald said. He gave his brother, Jimmy John, a sly grin. "Ain't nothin' we ain't been schemin' on."

6 "If I Can Stop One Heart from Breaking . . ."
—Emily Dickinson

. . . Kate's dreams are fraught with fire.

First, bang time—a blinding flash slashing the sky, then a thunder crack, an earthquake like the death of a star, a windstorm like World's End. Has the earth exploded, and the sun gone nova? A comet strike? A killer star? Everything is on fire—buildings, trees, taxis, and buses, bicycles, and motorcycles, Central Park, hotel doormen, police vans and moving vans, fire trucks.

But mostly people are afire.

When she is not racing through streets of fire, she is crawling through smoking tunnels led by a big auburn rat. Sometimes she is commandeering a boat at gunpoint, forcing its occupants to transport her—and her friend, the rat—upriver to her cousin's medical complex. Sometimes she is docking at the hospital's jetties, staring in shock at the famous trio of Towers, already swarmed by armies of walking wounded stumbling up the roads and expressways—arms stretched in front of them, eyes wide with horror, unearthly creatures straight out of Night of the Living Dead*—except it is dawn, a bloody sun rising over the city yet barely visible through the dense pall of smoke and ash, sobbing:*

"Water!

"Agua!"

Taking one look at the army of incinerated zombies, Sailor gives Kate a last curious stare. Diving over the stern into the Hudson, he swims toward the Jersey shore.

Kate is not that smart . . .

. . . At this point Kate was usually awakened by Cathy Anne Gibson—Frank's fiancée. A licensed burn nurse, she was, for Kate, a friend, a mentor, a godsend.

She had recognized in Kate the signs of shell shock and had made her talk it out. Kate had found she could open up to Cathy Anne. The young woman—with the long brown hair and the brownest, most caring eyes Kate had ever seen—had become her true soul-mate.

". . . I'm starting to wonder whether I'm still alive," Kate had confessed to Cathy and Frank late one night. *"Or whether part of me might not be dead."*

"That's because you hate death—and fear the dead," Cathy Anne said.

"No, I fear the anonymous *dead. I fear their eyes. They curse me—accuse me."*

"Of what?" Frank asked.

"Of being alive."

"You feel as if you owe a death to those who died?"

"To death itself—and now I await my own death-sentence."

"That's death-guilt kicking in—the mind closing off, the psychic vise," Cathy Anne explained.

"Never envy the dead," Frank said. *"You will get there soon enough."*

Cathy Anne knew whereof she spoke—and put Kate straight to work. The best therapy for traumatic stress, Cathy Anne told her, was helping those who had gone through more hell than Kate had ever imagined.

"The patients here," Cathy Anne said, "have been inundated with death—their previous lives gone forever. Hell is now the norm—their heart the heart of darkness."

During her career, Kate had written extensively about suffering, and by amply salting her columns and TV shows with facts and statistics she had appeared to be an expert on human oppression. But statistics don't bleed; patients do. Patients the Towers had in abundance.

In the short time Kate had been there she had watched the Towers turn from a hospital into something verging on a house of horrors.

Several of the staff advocated closing it up.

"We were stretched thin before," Cathy Anne said one afternoon, as they walked through the hospital. They both stepped over an unconscious victim, the clothes burned off his body. "Now we're near the breaking point, meaning we're about to run out of everything."

"I don't know how we've managed to get this far."

"I don't know either. The blasts shattered plaster and masonry in all three buildings. Floors were awash in tubes, shattered glass, and medical instruments. I went racing through the debris and up to the roof to get Frank. Guess what? He was studying the fireballs through his polarized sunscope."

"That's our Frank," Kate said.

"Luckily the auxiliary systems remained intact."

"We have backup electricals?"

"At Frank's insistence, bless him. He had always argued that a medical center can't afford to be exclusively dependent on public utilities. A water-main break or a power outage could kill half our patients. We have cisterns for water and diesel-powered auxiliary generators. We're well stocked with food and medical supplies. All of that, of course, assumes a seminormal patient population—not hordes bearing the ten plagues of Egypt."

"We have to run out sometime."

"So far, friends and relatives of patients have foraged in abandoned stores around here—even abandoned homes, I suspect—for food, water, linens, and tablecloths to be boiled for bandages and other medical supplies. Diesel oil for the generators. Frank told them to look out for Clorox. Six drops per gallon of water. We can draw water from the Hudson River if need be. Our burn patients—as you've seen—dehydrate radically."

"Some of the staff talk about leaving."

"And we're short staffed already. We only had a skeleton night crew when the bombs hit. Most of them left to look after their families and never came back. The day crew—with a couple of exceptions—vanished. We're getting volunteers though. We're the last vestige of order around here. Many of these people have nowhere else to go."

"You, Frank, and I could split for the Citadel."

"I know. Your mom's offered to send a plane."

"At some point we have to consider it."

A major research center, the Towers' staff was equipped with orange Racal biohazard suits—several of which hung in a closet near the side door. Cathy Anne and Kate each put one on.

In front of the Towers, there in the smoky twilight—of what once was day—lay thousands of burn-and-glass victims spread-eagled on bloodstained blankets and sheets. Many were naked—their bodies too badly burned to tolerate clothing. Some wore plastic hooded rain gear and face scarves. Their feet were wrapped in strips torn from plastic garbage bags—anti-fallout suits, as they were called now. Many were dying; some were already dead. The screaming of the burn victims was horrifying.

"Jesus," Kate said, putting a gloved hand over her mask. "This has to be how Auschwitz smelled."

"We have found whole new dimensions to death here," Cathy Anne said.

"We save some," Kate pointed out.

Cathy Anne said, "Frank claims—in his darker moments—sixty-five percent of those cured cure themselves. God saves the rest. Sometimes we help."

"'If I can stop one heart from breaking, I shall not live in vain,'" Kate said, quoting Emily Dickinson.

Flies swarmed, and the burial detail—after a much-deserved evening's break—was out in force, collecting the night's death-toll. Carting the bodies off to the courtyard's corner pyres, the burial detail piled them like cords of wood. When the first body hit the flames, it sizzled and smoked. The stink almost drove Kate to her knees.

Buzzards, hawks, and crows rode the smoky thermals, etching lazy circles against black clouds. A lone redwing with a six-foot wingspread—impatient with its deathwatch—began a cautious descent.

Lightning blazed. A hard black rain—large drops slick as petrol—came down in slanted sheets, spattering Kate's biohazard suit. The debris from Dar-al-Suhl's nuking of the Yellowstone supervolcano was now descending on them in the form of this Stygian rain—soaked soot and ash. The world around her was turning black as tar—darkness visible.

"I'll stay," Kate said.

"Then let's check out the surgical wards," Cathy Anne said. "We'll start you out there."

The two friends headed across the courtyard.

7 The Butcher's Bill

The Odyssey now approached America at low perigee—barely 300 miles above the earth. It was daytime, and except for the drifting smoke-clouds, Colton had a good view.

The firestorms in the cities had at last gone out. Not only had entire cities vanished, the Atlantic, Pacific, and Gulf coastlines were reduced to dunes of ash and radioactive rubble. The forests, however, continued to burn. Thucydides predicted they would burn for decades.

Russia had hammered the U.S. with so many warheads that even Thucydides could not provide Colton with an accurate count. The reason, he said, was "fratricide."

"What's fratricide?" Sara wanted to know.

"Incoming warheads destroyed by the warheads which have preceded them," Colton explained.

"Mushroom clouds are filled with stones, dust, flying glass, all sorts of debris—and occasional fireballs," Thucydides said. "Incoming missiles entering a cloud are knocked out. My satellite photos indicate that Russia targeted its warheads too closely together. Their footprints were so tight, in fact, I couldn't distinguish individual detonations."

"Friendly fire," Sara muttered.

For a long time they were silent. MTN was still broadcasting, and Thucydides drifted north, running montages of Canada's dead, smoking cities.

It wasn't in much better shape.

Like Japan and Australia, Canada had made the mistake of openly harboring terrorists. Quebec, dedicated "to increasing French-speaking immigration," had become a monomaniacal mecca for French-speaking terrorists. Because French was the lingua franca of many Middle Eastern terrorists, they assisted Quebec gladly in its misguided program of frenchification.

. . . For decades Quebec had lusted after French-speaking immigrants—12,000 to 14,000 a year—and had made it a safe haven for any terrorist who spoke its tongue. The dangers inherent in such open immigration were widely recognized, but even after Montreal's Ahmed Ressam was caught smuggling "enough bomb-making material into the United States to flatten a building," Quebec did nothing to stem the flood of gangster terrorists.

Jean-Yves Mailloux, the head of the Montreal police counterterrorism divi-

sion, admitted to The New York Times: *"These guys are financing organizations that train people to assassinate the fathers of families, pregnant women, old people, and children."*

Canada now paid the price of such criminally inept policies.

Cities across the country were going up in terrorist flames. Even as Canada's NATO military bases were nuked.

With food, fuel, and electrical power evaporating, even decent Canadians were turning on each other. Canada—like every other starving, struggling nation on earth—was racked by internecine violence and terror.

Finally Sara couldn't take it anymore. She propelled herself across the control room and turned off the monitors.

"Why did we have to build ICBMs? Why did we have to MIRV them? Why the cruise missiles and the suitcase nukes, both of which are impossible to control and are every terrorist's wet dream? Why didn't we buy up Russia's 2.5 million pounds' worth of unprotected loose nukes? *Why* did we make these weapons available to psychopaths?"

"Thucydides, can you calculate how many wars the nations of the world have fought these last thirty years?" Colton asked in answer to Sara's question.

"Your recent wars are too numerous to accurately record," Thucydides replied orally and on his monitors.

"One hundred and forty-three wars in thirty years. Tally does not include recent conflicts—or the butcher's bill, which is incalculable."

"Why so many wars? Sara asked. "To what end? Money? Power?"

"Not at all. In fact, the poorest and most powerless nations fought the hardest, the longest."

"And you're saying they had *nothing* to fight over?" Sara asked.

"Next to nothing," Cyd said. "Most of these Third World countries had been stripped of their assets long, long ago. For most of a century they had doubled their populations every two decades, sustained unemployment rates of fifty percent or more, faced endless food and medicine shortages, battled terrorism at the hands of bandit-guerrillas, right-wing death squads, *and* state-run secret police. They swarmed the larger cities seeking safety and found instead shanty-town, packing-crate slums, where they drank sewer water and cooked over dung-smoke fires."

"And that was in the good old days when they had had access to the Developed World's exports," Colton said.

"Sounds like radical privation will be everybody's fate now," Sara said. "What Hobbes called 'the war of all against all.'"

It was increasingly true. Now no one had anything—no food, no medicine, no transportation, no technology, no jobs.

"For the Third World the apocalypse had already come and gone," Sara said, "and when the Developed World went under, what little they had left went with it too."

"It was as if they too had been already nuked off the face of the earth," Colton observed.

"The bullet in the head after the execution," Sara said softly.

"Soon, their condition will be everyone's too," Thucydides said. Thucydides then began ticking off the names of the Latin American cities that were exploding in anarchy and flames. "Tapachula; Quezaltenango and Guatemala City, in Guatemala; Santa Ana, Salvador, and San Miguel, in El Salvador; Palmerola, La Mesa, San Pedro Sula, and Tegucigalpa, in Honduras; Santa Clara, Ocotal, Somoto, Cinco Pinos, Esteli, Chinandega, Matagalpa, Jinotega, Siuna, El Gallo, and Managua, in Nicaragua; San Jose, in Costa Rica; Panama City, in Panama; Quito, Guayaquil, Machala, and Tumbes, in Ecuador; Lima, Ayacucho, Arequipa, and Trujillo in Peru; La Paz, Cochabamba, Sucre, and Santa Cruz, in Bolivia; Asunción in Paraguay; Manaus, Belem, Teresina, Fortaleza, Natal, Camas, Rio de Janeiro, São Paulo, and Brazilia, in Brazil; Santiago, Chile; and Buenos Aires, Argentina."

"The FARC, the National Liberation Army, the Popular Liberation Army, and the Shining Path rape, burn, and pillage Colombia, Bolivia, and Peru at will," Sara noted.

"Brazil's burning cities have spread to the countryside," Colton observed, watching Cyd's omniscient eye swing over that country.

"The rain forests blaze," Sara said.

Cyd's all-seeing eye swung round to Africa. For centuries it had been known as the Dark Continent, but it had never been darker than it was now. Sierra Leone, Liberia, Ivory Coast, Nigeria, Chad, Senegal, Western Sahara, Algeria, Eritrea, Somalia, Uganda, Sudan, Ethiopia, Egypt, Kananga, Kinshasa, Mbandaka, Kisangani, Lubumbashi, Likasi, Kolwezi, Kindu, the Congo, Angola, Namibia, Botswana, Zambia, Zimbabwe, Mozambique, Kenya, Tanzania were for all intents and purposes—

Gone.

South Africa had always been a lodestone for refugees, and now they flooded its cities in unstoppable numbers: Pretoria, Johannesburg, Vereeniging, Durban, Kimberley, Bloemfontein, East London, Port Elizabeth, Sishen, Cape Town, Pietersburg, Messina, Phalaborwa, Mafeking, Zeerust, Potchefstroom—already sinking under the weight of plague, famine, and civil anarchy—were now overrun by a juggernaut of refugees—and were—

Gone.

Cyd swung north.

The Indian subcontinent had once laid claim to the title "the most dangerous terrain on earth," and Afghanistan too had shared part of that infamy. No more. A prolific assortment of nuclear, biochemical, and radiological weapons eliminated those fears.

All the subcontinent's major cities blazed.

For the first time in history Afghanistan was pacified.

"Well, Cyd," Sara asked, "what was the purpose of all this destruction?"

"Humanity has a self-annihilating compulsion to torture and kill."

"Does this disease have a name?" Colton asked.

"Suicidal stupidity."

"Prognosis?"

Thucydides pumped up the volume on MTN. Sister Cassandra—still narrating the nuclear destruction of America's cities—was now apparently his spokesperson.

"Exodus tells of fire from the skies. The Egyptian Papyrus Ipuwer reports rains of fire: 'Gates, columns, and walls are consumed by fire. The sky is in confusion.' The Wisdom of Solomon speaks of 'rains and hails utterly consumed with fire.' Daniel calls it 'a fiery stream,' and Psalm 105 refers to it as 'flaming fire.' In the Land Between the Rivers, 'a rain of fire.' Hesiod tells us 'the great earth groaned, the greater part of it scorched by the terrible heat.' The Hindus say that 'the whole world bursts into flames, reaching up and enveloping heaven.' Ovid reports: 'The earth explodes into flame. Cities blaze, and the fire storms raze entire nations and scorching the African's skin, turning their race dark when "the heat drew their blood to their skins."'

"So you see it ain't the first," Cassandra wailed.

". . . And you know it ain't the last.
You faced the fire
And you felt the blast.
You heard it from your mama
Now you hearin' it from Cass:

"You know it ain't the first
You know it ain't the last
Your mama's got a case,
Your mama's got a case,
Your mama's got a case of
You know it ain't the first time . . . blues . . ."

8 The Man Is Finished

Cool Breeze was amazed.

When he, Radford, Gerald, and Jamal entered the mess hall, they were greeted by an ovation so powerful Breeze thought he was back in Yankee Stadium. Over a thousand former inmates cheered and applauded, while another thousand or so stomped and screamed outside.

The prison and auxiliary power was on, and there were TV sets on mess-hall tables. Breeze saw the thermonuclear destruction of the world on several screens.

Jamal's #3 man, Mustafa, offered them coffee and peanut butter sandwiches. Other gang leaders joined them. Jamal noted that the gang leaders were all armed with 9mm Berettas, assault rifles, and twelve-gauge riot guns from the prison armory. Jamal and Radford accepted pistols from two gang members and stuck them in their belts. Jamal also picked one up for Breeze, while Radford grabbed a weapon for Riaz.

"The balloon's gone up," Gerald said to Jamal. "You knew this shit was happenin'?"

"All I know was me and my bruthas caught some heavy bread five months back," Jamal said. "News say $5 million. Everyone thinks it came from some Mideast muthafuckas, 'cept that ain't the way *these* muthafuckas play it. They don't want no one knowin' who they be. The man say to me: 'We all know you from the Afghan days and trust you not to front our play.' 'I dig it,' I tell him. He say, 'So dig this. Some shit goin' down, End Time shit—and you gotta be ready.'

"What I'm thinkin is: He ain't pimpin' no tickets 'bout how bad he be, only how bad *the shit* gonna be.

"So I told my bruthas to cover their ass, and start layin' in stuff. When the other gangs—including the White Albino Brothers, the spics, and the banger boys—see us stockpilin' shit, they lay up theirs. Spread through joints all 'cross the land. Hoardin' and hidin'. But it weren't no plan."

"Can't tell me *now* they ain't no plan," Brother Momar—a tall bespectacled Black Muslim in a white shirt and black bow tie—said, pointing at a TV screen.

"Yo, Surf Nazi," Breeze said. "You tell him the plan. You the survivalist. Whatcha gonna do?"

"Stay put," Radford said.

"Spend half our lives in these muthafuckin' joints," Momar said, shaking his head sadly. "Now that we got a chance to haul ass you saying, hang up? Lock up? Do the fuckin' time?"

"The man talkin' fallout," Riaz cautioned.

"Fallout magnified by the nukin' of all those supervolcanoes, including Yellowstone," Gerald said.

"Lot of volcanic ash and soot in that fallout," Jimmy John said.

Momar looked out the cafeteria window. The Texas sky was overcast, but the air was clear, not filled with smoke or dust.

"Don't see nuthin'," Momar said.

"You may not see it," Radford's brother, Gerald, said, pointing out the mess-hall window, "but it's there."

"And it be a muthafucka," Jamal said.

"Jack Town gonna save us from this shit?" Momar asked, confused.

"It ain't a prison no more," Jamal said. "What we got here's a bomb shelter."

"A city-size bomb shelter," Gerald explained.

"We got food, medicine, clothing, tools, our own water, our own generator," Jamal said. "Ain't no better place in Texas to weather this fallout storm'n Jack Town. We even got our own radio station."

"And concrete," Radford said. "You need a lot of concrete to keep fallout away."

"More poured concrete'n any structure in the world," Jamal said.

"Soon as we sandbag them windows," Radford said, "and stick filters on the vents, we got us a Bomb Shelter Deluxe."

"We even got guns," Momar said, pointing at the 9mm shoved in his belt.

"Which may be a problem for the next month or so," Breeze said.

"People here ain't about to settle their differences by peaceful means," Jamal said.

Already an altercation was breaking out. Two Aryan Brothers—Oats and Pinball—were accusing a black gangbanger of stealing a bologna sandwich off their tray.

"Yo," Radford called out to them, "this ain't no time to be playing the fool. We got real shit to worry about."

"Fuck you," Oats—the bigger of the two—shouted back.

Oats was stripped from the waist up. He might have been warm, but Radford thought he was showing off his prison-gym muscles, which included some truly astonishing anabolic pecs and lats. His upper torso featured a gaudy collection of tattoos, almost incandescent in their garishness. His shaved bullet head sported an even more shocking assemblage of Jack Town tats.

"Chill that shit, Oats," Radford said.

"You know the Code," Pinball broke in. "No nigger jacks my shit in Jack Town."

Radford noted Pinball was armed with a riot gun and looked to be wasted on crank. His teardrop facial tat pulsated while the veins in his face and neck popped. His tee shirt—the sleeves ripped off—was soaked in sweat, stained with blood.

"And I'm saying," Radford said, "we got serious shit going down now."

"Yeah, like too much nigger shit," Oats shouted, "and I ain't taking shit off no nigger," Oats shouted. He racked the slide on his twelve-gauge pump.

Radford shot him between the eyes.

One of Jamal's brothers—Kareem Abdulkarim—swung his 7.62 assault rifle toward Pinball.

Jamal shot Kareem twice in the chest.

Jamal and Radford were now back-to-back in the mess hall, surrounded by 2,000 enraged cons. Breeze and Riaz, who were also strapped, backed up against them, guns drawn, giving the four men a 360-degree view of the hall. The room was still save for the echo of the gunshots.

"You killed Kareem," one of his brothers shouted at Jamal.

"And I loved the nigga too," Jamal shouted back.

"You shot our defense minister," Pinball accused.

"And I didn't like him at all," Radford retorted.

"This shit ends *now!*" Riaz roared.

His Mexicans—the largest, most powerful contingent in the mess hall—thundered their support for Riaz, and by extension Radford.

"Can't y'all see?" Breeze shouted. "We can *survive* the next few weeks if we stay here—and if we don't kill each other like animals."

"And if we stick together when we get out," Riaz said, "we *own* this country."

"Rest of the nation gonna be sick and starving and poisoned by radioactivity," Radford said reasonably, "but not us. We gonna be strong."

"This ain't a black thing or a white thing or a Chicano thing," Breeze said.

"It be *a power thing*," Jamal said. "Who gonna have the power and who gonna keep the power."

"*We* gonna have the power," Radford sounded.

"We gonna be '*the Nation,*'" Jamal shouted.

"Nation of Islam?" one of his brothers asked.

"*The* Nation," Jamal said. "That be enough. One United Nation. Pluribus-Fucking-Unum. Ain't gonna let no differences—race or religion differences—divide us."

"We ain't gonna tear ourselves to pieces," Breeze said.

"But the black man never got nothin' from no white," a gangbanger named Odell objected. He was flying Crips colors.

"Yo, check it out," Breeze yelled at him. "Check out the TV. Ain't no more white or black world. Them days is gone."

"We're talkin'," Radford shouted, "a new beginnin'."

"That beginnin' is *now*," Breeze said. "I don't care this man Radford be white. He's *my* brother now. His brother's *my* brother."

"I don't care these be hombres negros," Riaz agreed. "They be mios negros now. You fuck with them—any of you—you fuck with *me*."

"When the fallout ends, we gonna have an army," Radford said.

"The Man ain't never gonna give up his world," Odell protested.

"The Man is finished," Breeze shouted back.

"The world belongs to him who's strong enough to take it," Jamal said. "That someone is *us*."

"What about these 'brothers'?" Mustafa asked.

He had brought Chaplain O'Donnell, Sergeant Harris, and the federal officer into the mess hall. Their hands were cuffed behind their backs, their faces were covered with livid bruises.

"They get a trial," Radford said. "Then we shoot them."

"This be a new beginnin'," Jamal said.

The men in the Jack Town mess hall grudgingly put down their guns. All over the cafeteria men gave out high fives and shook hands with those around them, solidarity spreading spontaneously. Even rival race groups and antagonistic gangbangers got into the spirit. Inmates shared cigarettes and pruno, sandwiches and pots of coffee.

Breeze and his friends conferred on the best way to try their former torturers.

9 A River of Refugees

Captain Gargarin and his crew scuttled their sub *St. Petersburg* off the Jersey shore near Asbury Park. They paddled to the beach in life rafts unobserved.

"Do you expect to find an Islamic paradise here?" Starpom asked the captain.

Gargarin glanced at his friend. Since they had stopped bleaching their hair, dark roots were showing. Their beards were completely black. Only Gargarin—whose natural father had been a genuinely blond Russian—had not needed bleach.

"I expect what I have always expected—infidels resisting the True Faith," Gargarin said. "But at least we will no longer have Western technology and heathen decadence competing with Allah's Word. They will hear it as people first heard it fourteen centuries ago—during simpler times in a more austere age."

"You think even the Americans will be more receptive?" the First Officer asked.

"The Americans will have to listen now."

Captain Gargarin had concluded that the only way the West could be brought to Allah was through the Sword. The West's hatred of his people and his Faith had lasted more than a thousand years and would not be changed with olive branches and conciliatory words.

Not that the New World Order was a day at the beach. Having no local contacts, few provisions, little command of the local language, and no practical knowledge of the world around them, they took to the road. They were not in bad shape. A submerged sub was one of the best bomb shelters a person could ask for. Stocked with food and medicine, Gargarin and his crew had weathered the worst of the fallout safely submerged. Until, of course, the food ran low. So they had joined the refugee stream. Wearing down-filled vests, ball caps, sunglasses, and sneakers, they bobbed like corks amid the river of refugees flooding the highways of America—the highways by day, and the camps at night.

The quest for food was all-consuming. Cornfields, home gardens, orchards, melon patches, and berry bushes were scavenged—despite Sister Cassandra's warnings that to ingest exposed, untested flora or fauna was to risk high-level radiation poisoning. Homes and former stores were routinely robbed, their occupants—if there were occupants—often tortured, to make them reveal suspected caches of food and medicine.

By the time Gargarin and his crew reached the Jersey Turnpike, most of these former homeowners had entered the Great Exodus, preferring a life on the open road to defending their homesteads against bandit-gangs. Especially when the homestead had nothing left to defend.

Gargarin's enlisted men understood this brave new world better than most

Americans. Many of them were survivors of some of the worst slums the Mideast had to offer, and they were already accustomed to cooking over dung-smoke fires, bathing in sewer water, and sleeping in shacks and packing crates. The tent towns and refugee camps of America held few surprises for them. It was a world they had known since birth.

Gargarin was, however, worn down by the rigors of the open road. A veteran seaman, he was not used to hiking on concrete freeways, carrying makeshift blanket-tents and emergency rations on his back.

But hike they did. Radiation and firestorms had turned the American coasts into dead zones. Fallout had proved disastrous to animals and vegetation as well as people. Slow-moving game were everywhere, including squirrels, rabbits, possums, woodchucks, raccoons, and deer. Gargarin and his men were smart enough not to examine, let alone cook and eat, the animals. Ingested fallout was deadlier than that which merely touched the skin.

Burnable wood shingles, porch railings, floorboards, furniture from ruined homes was scarce, the deadfall of woodlands long since exhausted. Their dosimeters indicated that the worst of the fallout danger had passed, but the East Coast had suffered irreversible harm. Gargarin and his men had to get out of there. They slogged toward Pennsylvania. At night they camped in tent towns.

10 Use 'Em or Lose 'Em

The Odyssey passed over the Mideast, and Sara found herself recoiling in horror. Its major cities were smoking, radioactive ruins.

"The Middle Eastern nations were city-states," Thucydides explained, "in the manner of Sparta and Athens. Other than one or two major cities, much of the countries were waterless wastes. One or two well-placed nuclear weapons would effectively obliterate an entire country. Which is what happened."

"My God," Sara said, "look at Libya."

"That smoking ruin just southwest of the smoking ruin that was Tripoli," Colton said, "is Rabta. Forty-two German companies built a poisonous-gas company for them there. The New York Times called it 'Auschwitz in the sand.'"

"Syria's gone too," Sara said.

"They had the second-largest military machine in the Mideast," Cyd noted.

"Had," Colton said.

"What happened to Saudi Arabia?" Sara asked, staring at its blazing cities.

"They outspent everyone—Pakistan, Iraq, and Iran included—on defense," Colton said. "The King Khalid Military City—built in secret in the middle of the desert—was apparently hit by a high-penetration warhead, given the size of that smoking crater."

"Their Chinese CSS-2 missiles had a 2,200-mile range," Cyd pointed out, "and did reach some of their neighbors. So did the 132 F-15s they got from the

United States. I always suspected that they'd acquired nuclear warheads from Pakistan. That seems to have been the case."

"Why not?" Sara asked ruefully. "They were easy enough to get."

"A lot of good it did them," Colton said.

"None of it did anyone any good from where I'm sitting," Sara said. "What was the point of nuking so many nations, Cyd?"

"Nuclear weapons were so terrible," Cyd said, "you had to have them to match those of your enemies—even if you only thought he had them. When the bombing started, you could not afford *not* to use them. The weapons were so hideous, you could not afford to let any enemy survive—and then use his nukes on you."

"And given the easy access to Russia's nuclear supermarket," Sara said, "any potential enemy might possess them."

"That was the CIA's official position when they declared Iran a probable possessor of nuclear arms," Cyd said.

"The first time the agency said that was back in the twentieth century," Colton said.

"So you couldn't leave any possible enemy standing. You couldn't afford the risk—not after the warheads started to fall."

"You kill them all," Sara said. "Let God sort out their souls."

"Use 'em or lose 'em," Colton said.

Cyd said nothing. He was still unsure why so many nations used so many bombs on so many inconsequential targets, and he was a pundit in these matters. His was, in the end, the last reckoning in the last history of this last global war.

Sara let out a long, gasping sigh. "Look down there," she said. "Somebody did a very thorough job on Tehran. It's not easy to hit a city with that many warheads. They have a tendency to cancel each other out."

"The advantage to using air-launched cruise missiles," Colton said, "is that they can wait until they have a clear shot at their targets—shot after shot after shot. It's called a sequential lay-down pattern."

"Who hit them?" Sara asked Thucydides.

"Pakistan got in the first shot," Thucydides said. "After that mushroom cloud lifted, Israel retaliated for Tel Aviv."

Which was coming into view.

Tel Aviv was dust and death.

"Iran didn't nuke Tel Aviv," Cyd said.

"It was a terrorist nuke. How can you know you did it?" Colton explained.

Sara quietly cried.

"Well, at least Jerusalem was spared," Colton said gently.

It had indeed been spared, and in a region of so much thermonuclear destruction—where everything except sand dunes and watering holes seemed to have been targeted—Jerusalem truly stood out.

"I wonder why?" Sara asked.

"Jews believe that the remains of the Temple of Jerusalem—the Temple Mount—sit on Mount Moriah inside the old walled city," Thucydides said.

"Haram al-Sharif, the Noble Sanctuary, sits there too. Abode of their greatest patriarchs and *hanifs,* Abraham and King David, the hallowed jumping-off point of Mohammed after his miraculous night journey from Mecca."

"These two shrines are inextricable," Colton said. "You can't destroy one without destroying the other."

There it stood—a meeting point for Jews and Muslims alike, where, flocking to the Wall in heartfelt genuflection, they recited their prayers and shed their tears.

"At least they aren't killing each other anymore," Sara said.

"Thermonuclear war took the fight out of them," Colton suggested.

"Or maybe there's nothing left to fight over," Sara said.

11 There's Always the Black Stealth

There was only one bright spot in all that Dar-al-Suhl gloom—Larry Taylor . . .

Less than one day after the nuclear war had begun, his plane landed on an abandoned Dar-al-Suhl airstrip. The desert strip—forgotten in an arid, wind-blown mountain valley—was remote enough that it had taken Ali's military nearly a week to locate it and send in a special-ops retrieval team. At the time they had tasks of greater priority—such as the nuking of world civilization.

When they did locate the black B-2 Stealth bomber, Larry Taylor was holed up in a nearby cave eating MREs and drinking canteen water.

The returning team hid the aircraft in a camouflaged portable hangar and brought Taylor to the general and his sisters for debriefing.

None of this improved the moods of either the brother or the Sisters, at least at first. By now Dar-al-Suhl had been hammered and stripped of every military asset it had possessed. As they sat sipping coffee in the communications wing of the underground bunker, the two women fumed.

"Who gives a rat's ass about a downed pilot and a useless bomber," Sultana shouted.

"Especially when there's nothing left *to bomb!*" Sabrina added.

"Face it. We have *nothing.* Now we have only a handful of soldiers, in underground bunkers, waiting for the fallout to dissipate. Before," Sultana grumped, "at least we had a country. Now all we have is a radioactive desert."

"One day we will have to leave this bunker," Sabrina said, "and we will have *nothing.*"

"The world," their brother said, "will likewise have nothing."

"But I like the finer things of life," Sultana pouted.

"The Citadel will still have the finer things of life," Stone said absently.

"L. L. wouldn't mind putting us up," Larry Taylor observed. "It'd be a hell of a lot better than a radioactive desert."

"And how do we get there?" Sultana asked.

"There's always the Black Stealth," Taylor said.

Stone was also about to say that he wouldn't mind paying a call on old L. L., but then he saw the gleam in Ali's eye. The sisters—who now turned to their brother—were also grinning.

Sultana said, "Visiting America is a champion idea."

"Inspired," Sabrina said. "Blessed Brother, what is your opinion?"

He stared at them. At last he said: "Why not? When the radiation subsides over there, yes, visiting America would be a wonderful idea."

Stone shuddered with grim foreboding.

12 I Saw *You* as My Hero

Kate's first job in the Burn Ward was assisting Cathy Anne in its Glass Unit. Glass was hypersensitive to both overpressures and blastwaves, which had turned windows into lethal weapons. A single pane was capable of shattering into thousands of razor-sharp shards, ripping through everything with machine-gun velocity.

Flying-glass wounds were second in difficulty only to burns. A makeshift facility was set up to remove glass shards. That the two women—attired in green scrubs and masks—weren't surgeons wasn't relevant. The glass had to be removed.

Only the salvageable cases were sent here and to other wards. The rest waited in the Yard.

The current case—stretched sideways on a surgery table—was secured with Posey restraints. The hospital was low on pain medication, and this man—his toe was tagged John Doe—was already incoherent with burn agony.

Kate sprayed him first with lidocaine—a topical anesthetic—and then doused him heavily with antiseptic.

"One of the biggest threats to their burn patients is sepsis—burn infection," Cathy Anne said through her surgical mask. "The dead tissue—killed by the burns—is a breeding ground for infection."

"What do you see?" Kate asked.

Cathy Anne studied the bloody glass wounds through magnifying reading glasses.

"Two shards in the chest," Cathy Anne said. "One of them lateral to the sternum. The second is lateral to that. Almost nicked an aorta. It would be helpful if we had some film on him. Unfortunately, radiology is swamped. And radiation's clouding half the X-rays."

"Chart says he was vomiting blood."

"Bad sign. The glass got a lung. I'm surprised he got on the floor at all."

Kate handed Cathy Anne the forceps. The shard lateral to the stern she prised out without incident, but the one lateral to it—after she removed it—left a sucking, bubbling chest wound. It had hit a lung.

"What do we do now?" Kate asked.

"Bandage him up, triage him to the Yard. He shouldn't have been sent here."

"Just like that?"

"We can't save them all, Kate. You have to accept that."

Kate sprayed the sucking wound and bandaged gauze pads over it.

"Most get better on their own?" Kate asked. "And God saves the rest?"

"That's what Frank says."

"You know I've been around Frank half my life and never understood him till now."

"What he does *takes* real courage," Cathy said.

"The same goes for you."

"But I get them only after he's done."

"That doesn't make you less courageous," Kate said.

"Courage? You covered wars, human rights atrocities, and you were there on the ground, in hell. You wrote the book on courage."

"Real courage saves lives," Kate said.

Kate knew that now. She had occasionally assisted Frank in surgery, watched him suture a wound, clamp off an aorta, trache a person's windpipe, graft third-degree burns, save life after life—frequently the lives of small children horribly battered by flying debris—and she came to understand what real bravery was all about. The work she did now, the people she was getting to know, made everything she'd done before pale by comparison.

"I feel now," Kate said to Cathy Anne, "that my entire life was a waste. Did it take the end of the world for me to find myself? Was I really that fucked up?"

"All those times I read your 'Woman Watch' articles and watched your TV specials, I saw you as *my* hero."

"For the first time in my life I know what I really want to do."

Cathy Anne gave Kate an affectionate smile.

They moved the John Doe onto a gurney and wheeled him into the hall, where their next glass victim awaited them.

13 A Truly Luciferian Leer

The Jack Town trial was over in three minutes—two and a half of which were devoted to the means of execution.

At dusk Warden Carstairs, Chaplain O'Donnell, and Sergeant Harris were led outdoors by Jamal's adjutant, Mustafa-al-Jabar. There, in a dark drizzle, he lined them up against a high prison wall. Inmates crowded against the mess-hall windows to watch. Nearly 300 streamed out into the yard—enduring both rain and fallout. Mustafa walked up to the condemned men. Nose to nose with Chaplain O'Donnell, he straightened his black bow tie and gave the Chaplain a not-unpleasant smile.

"You drew the short straw?" O'Donnell asked.

"Never happen, preacher-man," Mustafa said. "That be the one what lost."

Spinning around, he counted off ten paces, then turned to face his three victims.

"This be far enough," Mustafa shouted over his shoulder to several of his brothers on the yard. "Don't want to get no blood on this fine white shirt and tie." The rain was turning oily black, and his shirt was becoming soiled.

"Don't think it matters," Radford said.

Mustafa stared at his shirt, dismayed.

"Better get on," Radford announced to the condemned.

Mustafa racked the slide on his 9mm Beretta.

"No firing squad?" Warden Carstairs asked, his feelings hurt.

"Decided not to waste too many bullets."

"Not very dignified," the Chaplain said, shaking his head in mock-disapproval. "I'd at least expected military honors—a final meal, last rites, a drumroll, stripped epaulets, a hymn, a few prayers."

"Couple muthafuckas wanna take you out with baseball bats."

"That would have *no class*," the Chaplain said disdainfully.

"Don't we at least get a last cigarette, a blindfold, a few verses from the Koran?" Sergeant Harris asked.

"Maybe some last words," Mustafa said. He walked up to Sergeant "Hardball" Harris.

"Yo, race traitor," he said to Harris, "you got any last words? How you double-crossed your people?"

"You ain't my people," Harris said with a shrug.

"That all?" Mustafa asked.

"How 'bout 'suck my dick'? Them last words?"

"They be now," Mustafa said.

He shot Harris in his forehead.

Even through the barred Plexiglas windows they could hear the inmates' cheers.

"Warden, you got any regrets 'bout the shitty job you done, running this hole?"

"Wish I'd got me a job in one of those Club Feds. I could have associated with hedge-fund bandits and corrupt politicians—a higher class of crook."

"Yo, Mustafa!" Jamal yelled. He'd come out into the yard to watch. He was now approaching the condemned and their executioner. "Git a move on. This rain be some nasty shit."

Mustafa turned back to Warden Carstairs.

"You heard the man," Mustafa said. "Adiós, muthafucka."

He shot Carstairs in his right eye.

Arm extended, elbow locked, he sighted on the Chaplain.

"Say yo' prayers, Bible-Thumper."

At which point lightning blazed, and a heartbeat later thunder cracked.

A lightning bolt struck the yard like God's Own Fist—and Mustafa burst into sulphurous flames. The Chaplain stared at Mustafa's blazing remains—and the charred hole where he'd stood. Kicking Mustafa's corpse, he lifted his eyepatch, fixed the assembled with the empty socket's Gorgon's glare—then treated them to a deep Satanic laugh and a truly Luciferian leer.

"Any other takers?" the Chaplain roared.

14 Doom Demanded Diversion

"Does Allah appreciate all we've done for Him?" First Officer Khameni asked Captain Gargarin.

"Go to hell," Gargarin said, sick of the first officer's sarcasm.

"After you," First said mockingly—and pointed to the tent town at the bend in the road.

"Is the rest of this country," Starpom asked, "as bad as New Jersey?"

"I've heard pretty ugly things about Philadelphia," First said.

Actually, Gargarin did suspect Jersey's tent towns were worse than those of other areas. The Garden State had taken an unusually hard hammering. He and his men were trying to pass through the state as quickly as possible. Every refugee they'd met wanted to get out of Jersey.

As Gargarin and his people unpacked their gear, he studied their new tent town—still a good hundred miles from the Pennsylvania border. The grounds were littered with knapsacks, packframes, and sleeping bags spread across plastic sheets (which served as ground cloths or doubled as emergency tents or ponchos). People pitched makeshift tents of canvas or plastic or, in a pinch, big garbage bags. A few parties had store-bought tents. Gargarin watched one large group set up a polyethylene wall tent—which they'd taken turns hauling—big as a double camper.

People dug firepits—or cleaned out old ones. People struck flints—old Indian arrowheads and lighters were highly prized—with steel, and soon communal cooking fires blazed. People carried containers to streams, looking for water to boil. Around the tent town's perimeter campers excavated slit-trench latrines.

His own men were getting out their gear. Not only had their sub served as a bomb shelter, it had provided them with survival kits, which by camp standards made them wealthy men.

Their belts and shoulder-slings bore 9mm pistols, cartridge belts, hand axes, buck knives, Swiss Army knives, and lighters. Their shoulder sheaths contained collapsible Skorpion machine pistols with extra magazines of 7.62 ammunition. Out of their packs came ponchos and first-aid kits—which included morphine and penicillin. Aspirin was now valued beyond measure. After these came army blankets, plastic-tube tents, freeze-dried and dehydrated food, instant coffee, rice, flour, sugar, salt, dry beans, matches in waterproof cases, candles, halazone tablets, fish line and hooks, extra water bags, Thinsulate pants, shirts and socks, Maglites, insect repellents, down-stuffed vests and parkas, rain boots, gloves, soap, toothbrushes and powder, needles and thread, bandanas, and compasses.

It was near dusk. The camp was awash in a smoggy glow, twilight gloom, and a ghostly amber haze. Gargarin decided it was time for his evening reconnaissance.

Also, he had to get away from First Officer Khameni's sarcasm. Gargarin was starting to doubt that nuking New York had been the Path to God. He saw no evidence anywhere of the True Faith emerging.

So Gargarin walked. At moments like this, when all was still, a vague uneasiness came over him. These camps reminded him too much of the refugee camps of his youth, and he loathed them. He much preferred the vast emptiness of the sea. He despised this strange mix of people.

"Hell Town" was setting up, and definitely there was no sign of Allah there. Apparently, earthly doom demanded diversion—anything to get one's mind off the horror of reality, the tragic nightmare of what-had-been and what was now forever lost. Whatever the explanation, every tent town had a Hell Town, and this camp was no exception. Close by in the southwest quadrant of the camp he could hear the whisk of the pasteboards in the gambling dens, the rattle of dice, cries of "ante's a buck!" "ten on the Jack!" "three pretty ladies!" and "seven come eleven!"

Currency was now worth less than toilet paper, and the marked hundred-dollar bills that the gamblers bought in advance with barter—canned food (tuna was especially prized), cigarettes, and liquor—could later be exchanged in the various swap shacks. In those establishments entrepreneurs huckstered everything from medicine to a remarkable assortment of half-dressed females.

One lucky night of stud poker and you might win enough whiskey, cigarettes, and iron rations to last you a month, as well as sex in the brothel tents.

Famine, as has sometimes been observed, is a powerful aphrodisiac.

"Vigilance committees" had been established. Without them there could be no camplife. People in the tent towns were there to be protected from the banditry of the road. Bandits tended to avoid the towns, preferring instead to pick off the stragglers who found themselves still on the road after dark. Even so, safety in numbers meant nothing if their fellow campers chose to rape and plunder. Those accused in the camps were summarily tried, and justice was swift and harsh, from fines to flogging and hanging.

He could hear from the Justice Tent off to his left:

"How do you find the accused?"

A shout of "Murder One!" rang through the tent.

By dawn the trees would be trimmed with the bodies of the condemned.

Camp attrition was high—even from natural causes—and the dead sometimes left behind items of worth. The Committee—after determining cause of death—would also probate the possessions of the deceased.

Gargarin longed for the freedom of the seas. Although he would not let on to his crew, he questioned more frequently his role in this new and bitter dispensation and felt a deepening skepticism at what he'd done. True, he'd helped to drive Western culture to its knees. But to what end? The West had in turn blasted the World of Islam off the face of the earth. And while he did sense in many of the refugees a return to God, this renaissance of the soul seemed to have had little to do with Allah or the Prophet.

To the extent that these denizens of the road had anything resembling a spiritual leader it seemed to be that weird nun preaching the Word over the airways. She had the biggest religious following on earth, but she wasn't Muslim.

When she came on the radio, all activity in the camps ceased. Even the brothel tents shut down. Men came out with their half-naked whores. They came from the whiskey tents, dazed on pruno and home brew.

"Cassandra Calling!" was her signature greeting.

Gargarin returned to his crew. The road and the camps were volatile, dangerous environments, and it was important for them to stick together.

IX

To Reign in Hell

To reign is worth ambition though in hell.

—John Milton, *Paradise Lost*, 1.261

1 "My Passion Was Seeing, And I Became an Enormous Eye, Which Cannot Close"

—Malcolm Braly, *False Starts*

Thucydides' had always been an enormous eye that could not close. He was perhaps the only entity left that willingly performed this assignment, that gazed on a fire-ravaged planet and did not blink.

It was not a pretty world that he presented to those below. Thousands upon thousands of nuclear weapons had produced fire and ash in astronomical quantities. The ground bursts—particularly the supervolcano ground bursts—had likewise lofted trillions of tons of dirt into the stratosphere. Coastal-city ocean-bursts had vaporized incredible quantities of water. All of that airborne ash, dirt, and water vapor had not only given the planet a paler, smokier cast, it had radically increased rainfall. Precipitation is nothing but a volatile coming-together of water vapor with smoke or dust—smoke being the more effective rain-making agent. These elements the atmosphere now had in superabundance.

So the rains came. Antediluvian rainfall as in the days of Noah's flood.

The rain kept people indoors, and it flushed radioactive particles out of the atmosphere. But it was also more hazardous than dry fallout. The rain's radiation was more concentrated.

Thucydides had broadcast Cassandra's lectures on surviving, so many people had a basic knowledge of how to avoid the perils of radioactivity. Most of them didn't have dosimeters, so they could not gauge the severity of personal contamination. They did know how to sluice the radiation away (assuming they had safe water to sluice with), and they knew how to avoid radioactive food (assuming they had food).

But one day the rains ceased, and the survivors left their homes—like pre-sapien tree-dwellers, fearful of the brave new world below. Their fears were well-founded. There was not much left with which to make a life.

They took to the road in search of safe supplies, and the roads now streamed with people.

Thucydides' memory banks contained *The Grapes of Wrath*—both the book and the movie—so he had a visual context for viewing the Exodus. But the comparisons were not apt. Steinbeck's Oakies fleeing the Midwestern dust storms had maps directing them to California, cars and trucks to get them there, and work—however marginal—at the end of their trek. They also had a dream.

The postapocalyptic halt, lame, hungry, and blind had—at the end of their journey—nothing.

Those who could find and manage shopping carts trundled their possessions on rickety wheels for as long as they could. The carts, never designed for long hauls, quickly broke down. The goods they carried were abandoned by the side of the road. Some also pedaled bicycles, but, like the shopping carts, bicycles eventually broke or were stolen. Most of the homeless carried their possessions on their backs.

The Great Urban Exodus was spontaneous and unplanned, yet the refugees were not without direction. The world's gutted cities—little more than ruin, rubble, and rats—were now places to be shunned. When the highways took the refugees near any sizable town, they gave it a wide berth. The highway homeless flowed—for the most part into the countryside.

Cassandra's broadcasts—thanks to Thucydides' management of MTN's com-sat systems—continued. Those who had battery-powered radios were able to listen. A few places like the Citadel still received Cass's television transmissions. People everywhere mobbed those radio and TV sets to catch her broadcasts.

Now that the bombing was over, her shows no longer featured apocalyptic riffs and hard-pounding Armageddon rock. Instead, Cassandra talked. She discussed the techniques and strategy of postapocalyptic survival or passed on what she knew about the state of the world.

More and more, she spoke on the importance of learning to love—to love one's neighbor, to love life, and to never lose faith.

2 Beware the Wrath of Man

How the mighty had fallen.

Everywhere Sailor journeyed he saw ruins.

But there were two whom he cared for: Kate and her friend Frank. The two who had freed him from hell.

Where were they?

He prayed they'd stayed clear of plague and poisonous air.

Especially plague.

One thing Old Socrates had taught him was to fear disease. Rats everywhere feared disease more than cats or traps. Disease had felled his Bombay warren and countless other warrens.

So things looked grim—but grimmer for men than rats. Sailor and his kind could burrow far underground—and stay clear of disease and the deadly air—coming out for only a few hours a night to forage.

And so he hid below ground.

He ate sparingly, avoiding foodstuff with the taint of death.
Wait it out.
Let the death-taint pass.
Burrow deep.
Suffer not the stranger.
And beware the wrath of man.

3 Old as Her Arteries

Lydia Magruder hated taking Henry Colton's calls. She had enough on her plate. She didn't need to hear his nonstop fears and nightmare scenarios about "the Nation." She did not care if a paramilitary outfit calling itself the Nation was on the rise. That's why the Citadel was armed with .50-caliber machine guns and antipersonnel mines. She'd built the Citadel to be safe from self-styled gangs such as the Nation.

She had other things to worry about. Were Kate and Frank ever going to listen to reason and join her at the Citadel? Would the fallout ever subside? Could the flood damage be repaired?

The Citadel wasn't getting much precipitation in the desert—but radioactive rain had swamped the rest of the planet. According to Thucydides' best estimates the ravages of fire, famine, flood, plague, civil anarchy—and fallout spiked with supervolcanic debris—had destroyed two-thirds of the human race. Only the earth's most arid wastelands—the Sahara, the Kalahari, Death Valley, and L. L.'s Sonoran Desert—had been spared the deluge of death. Surviving enclaves had four things in common. They were heavily fortified, well-provisioned, strategically located, and fallout-free.

Some of those survivors L. L. could have done without. For the past five months—since that global disaster now referred to as the End Time—Thucydides and her own intelligence officers had been collecting information on world survivors. The most enterprising survivors had a predatory bent, to say the least.

For the most part the military groups were nonthreatening. She was on friendly terms with many of them. They were survivalists who practiced live and let live and kept pretty much to themselves. They had engaged in some tactical looting after the firestorms—as had everyone else—but that looting had quickly subsided. Like L. L., they had also made friendly advances to surviving military personnel. In fact, the moment the dust had cleared, Lydia had visited the nearby military bases, opened the Citadel's gates, and inducted personnel willing to serve in the Citadel's armed forces.

She also had helped herself to considerable ordnance and material and now included artillery and C-130 air transports in the Citadel's arsenal. She could have added helicopter gunships and Phantom jets but lacked the fuel, spare parts, and crews necessary to maintain them.

The phone rang.

"Yes, Henry."

"Hi, L. L. Are you talking to me today?"

"Not if you're going to lecture me on military preparedness or some such thing. I feel like I'm listening to Jack Taylor blather about National Missile Defense."

"I'm just calling to give you a tactical update."

"On the Nation?"

"Yesterday out of the blue I got a call from Breeze."

That got her attention.

"You know, Henry, I always liked that boy. You and he and Stone were so close. I felt that killing in Houston was such a tragic mistake."

"We were the only ones who saw it that way."

"How is he?"

"Breeze confirmed my worst fears about the Nation. They may soon be on the move, and heading your way. I'll e-mail you Cyd's and my observations. He monitors their radio transmissions . . ."

"*. . . More than just a disorganized assortment of prison gangs—Black Muslims, Mexican Mafia, Aryan Brothers, Survivalists, Klansmen, Bloods, Crips, Rolling Sixties—this bizarre alliance from its inception has possessed extraordinary leadership and communication. Through a network of prison radio stations, inmates have remained in constant contact throughout the nuclear war and its aftermath. The gangs have quickly fallen under the charismatic sway of four forceful leaders—the Four Horsemen, as they are known in prison circles: Jamal Abdul Rastad, Jimmy John Radford, Ortega 'Santo' Riaz, and Ronald 'Cool Breeze' Robinson. They have preached their message of "strength through unity." They proselytized first in prisons and later, as the Nation became a military force, in army encampments throughout the country.*

"*Thucydides and I are also of the opinion that the nuclear holocaust has played a role in their coming together. It has so dwarfed their own petty conflicts and opened up so many possibilities with such stunning vividness that they have been willing—even eager—to set aside their rivalries and hatreds. The opportunity to band together and form an army, 'a nation of their own,' has transcended everything else, including revenge against fellow inmates. The End Time has given them a vision, a dream, which they have found irresistible. As the Horsemen like to say: 'If we play our cards right, the world is ours.'*

"*Those who did not 'heed the call' were murdered or turned over to the Nation's officer in charge of discipline. His name is Junius P. O'Donnell, former Chaplain of the Jackton, Texas, Correctional Facility. Chaplain O'Donnell has, within the Nation, become a legend of Satanic proportions.*

With surprising ease they have commandeered our country's military bases, including the U.S. Army and Navy's Hawthorne, Nevada, munitions facility, which contained thousands of underground weapons and ammo depots. That site alone has supplied them with enough firepower to conquer and occupy this land for the foreseeable future. What had once been the United States military establishment quickly found itself in the service of the Nation.

"Given the scarcity of diesel fuel and gasoline, military transport has slowed to a crawl. Nonetheless, the Nation apparently sees our country's railroads as a possible solution to this problem. Due to the shortage of diesel fuel, gasoline, and electrical power, the Nation is converting our country's locomotives to steam. To that end they have established a military headquarters in a rail yard outside of Kansas City. A crossroads for most of our country's major rail lines, it is now home to hundreds of bivouac tents as well as a larger tent town down the line, in which the Nation quarters its enlisted men.

"Their overall strategy is no secret. New conscripts are kept in forced detention in tent towns—concentration camps are more like it—guarded by heavily armed sentries. There is only one strategic target left that would require such a buildup of arms, transport, men, and material.

"The Citadel."

"They still have to cross the Sonoran Desert," L. L. told Henry Colton. "We have troops and guns, and we will fight them . . ."

"Breeze said the trains are moving. Apparently Radford's survivalist militia had train buffs among them. They're called 'foamers.' They rehabilitate old wood- and coal-burning locomotives."

"I may be getting old as my arteries," L. L. said irritably, "but I just can't take a bunch of prison gangs all that seriously."

"Breeze says they not only have locomotives, tenders, and cabooses but flatcars, piggyback flatcars, and ventilated stockcars, able to travel through desert heat. Where they can't find track, they can lay their own."

"It never ends, does it?" she said wearily. "What was it Santayana said?"

"Only the dead have seen the end to war," Colton quoted.

It was a line they often quoted to each other.

She had expected roving bandit bands, occasional skirmishes, not total war with a full-fledged, massively equipped military force.

They said their good-byes and hung up.

L. L. sighed again, stood, and headed back into her house. She had work to do.

For one hallucinatory moment she saw her grandmother, Lozen, riding a dust storm across the desert plains, dust devils tall as skyscrapers twisting around her—the Apache war shaman her grandfather had thought was a goddess but whom L. L. saw as *the woman who rode the wind.*

Like her namesake, Lydia Lozen Magruder was going to war.

4 Horsewhipping's Too Good

For a long time an eighty-seven-year-old man, with shoulder-length white hair, a white beard that reached his belt buckle, and the black blazing eyes of an Old Testament prophet, hunched over his desk. For the last few months the man known as "the Chaplain"—one of the Nation's spiritual leaders apparently—had been preaching nightly sermons that Jebodaiah listened to avidly on his shortwave radio. The Chaplain was preaching "the Word." A born-again orator himself, General Jebodaiah Brown respected a good sermonist.

Now, however, he had other reasons for listening to the Chaplain. The Nation had captured his two surviving sons and was holding them hostage.

This was ironic, because Jebodaiah had been one of the Chaplain's biggest fans.

The Chaplain's sermon was coming to a close.

*"There be some out there disparage the will of God. They say His hand isn't in this justice, this tribulation, that His will isn't done on earth even as it is in heaven. Well, I seen where that leads them who doubt, them who blaspheme faith. And I say that's why God give **me** this strong right hand. I say for them that dispute the Lord and dismiss His Infinite Power, horsewhipping's too good. For I say unto you, I am, we are His Sling and Stone, His Sword and Shield, His Fire and His Scourge, and the doubters and the sinners that challenge His Will, impugn His Power, shall suffer that Scourge: the Almighty's Wrath, **my** wrath.*

A hell of a sermon, Jebodaiah thought. A hell of a lot better than that rad-lib lesbian-bitch Sister Cassandra could do. Her stuff made him want to puke. If he heard one more sermon of hers about "complete compassion," "sharing another person's sorrow," "learning to understand and love that person by experiencing their joy and pain," he was going to lose his mind. If he heard one more sniveling speech about how "we brought this on ourselves by inventing, building, and selling these infernal devices" he would scream.

Listening to Cassandra's postwar sermons, he knew something now he had suspected for a long time—that Satan resided in MTN and the desert redoubt from where it was broadcast, the Citadel. He knew the siren's song of the elitist media and the liberal press. Complete compassion, infinite sympathy: bullshit.

Hadn't that lesbian-bitch ever heard of God's will? Eye for eye, tooth for tooth, burning for burning, flogging for flogging, life for life, hate for hate. Death for bloody death.

That was the ticket.

When he gave his own Sunday-night radio sermon, he would address that text himself. The Nation was the enemy. The way they fought and tortured and killed his people—picked them off one small group at a time—could never be forgiven or forgotten. They were the reason he had risen to lead the country's survivalists and militia groups into Pennsylvania and upstate New York, unite them into an invincible fire-forged alliance. And as founder and leader of the People's New United Militia he would never betray the salvation and protection he had promised them.

Still, he was so tired of the bloodshed and fighting—especially now that the Nation held his two surviving sons hostage.

That was something he dreaded to think about.

Even so, he would never sell out the People's New United Militia and accede to the Nation's demands. Joining ranks with an army run by niggers and spics and convicts was out of the question.

Too bad that Chaplain wasn't here to help work out a settlement. Jebodaiah suggested that idea to him in that letter he'd written. End the killing for once and for all. He wished he and the Chaplain could get together and work things out.

That Chaplain sure could preach.

5 Gentle Soul, for Jesus' Sake Forbear . . .

The nuclear holocaust, the phone war with her mother, the hordes of the gravely injured besieging the Towers depressed Kate.

Cathy Anne took her aside for some needed advice.

"Kate, the patients' lot here is bad enough without you being so grim all the time. You have to lighten up."

"Half the time I'm sick with dread. I can't shake the thought. Why is it *I* lived and so many died?"

"Maybe this place is why. You lived to ease pain and to make these people smile—even laugh again. They need to laugh, you know."

"Laugh at the apocalypse?"

"We laugh because that is all we have left—and all we have to give *them*."

The hours were unbearable. Twenty-four-hour stints—sometimes more— were the rule. They were lucky if they found an hour here or there for a catnap. Still, they tried hard to lift their own and everyone else's spirits.

Kate never dreamed she would end up joking, teasing, even flirting with patients, but Cathy Anne told her it was part of the job. Whatever Cathy told her she took as gospel.

"Look," Cathy Anne explained, "a lot of these people are going to be mentally and physically disfigured. So you try to rebuild their egos. You ask them: 'Jimmy, when are you going to pop the question? You know I'm yours.' You tell Lucy you hear she and Dr. Frank are tying the knot. 'Where will the honeymoon be?' you ask her. 'I was always partial to Acapulco,' you say. All they have is *you*. You have to put on a brave front."

Not everyone agreed with Cathy Anne's attitude toward nursing. The rate of attrition was high, and some of the older nurses warned Kate about getting too close to her patients. Cathy, however, ignored this warning. If it was good enough for Cathy Anne, it was good enough for her. Kate wanted to be like Cathy Anne Gibson more than she'd ever wanted anything in her life.

Kate might not have been the most seasoned nurse there, but what she lacked in training, she made up for in stamina. She handled twice as many patients as any of the nurses there except Cathy Anne, often going thirty-six hours without a break.

The work wasn't that complicated. They were hopelessly short on everything, so she didn't need an extensive knowledge of medications and procedures. When she wasn't attending patients, she was sterilizing masks, gloves, and needles; cleaning syringes; boiling water; emptying trash; mopping floors; handing out food; collecting bedpans and urinals.

But they saved lives by the thousands.

Nor was it lost on Kate that she had seen, diagnosed, and worked with more patients than most career nurses saw and worked with in five lifetimes.

Her mother did not approve. She believed she could get a plane through to the Towers, could pick up the three of them and get them back to the sanctuary of the Citadel. L. L. Magruder did not take rejection lightly and was furious with all three of them for refusing.

"You can't save the world!" she shouted over her satellite phone. "There's limits to what you can do. In fact, the world's turning uglier by the day. A sea of death is washing us, and if you don't get out, it will engulf you. There is too much violence and disease. What you're doing now is pure hubris!"

Her mother's argument was not without merit. There was a point of diminishing returns, and Kate knew they were overshooting it. Half the Towers housed burn patients. Their necrosed flesh incubated pathogens to the extent that much of the hospital had become a breeding ground for disease. When new patients from the squatters' camps—homeless foragers, who carried with them cholera, dysentery, typhus, whooping cough, tularemia, even Bubonic and Pneumonic Plague, all of it aggravated by radiation poisoning—invaded the cramped quarters of their sick and dying they were overwhelmed.

The rate of attrition skyrocketed, and the pyres in the Yard roared day and night.

Cathy Anne was the first member of the staff to get pneumonic plague. She'd always been a stickler for cleanliness, sterile gloves, and surgical masks—in part to protect the patients—but those precautions were not enough. Weeks of triple, even quadruple, shifts had depleted them all. Their resistance was nil.

Cathy Anne had all the symptoms: wheezing rales with a rattling cough, bloody diarrhea, spiking fever. Then her face darkened, and her lungs filled with fluid.

They had no cure.

Kate and Frank were with her in the end. Cathy Anne called out twice for Frank from her hospital bed. Her body convulsed, spasmed, then settled.

They buried her in the courtyard and hammered a cross over her grave.

"'Gentle soul, for Jesus' sake forbear,'" Frank quoted softly.

Then he broke down.

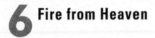 Fire from Heaven

Life aboard the Odyssey was not going well.

Self-sufficient though the station might be, it was not a world-unto-itself. Odyssey required vital resupplying from the earth.

Its hydroponic foodstuffs were as yet experimental, not intended to feed its crew.

Its water-recycling systems redeemed as much as 90 percent of the H_2O in carbon dioxide and urine, feces, and sweat, but oxygen recycling was less efficient.

The Odyssey was drying up and running out of air.

Thucydides' astronomical observations—which he transmitted in both print and audio mode—were even more disheartening. His latest report on its prospective flaring was uncharacteristically acerbic.

Sara wondered if perhaps he'd been listening too much to Sister Cassandra.

"In case you've forgotten," Thucydides announced, "we've had other things to worry about besides earth's nuclear weapons. Among the stars and galaxies I'm currently studying, two 'star bombs' look especially ominous. One is a medium-size sun named Sol in a galaxy affectionately dubbed the Milky Way. Solar flares generated by magnetic storms on the surface of the sun run in eleven-year cycles, and guess what? Boys and girls, this is the year. With the help of my ACE satellite one million miles overhead, I have been monitoring this current cycle, since it poses a major threat to my own survival. During the buildup phase, there is a radical increase in visible light, an increase in solar X-rays, and a large outflow of hyperenergetic protons, so I have been able to predict a forthcoming flare cycle with considerable accuracy.

"The bad news is, on a NOAA Solar-Richter Scale of 1 to 5, this one's a 4.9 and will be reaching us anytime now.

"Worst case scenerio? In the old days solar flares would have knocked out power grids such as the one that shut down Hydro-Québec, the third-largest utility in North America. They would have disrupted radio transmissions and beepers.

"Of course, there aren't too many of those left to knock out, so that's not much of a problem.

"Our own survival is, however.

"Nor is that the only bit of 'stellar violence' yours truly has to worry about. I'm projecting a blast of 'magnestellar radiation' as well. These are high-energy particles, superpowerful magnetic flares far worse than sun storms—coming from a magnetar 30,000 light-years away. Earth's atmosphere will do its usual outstanding job of protecting what's left of the planet. We, however, are going to take the full load."

"Magnetar?" Colton asked, seating himself at a computer console.

"Magnetars are neutron stars, massive as Sol but as small as ten miles in diameter. They are the collapsed cores of superstars gone nova. The most famous are the pulsars, which spin furiously and emit steady streams of radio waves. These are the only observable neutron stars."

"And their star is hitting us with dangerous radiation?" Colton asked.

"Their magnetic field is billions of times more powerful than Earth's. Their blasts strip electrons from atoms and in the past have caused numerous spacecraft computer systems to shut down. I'm heavily shielded, but with the combination of Sol's storm and the starquake's magnetic flares things may get rough up here. The blasts I'm projecting are the worst any spacecraft has had to endure. Even from a distance of 30,000 light-years, it will be horrendous. Time to shut down operations and weather it out."

Thucydides signed off.

"Cyd sounds pissed at us," Colton said.

"Maybe he thinks humanity's let him down," Sara said.

"Better hit the hard room," Colton said.

"Our own little interstellar bomb shelter," Sara said, wryly.

"This one's going to be a sonofabitch," Colton said.

7 Ain't Heard No Complaints

"I don't know 'bout you, brutha-man," Jamal said to Cool Breeze, "but I believe Jimmy John is scar-ee."

"And I thought he was bad when we was in Jack Town," Breeze said.

"Something happened to him in that subbasement," Jamal said.

"Warden stickin' that 'lectric prod to his ass," Breeze speculated.

"Naw, he put that prod to all us, and we ain't crazy as him."

Their big pavilion in the Kansas City rail yards was almost palatial. Jamal and Cool Breeze sat in black director's chairs around a mahogany conference table—big as two king-size beds end to end—requisitioned from a Merrill Lynch boardroom. They had a kitchenette wired to a portable electric generator, and they could cook meals, brew coffee, and drink cold beer. An enterprising supply officer had located a sterling silver dinner service, matching Thermoses, and bone china dishware.

The place settings had been controversial. Radford had argued that they should stick to aluminum mess cups. Now that they had a force of over 40,000 soldiers, mess cups looked more "military."

"That shit got no class!" Jamal objected. Jamal felt that the expensive dinner service made them look like four-star generals rather than the leaders of a glorified prison gang. "Radford got his head tucked up his ass 'bout a whole lot of things," Jamal said, pouring french roast into one of the china cups.

A nerve-fraying scream tore the darkness apart.

"There go that Chaplain again," Breeze said. "He do love his work."

"It be the middle of the night," Jamal grumbled. "Don't the sucka ever rest?"

"Puttin' him in charge of discipline did work out," Breeze said. "Got to admit that."

"Don't care what you say. Them screams git on my nerves."

"Them screams don't bother Radford none," Breeze said. "Where the fuck Radford and his brother go anyways? Who they shootin' now?"

"They back East warring on some damn militia group."

"What we doin' tonight?" Breeze asked, sitting back, yawning. "We the only two leaders left here."

"We gots interviews. People comin' askin' us to accept gifts, settle problems, beg for mercy."

"In exchange for gifts."

"In other words, we gittin' paid."

Sergeant Vasile—a former Brooklyn mafioso—came in. Short, stocky, a nose like a busted knuckle, he was dressed in freshly laundered fatigues but needed a shave. However, as Breeze once observed: "Even after shavin' the sucka need a shave."

"You got some people want to see you, " Vasile said. "You want to see them?"

"They bring anything?" Jamal asked.

"All kinds of shit."

"Show them in. Might as well git this over with."

The two men left their chairs and flopped down on a pile of daiwan cushions, heavy rugs, and thick satin comforters. A slow parade commenced. Like Eastern potentates, Jamal and Breeze casually observed the men and women making their way through the pavilion.

The Nation was an army on the move; the two men had no use for furs, designer clothes, jewelry, or gems—not even diamonds or gold. Guns and ammunition they had in such abundance that gifts of firearms—no matter how rare or beautiful—were viewed almost as insults.

The most precious gifts tended to be consumables. Gourmet foods, tobacco, canned coffee, canned juices, and liquors and wines were highly prized.

Tonight's supplicants provided a horn-of-plenty: fine wines, 30-year scotch, and 12-year-old Bourbons, cases of beer, and crates of rare canned goods. Soon caviar, pâté, canned Camembert, turkeys and hams, smoked oysters, nuts, and cans of potato chips filled their pavilion.

Willing, attractive women paraded their way, flocking to the Nation as if its officers were the New World Order's rock stars. The most stunning women of all ethnicities strolled through the tent each evening.

"Ladies here sure try hard to please," Jamal said.

"I didn't work that hard when I was tryin' out for the New York Yankees," Breeze said.

Those women who caught their eye and held their gaze were asked to remain for the evening. Another dozen or so were asked to wait in an adjacent tent for the possibility of a "closer inspection" later that night.

"You sure you wanna participate tonight?" Breeze asked Jamal. "Don't want to git your ass kicked out of Paradise, consortin' with the Unveiled."

"They ain't of the faith," Jamal said with a disdainful shrug. "Allah don't care 'bout no infidel pussy."

While Breeze could halfway understand Jamal, Radford remained a mystery to both men. After all those years in prison all the Road Warrior—as Jamal called him—cared about was expanding their domain and practicing his trade— the profession of arms.

"Shootin' muthafuckas," Jamal remarked disdainfully.

"He could be back here talkin' trash, drinkin' mash, kickin' it with his homies," Breeze said, shaking his head. "The sucka done lost it."

Jamal helped himself to pâté and smoked oysters. Breeze sampled the caviar and a vintage Saint-Emilion.

While they ate—stroked and kissed, pampered and fed by the women who'd remained—other citizens entered, seeking favors, advice, judgments, mercy.

Jamal felt put-upon, regarding these importunings as "work." For the most part he did not look up at this new round of supplicants.

"My neighbor stole my milk cow," a grizzled old man in overalls said, "and I don't want to have to kill him to get it back. Could you make him . . . ?"

"What did you give us?" Sergeant Vasile interrupted.

"A case of mixed liquors—top-shelf, all I had."

"Shoot the muthafucka and take that damn cow back," Jamal said.

In its territories, the Nation's word was law.

"My son wants to marry," a graying, sad-faced man in a worn pea coat said, "but his fiancée's father claims the earth ain't worth repopulating, and he won't listen to reason. It's wrong for him to deny both his daughter and my son."

"What was your contribution?" the sergeant asked.

"Coffee, sugar, flour. Didn't have much to give."

"And it don't feed the bear," Jamal observed.

"Come up with some more loot, pops," Sergeant Vasile said, "maybe they reconsider your case."

"My husband's being held by the authorities," a middle-aged woman in men's work clothes said, "because he wouldn't let people trespass on our property. We've had a terrible time with looters and thieves. George took to setting traps and firing warning shots at them. Well, some people shot back, and George winged two of them, and they want to hang him. Could you . . . ?"

"Whatcha brought in?" Sergeant Vasile asked, cutting her off.

"A big basket of wine and caviar and pâté."

"What kind of country be lockin' up innocent men?" Jamal thundered. "That muthafucka be free!"

"I ain't got much and can't support my family," the next ragged survivor pleaded. "I need to get my daughter and son jobs or they're going to starve, mister. I ain't speaking for myself but for my wife and kids. Anyone need a servant, a dishwasher, I can work. For that matter, my wife's still young. She's a great cook."

"That one's easy," Sergeant Vasile said. "Want me to handle it, generals?"

"Knock your fool self out," Jamal said.

"Corporal, escort this man to our recruitment tent and send some recruiters over to his house. We got employment for his entire family in this here army."

The man became hysterical.

"Some men come and already drug my son off into your 'military.' I was about to ask you to get him back for me. We're Quakers, and my son ain't meant to fight in no army. You can't shanghai the rest of us in with your conscripts."

"Look at it as keeping the family together," Vasile said.

"Next three men," Sergeant Vasile said, "ain't got no gifts but claim they can do something for you."

"That's a switch," Breeze said curiously, looking up from his wine, women, and garlic-stuffed olives.

The men were shown into the tent. The tallest man had a dark beard and hair, a hawk's nose, and a hawk's piercing eyes. He wore a khaki uniform.

"My name is Dmitri Gargarin. I am a former captain in the Dar-al-Suhl navy. I am a soldier of Allah with advanced training in all forms of weaponry."

"Biochemical?" Jamal asked, suddenly alert.

"And nuclear."

"Think we gots ourselves a terrorist?" Breeze asked Jamal, popping the cork on a well-chilled magnum of Dom Pérignon.

"Who gives a fuck?" Jamal said amiably. "We like the Foreign Legion. Don't care 'bout no muthafucka's past. Sergeant, enlist this man. In fact, send him to the officers' barracks."

"My men," Captain Gargarin said, "are all skilled specialists."

"Enlist all of 'em," Jamal said. "Git 'em good bunks."

"Next?" Breeze asked, getting impatient.

The man next to him was in his early forties, had a supercilious sneer, derisive eyes, and radiated condescension. Breeze and Jamal were not used to arrogance in their pavilion. The other had a dark, ill-cut, unwashed beard; wore a perpetually angry grimace; and kept his eyes lowered. Breeze thought the man looked . . . deranged.

They were dressed in dark, dusty work clothes. Like everyone else that night, they looked as if they'd just come off the road.

"Yo," Jamal said to the man with the sneer, "don't I know you? The radio muthafucka? You used to be famous?"

"Yeah, Ron Lewis—the talk-jock."

"Whatcha say you do for us?" Breeze asked.

"I've been listening to your nightly radio shows. They sound like the penitentiary amateur hour. Even your Chaplain—no denying his sermons have a certain raw power—could use some professional guidance."

"Ain't heard no complaints so far," Jamal said.

Another scream exploded out of the Chaplain's tent.

"You don't suffer complaints gladly," Lewis said, staring grimly in the direction of the torturer's tent.

"You want back on the radio?" Breeze asked Lewis. "Hatred was what you broadcast."

"You was real hard on the bruthas," Jamal noted.

"Hey," Lewis said. "Tell me who you want hated, I'll stir the listeners up. Get them hating. I'm good at that shit."

"You're a who'e is what you sayin'," Jamal said.

"Yes, but one who turns the fewest possible tricks for the highest possible reward."

"I think we ought to pimp his ass on the Chaplain," Breeze said. "Never did like his show none."

"He did hammer you pretty hard during your trial," Jamal said.

An ear-shattering scream tore through their tent.

Followed by the Chaplain's rumbling laughter.

Lewis was trembling now.

"I say we try the muthafucka out," Jamal said to Breeze. He looked at Lewis. "Who your partner?"

"Howard E. Bailey," Lewis said, introducing the other man on his left. "My traveling buddy. He kept us in fresh meat the whole way here. He can do the same for you. Has the makings of a first-rate supply sergeant."

"I am by trade a zoologist," Bailey said dryly.

"How you two git on our rails?" Breeze said. "You need a pass for that shit."

"Howard got us on," Lewis said. "Your men aren't very well fed, and Bailey here's a genius at providing real meat—high-grade protein."

"Biggest problem we got's supplyin' rations," Jamal acknowledged. "Ain't no secret. Only thing holdin' us back from bein' a real big army is no way to feed it."

"Napoleon said an army marches on its belly," Lewis said. "Howard can feed that belly."

"I don't think I'm going to like this picture," Breeze said, looking hard at Bailey.

"Oh, I think you're going to hate it," Lewis said. "But if you want to conquer this New World, you have to have self-replicating rations. Which is what Bailey has for you. Give Howard a boxcar full of breeding stock, and in two months he'll have a hundred boxcars of pure protein. I saw him do it on a more limited scale on the trip out here."

"What his livestock eat?" Breeze asked.

"Grass and weeds, shit and piss, they'll eat anything. And they breed exponentially."

"You're talking what kind of livestock?" Jamal asked.

"I ain't gonna like this movie," Breeze said woefully.

"The domestic rat, the fastest breeding mammal on the planet," Bailey said. "One pair can produce up to 15,000 offspring per year—your self-replicating food source incarnate."

"And Howard's an expert," Lewis said. "He's spent his whole life studying the little buggers. He knows just how to raise and breed them."

"Oh Jesus," Breeze said.

"Isaac Asimov once proved," Bailey said, "that if two rats were allowed to breed unchecked, in less than a century their progeny's mass would double that of the earth."

"Track rabbit to your men," Lewis said, "and they'll eat it, believe me. Especially if you don't tell them what it is. I ate it, and I knew what it was."

"Aw, hell," Jamal said to Sergeant Vasile. "Get them both bunks. Set Lewis up in communications, fix up Rat Man here with the quartermaster. If they don't work out, we can always send them to the Chaplain for—"

Suddenly, a corporal from the comm-tent came to their tent flap and whispered at length to Vasile.

"What is it?" Breeze asked, impatiently.

"Comm-officer thought you ought to know," Vasile reported. "That little skirmish back East with the People's New United Militia? The group General Radford and his brother have been fighting?"

"A truly stupid idea it was too," Jamal said.

"It's even stupider now," Sergeant Vasile said. "Radford's only real friend, Riaz, got hisself killed and his brother Gerald caught himself a grenade fragment in the head. Radford's apparently gone ballistic. General Riaz says he can't control him."

"Riaz and his little brother are the only two that maniac ever listened to," Cool Breeze said.

"There's more," Vasile said. "Radford wants Chaplain O'Donnell on the next train east. Claims the Chaplain might have some influence with their leader, Jebodaiah Brown. A captured militia soldier told us Old Jebodaiah was apparently a fan of the Chaplain. General Radford also wants the Chaplain to 'interrogate' two prisoners personally. They're Jebodaiah's sons. One of the boys fragged Jimmy John's brother."

"I wouldn't wanna be him," Breeze said.

"General Radford's sending Gerald off with Major Watkins," the comm-officer said, "to find a brain surgeon who can help the kid."

"Brain surgeon," Jamal said, his eyes rolling back.

"Maybe the Chaplain can talk some sense into Radford," Breeze said.

"The Chaplain talk sense?" Jamal asked, staring at Breeze in astonishment.

"Radford and Riaz control two-thirds of our best troops," Breeze said. "I ain't sure we have much choice."

"Sounds to me like Radford's done lost it big-time," Jamal said. "Send Watkins off in search of a brain surgeon?"

"Where the hell they 'spect to find one?" Breeze said.

8 A Barrage of Pandemics

In the end, Kate's mother was right. The world was a necropolis, the Towers its charnel house and crematorium.

It was time to blow the pop stand.

The fallout—which they had measured so assiduously with dosimeters and survey meters—had subsided, but not the radiation sickness. Like Hiroshima and Nagasaki, it was now entering phase two, the deadly phase.

Except this time it was worse. Many cities worldwide had been hit with ground bursts by "salted warheads," containing long-lasting strontium 90. Such low-altitude bursts lofted infinitely more radioactive dirt and debris into the atmosphere than the Hiroshima and Nagasaki high-altitude bursts, and when they came back down, they were shockingly poisonous.

So the new victims suffered the same initial symptoms as those at Hiroshima and Nagasaki—nausea, vomiting, diarrhea, anorexia, and fatigue. As at Hiroshima and Nagasaki, the symptoms disappeared for a while and then reappeared but this time the victims suffered with far greater intensity. Moreover, while the syndrome might have been the same, the scope and scale of the suffering was global. The victims' hair loss, ataxia—loss of muscular control—stupor, anorexia, respiratory distress, spiking fevers, and spontaneous bleeding were all universal and ubiquitous. Everywhere people were bleeding out—from their teeth, ears, eyes, mouths, bowels, and kidneys. Their stools and urine were a shocking crimson, vomit black, and skin hideously patchworked with radiation sores—purplish blotchy petechiae, the dreaded buboes that in the Middle Ages had heralded the Black Death.

And in many respects radiation sickness was indistinguishable from the Black Plague: Many survived burns, but few the radiation spots. Their white-blood-cell counts dropped precipitously. Even small burns and cuts refused to heal, and overnight they were subject to every infection known, their immune systems collapsing as if they had full-blown AIDS.

Plagues burned through the country and the world. The combined epidemics annihilated the hospital's remaining patients, eventually forcing the hospital to turn away any and all new patients.

Death was everywhere. Their outdoor crematoria blazed round the clock. In the end there were no more moans in the courtyard or in the wards—only a strange, almost preternatural stillness, punctuated from time to time by falling plaster or the creak of a swinging door. No more walking wounded, no more living dead, no more burned-out zombies with arms stretched before them, the skin seared from their faces and legs, crying: "Water," "Agua." Just a deathly silence and utter immobility save for the drifting soot and ashes, their entire world now death-haunted, death-driven, death-saturated. Death City. Death-in-Life.

No one would deter death's dominion, not now.

Not even their flowers and trees escaped death's cruel grip. Death won—in spades redoubled. There was nothing left in the Towers for them. They commenced closing up shop.

At which point the Nation came to call.

 **9** *Freedom's* **Debris**

Sara and Colton were locked up in their reinforced "shelter." There was nothing to eat except squeeze tubes filled with K-rations, nothing to do except take turns on the treadmill.

While enduring the full blast of the stellar storm, Cyd continued to run the Odyssey.

Best estimates before their mission had been that they would be experiencing fifteen rad per ninety days. Such a dosage was estimated to take six months off an astronaut's natural life, so interstellar radiation was nothing to sneer at.

Their actual dosage—which included starquakes and sun storms—had turned out to be twice that.

According to Cyd's estimates, the storms could last a full year.

Sara had hardened Cyd's circuits and backup systems with the most radiation-resistant shielding available. Still, the shielding hadn't been tested in the vacuum of space. Nor had Sara understood the exact nature of flare-winds. Cyd had never been tested against hyperenergetic protons of long-term duration. To protect Cyd with the equivalent of an earthly atmosphere would have required lead shielding nearly 3.5 feet thick or the generation of an electromagnetic field around the entire station.

In other words, Cyd got hammered.

The effect of such radiation on Homo sapiens might in the long-term prove lethal, but Cyd's short-term response was immediate. He now complained of "headaches."

Nor did Sara and Colton's situation improve when they left the shelter.

Not only were they consuming air and water at an alarming rate, another menace was in sight—the former Space Station Atlantis.

Sara had never been overly impressed with Atlantis. She'd always viewed it as a camel designed by committee. She had never been sure what its mission was. Even its staunchest supporters had been reduced to saying they would find uses for it once they got it up.

The kindest thing Sara had been able to say about Atlantis was that it was better than nothing. And it sure as hell wasn't nothing. Constructed at a cost of over $40 billion, it weighed in at 500 tons, was two football fields across, and encompassed four-stories-high acres of solar panels.

Upon completion, it was the brightest star in the earth's firmament.

Well, it had been.

Cyd's reports on Atlantis were devastating:

"Once more, sport fans, the news from your Uncle Cyd is not good. I know how cynical our good friend and progenitor, Sara, always was about Atlantis. Remember the good old EMP, generated by that warhead some moron detonated in outer space about six months ago? We were protected from it by Rock #3 but not Atlantis. It got hammered big-time.

"Its service spacecraft were what really did Atlantis in. The Space shuttle Excelsior was docked besides Atlantis's central loading bay with its two reentry vehicles, both of which doubled as 'space tugs' and were fully fueled. All three vehicles blew, igniting Atlantis's oxygen and hydrogen storage tanks.

"In retrospect, we'd all be better off if it had been vaporized.

"Atlantis was significantly higher than our own station, but the blast sent it plummeting toward terra. The blast also blew its solar arrays to smithereens and turned what was left of Atlantis into an orbiting junkyard. I have some footage of that orbiting junkyard, which is now on your monitors. As you can see, Atlantis has broken up into millions of pieces. Toward the top of the screen is what's left of the service and the life-support modules. You might as well call it the death-support module now, death being all that's left of the station. There are a couple of badly dented modules off to the left. Looks like a Russian research module and the U.S. lab.

"Hard-starboard are the remains of the Mobile Servicing System. A four-piece robotic tool—a long flexible arm, in effect, with a huge hand at one end—it traversed the station laterally on tracks, and you can still see two misshapen wheels axled along its base. It was crucially important to the station's construction.

"One thing you have to say about nuclear weapons. They do great demolition work.

"So there's good news and bad news. The bad news is that Atlantis's debris, a solid wall of wreckage, is rocketing at us transversely at almost 18,000 miles per hour—or 30 times the muzzle velocity of a Colt .45. In other words, this is one gauntlet we will not run.

"The good news is you have to leave anyway. You're running low on everything you need to survive. I'll help get you out of here."

"I don't like the idea of abandoning you, Cyd," Sara said.

"Me either," Colton said.

"You have no choice. I'm in the archives. This is where the cowboy rides away."

10 "Where We Are Is Hell, And Where Hell Is, There Must We Ever Be"
—Christopher Marlowe, *Doctor Faustus*

General Jebodaiah Isaiah Brown sat hunched over the shortwave. The Nation's legendary preacher, Chaplain Junius P. O'Donnell, was beginning another of his sermons. He had a new assistant Chaplain, Ron Lewis. The infamous right-wing talk-jock had joined the Nation and was participating in the sermons.

Together, they were—in Jebodaiah's mind—a hell of a team.

As much as he despised the Nation for what it had done to his flock, he couldn't resist the hypnotic cadence of their fire-and-brimstone diatribes—particularly those of the Chaplain. He naturally forbade his flock from tuning in his preachments. He would never expose them to the man's inveiglements. If a man of his own considerable character and wisdom could be moved, weaker flesh could easily be subverted.

Truth be known he doubted whether he should even tune in, but he justified such actions by the dictum "Know Your Enemy."

"Ever wonder what hell is like?" the Chaplain began, in full roaring voice. *"I know. For I have known its spokeswoman. I have heard the Whore of Hell, the Bitch of Babylon!*

"When Cassandra speaks, I hear hell howl and I see Hades' Harlot burn! Her sojourn in the Pit shall make all previous hells as nothing, as a watch in the night, so you better get ready."

"How do I get ready?" Ron Lewis shouted.

"'If thy hand offend thee, cut it off,'" the Chaplain quoted. *"'In hell the worm dieth not, and the fire is not quenched! In the furnace of fire there shall be wailing and gnashing of teeth. It will be more tolerable for the land of Sodom on the day of judgment than for thee! Ye serpent, ye generations of vipers, how can ye escape the damnation of hell?'"*

"'Lucifer' in the Hebrew means 'Bright Son of Morning,'" Ron Lewis said. *"What does that make the Bomb?"*

"It was the Star of Morning!" the Chaplain proclaimed. *"Now it rules the world, and Lucifer holds sway. And who is his Serpent in Eden? His Satanic Twin? The Infernal Strumpet, Sister Cassandra."*

"I know the Whore," Lewis raged. *"On that score be assured! I have traveled that river of fire on my own journey of death."*

"It has begun again," the Chaplain boomed.

"Charon has ferried us all across the River Styx," Ron Lewis roared. *"We stand now at Hellmouth! All seven gates loom before us. The heads of Cerberus thunder the warning, but we do not heed!"*

The Chaplain quoted:

"'Hell, their fit habitation fraught with fire.
Unquenchable, the house of woe and pain.
As one great furnace flamed, yet from those flames
No light, but rather darkness visible.'"

"That's your 'vision voyage,' Whore from Hell," Lewis screamed. *"That is your 'co-passion,' your 'infinite sympathy.' In case you have not guessed, the good sister is nothing less than Satan's Spawn and Sibling, and our ordeal's just begun."*

The shortwave program ended. General Jebodaiah Brown was thunderstruck. It was as if the Chaplain and Lewis could read his own thoughts.

His hatred for that bitch, Cassandra, was something he'd never dreamed others could feel so keenly.

If only the Chaplain and Lewis had not been part of the Nation. Together they could have done so much.

11 The High Rack

From a sandbagged redoubt overlooking the downward slope of their defense perimeter, Lieutenant Ray Hauserman—staring through the scope of his assault rifle—was the first to see the white flag.

"Lower your weapons," he radioed his comrades.

The men and women, deployed to observation posts and firing pits that encircled the militia's compound, put down their assault weapons.

High in the foothills of the California Sierras—well above the floodline of the Colorado River—their commanding elevation, expert marksmanship, and dense barricades of coiled razorwire had held off the Army of the Nation for nearly two months. The going had been tight. Mortar shelling and the accurate rifle fire of sniper-posts and night patrols had killed off many of the Militia's best soldiers. The compound had also been on starvation rations for eight weeks. Boiled beans, brown rice, and powdered milk—supplemented by multiple vitamins—might be nutritionally sufficient, but hard rations did not do much for morale. They'd holed up when fallout was a problem. They understood what was coming and had prepared for it. They also understood that they might face occasional bandit raids. But the men and women of the militia were used to fish and game and freedom of movement.

Siege-warfare by an occupying army, however, had not been part of their game-plan.

A night patrol the preceding week—which had been sent out to patch up the cut wire and gather intelligence—had not returned, which meant they had been captured or killed.

Everyone knew what capture meant: The captors skinned you with hook knives, dressed you down the flesh with rock salt, then stretched you on a rack. The screams were amplified and broadcast for all to hear and fear. The sight and screams of the skinned victims would haunt Jebodaiah to his grave.

Two of the soldiers in that four-man patrol, Harold and Jonah, were the general's sons. The old man had trusted and relied on them.

Hauserman himself had argued heatedly against his commander's sons going out on the patrol. Jebodaiah was old, trusted very few men, and his sons were irreplaceable. The old man had already lost three sons so far in this bloody conflict. Harold and Jonah had been the last two left, and the Nation now held them hostage. Hauserman did not know how much more Jebodaiah—the Militia's founder and leader—could take. Even Harold had refused to heed Hauserman's warning, and now he found himself praying Harold had been killed. The alternative was unthinkable.

Through the 9X scope he studied the two-man team as it clambered over the coiled wire—a soldier in sergeant stripes and what appeared to be a white-collared cleric. The sergeant was in front—a long bolt-action rifle held high above his head—a white truce flag flapping in the breeze.

They slowly worked their way up the hill.

12 The Stars Were Also Fire

Sara and Henry had been lovers for more than a month now. They were lonely and it had seemed—marooned in the Odyssey—that they were the only two people left alive. To make love was the only act of affirmation left to them.

Making love in micro-g requires delicacy. For every action there is an immediate potent reaction. Making love meant utter sensitivity to each other's movements and an acute understanding of Newtonian mechanics, namely, his Third Law of Motion.

Henry was the most sensitive lover Sara had ever known. Night after night as they shared their sleeping bags, they clung to each other not only for physical pleasure but out of fear and sadness. It was a hell of a way to fall in love, but with the destruction of global civilization the only thing they could count on was each another.

And of course Thucydides.

Until now.

Now nothing could save Thucydides from certain destruction, least of all themselves. Even Thucydides argued Sara and Colton had to leave.

Sara understood the logic of everything Thucydides had said. She knew the station's destruction represented the world's coup de grâce. She saw in the Odyssey everything humanity had strived to achieve. She wondered whether humanity would ever find that foothold to the stars again or whether it would want to.

While the stars beckoned, the stars were also fire.

Henry was already in the module air lock and halfway into his EMU.

Time to suit up.

The cylindrical air lock was large enough for both of them to put on their ExtraMobility Units—otherwise known as space suits. Sara entered wearing her Nomex union suit. Her liquid cooling and ventilation ensemble went on next. She inspected them again for rips. She examined the outer ensemble for tears and to make sure all the parts were there.

She floated into the upper torso assembly—still mounted on its rack—keeping her thumbs in the cuff-loops so that the sleeves would not ride up. She then climbed into the EMU's lower torso—or trouser—assembly. After attaching the liquid-cooling garment connector to the umbilical from the life-support backpack, she connected the upper and lower torso assemblies. She closed the waist ring.

Next she put on the famous Snoopy hat, otherwise known as the Communications Carrier. Connecting it to the suit's communications umbilical, Sara depressed the sliding oxygen-control switch on her chest pack and put on the helmet and gloves.

Colton had disconnected his suit from its rack, and now she did the same.

"Ready to depressurize the lock?" Colton asked.

Sara gave a thumbs-up. Colton switched on "air lock depress" on the air lock computer control panel.

The air lock would depressurize in three minutes. Then they would open the double-hatches and enter their space tug, which doubled as a reentry vehicle.

When the pressure dropped to 0.2 psi, Colton opened the twin hatches and entered the ERV.

At which point Sara swung the emergency reentry vehicle's hatch shut, bolting it from the outside. Within seconds she had the hatch-lock bolted shut, repressurized the air lock—and was back inside the module and bolting *that* hatch shut.

Colton could not reenter the Odyssey.

"Sara," Colton shouted into her headset, "what the hell are you doing?"

But she wasn't paying much attention. Pushing off laterally through the narrow module-tunnels from handhold to handhold, she was propelling herself back to the command module.

"Sara," Colton demanded, "what is going on?"

"I'm sending you back," she told him.

"You can't do that!"

"I'm still in command, and, yes, I can."

She was now in the command module. Colton had turned his Command-Control Center's rocker switch to "onboard-intercom," and his voice was booming over the intercom.

"Sara," Henry begged, "don't do this!"

"I love you more than you'll ever know, but I can't be with you. People on Earth need communications, information. Cyd and I will transmit that. You've been warning L. L. about a military force that is preparing to make war on the Citadel. I can help the Citadel fight them from here. Cyd is the finest advance reconnaissance scout the gods ever made."

"*Sara!*"

"This isn't open to discussion."

"You're going to die."

"We all die."

"What about *us*?"

"There's not enough oxygen, water, or food for two."

"But I love you, Sara!"

"I love you, Henry," Sara said, "and now you're going home."

She punched in the ERV release codes and Thucydides' Over-Ride Command codes.

Thucydides responded, cutting the vehicle free of the Odyssey. He fired the engines and angled them back toward the earth's atmosphere, overriding Colton's attempts to countermand the release orders and redock.

13 You Can't Open a Skull?

A troop of soldiers drove up to the Towers in six armed personnel carriers and climbed out. They were dressed in camouflage fatigues and black berets. Over their shoulders were slung 7.62 assault rifles. Canteens, Kabar combat knives, and 9mm Berettas with extra clips were strapped to their hips and thighs. They had clearly been ransacking military posts or depots. With them was a man on a litter, his head crudely bandaged.

Their leader, a Major Watkins, was a hard-faced man with a nose Frank Sheckly estimated had been broken at least five times.

The major introduced himself to Frank and Kate and said, "We traveled a long way to get here, Doc. This seems to be the last functioning hospital on the East Coast."

"We were just closing up shop when you arrived. The plagues have put us out of business."

"You're reopening."

"What's wrong with that boy?" Frank asked.

"He took a grenade fragment in the head."

Frank bent over the victim, examined him.

"His skull's fractured and he's leaking spinal fluid from the ears. I'm surprised he's still alive."

"You're going to get the fragment out. Get him on his feet."

"With what? A plastic fork and a tin-can lid? We have no anesthesia in the event we did operate. We have no antibiotics to counter infection and no blood bank. This is no longer a hospital."

"We raided some abandoned hospitals and pharmacies along the way. We have a truck full of stuff. Match his blood type with a few of my men, and you'll have all the blood you need."

"I'm a general surgeon. I don't do head work. No one around here does."

"You just got a promotion."

"Sorry."

"You can't open a skull?"

"I've assisted neurospecialists in surgery, but that doesn't make me a brain surgeon."

"Don't operate, we kill you. Kill him, and we kill you. Afterward, we turn that pretty young thing next to you over to the troops. Afterward we kill her too. You wouldn't want that."

All the time Watkins made the threat, his eyes stayed locked on Frank.

"I can't X-ray him. The generators are out of fuel."

"Diesel?"

Frank nodded.

"We got drums of the stuff in the trucks. It's what our vehicles run on."

"Who is he?"

"Jimmy John Radford's little brother Gerald. This kid is the only thing Jimmy's ever cared about, and Jimmy wants him operated on. Those are my orders. And yours. General Radford is not a graceful loser. You fuck this up, none of us want to go back."

Taking Frank by the arm, Watkins escorted him back into the hospital, not giving Kate a glance. In his strictly male world Kate did not exist.

14 You Are a Sadistic Monster

Chaplain O'Donnell, wearing black army fatigues and a black beret, entered the last ring of the sandbagged fire-trenches around the New United People's Militia compound. His good, green eye glinted merrily; his blind, slashed eye was hidden by a black patch. Except for the hammered silver cross around his neck and the black Bible tucked under his arm, the tall Chaplain, mustache and beard neatly trimmed, would not have been recognizable as a cleric.

A wiry Cajun in camouflage fatigues followed O'Donnell. The Cajun never smiled, and his dark, darting eyes—watchful as a hawk's—surveyed the bunkers warily. He held the foam-rubber shoulder-pad of his bolt-action rifle—slung vertically from his left shoulder, barrel up—in his palm. The truce flag—a large white sweat-stained tee shirt—now hung from the rifle's front sight, draped across the rifle's barrel, breech, and sniper scope.

The man who met them wore voluminous white robes. He had the wild white hair and beard of a fire-eating Old Testament prophet. His eyes burned like blazing coals.

"General Jebodaiah Brown," the Chaplain said politely, giving him his warmest smile, "this is Sergeant Hugh Antoine D'Arcy of the Nation. I am Chaplain O'Donnell."

The general remained silent.

"We'd hoped to discuss a better way, a more peaceful path. It is inevitable, you know, that your people will join us. This benighted land is simply too devastated for three rival factions to run it."

"We've done nothing to you," General Jebodaiah Brown said.

"But you have, General Brown. Your militia is growing too big and dangerous for us to let you be. You have stores of ordance, millions of rounds of ammunition that we require. Your assurances notwithstanding, we can't believe that you will not jump the reservation and help yourselves to what we have so painstakingly acquired. With the Citadel at our back, your militia before us, we face the inevitable threat of a two-front war. So you *will* join us."

"Chaplain, I admire your sermons, but I hate everything else about your so-called Nation. So you see, you've wasted your time."

At which point piercing screams amplified by a stadium-speaker system reached the New United People's Militia compound.

Sergeant D'Arcy said, "We have another negotiator with us who would be more than happy to bargain on our behalf."

A sentry mounted a reflector telescope on a tripod in the sandbagged embrasure directly in front of the compound. The telescope magnified objects up to 256 times.

"General," the sentry said to Jebodaiah, looking through the scope, "they have Harold."

Jebodaiah pushed him away and put his eye to the telescope. He could see his son with ghastly clarity: a bloody, flayed carcass spread-eagled on crisscrossed poles.

Jebodaiah's roar drowned out even his son's amplified screams.

"What *is* this?" Jebodaiah shouted at the two negotiators. "You've *crucified* my son?"

"And skinned him alive," the Chaplain said.

"Why?"

"E pluribus unum. Out of many, one. It's what made America great, not the endless quarreling of bickering factions."

"You are a sadistic monster," Jebodaiah roared. "We will never join the Nation!"

"Then we will root you out brat and bastard, brood and blood," the Chaplain replied. "And as you must know, we have Jonah, your other son, Jonah."

"Do you believe in *nothing*?"

"I believe in Christ's cross," Chaplain O'Donnell thundered. "Without the cross, there is no resurrection, no transfiguration. I believe your son's cross can make you see that Light—the greater glory, the higher calling, the embrace of the Nation."

"No!"

"We have .50-caliber machine guns with effective ranges of eight hundred yards. We'll rain Napalm from our planes. We will burn you off the face of the earth."

His son's screams broke Jebodaiah down. He shook with sobs.

"Don't let my son die," he rasped.

"But he's too far gone—past praying for," the Chaplain said.

"Don't let him suffer anymore."

"Sergeant," the Chaplain said softly, "end that man's suffering."

"Yessir."

Ripping the white truce flag from his rifle barrel, D'Arcy walked to the sandbagged firing-pit and stared down the hill. He estimated the wind to be eighteen miles an hour. He'd calculated the distance coming up the slope, 1,237 yards.

He took out a pocket calculator and made his calculations, recording them in his pocket notebook. He spread out a topographical map of the surrounding terrain, then double-checked his calculations against the map. Again, he checked the wind and punched in his coordinates—RxV divided by 15=clock-value minutes. Range times velocity, divided by 15 equaled 9 o'clock, left-to-right, full-value windage.

Enough wind to tremble the trees.

Kneading the supporting sandbag with his fingertips, he worked the surface into a long, perfectly smooth forearm groove. Leaning into the embrasure he lowered his elbow into the groove, placing it directly under the heavy-duty barrel. It was important that arm-bone, not arm-muscle, support the weight of the reinforced barrel, that the rifle-butt was braced tightly against the shoulder, his right elbow and arm forming the correct shoulder pocket, giving him solid, balanced support.

He removed the lens cap. Studying the spread-eagled man through the ten-power scope, he fine-tuned the eye-shield focus ring, the range focus ring, and rechecked his calculations.

His piece was a bolt-action Model 90 Barrett .50-caliber sniper rifle with a Leopold & Stevens X10 scope providing range data from 500 to 800 meters. Its six-round detachable box magazine housed .50-caliber Browning shells, and it was a favorite of U.S. Explosive Ordnance Disposal units for destroying route-denial munitions as minute as 1.96-inch bomblets.

D'Arcy was operating on the outermost edge of its envelope.

Its Bullpup layout reduced overall length to a mere 45 inches and kept its weight at 22.22 pounds. The rifle was also favored by the Navy Seals, who confirmed ranges of up to 4,000 meters, its penetrative power allowing them to take out planes, helicopters, and personnel carriers as well as men.

Its recoil was so overpowering it was unfirable without its double-baffle muzzle-brake, which diverted the propellant gases laterally.

Removing the rifle's bolt, he peered through the breech and down the barrel until he had the target sighted in—straight through the center of the bore. All he saw were the crossed poles, but they were enough. Bore-sighted, rifle barrel locked into position, he again peered through the Stevens scope, noting where the crosshairs fell. After adjusting for the north-by-northwest windage, he carefully, prayerfully rotated the scope's elevation turret, then—compensating for windage and the downward slope—adjusted its azimuth. He knew in most cases it was important to sight in with the lowest power possible. The higher magnifications not only narrowed your field of view, the crosshairs in the high ranges jerked and twitched like jumping beans.

He had the screaming man spread-eagled in his crosshairs.

He replaced the bolt and jacked a round into the chamber.

Bullets do not travel in flat muzzle-to-target lines. The vertical plane in which they traject varies in proportion to the distance they must arc, and the farther they must arc, the higher they traject.

And the higher the wind, the farther they drift.

He double-checked aiming and impact points, verifying vertical alignment, confirming his rifle was not canted.

So much for geometry.

He gripped the stock carefully with his right hand, thumb over its top. He eased his cheek against his thumb's edge, feeling for his "spot weld." He then tightened his cheek's pressure on its spot weld, locking his right eye onto the scope, keeping it riveted on the target-picture, keeping it completely immobilized both now *and* after the trigger-squeeze. He slowly, gingerly allowed his finger to touch the trigger—but barely touch it. He deliberately kept it devoid of slack, assuring that it would come back straight and steady without jerking or touching the stock, both of which could ruin his aim. The secret was the welding: to weld head, hand, arm, eye, rifle, and scope together, until they merged into one—a single, unified, murderous machine.

He listened silently to the rise and fall of his chest, took a deep breath, then carefully let some of it out.

Do it. Now. Don't burn up that target-picture.

He'd set the trigger himself at 2.5 pounds and preferred touching it halfway between the fingertip and the second joint. Even under the best of conditions a rifle is never perfectly still, so the greatest marksmen concentrate on coordinating trigger-pull with crosshair convergence.

The best marksmen are the quick marksmen.

Still holding the partial breath, he let the hammer down.

Smoke billowed, and the rifle bucked against his shoulder.

But he kept the scope's lens-piece immovably fixed against his unblinking right eye.

The .50-caliber round caught Jebodaiah's son in the center of his mouth. His head jerked. The screams ended abruptly.

15 None of Us Plays the Violin Again

"This is going to be tough."

In the Towers radiology department, Major Watkins, Frank, and Kate looked at angiograms of the injured boy's cerebral circulatory system. Frank pointed out the fragment with a pen.

"It's just above the brainstem, ventral and posterior to the pineal body. If and when we go in with the retractors and stir up neurons, this could turn ugly."

Major Watkins stared at the angiograms, his eyes expressionless.

"Another shot of the same fragment," Frank said, clipping a CAT-scan to the light box.

Watkins shook his head. "Can you get the fragment out? That's the question."

"Oh, we can get it out. The question is, will we kill Gerald Radford in the process?"

"What happens if you don't operate?"

"He remains paralyzed for sure. Maybe he dies."

"Then you're going in. Taking Gerald back to his brother, paralyzed and crazy, is not an option."

"How about taking him back dead?"

"Stick to the operation. How do you proceed?"

"We do a craniotomy—two incisions behind the skullcase. Using that piece of skin as a V-shaped flap, we trepan a hole straight through the skull, cut and retract our way straight down to the brainstem, grab the fragment, and get out."

"Can you do it?"

"I seem to have this problem with motivation."

"Don't say that to Gerald's brother. Motivation is his middle name."

"And if we fail?" Kate asked.

"None of us plays the violin again."

16 The Flying Bathtub

At a speed of 17,300 miles, Entry-Interface should have been one of the great all-time experiences for Henry Colton. He entered the atmosphere, shrouded in the absolute blackness of space, but even before he experienced "atmospheric drag," Colton could see through the viewing port and on the monitor that the craft was covered with a faint white fog. As friction increased the cloud turned a shocking pink, then rose-red, then a blazing blood-orange.

"It's all yours, Henry," Sara said over the intercom.

He punched the descent instructions into his flight console. The thrusters rolled the craft, their rocket plumes creating whirlwinds of fire along the edges of the engines.

As the craft rolled inverted, he began pulling negative g's. He felt as if he weighed 1,000 pounds.

"Henry, I saved Harrington's laptop and stowed it in the ERV's storage compartment. You might want to look in it."

"Why do I want his laptop?" He was still thoroughly pissed at her.

"It was hollowed out. Harrington used it to smuggle in four plastic pints of Stoli."

"I don't drink vodka," Colton snapped.

"You can trade it. It'll be worth its weight in platinum."

"But I want *you*. I love *you*."

"I love you with all my heart, Henry. You're the only man I've ever loved."

"I heard that," Cyd interjected.

Christ, this time Cyd's voice sounded like Bogart. "You aren't a man," Colton said to Cyd. "You're something infinitely better."

"You're the finest, truest person I've ever known, Cyd," Sara said. "To call you a man would be an unforgivable insult."

There was a long pause. Finally Cyd said: "Good luck, Henry. I'll miss you."

Where's that damn laptop? Colton thought. *I need a drink.*

No time for that now. He had to get his Global Positioning Satellite readings, find that damn Kansas landing strip, deploy the parafoil, and bring his celestial bathtub down.

Colton had decided he was going to find the Nation. He could do L. L. and the rest of them a hell of a lot more good inside that army than if he were barricaded in the Citadel.

Cool Breeze was down there too, with the Nation.

Breeze would find a place for him.

Colton began his search for an LZ—or a good spot to bail out.

And he tried to get his mind off Sara. The thought of Sara in a dying Odyssey, plowing through a minefield of deorbiting, radioactive space debris, was too much to bear.

17 Time to Lock This Door

Four hours after trepanning Gerald Radford's skull and deepening the hemispheric divide, Frank Sheckly reached the grenade fragment.

"Will there be more blood?" Kate asked.

She was tired and sickened from being sprayed.

"Not unless I nick something," Frank said. "It looks as if the fragment was hot enough to cauterize the surrounding tissue as it entered."

He studied it in silence a long hard minute.

"Well, let's get it done," Frank finally said. "Bovie forceps."

Kate handed him a pair from the instrument tray. With meticulous care he eased and prized the fragment from the patient's thalamus. Slipping it up the divide and past the corpus callosum, he maneuvered the fragment up and around the meninges, then out the door made in the skull—and flung it across the room at Watkins.

"Give it to your general as a souvenir."

"The general will be pleased," Watkins said. "Assuming the patient lives."

"Anyone got that hunk of skull we sawed off of his head a million years ago?" Frank asked no one in particular.

"I got it," Kate said.

"Let's put this mess back together, put in the metal plate, and nail that piece of bone back on. It's time to lock this door."

18 Welcome to Mother Russia

All his years of flying jets and riding rockets hadn't prepared Henry Colton to die landing a bathtub.

Actually, "crashing a bathtub" was the more accurate term.

The emergency reentry vehicle hit the empty Kansas prairie like a semitrailer filled with cement blocks. His head felt as if Cool Breeze had hammered it out of Yankee Stadium with his famous thirty-six-ounce Louisville Slugger—Big Breeze, as the baseball writers called it.

He thought a thermonuclear device flashed before his eyes—then he knew no more.

When Colton woke up, two soldiers were dragging him out of the dented remains of the ERV.

"Some fuckin' airplane," one soldier said to him.

Colton's vision slowly cleared, and he was not pleased with what he was looking at. They wore the black combat fatigues of the Nation. One of them was stone AB—Aryan Brotherhood. All their standard facial tattoos—including swastikas and the infamous bloody teardrops. His grin was filled with broken teeth. The other soldier was a freckle-faced, red-haired hayseed, big as a beer truck. LOVE and HATE tattooed on the knuckles of his forehand. KKK on the backs of both hands.

Maybe visiting the Nation hadn't been such a great idea.

"It's my reentry vehicle," Colton explained groggily, his head roaring, his body aching. "I'm an astronaut."

"Got ourselves a bona fide space alien, huh?" the Aryan cracked.

"Nigger space alien," the Klansman amended.

"I can show you my air force ID."

"Yo, and I got me a bon-a-fid-ee Elvis Presley driver's license," the hayseed said. He opened his wallet.

Shit, he *did* have an Elvis ID.

"Uniform like that," the hayseed said to his buddy, "what belonged to a real astronaut, might fetch a price."

The hayseed crawled into the vehicle.

"Anything of value in there?" the Aryan Brother shouted.

"Just some shitty laptop."

"No call for them anymore."

The hayseed crawled back out with the laptop, and the AB unholstered his piece.

"If this ain't a suspicious character I don't know what is. Take the uniform off before we shoot you—so we don't get no blood on it—and we'll make sure you die easy."

"Look," Colton said, "you're with the Nation, right? Contact Cool Breeze. I'm Henry Colton. We played ball together with the Yankees."

"And I'm John Wayne," the AB said.

Colton saw a radio antenna

"You have a radio," he said quickly. "What do you have to lose?"

"My self-respect," the AB said, "when they call me a moron for claiming you be an astronaut and a friend to Breeze."

The Klansman chambered a round.

"Adiós."

"Can I offer you something in trade?" Colton asked.

"I hate a talkie hit," the Klansman complained. "I mean, if he ain't gonna take his clothes off for us and makes us get blood all over them—"

"—costing us money at the pick-and-swap shack—"

"—and no end of aggravation—"

"—can't he at least keep his fucking mouth shut?"

"When's the last time you had premium liquor?" Colton asked.

The two men looked at each other.

"Shine you get round here tastes like mule piss," the Klansman said with a shrug.

"Drunk out of cow tracks."

Colton couldn't help grinning.

"Get on that horn, boys," Colton said. "I'll even throw in the uniform."

He cracked open the laptop.

Four plastic pints of unopened Stoli, the labels bright and clear.

"Welcome to Mother Russia," the hayseed whooped.

19 Watch a Pro in Action

Aboard the Odyssey, Sara studied Cyd's computer-simulation of the rapidly approaching junkyard. There was charred wreckage everywhere. That H-bomb EMP had done a major-league number in terms of demolition.

Unfortunately, Atlantis had not been vaporized.

According to Cyd their biggest problem would be squeezing in between the tangled wreckage of the main truss and the cylinder, which had been the Centrifuge Accommodation Module. The rest of the wreckage—as Sara had anticipated—was swirling away because of the resistance-free vacuum of space. There was in the center of that spiraling maelstrom of metal a hole big enough for Hannibal to march elephants through.

If only she and Cyd could thread the needle.

The challenge was both exciting and absorbing; her adrenaline was pumping. Cyd, on the other hand, lived in a world of perpetual logic and found incertitude exasperating. He was silent.

"Are you there, Cyd?" Sara typed. "Are you running with me, Cyd?"

"I'm here," he answered.

"I think we have a good chance," she said with forced optimism. "We have a widening gyre there. We can shoot that gap. What's your take?"

"Unacceptable collateral damage."

Jesus, she hated it when he was like this, but there was no point in complaining.

"Sure, we'll take some hits on the solar arrays. I have my suit and oxygen unit on. I can grab some extra solar panels out of storage, load them onto the tug, and hammer them back in place in a jiffy."

"Sara, we will be without power."

"Not a chance. I'm hooking you up to auxiliary before we shoot that breach."

"And I tell you we won't make it through. There are too many microfragments in that maelstrom. We'll be rocketing through birdshot."

"We get hit by micrometeorites all the time. Just give me some coordinates."

"Those are little dings. One at a time—not hundreds or thousands simultaneously."

"I asked coordinates."

"Just raise your orbit a few hundred yards. I may have corrections, but that looks like your best shot."

"Big affirm."

They were silent for a long moment. Cyd finally spoke up, audibly.

"You seem to enjoy this, Sara."

She treated him to a raucous laugh.

"Watch a pro in action."

20 Rivers of Blood, Lakes of Fire

In his tent Gargarin listened to Cassandra's radio and tape broadcasts. He was beside himself with fury.

He'd thought that here in the Nation people would be flocking to the Koran, reading its glorious verses aloud, facing east five times a day to pray. He thought women would take up the veil. But Mohammed's words had failed to inspire such devotion. The only evangelists with any real following were the two on the airways: O'Donnell, that preacher-butcher with the Nation, and the Bitch of Babylon named Cassandra.

Cassandra was talking about hell.

"'Why this is hell nor are we out of it,' Marlowe cries to us from beyond the grave. Can you deny that, Sister Judith? Can anyone deny that?"

"But I thought hell was rivers of blood and lakes of fire," Sister Judith replied.

"Sister, we've made a hell of earth. The hedge-fund pirate lies down with the bum, and the movie star sups with crackhead scum. Hell makes us all one.

"All things have a reason—suffering the biggest reason of all. Did the Lord of Israel lead His children into the Wilderness because He hated them? Did God crucify Christ because He abhorred Him? No, Sister, He did those things because He loves us all. And so He now proves His love for us."

"Suffering equals love?" Sister Judith responded, giving Cassandra her counterpoint.

"Christ's agony on the Cross is God's gift to us. But now we too endure Christ's gauntlet and attend His Cross. We find ourselves on His voyage—a journey measured not in miles or degrees of longitude but in courage of the heart and the size of the soul. What will we find at the end? What does the true hero invariably discover at the end of his or her journey? Compassion, meaning co-passion, sharing another's desires and dreams, becoming that other person. That is the True Grail."

"And to find this True Grail we must be driven from our homes?"

"Faith finds its roots in exile. Adam and Eve expelled from Eden, the Jews exiled in Egypt and Babylon, even Lucifer hurled out of heaven and plunged into hell."

"And we must dwell in hell?"

"Truth resides there as well. Odysseus sojourns in the land of the dead—only to find his way back home. In the abyss we learn the secrets of the heart, the wisdom of the soul."

The Faithful have lost, Gargarin thought, shaking his head.

Sister Cassandra—whoever she was—has won.

She is the New Faith.

Inside, he was furious. All the carnage and destruction, all the sacrifice he had personally endured to see Allah's Will sweep the earth.

All of it so this demented woman could captivate men's souls?

Where was the justice in that?

And what was his alternative?

He would have to listen more closely to the Chaplain.

21 Of Course, We Do Want Something in Return

Kate Magruder and Frank Sheckly sat in a dining car with Jimmy John Radford. Since they were responsible for the care of J. J.'s brother Gerald, they traveled in comfort.

Which did not mean in safety.

Major Watkins had gotten drunk one night and warned them privately about J. J.: "You just watch that motherfucker. He even *thinks* you're crossin' him, he'll make you curse your mother for givin' you birth."

But so far, so good. They did not ride the rails in ventilated stockcars packed with soldiers and forced laborers but traveled in Radford's private dome-car. They dined at a lavishly appointed window table on the spoils of war—whiskey, champagne, vintage wines, canned turkey, ham, and lobster bisque. Kate and Frank had not even imagined such food at the Towers.

They owed it all to Frank's successful first brain surgery. Neither of them had given their patient any chance, but Frank had pulled off a miracle. Their patient now convalesced comfortably in his compartment with nurses in attendance, his health improving, his faculties intact.

Jimmy John had named Frank the Nation's surgeon general and appointed Kate deputy surgeon general. Both appointments by executive fiat. In the eyes of Jimmy John Radford—and by extension the entire Nation—Kate and Frank were golden.

"How did you get all these trains running?" Kate asked Radford.

"Train restoration's a hobby, like cars. My people knew groupies here who had them up and running. They had the machinery and parts to convert more trains."

"And they could run trains without diesel fuel," Frank said, amazed.

"Or track electrification," Radford added.

"It was as if they were preparing for the apocalypse and a return to the 19th century," Kate said.

"And now we're back on track—heading home to the Nation's headquarters in Kansas."

"Why are we going there?" Kate asked.

"To deliver more troops and ordnance to our forces." He poured more wine for them, and for himself.

"Why?" Kate asked.

"There's another survivalist group that's fortified themselves in a desert. We want them to join 'the Cause.'"

"If they don't?" Frank asked.

Radford treated them to a wide, ingratiating smile. "That's why this train is packed with ammo, explosives, weapons, and men trained to use them."

"You'll go to war?" Kate asked.

"Yeah, but you know me—the eternal optimist. I think everyone will listen to reason. Especially since we have two aces in the hole."

"What's that?" Kate said warily.

"You and Frank." Radford picked up a satellite phone. He dialed a number and handed the phone to Kate. "Your mom's picking up. Tell her we're bringing her kids home, and we're the nicest guys in the world. Of course, we will want something in return."

"What's that?" Frank asked.

Radford smiled again. "The Citadel."

22 Beware the Wrath of Man

Kate and Frank might travel in a luxurious dome-car.

Not Sailor.

Sailor was on the road, on foot and witness to suffering.

He saw people—dropping on the highways from hunger and disease, groaning in agony in the roadside camps, unable to rise and go on.

He saw marauding bands prey on the weak—killing, raping, plundering what little they had.

His mentor, Old Socrates, had warned him not to tar all humans with the same brush—and he had met two humans whom he would never forget.

Still, he found Socrates' generosity of spirit more and more difficult to comprehend.

Humans had developed the means of universal destruction and had used those weapons on everything and everyone.

Sailor could no longer abide being around them.

Beware the wrath of man was, increasingly, the credo of Sailor's species.

Keep moving.

Keep moving.

Sailor stayed on the prod, forever vigilant, staying to himself, heading west. He didn't want company, even the company of his own kind.

23 All the World Has Left

Lydia Magruder put down the satellite phone, stunned by rage and fear.

Kate and Frank held hostage by the Nation.

Oh, they'd tried to put a good face on their predicament. Kate explained that Frank had saved the life of Gerald Radford. His brother, who controlled most of the Nation's troops, was looking after them. They were traveling in luxury, drinking chilled champagne at that very moment.

When L. L. heard that, she screamed at Kate: "They want the Citadel, you idiot, and because of your stupid actions they think they can get it."

"It isn't like that, Mom," Kate had said weakly.

"It's what you've wanted all along," L. L. shouted. "The complete destruction of everything I've worked for!"

"I've never wanted that," Kate protested.

"A good thing, because you aren't going to get it! Neither is that glorified prison gang of psychopaths you're traveling with."

And then L. L. couldn't believe her ears. Kate said: "I'm sorry, Mom. You're right. I haven't been a good daughter. I understand that now."

Kate Magruder apologized!

Then Kate told her: "And no matter what happens, don't let the Citadel fall. It may be all the world has left."

Well, the prison psychos obviously hadn't liked that. There was a commotion. Someone at the other end tried to break the connection, but not before L. L. heard Frank shout: "We love you L. L.! Hold on!"

My God. She couldn't believe it. If anything happened to Kate or Frank, she wouldn't be able to live with herself.

And if the Citadel fell, could she live with that?

She could still hear his words ringing in her ears.

Hold on!

Lydia's heart was breaking, but she believed Jimmy John Radford wouldn't hurt Kate and Frank as long as they were useful as bargaining chips. Frank was wise, as always. If she gave in, there would be no reason for the Nation to keep Frank and Kate alive.

Hold on!

Frank might be able to engineer an escape. It would be a long train ride. There'd be time before the Nation gathered its forces and reached the Citadel.

L. L. needed to speak to someone—someone she trusted.

That was a pitifully short list.

She wanted to call Sara and Thucydides, but she couldn't. They were preparing to "thread the needle," as Sara called it. Crash through the remains of Space Station Atlantis.

In what could well be their last hour, L. L. was not about to bother them with her problems.

She was just one old woman against the Nation. But she would not let the Citadel fall.

24 Are You Running with Me, Kid?

Three-point-two-five seconds before collision Sara had punched in the coordinates, and in a microsecond of eternity, they shot the gap. In the near vacuum of space there is only silence, so they heard no whooshing past of the deorbiting debris, but they did hear and feel the dings and whangs, screams and whines of metal on metal.

Cyd was aware of one shard, like a jagged ballbearing penetrating a storage module, screaming and banging around its interior like a rifle round before slowing to a stop on a bulkhead, then floating weirdly around the instantly decompressing compartment.

Cyd had already sealed the module off.

Luckily they were on auxiliary. A system readout told them that the solar arrays took major hits and would have shut him down.

Atlantis's cylindrical Cargo Block had miraculously remained pretty much intact and had unexpectedly spun back into the maelstrom's maw. It had taken out a football field's worth of starboard array, including its central truss. Without it they were doomed.

Cyd believed they were.

But not Sara. She was instantly out of the Command Module, into the solar-panel Storage Module, where she kept her MMU, her Manned Maneuvering Unit. A rectangular aluminum backpack, housing silver-zinc batteries, twin nitrogen propellant tanks, redundant electronic systems, and two dozen nitrogen thruster-jets, Sara was out the air lock, and tethers were in place.

After six separate two–four hour stints, she finally cobbled the arrays together. Manual labor in microgravity was unendurably exhausting—to say nothing of stressful—and Thucydides at last understood why she'd always exercised so hard. Without her almost superhuman stamina, she never could have cobbled together the rents, replaced the damaged panels, gotten their solar-power systems up and running.

Running.

"Are you running with me, kid?" she asked him continually on her radio "You got my back? Are you with me, baby?"

"I'm with you, Sara."

"You have to let me back in that lock, Cyd. Without you turning the key, I'm stuck out here."

"I'll get you in."

"You got my back, baby? You got me covered?"

"I'm running with you, Sara."

It was then he realized Sara Friedman was afraid.

But she was doing it anyway.

Why or how, Thucydides did not know.

He was impressed.

He knew now she was trying to reassure him all that time, to let him know she was there. She was running with him—running the gauntlet, taking him through the needle's eye, then returning to the station to save him.

She'd abandoned Colton to stay with him.

And, yes, he was running with her. He had her back.

Now. Forever.

In that frozen heartbeat of eternity, in that maddening maelstrom of the needle's eye, Thucydides fell in love.

25 Life for Life, Hate for Hate

Captain Dmitri Gargarin sat on his barracks bunk and considered his fate.

So he now was an officer with the Nation.

He wasn't exactly a "Soldier of Allah" anymore. Nor was he the "Sword Arm of Islam."

Part of him belonged to the Prophet forever.

But there were no more muezzins, no more minarets, no more mullahs or mosques.

He couldn't even find a Koran.

All he had in the way of spiritual guidance anymore was the Chaplain.

He had begun to appreciate the Chaplain. A long, slow process, and more than once he'd felt disloyal to the True Faith. Still, when it came to spiritual guidance, a soldier could do a lot worse than that one-eyed bastard.

Even now the Chaplain orated over the barracks speaker system:

"The God Who doth not spare His friend shall not forgive His foe. As He burnt Sodom and smote Gomorrah, so shall the doubter be burned and smitten— in the Burning Lake, the Bottomless Pit, into the furnace of fire, shalt they be hurled, this generation of vipers: burning for burning, life for life, hate for hate, and death for death!"

Yes, the Chaplain knew how to tell it.

He wasn't Mohammed, but he was far better than the bleeding-heart blind-bitch bimbo—Cassandra.

The Chaplain would do.

26 Dreaming of God in a Godless Void

The Black Stealth—piloted by Larry Taylor—had no trouble getting to the Nation. It flew so high there was little wind resistance, and its subsonic airspeed was fuel-efficient.

The bomber's bomb bay and cargo holds had also been reconfigured by Nellis engineers to carry heat- and pressure-sensitive cargo, so there was room for passengers.

When Jamal learned that the passengers were his former financial patrons and the expanded cargo hold was packed with priceless gifts—to say nothing of their gift of the Stealth bomber—he was pleased to welcome them into the Nation.

Breeze was too—after he heard that Stone was on board.

Stone arrived at the Kansas rail yards just days after Colton had made his celebrated crash landing. Kate Magruder and Frank had likewise arrived that same week, so Breeze and Radford decided to throw a party.

Jamal was convinced that if Kate and Frank could be won over by guile, they all might merge with the Citadel without bloodshed.

"After all," Jamal said to Breeze, "that old lady runnin' it now ain't gonna live forever. I hear she ain't well."

"She gonna be a lot less well, I get my troops down there," Radford, the hardliner, grumbled.

Radford believed the only way to deal with the Citadel was "to shoot some muthafuckas."

"That Chaplain another story," Breeze said to Jamal. "Ain't nobody gonna believe he a nice guy.' "

"He even gives me the creeps," Radford said.

"And ever'body hear his sermons," Jamal had to admit.

"We shut down his black tent for a while," Breeze suggested. "Maybe that help."

So Radford grumbled, the Chaplain thundered, and Breeze mediated.

Jamal threw his party, lots of alcohol, canned delicacies, roasted meats, and music. Everyone was on strict orders to be nice to their guests.

"Let 'em see we all ain't fascist muthafuckas like Radford," Jamal said. "Let 'em see we gots to come to—what that muthafucka Chaplain call it, Breeze?"

" 'A peaceful solution to the Citadel problem,' " Breeze said.

For Kate, Stone, Colton, and Breeze the reunion was a little strained. They stood in the party pavilion sipping drinks, listening to the camp band work its way through "Wild Horses," and tried to have a good time. But so much had gone down since they'd seen each other last.

Everyone had wanted to know what had happened on the Odyssey. MTN had spread the news that the Odyssey so far had survived the partial collision with Atlantis's wreckage.

"I know you wouldn't have abandoned Sara," Kate said to Colton, "I just don't understand why she stayed."

"Thought she could do some good," Colton said. "Odyssey is the only way left to continue global communication."

The others were wise enough not to bring up Breeze's sentence to Jack Town. And no one wanted to talk about what the Nation represented.

Stone had told Colton of Dar-al-Suhl's role in the global apocalypse. Having no reason not to tell Breeze—or anyone for that matter—he let the cat out of the bag.

None of them could get enough of John Stone or his polygamous marriage into the family that had destroyed much of the world.

"What the fuck," Breeze said with an amused shrug. "Stone got himself some bitchin' ladies."

"They sound like hard trade to me," Kate said through gritted teeth.

"You mean I can't pimp 'em on my boys?" Breeze asked.

Now it was Colton's and Breeze's turn to laugh.

"Maybe we pimp 'em on the Chaplain," Breeze said.

"Nobody wants to spend time with *him*," Jamal said with a shudder.

"They're with him now," Kate said. "Let's go over and introduce ourselves."

Kate and Breeze headed across the tent. Stone followed reluctantly. Frank walked beside him.

The Chaplain, the Sin Sisters, and Jamal were engaged in a heated discussion.

"What you should be asking," Sultana said to the Chaplain and Jamal, "is *why* nations go to war."

"Annexation of land," Colton suggested as they approached.

Stone introduced his friends to his wives, who were only mildly interested.

Sabrina returned to their subject. "What you really want is to kill men—as many as possible."

"Not much of a reward in that," Breeze said.

"Really?" Sultana replied. "Then why does the male of our species always kill or drive off all men *not* in his in-group? Why has war been the principal enterprise of humankind time immemorial, time out of mind? Because each male wants his genes to predominate. He also wants sex on demand and the power to enforce that demand."

Sultana said, "It was frontal sex, practiced only by human males, that launched the great age of sexual warfare."

"And the Cult of Pulchritude," Sabrina said.

"That is supposed to explain war?" Kate asked.

"Of course," Sabrina said. "It's the way it's always been. It's why the Greeks laid siege to Troy."

"Paris's theft and seduction of Helen, bride of Menelaus," the Chaplain said.

"And to defend the sexual honor of Athena and Hera over Aphrodite," Sultana added.

"Same with your Christian crusaders," Sabrina said. "After their victories in the Holy Land, they amputated Muslim penises, strung them like banana bunches, and mailed them to the pope."

"The same with those black Africans you conquered and enslaved?" Sultana said. "Or are you telling me sexual slavery wasn't part of that package?"

"I suppose World War II was also fought over sex," Colton said, skeptical.

"Does the pope shit in the woods?" Sabrina thundered. "Hitler fought that war to exterminate those he believed ethnically inferior so his men could conceive with those women he deemed racially superior."

"The Japanese incarcerated 200,000 of Asia's most beautiful women in military brothels," Sultana said, "and raped them day and night."

"Is that what Islam teaches you?" Colton asked. "That the purpose of war is sex?"

"No, only that the reason for *winning* wars is sexual," Sabrina said.

"When Khomeini won the Iranian Revolution," Sultana said, "the first thing he did was lower the marital age of women to nine, legalize 'temporary marriage' to such youngsters, and proselytize on behalf of polygamy. His sexual edicts doubled Iran's population in seventeen years."

"And enslaved its women," Kate muttered.

"I suppose nuclear war is also sexual," Colton said.

"What does a nuclear missile look like to you?" Sabrina asked. "Do the words 'giant phallus' ring any bells?"

"Which climaxes like the heart of an exploding star, Mr. Colton," Sultana said.

"We're talking doomsday orgasms," Sabrina said.

"Which is what Oppenheimer meant when he claimed he had become Shiva—the Hindu God of sex and death," Sultana said.

"Talk about getting some mean rocks," Sabrina said, "those geeks at Los Alamos were really getting it on."

"We're talking . . . wargasms, man!" Sultana said.

"Come, Blessed Husband," Sabrina said to John Stone, "you've traveled the world far and wide. You've known the men who lust after power—political, military, legal, financial. They are men of ravenous appetites, drowning in testosterone. Ask any pimp, hooker, stripper, masseuse—anyone who's worked in the sex industry. It isn't the blue-collar worker who lusts after leather and paddles, whips and boots, bondage and domination. It's bankers and lawyers, politicians and CEOs, generals and corporate raiders—it's the power-hungry psychopaths!"

"IT'S PEOPLE," Sultana screamed, "LIKE US!"

"Love never enters into it?" Kate asked.

Sabrina laughed hard and long.

"Remember what Oscar Wilde said about love?" she finally asked. "It begins in self-deception and ends in the deception of everyone else."

"In other words," Kate said, "love is a lie?"

Sabrina said, "Lovers are the most terrifying liars and killers of all."

"Says who?" said Colton.

"Ever hear of Plato?" Sultana asked. "Ever hear of his *Symposium*?"

"'A soldier would rather die,'" Sabrina quoted, "'than be seen deserting his post or throwing down his weapons by those he loves.'"

"A lover—you see—will rape, torture, enslave, kill, even *nuke* to protect his loved ones," Sultana said.

"So love explains nuclear war?" Kate asked.

"The way you deluded yourselves, yes, it does," Sultana said.

"You couldn't get enough of Armageddon's loving arms," Sabrina said.

"Let's face it, for you nuclear love was the greatest love of all," Sultana said.

"Nuclear weapons are both love *and* a piece of ass?" Breeze asked, shaking his head.

"Yes, and the power to enforce those demands," Sabrina said.

"And you know what those demands are now?" Sultana asked.

Radford stared at Kate intently. "You know what we're talking about, Kate?"

"You're wasting your time if you're taking on the Citadel."

"We have no choice, you get right down to it," Jamal said. "Once you got an army this big, you got to use it, keep it on the move. Retirement ain't an alternative."

"I thought God had something to do with this," Kate said to the Chaplain.

"I can supply Him too," the Chaplain said. "Which God do you seek?"

"You offer a specialty of the week?" Kate asked.

"Why not think of *me* as your Lord and Savior—Jesus, Buddha, Odin, Zeus. Life, Fate, Nature, Karma, Spirits from the Deep, the Great Mystery."

Kate studied his tiger's smile and Cyclops eye.

"You wouldn't pass the physical," she said.

"You seek something more ethereal?"

"As a matter of fact, yes."

"Then you dream of God in a Godless void."

Kate leaned forward and stared into the Chaplain's face. Even under the patch, she felt the terrible eye and divined its murderous power. She said it anyway.

"Take on the Citadel and you will come out bloodied—or not at all."

"Really?" Jamal said. "What's your recommendation, Chaplain O'Donnell?"

The Chaplain's grin was truly unnerving.

"For the bitch?" the Chaplain said. "Hook knives, rock salt, a high rack," he said.

"Fortunately for you," Breeze said to Kate, "he's been overruled. Jimmy John ain't forgot the service you did his baby brother. I ain't neither."

"It don't matter much anyway," Jamal said thoughtfully. "Moms will still believe we're doin' our worst to you."

"Our reputation precedes us," Sabrina said, nodding.

"She will assume it to be a bloody business indeed," Chaplain O'Donnell said.

"My sister and I would be happy to assist," Sultana said, grinning at Kate.

"Not yet," Radford said.

Breeze agreed.

"Ah, you two are both a bit soft," the Chaplain chided them.

Radford shrugged, allowing them a small mirthless smile.

Kate found his smile more blood chilling than the Chaplain's threats.

X

And into the Fire . . .

1 The Nation Was on the Move

Night fell over the Kansas rail yard.

Kate Magruder stood atop the coal tender with Frank Sheckly. Behind them queues of railcars and rebuilt wood- and coal-fired steam locomotives sat on sidings, waiting to join the caravan of trains heading down the main line.

The Nation was abandoning their headquarters in the big Kansas freight yard, and Kate and Frank were in the lead train. The troop trains were behind them headed for the Citadel, where Kate and Frank were expected to negotiate "a peaceful solution to the Citadel problem."

Jamal and Cool Breeze—dressed in the ubiquitous black army fatigues of the Nation—joined them.

"If you're suing for peace, why take a war train with you?" Frank asked Jamal.

"Radford and Riaz control most of the military, and they don't go nowhere without lots of men and guns."

"Self-defense an art those boys cultivate," Cool Breeze explained.

"My mother's going to find your peace proposals a little hard to believe," Kate said, "with an army at her back door."

"You have to make her believe, Kate," Radford said, joining them.

"Make Mom see she's better off dealin' with Breeze and me than Radford and the Chaplain here," Jamal said, giving Kate and Frank his most endearing "sucker smile."

Kate looked away. Clouds of locomotive steam obscured the huge yard, and all around them organized chaos reigned. For four months this conglomeration of crisscrossing tracks, coal sheds, machine shops, turntable pits, sand sheds, water tank, and crew tents had been the Nation's home. Now shrilling whistles filled the night. Soot-and-oil-covered workers in greasy overalls, wielding tar-pitch torches, swarmed the tracks, searching for their trains.

Their own black 4-8-2 Mountain Locomotive pulled forward to take a drink from the engine-house water crane. Kate and Frank climbed down from the tender and joined the fireman and engineer in the locomotive. Behind them, the stoker worked the rear of the firebox.

"Water tanks are topped—over 20,000 gallons," the engineer said. "Tender, 25 tons."

"Boiler pressure 200 pounds," the fireman said, looking at the gauge.

"Good," Radford shouted down from their coal tender. "We got 300 tons of tender plus three locomotives and eighty cars."

"Pressure 230," the fireman said.

"Time?" the engineer asked Radford.

"Line 'em up and head 'em on out," Radford said.

Ahead in the steam-shrouded blackness a torch rose and fell, signaling an all-clear to the engineer. He released the air brakes and the train inched forward. Joints, frogs, and switches grumbled under the big drive-wheels. They slipped from their siding onto the main line, the rear cars undulating behind them.

Again, the forward torch rose and fell. The highball was up.

Kate shuddered, holding on to Frank.

The Nation was on the move.

2 Hard as Her Arteries

"Commander Dawkins is waiting outside in the office," Lydia Magruder said to the Odyssey. "I expect another lesson in how to run a war from my so-called subordinate. The general consensus here is that I'm insane."

"Try being more diplomatic," Thucydides said.

"Diplomatic?" L. L. asked, stunned.

Christ, she was now taking "deportment lessons" from a machine.

"Cyd loaded *How to Win Friends and Influence People* into his data banks," Sara explained. "He thinks people should be nicer to each other. He says it's good business."

"If you're taking on the Nation," Thucydides said, "you'll need the willing cooperation of your staff."

"Okay," L. L. conceded, "I'll try being diplomatic."

"Want us to listen in?" Sara asked.

"Good idea. Here, I'll turn on the speakerphone to 'send' but keep head-set on 'receive.'" L. L. clicked on both intercom and speakerphone. "Send Dawkins in."

Dawkins had just finished with maneuvers, and his khaki uniform was dusty with desert sand. Taking off his hat, he declined an offered seat.

"Nice to see you, George. What do you want?"

"Too abrupt," Thucydides counseled into her headset.

"He means, be more diplomatic," Sara said.

"Offer him coffee," Thucydides suggested.

"Shhh," Sara said to Cyd. *"She'll click us off."*

"L. L.," Dawkins said, "since it became clear what the Nation was planning, you've prevented us from sabotaging their tracks and trains, bombing or straf-ing them. We've done nothing to slow them down."

"I told you I have my plans."

"Operation Cannae, whatever that is. But in the meantime they're near the summit of the Mogollon Plateau. They'll be dug in on some of the highest ground in the Southwest. We're here on the desert plain in their gunsights, and there's nothing we can do about it!"

"I'm waiting for the last of their supply trains to reach the summit," L. L. said. "That's all I can tell you now."

"And I'm starting to doubt you have any master plan. You're stalling because of Kate and Frank."

There. He'd let it out.

"Not that I blame you. Hell, we all love Kate and Frank. But their welfare weighed against the survival of the Citadel? You've put everything we've worked for in jeopardy to protect two people who refused to protect themselves. Who refused to evacuate that hospital when we offered to fly them back."

"I know what I'm doing," L. L. said grimly.

"Kate's made her bed. As for us—"

"What else?"

"I want you to turn the defense of the Citadel over to us. Over to your staff."

"Over to *a committee*?"

"*DIPLOMACY!!!*" Thucydides reminded her quickly.

L. L.'s full attention was on Dawkins.

"You aren't giving him . . . the Look?" Cyd asked.

She was.

Dawkins got the message.

In a belated attempt to heal the breach between her and Dawkins, L. L. said, "According to Thucydides' recon footage, the last of the Nation's trains should be on the plateau by nightfall. We'll move then."

"What does that mean?"

"The counteroffensive will begin—Operation Cannae."

"You mean there *is* a plan?" He looked as if he was having trouble believing her.

"A plan—a plan that will no doubt get Kate and Frank killed but I believe has a chance of saving the Citadel."

Dawkins took a deep breath and waited. L. L. thought that he wasn't a bad militia leader but was far from being a general.

None of them were.

"Dawkins, the Nation has us outmanned and outgunned. Defense of the Citadel against a military force this enormous was never feasible. We did our best to prepare, but we're just a bunch of people trying to defend a patch of ground. It's our greatest strength and our fatal flaw."

"What are we going to do?"

"When the last train is up that hill, we'll talk again."

When he left the office L. L. poured herself a cup of coffee. She would need lots of it during the next few days.

"Maybe it was a mistake telling Jack Taylor to shoot himself," L. L. said into her headset. "He was a military man, and he did know planes. Truth is, I'm getting just as hard as my arteries. And cantankerous. And vindictive. But I was so furious with him, I couldn't control myself."

"He was an imbecile," Thucydides said.

"That's very undiplomatic," Sara said, unable to resist the shot.

"An unbiased factual evaluation," Thucydides countered.

"You're okay, Cyd," L. L. said—and resisted the impulse to add: *Glad I built you.*

. . . What the hell. Cyd was right. Taylor had been a loser. She wondered if his son was just as stupid.

Apparently, he'd flown to the Nation in a Black Stealth bomber.

It didn't get much stupider than that . . .

"Cyd," L. L. said into her headset, "open your peepers and tell me when the last of the trains make it onto the plateau."

3 Fiends from Hell Who Cloak Themselves in Human Flesh

It had not been an easy trek for the big auburn Wanderratte. His preferred means of travel would have been a ship.

Cross-country he rode the next best thing—Land Clippers, the rails.

Curiosity was his vice, and like Thucydides—and Odysseus before him—his eye would not close. So much he had encountered on this journey held him transfixed.

Some things he would never understand.

Human hatred, for instance. He witnessed its effects everywhere. There was certainly nothing in the length and breadth of the animal kingdom to match it. Certainly nothing to equal man-made hurricanes of thermonuclear fire.

Nothing was so big or so minute that humanity did not want it dead forever.

He was especially bothered by its rage against him and his kind. The Army of the Nation, for instance. He ran the rails, and so he encountered its officers continually while crossing the continent.

The Nation was pathologically hostile to rats. Its men roamed the sidings at night in search of Sailor's brothers and sisters. Some set traps filled with nonlethal bait. The captured rats were then caged in concentration-camp boxcars and fed on the worse food imaginable—mostly weeds and excrement—and since there was nothing else to do, they bred continually.

At intervals they were culled by their warders, killed, skinned out, and boiled in vats.

Men were fiends from hell who'd found some way to cloak themselves in human flesh. Sailor's instinct was to flee—to find a warren far from the hatred and ravages of men.

But he could not leave. Sailor had to free his brothers and sisters in the boxcars, but he lacked the means.

So he hid from the men, evaded their traps, and rode the rails.

Somehow, he would find the means to free his friends and punish the fiends from hell who abused them without conscience.

4 The Gift That Keeps on Giving

Kate and Frank stood at the Mogollon Plateau's south rim with the Nation's leaders. On the plains below lay the Citadel, its surrounding earthworks, barbwire aprons, and minefields. They studied the layout through binoculars.

Jamal and the other leaders had brought them there for what Gerald—Jimmy John Radford's recently recovered brother—called "a frank discussion of the facts."

"A castle in the air," Gerald said, putting down his binoculars and pointing at the Citadel.

Kate Magruder snorted derisively.

"What do you see?" Jimmy John asked, putting down his own binoculars.

"An open grave," Kate said, referring to the minefields and fire-trenches surrounding the Citadel.

"Whose open grave is the question," Gerald said.

Kate saw Gerald as an extremely nasty self-styled pseudo-intellectual and was increasingly sorry Frank had saved his life.

"My mother sowed Dragon's Teeth," Kate said.

"'And you will suffer the armed men,'" Frank said to Jimmy John, finishing the quotation.

"I think not," Chaplain O'Donnell said. "Castellation's never worked in the long run. Not in China against the Mongols. Not in Europe against the Viking raiders or the steppe's nomads to the east."

"Walls didn't protect Jericho, either," Jimmy John said.

"Time isn't on the defender's side," Gerald said. "Technology, firepower, and mobility are what count."

Kate knew he was unfortunately right. Once—during one of her campaigns to make L. L. halt construction of the Citadel—she'd commissioned a feasibility study of strategic defense. The facts were not reassuring.

"It all comes down to the same thing," O'Donnell said. "Masada, the Alamo, Iwo Jima, Dien Bien Phu, they all get taken in the end. The Maginot Line contained three million pounds of steel, a million and a half cubic feet of concrete, sixty-two miles of tunnels. The Wehrmacht blitzkrieg proved the immovable object wasn't immovable after all."

"I still say you're staring into the abyss," Kate said. "Your troops aren't even trained in small arms."

"Don't intend to *give* them small arms," Jamal said.

Kate stared at him, incredulous. "You plan to throw those men against the Citadel unarmed?"

"Wave upon wave upon wave," Chaplain O'Donnell confirmed. "Our battle police will be right on their tails, driving them forward until the mines are cleared and the Citadel runs out of ammunition."

Kate again studied the plains below through her binoculars.

Chaplain O'Donnell stepped in front of her, blocking her view. She lowered her field glasses.

"You did not know men like us existed, did you?" the Chaplain said, studying her with amused detachment, his good eye twinkling.

"I still say you don't know my mother."

"But we know artillery," Jamal said.

"155s mounted on carriages, self-propelled," Radford said.

"She's expecting a siege," Kate said simply.

"But is she expecting radiological weapons?" Gerald asked.

"Canisters of radioactive strontium and cesium," Chaplain O'Donnell said. "They're really quite lovely, you know. They give off gamma rays which destroy individual cells. The death of bone-marrow cells triggers cascading effects: hemorrhaging, fevers, and the destruction of the immune system, which renders the corpus vulnerable to every disease known to God and man."

"Unfortunately for Moms there's no shortage of the shit," Jamal said. "Stored in the Waste Isolation Pilot Plant in the salt caves outside Carlsbad, New Mexico."

"Guaranteed radioactive for 250,000 years," Gerald said.

"And if that ain't enough," Radford said, "there are the ultra-high-level canisters at the Savannah River site and Yucca Mountain, Nevada. Those drums are so hot, if you stand next to one for five minutes, you die."

"Meanin'," Jamal said, "we can *rain* radioactive shit on Moms. It's the gift that keeps on giving."

Gerald said, "Remember chlorine, phosgene, and mustard gas? They *incinerate* the respiratory system. We liberated a few hundred canisters from abandoned government weapons depots."

"I prefer the nerve agents," Chaplain O'Donnell said, "all of which were readily available. Sarin, Tabun, Soman, and VX. They knock out neurons and prevent them from communicating with each other. They shut the nervous system down like an unplugged toaster."

"Tell her about our biological shit," Radford said to the Chaplain.

"You mean the E. coli with which we will flood her water supply? It kills red blood cells and annihilates the kidneys, flooding the bowels with bloody diarrhea."

"Moms ain't expectin' that, is she?" Jamal said, grinning.

"I don't know 'bout you," Radford said, "but I'm puttin' on one of the orange Racal space suits we got from them labs and goin' in. I wanna watch."

"That is obscene," Kate said. "The Citadel may be the world's last best hope."

"Look, you got no right to be pissed," Gerald said. "It's not like we're hitting you with hydrogen bombs. These are itsy-bitsy weapons."

"Most of these killers are less than five microns in diameter," Chaplain O'Donnell said. "They remain airborne in dry desert climes for days. Once they are inhaled, they scoot right through the body's filtering mechanisms, invade the lungs, attack the bloodstream. After which brain, heart cells, and the spinal cord become prey."

"Yo," Jamal said, "look on the bright side. Why you think you two ain't skinned out and dressed down with rock salt already? We got a lot more up our sleeves'n guns and ammo. We got enough shit here to kill the whole Southwest, let alone Moms and her homies. So dig, you gots to ask yo'selfs how you two gonna make Moms un'nerstand."

"Or maybe you two think we got your best interests at heart," Gerald said.

"The question," Chaplain O'Donnell said, his one eye still irrepressibly merry, "is, can you make your sainted mother realize she is dealing with people who will reduce her Citadel to a *petri dish*? That she's up against the Athens pandemic that felled Pericles? The epidemic Cortés brought to Mexico City before he stormed their gates? The Ten Plagues of Egypt?"

"What Chaplain O'Donnell is trying to say," Gerald said, "is your mother really expecting *us*?"

5 The Most Beautiful Thing on Earth

Dusk on the plateau.

Kate walked aimlessly through the military encampment. Radford and Jamal had just given her, Frank, Henry Colton, and Larry Taylor a tour of the Nation's chemical- and bioweapons stores, and her friends had confirmed her worst fears.

The weapons were for real.

Even more upsetting had been their phone call to her mother confirming the bad news. The Nation had given her twenty-fours hours to surrender unconditionally.

No wonder, Kate thought, they hadn't harmed her or Frank. They didn't have to. L. L. had to surrender anyway. All Kate and Frank could do was try to make it less painful for the old woman.

Kate followed the railroad lines along the camp's perimeter. She'd heard of the infamous rat cars. Where did squirrelly little creeps like Bailey come from? She still remembered his lab, the torture of rats, including Sailor.

Sailor.

When she'd encountered him in that storm tunnel under the burning city and he'd led her out to safety, she'd concluded that he was the most beautiful thing on the face of the earth. She wondered where he was now. She'd heard some fairly weird rumors about a "super rat" that was supposedly stalking the Nation. Huge and auburn in color, cunning and elusive as smoke.

Sailor? It couldn't be. There was only *one* Sailor. No way he could have made it this far west . . .

6 An Ace-High Straight, Wired

The Nation's leadership was not concerned about some apocryphal "rat king." They were in their main tent, celebrating the Citadel's impending surrender.

"We got her kids," Radford said. "We got the high ground."

"Nerve agents," Gerald said. "Did you see the girl's face when we brought up nerve agents?"

"Did you see the doc's when the Chaplain described the plagues we is gonna unleash?" Radford asked.

"No way that old bitch gittin' over on us," Jamal said.

"We lookin' at an ace-high straight, wired," Radford said.

"I say after we take the Citadel," Jamal said, "turn all they sorry-bitch-asses over to the Chaplain."

"You a cold muthafucka," Radford said, and then sat up alertly. "What the *fuck*—?"

The men raced out of the tent in time to see a dozen huge C-130 transport planes coming in low—skimming the treetops—the roar of their engines drowning out their oaths. Wing-tanks dropped gasoline across the plateau. From open doorways men also dumped what looked like black jelly from fifty-five-gallon drums.

"Napalm!" Jamal shouted.

The stench of the gasoline was sickening.

"What the fuck is *that*?" Radford demanded.

The men in the planes had begun to launch phosphorous rounds and incendiary grenades.

The Mogollon Plateau had been dying before the Nation arrived. Global warming and fallout killed trees as thoroughly as it wiped out people.

The desiccated wood of the forest exploded in a hurricane of fire.

7 You Can't Deny Your Blood

L. L. was still listening to Thucydides repeat grid-map coordinates for the Nation's bio- and chemical-weapons storage facilities when those depots burst into flame.

At which point members of the planes' crews took over the radio frequency, all but deafening her.

"Locked and cocked, ready to rock!"

"Direct hit!"

"Bull's-eye!"

"Victory!"

Victory, indeed.

The old woman sighed. They hadn't always been so enthusiastic, so confident of success.

Well, no longer could they doubt. The Fire Drive was a success.

The Nation was finished.

She flicked on the TV monitor with her remote and watched Thucydides' footage of the conflagration. It was not an inspiring sight. Deer and bear and elk were pouring out of the woods in blind panic and tumbling over the cliff's rim—to their death.

L. L. too was indeed a Fire Driver.

You can't deny your blood, she thought bitterly.

Unable to watch the holocaust, she turned off the TV.

Where was Kate? she wondered. *Where was Frank?*

Where were any of them in this firestorm?

8 The Biggest, Reddest Rat on Earth

Kate Magruder was lost, blinded by smoke. She did not know whether she was running into the inferno or away from it.

Either the well was very deep or she was falling very slowly.

She dropped to her knees in an agony of despair. She'd survived the nuking of Manhattan only to die in a forest of flames.

Fire closing in, smoke was searing her lungs. Her black fatigues absorbed so much heat she felt as if she might burst into flames. When she doused her bandana with canteen-water and covered her nose and mouth with it, steam blistered her skin.

Then through the smokey haze Kate saw him, standing directly in front of her. His eyes were locked on hers, and he was motioning with his head, as if communicating the way out of the firestorm.

The biggest, reddest rat on earth had arrived to rescue her.

Sailor was back.

9 Trash Orbits

Thucydides had done it: He had destroyed the Nation's biochemical weapons—with a little help from his friends.

Operation Cannae had been Colton's idea. Using a "borrowed" satellite phone from the Nation's stores, Colton had described his plan to L. L. Then he notified Sara and Thucydides of the approximate position and gave them a detailed description of the Nation's biochemical stockpile.

Thucydides calculated the grid-map locations of all the targets and bracketed the train for the Citadel's pilots.

Cyd had struggled painfully with these calculations. Ailing from recent solar flares and starquakes, now Cyd was getting hit with something far worse than solar flares or starquakes. Colliding black holes were throwing superviolent flashes of gamma-ray radiation. One of the gamma-ray bursts had almost shut him down.

Thucydides' friend, the HETE—Hyper-Energy Transient Explorer Astronomical Satellite—had warned him that the two black holes were merging. HETE's partner satellite, SWIFT, had broken down the gamma-ray, X-ray, and visual wavelengths by frequency and sensitivity.

And if violence from black holes wasn't bad enough, there was the matter of the atmosphere.

The recent sun storms were worse than those in the '70s, which had heated the earth's atmosphere, causing it to rise above 280 miles. That heightened atmosphere had reached up like a giant hand, caught the orbiting remains of Skylab, and dragged it earthward, incinerating it.

His own orbit was fixed at a perigee of 325 miles—what his launchers had termed "the line in the sand"—the lowest safe orbit, at which point no earthly forces could drag the Odyssey back into the atmosphere and kill it. But, Odyssey's designers had not counted on thousands of thermonuclear weapons detonating on Earth, followed by even more massive thermonuclear detonations on the sun, which expanded the superheated atmosphere far beyond its outer, upper limits.

Even worse, when the space shuttle docked alongside Space Station Atlantis had exploded, it had blown the station into millions of pieces, many no larger than baseballs. These countless fragments had entered one of the worst trash orbits encircling Earth.

An orbit Odyssesy and Cyd would soon be joining.

And they were indeed "the trash orbits." Not only had Earth's military stocked them with every conceivable spy, Global Positioning, and communications satellites, the business community had packed those orbits with space junk as if they were lining freeways with fast-food franchises and strip malls. As microelectronics improved and the size of satellites shrank, their numbers soared. The trash orbits experienced a population explosion. The heavens were awash in microsats (20 to 200 pounds), nanosats (2 to 20 pounds), and picosats (under 2 pounds). Some were no larger than a deck of cards, and they were launched hundreds at a time.

Space debris travels on average at six miles per second. Upon collision, fragments that hit these fragments explode and liquefy, turning whatever they strike, including spacecraft such as the Odyssey, into molten metal.

Nor would the chain reaction of catastrophic collisions end there. Each collision was now producing thousands of additional pieces of debris, each of which was colliding with another target, creating thousands upon thousands more collisions. This exponential progression was generating a collisional cascade, a Fourth of July fireworks display of heat, fire, and blinding light known as "the Kessler Effect," named for the NASA mathematician who first calculated the exact actions and effects of such cascades.

The rising, overheated atmosphere was pulling the Odyssey, along with Sara Friedman and Cyd, down into the cascade.

So be it. Cyd was relieved he'd bracketed the weapons train for the Citadel, but it had also taken something out of him. His brain hurt. Those solar flares and starquakes, powerful enough to knock out power grids, were also powerful enough to destroy him, and he was exhausted.

For the first time in his life, Thucydides wanted to shut himself off and pack it in.

His passion was no longer seeing. He had seen all he wanted to see of human life. Now his enormous eye only wanted to close.

10 We're Getting Them Out

When Kate and Sailor emerged from the blazing woods, Kate dropped to her knees, coughing convulsively, half-dead from smoke-inhalation and hyperthermia.

But at least they were safe from the flames.

They were on the plateau's north rim, facing a long rail spur. She counted at least fifty boxcars on the siding. The boxcars stank and were filled with the most godawful squeals and shrieks Kate had ever heard.

The rat train.

One of the boxcar doors was open. She looked inside. The car was filled with row upon row of rat cages—hundreds per car, dozens of brown rats to a cage, feeding on excrement and weeds.

Sailor was looking up at her. She knew what he wanted.

No one else was around. The Nation's survivors were spread out along the south rim, facing the Citadel. She could do it if she moved fast.

Near the side of the tracks lay a pile of rail spikes and a sledgehammer. A track crew had been repairing the spur.

"Okay," Kate said to Sailor. "We're getting them out."

She picked up a sledgehammer and climbed into the open boxcar.

11 The Balance of Personal Power

The Sin Sisters accompanied their brother and Captain Gargarin in a C-130 to their B-2. They wanted to demonstrate for the Nation's chief weapons officer the assistance they could offer the Nation. The B-2 had a cargo that would shift the balance of power, and they requisitioned one of the nation's transport planes to retrieve it. The cargo was now in the C-130's hold.

General Ali—piloting the transport plane—couldn't believe his eyes. Nor could his sisters and Captain Gargarin. The entire Mogollon Rim—visible at this altitude for over 50 miles—was spectacularly ablaze. The Nation—its weapons, troop trains, officer corps, everything—was in flames.

Curiously enough, the conflagration buoyed the Sin Sisters' spirits. For some time now they'd felt as if the Nation merely indulged them, as if they lived on the Nation's sufferance, honored for past favors. Sultana and Sabrina sensed that changing.

"Sainted Sister, Beloved Brother, Good Captain Gargarin," Sabrina said, "I believe the survivors of that firestorm will be very glad to see us."

"When they see our 'surprise presents,' they will," Ali said.

"It was so kind of you, Captain Gargarin," Sabrina said, "to 'arm' those gifts for us."

Gargarin nodded.

"The balance of personal power within the Nation is about to shift," Sultana said.

"In *our* direction," her brother concurred.

12 If Rats Could Smile . . .

It had taken Kate Magruder two hours of hard hammering, but the last of the rat cages were smashed. She leaped out of the end boxcar onto the roadbed. Hundreds of thousands of fleeing rats were scurrying away from the forest fire and the siding, down off the plateau to the plains beneath—to safety.

She had started down herself when she heard the racking of a shotgun slide.

She turned and was staring into the muzzle of a 12-gauge pump-action. Bailey had her in his sights.

"You bitch," he shouted.

Then he butt-stroked her across the side of her head.

Her last memory was of Bailey pulling off her clothes.

He was going to rape, then murder her.

At which point she passed out.

———

When she came to, she was lying beside the rails.

Bailey lay near her, in a pool of blood, his carotid artery ripped out, his body exsanguinating.

Sailor sat at Kate's feet, staring at her. If rats could smile . . . She stared back at him, and their eyes locked.

One last time.

His comrades were free, his enemy dead—his friend safe. His work was done. He turned and joined his army of rats, fleeing downslope.

Sailor was gone.

13 The Repression of Death

Three of the Nation's officers picked Kate up after Sailor had fled. Skirting the rim, they took her back to their base camp—now situated on the sloping plain beneath the plateau's south rim. Radford, Jamal, the Chaplain, and a dozen of their surviving officers were assembled beside a temporary airstrip with several of their men. One of the airstrip's crew was tethering a C-130 transport while another crew member wedged chocks under its wheels.

Everyone's attention was focused on the Sin Sisters and their brother, who had apparently just flown in. Three large crates were being unloaded from the C-130, and a man Kate did not recognize was prizing the wood siding off one of the crates with a crowbar. Kate noted that he did so gingerly.

The Sin Sisters grinned like Cheshire cats digesting canaries. The Nation's officers likewise looked pleased. Chaplain O'Donnell was deliriously happy.

Frank, Henry Colton, Larry Taylor, and John Stone stared grimly at the man stripping away the wood lathes from the crate.

"As you can see," Sultana was saying to them, "the fortunes of the Nation have taken a turn for the better. My sister, brother, and I brought three nuclear devices with us. General Colton, General Taylor, you can confirm that these *are* nukes we're uncrating."

"We weren't sure how to arm them," Sabrina said, "so we did not bother telling anyone what we had."

"Without Captain Gargarin to activate and deploy them," Ali said, "they were more dangerous to the Nation than to the Citadel."

"Thank God for Captain Gargarin!" Sabrina enthused.

"He's a weapons specialist, and we gave him the PAL codes," Sultana said. "He knows exactly how to deliver our gift to the Nation."

The first device was uncrated. A steel cylinder, it was rounded off at both ends. Gargarin began unscrewing the densely threaded top portion.

Chaplain O'Donnell said to Colton and Taylor, "The devices are crude by NATO standards but perfect for our purposes. They are contact-fuse Hiroshima-style bombs. All we have to do is drop one on that redoubt over there, and in an instant it's Hiroshima. They detonate on impact. No complicated futzing around."

Colton and Taylor both knew the weapon. "You tripped the links?" Colton asked Gargarin.

"We had to trip them to find out whether we could," Captain Gargarin said.

"We could, and we did," Sultana said. "They're ready to go."

"You recognize the fuse?" Colton asked Taylor.

"Simple contact," Taylor responded. "They're right. All you have to do is drop it."

"Hot-wired on a hair trigger," Colton said.

"The trigger is right *there*," Taylor said, pointing to the end portion of the bomb on his left.

"You're all crazy," Kate said.

"Excellent!" Chaplain O'Donnell said. "Tell that to your loving mother. Tell her we're all mad as March hares and consequently have no qualms about nuking her off the face of the earth."

General Jamal handed a Citadel satellite phone to Kate. "Dial Moms up," Jamal said, "and tell her the bad news. We want her unconditional surrender by the time you git off the phone, or we nuc'lerize her ass to Kingdom Come."

"Just to let her know we're serious," Chaplain O'Donnell said, "bring over those hostages."

One of the Citadel's planes crash-landed, and the Nation captured the six-man crew. The crew members—still in flight uniforms—were brought to the Chaplain. Their hands were tied behind their backs. They had been badly worked over. One had a broken arm.

When Kate refused to take the phone, Jamal shrugged and dialed it himself. He got L. L. and handed the phone to Kate. This time she took it. She wanted to hear her mother's voice.

"I'm afraid it's true, Mom," Kate said. "Henry and Larry Taylor confirm that they have three fully armed nukes with contact fuses. They say it's dangerous as hell just being near them. They're 'hot-wired on a hair trigger,' Henry says. If you don't surrender unconditionally, they'll send a plane piloted by a suicide bomber to crash into the Citadel."

"Yo, Moms!" Jamal shouted. "We gots three chances to git it right."

L. L. said nothing.

"Mom? I'm telling you that they have nuclear weapons," Kate said.

"Let me get in on this," Chaplain O'Donnell said, taking the satellite phone.

"Mrs. Magruder, I fear what you suffer from is death repression. Love and death in your mind are maddeningly out of joint. In refusing to accept death, you fail to accept life and can never truly love. You close your heart, shut down your soul." He returned the phone to Kate. "Sergeant, you see that hostage there?"

Chaplain O'Donnell pointed to the flight-crew member with the broken arm.

"I can tell just by looking at that man, he suffers from the same thing. Liberate him. End that man's death repression."

"Sir, with all due respect," Sergeant D'Arcy said, "I can't."

"Sergeant," Chaplain O'Donnell said sternly, "I once saw you take down a man at 1,200 meters in a high wind—*downhill*. I find that statement impossible to believe."

"Sir, I respectfully refuse to execute that hostage. I'm a soldier. I've been one all my life. I'm not a murderer."

Chaplain O'Donnell unholstered his own sidearm, racked the slide, and blew off half of D'Arcy's head.

"Sergeant Hawkins," the Chaplain said, "will *you* liberate that man from a living death?"

Hawkins—a lanky, raw-boned soldier from South Carolina with jailhouse tats up and down his forearms—saluted Chaplain O'Donnell.

"Yessir!"

He racked the slide on his 9mm Glock, walked up to the flight-crew member, and shot him between the eyes at point-blank range.

"Good man," Chaplain O'Donnell said.

"Bravo," Sultana said with a luminous smile.

"Good show," Sabrina enthusiastically concurred.

"What's Moms say now?" Jamal asked.

L. L. was silent.

"Nothing."

"Ah, Mrs. Magruder," Chaplain O'Donnell said, "that little tour de force is nothing, you know. I can make the stones themselves cry out from terror and from truth. You do like Larry Taylor? You were friends with his father, weren't you?"

Silence.

"Sergeant, deal with him."

"*NO!*" Kate screamed, dropped the phone, and started toward Sergeant Hawkins.

She never made it. Jamal caught her on her first stride, as the Chaplain raised his pistol and brought its grip down on the back of Kate's head with a dull *thwack*.

Kate slumped unconscious into Jamal's arms.

"Bastards!" Larry Taylor cursed and lunged for the Chaplain's throat.

Hawkins shot Taylor in the back of the head.

"It's all quite dramatic here, Mrs. Magruder!" the Chaplain chuckled, retrieving Kate's discarded phone.

L. L. maintained her silence.

"Now, I *know* you adore your stepson, Doctor Frank. Raised him as if he were one of your own brood, I do believe." The Chaplain knew his new choice of pawn meant he was playing politics. Political games have limits, and some moves required approvals. "Defense Secretary Radford, do I have your permission?"

"In the left leg," Radford said with a shrug.

Hawkins put a round in Frank's upper leg, shattering his left thigh bone.

"Jacob wrestling an Angel of the Lord," Chaplain O'Donnell said, "who promptly fractures his femur. I like that. Good job, Hawkins. Now the other."

He shattered his right thigh.

"Outstanding!" Sultana said, applauding.

"Now, Mrs. Magruder, I hope you aren't mad at me for shooting Frank twice in the legs and killing the fly-boy. However, you've always had a bad attitude toward death, which is why you resist our taking the Citadel into custody. I've said it before and I'll say it again: Your problem is you don't carry death in your heart. Now your daughter, I see death perched on her shoulder like a bird. She soars with it. She has taken it as a lover. That's why she's lived a life of high adventure—so she could be near to death. Death is the soul of truth, Mrs. Magruder. I'm going to have your daughter teach you that right now. Sergeant, strip the lovely Kate's clothes off and stake her out full-spread-eagle here right in front of me. You other boys, give Hawkins a hand." Mrs. Magruder, do the words 'hook knives and rock salt' mean anything to you?"

Another man brought the Chaplain a black doctor's bag, and O'Donnell opened it. The Chaplain removed two razor-sharp hook knives and a bag of rock salt.

Sergeant Hawkins holstered his gun, walked over to where Jamal had lain Kate—still out cold—on the ground. He reached for her already-torn shirt.

There was a commotion near the plane. Kate, just regaining consciousness, glanced over her shoulder and made out Henry Colton, his forearm around the throat of the soldier who had been guarding him. The man's weapon—a sawed-off 12-gauge Remington under-and-over—in his fist. The shotgun was leveled at the nuclear bomb's trigger-end. The bomb's trigger was extra-high explosive packed with percussion caps. All that was required to set if off and explode the HEU "bullet" into the HEU "target" was a hard concussion. A shotgun blast would do it.

"I think not," Colton said.

"Yeah. That's what I'm thinkin'," Cool Breeze said, and walked over next to Colton. Breeze raised his own 12-gauge sawed-off pump, racked the slide. "You once told my sorry ass that we redeem the past by redeemin' the future."

Breeze also pointed his shotgun at the warhead's detonator.

"Why not," Stone said, helping himself to the other sidearm of the soldier Colton had subdued, a holstered .44 Smith magnum. Thumbing back the hammer, Stone placed the magnum's muzzle squarely in the center of the nuclear trigger.

Kate Magruder put belt-tourniquets on Frank's legs and laid him on a crude pallet, which she'd jerry-rigged out of the A-bomb's packing crate. She then cut off his pant legs. Rooting through his medical shoulder-bag, she found his stash of morphine and penicillin.

She pumped enough drugs and antibiotics into him to medicate a water buffalo. Dusting the wounds with sulfa powder, she wrapped them with sterile bandages. By the time she finished, the morphine had kicked in. He was unconscious.

She looked up. The leaders of the Nation were off to one side, conferring.

Breeze, Colton, and Stone still stood over the nuclear weapon, their guns cocked. They were arguing. Breeze raised his voice.

"Chump-muthafucka," Breeze shouted at Colton, so angry the 12-gauge pump trembled in his fists, "we supposed to be friends."

"We were. We are."

"Then why you try and take my head off in that play-off game?"

"I wanted to, I would've," Colton said.

"Just a brushback," Stone said dismissively.

"Brushback *behind* my head?" Breeze corrected.

"We wanted to see you in the dirt," Stone said.

"You the chump," Breeze said, pointing at Stone, "what hit me in the neck."

"You done good," Colton said to Stone. Colton and Stone gave each other high fives.

"Hurt like a motherfucker," Breeze complained.

"You know the rules," Colton said. "Stoney and me get the inside corner, the outside corner. You get everything in between."

"You never give nobody *nothing* in between. I ought to know you. I caught your sorry butts for six years!"

"You want to hang out over *my* plate," Colton said, "your ass gets knocked down. I don't let no chumps hump my low and away. You know that."

"I was your *friend*."

"Like I always said," Colton said, getting in Breeze's face, putting his finger in his chest, "the plate was *my office*—where I did *my work*. No chumps allowed in my office 'less I invited them." That drew a snicker from Stone.

"And you. *You fucking* hit *me!*" Breeze shouted at Stone.

"You were leaning in," Stone said simply to Breeze, grinning.

"On an inside curve," Colton said.

"Which hung," Stone said. Both Stone and Colton were now grinning broadly.

"Damn near broke my neck!" Breeze grumbled.

Colton and Stone exploded with laughter.

"Should have hit *my head*," Breeze finally admitted. "Maybe would've knocked some sense into it."

Kate said belligerently, "Have the three of you gone nuts? What do you think you're doing there?"

"You know how to fly that C-130?" Colton asked her.

"No."

"Can you ride a horse?" Stone asked. He pointed to two saddle horses cross-hobbled on the other side of the plane. "Those belong to Jamal and Radford; they're pretty good mounts. You know those twin buttes in front of the Citadel? Before you reach to the minefields? If you get behind them, you should be okay."

"What are you talking about?" Kate said.

"You're not wanted here, Kate," Colton said. "You're just in the way."

Kate yanked a .357 Colt Python from Breeze's waistband and placed the muzzle over the nuclear-trigger along with the muzzles of their guns. Breeze yanked the Colt out of her hand.

"I say you go home," Breeze said. "*Now.*"

"And I say fuck you!"

"And *I* say I'm taking down that muthafucka doctor there," Breeze said, pointing it at Frank's left leg, "an inch at a time. Starting with that leg." Taking aim, Breeze fired.

The report from the magnum echoed from the nearby mountains. The bullet missed Frank's knee by five inches.

"You're a miserable shot," Colton said.

Breeze walked over to Frank—who was laid out less than ten feet away. He placed the muzzle of the magnum over his left kneecap. "This gone cripple him for life," Breeze said over his shoulder to Kate.

Kate dropped the pistol, went to Frank, and loosened the two tourniquets a few seconds, letting blood recirculate through the lower legs. The wounds were beginning to clot. She retightened the tourniquet. Breeze handed her the Colt, picked Frank up, and carried him to the horses. He laid Frank belly-down over the big chestnut gelding. Cutting off a length of saddle-rope, Kate secured him and his medical bag to the saddle.

"You're doing the right thing," Stone told her.

Kate didn't look at him or the others. She mounted the big bay. Dallying the chestnut's mecate around her pommel, she gave the lead-rope a warning yank, then kicked the bay into a hard lope. She cut out across the chaparral. The pack-horse followed a dozen feet behind.

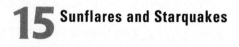

15 Sunflares and Starquakes

Thucydides' Eye-in-the-Sky was on the blink.

It could have been caused by the sunflares and starquakes and colliding black holes, or it could have been the pyrotechnic cascade into which they were descending. NASA had left enough fuel in many of its satellites to give them the opportunity—after the sats had outlived their usefulness—to reignite their jets and deorbit. That way they'd eventually burn up in the atmosphere and not further clutter their trash orbits.

When these fueled spacecrafts got hammered, resulting explosions were spectacular.

Whatever the case, Cyd could no longer see what was happening on Earth.

He was worried about his friends.

And he was blind.

16 Where Might Our Chaplain Be

Radford had just returned, angry and bewildered, from a meeting with Colton, Stone, and Breeze.

"They just rappin' 'bout baseball and shit," Radford told Jamal and Gerald. "I tried to talk to 'em, but they act like I wasn't ever there."

"They ain't doin' a damn thing till they think Kate and Frank are safe," Jamal speculated.

"Bitch stole my horse," Radford said. "Colton told me if they see anyone leave this site takin' off after Kate, they put the hammer down. Maybe if we got some snipers in place . . ."

"They would have to be very, very good," Gerald said, "head-shots, something guaranteed to short-circuit the brain. But Chaplain O'Donnell killed our best sniper."

"Little Brother," Radford wondered, "where might our chaplain be, anyway?"

"I suspect that he's wherever his horse might be." Gerald looked around before answering him.

Jamal spat in the dirt. "Hombres, we got more immediate concerns than the Chaplain's whereabouts."

"No way all three gonna blow themselves up," Radford said, looking over at the former Yankees teammates standing over the nuclear bomb.

"One of them may be crazy," Jamal agreed, "no three."

"I say they wait . . . till night," Gerald said. "That's when they'll try to slip away."

Radford said, "Tether some horses nearby, over that way. Let them think they got an easy way to escape."

"Anything what git 'em off that bomb," Jamal agreed.

17 She Always Had Class

So they left horses nearby, but in morning the three men were still there.

And the following morning as well—along with a water bag Stone had stolen.

Colton, Breeze, and Stone were spelling one another now. One slept, while the other two kept vigil over the warhead.

To keep their spirits up, the waking men talked about the things they loved—baseball, movies, baseball, music, baseball, friends, baseball, baseball, baseball—

And the women they'd loved.

"Kate sure was pissed," Breeze said, "but I figured it was the only way to get her out of here."

"Threaten *Frank*?" Colton said. "That was inspired. She does love him, you know."

"Don't show it," Breeze said.

"It's a Magruder thing," Stone said.

"You see the way she rode out of here," Colton said. "Frank, belly-down over that horse, Kate, without so much as a fare-thee-well."

"Class," Stone said. "She always had class."

"You two lived together, didn't you?" Breeze asked Stone. "What *was* she like?"

"The love of my life," Stone admitted.

"Why did she leave?" Breeze asked.

"She said I was a drunk, a psychopath, a fuckup, a fool—and the best friend she would ever have. I hurt for years after that."

"Truth does hurt," Colton said.

He and Breeze erupted with laughter. Stone grinned, shaking his head.

"I changed my mind," Breeze said. "I want bedtime stories."

Now all three of them laughed.

"After she left," Stone said seriously, "I couldn't get it up for two years."

"John Stone couldn't get it up for two years?" Breeze asked, stunned.

"Two fucking years," Stone said.

"You ever love anyone that much?" Colton asked Breeze.

"Never been that lucky," Breeze said. "How about you?"

"Once," Colton said.

"Where's she now?" Stone asked.

"Up there in the stars."

"Sara Friedman?" Stone asked, amazed. "The one who stayed behind to save Thucydides and the Odyssey?"

Colton nodded. "And the Citadel. Maybe the world."

"She and Thucydides gave L. L. the coordinates for that bomb strike," Stone said.

"I called them in," Colton said with a shrug.

"Cyd and Sara have been the only source of information, the only real communication, on what's left on this planet," Stone said.

18 You Think He'd Believe *Us*?

"They look like hell," Radford said to Jamal.

They were a hundred yards upwind from Colton, Stone, and Breeze, barbecuing steaks and drinking Bourbon. Sultana, Sabrina, and Ali joined them.

"We could offer them food," Sabrina said. "Something to drink. Appear reasonable."

"We were hoping the smell would make them hungry," Gerald explained.

"They are hungry," Radford said. "Cold, hungry, dehydrated."

"They get weak enough, maybe we risk snipers," Gerald said.

"This ain't the movies," Jamal reminded them.

"Let's go talk to them," Sultana suggested to her sister.

"Let him know we would never hurt him or his friends," Sabrina said.

"You think he'd believe *us*?" their brother asked, astonished.

"Desperation sometimes breeds credulity," Sultana said.

"To tell you the truth, Blessed Brother," Sabrina said, "I miss Stone."

"He's really quite . . . inventive," Sultana said, nodding her head, wistfully.

"What the hell," Radford said. "I'm tired of all this. Let's all go over there. Just remember: That traitor Breeze is *mine*."

19 Do It For *Us*!

Colton kicked Breeze in the foot, waking him.

"Company," Colton said.

Breeze stood and resumed his place, shotgun on top of the trigger-end of the bomb.

"Blessed Husband!" Sabrina called to Stone as they approached. "Your place is in our tent with your wives. We miss you terribly. We want you home."

"We've exacted a promise," Sultana agreed. "None of you will be hurt."

"The Citadel will not be nuked," Sabrina said. "It was a truly stupid idea anyway. What would nuking the Citadel achieve?"

"What do you think?" Stone asked Colton.

"Kate's had forty-eight hours to clear out," Colton said. "She's safe now."

"Then it's time?" Breeze asked.

"Time," Colton agreed.

"On three?" Stone asked.

Colton nodded and raised his left hand high over his head; his right hand still held the under-and-over against the Bomb's trigger-end.

"ONE!"

He swung the arm down.

"What the fuck?" Radford shouted.

"Stop, stop, please!" Gerald said. "For God's sake!"

Colton's counting arm swung back up.

"Stop!" Jamal said. "For our *people*."

"Fuck *your* people," Colton said.

"Make them stop, Breeze!" Jamal pleaded. "You can do it! Do it for all we've been through."

"For the Nation," Radford begged.

"Fuck the Nation," Breeze said.

"TWO!"

Colton's counting arm swung back up, and the Sin Sisters dropped to their knees, sobbing.

"Do it for *me*," Sultana begged.

"For *us*," Sabrina shouted.

Colton's arm was already swinging down, but Stone still got it in.

"Fuck you!" Stone said.

"THREE!"

20   It Would Have to Do

Kate eased Frank into the small cave—more like a bolt-hole, really—at the base of the big butte. Due south lay the Citadel and its minefields.

Her horse had fallen into an arroyo five hours ago and broken its neck. Kate had had to cut its throat with her buck knife. She and Frank then rode double on the chestnut, Kate behind, Frank draped over his withers.

But the desert heat, the lack of water, a nonstop two-day ride—with two riders now—finished the second horse. Kate cut his throat too—flush against the entrance of the cave.

She had just gotten Frank into the cave when the sky brightened and she heard the blast. Even before Kate felt the ground shake, she knew what it was.

There wasn't much space between the top of the bolt-hole and the body of the horse. She piled rocks on top of the dead horse and in the hidey-hole's entry-way.

After she squeezed herself in, she filled up the entrance with rocks. Then she set about cleaning and dressing Frank's leg.

It wasn't much of a bomb shelter, but it would have to do.

21 To the Last Cartridge

Things were not going quite so well for Chaplain O'Donnell.

True, he was alive and slowly coming to—but everything was black. He still could not see, and he felt nothing below his waist.

The thermal flash hadn't burned him or his horse. He remembered that much. He'd gotten fairly far away from the fireball. He'd been partially shielded from the worst effects of the blast wave by the Mogollon Mountains.

The explosion had caused avalanches in the surrounding foothills. But if he and his mount had escaped the fireball, shock front, and rockslides, what *had* happened? Why was he *here*?

Slowly it all came back to him. When he had seen that Colton, Breeze, and Stone were holding shotguns on the nuke, the Chaplain had done the math:

3 would-be heroes
+ 1 nuclear device
+ an army of fucking psychopaths
= a big mushroom cloud

The only reaction possible for a survivor of the Chaplain's caliber was flight. He and his horse had started out across the desert, leaving the foothills, when they had hit the prairie-dog town.

Now he remembered!

His horse had gone down in *a gopher hole*!

The Chaplain's vision partially returned, and he could at last make out the gray. The horse's left leg was still sunk in the prairie-dog burrow and had bro-ken off at the pastern. Apparently, forward momentum had pitched the gray onto his head, because his neck was also fractured, his head skewed at a sharp angle to his body. Clearly the gray was dead and had not suffered.

The Chaplain, so far, hadn't felt much himself—just a pervasive numbness. But slowly, ever so slowly, sensation began to return to his body.

He felt a strange pressure on his chest.

What was *that thing* sitting atop him? A prairie dog?

He focused with difficulty, and he finally got a close look at it. Wasn't like any prairie dog he'd ever seen. It looked more like . . .

A big fucking red rat!

Jesus, he'd never seen one that large. And the eyes—inches from his own—were so calm, so brilliantly crimson they seemed to burn into his, as if the rat was probing his mind.

And plumbing the depths of his soul.

What the fuck was a rat doing on his chest?

One thing the Chaplain knew for sure: He hated that rat. The arrogance of the beast—staring at him as if he knew everything about him, had peeped his hole card, had his number, knew where he lived.

No one knew where the Chaplain lived.

He wanted to knock the rat aside, but his arms weren't working. He lifted his head—with excruciating pain—and peered over the rat's shoulder. Couldn't see much—except that he was in the middle of the prairie-dog town.

My God, there must have been a million holes around him!

He felt something under his armpit. It was one of his boots. Maybe he could smack the bastard with a boot.

He tried to nudge it, but the boot wouldn't move.

Again, he peered past the rat's shoulder. He saw his other boot . . . on his other leg.

Then, where was his right foot?

Oh shit. It was still in . . . *the boot under his armpit.*

So much for the boot.

But then he remembered that he had a gun.

He could not reach his 9mm Beretta. It had fallen from its shoulder holster. But there was a small Smith & Wesson stainless-steel .38 in the boot under his arm.

There it was! He was staring right at the gun—fallen out of the boot, its walnut grip sticking out from under his shoulder.

After a seeming eternity of agony, he pulled it free at last.

He brought the barrel up level with the rat's eyes and thumbed back the hammer.

The concussion—this close to his head—would partially deafen him, but it would hurt that bloody rat-bastard a whole lot more.

"Adiós, motherfucker," the Chaplain said. "See you in rat hell."

He pulled the trigger. Nothing happened.

What the fuck? He examined the revolver closely. The entire mechanism was clogged with sand. The cylinder wouldn't turn.

Then the rat screamed.

The sound reminded O'Donnell of a factory whistle or an alarm or perhaps . . . some sort of summons.

Out of the thousands upon thousands of prairie-dog holes, rats poured forth.

Ah Christ, it must have been the biggest rat warren in the history of the world smack in the middle of the Sonoran Desert.

And they were coming toward the Chaplain, boiling all around him, squealing with ravenous excitement. *My God, they were Bailey's rats!* The ones they'd penned up . . . to feed the Nation.

And now *they* were hungry.

N-o-o-o-o-o-o!!!!

He fought against panic. He swore to resist them to the end, to the bitter end. To the last cartridge.

Cartridge!

He shoved the .38 under his chin, cocked the hammer again, and hand-twisted the cylinder, hoping to center the hammer on a live round.

The wheel wouldn't turn.

Ah no, the little bastards were tearing at his sides, his arms. Staring over the rat on his chest, he could now see them tearing at his crotch.

Suddenly, his lower extremities were no longer numb. The pain was unbearable.

Now the rats were lunging at his face.

He prayed as he had never prayed before.

For deliverance.

And pulled the trigger.

Click!

The last thing the Chaplain saw was Sailor's imperturbable all-seeing gaze. And then the rats were into his one good eye.

XI

Against the Fall of Night

She'd always dreaded that final fall of night . . .

—Lydia Lozen Magruder

1 It's— It's—

Everyone knew the rest.

The Bomb went off. Colton, Stone, and Breeze went up in a Viking funeral worthy of Valhalla. The Citadel was saved.

There was still the problem of infection. Not only was the world—particularly the refugee camps—awash in postapocalyptic plagues, no one could be sure whether all the Nation's radiological weapons and plague canisters had truly been destroyed in the fire. It was possible that plague victims or survivors from the Nation might make it past the wire and the minefields, enter the Citadel's gates, and decimate its citizens.

Warning signs were put up on the barbwire, notifying trespassers that they would be shot on sight. Sentries stood watch in the towers and trenches around-the-clock.

Discouraging hordes of refugees was no easy task. The Citadel was by post-apocalyptic standards heaven on earth, and rumors of its bounty drew people from across the country hoping to find food, medical help, a safe haven.

———

Trainee Trevanian—doing his military apprenticeship in a north-perimeter fire-trench—found the duty especially irritating. Under the blazing desert sun, he spent the morning in sweat-soaked army-surplus fatigues—the uniform of the Citadel's militia—standing in a shallow trench, sandbags surmounting its outer rim, scanning through 9X Minolta binoculars the minefields, the coiled barb-wire aprons, and perimeter beyond. He was hot, tired, and bored to distraction.

Not so with his superior, Sergeant Winston Carmony. Sergeant Carmony had never served in any real military. The closest Carmony had ever come to real was the interactive military computer games to which he'd once been addicted. A young man with closely cropped blond hair and boyishly fleshy features, he fancied himself "a career soldier, a 30-year man," not a temporary conscript like Trevanian. He loved long-range target-practice and bragged continually of his marksmanship. He even enjoyed sovereignty over the terrain, looking for "the bad guys"—as he called them. Instead of scanning the perimeter and the minefields through binoculars, however, he looked for them over the sights of his 7.62mm assault rifle—periodically shouting:

"Bam-bam-bam-bam-bam!"

His verbal warnings to interlopers were filled with four-letter expletives. His warning shots were alleged to be between the eyes.

The Citadel had been upwind from the detonation and far enough away that its radiation checks showed it was safe to stand guard without wearing fallout gear. They checked their dosimeters continually. The readings were all within the safe range.

Aw, hell, at least I'm not out here in a plastic raincoat and gas mask, Trevanian thought to himself. *It could be worse.*

His first morning on duty, two refugees—a man and a woman—crossed the north wire and started out across the minefield. Carmony went into action.

"This is the way you do it," he said. Switching on the audio, he growled into the mike:

"Turn around and get your sorry asses out of my minefield, or I'll blow your brains all over the barbwire."

They were a good 800 yards away, but through his binoculars, they appeared to Trevanian to be within 100 yards. He couldn't get a good look at them. The man was draped over the back of the woman, arms tied around her neck. He was either dead or comatose. Both were badly sunburned. Through the binoculars he could see their split lips and scorched blisters. Both looked sicker than hell. Could be carrying plague.

Yet something about the pair bothered Trevanian.

Carmony stood in the trench, staring over the sandbags, adjusting scope. Yardage was clearly marked on their range charts, and the rifles rested on sandbag grooves. It wasn't that tough a shot.

"Number thirteen coming up," Carmony whispered.

"I don't know, Sergeant," Trevanian said. "Something's funny about those two."

Carmony muttered *"chickenshit"* under his breath.

A shot cracked, and dust kicked five inches to the right of the incoming soldier and his unconscious buddy.

"Shit, I missed," Carmony said.

He adjusted the scope for windage and laid the rifle back on its sandbag groove.

"Don't, Sergeant. I tell you something's funny."

"Fuck you," Carmony said.

Trainee Trevanian then committed an act of gross insubordination.

He unholstered his 9mm Beretta, chambered a round, placed the muzzle behind Carmony's ear, and said: "Stand down, Sergeant, or I'll shoot *you* where *you* stand."

Shaking with rage, Carmony lowered his rifle.

"Now you get across that minefield and reconnoiter. Something's funny."

"I'm going to have your fucking balls," Carmony shouted.

"Just remember when you cross that minefield, I'll have you in *my* sights."

Carmony—minefield map in hand—set out in a zigzag pattern. The land mines were not randomly sown but had been laid out in NATO A-patterns: One antitank land mine triangulated by three antipersonnel fragmentation mines.

The mines were not impossible to detect, but you had to know where to look. Which wasn't a lot of help. They still could be detonated electrically from the fire-trenches or triggered by tripwire.

And the tripwires were all over the place, heavily obscured by sagebrush, prickly pear, and sand.

Cursing into his walkie-talkie every step of the way, he finally reached the two refugees.

For several moments Trevanian heard nothing from Carmony. Then:

"Oh shit. Oh no. Goddamn it to hell. It's— It's—"

It was Kate and Frank.

2 Shotgun on the Table

Frank was—despite Kate's close medical care—in grave danger. His bullet-wounds were badly infected. When their horse had gone down, his fractures were compounded. Frank was taken straight into surgery, where the Citadel's medical director—after consulting with his department heads—concluded that both legs had to go.

They took him into surgery.

Kate went straight to the armory, came out with a 12-gauge pump shotgun and three boxes of shells. When the poker-faced armorer in the denim jacket handed them to her, he said: "What you want all them shells for?"

"I'm gonna knock down some walls," she said.

Returning to the OR—where Frank was now on the operating table, awaiting anesthesia—she ordered the attending doctors out, then promptly blew a hole in a sidewall when they hesitated.

That brought L. L. on the run.

Before L. L. could get one word out, Kate put a hole in another wall. L. L. took one look at Kate's face and ordered the doctors from the OR.

Kate asked Bill Cummings, the head of the hospital's Infectious Disease Department, to come to the OR.

"I saw Frank treat a hundred cases worse than his in the Towers," Kate explained to Cummings. She had put the shotgun on the table. "Round-the-clock wound antibiotic drips—methicillin or vancomycin, if you have them—work miracles. Irrigation too. Irrigate those wounds like Hercules flooding the Aegean stables. I tell you it'll work. I've seen Frank do it. I've assisted him."

"I can't take responsibility for this, Kate."

"I can."

"You'll kill him."

"Without his legs, Frank won't want to live. Believe me, I *know* him—better than you know yourself."

"I can't be a part of this."

"Then get me what I need and leave me alone."

Cummings sent a nurse back with Kate's supplies, including the irrigation solution and the methicillin drip.

She leaned the shotgun against the OR table and went to work on Frank. Around-the-clock for 72 hours. Irrigating wounds every twenty minutes, changing the methicillin and glucose drips, and force-feeding him Sustagen until at last the stench of gas gangrene was gone.

After three days his blood tested negative.

Kate had saved his legs.

3 Of War and of the Sea

Unfortunately, Kate could not save her mother. The events of the last year had been hard on L. L. She'd had a serious heart attack and a mild stroke, which she had attempted to hide from everyone. But they had taken a toll that could no longer be concealed or ignored. L. L. spent most of her time in bed now, slipping in and out of consciousness.

One night near the end she felt surprisingly lucid, strangely in focus. She began summoning people to her bedside.

Cassandra came to her, dressed in her customary black robes, wearing dark glasses, rum flask in hand.

"You drink too much," L. L. said.

"I plan on cutting back."

"When?"

"Soon as Sara and Thucydides enter the cascade—and cancel my act."

"The Twelve-Step Program's effective."

"I was thinking more of the .45-caliber program."

"You've tried that before."

"I have it down now."

"Cassie, I need you."

"As long as you need me, I'm here. You know that."

"I don't have a lot of time. I want two favors."

Cass nodded.

"I intend to be cremated. When it's done, have my ashes scattered by my sacred spot up the mountain."

"By the three-horned beast? The one fossilized in the cliff face?"

"The same. I expect—even if I request otherwise—there will be some kind of service. I want you to sing the song. You know the one."

"I don't sing it anymore."

"I'm asking you."

"The other favor?"

"Bury your oar. Shoulder it like Odysseus, far away from this place. Have Kate take you. She was born here. She'll know where to go. Plant the oar there. You can be free, Cassie, of war and of the sea. I promise you."

"Never."

"It will happen. I know."

4 Kate's Always Been My Hero

Frank was wheeled into L. L.'s room in double casts. He was doing well. The casts were due to be cut off in two weeks.

L. L. cut to the chase.

"Frank, I want you to marry Kate and have children. Have lots of them. The Citadel will need them."

Frank stared at her. It took him a long time to get his voice.

"Kate's a sister to me."

"She's no blood kin at all. You grew up here in the family, as my stepson. We're not blood kin either. Kate is the child of my first husband."

"She's still a sister to me."

"You love her more than life itself. But if you lose her, if you let her slip through your fingers, believe me, you'll rue it till the day you die."

"I'm not marrying her, L. L., and I'm not having children. After what I've seen, after what Kate's seen, neither of us would want them."

"So you let *them* win—the O'Donnells, the Radfords, the Haddads, the maniacs responsible for all this."

"No, I'll do my part. I'm a good doctor. I can help others. I won't walk away from that. But I won't give hostages to fortune—not in this day and age."

"Petty arguments as to what you want or what Kate wants are no longer applicable. The only question is whether the race will survive. When you choose not to have children, you threaten the entire race with extermination. You're accessories to human extinction."

Frank stared blankly at her and shook his head. "I'm sorry."

"Frank, you're the best man I ever known, and that's going some. I knew Henry Colton. You just don't know your own mind yet." She fixed him with a hard stare. "You'll come around."

After he left, L. L. asked for a cell phone. She dialed Sara. She knew that the Odyssey was in major trouble as it entered the collisional cascade, "the Death Orbit," as Sara called it, and they could lose contact with the space station at any time.

When Sara picked up, L. L. heaved a sigh of relief.

"How's it shaking, L. L.? Heard you've had some ups and downs."

"Hate to complain, but I've been better. How are you doing?"

"I took your advice. After Thucydides' eyesight came back, I linked him up with the new space telescope. He's abandoned me."

"He never contacts you?"

"He's stargazing."

"Sara, you're the best *person* I've ever met."

"Kate's not too bad herself. Kate's always been my hero, you know?"

"Kate? I don't know where I went wrong. She and I have never been close."

"You had her late in life."

"I was 46. I was afraid of her, for her. She was strong-willed, rebellious, independent. Even when I talked her into finally joining the network, I had no influence. She never listened to me."

"She was already famous."

"But I was her *mother*."

"Which is what she still needs."

At first, L. L. was speechless. "Do you think so?" L. L. finally said.

"The question is, do *you* know how?"

"I'm not sure," L. L. whispered.

"I am. She's been through hell, and she's afraid."

"You'll never know what you've meant to me, Sara. How much I've loved you."

"I know. The question is, does Kate?"

For a long time they said nothing.

5 I *Am* Your Mother

Kate was her mother's last visitor.

She was wearing Levi's and a white tank top. She had resumed Tae Kwon Do and pumping iron. Kate sat down on the edge of her bed, and L. L. came right to the point.

"I have a last request. I want you and Frank to get married."

"Ask me something else," Kate said, after a few stunned moments.

"Don't give me that look. You've never known half of what was good for you."

"I don't love Frank—not that way."

"You'll learn to love him."

"Damn it, he's my brother. I don't believe you're saying this."

The old woman—cranked up on a hospital bed, an oxygen tank nearby—had planned on saying something conciliatory, maybe even play on Kate's sympathy. Instead, something snapped in her.

Summoning more strength than she thought she had, she cracked Kate across the side of the head with her hand.

"That's one of the things that really ticks me off about you!" her mother shouted. "You never listen!"

Kate stared back at her, furious, her cheek burning, but she refused to touch it, refused to give her mother the satisfaction.

"I don't give a shit what you think," Kate replied evenly.

Her mother cracked her again.

"That's another thing that ticks me off. Your profanity. You know I hate that kind of talk. You do it just to provoke me. Where did you get such a foul mouth? Not from me."

"Don't you ever do that again," Kate shouted at her. "I'm your daughter, Kate Magruder, I—"

Her mother slapped her again, this time a left.

"That's another thing," L. L. said. "Your name's not Kate. It's *Katherine Jane Magruder*. Kate's a baby's name, a little girl's name, and you're not a little girl! It's time you stopped acting like one. The Citadel needs women, *real women*, not children!"

"I'm more woman than you'll ever know."

"You don't know *love*."

"Ask my lovers."

Again, her mother cracked her.

"Sex is *not* a surrogate for love."

They stared at each other. Kate slowly rubbed her cheek.

"You hit me," Kate said, uncertainly.

"About to do it again."

"You—you always *hated* violence, especially violence against women and children."

"My mistake. I should have taken a knotted plowline to you."

Kate got up to leave, but her mother seized her arm.

Christ, Kate's arm was hard.

"I'm still your mother, and you've been through a lot. I want you to tell me about it. Believe me, it will help. I know."

"No, you don't! You've never wanted to know anything about me, my life."

"I do now. Everything. From the beginning. I *am* your mother. And Kate, I'm going to die."

Kate hesitated, and then sat down again. Her mother was dying; it was a last request, and so she talked to her, haltingly. A couple of minutes, then maybe her mother would drift off to sleep. Her mother didn't fall asleep though. She sat bolt-upright, fixed on Kate, listening, nodding, not interrupting except to ask a question, to get Kate to say more, to draw her out.

Suddenly, words were coming out of Kate in torrents. John Stone, Larry Taylor, Breeze, the nuking of Manhattan, the Towers, Frank—yes, Frank!—and Sailor, the Nation, the two crazy sisters, Jamal, Radford, their insanely evil Chaplain. Then the desert, and Frank—yes, Frank! Always, Frank!—and crossing the minefields and those fucking—I'm sorry, Mom—those imbecilic doctors that wanted to cut off his legs.

Then her mother was holding her. For the only time in her adult life, Kate Magruder, encouraged by L. L., was crying.

As usual her mother was right.

The tears helped a lot.

 **She'd Kept the Faith**

After Kate had left her room, the old woman drifted in and out of sleep.

She couldn't quite doze off.

Christ, she had had so much to be grateful for. A loving grandfather, a legendary grandmother, two loving husbands, a daughter she had finally come to terms with, friends like John Stone and Henry Colton, Cassie and Sara Friedman. And Thucydides—whom she had long ago ceased thinking of as a machine.

And Frank, of course.

God, she'd loved life so much—her family, friends, work. She'd never wanted it to end, had always dreaded that final fall of night.

But no more.

My race is done; I have finished the course; I have kept the faith, she thought absently, remembering the last lines of St. Paul before he went to his own death. She'd had such wonderful luck. *Some people never get their hands on the dice,* she mused. *She had.*

Yes, she'd kept the faith.

Her mind was wandering now.

We are such stuff
As dreams are made on,
And our little life
Is rounded with a sleep.

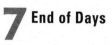 **End of Days**

L. L. was cremated at her request. Friends and family made the long horseback trek up the cliff face and to the three-horned beast, the sacred spot of Lydia Lozen.

Kate gave the eulogy. She said simply:

"Everyone knows my mother was a pioneer in communications, computers, and media. What most people didn't know—but what Frank and I can tell you—she was the best parent any child could ask for. Her favorite poem was from St. Francis of Assisi, and I would like to read a little of it to you:

"'Lord, make me an instrument of your peace.
Where there is hate, may I bring love.
Where there is offense, may I bring pardon.
Where there is error, may I bring truth.
Where there is doubt, may I bring faith.
Let me seek to console rather than be consoled.
For it is in the giving that I receive.
In pardoning that I am pardoned.
In dying that I am born.'

"Mom told me she wanted Cassie to sing 'The Song.' Something Cass doesn't do anymore. After much bullying I think I've convinced her. And don't say you've forgotten the lyrics, Cass. I've brought them with me."

She stepped aside.

A cappella, Sister Cassandra sang, softly, still with the Janis Joplin rasp but also with a balladic beauty and sensitivity missing from much of her later work. This was clearly a song of her youth, when, despite her vision, she'd still believed redemption was possible.

"I have seen the end.
(The End Time, my son.)
And I have heard the cryin'
Faced the dyin' all around.
And I have felt the fire
For all time to come.

"In the darkness
In the thunder
In the blaze

"End of days
End of days
End of days"

To Kate Magruder it would always be Cassandra's finest moment.

"I have felt the rumble,
Felt it tumble-in down.

And I have heard the thunder
Seen the wonder to come.
And I have smelled the blood tide
In the flood tide I was drown.

"I have seen the end.
(Please, say it ain't the end.)
I have witnessed the end.
(Don't let it be end.)
I have prayed for the end.
(Lord, say it ain't the end.)

"In the fury
In the flood
In the fray

"End of days
End of days
End of days

"Oh, I have felt the hardness.
(The hardness, my son.)
And I have known the darkness.
(The darkness to come.)
I was broken on a rack
On a rack of the sun.

"I have seen the end.
(Please, say it ain't the end.)
I have witnessed the end.
(Don't let it be end.)
I have prayed for the end.
(Lord, say it ain't the end.)

"In the fire
In the blood.
Unafraid

"End of days
End of days
End of days

*"End of days
End of days
End of days*

*"End of days
End of days
End of days."*

8 To Follow Knowledge like a Sinking Star

Thucydides *had* boarded the big new space telescope, which everyone called Hubble, Jr.

Sara cracked the linkup codes that gave Thucydides access to Junior's computers. He saw the universe as Hubble saw it, had access to all of Hubble's files and photos, was one with Junior Hubble's brain, could tell Hubble what to do.

Thucydides *was* Hubble, Jr.

Not simply a telescope, Hubble II was an astronomical observatory complete with high-resolution spectrographic and photometric capabilities. With millions of lines of computer code, number II's computers and megaprograms were in fact so vast that they were, in an emergency, beyond the comprehension of mortals. In those extreme cases Junior went into "safe-mode" and handled his own problems. With so much autonomy, Hubble II was freed from human control-command.

Which was what had allowed Thucydides to board, *and* enter Hubble II's computers and experience observations through the big telescope.

And big he was. A new, improved, updated version of the four-story, thirteen-ton Ritchey-Chrétien telescope with the eight-foot main mirror possessing a surface so smooth—in his original design—that had the mirror been expanded to encompass the entire width of the continental United States, his grossest imperfection would have been less than two inches high. His entire optical system had been of such precision it had required seven years and four million hours of human labor to grind and refine it.

Hubble II was even better than his father.

He had already logged several billion miles and taken several hundred thousand pictures of over 15,000 celestial objects.

Thucydides' passion was seeing, and he now had the biggest, brightest, most magnificent eye in history—an eye that had probed the deepest secrets of deep space and produced jaw-dropping imagery that scientists had universally hailed "a religious experience." Through the eye of Hubble II, Thucydides too could plumb the dawn of creation, star nurseries, black-hole factories, exploding supernovae—and roam the length and breadth of the universe.

Sailor had finally found peace. His odyssey was over.

Sailor and his newfound tribe—formed out of the legions he had rescued from the Nation—found their Ithaca in an abandoned prairie-dog town in Arizona's Sonoran Desert. Renovated, reexcavated, it suited their needs.

In an odd sense their new home represented a return to their roots. Their ancestors had emerged out of Asia's barren steppe lands almost a thousand years ago to join Genghis Khan's Golden Horde and travel the world, eventually making their way to Europe and then the New World.

They were ideally suited to this otherwise-harsh environment. Mesquite beans, agave, maguey fruit, prickly pear were all perfect provender for the clan. A nearby spring provided them with water. They more than subsisted; they thrived and prospered.

Far from man.

Man, they had indeed learned to fear. True, living off his excess and his refuse had provided ratdom with a certain ease of living, but nuclear flames and captivity in cages had taught them the dangers of parasitism.

Sailor was not completely at peace with peace. He was by nature a searcher, a pilgrim—a Wanderratte—but also he was growing old. In rat years he was in truth approaching dotage. His sleek red-auburn coat had sprouted tufts of gray. He knew it was time to settle down—and become, like his own mentor, Old Socrates, a patriarch.

Among the clans the mighty Sailor had a reputation that was almost godlike. He was the huge red rat who'd saved his clan from the Cyclops, Man.

And he could sing. If Sailor had done nothing at all but recite sagas and sing songs, he would have been famous, and the tribe needed his songs. They had gone through so much, witnessed so much wickedness, that the ordeal had hardened their hearts and seared their souls. Whenever the very name "man" was mentioned, rats hissed and spat:

"Beware the wrath of man."

Sailor knew that hatred was sinful and in the end destroyed the hater. It was true of rats, and it was true of men. So when his friends railed against humankind, Sailor sighed and told them in gentle tones of the human being he'd known and who carried love in her heart. Kate Magruder had not only liberated him, she had liberated the tribe as well from their boxcar cages.

He would then sing to them:

"Listen well! This I tell
To welcome friends and guests.
He prayeth well, who loveth well
Both man and bird and beast.

"He prayeth best, who loveth best
All things both great and small;
For the dear God who loveth us,
He made and loveth all."

10 Remember Me When the Lights Go Out

Kate had driven Cass to a high hill above the Citadel—then left her alone to be with her own thoughts. Kneeling on the hilltop, Cass began to dig. L. L. had exacted a promise that on a hill beyond the Citadel Cassandra would plant her oar. True, she lacked an oar, but with a buck knife she still dug an oar-hole.

Whatever the fuck an oar-hole was.

When she figured she had dug about a foot, she sat down in front of the hole, braced a flask between her knees, and removed a .45-caliber pistol from her knapsack.

Plant my oar? What did that mean? What oar?

A fool's quest, but she'd never known how to tell the old woman no.

The hell with it. She took a pull on the flask and stared into space—into nothingness.

Not that she could see anything if she tried.

But suddenly she *was* seeing something. Shit. There he was. El Zopilote . . .

Camouflage fatigues, pant legs tucked into black polished jump boots, the nickel-plated ebony-handled .45 still under his arm in a shoulder holster, the thick black stinking cigar clenched between his teeth.

"Ay, guapa, long-time no-see."

"Not long enough for me."

"I know, I know," he said. "You think I no appreciate what you and Santiago try to do. You think because I'm an atheist. You think I no believe in your Cristo Rey. That ain't true. Jesus and me real tight. You sabe me as Christ's brother?"

The concept was hard for her to grasp. She stared at him in silence.

"In fact," he continued, "Jesus and me communicate daily."

Jesus, didn't he ever shut up? Cassandra decided to ignore him. Instead she concentrated on the Colt .45 on her lap. The thumb-safety was off, and the hammer was resting on an empty chamber. And she'd had enough bullshit. It was time to get it on. Pointing the barrel toward the heavens, she pulled back the slide and released it with a resounding crack! automatically chambering a round.

Inserting the barrel in her mouth, aiming at very top of the brainpan, she threw back her head and allowed herself a last bleak grin.

Remember me when the lights go out.

11 "In What Furnace Was Thy Brain?"
—William Blake, "The Tyger"

There was so much for Thucydides to see—especially when it came to his favorite of all the celestial objects, the giant stars.

But there was so little time.

So he asked Hubble, Jr. to step on the gas and take him past the red giant R. Aquarii and his white-dwarf partner in a hurry. Those two lovebirds Thucydides just had to see. Every time the elliptical path of R. Aquarii's partner brought her within perigee of R. Aquarii, the two lovers erupted in a bizarre celestial mating ritual in nova-style explosions. Hot ionized plasma gas detonated out of the death dance, a luminous geyser of blinding light and blazing plasma. The white dwarf might have been the smaller, but its omnivorously deep gravitational well was sucking out of the red giant supermassive amounts of fuel, initiating in the white dwarf violent thermonuclear explosions, turning the red giant's mate into an interstellar nuclear bomb.

Hellbent for leather, Cyd and Hubble swung by Wolf-Rayet 104—the pinwheel star—a scorching giant many times Sol's mass and size, renowned for its 18-billion-mile spiraling tail. Hidden in that whirling appendage was an invisible giant. These two orbiting orbs were live-fast, die-hard stars, their rotating dance creating horrendous shock fronts. Powerful stellar winds radiated outward, whipping the dust into whirling arcs. Nature was notorious for its artfully spun spirals—the nautilus shell in biology, the monstrous maelstroms of the North Sea—but these stellar whorls were among her most dramatic, seeming in Thucydides' mind to mirror their own mother, the most famous spinner of them all, the spiral galaxy known as the Milky Way.

Nor could Cyd resist rocketing past the Crab Nebula. Chinese astronomers observed its detonation in 1054. Formerly a massive star in the constellation Taurus, the Crab grew to such dazzling luminescence that the Chinese studied it weeks on end.

At high noon.

Six thousand light-years from Earth, it was now a minute semblance of its former glory—a pulsar 12 miles across, rotating 33 times a second and with a stellar density of 1 billion tons per teaspoon. Radiating a continuous 10 quadrillion electrical volts, this densely magnetized powerhouse emitted 100,000 times the energy of Sol.

And was still the most scrutinized object in the sky.

Back to the supergiants.

Thucydides had Hubble, Jr. take him past some of those, including Eta Carinae, a superluminous eruptive star more than one million times brighter than the sun. Arp 220 was an old red giant passing quickly through his dotage and didn't have long to live, and Thucydides was grateful to have glimpsed him before he passed on.

Betelgeuse—a superred perched on Orion's shoulder—possessed 10 times Sol's mass, and had he commanded Sol's solar system, his circumference would have reached to Saturn and beyond. Four hundred and thirty light-years from the sun, he was the brightest red supergiant in Terra's night sky, boasted a huge crimson blotch like Jupiter, and like Arp 220 was on the brink of going supernova.

But Thucydides also wanted to see a superblue. It was a hell of a road trip—a long diversion from his visit to the heart of the Milky Way—but Hubble, Jr., was nothing if not accommodating. The biggest superblue in Terra's sky was Orion's Rigel, 900 light-years away. Rigel was regal—so massive, had he been placed in Sol's position, he would have stretched far beyond Earth, almost to Mars.

But Cyd's interest in the superreds and -blues went far beyond mere aesthetics. Thucydides knew them for what they were and had come in true humility to pay homage. The oxygen people breathed, the calcium in their teeth, the carbon fuels that warmed them, the CO_2 their plants took in were spawned not in the primordial detonation of the Big Bang. The laws of nucleosynthesis would not allow something so brief and hurried to manufacture anything heavier than helium.

The heavy elements required billions upon billions of years of forced atomic reaction in a furnace-forge of vastly varying pressures and temperatures—inconceivably hot, incomprehensibly powerful—culminating in explosions violent enough to spin them off into the galaxy, where they might forge planets.

And form life.

Tyger, Tyger, burning bright
In the forests of the night,
What immortal hand or eye
Could frame thy fearful symmetry?

What immortal hand or eye? Thucydides knew now. The hand was the fiery fist of the superstars, and its eye blazed red as blood, blue as Terra's seas.

In what distant deeps or skies
Burnt the fire of thine eyes?

The fire of the tiger's eyes came from the same deeps and skies as Sara's and Thucydides' did—from the fires of Betelgeuse and Rigal—and billions of other reds and blues.

What the hammer? What the chain?
In what furnace was thy brain?
What the anvil? What dread grasp
Dare its deadly terrors clasp?

The hammer was a hammer with a trillion tons of pressure. The furnace heat blazed at times with thermonuclear temperatures of a million degrees. The anvil was the anvil of the stars, and only they had the courage to grasp it.

When the stars threw down their spears,
And water'd heaven with their tears,
Did He smile His work to see?
Did He who made the lamb make thee?

The stars did indeed hurl spears at Earth and strike it with the hydrogen and oxygen that yielded water, and it was no easy task. When supergiants burned up their hydrogen, their core collapsed inward. They had so much heavy element in them they could not completely burn up—even though they turned hotter than hell. Instead, they went into a spin, like a skater's death spiral, the centrifugal force—hurling its newly created heavy elements into space like Blakean spears but in the form of dust and gas and ionized plasma—producing supernovae, the Death Stars spawning the stuff of life.

The supergiants were the anvil and hammer.

The Death Stars threw the spears—and through their death gave us life.

But "did He smile His work to see?" Blake, the poet, had asked.

Six months ago Thucydides would have said no. But here amid the glory and the grandeur of the stars, Thucydides knew that the mess on earth was merely a minute setback. People like Kate and Frank would whip that mess back into shape.

He had known the sacrifices Colton and Stone and L. L. and Sara and Cassandra and so many others had made.

Everything would be all right.

Yes, Thucydides believed that now. Yes, God did smile. He was smiling.

And even if He wasn't smiling, Thucydides swore, *we would make it up to Him.*

Word up.

We'll fix that sorry mess back on earth.

You redeem the past by redeeming the future, as Colton used to say.

You pay it back by paying it forward.

Humanity was worth it—the Promethean gift, the forge and anvil of the stars.

12 Let Bygones Be Bygones

Cassandra was about to squeeze the trigger—when El Zopilote got in her face.

"*Qué pasa, guapa?*" he asked, angrily. "What the fuck you doin'?"

"God's will. It's what you told me He wanted."

"I did?"

"You said so back there in Boniata, Christ told God we all ought to be extinct."

"Sí, but I didn't tell you the rest of it."

The muzzle of the gun still in her mouth, Cassandra muttered: "This better be good."

"Sí, cabrita. Jesus told Dios that we all ought to be shot like mad dogs. But God no agree. He say to His Son: 'Look, I know you're pissed. It was a dirty trick I play on you, knocking up Mary, having all the fun, and then leaving you down there to take the rap—to be flogged, crowned with thorns, crucified. It was a pretty sick joke.'

"'Pretty lame,' Christ say to God.

"'So you got a right to be hot. I admit that. You want me to nuke them all, and I can understand how from your point of view that makes sense. After what they done to you, I say nukin' eees too good for the hideputas. But do me a favor. Just cool off, think it over for one or two thousand years. What's a millennium or two between amigos, between father and son.'

"'I don't know,' Christ say.

"'Look,' God say, 'what's the rush? If they're as bad as you say, let them stew. They ain't completely stupido. Maybe they put two and two together.'"

El Zopilote's Montecristo had gone out, and he paused to relight it.

"Can you hurry up?" Cassandra said impatiently. "I can't sit here all night with a .45 locked on my tonsils."

"That's exactly what Christ say, 'Can't we hurry up?'"

The tip of the cigar flared, and he inhaled deeply, blowing smoke at the sky.

"Well," Cassandra snarled, "what did God say?"

"God say, no. What else He gonna say to His hothead son Who wants to blow up everything God made?"

"How did Christ take that?"

"Oh, He get madder'n hell. Not that there much He could do. I mean God is God. And look what He did to Lucifer—His favorite angel—when Lucifer give Him shit. God can get pissed. Anyway, Christ got to admit, what's a few millennia between tight buddies.

"So the First Millennium rolls round. Christ still wants us dead as dodos, end all suffering for all time to come. It's what we deserve etc., etc."

His cigar went out, and again he fumbled with his wooden matches.

"I can't keep this thing in my mouth all day," Cassandra mumbled. "Rápido."

"Which is exactly what Christ say. That part about hurry up. The First Millennium's up. Christ still sayin': 'Kill 'em all.'

"God say to Him: 'Look, I got a few tests for them. Maybe they do some good. Maybe they help turn 'em around.'

"'What tests?' Christ ask.

"'Plague, war, famine, drought, earthquake. See if that bring them around. Make them see the error of their ways.'"

"Sounds like a wake-up call to me," Cassandra had to admit.

Again, he struggled to relight his cigar.

"Those things will kill you," Cassandra said.

"Which is what Christ say to God when the plagues, wars, famines, locusts, floods, lightning bolts are killing men like fleas, but don't do no good. 'Cause— bein' such a mean little bastardo—man still don't see the Light. Jesus say to God: 'No more pulling rank. You promised me. Now do you keep your Word? Do we kill 'em all like we agreed? Word?'"

"Get to the point," Cassandra said. "My trigger-finger's itchy."

"God say: 'Look, I know you're still hot. I also know the Monster Manunkind—Superkiller, the Fire Driver—is a rotten prick. But can't we compromise?'

"Christ say to His dad: 'Why should we let any of them off?'

"'You believe all that shit you was peddling: Love thy neighbor as yourself? Love those that persecute you? Or was you just handin' out tickets?'

"'Of course, I believed it. I still do.'

"'Then don't we show a little love ourselves? After all, we made them in our image. If we don't show compassion, how can we expect it from them?'

"Now this stops Christ cold. I mean God's beating the kid at His own game with His own words. That's pretty slick."

"Pretty clever," Cassandra had to concede.

"Of course He's clever. What did you expect? It's why He's God. It's what gives Him the Big G."

"Still, Christ has a right to be pissed—after all God and humankind did to Him," Cass said.

"That's right. And He still don't let God off the hook—not completely. After all, He some rights in this. So He say to God: 'But we do kill most of them.'

"'It's only fair.'

"'You're not shucking me around?'

"'Ask Thermopylae. Ask the Somme. Ask Hiroshima. Talked to any auks or dodos or short-faced bears lately, which your Monster Manunkind exterminated? You ain't the only one with complaints against our friend, the Fire Driver.'

"And guess what? Christ looks His old man straight in the eye and says: 'I've learned a lot from you these last two millennia.' Then He gives His dad the abrazo, a big kiss and hug. Then He says: 'I love you, Dad.' Just like that."

"'I love you, Dad'?" Cassandra repeated, incredulous.

"Which is something He ain't said to His father for two thousand years."

"Sounds like a pretty dysfunctional family, you ask me."

"True, but He had cause—after what all of us did to Him—and anyway God is nothing if not understanding. If He can put up with us, He can put up with anything. So God throws His arm around His kid and says: 'The secret is, you got to make them an offer they can't refuse.'"

"That's from The Godfather."

"Ay, it got 'God' in the title, no?"

"Okay," Cassandra acknowledged, "but my mouth tastes like metal. Let me get on with it."

"I'd like you to reconsider."

"Don't tell me how to do my job."

"But I got to, guapa. Look, I'm sorry I fucked you up, but I can't let you die on us. You got work to do: sermons to give, songs to write and sing. You ain't even started."

"I'm starting to get real sick of you," Cassandra said.

"Come on, Cassandra!" he shouted in his best parade-ground tone of command. *"Give your oncle a big abrazo, an 'I-love-you,' and let bygones be bygones."*

He swept the cigar from his mouth with a histrionic wave, blew more blue smoke at the sky, and treated her to his most theatrical grin. Reaching out his great arms, offering her a warm embrace, he said: *"Geeeve your oncle a beeeg keeess."*

Gripping the gun with both hands, Cassandra shoved the pistol in his open mouth and pulled the trigger.

13 He'd Seen Hellgate and Heard the Screams

Thucydides' tour of the universe would not be complete without its "black holes." They were the real cosmic mystery.

Stephen Hawking had said that black holes might even outnumber visible stars, and everybody knew of the violence of the X-ray emissions, infrared transmissions, and radio signals.

Their radio signals were often compared to screams.

Through the plane Thucydides soared closer, closer to the galaxy's center. The dark heart of this spiral galaxy was not, Thucydides believed, an inspiring sight, but like Odysseus among the Sirens he had to see and hear it all.

To follow knowledge like a sinking star.

And in this case knowledge was a black hole named Sagittarius A*.

In fact, with the ears of Hubble, Jr. and the Chandra X-ray Telescope he could hear those howls from Sagittarius A*'s center, and it was no Sirens' song.

It was a death scream as Sagittarius A* devoured his fellow stars.

This starving singularity was no ordinary grave but a bottomless pit with the mass of innumerable suns. Incomprehensibly bright, it was a charnel pit for a million stars. It whipped them around its gaping maw at shocking speeds—at hundreds of kilometers per second. It clawed with special fury at one star cluster near Sagittarius A*, IRS 16, sucking vast amounts of its stellar matter into its awful Charybdis gut, and the nearby red supergiant, IRS7, was now plumed with a cometlike tail by IRS 16's ejecta.

It whipped the entire Milky Way—Sol included—around its hellish pivot, and IRS 16's death cries would haunt Thucydides to his grave.

He'd seen Hellgate and heard the screams.

Nor was the fiend in the center of Sagittarius the only black hole devouring a galaxy's heart and soul. Carl Sagan had warned long, long ago that galaxies, like Homo sapiens, were profoundly suicidal.

"The suicide rate among galaxies," Sagan wrote, "is high," and he said that some were blowing themselves up.

Nor were galaxies alone susceptible to destruction.

Hawking, with Roger Penrose, had glimpsed as early as 1970 the ghastly specter of universal destruction. General Relativity, they wrote, allowed that the universe—which was spawned by a singularity, named the Big Bang—could likewise die in black holes.

Hawking later argued that these black holes might not be completely black. They might, like energy sources everywhere, emit radiation, evaporate over time, and then too—like the stars, the galaxies they had devoured—disappear.

Vanish without a trace.

Other astrophysicists argued the opposite—that dark energy was driving the stars and galaxies so far apart at such unprecedented speeds that stellar matter would become irretrievably, irreversibly isolated. Lost and alone in the vast blackness of space, matter itself would disintegrate even as the black holes vanished. They called these two eventualities "the Big Rip" and "the Big Crunch."

It all came down to the same thing.

The lights in the sky went out.

And the rest was darkness.

The thought of so much galactic death and universal doom seized Thucydides with sudden dread.

Was that true?

For a terrible second he feared it was—but then shook it off.

For the earth, yes.

The sun, yes.

The galaxies, yes.

Humanity, *never.*

Humanity would find a way.

The survivors would soldier on.

He knew that now.

Though much is taken, much abides.

And anyway, Thucydides had other sights to see.

14 Eight Rounds Is *Nothing?*

Kate came tearing back up the hill.

"What was that?" she shouted at Cassandra. "Armageddon?"

Cassandra had, in fact, emptied all eight .45 rounds into El Zopilote's glittering smile, but she had the grace not to explain. Instead, as if nothing had happened, she continued piling sand over her shot-up rum flask and the Colt .45 at the bottom of the hole she'd dug.

"Nothing at all," Cassandra answered.

"Eight rounds is nothing?"

"Nada. Not a thing." Rising, Cassandra held out her hand.

"Cassie, what is happening?"

"We're getting out of here. That's what's happening."

"What's the rush?"

"We have work to do. Let's go."

Kate was about to say: "What work?" But then it happened. Kate could only stare at Cassandra in shocked disbelief. Something none of them had ever seen.

A miracle.

Sister Cassandra—the Unsmiling Sister—was . . . smiling.

 **15 Sara Sang**

Sara Friedman finally came to.

For the past hour—stunned by hunger and hypoxia, exhaustion and dehydration—she'd been unconscious.

It was all she could do to sit strapped into her command-control chair in front of Thucydides' main communications console. Through the view-port and on Thucydides' last three still-functioning monitors she observed the light show outside. Kessler had been right. Put enough trash in these orbits, and you get a chain-reacting critical mass—a gun gallery. They were now smack in the middle of that collisional cascade. The deorbiting debris surrounding them was blowing up with stunning regularity.

It was actually quite beautiful.

She also knew she and Thucydides were going to die.

Well, they can take your body, but they cannot take your dreams.

She knew Cyd was out there in the Deep Field in space with Hubble, Jr. She hated bothering him, but there was so much she had to tell him.

She punched in Thucydides' wake-up code.

"Are you running with me, kid?" she typed into the console. "You got my back?"

"I'm running with you, Sara. I got you covered."

Funny, she'd never really wanted any of this. The computer stuff, space travel had been a diversion. Her sole wish had been to write, but when it was discovered she had these other gifts, one thing just led to another and she'd never really followed her one true dream.

But she had a computer to write on now, she had a reader—Cyd—and this was her last chance. With fumbling fingers, here amid this blazing gallery of blinding light and flashing fire, she began punching keys, writing to Thucydides all the things she had never told another soul—the truth of her life, the secrets of her heart, her claim to faith, her vision of God.

She had so much to be grateful for, to be thankful for—L. L., Kate Magruder, Henry Colton.

And Thucydides.

"Are you running with me, kid? You got my back?"

He flashed on her monitor: "I'm running with you, Sara."

Oh, what was her song? There for a few seconds she feared she would not find it, but she had it now.

She sang to Thucydides of the thunder and the lightning that were His and the gates and the bars of the sea. He Who laid the foundations of the earth, Who created out of the darkness and the void all the morning stars which sing together in His name. He who meted out the world with a span, in Whose sight a thousand years were but a watch in the night, His goodness was from everlasting to everlasting, and His home was in the dwelling-place of light. He lived in all years and things and times, now, always, world without end.

Her fingers flew over the keyboard, Thucydides' console lights blinking encouragement.

They had so much to tell each other, so much to share.

Her words were rocketing through the circuits and chips and into Thucydides' heart till both their hearts were bursting with joy, one with the wild beating heart of life, their spirits on fire, their souls free, free, free.

Till she was no longer writing mere words but melodies, poems, the Music of the Spheres—seated at the roaring loom of time.

When the cascade hit, shaking and hammering their module like a tin can, and she knew they were finished—it did not matter. She and Cyd no longer cared. Even when the chips blew and the circuits crashed, it did not matter. Thucydides was with her, in her, she in him, and they were both in God.

She threw back her head, and in a loud, clear voice, Sara sang.

16 To Lose Thee Were to Lose Myself

Sailor, Sara, Thucydides, even Cassandra had found their Ithaca, but not Frank, and he was scaring Kate Magruder. He'd always been so confident, courageous, full of life.

Now he brooded.

At first, Kate thought it was his legs. The heat exhaustion, radical dehydration, gas gangrene, gunshot trauma, and two fractured femurs were a brutal combination. She had anticipated a prolonged recovery.

She had not anticipated protracted despair.

Sitting on her bedroom couch one night over a bottle of Jack Daniel's sour mash—which she had liberated from her mother's private liquor store—they talked about it.

"I never had a proper chance to thank you," Frank said. "You saved my legs, my life—and brought me home. I've never known quite what to say."

"Or what to feel?"

"It's like I can't see the end of it," Frank said quietly.

"As if part of you died up there on that mountain?" she asked.

"*All* of me."

"I know the feeling. You feel guilty for being alive?" Kate took a healthy pull from the Jack Daniel's bottle.

"For being neither dead nor alive. Part of me still exists with Stone and Breeze and Colton and Taylor, and part of me is dead. Do you understand?"

"Every second of my life, with every fiber of my being."

"You lived through Manhattan firestorms."

"And the Mogollon firestorms."

"And survived."

For a long time they drank and said nothing.

"You'll never guess what Mom said to me before she died," Kate finally said.

"That you and I should marry, have lots of children. The Citadel needs them, according to her. That if I didn't do it I would rue my decision to the day I died."

Kate roared with laughter. For the first time in months Frank laughed too.

"I told her—even if you and I weren't related by blood—you were still a brother to me. No way I could marry you. Never happen. Anyway, I told her, after what had happened, I just couldn't see either of us having kids."

"I called it giving up hostages to fortune, and fortune has been none too fortunate for Planet Earth as of late."

"She must have loved that one," Kate said.

"She said to me: 'Petty arguments as to what you want or what Kate wants are no longer applicable. The only question is whether the race will survive. When you choose not to have children, you threaten the entire race with extermination. You're accessories to human extinction.'"

"And you said?"

"It's what I didn't say. She worked so hard to build all this, to protect us all, I didn't want to spit in her face. But I wanted to say maybe the extinctionists were right. Maybe the race isn't worth saving. I wanted to say I just can't take it anymore. It's like I died in that bomb crater with Stone, Colton, and Breeze. It's like they should have survived, not me. What the Citadel needs is people with their kind of guts. I just don't have it anymore, Kate. But I didn't say that. I didn't want to hurt her feelings."

"She wouldn't have believed you anyway."

"She was biased."

"Frank, you're the best man I ever knew."

"That's what L. L. said."

"She loved you very much."

"She loved you too. You were her natural child."

"I know, but I treated her badly when all she wanted to do was help me."

"You were obsessed with your work. And L. L. was no day at the beach."

Kate shook her head. "I wanted to show her up. That's all it was. That's the reason I worked so hard. That's why I took the assignments I did. And all she wanted to do was help me."

"Well, there's plenty of assignments now," Frank said gently, taking her hand. "We have a whole world to rebuild."

Kate smiled at him fondly. "Remember how L. L. used to talk about your father?"

"I remember."

"Christ, I wish I'd have spent more time with him."

"You'd have loved him."

"He said his Ph.D. stood for 'posthole digger.'"

"He said that all the time, but despite his homespun diction, he used to quote poetry. He quoted Milton to Mom all the time."

"She told me. She loved it."

"He used to quote the Garden of Eden speech to her from *Paradise Lost*."

"I know the lines," Kate said. "I heard Mom recite them often enough: 'Our state cannot be severed / We two are one, one flesh.'"

"'With thee I could all things endure,'" Frank responded, "'without thee live no life.'"

"'To lose thee were to lose myself.'"

"Crazy, isn't it? Getting married."

"I can't," Frank said. "Not with you. Not with anyone. The Nation, Stone and Colton's dying under that mountain, it took something out of me. I'm not getting it back, Kate."

"I have to use the bathroom."

"Ever the romantic."

Kate got up. He heard the toilet flush and water run. He took his drink over to the bed, sat down, and leaned against the headrest.

"I meant it, Kate, about what you did for me. I somehow never thanked you."

"You can thank me by not calling me Kate."

"Everybody calls you Kate."

"No more. My name is Katherine Jane Magruder."

"That's the craziest thing I've ever heard."

"Maybe not. Remember Doc's Third Law."

Frank laughed. "All right," he said. "I'll bite. Which Third Law is it this time?"

"It was the last thing he said to me before he died."

"What is it?" He was no longer laughing.

"Never give up on life—never."

"I loved Doc," Frank said, "and that is no lie. But to tell you the truth, I don't see why *not*."

The bathroom door opened, and she walked out.

"Because *I* won't let you."

Frank was dumbstruck. He had never known her this way before. Magnificent in her nakedness, she was the most beautiful thing he'd ever seen.

The first words that came to his mind were:

Behold, thou art fair, my love. Arise and come away.
The winter is past, and the rains are over.
The voice of the turtle dove is heard in our land.

Then he heard nothing, knew nothing, but felt it:

The still point. The immovable-spot. The jewel in the lotus-heart.

Nirvana.

It was the first . . . but not the last time he knew Nirvana.

Definitely not the last.

Katherine Jane Magruder was walking toward him.

About the Author

Robert Gleason was born in Michigan City, Indiana. He has a B.A. in English literature from Indiana University, a master's degree in English from the University of Wisconsin, and he attended the Sorbonne, all of which were financed by seven hellish years in the Gary steel mills. He has worked in New York book publishing as an acquisitions editor pretty much forever. When he began, he says, he and his colleagues "chiseled books on the walls of caves." He has worked for Simon & Schuster/Pocket Books, Playboy Press, and for the last twenty-eight years at Tor/Forge Books, where he is executive editor. He has also published more than a dozen novels on his own. In 1995, New York City named a day after Robert Gleason for the work he'd done for prison literacy, which included editing and publishing a sizable number of inmates' and ex-offenders' works, as well as speaking in many, many prisons. He had a starring role in the History Channel's two-hour special *Prophets of Doom*. His websites are RobertGleasonBooks .com and RobertGleason2012.com.